Roland Eagles –

he lived for vengeance, power ... and the love of one woman. Orphaned by a German bomber, he learned to live by his wits early in life. And as he built a financial empire in the bloodied aftermath of World War II, he used the hard-won skills of his childhood to ruthlessly take what he desired – in business, and in bed – never realizing how easily, how suddenly, all his victories could slip away.

From the horrors of London under siege, to the splendours of New York high society, from the struggle to build a dynasty to the battle to save it, this is the story of a man ruled by anguish and ambition, destined for tragedy and triumph!

EAGLES

Lewis Orde

CORGI BOOKS

EAGLES

A CORGI BOOK 0 552 12669 1

First published in the United States of America by Arbor House
Publishing Company and in Canada by Fitzhenry & Whiteside
Ltd in 1983. Originally published in Great Britain by Judy
Piatkus (Publishers) Limited of London.

PRINTING HISTORY
Judy Piatkus edition published 1985
Corgi edition published 1986

This book is set in 10/11pt Sabon

Corgi Books are published by Transworld Publishers Ltd.,
Century House, 61–63 Uxbridge Road, Ealing, London W5 5SA,
in Australia by Transworld Publishers (Aust.) Pty. Ltd.,
26 Harley Crescent, Condell Park, NSW 2200, and in New
Zealand by Transworld Publishers (N.Z.) Ltd., Cnr. Moselle
and Waipareira Avenues, Henderson, Auckland.

Printed and bound in Great Britain by
Cox & Wyman Ltd., Reading

For Big Ears, Flossie and Minnie

EAGLES

PROLOGUE 1970

The couple moved slowly to the center of the dance floor at Claridge's, the bride, slender and graceful in a flowing white silk-and-lace dress, the groom, stiff and erect in a tailored formal suit at her side. For an instant they stood motionless gazing at each other until the orchestra began to gently play the first bars of 'My Way'. A burst of applause erupted from the wedding guests as the couple began to dance, only to be swallowed up moments later by other dancers.

Off to one side observing the scene stood a very tall, distinguished-looking man in his middle forties. His gray hair was thinning and his sharp blue eyes were set in a round, open face. Only now, as he watched his older daughter, Katherine, dancing with Franz Kassler, her husband of just a few hours, could Roland Eagles finally make himself accept that she was married. Even during the church ceremony the realization had not struck home completely. At the reception and dinner that followed he had deliberately pushed it from his mind. But at this moment, as he watched Katherine being swept around the floor in the arms of her husband, Roland forced himself to admit sadly that his little girl was no longer little, and no longer his.

He lit a Davidoff cigar, hoping to divert himself from the sentimental thoughts that threatened to bring his emotions to the surface. It would never do for a man who controlled an empire like the Eagles Group to be seen misty-eyed. Then, with an angry, impatient gesture, he stubbed it out. What did he care what anyone thought? As the father of the bride he was entitled to enjoy this

11

particular day in any way he saw fit. If tears were the measure of his happiness it was his concern and no one else's.

Watching his daughter, Roland recalled the first time *he* had ever danced at Claridge's . . . He was with Katherine's mother, in white tie and tails amid all the pomp that surrounded a diplomatic affair. Had twenty-one years really passed so quickly? Surely not. The memories of that night were still so sharp, so poignant. It could have been last week . . .

Katherine and Franz passed close to where Roland stood and she blew him a kiss. He responded with a wave and wondered if her new husband would be jealous of her affection for her father. Could a man be envious of his father-in-law for that reason? It was an intriguing question, but Roland knew that Franz had no cause for concern. Katherine was like her mother: the man she chose to love would be the man she would love forever, with a loyalty and strength that was all-consuming. If Roland could find any dissimilarity between mother and daughter it was in physical appearance alone; Katherine's mother had been petite with dark skin, jet black hair and dark flashing eyes, like those of a gypsy. Katherine had taken after Roland's own mother, tall and blonde, with a creamy, clear complexion. Like a young Grace Kelly, Roland had often thought. Her temperament, though, was a legacy from both her mother and himself – a fiery spirit and an indomitable will. In family disagreements, sparks always flew.

The first dance ended and Roland stepped onto the floor. 'May I?' he asked both his daughter and son-in-law.

Franz Kassler relinquished his grip on Katherine. 'Only for you, sir, would I give Katherine up. But for no more than one dance.' The German-accented English was clear and crisp, the delivery – despite the intended humor –

12

almost curt. In another time and place Roland might have mistaken it for an order.

Roland took his daughter in his arms and gazed fondly at her. 'You look absolutely radiant, Kathy.'

She lifted her head to kiss him on the cheek and he saw tears glistening in the blue eyes that were every bit as vivid as his own. 'Thank you for a wonderful day.'

'You made it wonderful all by yourself.'

'I'm so glad you did it this way, with the reception, banquet and ball following the church service. It's so much nicer than the customary wedding breakfast. It's almost like . . .' Katherine struggled for a few seconds to find a suitable analogy '. . . like a Jewish wedding.'

'They believe in big weddings. So do I,' Roland replied, grinning. He looked over his shoulder at Franz Kassler, who stood on the edge of the dance floor, waiting impatiently for the music to end. 'He loves you so much he won't even let you out of his sight. You chose well.'

'You approve?'

'Of course. You always knew that.'

'And if you hadn't approved? Would you have stood in my way? Denied me my happiness?'

Roland smiled at the memories those questions triggered. 'Would you have defied your own father?'

'Yes.'

'I know. Which is why I'm glad it never came to that. I would never have found the strength to fight you.'

A camera flash exploded nearby causing Roland to blink. He recognized the man as a photographer from his own newspaper, and wondered briefly if that would be the photo used in the society column the next day. He mused at what the caption might read: Daughter of British tycoon marries son of German industrialist . . . wealth weds wealth? He never tried to exert any influence over the newspaper, and hoped in exchange that the editorial staff would be kind to him. Had he been smiling when the photograph was taken? Or had his brow been creased in thought? There was so much to think about today . . . the memories of Claridge's itself . . . Katherine . . . Franz Kassler's family . . . He was surprised that his daughter's wedding had brought back so many memories, some he would just as soon forget.

When the dance finished Roland held his daughter, reluctant to let her go. He felt a tap on his arm. 'May I have my wife back, sir?' Franz said, standing next to him.

'You may.' Roland kissed Katherine, patted Franz on the shoulder and walked away, heading for the table where Franz's father sat alone. He wondered if Heinrich Kassler was reliving memories as well . . . Was he, too, trying to unravel the intricate maze that had led to this union?

'A truly handsome couple,' Kassler said as Roland joined him at the table. 'I am thrilled that my son should have chosen such a wonderful girl for his wife.'

'You know, it was only ten minutes ago that I could make myself believe they were married,' Roland replied. 'She's just turned twenty, he's twenty-four. Children. It doesn't seem possible.'

'When we were their age we were preoccupied with other things, eh, Roland?' Kassler's voice carried barely any accent at all, as if he had worked hard at perfecting his English. 'Circumstances dictated that we could not enjoy such innocent happiness.'

'Too true.' Roland pulled another Davidoff from his pocket, lit it carefully from a gold Dunhill. 'I think we're getting old, Heinrich. Another generation is preparing to take our place.' Through the cigar smoke he studied Kassler, the lined face, the strands of silver hair smoothed across the scalp, the blue eyes dimmed by time. Roland knew he had only to look out over the dance floor at his son-in-law to see how Heinrich Kassler had once been: straight-backed with a platinum blondness and pale blue eyes that seemed to hold a trace of steely arrogance . . .

the same as when Roland had first met him twenty-five years earlier. Now they were both middle-aged.

'Roland, you and me, we will never grow old. Other people, perhaps, but we have been through too much – we have created too much – to be affected by nature's perfidy. This' – Kassler touched his thin silver hair – 'is just camouflage.'

'Are you implying that we're too rich to become old?'

Kassler shook his head. 'No one is ever that wealthy. Even the combined power of Eagles Group and Kassler Industries cannot fight the onset of age. But we have been raised the hard way. We've been toughened against the natural processes that afflict ordinary people.'

'Listening to you, I can almost believe it.'

Another man joined them, a burly, dark-haired man with a square block of face, a heavy nose and a shadowy beard that seemed to resist the efforts of any razor. If what Kassler said was true then Alf Goldstein would never grow old either, Roland decided; he had also been raised the hard way.

'Congratulating each other or just reminiscing?' Alf Goldstein asked.

'A little bit of both,' Roland answered. 'Sit down and join in.'

Goldstein pulled out a chair and sat down heavily, uncomfortable in his tuxedo. But then his heavy frame tended to look distresssed in any kind of suit. Even now Roland could recall the man who was his chauffeur and personal assistant as he had been twenty-one years earlier: a taxi driver content to sit behind the wheel of his cab, exhibiting a knowledge of London that surpassed any map or tour guide.

And four years before that, in 1945, wearing a British army uniform, filling it out until the seams threatened to burst.

They had all been in uniform then, when they had first met. Alf Goldstein. Heinrich Kassler. Roland Eagles.

Only Kassler's uniform had been different – he had been wearing the colors of the other side. And his perfect command of English had brought Roland to within a hair's breadth of killing him out of hand . . .

Just as it had brought Roland face-to-face with a heritage he could no longer ignore.

CHAPTER ONE

By the spring of 1945, the German war machine lay in ruins. On all fronts, allied forces surged forward against ever weakening resistance. In the east, the Russians advanced; in the south, the Americans; and in the north, the British. Each victorious army uncovered its own share of atrocities to shock a watching world.

In the middle of April, Roland Eagles was a captain in a British anti-tank regiment in northern Germany, a veteran of almost five decoration-studded years. As a corporal at el-Alamein he had been awarded the enlisted man's Military Medal. In 1944 he had been given a field commission, jumping from sergeant to second lieutenant after his company commander was killed on Normandy's Juno Beach; and before the unit got off the beach that day Roland had been put forward for the Military Cross after destroying a German machine-gun emplacement. None of this action, though, could have prepared him for the horror he would encounter in Germany itself.

During a respite in the fighting, orders came from headquarters that Roland's unit was to participate in an operation organized by the Red Cross. Faced with an outbreak of typhus, the retreating Germans were willing to turn over a prison camp to British forces. The name of the camp was Bergen-Belsen.

Through a red veil of barely suppressed anger, Roland watched German troops march away under the protection of a white flag. He understood only too well how fragile the line was that kept him from ordering his men to open fire; he hated this enemy with a passion that bordered on madness. Perhaps the only thing that restrained him from breaking the truce was the knowledge that another British unit was waiting close by, and there the Red Cross and the white flag would be of little use to the retreating Germans.

When the last of the Germans had marched away, Roland led his men into the camp. No joyful crowds rushed forward to greet the liberating force, as had happened in the towns and cities along the route to victory. In Bergen-Belsen, there was no celebration – only lethargy and resignation to dying among the hapless human refuse which had been transported from other camps in the east as the Germans had fled before the Red Army.

Sixty thousand survivors crowded the Old Camp, barely able to recognize the difference between German and British troops. Men and women with shaven heads, sunken faces and stooped skeletal frames limped around in grotesquely flapping striped uniforms that offered little protection against the weather. Others lay on the ground or on stacked narrow cots, too weak to move. Arms and legs bore signs of rat bites. Typhus was rampant. For thousands, liberation had come too late; only now it would be German prisoners who pushed the dead to their mass graves.

Roland was like a man with a holy mission. He searched among his own soldiers for an interpreter, someone who could communicate with the survivors in either German or Yiddish. He found a sergeant who could speak both passably, a heavy-set, dark-haired man named Goldstein. The sergeant became Roland's constant companion as food rations were passed out and adequate bathing and toilet facilities were erected. Extra accommodation was found in the New Camp, which before the liberation had been military barracks. Typhus sufferers were quarantined. The healthy were disinfected with DDT and issued fresh clothing. Those for whom it was too late continued to die.

With Goldstein, Roland toured his sector of the camp, attempting to reassure the inmates that everything possible was being done to ease their pain. But even with Goldstein's help Roland was unable to communicate with many of the survivors, who spoke only Hungarian or Russian; then the survivors themselves had to be pressed into service as part of a complicated chain of interpreters.

'Why do they only eat part of the food?' Roland asked Goldstein after supervising the distribution of rations.

Goldstein relayed the question to a group who had been seen hiding unfinished cans of combat rations in their clothes. 'They're saving it for tomorrow sir.'

'For God's sake, why?' Roland gasped in disbelief. 'They'll get more food tomorrow.'

'That's not the way they've been living, sir. If they eat everything at once there might be nothing more for two or three days.'

'Tell them that the British will ensure they have more food, sergeant. They are to eat everything they are given each day.'

'Yes, sir.'

Shortly after the command was given Roland and Goldstein watched in helpless horror as the survivors became violently sick from cramming so much food – though it was only a can of combat rations – into pitifully shrunken stomachs.

Two days after the British had taken control of the camp a patrol brought in a man who had been found hiding in the nearby pine forest. Although wearing the dirty, ragged uniform of a Wehrmacht corporal, the man had a healthy, well-fed appearance. In his late twenties, his fair skin gleamed with a shining vitality, his blond hair was almost clean. While searching him the patrol had discovered a small tattoo beneath his left armpit, his blood group. The prisoner was not a simple army corporal but a member of the SS.

19

The moment the prisoner was brought into his office, Roland sent for Sergeant Goldstein.

'Sergeant, ask the prisoner what his name is.'

'*Wie heissen Sie?*'

'An interpreter will not be necessary.' Standing between his escort of two soldiers, the blond-haired German addressed Roland in English. 'I speak perfectly adequate—'

At the sound of the man's voice it was as if a plunger had suddenly been pressed inside Roland's head. He kicked back his chair and pulled his service-issue Webley revolver from its holster, pointing it at the German with a hand that was suddenly white and trembling. 'Shut up ! I don't want to hear my language coming out of your filthy Nazi mouth!' He swung around to glare at his interpreter. 'Goldstein – make the bastard speak German!'

'*Wie heissen Sie?*' Goldstein repeated, his eyes leaving the prisoner just long enough to steal a quick glance at Roland as he slumped back into the seat, dropping the Webley to the desk. The sergeant was stunned by the abrupt explosion of his normally calm commanding officer.

Pale-faced and visibly shaken by the outburst, the German answered: 'Kassler, Heinrich.'

'Rank?'

'Corporal.'

This time Roland's anger was controlled, his voice cold and level.'Your real rank, before I order these soldiers to take you outside and shoot you.'

The German glanced nervously at the escort; they stood at strict attention, rifles gripped tightly. '*Kapitan.*'

'You are a member of the SS. Why are you wearing the uniform of a common German soldier?' Roland stared belligerently at the prisoner while Goldstein translated in slow, halting German.

'The *Schutzstaffel*, like the entire National Socialist regime, is responsible for crimes of great magnitude,'

20

Kassler replied softly. 'I did not wish to take my chances on being captured and summarily executed.'

At first Roland was amazed by the answer. Then he became intrigued. Why would an SS officer speak so openly? Why would he incriminate himself in this manner? 'What was your role in this carnage?' he said, making a sweeping gesture to encompass the entire camp.

'I had no part in this misery. I was responsible for saving lives here, not destroying them.'

'You were responsible for what?' Incredulous, Roland waved away Goldstein's attempt to translate. The prisoner had *made* Roland want to hear his own language spoken by the German.

Kassler switched to English. 'For saving lives. I loathe the Nazis as much as any decent man—'

'Is that why you joined the SS?'

Kassler's steely eyes froze at the sarcasm. 'I joined the *Schutzstaffel* to protect my family and fight against the evil which had enveloped my country.' He paused to see what reaction his words would provoke. Roland ordered him to continue. 'Before the war my father owned a factory near Stuttgart. He manufactured components for motor engines. In 1938 he was ordered to switch production to components for tank engines. He refused and was thrown into prison. The factory was taken over, given to others faithful to the state. My father died a year later, in Buchenwald, two weeks before Hitler invaded Poland with tanks containing engine parts manufactured at my father's factory.'

'Then what happened?'

'To protect the rest of my family I had to pretend to be the exact opposite of my father. Naturally, because of the stand he took we were all suspect. I became a party stalwart by joining the *Schutzstaffel*. When I made my vow of loyalty I took another oath, a silent one that I would keep. I swore to do all in my power to work against the evil of Adolf Hitler and the criminals who supported him.

21

I am heartbroken now as I see the disasters which have befallen my country, but I am also proud that I kept my promise.'

Roland dropped his eyes to the desk, fixed them on the Webley. He became fascinated by the cold impersonality of the weapon as he considered Kassler's words. What if the German was telling the truth? Such a possibility was out of the question, Roland reasoned. No man, not even a saint, could accomplish good in the midst of all this horror. Or *was* it possible? Could it be, by some miracle, that Roland had stumbled on one decent German, a man of high principle who had used the system in an attempt to wreck it? Roland didn't know the answer, but he couldn't dismiss the question; he had to find out. He slowly lifted his gaze from the desk to the escort. 'Remove the prisoner. Bring him back when I call you.' He waited until Kassler had been taken outside, then he turned to Goldstein, anxious to hear his opinion. In the few days since they had arrived Roland had become closer to Goldstein than to anyone he had encountered in his five years in the army. He knew it was the horrors at the camp that had drawn them together. 'What do you think about all this, sergeant?'

Goldstein nodded toward the Webley. 'Let me have that for five seconds, sir. I'll shoot the bastard and save us all the bother of disproving his lies.'

Roland considered Goldstein's blunt reply . . . Two minutes earlier he had almost impulsively done what Goldstein was suggesting, even with Goldstein and the escort as damning witnesses. Now he was having second thoughts. 'I'm not certain that acting as judge, jury and executioner is the answer, sergeant, although I can understand perfectly how you feel.'

'Can you, sir? With all due respect, I don't think you've got the vaguest idea how I feel. I know you've done everything you can for the people here, but you've just done what any decent human being would do. My feelings go a bloody sight deeper than common decency, sir. Forty years ago, my family came to England from a small village on the German-Polish border. For all I know, some of those skeletons out there could be my cousins.'

'Sergeant . . .' Roland took a deep breath and let it out slowly. 'I understand a lot more than you think I do, because any of those poor bastards out there could be my cousins as well.' Even as he said it, Roland wondered whether he had made a mistake. Despite the closeness that had grown between them, Goldstein was still virtually a stranger, and Roland was telling him something he had never admitted to anyone before – in fact, it was something he could scarcely acknowledge to himself. 'My old man was a Jew.'

'I wasn't aware of that, sir.' Goldstein had become very stiff, as if embarrassed by his own display of emotion and Roland's confession.

'Neither was I until I came to this place. I never gave a damn for it one way or the other. But after seeing what's gone on here, I can't stop thinking about it. Does that make any sense to you, sergeant?'

'Yes, sir, it does.' The sergeant watched his young captain carefully, uncertain of what was going through his mind. He seemed to be wavering on a tightrope. On one side was the present, on the other side – yawning like a chasm – a portion of his past he had previously denied. It was as though he was trying to balance himself between the two . . .

Goldstein knew he wouldn't be able to do it – not for long. Bergen-Belsen had opened up that past and now Roland had not only to recognize . . . he had to learn to live with it.

The siren began as a faint chilling whisper, greedily sucking air into its lungs, gathering strength until it finally pierced the sky with its warning.

By the middle of September 1940, the mournful wail

23

was such a familiar sound along the Kent coast that reaction to it was automatic, almost unhurried. Families with houses that had cellars went below ground. Others trooped in orderly fashion as they'd done many times before to communal shelters, waiting until the all-clear sounded. A few diehards stayed put, obstinately daring the Germans to bomb them. In London, where the Luftwaffe was usually headed, there might be panic; but in genteel seaside resort towns like Margate, Ramsgate and Cliftonville the siren was little more than an annoying interruption to the day's routine.

The Eagles family home in Margate had a cellar. As the siren sounded in the late afternoon, Henry Eagles, his wife Betty, and their three children – Roland, Maureen and Neil – went into their rehearsed routine. Windows were fixed open to lessen the chance of glass breaking from concussion should any bombs be dropped nearby. Roland went out into the garden to fetch the cat. Then the family trooped downstairs to the cellar, which Henry Eagles had fitted up as temporary living quarters with a collapsible table and chairs, cooking facilities from a primus stove, canned food and water, and five bunks attached in tiers to the walls. In one corner of the cellar, hidden by a screen, was a chemical toilet. When the door to the rest of the house was closed, the sound of the siren barely penetrated.

'Here we go again,' Roland muttered as the first sound of the approaching bombers vibrated through the ground. With newspaper in hand, he perched himself comfortably on the edge of one of the bunks. It did not escape his father's attention that the paper was folded open to the racing page.

'Didn't you bring any homework down with you?' Henry Eagles asked.

'I did it all during the sports period this afternoon.'

'You managed to avoid getting picked again?'

'No one ever picks me because I'm a jinx to whichever team I play for.'

Henry laughed. 'You go out of your way to be a jinx.' He knew his oldest son hated team competitions. Roland saw no logic in it; it meant nnothing to him o be on the winning side in a game of soccer or cricket. Where mental prowess was called for, however, he was an outstanding competitor. He shone at chess, winning the school trophy for the past two years, just as he excelled in his academic studies, attacking each subject with a cold, methodical efficiency while seeming not to work at all. But sports, where he should have done well because of his height – three days short of his sixteenth birthday and already one of the tallest boys in school – raised no enthusiasm what-soever.

Henry understood his son's aversion to sports, because they didn't come as naturally to him as did his mental capacity. And if Roland could not effortlessly shine in any subject of activity he saw no reason to waste his time and energy trying to do so. For Roland it was an all or nothing proposition – mediocrity had no place in his life.

His attitude, particularly toward sports, dismayed his father. Though in his early forties, Henry Eagles was tall and trim, firm-muscled and athletic. He still found time to play cricket in the summer and rugby in the cooler months. It was a healthy break from the humdrum routine of the accountancy firm in Margate where he was a partner, and it was a disappointment that his son wouldn't join in with him . . .

The noise of the bombers increased, drowning out the wail of the siren. The house shook, causing all five mem-bers of the family to stare up at the cellar ceiling. How safe was it down here? What if Margate was the target this time? Would the cellar withstand the explosions? Roland dropped the newspaper and pulled his younger brother and sister onto the bunk with him, arms protectively around their shoulders. Neil tried to act like he thought an adult would, sitting upright, unafraid, but Maureen was visibly shaken by the sound of the aircraft. Roland held her tighter, reassuring her that he wouldn't let anything happen to her. He glanced at his parents, who were sitting by the table. His mothers's fists were clenched nervously; her blue eyes fixed on the crucifix on the wall. His father sat holding the cat, absently stroking its fur.

The drumming of the bombers seemed to last forever, as if the entire Luftwaffe was passing overhead. The family was silent until, at last, it began to fade, then finally died away.

'London again.' Roland's mother said. Relieved, she ran a hand through her long blonde hair, stood up and walked across the cellar to touch the crucifix.

'Poor devils.' Henry murmured. 'It must be hell there.'

'Are you worried about your family?'

Henry looked sharply at his wife. 'I have no family in London. The only family I have is right here, in this cellar.'

Betty Eagles dropped her eyes, wishing that she hadn't mentioned her husband's family. He hated them as much as he hated the German bombers which flew over the house almost every day. Sometimes she wondered if Henry was secretly praying that one of those bombers would someday find his family and drop its load right on their heads. What made it worse was that Betty knew she was the reason for the ill feelings on both sides. If she had never met him, never married him, he never would have fallen foul of his family. There were times when she wondered if he blamed her as well . . .

'There's the all-clear.' Roland said the moment he heard the siren pick up again, the long one-note blast that signified the danger was over. As far as he was concerned, it couldn't have come at a more timely moment. He hated it when his father spoke of his family like that. Regardless

26

of what had happened, it was still his family . . . His mother should never have mentioned them. He stood up and began climbing the stairs to the ground floor. 'I'll close the windows.'

'Don't turn lights on until you've got the curtains drawn,' his father called after him.

'I know the rules.' Roland walked around the ground floor, closing windows and drawing the heavy drapes, then repeating the chore upstairs. All the while he thought about his parents, the anger in his father's voice . . . Maureen and Neil were still too young to understand the turmoil caused by their parents' marriage, Catholic to Jew. Although Roland could intellectually understand what caused the split, he knew he would never understand in his heart how a family could cast out one of its own – especially when the only crime committed was that his father had fallen in love. . .

In his own room he opened a drawer and pulled out an old cigar box that held his personal treasures – a diary he had once kept through an entire year, scout achievement badges, a silver ring he had found on the beach two summers ago. At the bottom of the box was a small, flat, rectangular metal casing with a hole at each end for a nail. His father had given it to him years ago, telling him it was a Jewish good luck charm. Roland couldn't now remember the strange name by which his father had called it. Opening the back, he extracted a small piece of parchment, unfolded it and stared uncomprehendingly at the minute Hebrew printing. It was supposed to be a prayer but it meant nothing too him. If it rally *were* a lucky charm, he reasoned, then maybe there was a chance that his father could become friendly with his family again. He slipped the charm into his pants pocket, replaced the box in the drawer and continued closing the windows.

Later that night, when Maureen and Neil were in bed and Betty Eagles sat reading, Roland and his father played chess at the dining room table. The curtains were securely fastened, taped at the sides to prevent light leaks. Not all the neighbors were as conscientious, though, and every so often Roland would hear an air-raid warden shout 'Get that light out!' as he patrolled the area seeking blackout offenders.

'You've got your O-levels this year,' Henry Eagles said as he pondered a move. 'I think you should spend more time studying than you do.'

'Why should I pretend to study hard when it comes so easily?' Roland reached out and grasped his father's hand as he was about to move a piece. 'I wouldn't do that – it'll be mate in three if you make that move.'

Henry surveyed the board, shook his head with a feigned weariness and changed his mind. 'I wish you wouldn't be so bloody patronizing when we play.'

'I like our games to be competitive.'

'Even if you have to provide the competition yourself?' Henry said with a friendly edge to his voice. He hadn't beaten Roland in over a year. 'What do you want for your birthday?'

Roland considered both the board and his father's question carefully. 'How about a new bicycle?'

'Too expensive. Lower your sights.'

'All right.' Roland moved one of his own men. 'I was going to buy one for myself, but I thought I'd see if I could con you out of the money instead.'

'Are you that wealthy these days?'

Roland reached into his back pocket and pulled out a well thumbed post office savings book. 'Forty-seven pounds, eighteen shillings and threepence.' He was particularly proud of his post office account – it represented his winnings at the track.

'You just make sure you don't get caught betting,' Henry warned. 'Either by your schoolmasters or the police.' Roland had been playing the horses for more than a year, ever since he had sat down to study form sheets

28

with the same single-minded efficiency with which he mastered everything else. His bets were modest, a shilling or two placed with a bookmaker in Margate who didn't object to doing business with schoolboys . . . And while Henry himself had no interest in placing bets on horses, he knew there was little point in forbidding Roland to gamble; the boy was simply too strong-willed to be thwarted. Besides, Henry was secretly impressed with his son's winnings, particularly the way he kept an account of everything he won or lost, entering it into a ledger like a man running a company. He thought that the experience might be useful some day . . . in another two years Roland would be finished with school altogether and could join him in the accountancy firm, starting out as an articled clerk. He had the mind for it, a brain which naturally divided figures into profit-and-loss columns. He'd fit in well, Henry thought, as long as he didn't get dragged off to war. God forbid . . .

'There are a couple of good horses running tomorrow — make a nice double. Want to come in with me?' Roland asked cheekily.

'No thank you. I make my money honestly.'

Roland studied the board for a few seconds, then asked, 'Why don't you make up with your family?'

The question was unexpected and Roland's father was clearly not happy to have the subject broached again.

'What makes you ask that?'

'You were worried tonight about the bombers, even if you claimed you weren't. You worry every night London gets bombed.'

'Roland, my family stopped speaking to me. I never stopped speaking to them. It was their choice, not mine. I merely accommodated them.'

'Do you think you'll ever see them again?'

'Who knows?' Henry gazed at the board and tried to focus on the game but found it impossible; his son's nagging questions had wrecked his concentration. He

29

reflected on how, at times, Roland seemed mature beyond his years, while other times he could be so utterly naive. He refused to accept that a family could be split up, nor could he comprehend the bitterness that resulted in a family of orthodox Jews when a son married a Catholic. Perhaps when he grew older he would understand better how families sometimes work, Henry thought sourly . . . after he'd accumulated enough cynicism and bitterness in his own life.

'Will you ever see them again?' Roland repeated.

Henry glanced at his wife and saw that she was staring at him. 'Roland, do me a favor and don't ask so many questions, eh?' He pushed the board away, toppling the pieces. 'I give you the game. Now you'd better get to bed, you've got school in the morning.'

Roland kissed his parents goodnight and went upstairs. Before going to bed he looked in on his sister and brother, pulled the covers up and kissed them both. He loved his family – nothing could ever separate them – and it grieved him that his father's family was not as strong, or as forgiving.

Roland's final class before lunchtime the following day was the subject he hated most: religious instruction. He took just enough interest in the lessons to learn the names, dates and places he needed in order to pass the exams. Had the class been taught by anyone other than the school's headmaster, Mr Spott-Mandray, Roland wouldn't have bothered at all. But Spott-Mandray, known to generations of students as Old Spotty, still inspired fear.

As the tall, gauntly thin headmaster paced the front of the classroom, black gown billowing out behind him as he recited facts about the children of Israel fleeing from Egypt, Roland checked the racing page spread across his knees. Occasionally he looked up, just to make certain that the headmaster wasn't taking any undue interest in him.

'Eagles!' Spott-Mandray suddenly called out. 'What was the fifth plague visited by God upon the Egyptians?'

'Boils, sir,' Roland fired back, caught momentarily off-guard. Looking at the headmaster's beaked nose, pale face and prominent widow's peak he couldn't help thinking that with the black gown Old Spotty resembled a huge vampire bat.

Spott-Mandray glared across the classroom at Roland. 'That was the sixth plague. Pestilence was the fifth. Pay attention, boy.'

'Yes, sir.' Roland held Spott-Mandray's gaze for a moment then dropped his eyes to the desk. School rumor had it that Old Spotty was waiting to be called into the army. He had been in the first World War and had retained a reserve commission. The day Old Spotty returned to active service couldn't come soon enough for Roland; the old martinet would get the shock of his life when he tried to treat grown men as if they were school-boys.

Mercifully, the class finished, and Roland slipped the racing form into his blazer pocket. As he was passing through the door, clutching the bag of sandwiches he always brought from home in preference to school lunches, Spott-Mandray called him back.

'Eagles, it is a great pity that you do not apply yourself as diligently to religious instruction as you do to other subjects.'

'I do, sir,' Roland lied. 'I just find other subjects easier.'

'Easier – or more important?' Spott-Mandray countered, and Roland knew that he was about to launch into one of his sermons. Old Spotty's life seemed to be ruled by religion; his favorite time of day was morning assembly when he led the school in prayers. 'The Bible, Eagles, is the most important work of literature ever written. We can all learn to live decently from its teachings.'

Roland recalled the episode in the cellar the previous evening. What did the Bible teach? That you could only associate with – only marry – your own kind or forever

31

be damned? In that light, the Bible taught hatred and bigotry, and Roland wanted none of that.

Spott-Mandray was far from finished. 'Do you study the scriptures at home? Are the members of your family churchgoers?'

'We belong to a church, sir.' That seemed to be the easiest way to answer. In truth only Roland's mother and younger brother and sister ever went; his father refused to have anything to do with religion, and Roland followed his lead.

'How often do *you* attend?'

'I don't sir.'

'Why not?' Spott-Mandray said in an angry tone, challenging him.

'Because my father taught me that it's what's here that counts,' Roland said, pointing to his heart. 'If there is a heaven you'll get there by your actions, not by regular church attendance.'

Spott-Mandray's pale face turned even whiter. Roland thought he might be summoning up one of the plagues they had discussed during class, but all the headmaster could manage was a disgusted wave of dismissal. Roland needed no urging; he turned and left quickly before the headmaster could change his mind.

Sitting in the playground, Roland gulped down his lunch. After throwing the empty bag into the trash can – cleanliness was another thing Old Spotty was crazy about, constantly posting notices that it was next to godliness – Roland left the school and walked across a busy intersection to a small, dingy tobacconist's shop located on the opposite corner. Two customers were in the shop and Roland busied himself by pretending to look at newspapers while they made their purchases. After they'd left he approached the middle-aged, balding man behind the counter.

'Hello, Lenny, how's business?'

The shopkeeper acknowledged the greeting with a dismal shake of his head. 'Could always be better. Have you come here to place a bet or pass the time of day?'

Roland pushed a sheet of paper and two half-crown coins across the counter. 'Five-shilling win double on Turkish Delight in the one-thirty and Queen Bess in the two-forty.'

Lenny who acted as a commission agent for a local bookmaker, dropped the sheet of paper and the coins into a special drawer. 'Got a tip direct from the stable, have you then?'

'From the horses themselves,' Roland said cheerily. 'I'll see you after school for my winnings.'

'Some hopes, Roland. You've got two chances with that pair – slim and none. Seriously, did you get a tip?'

'Where would I get a tip, from one of the prophets we talk about in religious instruction?'

Lenny's laughter followed Roland out of the shop. He didn't need to hear tips; he could handicap efficiently all by himself . . . Turkish Delight had finished second in its last three races; today it would be wearing blinders for the first time to break it of its habit of being distracted by other horses. And Queen Bess was a derivation of his mother's name, Betty, which was short for Elizabeth. Intuition and superstition – the perfect basis for a two-horse bet – and Roland's own formula for success at the track.

At one-thirty that afternoon during history class, Roland looked at his watch and then closed his eyes, picturing the race in his mind, silently willing Turkish Delight to win. He repeated the action at two-forty, during geography, this time urging Queen Bess across the line. The remainder of the afternoon he devoted to his studies, free of distractions.

When the last class finished he ran down to the playground. Instead of jumping onto his bicycle and heading home, he raced across the street to the tobacconist's shop. Lenny gave him a doleful look when he entered.

33

'What have you got, a crystal ball or something? Or do they teach fortune-telling in school these days?'

Roland grinned at the complaints, figuring that his hunches must have paid off. 'What were the prices?'

'Turkish Delight came in at four-to-one. Queen Bess paid nine-to-one.'

'That's twelve pounds ten you owe me.'

'I know. Mind like a bloody adding machine you've got.' Lenny handed across a brown envelope. Roland ripped it open, counted the money, then passed half a crown across the counter.

'Have a drink on me.'

'Thanks. Next time come back when you've got a loser.'

Holding the money, Roland left the shop and looked around the intersection. Another day, another profit to be entered into his ledger and more money for his post office account. Careful research and deserved luck, Roland thought, congratulating himself, that was all success needed. He was about to cross back over to get his bicycle when he noticed an elderly woman standing at the curb, testing the ground with a white stick. Roland hesitated, then stepped forward.

'Want to cross with me?' he asked.

The woman held out her hand and Roland allowed her to grasp his arm. He waited patiently for a break in the traffic, then slowly crossed the road toward the corner next to the school entrance. His eyes trailed downward to the tip of the white stick, fascinated as it leaped around like a snake's tongue discerning obstacles.

'All right now?' he asked as the woman stepped onto the curb.

'Yes, thank you.' The woman released Roland's arm and started forward confidently. Roland stood transfixed with horror as she walked straight into the railings surrounding the school. He moved toward her to help her recover her bearings, then froze as the woman swung at him.

'You little fool!' she screamed at where she thought he stood. She lashed out with the white stick, catching Roland painfully across the hands as he raised them in protection. 'You took me to the wrong corner!'

Roland felt his face redden as people turned to look. Uncertain what to do, he chose flight. He spun around, brain pounding in panic as the woman's furious screams followed him and ran toward the school entrance, wanting only to be on his bicycle heading home. Instead, he ran straight into Mr Spott-Mandray.

'What the devil's going on, Eagles?' The headmaster had been about to get into his car when he had heard the woman's screams. Roland struggled against his grip, surprised that Old Spotty had the strength to hold him. 'What did you do to that blind woman? Where did you get all that money you've got there?'

Roland stared down at the fistful of money he had taken from the bookmaker's agent, then at the woman who was still standing on the sidewalk screaming in his direction. A crowd had gathered around her but so far no one had offered to help. Suddenly he realized what Old Spotty must be thinking . . . what he could only be thinking about a boy who confessed that he thought going to church was a waste of time . . . that he had stolen the money, robbed an old blind woman!

'It's mine!'

'Then why is that poor woman screaming at you?' Spott-Mandray swung Roland around and marched him back to the woman.

'Madam, what did this boy do to you?'

'He thinks I stole your money!' Roland blurted out.

'He took me to the wrong corner!' the woman screamed, unconcerned about any money. 'He could have gotten me killed! I don't know where I am now.' Someone from the crowd finally stepped forward to offer assistance. Spott-Mandray refused to let go of Roland's arm and demanded again to know where the money had come from. He snatched it away and counted it.

'Twelve pounds ten – that's a working man's wages for a fortnight!'

'Give it back to me, it's mine!'

'We'll get to the bottom of this.' Pushing Roland ahead, Spott-Mandray returned to the school, up to his study where he closed the door. 'Now, do you tell me where you got that money or do I bring in the police?'

Police? The idea appalled Roland. What would his parents say if they knew he had been in trouble with the police? But he had done nothing wrong, he had nothing to hide. Of course he did, he realized dejectedly. Bookmaking was illegal – just as a boy not yet sixteen making bets must surely be. Damn that blind woman, why did she have to be standing there? A minute earlier, a minute later, and he would have been well on his way home by now, happily cycling away the three-mile journey.

'Well?' Spott-Mandray prompted. 'You are not leaving here until I get to the bottom of this.'

'That twelve pounds ten is mine, sir. You have no right to hold on to it or to question me about it.'

'First you'll tell me where you got it,' the headmaster said, ignoring the remark. 'If I am satisfied, I will return it to you.' The headmaster set the money on the desk.

'I won it,' Roland stated flatly, eager to finish the confrontation and pushed by a perversity to see how Old Spotty would react to *that*.

'Won it? Gambling? Gambling in this school is expressly forbidden. And how could you win such a fortune pitching pennies?'

'I did not gamble in school, sir, I won it on the horses.'

Roland's admission was rewarded by an almost imperceptible arching of the headmaster's thin eyebrows. 'You ... bet ... on ... the ... horses?'

'Yes, sir, I did.' Seeing his chance Roland snatched up the money from the desk and jammed it into his blazer pocket. His fingers came in contact with the Jewish good luck charm he had taken from the cigar box the previous night; maybe it really was lucky.

'Where did you make this bet?'

'I can't tell you that, sir.' He refused to implicate Lenny.

'Can't you? We'll see about that.' Spott-Mandray opened the wide center drawer of his desk and Roland flinched. He knew that inside were four curved bamboo canes. The headmaster selected the heaviest, drew it out and cut the air experimentally. 'Bend over the desk.'

Roland backed away. He had bent over that desk once before, in his second year at the school. The memory of his humiliation still burned, even if his buttocks had recovered. He wasn't about to repeat the scene willingly.

'Bend over that desk.'

'No. You have no right. I did nothing wrong either in school or during school hours.'

'I have every right. I will not tolerate any of my students gambling. Now, for the last time, bend over that desk or it will be the worse for you.'

'No, sir.' Roland retreated to the door and opened it.

'If you disobey me, you will never return to this school, Eagles. I will begin expulsion proceedings against you tomorrow.'

Roland took a final look at Spott-Mandray holding the cane and then ran through the door, slamming it behind him. He raced all the way down the stairs and out into the playground to the bicycle racks. He'd be damned if he'd accept a beating from Old Spotty. He would rather face his own parents and tell them why he was being expelled.

It was four-thirty when he finally wheeled his bicycle out of the school playground, thirty minutes behind his normal schedule. His parents would be wondering what had happened to him. His father would be home already

37

since his office had begun to close early each day, now that the bombing raids were so regular. Pedaling furiously, Roland set off through the center of Margate toward his home on the southern edge of town.

He was so wrapped up in thoughts of school and Old Spotty that he didn't even notice the air raid siren until he stopped the bicycle for a red light. He looked around and saw that the few cars on the road had stopped. Their passengers joined the steady rush of pedestrians toward the shelters. Gripping the handlebars of the bicycle, Roland debated whether to run for cover or try to make it home, still two miles away.

'You on the bike!' a man shouted. 'What the hell do you think you're up to?' Roland glanced left and saw an air raid warden wearing a flat tin hat and gas mask. 'That's right . . . you! Are you deaf?'

Despite the warden, Roland was reluctant to join the others moving toward the shelters. His parents would be sick with worry – it was more important to get home and let them know he was safe. Excitement churned in his stomach as he looked skyward. Over the English Channel he could see a Spitfire squadron as it climbed to meet the oncoming threat. This was the first time an air raid had caught him out in the open and he didn't want to miss this one chance to witness history. Damn!

Ignoring another shout from the warden Roland pushed off toward home, looking alternately from the road to the sky above. As he cycled, the noises of the engines grew steadily louder – a combination of the menacing snarl of the Rolls Royce engines in the Spitfires, the heavy throbbing of the massed German bombers and the high rasping note of the Messerschmitt 109-Es which flew escort duty for the pack.

The sky became black with planes as both sides maneuvered for advantage in a deadly aerial ballet. Roland stopped again and let the bicycle rest in the roadway while he craned his neck and shielded his eyes from the sun. Not once did he consider that he was standing exposed in the street as the aircraft passed overhead . . . all he had eyes for were the elegant Spitfires as they darted in and out of the bomber pack, evading the attempts of the Messerschmitts to protect their charges. Roland knew how unfair the battle was to the Germans and reveled in it. The Spitfires could freewheel all over the sky but the Messerschmitts had to preserve their scanty fuel ration. Half of them would probably run dry on the way home anyway and be forced to ditch. With this kind of patchy protection the bombers had to move on to London as best they could. Even as Roland watched, smoke poured from stricken bombers as the raiding party crossed the coastline and pressed inland.

Roland fixed his gaze on a lone Spitfire as it bore down on a trailing bomber, a Heinkel 111-H. The Heinkels were antiques, first flown in the Spanish Civil War. Now they were hopelessly outdated, no matter what modifications had been made. Like a lioness separating its prey from the herd, the Spitfire forced the Heinkel away from the main body of bombers. At less than a thousand feet the two planes roared past Roland, who stood with his arms above his head, fists clenched in victory as bullets from the Spitfire's eight machine guns fired into the bombers's port wing. The Heinkel's port engine gushed thick black smoke, then flames poured out as the battle continued southward toward the area of town where Roland's family lived. How his family would envy him, he thought. They were stuck safely in the cellar while he was enjoying a grandstand view of the Heinkel's last moments.

Still pursued relentlessly by the fighter, the Heinkel dropped lower and lower until at last Roland lost sight of it altogether. All he could see was the Spitfire. Moments later there was a thunderous explosion. Even from where Roland stood, a mile and half away, he could feel the ground shudder. The Heinkel was down!

He picked up his bicycle, prepared to continue the journey home. Then suddenly he saw the Heinkel reappear, climbing by some miracle, its port engine ablaze, heading groggily out to sea with the Spitfire still on its tail.

Panic froze Roland where he stood. What had exploded?

And where?

In that fraction of a second Roland's excitement turned into fear and a numbing certainty that filled him with dread. He started pedaling as fast as he could toward home. Ahead of him a pall of gray smoke rose into the air. It spoiled what was otherwise a clear blue sky, pinpointing – Roland was certain of it – the exact location of his family's home. Tears filled his eyes. His heart pounded and his lungs felt ready to burst. He tore blindly across street intersections, ignoring red lights and traffic. When he arrived he vaulted off the bicycle before it had even come to a stop. The street was already blocked by fire engines and ambulances. A dozen houses were in flames, and huge craters pitted the street where the Heinkel's bombs had fallen. Clouds of steam rose to mix with smoke as water from hoses evaporated in the heat. Roland ran toward the inferno that had once been his family's home, but his desperate attempt to reach his family was stopped by the strong grip of a fireman.

It didn't matter to Roland that the crew of the crippled Heinkel had held no personal animosity toward his family, that the bomber's original target had been the East End of London, that the Heinnkel had only emptied its bomb racks in its need to quickly shed weght. With one engine on fire, jettisoning the bombs was its only slim hope of escape. It had also proven to be a futile one . . . The next burst from the Spitfire had ripped through the bomber's cockpit, sending the Heinkel swaying drunkenly over the beach to crash into the sea. Roland cared for none of this . . . all he knew was that his family was gone

40

. . . that as he had stood staring at the blaze, caught in the realization that the warmth and affection they had always shared – the love – was gone. For the first time in his life he was totally alone, not even considering that had he not been detained at school, had he not stood gaping at the aerial battle, he, too, might be dead.

Roland spent the entire night at the bombsite, watching as the firemen and rescue workers cleared enough of the rubble to bring out the bodies. His face streaked with tears, he forced himself to look at the broken bodies of his parents, his brother and sister. Before they could be loaded into an ambulance, Roland removed the identical gold wedding bands from the remarkably unscathed hands of his parents. He slipped his father's ring onto the middle finger of his right hand and pressed his mother's, much smaller, onto his little finger.

The following morning, hollow-eyed from grief and lack of sleep, Roland went to the post office and closed out his account of racing winnings. In the afternoon he attended the funeral services for his family at the local Catholic church, strengthened by the attempts of aunts and uncles from his mother's side to console him. As the priest searched for comforting words, Roland caught himself wondering if anyone would ever tell his father's family what had happened. As he followed the caskets to the cemetery he experienced a wistfulness that his father's family would probably never know; then he felt resentment, a deep, burning hatred growing inside him. They *should* never know. They didn't deserve to know, not after the way they had treated his father.

Roland watched as the coffins were lowered into the ground, the priest's final words breaking the silence. He took a spade and shoveled earth onto the coffins containing his mother, brother and sister. By his father's coffin he stopped, reached into his pocket and dropped the good luck charm into the grave, following it quickly with earth.

When he straightened up and looked around, he saw that no one had noticed his surreptitious act.

Later that day, after having evaded his relatives' well-intentioned questions about his plans, Roland traveled by train to London. He spent the night on the platform of an underground station where hundreds of Londoners sought refuge from the Blitz. No sound of the battle penetrated into the bowels of the earth where Roland lay on a cold, stone platform, but anger kept his own vengeful visions alive. While those around him sang Vera Lynn songs to buoy their spirits, Roland imagined German bombers trapped in searchlight beams, unable to escape the piercing columns of white light. In his mind he saw bursts of anti-aircraft fire, followed by the planes plunging to earth in a trail of blazing debris, their crews trapped inside to suffer the same fiery death his own family had known.

At five in the morning, on the dawn of his sixeenth birthday, Roland emerged from the underground station. While his companions of the night returned to their homes, Roland wandered around the heart of the city. It occurred to him that he should return to Margate . . . his family's affairs needed to be put in order, and his mother's family would be anxious to know his whereabouts. But something even more pressing urged him to ignore these responsibilities – above all he wanted revenge; everything else could wait.

At nine o'clock he entered a menswear shop and bought a brown, Prince of Wales checked sportcoat to replace his school blazer, which he rolled into a bundle and dropped into a garbage can. Next he walked into an army recruiting office to volunteer. He lied about his age by adding two years and hoped that his above-average height would convince the recruiting officer that he was eligible. The officer looked over the boy who stood in front of him and asked for a birth certificate. When Roland replied that he didn't have one, the officer asked for a letter from his parents to verify his age. Roland countered by saying his parents had died two days earlier in an air raid. The officer asked about schooling. Roland, in keeping with his claim that he was eighteen, replied that he had just passed his A-levels and was about to begin accountancy articles. When the officer asked if he wanted to join the Pay Corps, Roland shook his head fiercely. He wanted to join the infantry.

The recruiting officer regarded Roland thoughtfully. Despite the boy's obvious fatigue, his eyes reflected a steely determination. Perhaps he was telling the truth, perhaps not. But if he was rejected here he would continue trying until he found a recruiting office that would accept him. Here was a boy who refused to let the grass grow under his feet. His family was barely cold in the grave and he was ready to wipe out the entire German nation in revenge.

Two weeks, the recruiting officer decided as he began to write down the necessary information. Two weeks in action and this Roland Eagles would become either a hero to King and country, or another fatality . . .

'No, I never gave a second thought to what my old man was until I came to this damned place,' Roland said to Sergeant Goldstein, aware that he was repeating himself. He paused to light a cigarette, using the time to collect his thoughts, uncertain now why he had even broached the subject. Of course, to show that he was just as concerned as Goldstein about the survivors in the camp. 'My father changed his name when he converted to Catholicism and married my mother. At least, I assume he converted. I buried him with the rest of my family in a Catholic cemetery, after a German bomb hit our house. No one seemed to object. He never had much time for religion, though – I guess I picked that up from him – but just to be on the safe side I dropped one of those good luck pieces into his grave.' He closed his eyes for a few seconds as the dismal scene came to mind. He quickly shook the memory and saw that Goldstein was staring at him. 'You know what I mean, sergeant – what do you call them, the things Jews nail on doorframes?'

'A *mezzuzah*, sir?'

'That's the word. My father gave it to me years earlier and I'd hidden it away for luck. It's odd, but the night before my family was killed, I'd dug it out and carried it around with me the next day. Not only did I live while they died, but earlier that same day I'd won twelve pounds ten from a local bookie on a five-shilling win double. Biggest single win I'd ever had.' Roland paused, reflecting on how fate – if you could call it that – had spared him.

'Why did your father change his name, sir?'

'A symbolic gesture.' As he answered, Roland again felt the same mixture of wistfulness and resentment about his father's family, just as he had on the day of the funerals. 'He cut himself off from his family after he married my mother – they acted like he didn't exist. I never knew any of them – this all happened long before I was born – but my father told me about it when he thought I was old enough to understand. He wouldn't admit it, of course, but it broke his heart, what they did to him. I don't think they even know he's dead, or that I exist. They never cared enough to find out anything once he'd decided to marry my mother, and I believe that's the way he wanted it to the end.'

'That's rough, sir, but it's happened a lot of times. And both ways.'

'I know, but that doesn't make it any easier to accept.' More painful memories surfaced which Roland forced himself to fight back. 'I would appreciate it, sergeant, if what I just told you goes no further than this room.'

'You have my word, sir.' Goldstein said and thought he knew why. It was one thing for the captain to confide in him to demonstrate his concerns. It was another matter

44

entirely if he'd given any thought to making the military his career; then his background could be a hindrance.

'Thank you. Believe me, there's nothing I'd like better than to put a bullet between this SS bastard's eyes,' Roland said, remembering the prisoner outside. 'But what if he is telling the truth?'

'What? That he joined the SS to protect his own family and work against the Nazis?' Goldstein's cynical chuckle revealed exactly what he thought of Roland's question.

'Stranger things have happened.' Still, why should he even think of giving a German the benefit of the doubt? Roland asked himself. All he had to do was recall that September day in 1940 to remember how generous the Germans could be . . . or to think of what he'd witnessed at Bergen-Belsen itself. Yet there was a quality about Heinrich Kassler which set him apart; something which Roland couldn't quite name. The man had been unafraid to talk about his membership in the SS and his reason for joining. The acts of mercy he claimed to have performed within the camp could be easily checked . . .

'Lets confront Kassler with some of the camp inmates, sergeant. If they don't rip him to pieces then we'll know he might be telling the truth.'

'I'll fetch a few, sir.' Goldstein saluted and left.

Roland called for Kassler to be brought back in. The German officer stood at attention for five minutes until Goldstein returned with two young men whose frail bodies and wizened faces made them look three times their age. All of the camp uniforms had been burned, and the two inmates wore British uniforms without rank or insignia. Roland thought they looked like a ghastly parody of a recruiting poster.

'Do you know this man?' he asked through Goldstein.

Both men nodded as they stared at Kassler; the German returned their gaze calmly.

'Who is he?'

'*Kapitan* Kassler.'

45

'He was a member of the SS assigned to this camp?'

'Yes.'

'Did he ever mistreat you?'

'No.'

'Did you ever witness him mistreat anyone?'

'No. *Kapitan* Kassler was a decent man. Whenever possible he treated us well.'

'In what manner?'

'When he was in charge of work details it would be his responsibility to report any prisoner who was too ill to work.'

'What would happen then?'

'The prisoner would be . . .' The inmate stopped in mid-sentence; the words were unnecessary.

'What did Captain Kassler do that was so fair?'

'He devised methods to let sick men rest. He falsified the *Appel* so that men missing because they were ill would be accounted for. Sometimes he managed to arrange for extra food rations by diverting food from the guards. He saved many of our lives at risk to his own.'

Roland leaned back in his chair and thought about the war, from that moment when his family had died to this very instant, apparently confronted by a German officer who had managed to perpetrate a little good amidst the unconscionable filth. He looked at Kassler, still at attention, flanked by the two British soldiers in their tin hats. Was it possible? His gaze fell on the two inmates, and he couldn't help but wonder what the future held for such human tragedies. And Sergeant Goldstein, who stood by the desk awaiting orders . . . what did he think of the German officer now? Did he still want to borrow the Webley? 'Sergeant, see if there are any inmates who are willing to sign affidavits about Captain Kassler's behavior. When you've done that, arrange for him to be escorted to headquarters. Intelligence will be interested in his story; we'll see if he can be of any help to them.'

As the escort about-faced, Kassler saluted; not the Nazi straight arm but a military salute, right hand brought up crisply to the forehead. Roland returned the salute and was surprised to see Kassler offer his hand. 'I hope that we might meet again, Captain' – Kassler glanced quickly at the makeshift nameplate on the desk – 'Eagles. I am sure that in years to come we will both treasure this moment as an instant of sanity in a world gone mad.'

Roland stared at the outstretched hand, hesitated. Finally, wearily, he grasped Kassler's hand. His hatred had brought him here, but now it was slowly burning itself out. Here, in Bergen-Belsen, it was time to think about putting his rage to rest. Time to consider how to pick up the pieces of his life, if it were possible . . .

When the European war finished, Roland's unit was still at Bergen-Belsen, its role changed from one of combat to administration. While other soldiers complained about the duty, wanting to be home with their families, Roland made the camp his home. Off-duty, he took it upon himself to work with the Red Cross on behalf of survivors searching for relatives who had been at Auschwitz and the other camps. He wrote letters for those who had relatives in the United States, and for others he tried to get the paperwork started for entry visas. While on duty, he deliberately turned his back when groups of young inmates, mostly Russian, wandered from the camp to plunder nearby German villages. As far as Roland was concerned, they were entitled to anything they could take from the country which had been their barbaric host.

In August, when the war in the Far East ended, Roland's company was transferred to Berlin as part of the British garrison. He spent his twenty-first birthday the following month walking around the allied sector, inspecting the bombed-out hulks of the once proud city. Although his hatred for Germany had dimmed since he'd met Heinrich

Kassler five months earlier, he couldn't help but feel a sense of gratification, pleased that he had been responsible in some small way for the destruction. It was then that he realized how deep his emotional scars were. He wanted to harbor none of the self-destructive hatred that had consumed his father, but if he could find some degree of satisfaction in the wreckage of a country – no matter what the country had done to the world, to him personally – then he was suffering from a sickness that might take years to cure.

He thought about his father's family as well, the resentment he had felt toward them. Now, he didn't feel resentment as much as curiosity, because he realized at last that his father was to blame in part for the split. Not by marrying his mother – good Lord, no! – but because he had never made the slightest attempt to heal the rift. He had adopted a belligerently unforgiving attitude that made a reconciliation impossible. He'd never given them the opportunity to change their minds, nor did he try to win them over. No, by damn . . . he had resolved to be just as bigoted and full of hatred as they were.

Now that his father had been dead for five years. Roland wondered whether he could introduce himself to his father's family and finally mend the split? He wanted to. He was curious about them, about the kind of people they were. He was no longer content to see them through his father's twisted perspective; he needed to see them for himself.

Although he knew their names, knew where they lived, he didn't intend to simply knock on their doors and explain who he was – that would be like an outcast begging for admittance. Roland resolved that he would meet them one day – but he would do it with style.

He wanted, one day, to meet them as equals.

CHAPTER TWO

Roland remained in the army for another two years. He was eventually transferred from Berlin to Aldershot Barracks in the south of England, where he commanded training companies of young inductees doing national service. For the benefit of his superiors he announced his intention to make the military his career, but he was honest enough with himself to know that the uniform provided an easy, if temporary escape from responsibility. He knew that one day he would have to make a decision about his life, but he didn't yet feel pressured by time . . . too much had happened to him during the war and he felt entitled to the rest. A commission in the peacetime army was a comfortable way of life, and after years of frontline service, Roland was learning to enjoy comfort.

In the early autumn of 1947, at a regimental dinner in the officers' mess, Roland's complacency was jolted sharply enough to force him into a decision. After the dinner, he stood to propose the loyal toast to King George the Sixth, an honor bestowed upon him by Colonel Milburn, the regimental commander. Following the toast, permission was given to smoke. After pipes and cigarettes were lit, Colonel Milburn – a trim, wiry-haired Scot with a pencil-thin moustache – rapped on the table for attention.

'Gentlemen, I have news which you will be delighted to hear, I know you're all fed up to the teeth with training duties, that you all would like to get back to the real work of the military. Well . . .' he paused, knowing he had their full attention, '. . . when the current training cycles are over, that's what we'll be doing. The entire regiment is being posted to Palestine. They've found out they can't do without us over there, and we're going to show them how to keep the peace.'

The men greeted Milburn's announcement with an enthusiastic round of applause, except for Roland, who clapped politely. He had always known he might be transferred to Palestine, but as time had passed the odds of it happening had grown longer. He'd gradually allowed himself to believe that the British would be out of Palestine before he could be sent there . . .

'Something wrong, Eagles?' a major sitting on his right asked. 'You look like you've lost a pound and found sixpence.'

'I'm all right. Just a bit stuffy in here.' He looked back to Colonel Milburn, who was speaking again.

'Gentlemen, I give you the toast – the finest regiment in the finest army in the world. That's why we've been chosen for Palestine.'

Roland waited for the excitement to abate before excusing himself and going over to where Colonel Milburn sat. 'Sir, could I have a word with you please?'

'Now? Is it so important?'

'I think so, sir.'

'Very well.' The colonel rose from the table and followed Roland outside. 'What is it?'

'I wish to resign my commission, sir.'

'You wish to *what*?' The colonel was so shocked that he never even wondered why Roland had chosen to break such news at a regimental dinner. Roland was the finest junior officer they had. His efficiency reports were impeccable, his companies always had the highest training scores. Most of the other junior officers were young, inexperienced, doing their national service the same as the men they commanded. Roland had served brilliantly, he was a hero, for God's sake. Why would he even consider resigning? 'You've been in the army seven years, Eagles. Outstanding service. Doesn't that mean a thing to you?'

'Sir, they were seven of the proudest years of my life.'

'Then what brings this on?'

'Your announcement inside, sir. Going to Palestine. I consider reprehensible the idea of going over there and continuing under a Union Jack what the Germans tried to do under a swastika.'

The colonel glared at his subordinate. 'You're acting like a sentimental fool, Eagles. Damned disloyal, too. Do yourself a favor by forgetting this ridiculous idea. Go over there, keep the Arabs and the Jews from tearing out each other's throats until we're out of that infernal place and you'll be well on your way to your majority. You're a young man, you've got a wonderful career to look forward to in the army. I wouldn't even be surprised if you've got a brigadier's baton tucked away in your knapsack. Don't turn your back on all of it.'

It was as if Milburn hadn't uttered a single word. 'I'll have my letter of resignation for you in the morning, sir.'

'You do that, damn you!' Milburn watched as Roland turned and walked away, his lips stretched in a thin, angry line. And to think he'd given him the honor of toasting the King!

Promptly at seven-thirty the following morning, Roland presented himself to Colonel Milburn, saluted sharply and handed over a sheet of paper on which he had written his resignation request. Milburn took the document, glanced over it. 'You're an idiot, Eagles. That's all I've got to say to you.'

'Yes, sir.' Roland saluted again and prepared to leave.

'Not so fast. I want to know why you're resigning.'

'I told you last night, sir.'

'Now tell me the remainder of it. I think I'm entitled to know that much.' Milburn picked up a folder which lay on the desk in front of him. 'I went through your records

51

last night. There is nothing in them that connects with this decision. It doesn't make any sense.'

'Sir, there is one piece of information missing from those records. My parents are both listed as Catholics, the same as myself. My father, in fact, was a Jew. What I saw in those camps won't allow me to forget that fact.'

'I see. Do you think that makes any difference? You're still a soldier, you still obey orders. Or are you hoping that I'll have your orders changed now that I know your reason for not wanting to go to Palestine?'

'No, sir. I would never expect you to.'

'Good. Because I have no intention of doing so. If you want to throw away a promising career because you're having what you think is an attack of conscience, that's your privilege. And if you need a clean conscience that badly, you can damned well pay the price.' Milburn read the letter of resignation again. 'Have you given any thought to what you'll do on civvy street?'

Roland had asked himself the same question all night long. He would be starting from scratch, but he wasn't about to let Milburn know he harbored any reservations. 'No doubt I'll be able to find some kind of business to interest me, sir.'

'Very sure of yourself, aren't you? How about money? How are you set up?'

Roland was surprised at the turn of the conversation. He had expected nothing more than a curt interview, yet now Milburn seemed genuinely interested in his plans. 'I'm adequately funded, sir.'

'Not from your army pay, you can't be. Your mess bills are among the biggest I've ever seen.'

Roland held back a smile at this remark. During his time at Aldershot he had hosted some of the biggest parties the base had ever known. He liked parties and he liked his friends to share them. 'I've had some luck, sir.'

'Your racetrack outings and your card games?' Milburn asked, aware of Roland's fondness for gambling, which hadn't diminished over the years. 'You've become quite a legend at Aldershot, but even your good fortune can't have made you that rich.'

'I've also been moderately successful in the stock market, sir. I had an inheritance to safeguard.' Roland had carefully invested the entire family legacy in chemical and engineering companies and estimated himself to be worth a little more than fifteen thousand pounds, a very tidy sum. He could have made even more, he thought wryly, recalling the letter he had received almost two years earlier from Sergeant Goldstein. Once out of the army, Goldstein began collaborating on a book about the relief of the camp and had wanted Roland's help. Roland had never replied, feeling irritated that anyone should profit financially from the ordeal. His own lack of interest had made no difference. The book was published in the spring of 1947 and, as far as Roland could ascertain, was moderately successful. Although he had never read it he had been told that he was mentioned, praised by Goldstein for his swift action to ease the suffering.

'I still think you're a fool, Eagles, although I can understand now why you're doing it. You've got courage, I'll say that for you, giving up everything for a principle. I'll get the paperwork started but maybe you'll come to your senses before it's too late.'

'Thank you, sir, but I don't think I'll change my mind.'

'No, I don't think you will.' Milburn returned Roland's salute with a perfunctory nod. Perhaps it was just as well, he decided as the door swung closed behind Eagles. The army had no place for an officer who questioned his government's policies. Just as it had no place for an officer who, he'd just noted, wore two gold wedding bands on his right hand when he wasn't even married.

In early November, as one of the most bitter winters in British history began, Roland put on his uniform and captain's pips for the final time and took a taxi from the

53

army base to Aldershot Station where he could catch a train to London.

The first-class coach he entered was occupied by one other passenger, a woman in her mid-twenties with long auburn hair, wearing fur-lined brown boots and a dark green coat that almost matched the green of her eyes. She glanced up from the book she was reading as Roland closed the door and placed his leather suitcase and coat in the overhead rack. The annoyance that glinted in her eyes on first noticing the uniform turned to interest when she realized that her fellow traveler was a tall, imposing-looking captain.

'Going on a well-deserved leave?' the woman asked conversationally as Roland settled into a window seat.

'A well-deserved permanent leave,' Roland answered, setting aside the copy of *The Times* he had been about to read. 'I just severed my association with the army.'

'How long were you in for?' The woman had a soft yet assertive voice which asked questions in a manner which, while demanding answers, caused no offense.

'Two months over seven years.' A whistle sounded; the train belched steam and jerked into motion. Roland glanced out the window to bid farewell to Aldershot and the army.

'That's a long time, must be quite a wrench.' The woman leaned forward to study the ribbons on Roland's jacket. 'Excuse my curiosity, but is that the Military Cross *and* the Military Medal?'

'I came up through the ranks, got the opportunity to be a hero as both an enlisted man and an officer.' Roland felt quite flattered that she had recognized the decorations. 'For a woman you've got an excellent eye for ribbons.'

'I should have,' she said, smiling warmly. 'My husband was in the army.'

'Was? He resigned?'

'No. He died at Arnhem, a lieutenant in the paratroopers.'

'I'm sorry.'

'So am I. We were only married three months. When he was first drafted he was a mild-mannered man. But the army changed all that – he suddenly got smitten with the glory of it all. By the time we were married, just after D-Day, he was completely different . . . totally wrapped up in the military.'

'So what did you do?'

'Me? I continued his war effort the only way I knew how, by covering the war from a woman's angle – human interest stories, articles to boost the morale on the home front.'

'Journalist?'

'Sorry, I should have introduced myself. Sally Roberts, *London Evening Mercury*.'

'Roland Eagles, civilian,' Roland countered, and they both laughed. Roland knew the *Mercury* well. Although it didn't have the massive circulation of the *Star* or the *News*, it was a highly respected newspaper. Roland's regard for it came not from its liberal platforms but from its racing coverage; the *Mercury's* tipsters were among the best in their field.

'Might I be terribly nosy and ask why you're getting out?' Sally asked. 'Seven years seems such a peculiar number.'

'It was time, as simple as that.' He offered her a cigarette from a gold case and held out a matching lighter. 'What are you doing out here? Big story?'

'No, it's my day off. I'm visiting my family on their farm near Aldershot.' She accepted the light and gazed at his right hand. 'Why do you wear two identical gold rings? Two wives? That's against the law, you know.'

Roland looked down at the rings and explained their significance to Sally. She asked him again why he had chosen to resign when he had and, as the train rolled steadily toward London, he began to talk easily, barely realizing he was being interviewed in a skillful, sympathetic fashion. Sally seemed especially interested to learn that he had been part of the British force at Bergen-Belsen and questioned him extensively about the camp. As he related his conversations with survivors, his desire to help them, he understood that this was the first time he had ever spoken at length with anyone about the concentration camp. It was like washing his soul clean, shedding the last vestiges of horror that remained. Suddenly he was grateful that he had chosen this particular day to leave the army, had caught this train, had entered this very compartment.

For Roland the short journey was over too soon. At Waterloo Station he parted company with Sally, but not before writing down her address in Hampstead and telephone number. From the station he took a taxi to a small hotel off Leicester Square where he had stayed frequently during weekend trips to London. He checked in for a week, estimating that to be enough time to get settled. After unpacking he dialed the number Sally had given him.

'I didn't expect to hear from you quite so soon,' she said. 'I just got in the door, haven't even had time to take my coat off, and the phone was ringing off the hook.'

Roland grinned at his timing. 'I find myself with a night in London, my very first night as a civilian, and nothing planned to celebrate it. How about helping me out?'

'I thought you were looking for somewhere to live.'

'That can wait until tomorrow. Will you have dinner with me?'

Sally smiled. All the way home from Waterloo Station she'd been hoping he would call her. 'I'd love to.'

Roland offered to pick her up at seven-thirty. Sally suggested that since she had a car, she could come into town and save him the bother of traveling out to Hampstead. Attracted by the idea of being driven around, Roland accepted immediately.

Precisely at seven-thirty, a red prewar MG pulled up outside the hotel where Roland waited, snuggled against the chill in a bulky sheepskin coat. He had to bend almost double to get in, finding it difficult to maneuver his six-foot-two frame into the sports car. Sally waited for him to get comfortable before she sped away, changing gears with a swift dexterity that Roland couldn't help envying.

'You drive as well as a man.'

She flashed him a quick, angry look. 'Don't you mean that some men drive as well as I do?' Before he had the chance to reply, she added, 'That's the second time you've made that comparison. You mentioned on the train that I had an excellent eye for ribbons – for a woman. Don't tell me you're one of those unenlightened buggers who believes that a woman belongs in the kitchen, Roland Eagles. I thought the war finally put that Neanderthal philosophy to rest for good.'

Roland gave himself a mental kick. Damn it – he *did* think that way, but so did every career army officer – it went with the uniform. Men fought the wars and women stayed home. Well, he reminded himself, he wasn't an army officer anymore. It was time to change. 'You're perfectly right,' he said. 'Some men drive as well as you do. I apologize.'

'Accepted.'

'Where are we going?'

'To a tiny restaurant in Bayswater which does gastronomical wonders with the little food tthe government allows.' She double-declutched from fourth to third and acelerated past a line of slower traffic along Regent Street. Roland caught a glimpse of the Cafe Royal on the right and Adler's department store to the left. 'Or do you have any better ideas?'

Roland confessed that he did not and allowed himself to be led. After so many years in command it might make for a pleasant change . . . Besides, Sally was unlike any woman he had dated while in the army. The others had all been thrilled by military tradition. He sensed that Sally didn't give a damn for it.

In Bayswater, she pulled up outside a dimly lit restaurant called Antoine's and led the way inside. It was a family establishment where the middle-aged French owner and his wife acted as both cooks and waiters. From the way they fussed over Sally, Roland could see that she was a regular customer. With a faint twinge of envy he wondered how many other men had been there with her.

'What do you recommend?' he asked once they were seated at a cozy corner table. A candle set in a wall bracket above the table sent shadows flickering across her face.

'Everything. Just make sure you don't leave a scrap. With decent food being so scarce these days, Antoine gets very upset to see it wasted.'

'Don't worry. I've been told that I'm a voracious eater.' Roland was true to his word. He left neither a drop of the onion soup, a crumb of the home-baked rolls, nor a sliver of the chicken cordon bleu. And while Sally struggled to match his hectic eating pace, he eyed her plate and deftly picked off a slice of veal.

Sally was wide-eyed with amazement. 'Is it your habit to take food from other people's plates?'

'Only when it appeals to me,' he answered with a quick, infectious grin. 'Really, this is very good, you should try some,' he added, helping himself to another slice.

Sally surrendered the battle, setting down her knife and fork and allowing Roland to finish her meal; she had eaten enough already. 'Would you like to order your own dessert, or should I order two servings and two forks – both for you?'

'Would you believe that during the first week in

Bergen-Belsen I lost ten pounds? That place made me so sick I couldn't eat a thing.'

'I do believe you.' She reached across the table to clasp his hand, welcoming the streak of compassion she sensed in him. It was an odd trait, she thought. If anything the army usually hardened a man, not softened him . . . She studied him in the unsteady light of the candle. Even though he was relaxed, his face reflected a sadness as if it mirrored the tragedies he had witnessed. Despite the sharpness of his blue eyes there was also a warmth and an easy familiarity about him that made Sally feel she'd known this man for much longer than she had.

'What would you have done if you hadn't called me, Roland? Or if I'd been busy? Or if we hadn't even met?'

'Probably gone to bed with a book and spent the night wondering whether I'd done the right thing by leaving the army. That's why I'm exceptionally glad I caught that train.'

Sally was surprised to find herself blushing, not something she did with any frequency. Even the soldiers she had interviewed at the front with their unintentional vulgarities had never caused her face to redden. 'Thank you. And as far as I'm concerned, I think you did make the right decision.'

They left the restaurant a short time later and returned to the hotel. As they walked hand-in-hand through the lobby toward the stairs, the night clerk gave them no more than a passing glance, lifting his head from his newspaper just long enough to recognize Roland.

'Who's the picture of?' Sally asked as Roland turned on the light and closed the door. She pointed to a small framed snapshot on the mantelpiece and walked across for a closer look.

'A family picture taken in the summer of 1940. It was only a few weeks before . . . before I lost them.'

'Where are you?' Sally scanned the photo, seeking a

younger version of the handsome, articulate man who had taken her to dinner.

'Someone had to press the button.'

'Oh, I see.' His casual reply made her laugh, but as she turned away from the mantelpiece she felt a momentary awkwardness at causing Roland's memory to wander down an unwelcome avenue. She quickly searched for a way to lighten the mood, to bring their relationship back to the bright footing it had enjoyed before. 'And there you are, in all your fearsome glory,' she said, picking up a larger photograph from the chest of drawers. 'Why do you display a picture of yourself in uniform? Could it be vanity to complement your healthy appetite?'

'Just to remind myself of what I was, I suppose.' He took the photograph – taken a year earlier at Aldershot – from her and studied it. Was it just an unflattering pose or did he really look that old, the hair starting to thin at the front, gray showing around the temples, lines at the mouth. God, he thought, where had youth gone? And what would this woman think if she knew his true age?

'How old do you think I am?' The question flew from his lips before he realized what he was saying.

'About twenty-eight, thirty maybe,' Sally answered as she removed her coat.

'Try twenty-three.'

'Are you serious?'

'Never more so.'

She stood in the center of the room, coat trailing from her hand, staring at him. Perhaps she had made a mistake, but surely not by that much. 'Twenty-three? You told me you were in the army for a little over seven years. How old were you—?'

'I enlisted on my sixteenth birthday. I lied about my age.'

'Right after your family was killed?'

He nodded. 'Some birthday present, eh?'

She folded her coat across the back of a chair, walked

toward him, stood on tiptoe and wrapped her arms tightly around him. As he bent to kiss her he noticed the faintest trace of garlic, but instead of repelling him it was like an aphrodisiac; the taste and smell of a healthy, beautiful woman who had just dined well and now yearned to satisfy another, deeper hunger.

'Somewhere inside this slightly older woman, Roland Eagles, is a tiny voice crying out that I should feel like a cradle snatcher. But I don't. Why?'

'You tell me.' His hands slid down her back until they rested on her buttocks; as he drew her closer he could feel her thigh pressing gently between his legs.

'Maybe it's because you're by far the most mature twenty-three-year-old man I've ever met. Is that why you asked me how old I thought you were? Is that what your vanity wanted to hear?'

'Is vanity such a sin?' Roland had never considered himself vain, but if Sally wanted to label him as such he'd play along.

'That would depend on whether you've got anything to be vain about,' she said, then kissed him passionately, forcing his lips to open with her tongue. Slowly she drew back. 'And I think I'm most capable of judging that.'

Roland awoke just after seven the following morning, momentarily disoriented as he tried to identify the unfamiliar surroundings. At last he remembered: he was out of the army. Today was his first full day as a civilian, the beginning of a new life. On his last day as a civilian, he had been a fifteen-year-old boy burying his family; now he was a twenty-three-year-old man who had put the past firmly behind him.

The sound of movement from the bathroom startled him until he remembered Sally Roberts as well. He turned his face into the pillow and breathed in a faint but tantalizing trace of her perfume. He buried his face in it and relived for an instant the previous night.

'Are you getting up or are you going to stay in bed all day?'

So engrossed was he in his thoughts that he hadn't even heard Sally's footsteps as she returned from the bathroom. He lifted his head and saw her standing by the bed, wearing his red silk dressing gown. His eyes wandered over the contours of her body where the flimsy gown clung to her, then up to her face. The green eyes no longer flowed with the passion of last night; now, as they regarded Roland lying in bed, they were serene.

'Where are you off to so early?' he asked.'

'Some of us have jobs to go to. What about you?'

'I'll get up soon.'

'Must be nice to be idle.' She dressed, slipped on her coat and leaned over the bed to kiss him tenderly on the forehead. 'Telephone me when you've got a place of your own, Roland Eágles. I'm afraid that having a night clerk look me up and down, no matter how tactfully he does it, makes me feel cheap.'

Roland watched the door swing shut behind her, closed his eyes and went back to sleep. When he awoke forty minutes later, the first thing he noticed was that the portrait photograph was no longer on the chest of drawers. He felt flattered that Sally would want such a memento.

Roland found a place to live that day, a cheery, well furnished, two-bedroom flat close to Regent's Park, just a few minutes from Baker Street. It afforded him the best of both worlds: a view of the park, enough to let him feel he was in the country, while at the same time he could be in the center of London in little more time than it took to hail a taxi. He paid the first month's rent and arranged to move in at the end of the week. Feeling pleased with himself he went out for a leisurely dinner, then took a taxi back to the hotel. As he passed through the lobby the night clerk called him over.

'Have you seen this, Captain Eagles?' The man held out the late edition of that day's *Mercury*, and Roland could see immediately why Sally had taken the army portrait. He cursed himself for being foolish and egotistical enough – *vain* enough – to believe that she had only wanted a souvenir.

On the front page of the newspaper, under a two-line heading which read, 'Army Hero Resigns Over Palestine,' was the photograph and a six-paragraph story about Roland leaving the army because he disagreed with British policy in Palestine. Also included in the piece was biographical information about his decorations and how he had lied about his age to enlist. The article ended by mentioning the fact that an army spokesman had no comment to make. The byline of course, was that of Sally Roberts. Angrily, he flipped through the newspaper until he found the editorial columns. There he was again, used by the *Mercury's* editorial writers as the focus for an attack on the government's foreign policy. The editorial ended with, 'When our own decorated military men perceive the error in British action, why does our government remain so blind?'

'Let me use your telephone!' Before the night clerk could respond, Roland grabbed the receiver and dialed the number of the *Mercury*. When told Sally had left he slammed down the receiver and dialed her Hampstead number.

'You've got one hell of a damned nerve!' he yelled into the phone when she answered, disregarding the night clerk standing next to him. 'Do you realize I could press libel charges against you and your newspaper?'

'Libel?' Sally queried calmly. She had been expecting Roland's call for a couple of hours, ever since the late edition of the *Mercury* had gone onto the streets. 'I don't think libel enters into it, Roland. Every word in that story is true, just as you related it to me.'

Taken aback by Sally's composure, Roland calmed down slightly. 'All right then, how about theft?'

'Oh, Roland, do come on. I'm a journalist and I've got a living to make. You're good human interest copy.

Besides, it's not theft. I'll have the photograph returned to you. I only borrowed it to get a block made. I had no intention of keeping it.'

'Was that why you spent the night with me?' Roland shot a look at the clerk who, diplomatic man that he was, walked away. 'Did you do it for your precious story? So you could *borrow* the photograph?'

A long pause followed. For a moment Roland thought Sally had hung up. Finally she said, 'You really are only twenty-three, aren't you?'

'Just what is that supposed to mean?'

'Precisely what it sounds like. You're acting like a child.'

'A child? I've commanded men in combat . . . who the hell do you think you're calling a child?'

'Roland, do you think we could discuss this on a more personal level, say over dinner, before you burn out the entire London telephone system?' Sally's voiced remained infuriatingly level.

'I've already eaten, thank you. Besides, I've no idea what you'll take next.'

'I didn't mean tonight.'

'Well I did. Get that photograph back to me right now.' It sounded like an order he might have given to recalcitrant recruits.

'I've just run a bath, for God's sake.' Finally her voice showed animation.

'Then I suggest you empty it.' He hung up, not interested in her excuses.

'Are you finished, captain?' the night clerk asked, cautiously returning to his position.

A wave of embarrassment swept over Roland as he realized what a spectacle he had made of himself. 'Yes, thank you. This is for letting me use your telephone.' He offered the clerk a ten shilling note.

'Thank you very much, Captain Eagles.' The note disappeared into the man's pocket in a movement so swift

Roland had difficulty following it.

'*Mr Eagles*,' Roland muttered gruffly as he walked toward the stairs. 'Didn't you read the story?'

Sally Roberts arrived at the hotel shortly before eleven, but she wasn't alone. With her was a man in his late thirties with deep-set brown eyes, wavy black hair brushed back from his forehead and a well-trimmed Van Dyke. His tall, slender build was accentuated by the closely fitting beige cashmere coat he wore.

'Sorry I'm so late,' Sally greeted Roland as he opened the door to his room, 'but I had to go to Fleet Street and turn the blasted blockmakers upside down to retrieve your stupid photograph.' She thrust a large brown envelope at him with such force that he nearly dropped it. 'Now you can stop all this ridiculous nonsense about having me charged with theft and libel and God only knows what!'

'Were you so frightened to come by yourself, you had to bring a bodyguard?' Disappointment shaded Roland's taunt. He had hoped that when Sally arrived they could continue their lovemaking of the previous night and soothe their differences in bed.

The man with the Van Dyke gave a faint smile before speaking with a slight accent that Roland had difficulty identifying. 'I'm very flattered that I could be considered anyone's bodyguard, Mr Eagles. I am just someone who wanted to meet you.'

'Roland, this is Simon Aronson. He's a member of a political group which is trying to persuade the British government to ease its restrictions on refugees being allowed into Palestine. Simon, this is Roland Eagles – in between making threatening phone calls he steals food from other people's plates.'

Simon Aronson offered a hand which Roland took. 'We are very grateful for the stand you took, Mr Eagles. If the British public can see that even some of its military men are unhappy with the situation, perhaps the government will be forced to amend its rigid stance.'

Roland suddenly realized that his two visitors were standing in the doorway and invited them inside. 'What I did was not for public consumption, Mr Aronson. I did it because of my own moral convictions, not because I wished to become a pawn in some political chess game.'

'In these instances, personal feelings matter very little. Once you decide to take a stand on a controversial issue you no longer have the choice of how public a figure you become.' Simon looked around the room and sat down in an overstuffed armchair, carefully straightening the cashmere coat. 'Might I ask what your moral convictions are based upon?'

'Is this another interview, a follow-up story?'

'No.' Simon shook his head. 'Personal curiosity.'

Roland lit a cigarette while he thought about an answer. 'Seeing Bergen-Belsen, I suppose. Those poor devils were the responsibility of us all – not just the barbarians who put them there, but the rest of us who allowed such things to take place. And I guess the fact that I'm half-Jewish has a lot to do with it.'

'I didn't know that,' Sally said, obviously surprised.

Roland swung around to face her, unable to keep from grinning slightly. 'Are you upset that you didn't wheedle everything out of me?' She returned his question with a cold stare.

'Before the war it was never something I gave much thought to,' Roland said, turning back to Simon. 'Since Bergen-Belsen, though, I keep noticing little things that remind me – this Palestine business, overhearing people talking.'

'You've become sensitive to it. There is an old saying – and I hope Sally will forgive me for bringing it up – but a Jew should never worry if he forgets he is a Jew, because sooner or later a non-Jew will remind him.'

'Very apt.' Roland nodded in appreciation. 'But it still

doesn't ease my resentment about having my life spread over the front page of some cheap tabloid.'

'You can't blame me because you've had the kind of life that makes interesting reading,' Sally broke in, ignoring the remark about the *Mercury*. 'For a twenty-three-year-old you've achieved a remarkable amount.'

'Even if I did it in a remarkably childish manner?'

Sally could feel her face turning crimson. That was twice he had made her blush . . . 'I apologize for making that comment. Anyway,' she added quickly, anxious to get over the incident, 'the *Mercury* is a newspaper which believes the British government must act in a more humanitarian manner toward Jewish refugees who want to enter Palestine. Your action in resigning from the army was helpful to our case.'

'Is that the connection between you two? Palestine?'

Simon answered. 'Not quite. We – my family, that is – own the *Mercury*. We bought it a few years before the war. For us it's been a way to fight against the rise of fascism in this country.'

Roland laughed, 'I suppose I should feel somewhat flattered, the owner of the newspaper coming to see me as well as the suitably repentant reporter.'

'Repentant!' Sally exploded. 'Does your vanity know no bounds? What I did was for the greater good.'

'What else does your family do?' Roland asked Simon, now more interested in Sally's companion.

'We're in banking.' Simon said it quietly. 'Before the war we were solely in Paris—'

'Your accent, I was trying to place it.'

'French,' Simon acknowledged. 'Many Frenchmen believed that another war with Germany was impossible, even when Hitler came to power. My family didn't share this optimistic view. In 1934 we moved to Britain and set up our base of operations here. We're back in France now, but our main strength remains in London. What about yourself?'

'I'm looking to invest a sum of money. I want to study

67

the market first, though, get my bearings. Civilian life is different from the army. When I give an order here, no one listens.'

Simon laughed. 'It seems to have worked very well just now. Sally returned your photograph rather hastily.'

Roland turned to Sally, wondering whether she was still angry with him. 'I'm sorry I shouted at you over the phone, but seeing myself in the newspaper came as quite a shock.'

'You're right. I should have asked for the photograph, been more honest.'

'It's over with now, let's forget about it.'

Simon stood up and straightened his cashmere coat. 'I hate to break this up but my family is waiting for me. When you've decided what you want to do, please give me a call. There might be some way I can help you. Perhaps I can recompense you for any inconvenience you believe the story might have caused.' He handed Roland a business card with an address in the city. 'We're just off St Swithins' Lane.'

'Aronson Freres?'

'My great-great-grandfather and his brother.'

'I'll keep it in mind.'

'Please do.'

As his two visitors were leaving, Roland pulled Sally back. 'I need to know something about last night – did you stay here just because you wanted a story?'

Sally's face tightened and Roland expected another onslaught. Then she smiled, 'I could have written that piece from what you told me on the train, and I probably could have gotten a picture of you from the army information office. I spent the night with you because I wanted to. Can your suspicious mind believe that?' Without waiting for a reply, she kissed him on the cheek and walked quickly after Simon Aronson, who was already halfway down the stairs.

Roland remained in the doorway until he could no longer hear their footsteps. As he closed the door, he promised himself that in the future he would be very cautious if and when he ever had to deal with the press again . . .

Winter was vicious, the coldest Roland could remember with knee-high snow and icy winds, but it was of little concern to him. He was far too involved in learning how best to use his family inheritance to worry about the weather. He had no training in any particular profession, barring the accountancy basics he had learned from his father, and the military. No matter what he did he would have to start at the bottom. At twenty-three, Roland felt there wasn't time for that. He wanted to begin with a company of his own; that was the first step to meeting his father's family on equal terms.

He spent the following two months cooped up in the spare bedroom of the flat near Regent's Park, which he had turned into an office. He studied financial newspapers and magazines as he conducted his own crash course in business, researching those industries which seemed to have the most promising future in postwar Britain. In the beginning he ventured out only to eat, leaving the purchase of household necessities to the woman who came in twice a week to clean. Later, as his research progressed, he made appointments to see management people from the companies that interested him on the pretext that he had a considerable amount of money to invest. Little did they know that his sights were set much higher . . . he was going to buy one of them out.

Once or twice a week he saw Sally Roberts for dinner. Occasionally she would spend the night at his flat, and when she had gone he would diligently return to his work. The only break he took was on Christmas Day, when he attended a party Sally was giving to celebrate both the season and her promotion at the *Mercury* to editor of the women's page.

At the beginning of February, Roland made an appointment to see Simon Aronson.

Carrying a bulging briefcase, Roland followed a secretary through a maze of narrow paneled corridors to Simon's office in the bank, a square, compact room with beige carpet, furnished with a walnut desk, a low coffee table, a deep brown leather divan and two easy chairs. On his desk was a framed picture of his wife and two daughters. Two paintings, both of men with beards, hung from a picture rail. Roland spotted a family resemblance in the deeply set brown eyes and assumed from the clothes that they were Simon's father and grandfather.

'Mr Eagles, what a pleasure to see you again.' Simon rose from behind the desk and shook Roland's hand warmly. 'What can I do for you?'

'I was thinking along slightly different lines.'

'Oh?'

'Actually, I was wondering what I could do for you?'

Simon chuckled delightedly. Since their first meeting he had been looking forward to seeing the former army captain again. Despite the initial awkwardness of their earlier encounter, Simon had taken to Roland. Not because of his views regarding British policy in Palestine, but because Simon had sensed a positiveness – an unusually confident strength about the man. He had achieved a great deal for someone his age, even if his momentum had been assisted by the war, and Simon was certain that it would carry through in civilian life. The mere fact that he'd taken Simon up on the offer he'd made was proof of that.

'All right, what can you do for me?'

The question was answered with another question. 'What do you need doing?'

'The same as every other bank. We need profitable projects to invest our funds in. Sally tells me you've been working day and night on one. It shows, if you'll pardon my saying so. You have the coloring of a man who hasn't seen fresh air for a year.'

Although the remark was made lightly, Roland touched his face, suddenly aware of how pale he looked. The months spent in the flat poring over papers had taken their toll.

'Once I get my business off the ground I'll relax with a couple of weeks in the south of France.'

'Good, the words of a confident man.' Simon opened a desk drawer and reached inside. 'Do you play?' He asked, bringing out a backgammon board.

'I prefer poker,' Roland replied, holding back his surprise at the banker's suggestion.

'I don't keep cards in the office. This is for relaxation.' Simon set out the board on the coffee table and invited Roland to take one of the easy chairs.

'Is this how Aronson Freres normally conducts its business?'

'Would it bother you tremendously if it were?'

'No. It would just destroy a few of my cherished illusions about bankers.'

'That we're all a bunch of stuffed shirts?' Simon asked with amusement. He passed a die to Roland, who threw a six. Simon threw a one, and Roland took the move.

'I envy you your luck,' the banker said.

Roland grinned as he watched Simon play a three and a two. 'Wasn't it a compatriot of yours who said something about not wanting brilliant generals, only lucky ones?'

'Napoleon,' Simon acknowledged. 'I believe one of my ancestors financed his attempt to plant the *Tricouleur* in every corner of the world. Possibly not one of our wiser investments,' he added ruefully. 'All right, Roland – it is acceptable if I call you Roland, I hope – what do you intend to do that will benefit Aronson Freres?' He watched closely while Roland moved. 'Surely you would be better off covering your man, you are leaving him wide open.'

'A moment ago you envied my luck. I'm counting on it for you not to throw a one or a four.'

71

Simon threw a six and a three, and Roland covered the open man on his next move. 'Your luck is holding, Roland. Let me hear your proposal, please.'

'Four fields are doing well right now – engineering, motor cars, chemicals and pharmaceuticals. Soon there'll be a fifth – electrical goods. My research leads me to believe that there's going to be an absolute explosion of gadgets and appliances, first in the kitchen and then in the leisure areas. We're very slowly emerging from a period of austerity and people are going to want things. Christ, after what they've been through they're entitled to everything under the sun. That's the business in which I'm interested – electrical products.'

'What do you know about this particular business?'

'Only what I've learned in the last few months,' Roland said, 'but my main interest is in being able to read a balance sheet.'

'You have to be doing business before you need to read a balance sheet, Roland.' Simon pushed the men around automatically, unimpressed with what he had heard so far. Disappointed, too. He had expected something more adventurous, more in keeping with the way Roland played backgammon. Simon always liked to use the game as a means of judging a person's character, and Roland was an easy man to define – he had a strong sense of daring backed by an almost infallible belief in the power of his own luck. But now he seemed like just another prospective borrower, a man trying to persuade a bank to finance his dream. A dream which if it failed, would leave the bank to explain the loss to its shareholders. 'How do you hope to build this company?'

'Not from scratch, that's too long and laborious a task.'

'Acquisition?' Simon's interest increased a fraction.

Roland nodded. 'There's a company in Wembley, near the stadium, that's in receivership. Mar-Cross, Limited. It manufactures plugs, wall sockets, electrical fittings. It's a small, well-established firm that was rocky before the war. The war gave it a new lease on life when it manufactured under contract to other companies involved in government work. Now the business has dried up and it can't meet its obligations.' He opened the briefcase and took out a folder full of papers. 'Of all the companies I've been looking at over the past few months, this is by far and away the most promising. With the right management, the right new direction – and an injection of capital – I think it could be very profitable.'

'Bottom line, Roland. How much are we talking about?'

'Approximately fifty-five thousand pounds to buy Mar-Cross.'

'That is a considerable amount to pay for a bankrupt company just to begin with. How much will operating costs devour before the company is able to support itself? Assuming it will ever reach that point.'

Roland smiled to himself. He knew he had not broken through yet, but now he had him: 'Absolutely nothing. Not a single penny.'

'Nothing?' Something about Roland's expression arrested Simon's attention completely. He pushed the backgammon board aside, suddenly absorbed in what Roland had to say.

'Mar-Cross owns two tiny but quite profitable subsidiary companies in the Midlands. One manufactures leads and terminals for car batteries, the other makes insulation for heavy-duty cable. It's Mar-Cross itself which has dragged the whole thing down. I'm not interested in either of the subsidiary companies because I want to concentrate on products which will be used in the home. I've already contacted allied firms with an eye toward selling those two subsidiaries should I buy Mar-Cross. There's enough interest to make me optimistic.'

'Why don't these allied firms buy Mar-Cross and take control of the subsidiaries that way?' Simon asked, testing him.

'Large companies either don't have the time to do it in a roundabout manner like that or else they can't be bothered. If the companies are handed to them on a silver platter, however, they'll pay. I estimate that I'll be able to realize forty thousand pounds from the sale of those two subsidiaries, which will leave me – for an initial outlay of some fifteen thousand pounds – with a viable company ready for expansion. A company which, incidentally, owns the land in Wembley on which its factory stands. All the figures are in the presentation I've made. They're in that folder.'

'What kind of collateral will you be putting up? How much of your own money?'

'Everything I own, about fifteen thousand pounds' worth of stocks which I'll liquidate. And, of course, myself.'

Simon weighed the answer. 'I'm not certain that will be enough to persuade my board to back your venture. If the company went under because you went into a business which, as you say, you know very little about, what would we do with a mountain of plugs and electrical products?'

'You're forgetting the factory building and the land. Mar-Cross is worth more stripped and sold in separate packages than I'll pay for it.'

'Roland, Aronson Freres is a bank, not an estate agent or a factor. It deals in lending money to carefully assessed risks. It doesn't deal in land and electrical goods. That's how my board will see it when it considers your proposal.' He took the folder and leafed through the contents quickly, casting an experienced eye over the figures and data Roland had prepared. 'Leave it with me. Give me time to study this and I'll present it to my board at the earliest opportunity.'

'When do you think that will be?' No matter how hard he tried, Roland was unable to conceal his impatience.

'I've already put in an offer to the Official Receiver. It won't be good forever.'

'Thursday afternoon, two days from now.'

Roland closed the briefcase, which now felt light and unfamiliar. 'Simon, never mind about your fellow directors – what are your feelings?'

'I haven't had time to go through this yet.'

'Just as I've explained it to you.'

'All right, I like your thinking. If you did buy Mar-Cross, carved it up and sold it piecemeal you would probably show a quick profit on your original investment. There is something to be said for that kind of approach. But then, of course, you would not be a businessman; you would be a hatchet man. And I think you want to build, not take apart.'

'Will you support me?'

'I will support you. More than that, though, I cannot promise.'

Simon telephoned Roland shortly after four on Thursday afternoon, ten minutes after the meeting at the bank ended. But instead of telling him the board's decision, he invited him to his home for dinner that night. Roland, with a sinking sensation in the pit of his stomach, immediately knew what the bank had decided.

He arrived at Simon's three-story house in South Kensington at seven o'clock. A maid opened the door and led him through to the dining room where Simon sat playing backgammon with his two daughters on a corner of the table that was set for dinner with elegant silverware, crystal and china. On seeing his guest, Simon excused himself from the game.

'Welcome to my home. Miriam and Sharon have been looking forward to meeting you ever since I told them how well you play this game.'

'We never finished ours.'

'True, but the way we left it I would not have bet against you.' He introduced Roland to the girls: Sharon, the older at thirteen, had her father's slim build and deep brown eyes, with long black hair and a quick, spontaneous smile. As she formally shook Roland's hand, he had the premonition that in only a few years she would be breaking a lot of hearts. The younger of the two girls, Miriam, had hazel eyes and long blonde hair tied in braids. At ten, she still retained her puppy fat and showed no signs of her older sister's graceful manner. Roland couldn't help wondering if she was at all jealous of her older sister's blossoming beauty.

'Where's your wife?'

'Nadine? In the kitchen. No one else is allowed to cook but her, that's the one iron-clad rule of the house. I consider myself fortunate,' Simon said with a smile, 'that she allows me to make myself coffee when I work late.' Sensing Roland's anticipation he added, 'After dinner we can talk. I have a proposition which I think will be of interest to you.'

Simon's wife joined them a few minutes later, a dainty woman with an apron tied around her waist. Like her younger daughter, Nadine's hair was also blonde, cut short in a style that clung to her head like a cap, and her lively eyes were almost violet in color. Although she was tiny compared to her husband, Roland had little doubt it was she who organized the family. At the bank Simon might be a powerful director but here he did as he was told. And, Roland guessed, he would probably have it no other way. Considering his wife and two daughters, Roland thought, he couldn't blame him.

After dinner, Nadine allowed the girls to play one game of backgammon each with Roland, both of which he purposely lost, before telling them to say goodnight. Miriam dutifully kissed her father and mother, waved a quick farewell to Roland and disappeared upstairs. Sharon kissed her parents first, then stood solemnly in front of Roland.

'It was a pleasure to meet you, Mr Eagles. Please be our guest again.' Then, before Roland knew what was happening, she brought a blush to his face by leaning forward quickly and kissing him on the cheek.

'I think you made quite an impression,' Nadine laughed after Sharon had left the room.

'Throwing away the games didn't hurt your chances,' Simon joined in. 'I saw the way you played, making a liar out of me after I told them how good you were.'

'It was a tactful gesture,' Roland said good-naturedly.

'And it was appreciated,' Simon replied, then turned to his wife. 'If you will excuse us we're going into the drawing room to talk.'

'Of course.'

'I assume your bank turned me down,' Roland said when he sat down in the drawing room. It was more like a library, Roland thought. Books lined two of the room's walls. He looked around with interest, wondering if Simon ever found the time to read them, or were they just there for show? One complete section which had caught Roland's eye was devoted to legal volumes in both English and French.

'I qualified at the Bar in both France and England,' Simon offered, noticing his guest's interest.

'A sideline?'

'Not at all. I represent Aronson Freres. And you are perfectly right – Aronson Freres turned you down.'

'Any particular reason?' Roland asked, trying not to reveal his disappointment . . . it was one thing to guess that the bank had rejected his proposal; it was far worse to actually hear it.

'The general feeling was that you represented a risky investment because you have no experience in the field.'

'I see. What's your proposition?'

'I told you on Tuesday that I would support you. I am still willing to do so, but on a personal level. Despite your own lack of experience in this particular field, you have put forward a very thorough presentation. I'm impressed with your determination to see it through, and with the fact that you are willing to invest every penny you have. Therefore, I am prepared to put up the money from my own pocket—'

'As a personal loan?' It didn't seem possible to Roland that a man he was meeting for only the third time would make such a gesture . . .

'Most certainly not. We're discussing a sizable sum of money here, not a few shillings. If I loan you the money and you go under I would be deeply out of pocket. You put up your fifteen thousand pounds, and yourself, and I will supply the remaining capital – for a fifty-fifty partnership.'

'So if I go under you can claim a healthy tax loss.'

'If it should come to that, yes.'

'Forty-nine percent,' Roland countered.

'No.'

'Simon, I'm the one doing the work. I want control.'

'And if I am contributing the lion's share of the capital I also want some control over what happens. I think I'm entitled to it.'

'You pointed out the other day that you were a banker, not in real estate or the electrical business. Aside from money, how could you help?'

'Quite possibly I could not, but I want some say.'

'I can't do it, Simon. I'm sorry.'

Simon stroked his beard with his thumb and forefinger while he studied Roland. He found Roland's obstinacy amusing – like a young horse champing at the bit without realizing that the jockey also contributes to winning. 'What will you do, try other banks? Aronson Freres rejected your proposal and I was supporting you to the hilt. What chance do you think you'll have elsewhere? If you don't know the answer to that I'll tell you. Absolutely none. Surely you can see that fifty percent of something is worth a damned sight more than fifty-one percent, or even a hundred percent, of nothing.'

78

Roland understood how much sense he was making. Simon was his only entrance, even more so with the time limit he had to buy Mar-Cross from the Official Receiver. In another couple of days, a week at the very most, some-one else would step in and snap up the company. But if he owned only fifty percent how could he be confident of directing it the way he wanted it to go? 'I don't want to have to fight with you over every decision, Simon.'

'You won't have to, just as long as your decisions make sound economic sense.'

'I'm curious. Why would you want to help me this way?'

'I told you. I liked your presentation, the whole idea. And I believe you have the right combination of aggres-sion and luck.'

Luck? Roland marveled at the word. How much luck had he enjoyed in his life? Not that much that he could remember. Perhaps Simon saw it differently. 'Would you like to back my luck to prove your point?'

'How?'

'One hand of poker, five cards open. You back my hand, I'll back yours. If my hand wins, we're fifty-fifty. If your hand wins, then I get fifty-one percent.'

Simon appeared intrigued by the proposition. 'But then your luck would be with my cards, would it not?'

'Tough problem, isn't it? Even Einstein would have trouble figuring it out.'

'All right. I'll back your hand for an equal partnership.' Simon took a fresh pack of cards from the drawer of a mahogany secretary, broke the seal, removed the jokers and started to shuffle. Roland watched in fascination as the cards riffled quickly through the banker's long, slen-der fingers. 'Cut for deal.'

Roland cut a six, Simon a jack. Simon shuffled again, then offered them for Roland to cut. Roland shook his head. 'Just deal.'

Simon turned up the first two cards: a four of hearts for

Roland and eight of clubs for himself. The second cards were dealt: a nine of hearts for Roland, a king of spades for Simon. Then the third cards – an ace of diamonds for Roland, a four of spades for Simon. The balance shifted toward Roland's hand.

As he waited for the fouth cards, Roland suddenly realized that he was no longer bothered by the outcome of the hand. If Simon had this much faith in him then he would go along with any decisions Roland made; it seemed unnecessary to challenge the luck he placed so much importance on. The poker hand was an exercise now, nothing more than a means for Simon to further cement his belief.

Slowly, Simon turned up the fourth cards: a four of diamonds for Roland – a pair! – and a three of hearts for himself. The odds had shifted dramatically in favor of Roland's hand. 'My luck seems to be holding out for you,' Roland said.

'I expected it to. But there is still another card.'

'Don't bother. You've proven your point. Fifty percent.'

Simon smiled, glad of Roland's surrender with good grace. He hadn't wanted to take a chance on that last card; he still wasn't certain which way the luck would run when they were playing each other's hand. 'That wasn't what I was playing for, Roland. Anyone with an eye for a quick profit could spot a company in trouble, carve it up and sell off its assets. But you have the confidence to rebuild it. I was playing for fifty percent of Roland Eagles. I'll have the check for you tomorrow. Will you be using the Mar-Cross name or will you be forming a holding company?'

'I was thinking of R.E. Electrics, if that's okay with you.'

'Fine. I'll register it at Companies House. Two directors, you and me. A brandy to toast our union?'

'Please.' As Simon turned away Roland picked up the

cards and straightened them, unable to resist looking at the top cards. The first was the two of clubs, which meant nothing. The second was the king of hearts – a card that would have made Simon's hand a winner and given Roland control of the company. Simon had been right about Roland's luck, except it had been sitting beside the hand he was backing, not the hand he was holding. As he slipped the cards into the box he felt satisfied that the game hadn't been played through. With the faith Simon had in him he would make an ideal partner.

Simon returned with two brandy snifters, passed one to Roland and raised the other in a toast. 'To R.E. Electrics and its takeover of Mar-Cross.'

'To a profitable partnership.'

'It will be,' Simon responded. 'Any venture with a man as determined for success as you could be nothing less.' He smiled as he paid Roland the compliment, but a nagging question played on his mind: every man had a reason for ambition, aside from the obvious need to make his way in the world. What was Roland's? Sally had mentioned his single-mindedness, how he had locked himself away, willing to forego the usual comforts while he concentrated on a single objective.

Sally thought it was because of the sudden, cruel way in which he had lost his family. That was what drove him, she claimed, the desire to substitute family love with money and power. But Simon wasn't so sure. He couldn't put his finger on what motivated this remarkable man, but he was inclined to think it went much deeper than that.

CHAPTER THREE

Within eighteen months of forming R.E. Electrics and acquiring Mar-Cross, Roland had the company securely in the black. The two subsidiaries had been sold off, and to raise additional working capital he had suggested to Simon Aronson, as he had when he first presented his idea, that they sell the factory building and the land it occupied, then lease it back on a favorable long-term basis from the new owners. Simon agreed, and when the deal was made it meant that R.E. Electrics had taken control of Mar-Cross for virtually nothing; Roland had purchased the company with its own money.

Simon watched with admiration as Roland set about the task of building the company. Although well aware of his young partner's determination, he was still amazed at the ruthless speed with which Roland was able to accomplish his work. A new technical team, lured from other companies, expanded the original range of plugs and fittings to small appliances incorporating heating elements – electric kettles, irons, immersion heaters. Instead of advertising the products initially, Roland chose to offer special terms to carefully selected, highly visible small shops in London, selling at virtually his own cost and supplying attractive point-of-sale promotional material, which the shop owners welcomed. Once he had established that foothold he spread his net wider, advertising in the trade press. Sales picked up immediately as larger shops became interested in the new products from an old firm under young management.

So rapid was the buildup that one of the trade publications in which Roland advertised requested an interview.

Roland accepted, inviting one reporter to lunch at Eldridge's, a restaurant he frequented in Knightsbridge.

Choosing his words carefully, and knowing the reporter was happy to make the most of a free lunch at one of London's finest restaurants, Roland explained how he had taken over a company in receivership and turned it around. He astounded his interviewer, who was at least twenty years older than himself, by freely admitting that at the time of the takeover his own knowledge of electrical goods went little further than 'being aware that you had to plug them in before they would work.' He followed this admission with a carefully prepared quote: 'I am strictly a businessman who is capable of building a company – any kind of a company – because my strength lies not in technical knowledge but in being totally unafraid to surround myself with people who know considerably more than I do.' When the article appeared in the magazine, the headline referred to Roland as a flamboyant entrepreneur, the forerunner of a new breed of business executives created by the war. It was a description Roland quite liked.

One of those men who knew considerably more than Roland was Lawrence Chivers, a dour, black-haired Yorkshireman in his late thirties who never appeared anywhere without an enormous pipe jutting out of the side of his mouth. Chivers, a disgruntled sales representative with a vacuum cleaner company since leaving the Royal Air Force at the end of the war, had approached Roland as soon as he had taken over Mar-Cross. Impressed by the man's contacts within the retail industry, Roland immediately hired him as sales manager, and his instinct about the man quickly proved correct.

It was Chivers who made the major breakthrough Roland hungered for. After months of keeping appointments with buyers at London's largest department stores, pitching the new kitchen products, if only on a trial basis, Chivers finally received a positive response. With a showman's timing, he saved his announcement for the last moment of the regular Friday afternoon sales meeting in Roland's office.

'Any more business?' Roland asked, looking first at Simon, who always attended the meetings, then at Lawrence Chivers. 'No? I guess that just about finishes it then.'

'There is one minor point,' Chivers said, puffing contentedly on his pipe to surround himself with a cloud of gray, pungent smoke. A spark jumped from the massive bowl to burn a small hole in his tweed houndstooth sportcoat before he could brush it away.

'How minor?' Roland asked as he saw Simon glance at his watch. The banker had to return to his office in the city before he could go home to his family for their Friday night dinner.

'Well, you know we've been bashing away at all the big stores in the West End – British Home Stores, John Lewis, Gamages, et al. – I think Adler's may have bitten.' Chivers removed the pipe from his mouth for a moment while he explored the end. 'Not drawing properly,' he explained, as if anyone might be interested, and Roland felt like yelling at him to put the damned pipe down. 'Wasn't easy, though. No one seems prepared to make any decision at that place, certainly none of the buying staff. The buyers just hem and haw, and finally everything has to go right on up to the top.'

'To old Montague Adler,' Simon broke in. 'He still runs that company like it was his father's original stall in Petticoat Lane.'

'You know the family?' Roland asked.

'Not closely.'

'You say that like you're relieved.'

Simon laughed. 'I am. Montague Adler – or Mr Monty as he's called – is the original Jewish patriarch, Abraham reincarnated. He started Adler's with a small shop in the East End of London after his father had operated a stall in the Lane. Multiplied it to three nice stores. The old devil must be nearing eighty now.'

'Eighty?' Roland whistled. 'And he's still working?'

'He retired about ten years ago, from what I understand, although he kept the title of chairman. He used to attend the occasional meeting, wander around the store to see what was happening, but he didn't get too involved because his wife wanted him to ease up. She was worried about his health. Ironically, it was she who died. When that happened old Monty decided to become active in the business again. His son, Albert, had been managing it. Titles don't mean much in that company because everyone is scared to death of the old man. His word is law where his family is concerned, whether inside Adler's or out.'

'Albert's a bit of a louse, if you want my opinion,' Chivers chimed in. 'Monty might be an irascible old devil, but he's entitled to it. He's the one who built the business up. Albert likes the money and the prestige, but he hasn't got one-tenth of the old man's drive. I think that's why Monty came out of retirement. He didn't want to see the business ruined while he could still do something about it.' The pipe had gone out and Chivers paused to relight it. 'Deep down, I reckon old Monty believes it was the wrong son who died.'

'Pardon?' Between the pauses for relighting the pipe and the abrupt changing of subjects, Roland had difficulty following Chivers. He knew his sales manager acted the same way on business calls, interspersing his pitch with jokes and his own philosophical comments on life. It seemed to work with the buyers, but Roland often found it irritating.

'Monty had another son named Meir, older than Albert by a year or two. Went off to America in the early twenties to try his luck and got killed in a car crash. Was a bright fellow from all I've heard.'

'I see,' Roland glanced at Simon, knowing he was

impatient to go. 'How did you leave it, Lawrence?'

'Simpkins, that's the buyer, is definitely interested in us. Adler's used to be china, glassware, furniture, clothing. Now they're expanding into electrical goods. They're looking at Christmas as their first test for the new direction. Now Simpkins wants us – you and me, Roland, because they won't deal with just a lowly sales manager the first time – to make an appointment to see the old man. If he likes the look of us, we'll get the order.'

'That personal, eh? Then what are we waiting for? Telephone them right now for an appointment.' While Chivers dialed the number, Roland sat back, thinking. Three stores, the big one on Regent Street where the buying offices were, and the other branches in Manchester and Edinburgh. Get your goods selling there and you were made.

'Is next Wednesday any good, three o'clock?' Chivers asked, his beefy hand held over the mouthpiece.

Roland glanced at the diary on his desk. He had an appointment at six-thirty. 'All right, as long as we're out of there by four-thirty.'

'Where do you have to go?' Simon asked as Chivers confirmed the appointment at Adler's.

'I've got a dinner to attend with Sally.'

Simon feigned disappointment. 'Sharon will be jealous.'

Roland smiled as he pictured Simon's older daughter. His first impression of her hadn't been wrong. Each time he saw Sharon, which was about twice a month when he went to the Aronson home for dinner and an evening of backgammon, she looked even more lovely. At fifteen her body was already that of a woman's and she conducted herself with a dignity and elegance that seemed out of place in one so young. Simon and Nadine had mentioned the possibility of sending her to the Sorbonne in Paris, but Roland doubted that a finishing school could teach her anything she didn't already know.

'Tell Sharon not to worry. It isn't a date, it's for your

blasted newspaper. Sally's covering some big do for the new Argentinian ambassador, a banquet at Claridge's. She's asked me to escort her.' Though Roland sounded disgruntled at the prospect of the evening, he actually found himself looking forward to it – he hadn't seen Sally for almost a month. The ardor of their early relationship had cooled, but neither seemed to mind. Now they were friends – good friends – who got together every so often to exchange news. Roland was initially surprised by her invitation, thinking she'd been seeing someone regularly. Obviously that had finished.

'Tell Sharon,' he said, interrupting his thoughts, 'that if she ever needs an escort to Claridge's, I'll be more than happy to oblige.'

'I'll be sure to tell her.'

'It's confirmed,' Chivers said, hanging up the phone. 'Three o'clock on Wednesday afternoon.'

Under the desk, Roland clenched a fist in triumph.

Adler's was situated opposite the Café Royal at the bottom end of Regent Street, part of the row of Regency buildings which sweep gracefully northward from Piccadilly Circus and the statue of Eros.

Lawrence Chivers was carrying a bulky sample case when he and Roland arrived at the store for their appointment with Montague Adler. They took the elevator up to the fifth floor where Bruce Simpkins, the buyer with whom Chivers had been dealing, was waiting for them.

'Gentlemen, gentlemen, welcome to Adler's.' As Simpkins spoke he nodded his shining bald head and rubbed his hands together nervously. Roland recalled Simon's description of how the store operated and guessed that Simpkins was more than a little frightened of appearing before the old man to show merchandise he recommended the company buy. 'Please come this way.'

They followed Simpkins towards the buying offices, past the restaurant which took up half the fifth floor.

Roland looked through the heavy glass doors and could see waiters clearing up after the midday rush.

'Here we are, gentlemen.' Simpkins stopped so abruptly that Roland, still gazing at the restaurant, stumbled into the back of him. When he looked up he saw that they were at Simpkins' own office, the first in a short row that occupied the length of the hall. At the end were two heavy oak doors. In ornate gold script, one was marked 'Mr Monty' and the other 'Mr Albert.' Seated at a desk between the two doors, like an alert sentry, was an elderly woman with a grim face and tightly waved gray hair. Although she was equipped with only a typewriter and two telephones, she couldn't have looked fiercer had she been armed with a machine gun. Suddenly Roland had the urge to grab hold of Chivers and run. This wasn't a retail business . . . it was an empire . . . and they were about to meet the king!

'I trust that you've brought the samples we discussed,' Simpkins said to Chivers.

'Mar-Cross irons and kettles.'

'Good, good. Now remember, it must be a straightforward presentation. Keep your conversation to answering questions. Neither Mr Monty nor Mr Albert has time to waste on frivolities.'

Chivers nodded, and Roland wished that he had persuaded Simon to come as well . . . he had dealt with Monty Adler before, persuaded him to contribute a considerable sum of money to the Jewish National Fund to plant trees in Israel. When Roland reminded him of it, Simon cited that experience as his reason not to come, insisting that he wouldn't exploit an association based on philanthropy to gain profits for his business. Roland understood and respected him all the more for it.

'Shall we go?' Simpkins led the way toward the gray-haired woman who looked up as the three men approached, regarding them coolly. Simpkins introduced

Roland and Chivers, and the woman stood up and rapped on the door marked 'Mr Monty.'

'Enter!' a man's gravelly voice called out.

The woman opened the door gently. 'Mr Monty, Mr Simpkins is here with a Mr Eagles and a Mr Chivers from Mar-Cross.' She stepped back and, as the three men filed past, made an effort to smile, though the expression scarcely materialized.

Roland entered the office first, immediately stunned by its spaciousness. In comparison, his own office in Wembley was a slum, shoved away in an unused corner of the factory. Next to its size, the most striking thing about Montague Adler's office was a large picture window that looked out over Regent Street to the Café Royal. The floor was completely covered in rich brown carpet, and two exquisite Persian rugs hung from the walls.

'Come in! Come in! Don't stand there with your mouths hanging open like bloody American tourists!'

Roland snapped around to face the man who had spoken. Monty Adler, a stocky barrel-chested bull of a man with a mane of snow white hair and piercing blue eyes, sat behind an enormous, leather-topped desk. Dressed in a single-breasted black jacket and gray-striped pants, he wore a shirt with a stiff separate collar reminiscent of an age gone by. What Roland found most remarkable about the man was the size of his head – he was barely five foot three, yet the massive head would have seemed normal on a man a foot taller.

'Albert, come in here!' Monty Adler's voice bore the mark of a man unaccustomed to being ignored.

A door joining the two offices opened almost instantly and Albert Adler appeared. He was also dressed formally but, unlike his father, Albert appeared distinctly uncomfortable, constantly running a finger between the stiff shirt collar and his neck. Albert was much taller than his father and thin to the point of looking undernourished.

Even his lips were thin, Roland thought, and seemed to be permanently set in a pale, mean line. Roland chided himself for taking such an instant dislike to the man solely on the basis of his appearance.

'Come on then, show us your goods,' Monty ordered. 'No, not on my desk. On the floor.' He stood over Roland and Chivers as they knelt on the carpet with the sample case. Chivers opened it and brought out two electric kettles and two irons. 'Haven't been in business very long, have you?' Monty picked up one of the irons and examined it closely. 'Nice finish.'

'Eighteen months,' Roland replied. 'We took over—'

'I know perfectly well what you took over, what you did with it and who your partner is.' He replaced the iron and turned his attention to the electric kettles. 'What have your returns been like?'

'For guarantee work?' Chivers asked. 'Very low.'

'Albert, fill these kettles with water. I want to see how long they take to boil.' Monty passed both kettles to his son. 'And when you've done that get me a couple of tablecloths from the restaurant. We'll see how the irons work as well.'

Roland glanced at Chivers as Albert left the office with a kettle in each hand. The sales manager just shrugged his shoulders in an I-told-you-so attitude.

'What did you do before you took over Mar-Cross?' Monty asked.

'I was in the army for seven years.'

'Oh, of course, I remember you now. You're the army captain I read about, resigned because you didn't like what Ernest Bevin's little bunch of Arabists were up to. Can't say I blame you. Where are you from?'

'Margate.'

'Never been there in my life.' He swung toward the door as Albert reappeared, took the kettles and plugged them into wall sockets. He tapped his foot impatiently as he studied his watch and waited for the water to boil.

'They work,' he grunted when steam issued simultaneously from the spout of each kettle. 'Now let's see about your irons.' He lowered his eyes and studied the trousers each man wore. Finally he pointed at Roland. 'Give them here.'

Roland turned red at the prospect of undressing. 'Come on,' Monty pressed. 'Are you scared of your legs being seen or is your underwear dirty?' Without waiting for an answer, assuming he would be obeyed as he always was, Monty picked up the two tablecloths Albert had brought from the restaurant. He set one across the desk as a pad to protect the leather top. The other he sprinkled with water from one of the kettles. When he finished his work he looked expectantly at Roland. 'What are you waiting for, sonny? Surely it's worth showing your legs to prove how good your irons are.'

Very slowly, Roland removed his trousers and stood in jacket and shorts. He looked at Chivers, who had turned away, but it was obvious from the way his body shook that he was bursting with laughter. If you tell anyone at the factory about this, Roland thought, so help me God . . .

Monty paid no attention to the two men as he took the trousers and set one leg neatly across the desk. He plugged in one of the sample irons and, with the familiar manner of a housewife, touched his tongue and flicked his finger across the base of the iron to judge for heat. When the saliva sizzled, he nodded in satisfaction.

'Are you any good at pressing trousers?' Roland asked. He was still unable to believe he had undressed at the old man's command.

'Just watch and learn,' was Monty's only comment. He set the damp tablecloth on top of the trouser leg and pressed down gently with the iron. Steam rose as he worked carefully up the leg, exerting just the right amount of pressure. Satisfied, he rearranged the trousers and started on the second leg. When he was finished, Roland's trousers had knife-edge creases.

91

'Nice job,' Roland said as he dressed.

Monty unplugged the iron, tossed the two tablecloths onto the floor and gave Roland a smile that creased his face like a white prune. 'Sonny, I was pressing trousers in a tailor's shop in the East End of London before your grandfather was even born.'

'What do you think, Mr Monty?' Chivers asked. He glanced at Roland and winked.

Monty passed the question on to his son. 'What are your feelings, Albert?'

Roland studied Albert as he answered. Suddenly he could understand why the son was so thin. He probably had an ulcer from having to put up with his father all week long, especially after he'd managed to get rid of him once . . .

'Simpkins recommends the products. Isn't that what we pay our buyers for – to buy?' Albert's voice was like the rest of him, thin and reedy.

'You mean, what's the point of having a dog and barking ourselves?'

'That's another way of phrasing it.'

'Because this business was not built up that way. It was built because I take an interest in everything that goes on. You should, too, if you want to keep it making money once I'm gone.' Monty turned back to Roland and Chivers. 'You'll work out the size of the order with Simpkins. We'll want delivery by the middle of November, two months from now. You'll have the merchandise delivered here and we'll arrange for its distribution to our other stores in Manchester and Edinburgh. One other thing,' Monty added as Chivers began to repack the samples. 'Adler's believes in promoting itself to its customers. We don't believe in promoting our suppliers unless they are very, very special.'

Which we are not, Roland concluded to himself.

'On each piece of merchandise,' Monty continued, 'we want you to stamp: "Made expressly for Adler's of Regent

Street." The same message will be printed on the packaging.' He turned around and went back to his seat behind the leather-topped desk. 'Thank you for coming, gentlemen.'

Roland looked around. Simpkins was already standing by the door, holding it open. 'I'm glad we could do business,' Roland said, shaking hands first with Monty, then Albert. 'I hope this is the beginning of a long and rewarding relationship between our two companies.'

'Perhaps,' Monty concurred. 'Now go on with Simpkins. I've got work to do, even if you haven't.' With that said, his visitors passed through the door.

Roland and Chivers returned to Simpkins' office where the buyer wrote out the order. Every so often he stopped to wipe perspiration from his forehead until his large white handkerchief was soaked through.

'Did we behave ourselves satisfactorily?' Roland asked, amused by the effect old Monty Adler had on the buyer.

'You got the order, didn't you?'

The moment they were outside the store, standing in Regent Street, Chivers set down the sample case and lit his pipe. Roland took it as a cue and brought out his gold cigarette case. 'Quick cup of tea somewhere?' the sales manager asked.

'I think something stronger's more in order.'

'I agree. At least now we know why Albert's brother ran off to America, don't we?' he said with a grin.

Sally Roberts picked Roland up in a taxi at six-fifteen. He was relieved she had decided not to drive her old MG which she refused to trade in for a newer, more practical model; in her long turquoise evening dress and he in white tie and tails they would have arrived at Claridge's looking like someone's poor relations.

During the ride he related what had happened that afternoon at Adler's. It wasn't until the taxi neared the restaurant that he stopped talking about himself long enough to ask Sally why the new Argentinian ambassador was hosting the function, and why she had been invited.

'Nicanor Menendez is an Anglophile,' Sally explained. 'Maybe that's why he landed the plum of all diplomatic positions – the Court of St James.'

'Sure, that and all the money from his ranches, his copper mine and his hotels. He probably paid Perón a fortune for the position.'

'That's the way it's done over there, so don't criticize.'

'Do I hear Sally Roberts the socialist saying it's all right?'

'Not at all. But why should you, of all people, question it? When you're as wealthy as Menendez, won't you use the power?'

'I would hope we never have a Perón in this country I'd have to bribe.'

'Menendez went to university here at Oxford,' Sally continued. 'Now that he's back he wants to begin his tenure with a big splash. What better way than to play host to all the upper crust at Claridge's? The press is invited to make sure he's not ignored in the society and gossip columns.'

'Conceited bugger.'

'Actually, he's doing it for his son and daughter, Juan and Catarina. He's hoping, can you believe this?' – Sally started to laugh at the thought of it – 'He's hoping that they'll meet some members of the British aristocracy. Then Nicanor Menendez will be able to boast that he's got an earl or a duke for a son-in-law and a princess for a daughter-in-law. Can you imagine British aristocracy welcoming South American Catholics into the family?'

'For a share of Menendez's wealth, yes. Some of our titled chinless wonders aren't so well off anymore.'

'Roland Eagles, you're beginning to sound like a cynical socialist yourself.'

'Maybe I learned it from you. I take it you're covering

94

this bash for the women's page – ambassador's daughter makes London debut?'

Sally nodded. 'Juan Menendez already has a reputation as a playboy, Latin man about town. But Catarina is supposed to be something worth writing about. Barely eighteen years old and already the toast of the pampas. I'm looking forward to finding out for myself.'

The taxi turned into Brook Street which was already jammed with Rolls Royces and Daimlers depositing their elegantly attired guests. Never before had Roland seen so much jewelry in one place; wherever he looked, diamonds sparkled. He and Sally might joke about the ambassador's conceit, but his real guests were taking it all very seriously indeed.

Holding Sally's arm, Roland entered Claridge's and joined the stream of guests waiting to be announced by the red-coated toastmaster, then greeted by the receiving line made up of the ambassador and his family. Nicanor Menendez – his black hair streaked with gray, brown eyes overshadowed by bristling brows – wore a cluster of medals and decorations which reflected flashes of light from the chandeliers. To his left, his wife – a portly, dark-haired woman wearing a glittering tiara – offered her hand with an affected limpness. Next was Juan Menendez, the ambassador's twenty-one-year-old son, a slim, dark, intense-looking youth who would be spending his time in England working at the Savoy, preparing to enter his father's hotel business when he returned to Argentina.

But Roland paid scant attention to the first three people in the receiving line. He was too captivated by Ambassador Menendez's eighteen-year-old daughter to look anywhere else . . . Slender, with flawless olive skin, her flashing dark brown eyes were framed by flowing black hair that tumbled down in gentle waves onto her shoulders, accentuating the simple, but elegantly styled white silk gown she wore. On Catarina Menendez the diamond

95

tiara and bracelet seemed fitting. The jewels only served to emphasize her looks while on other, plainer women, they removed attention from their less than perfect features.

'Miss Sally Roberts and Mr Roland Eagles,' the toastmaster announced.

As they walked forward to have their hands automatically shaken by the ambassador and his wife Roland realized that Menendez hadn't the faintest idea who they were.

'We're so glad you could come,' Menendez said, his eyes flicking over Roland and Sally before moving on to the next guests. 'I hope you both have a wonderful time.'

'Thank you, sir.'

They passed Juan Menendez, again receiving the same handshake and greeting. In front of Catarina, Roland stopped as if mesmerized. Never before had he been so struck by a woman's beauty, and for a brief instant he forgot about Sally holding his arm, the other guests waiting in line behind him . . .

'Is this your first time in England, Señorita Menendez?'

'Yes.' The girl appeared startled by the question, at having one of her father's guests take the time to speak to her. This man seemed different from the countless others who had politely greeted her. She had noticed him staring at her when he was still three guests away from being announced – very tall, perfectly at ease in his white tie and tails, a disarmingly frank face with piercing blue eyes, and a touch of gray around the temples that made him seem distinguished. Catarina wondered about the woman with him. She wore no rings, although the man wore two. And their names were different. Though she wasn't sure she understood why, this pleased Catarina immensely. 'Are you a friend of my father?' she asked in lightly accented English.

'At this moment I wish I were.' He looked down and saw that he was still holding Catarina's gloved hand; he couldn't recall taking it in the first place, but he made no move to let go. 'What will you be doing in London?'

'My father wants me to attend school. A finishing school for very proper English ladies.'

Roland felt Sally gently tug his arm but he paid her no attention. 'How do you like London so far?'

The young woman warmed even more to the tall Englishman with the arrogantly clear blue eyes. She hadn't wanted to attend her father's banquet. She wanted no part of his social ambitions for her. But now, suddenly, she was glad she had come. 'The embassy is stuffy, everything is very formal. But I hope school will be more fun. What do you do?'

Roland was about to answer that he was with the press, otherwise how could be explain his presence at the banquet? Before he could open his mouth, though, he felt someone pushing him in the back. He turned around and saw the next group of guests waiting impatiently, annoyed by the delay. 'Perhaps I'll see you later.'

'I do hope so.' Catarina gave him a bright smile and Roland would have risked another push in the back but Sally dragged him away.

'I could say I'm offended,' she murmured, 'but I guess it's just a waste of time.'

'How do you mean?' He followed her to a notice board which held the seating plan. They were at a table reserved solely for the press, close enough to hear any speeches and distant enough from the top table not to be considered too important.

'You came here as my escort, remember? It looks like I've lost you already.'

'I'm sorry.' he said, kissing her on the cheek. 'Was I very rude?'

'Not really.' If anything she was amused by his infatuation with the Argentinian girl. She had never seen anyone smitten that quickly. She couldn't blame him, though. The girl was a real beauty. No wonder the ambassador had high hopes of marrying his daughter off to some English aristocrat; looks like those could alter a lifetime of anti-Catholic prejudice.

They sat down at the press table where Sally introduced Roland to journalists from the other newspapers. Conversation centered around the Menendez family and gossip about the real wealth in the clan coming from the ambassador's wife; it was her grandfather who had discovered the copper mine on which the family fortune was based. Roland found himself unable to concentrate on the talk. His eyes kept wandering to the main table, where Catarina sat with her family. Even Claridge's cuisine failed to interest him. Dishes were placed in front of him and removed, hardly touched. Had Sally not known what was occupying his thoughts she would have been concerned for his health.

After dinner, when the ball began, Roland tried to approach Catarina. To his stinging disappointment he learned that a dance card had been organized for her, filled with a long line of socially acceptable young men. So Roland settled for dancing the entire evening with Sally, with one eye constantly searching out Catarina. Whenever she passed close by he nodded a greeting and was rewarded each time with that same lively, impish smile she had given him in the receiving line. Sally quickly picked up on Roland's frustration and responded magnificently. She waited until Catarina had begun to waltz with a young, fair-haired man, then guided Roland so that the two couples collided in the center of the floor.

'Excuse me!' both Roland and the fair-haired man exclaimed together.

'Aren't you Giles Prideaux, the artist?' Sally burst out, focusing on Catarina's partner.

The man nodded. 'I'm afraid you have the advantage of me.'

'I interviewed you a year ago for the *London Evening Mercury*.'

'Of course, forgive me. Sally, Sally—'

'Sally Roberts.' She stepped hard on Roland's foot. 'I understand you're putting on another exhibition soon.'

'Yes, in a couple of months as a matter of fact. Hold on a moment—' Prideaux swung around to his partner, frightened that she might think he was neglecting her. He did so just in time to see her waltzed away in Roland's arms.

'Seems to have been a bit of a mix-up,' Sally offered apologetically. 'Shall we continue this dance together, Giles, or shall we stand in the middle of the floor like a couple of fools?'

Struggling to conceal his irritation, Prideaux took Sally in his arms. He had waited half the night for one dance with Catarina Menendez, only to have her stolen from him. As the two couples passed each other, Prideaux glared furiously at Roland. Sally, though, gave him a secretive wink.

Roland returned the wink and chuckled softly. 'What is so funny?' Catarina asked, having missed the exchange.

'Your former partner. He's still wondering what happened, how he began this dance with one woman and is finishing it with another.'

'Serves him right. He ignored me to talk to your friend. Anyway he is no terrible loss. He kept talking about his paintings and I didn't understand a single word. What do you do? Something more interesting than painting, I hope.' She was certain he did. Not for one moment could Catarina imagine the man who held her being able to stand for hours in front of an easel.

'I own a company that manufactures small electrical appliances for the kitchen – kettles and irons.'

'Are you very wealthy?'

'Not at the moment, but I hope to be.'

'Are you related to the King then, a duke of something or other, a viscount?'

'If I am, the Royal Family keeps it a big, dark secret.'

'Pardon?' Catarina was mystified by the flippant answer.

'No, I'm not.'

'What a shame. That means my father will not be interested in you. He wants to marry me off to some noble lord.'

'Do you want to marry a lord?'

'Not any I have seen here tonight.' She made such a disgusted face that Roland burst out laughing.

'What kind of man do you want to marry? Or am I being too inquisitive?'

'Not at all.' Catarina was delighted by his questions; everyone else she had danced with had either talked about her father or himself. 'When I marry it will be because I have found a man I love, not because of my father. And then' – she grinned and lowered her voice to a whisper that Roland could barely hear – 'I want to be surrounded by a mountain of dirty — what do you call them? – diapers.'

'We call them nappies over here. Americans call them diapers.'

'English in Argentina is full of American words. But you know what I mean.'

'You could always find a job in a laundry.'

She stuck her tongue out in a most unladylike manner and Roland almost yielded to the urge to bite it gently, forgetting what the other guests would think.

'Who is the woman you came with tonight?'

'A friend of mine. She works on a newspaper.'

'How much of a friend?'

'A very good friend.' Roland was uncertain why Catarina asked – was she interested in him or just curious? Sally had been the same way when they first met, only she had wanted the information for a story.

'She must be a very good friend to arrange for you to dance with me.'

They passed close to where Catarina's father and

mother stood. The ambassador gazed curiously at Roland, uncertain whether he was one of the young men he had wanted Catarina to dance with. Roland smiled at him and said: 'A wonderful evening, sir. Just wonderful.' Ambassador Menendez smiled back, ever the gracious host, but still unsure.

The waltz ended. Reluctantly, Roland relinquished his hold on Catarina to the next man on her card. 'Thank you.'

'Thank *you*,' she responded. 'I enjoyed it immensely. You're much more fun than my father's idea of the perfect escort.'

'Will I see you again?'

'You can reach me at the embassy.'

'I will.' He turned away to find Sally waiting for him. 'Thank you as well.'

'Glad to know I'm appreciated. How did it work out? Did you get as far as proposing marriage?'

'Marriage?'

'You heard me. The last time I saw anyone as glassy-eyed as you was at a boxing match. And he was being counted out!'

'Maybe he had a glass jaw.'

'And maybe you've got a glass heart, Roland Eagles.'

They returned to their table for a drink. While Sally talked to the other people Roland watched Catarina being taken around the dance floor, feeling envious of each successive man who partnered her. When she passed by his table, though, her eyes always locked with his.

Dirty diapers . . . dirty nappies . . . he thought with a smile. What a subject to talk about during a dance. And yet the raven-haired girl with the lilting accent had managed to make a mountain of dirty diapers sound like the most attractive proposition in the whole world.

The evening ended with the playing of both the British and Argentinian national anthems. As the last note died,

Roland looked around for Catarina but she had already left with her brother. At the door he and Sally said good-night to Ambassador Menendez and his wife, then went outside to search for a taxi. Beyond the cluster of limousines Sally spotted an empty cab and waved for it. Roland helped her in, dropped down on the seat beside her and gave the driver Sally's address in Hampstead.

'Is that where you're living these days, Captain Eagles?' the driver said.

Roland stiffened in shock and stared through the glass partition at the back of the man's head. 'Do I know you?'

The driver flicked on the interior light, removed his flat cap and turned around. Roland gazed in disbelief at the square solid face, the thick dark hair, the five o'clock shadow. 'Alf Goldstein, Captain Eagles. Bergen-Belsen, remember?'

'Goldstein!' Roland slumped back in the seat, amazed at meeting the former sergeant after four years. 'What are you doing still driving a cab? I thought you'd be living high off the hog by now.'

'Don't know what you mean,' Goldstein replied as he flipped the meter and drove slowly away from Claridge's. 'Cabbing's my livelihood. Always has been.'

'But that book you wrote – didn't you make any money from it?'

'Money? I didn't do that for money. Anything that book made went into a fund for survivors.'

Roland felt a sharp sensation of disgust at himself. 'I owe you one hell of an apology.'

'For what?'

'The reason I never replied to your letter was because I felt sick that you should profit from helping those poor wretches at the camp.'

'You thought I—?' Goldstein laughed and shook his head. 'Forget it, I should have said something in the letter. When you never replied I just figured you didn't want to be reminded of that place, not that I could blame you, or else the army lost the letter before it reached you.'

Roland remembered Sally sitting next to him and introduced Goldstein to her, explaining how they had been together at the liberation of Bergen-Belsen. When they reached Hampstead, Roland told Goldstein to wait while he saw Sally inside.

'I feel like I've exploited you tonight,' Roland told Sally as she opened the flat door. 'First you introduce me to Catarina Menendez, and now I've met Goldstein again because of you.'

'Maybe I'm your lucky charm. Sweet dreams of your Latin lady.' She kissed him on the cheek and watched him walk down the stairs to the street door. Sally had no doubt that Roland was already planning how he would win over Catarina Menendez. Nor did she have any doubt that he would succeed, no matter whether the Argentinian ambassador thought he was high enough up the social ladder to be a proper suitor or not. One thing Sally had learned about Roland was that once he made up his mind to do something, nothing could stop him.

Downstairs, Roland climbed back into the taxi and gave Goldstein the address in Regent's Park. Goldstein drove slowly, happy for the chance encounter with his old army captain. 'Remember Kassler?' he asked.

'Who?' Roland's thoughts wandered momentarily to Catarina and he had difficulty in placing the name.

'Heinrich Kassler – that SS officer we captured?'

'Christ, yes,' Roland said as his mind flashed back. 'What about him?'

'I'm glad you never did give me your Webley that day. They investigated him pretty thoroughly and it turns out he did a lot of good in that place. Inasmuch as anyone could do any good.'

'How did you find this out?'

'That fund for survivors I told you about. It's part of a group I belong to. We didn't only help the survivors but we kept an eye on those bastards who ran the camps.'

'What happened to Kassler? Do you know?'

'He didn't get caught up in the red tape for too long.

103

He was back home by the end of forty-five. I even mentioned him in the book.'

'What's he doing now?'

'Went straight back into the family business. Took over what was left of his father's factory near Stuttgart. Got a clean bill of health in the denazification program, and now he's one of the leading lights in trying to rebuild Germany. Then they can start World War Three in another twenty years or so, as soon as someone composes the right marching music.' Goldstein added bitterly and Roland laughed; his former interpreter hadn't changed his opinion of the Germans in the past four years.

'By the way,' Goldstein said, 'that was quite a write-up you got when you left the army. Quite proud of you, I was. Showed it to all my friends and family, told them you were my old commanding officer.'

'Sally, the woman we dropped off in Hampstead, was the one who wrote the story. Why didn't you drop me a line if you were so proud?'

'Because you never answered the last bloomin' letter,' Goldstein answered with a chuckle. 'This your place?' He pulled up outside Roland's building.

'This is it. Will you do me a favor?'

'Sure.'

'Make a delivery for me first thing in the morning. A bunch of the finest long-stemmed red roses you can get your hands on. Take them to Catarina Menendez at the Argentinian Embassy. Know where it is?'

'Nine Wilton Crescent, South West One,' Goldstein said. 'Any message to go with the roses?'

'You bet there is. "To Catarina, the prettiest Kate in Christendom . . . Shakespeare's words but my sentiments." Get it signed by me, with this telephone number.' He gave Goldstein his office number in Wembley, then passed him money to cover both the roses and the cab fare. 'Where do you live?'

'Stoke Newington, with my wife and two children.'

104

Goldstein passed a slip of paper to Roland with his own telephone number.

'Thanks. Never know when I'm going to need a taxi.'

'Thought you would have a car of your own.'

'Too much aggravation. I don't like driving to begin with and you have to be a masochist to drive in the West End. I take a train to work and taxis everywhere else. Good night, Alf. Nice to see you again.'

Roland stood on the pavement, watching the taxi move off into the night. Funny, he'd never even thought of Goldstein having a first name, even after going through something like Bergen-Belsen together.

Roland arrived at the factory at eight-fifteen the following morning, eager to meet with Lawrence Chivers and the factory manager to ensure there would be no hitches with the Adler's order. By nine-thirty the meeting was over and he was in his office, a cup of tea growing cold in front of him, a cigarette burning untouched in the ashtray as he stared at the telephone and willed it to ring.

Should he call Goldstein at home and see if the roses had been delivered yet? Maybe he should remind him, just in case he'd forgotten. Or had he worked late the previous night, got home at three or four in the morning and was still asleep?

The telephone rang and Roland snatched at it. 'Eagles!'

'Good morning, Roland.' It was a woman's voice and his heart leaped, until he realized it was Sally Roberts. 'I just wanted to make sure you'd recovered from last night.'

'Recovered from what?'

'Hey, you were flying so high that I was worried you might come down to earth with a big thud.'

'I'm still up there.' He told Sally about the roses and she laughed.

'You never sent me roses, you louse. But you can do something else instead. You just make damned sure you

105

give the *Mercury* and me preferential treatment when the greatest romance since Mrs Simpson unfolds. That's the *Mercury*'s price for taking you to Claridge's last night, and my price for having to put up with that twerp of an artist for one dance.'

'You'll get preferential treatment, I promise. I've got to go, speak to you later.' He hung up and turned away from the desk as his secretary entered the office. The telephone rang again. 'Eagles!'

'Roland, is that you?'

This time he knew there could be no mistake. A shiver ran down his spine and his cheeks burned with anticipation. He waved at the secretary to leave, waiting until the door was closed. 'Catarina?'

'Thank you for the roses, they're very beautiful.'

He tried to picture her. What was she wearing? A simple cotton dress? White, as she had worn the previous night? White, yes, that would set off her dark Latin beauty to perfection. 'I tried to find roses that were as beautiful as the girl I wanted to give them to,' he said. 'I'm sorry if I failed but the task was impossible.'

'Are you trying to embarrass me?'

'The furthest thing from my mind.'

'Where does the Shakespeare quote come from?'

'I'll tell you when I see you. May I see you?'

'Of course.'

'Tonight, for dinner?'

'No,' she replied. Had he detected disappointment in her voice? 'My father is having guests.'

'More lords and ladies for you and your brother?'

'Heaven forbid. Can we meet for lunch instead?'

'Where would you like to go?'

'Someplace quiet.'

'I'll pick you up outside the embassy at noon.'

Their date set, Roland quickly made plans for their lunch – he wanted his first meeting with Catarina to be special. He first phoned Goldstein's home, only to learn from his wife that he was out. He next left a message at the number for the cab rank Goldstein's wife said he worked out of, then phoned Eldridge's, leaving special instructions for their luncheon. When Goldstein returned his call he arranged to hire the cab for four hours.

Shortly after eleven Roland stood outside the factory waiting for the cab driver. When he arrived they went on to Eldridge's, where Roland picked up a large wicker hamper. With everything in place, they set out for the Argentinian Embassy in Wilton Crescent.

'Is that your lady friend I delivered the roses to?'

'I'm working on it. Did you have any trouble?'

'No. I took them to the embassy like you said, showed the card. A whole stream of people came out to look at me, then finally your friend came. She doesn't live at the embassy, she lives in the house next door.'

'You know more about her than I do, Alf.'

They turned into Wilton Crescent and Roland glimpsed Catarina standing outside the embassy. And she was wearing white! Even dressed in a white cotton dress with a white cardigan slung loosely around her shoulders she looked as lovely as she had the night before. In one hand she held a single long-stemmed rose.

Goldstein drew into the curb and Roland opened the door. 'Your carriage awaits you, m'lady.'

'I've been looking forward to seeing you all morning,' she said after sitting next to Roland in the cab's spacious interior. She toyed with the rose, lifting the half-open bloom to the tip of her fine, straight nose. 'No one has ever sent me roses before.'

'I feel honored to be the first.'

'What is in there?' Catarina pointed to the hamper on the floor. Instead of looking down, Roland gazed at her hand, the long slim fingers, her nails filed carefully and free of polish. The innocent hand of a child, he couldn't help thinking.

'Lunch,' Roland replied, momentarily distracted.

107

'Are we eating *al fresco*?'

'In a manner of speaking. You'll see.'

Goldstein drove the taxi deep into Hyde Park before pulling up in a secluded, tree-lined area. Without a word to his passengers he got out and walked away. Roland pulled down the jump seats to make impromptu tables and placed the hamper on one of them. When he opened it, Catarina gasped in pleasure. 'Do you own a restaurant as well as an electrical company that does not make very much money at the moment?'

'No. I just like good restaurants. Perhaps I should own one.'

'Perhaps you will one day.'

'Would your father approve of me then?'

'No,' she answered with a smile.

'What if I owned half a dozen restaurants? And a chain of hotels?'

'Mmm . . .' She made a great show of considering the question. 'Perhaps, but only if you were the King's cousin as well.'

'Did anyone ask who sent you roses?'

'My mother wanted to know who my admirer was.'

'What did you tell her?'

'I gave her your name, then I hid in my room with your flowers so she couldn't ask any more questions.'

Roland turned his attention to the hamper. From an insulated compartment he withdrew a bottle of Dom Perignon, still chilled from the restaurant's refrigerator. He followed this with two long-stemmed champagne glasses, china plates, silver tableware, Irish linen napkins. Carefully packed in the hamper was smoked salmon from the streams of Scotland, caviar, bread cut into tiny triangles. He opened the bottle of Dom Perignon, easing out the cork to avoid the expected wasteful gushing of champagne down the sides. Filling both glasses, he offered one to Catarina.

'To you.'

She clinked her glass gently against his. 'To us,' she

said, falling totally under the spell of the man she'd only briefly met the night before. 'To us. And to a veritable mountain of dirty diapers.'

'Nappies. Why a mountain?'

'Because I want many children. All good Catholic women have lots of children.' She studied him for a moment. 'Are you Catholic?'

'Half. My mother.'

'That's the important half. What is your father?'

'Was . . . my parents are dead. He was Jewish.'

Catarina dropped her eyes and Roland asked if there was something wrong; for the first time he seemed to notice the slim gold cross around her throat, the only piece of jewelry she wore. She took a long time to reply. 'My father—'

'He would approve of me even less?'

'You have to understand that he is a very close friend of Juan Perón. Since 1946, when Perón and his painted little whore of a wife took control of Argentina, many German refugees have been welcomed to my country. They have brought their hatred with them and the Jews of Argentina have suffered. Not like they did in Europe,' she added quickly, 'but when they criticize Perón for befriending such people they are reviled. Perón has made a fortune being hospitable to German refugees, and if he is to continue filling his coffers he can't afford that kind of criticism.'

'German refugees? You mean Nazis.'

'If you wish to use that word.'

'Does it bother you that my father was Jewish?' Roland wondered what he would do if Catarina answered yes. Throw her out of the taxi and let her find her own way home? Or would he ignore such bigotry because he was so captivated by the girl? 'Well, does it bother you?'

'No. I am too young to have formed such hatreds.'

'And if your father disapproved of me, would you defy him?'

'For my own happiness I would,' she answered, her

voice firm with conviction. 'But I don't think he would stand in the way of my happiness. After all I am his only daughter – how could he deny me?' She smiled suddenly, showing perfectly even white teeth. 'Besides, I could always argue with him that Catholics are really the first lapsed Jews. My father was in the Oxford debating society, he appreciates a well-constructed argument.'

Roland reached for the bottle and refilled their glasses. 'Denying and defying, you're making it sound like Romeo and Juliet.'

'Perhaps it is. Which play does that Shakespeare quote come from . . . the one you sent with the roses?'

' "The prettiest Kate in Christendom"? I'll tell you as long as you promise not to hit me.'

'Hit you? Why would I hit you?'

'It's from *The Taming of the Shrew*.'

She dipped a finger in her glass and flicked champagne into Roland's face. He laughed, and did the same to her. Then, before it could dry, he kissed it from her forehead, her cheeks, her lips.

During the ninety minutes Alf Goldstein was away – dawdling over a cup of tea and a cheese sandwich in a nearby cafe – two young people shared an extravagant lunch in the back seat of a taxi in Hyde Park.

They ate. They drank. And they talked. Roland, about his past, the sudden loss of his family, the bigotry he'd known that had tainted his father's life. Catarina, about the restrictions of being a diplomat's daughter, her dislike for the way her father was trying to arrange socially advantageous marriages for his children.

And as they did so, the eighteen-year-old daughter of the Argentinian Ambassador to the Court of St James and the ambitious twenty-four-year-old son of a Catholic mother and a Jewish father began to fall in love.

CHAPTER FOUR

During the next four weeks, Roland's priorities under-
went an abrupt change, from being the last to leave the
factory to being the first, rushing home to bathe and
change on the evenings he had a date with Catarina. He
kept two photographs of her on his desk – one taken on
the night of the Claridge's ball, the other a photo of them
together at a nightclub. During the week they kept their
dates simple, dinner or a show, always returning early
since Catarina had school the next day. On Saturdays,
though, when they could be together for the entire day,
they went racing, catching the last few meetings of the flat
season.

On their first outing to the track, Roland had worried
that Catarina would find little to interest her, that she
would only pretend to enjoy the excitement and color he
found there. He was wrong. She took to it immediately,
stressing how much more fun it was than any of the more
ladylike pursuits her father preferred for her. Roland was
amused when she wanted to know why there were no
Sunday races as well. In between explaining the Lord's
Day Observance Society, Roland considered Catarina's
father . . . Roland rarely saw the ambassador when he
called for her. When they did meet, Menendez's greetings
were always courteous, cool and formal, and Roland
could see that he was less than pleased that his only
daughter was being courted by a . . . what word would
the ambassador use? . . . by a commoner, damn it!
Roland couldn't help feeling that Menendez's faint, aloof
disapproval was like a dark cloud gathering on the horizon, and he wondered when the storm would erupt.

The trip from Brighton back to London took almost three hours because of a signal failure that stalled the train for fifty minutes. Catarina used the delay to lecture Roland on all the mistakes she thought he had made at the race where he'd lost all six races and forty pounds. Huddled in his sheepskin coat in a corner seat of the crowded first-class compartment, Roland listened in apparent agreement, smiling, nodding his head and continually telling Catarina she was perfectly right because he knew it drove her wild when he humored her this way.

'Got it all out of your system?' he asked, when she paused. He looked at the other passengers, wondering if they had been eavesdropping. No – there was never a need to eavesdrop when Catarina spoke her mind. She did it too loudly and too clearly. 'Now that you've had your say, let me explain the science of handicapping to you, young lady.' That also irritated her, being called *young lady*. But he enjoyed irritating her, watching the dark eyes flash dangerously, just as she enjoyed trying to make him mad. 'The only proper way to select a horse is because of its record, the kind of surface it's running on, the jockey and trainer, and the weight it's carrying. I would never pick a horse the way you do, just because you happen to like its name or the colors the jockey's wearing.' He turned to the other passengers. 'Am I right or wrong?'

One elderly man sitting next to Catarina had the temerity to nod. The others looked away quickly as if they hadn't been listening.

'Really?' Catarina demanded, rising to Roland's bait. 'And what did your scientific study of the records, the track conditions, the jockeys and trainers prove today? Six losers!' Satisfied that she was right, she sat back smugly in the opposite corner seat.

Roland wasn't about to give her the last word.

'What makes you such an expert? You'd never even been to a racetrack until I took you.'

'That doesn't make me any less of an expert than you. Besides, in Argentina I grew up on a horse. I know more about them than you ever will.' She turned to the elderly man who had nodded agreement with Roland. 'I gave him the names of three horses I thought would win. Did he listen to me? Did he even put one halfpenny on any of them? Oh oh, he knew better. Ask him,' she urged the man, 'what happened to Fat Fanny.'

'All right, so Fat Fanny managed to crawl in first,' Roland admitted grudgingly.

'And at what price did Fat Fanny manage to *crawl* in first?'

'Thirty-three to one,' Roland mumbled into this coat.

'I didn't hear you!'

'Thirty-three to one!' Roland fairly shouted. 'It was a poor field, you were bloody lucky, that was all.'

'Which is *bloody* well more than you were,' she retorted, mimicking his speech. 'But of course, you are too proud – too full of your precious masculine ego to listen to advice from a woman.'

Had such an argument been with anyone else, Roland would either have shrugged himself deeper into the sheepskin coat or stormed out of the coach, embarrassed by the scene. Instead, he secretly reveled in it. The tenderness and innocent, childlike quality which had attracted him to Catarina had masked a spirit and temper as quick and fiery as his own. When she thought she was right – which, disconcertingly for Roland, was as often as he thought he was right – God help the person who disagreed. Roland found her obstinacy, her willingness to stand up for herself, a challenge he welcomed. He had never met a woman quite like her before; they were, in his mind, a perfect match.

'Excuse me, sir.' Catarina softened her tone and turned to the elderly man sitting next to her. Roland had sought allies; so would she. 'Would you take advice from a woman?'

113

'If she guaranteed me a thirty-three-to-one winner I reckon I would,' the man replied, flattered by the attractive young woman asking him. When he noticed Roland glaring at him he decided to be more neutral. 'Of course when I go to the races I always leave my wife at home.'

'Clever man!' Roland applauded, turning to Catarina. 'Did you hear that?'

'All right, if that's how you feel I'll stay at home the next time. And *every* time. You can go and lose all your stupid money on your own. See if I care.'

Roland couldn't help grinning when he saw the fire glazing in her eyes, the tight set of her mouth. He impulsively made a face, jamming his top teeth down onto his lower lip. Catarina suddenly burst out laughing and reached across the narrow aisle to grasp his hands, oblivious now of the other passengers. Just then, the train jerked into motion and she slid from her seat, stumbling awkwardly in the aisle and landing on top of Roland. He held onto her tightly and kissed her, unwilling to let her go even when he noticed the other passengers and their indulgent smiles. He and Catarina were young and in love; such marvels deserved an appreciative audience.

In the month since their first date they seemed to have shared a thousand arguments just like this one. Over anything and everything: about racing, about the way he ate, about the fact that he didn't have a car when he could easily afford one. Only a week earlier, as a hint, Catarina had given him a present of a model racing car. It made no difference to her that Roland would rather be chauffeured around. She believed her man should own a car – and Roland was most definitely her man now – then they would have privacy for their intimate quarrels. Although, Catarina thought mischievously, witnesses *did* add spice at times, especially when she could pull them in to support her side. She knew it infuriated Roland when she turned their spats into public debates, but angering each other was fun; it made conciliation so much sweeter.

114

When the train reached Victoria Station in London, Catarina couldn't resist one final scene, one extra memory from the day's outing. She turned to the elderly man once again. 'Sir, how dare you disagree with my friend by saying you would listen to your wife — even for a big winner?' Then she grabbed Roland's hand and jumped onto the platform, laughing happily. Inside the compartment, the elderly man looked at his fellow passengers and touched a finger to his head. All the young people were crazy these days. The war had done it.

Catarina was still laughing when she and Roland reached the Menendez home next to the embassy. 'Wait in the drawing room. I'll be ready in a few minutes.' Before Roland could protest that there was no need for her to change, she ran from the room, closing the door and leaving him alone. He lit a cigarette and dropped down into a leather wing chair, studying a painting of Ambassador Menendez that hung on the wall above the fireplace. Next time he would let Catarina choose the horses, and then *he* could start the argument on the way home.

The drawing room door opened and Roland swung around, expecting to see Catarina again. Instead, Ambassador Menendez filled the doorway. 'Good evening, sir.' Roland stood up and dropped the cigarette into an ashtray. 'How are you?'

'Very well, thank you, Mr Eagles.' Menendez entered the room and closed the door, standing with his back to the fireplace, hands clasped behind him. 'Where are you taking my daughter this evening?'

'We're going to a play, sir.' Roland looked from the ambassador to the painting and back again. The artist had injected a warm humanity into the man's florid face; none of that warmth was evident now. 'Olivier in *Richard III* at the Old Vic.'

Menendez nodded. 'Catarina mentioned that you went to the races in Brighton this afternoon.'

So she was still at it, continuing the performance she had started on the train. 'Did she also mention that if I had listened to her advice I would have come back with my pockets bulging with money?'

Menendez appeared not to hear the question. He gazed coldly at Roland, frowning, the bushy eyebrows drawn together to form a shallow vee. 'Mr Eagles, when I decided that my daughter should complete her education in England, I did not intend for that education to include a course on handicapping horses. Do I make myself clear?'

Roland's amusement faded as the reason for Menendez's appearance became uncomfortably clear. 'You don't approve of my taking Catarina?'

'I entirely *disapprove*. Racetracks are populated by riff-raff. My daughter does not need to be exposed to such elements.'

Roland's voice took on an abrupt edge. 'Am I included in that description, sir?'

A bleak, humorless smile spread slowly across his face. 'Only if you wish to include yourself.' Menendez was never able to make up his mind about Roland, and this disturbed him deeply. From that first moment he had seen Catarina dancing with Roland at Claridge's, Menendez had been concerned. He was sure that Roland had not been included on Catarina's dance card; somehow he had bluffed or forced his way upon the girl. Then the roses the following morning. And that inane Shakespearean message . . . now these regular meetings, with Catarina so obviously captivated.

Roland was elegant, charming, apparently well off, although Catarina refused to divulge much information about him to her parents. But there existed about him a sharpness which worried the ambassador, the fine cutting edge of a confident adventurer. Or a fortune hunter. Menendez sensed these qualities and feared his daughter

116

was swimming in water far too deep for her own safety. She was too young, too inexperienced with people to know whether a man wanted her or the money she represented. 'I would appreciate it, Mr Eagles, if you would see less of my daughter. Your constant companionship of late is interfering with her studies.'

Roland glanced down at the floor, uncertain what to say. Should he defend himself by stating that Catarina's desires were most important to him – what she wanted, not what the ambassador wanted? Or should he try to salve a father's anxiety, no matter how ill-placed he felt it was, by appearing to heed Menendez's wish?

'After your visit to the theater tonight,' Menendez continued, taking Roland's silence for agreement, 'your less frequent visits to my home would be most welcome.'

Roland was saved from saying anything when the door opened. Catarina entered the drawing room, looking fresh and new in a tailored beige dress, a lightweight coat slung over her arm. When she saw her father with Roland she stopped, unsure; the room was filled with a tension she didn't understand.

'You look lovely,' Roland greeted her, eager to dispel the fear he could see in her face. 'All ready?'

'Yes.' Her eyes flicked from Roland to her father. 'Is there something wrong?'

Menendez turned from Roland and looked at his daughter. His frosty expression disappeared instantly. 'Enjoy your evening, my dear. Your mother and I will wait up for you.'

Catarina kissed her father. Roland wished him good night, then led Catarina from the house. The moment they reached the street, Catarina asked again what was wrong.

'Your father's very unhappy about me taking you to the races. He didn't like the way I exposed you to all the riffraff.'

'Oh, so that was what your big meeting was all about.' Catarina seemed relieved that it was so trivial. 'By tomorrow he will have forgotten all about it.'

Roland waved for a passing taxi. 'I don't think so. He's unhappy about me seeing you altogether, told me I was interfering with your studies, and that my less frequent calls on you would be most welcome.'

'He's never said anything like that to me.' She climbed into the taxi, waited for Roland to settle down beside her. 'If my father doesn't like me seeing you, he should speak to me about it.'

'Maybe he doesn't want to argue with you. You're his only daughter, remember?'

'So he tries to stay out of it by trying to make you stop seeing me. Did you agree with him?'

'Would I want to stop seeing a woman who can pick thirty-three-to-one winners?' He grasped her hand, holding it between his own.

'Is that the only reason?'

'I also happen to be in love with you, which is why I think we should find a way around him for now. This doesn't seem a good time to antagonize him.'

'I've made a lot of friends at school,' Catarina offered. 'I'm sure they would lie convincingly for me.'

Roland wasn't sure whether he liked the idea or not; he wasn't even sure that he relished the prospect of Catarina taking on her father in this manner; it could drive a split into a family if he persisted. Christ – he didn't want to do that . . . 'If we did that and your father happened to learn the truth, he'd be flaming mad.'

'How could he learn the truth? By seeing us together?' Catarina seemed more concerned about losing Roland than she was about enraging her father. 'I'm certain my parents would never visit racetracks or nightclubs, though my brother might.'

'Some double standard, eh?' Roland laughed. 'Your father turns his head at what Juan does but objects when you do the same thing. I wonder if somewhere there's a girl's father telling Juan exactly what your father just told me.'

'I wouldn't doubt it for a moment. Juan wouldn't listen. And neither will we.'

'Catarina, the last thing I want to see you do is fall out with your family . . .'

She gazed at him, concern in her eyes, uncertain about the change that had come over him. 'I won't fall out with them, Roland. My father will get over this. I'll persuade him.'

'How?'

'First, I'll get my mother on my side. With two women against him he'll be helpless.'

Faced with Catarina's determination, Roland could do nothing but smile. 'Okay, we'll use your friends as alibis until you can bring your father around.'

'I would be willing, tonight, to use Olivier for an alibi, Roland. Throw away the tickets. Let us go to your house instead.'

Roland didn't need any second bidding. He rapped on the glass partition and gave the driver the change in directions.

When they entered the flat Catarina looked around with impatient curiosity, wandering from room to room with Roland trailing behind. She stood in the center of the second bedroom, slowly turning around. 'This will make a wonderful nursery – once you get rid of all this garbage.' With a flourish she indicated the desk and chair, the cabinet, the piles of paper that seemed to be everywhere.

Roland watched with amusement. 'That, young lady, is not garbage. You're standing in my office away from my office.'

She picked up a piece of paper from one of the piles. 'Dear Sir, this is to confirm your order – boring!'

'Boring pays the bills around here. And put it back

119

where you found it,' he said as Catarina let the piece of paper drop from her hand. He'd spent hours sorting through orders and correspondence he'd brought home from the factory. Now that he didn't stay so late any-more, he had to work at home, often putting in two or three hours at night after returning from seeing Catarina; perhaps it was the price of becoming successful and falling in love simultaneously.

'And what is this?, Catarina plucked a sheet of paper from another stack, scanned the words. Her eyes opened wide as she read it. 'A strike?'

Roland took the piece of paper from her hand. It was a copy of a memorandum he had just sent to Simon Aronson, who had missed the previous day's sales meeting. 'One of our suppliers – a company by the name of Carters – has got labor problems at the minute. We get our heat-resistant plastic products from them, handles for irons and kettles. If Carters is struck, our people are threatening to black all their products, which will put us right up the creek.'

'When will you know whether they'll go on strike?'

'Management and union are talking right now. Management has offered so much and the union's demanding more. It could happen next week, the week after. I'm just hoping it doesn't happen at all.' Roland realized this was the first time he had ever spoken seriously about his business with Catarina. He had always kept it out of their conversations, not wanting to dull a single minute of their time together. But Catarina seemed interested in his business concerns . . . A lot of bridges were being crossed tonight.

'Can your people go on strike like this, just because others have?'

'They can, but they'd better not. It's one thing for them to strike against me because I'm a lousy employer. But striking because of something that's happening elsewhere is a situation I won't tolerate.'

'What will you do?'

'Sack the bloody lot,' he answered immediately. 'That's what I've suggested in the memo to Simon.'

She looked at the piece of paper again. 'Who is Simon?'

'My partner. He's a banker who put up most of the money. He also owns the newspaper Sally Roberts works on.'

'And how is Sally Roberts?' Catarina came closer, held his hands.

'Fine, the last time I spoke to her.'

'Do you not see her?'

'Not since your father's banquet. Surely you're not jealous of Sally?'

Catarina released his hands and turned away. She *was* jealous of Sally, jealous of any woman Roland knew.

'I still say this will make a wonderful nursery.'

'Only for a baby who wants to learn office procedure,' Roland answered, smiling at the way she had changed subjects.

'Roland, for a family you must make sacrifices. All this will have to go.'

'For a family I'd be willing to make a thousand sacrifices.'

She took his hand again and led him from the second bedroom to the master bedroom. A few seconds passed while she stood in the doorway, surveying the neatly made bed, the plumped-up pillows and comforter, the freshly laundered sheets. The chest of drawers and bed-side tables were free of dust; the nap of the carpet stood up where a vacuum cleaner had been to work. 'You keep your home spotless.'

'The cleaning woman was here this morning.'

'Is she attractive?'

'Tremendously so,' Roland answered, playing up to Catarina. 'In her sixties, as fat as a barrage balloon, has a cigarette dangling permanently from the corner of her mouth, and she needs a shave. And I wouldn't change her for the world.'

'What is this charming woman's name?'

'Mrs Smith.'

'Very likely. That's probably the name you insist she uses when you go away with her for the weekend.' Catarina entered the room, folded back the comforter and sat on the edge of the bed. 'This flat won't be big enough after all,' she said sadly. 'We'll need room for a housekeeper as well.' Suddenly she reached under one of the pillows and pulled out a pair of red-and-white-striped pajamas. 'Do you really wear these?'

'Yes, I do.' He grabbed them, embarrassed at having his pajamas not only put on public display but criticized as well.

'You must look like a stick of candy when you're asleep.'

He sat down beside her on the bed, arms around her. 'What do you wear to bed?'

'A very proper nightdress. Until' – she buried her face in his neck, nibbled gently on his skin – 'I think of you. Then I take it off and cuddle my pillow, smother it and pretend it's you.'

'Lucky pillow.' His fingers played with the buttons on her dress, then he slid it back from her shoulders and dropped it onto the bed. His lips traced the outline of her delicate shoulders, and, as she fell back onto the bed, arms outstretched to receive him, he noticed the thick clumps of curly black hair underneath her arms. A picture of Sally flashed in front of his eyes, clean-shaven, the modern woman. But at this moment Catarina was infinitely more desirable.

Her hands worked feverishly at Roland's shirt, his trousers, tugging clumsily at the buttons in her haste. She ran her fingers through the thick mat of hair on his chest, scraping his skin with her nails. Their mouths met; tongues teased, tantalized. The final restraining garments were ripped off, tossed aside.

Finally their bodies joined. Roland felt a sensation he had never experienced before – fulfillment as both a man and a person. After years without love, years of living a fragmented existence, he felt complete. Other women had simply afforded a physical release. Catarina had added an emotional, spiritual plane, draining him completely, yet at the same time filling him with a surging elation.

But his joy would have been dimmed had he known the torment that plagued Catarina as she lay in his arms. Even the warmth of Roland's closeness, the protective security he offered, failed to shield her from the distressing knowledge that in making love to him she had defied not only her father but her beliefs, the church that had been such an important part of her family life. Her mind dwelled on it with such unrelenting ferocity that the mental pain became physical. A headache began to hammer her skull above her right eye, causing her to cry.

'What is it?' Roland asked when she moved listlessly on the bed, holding her hand to her forehead, tears spilling down her cheeks.

'Just a headache.'

'What brought that on?' He was already halfway to the door, heading for the medicine cabinet and aspirin.

'Excitement. I get them sometimes.' She forced a smile, tried to stop the tears. Roland shouldn't be made to worry about her, she thought; she wanted to bring him love, not anxiety. She would have to work this out for herself.

He returned with two aspirin and a glass of water, standing over her as she took the medicine. 'This isn't going to happen every time, is it?' he asked, attempting a feeble joke.

'I hope not.' She stood up and started to collect her clothes. 'I think I'd better go home before I fall asleep here.'

Roland returned Catarina home before ten. She explained to her parents that the headache had forced her to leave the theater early, then she went to bed. Ambassador Menendez smiled to himself; perhaps this was an omen, the beginning of the end of her relationship with the Englishman.

On Monday morning, Simon Aronson visited the factory, disturbed by the memo he had received from Roland. Normally Simon's visits were confined to the weekly sales meeting, but the possibility of a strike that would wreck the delivery timetable for the increasing orders they were getting was cause for grave concern.

'We dare not be late with any of these orders,' Lawrence Chivers said in a meeting between the men. 'We're too new to take any liberties. Customers can quite easily go somewhere else because there hasn't been enough time for us to gather loyalty. And there are plenty of firms out there who'd love to pick up our business. They'd like to knock us right out of the game because we're scaring the hell out of them.'

The factory manager, Alan Winters, was also at the meeting. A short stocky man with thinning brown hair and watery blue eyes, Winters was responsible for the thirty men on the factory floor. He was another of those whom Roland had lured from a competing company. Now Roland turned to him and asked about outstanding orders. Although he already knew the answer, he wanted Simon firmly in the picture.

'The biggest problem you've got is Adler's,' Winters said, running his eyes over the clipboard he held. 'They're your major order sitting out there. Perhaps we can afford to risk a couple of the smaller ones, even plead with them for extra time and offer them something in return, but we daren't play around with an order the size of Adler's.'

'How far along is it?' Roland consulted his desk calendar. 'It's due in a month.'

'Heating elements, casings, wiring, switches . . . that's all in hand. We're waiting for the plastic components from Carters.'

124

'When will you have them?'

'Shipment's due in ten days. Then we can get right on it.'

Ten days, Roland thought, and Carters was already on the verge of a strike. He'd been on the telephone to them before the meeting; management and union were still far from agreement. Even if the components were ready, even if they were shipped, once Carters was struck Roland's own people wouldn't touch the stuff.

'Who is agitating for action?' Simon wanted to know.

'Bert Phillips,' Winters replied. 'The shop steward.'

'Have you spoken to him?' Simon asked Roland.

'Just the once, before I sent you the memo. I told him I wouldn't stand for any sympathy action.'

'Have him come here now. Perhaps we can sort out this problem immediately.'

Winters went to the factory to find the shop steward. While he was away, Simon asked Roland if he were serious about the step he had mentioned in the memo – firing any man who blacked Carters.

'What would be the difference?' Roland asked in return. 'Either way, whether they're blacking Carters or whether I fire them, we'll have no production. So we might as well get rid of them and try to start afresh when everything's sorted out.'

'What about going to another supplier?'

'All the others are tied into our competition. There isn't any way I could fill those orders in time.'

'If we get the shipment I could probably find people to do the assembly work,' Chivers offered. 'They'd work nights, on the quiet. And you'd have to pay them well.'

'Strikebreakers.' Roland mused. 'Then everyone would black *us*."

'Do you want to honor the orders?'

'Damned right I do. But I don't want to be shoved clean out of business by union bloody-mindedness.' He swung around as Winters returned with Bert Phillips, the shop

125

steward, a beanpole of a man with greasy iron gray hair and grimy blue overalls. 'Sit down, please, Mr Phillips.' Roland indicated one of the folding chairs that crowded the office.

Bert Phillips looked around, somewhat taken aback by the number of people; he had only expected to see Roland. He knew Lawrence Chivers, but he had seen Simon only rarely. Nonetheless, he knew that Simon was the man who controlled the company's finances. They must be really worried, he thought, and such knowledge gave him confidence.

'Mr Phillips, what is the position on the factory floor regarding Carters?'

'If Carters is struck, the men I represent as shop steward will refuse to handle any of their goods.'

'Even goods that have been completed before strike action begins?'

'It's immaterial when the goods are completed, Mr Eagles. If they come from Carters, and Carters is struck, then those goods are black.' Phillips was enjoying himself, putting his points to the men who paid him. He reveled in this kind of situation, where the roles were reversed and he had the power.

'Mr Phillips, your union members have no valid reason to act against me,' Roland pointed out. 'I have been more than fair with your people, their reasonable demands have always been met. If Carters should go on strike and your men disrupt any part of this business because of a misaligned loyalty, I will have no hesitation in ending the employment of any or all of them.'

'I don't think that would be very wise, Mr Eagles.'

'Why not?' Simon asked the question.

'Because you'd be closing your own doors. It's very hard to run a factory without anyone working for you, and if you sacked men with a justifiable grievance the union would take a very dim view of it.'

Roland ignored the threat in favor of continuing

126

negotiations. 'There's no way of filling our orders without these components from Carters. We're too late to go anywhere else. Besides — and in my view this is damned important — Carters has never done anything to us to warrant our going elsewhere.'

'That's not the employees' problem.'

'What do you mean it isn't the employees' problem?' Roland yelled with sudden anger. Christ, what was he dealing with here, a shop steward or a blockhead who was unable to see beyond the end of his nose? 'Isn't it the employees' problem if the company they're working for goes under? Where the hell are your brains, man? We're in this thing together.'

'Our priority is to stand by our fellow workers in their hour of strife.' Phillips sat back, pleased with himself. See what management had to say to that. The shop steward had always thought he would make a fine politician — Labor, of course. To his everlasting chagrin, however, he'd never been asked to run for election, even for local councillor. Those who did the asking suspected that Bert Phillips had a streak of larceny a mile wide — and they were right. Now Phillips waited expectantly, feeling that the time had arrived when an offer might be forthcoming — if not for the benefit of his fellow workers, at least for himself. He wasn't disappointed.

'Is there anything we could do to alter your position on this matter?' Simon asked.

Roland held up a hand quickly before Simon could continue. He wasn't about to bribe men to work for him when they were already paid to do so. 'You can return to the floor,' he told Phillips.

The shop steward got up slowly, unwilling to leave. The offer had been forthcoming, but it had been cut off before he could respond.

'Go back to work,' Roland said.

There was complete silence in the office until the door had closed behind the shop steward. Simon was the first to speak. 'We could pay him off. I swear I saw a gleam in his eyes when I broached the possibility.'

'You did. But we're not going to do business that way. We're going to ride this thing out come hell or high water.' He looked to the others for affirmation. 'Nice to know we've got a crook for a shop steward, though.'

'No one else wanted the bloody job,' Chivers said. Even Roland laughed at that.

By the next Friday afternoon sales meeting, the threatened strike had not yet materialized. Mar-Cross had been promised its complete shipment for Wednesday afternoon of the following week and Roland estimated that assembly of the Adler's order could begin the Monday after that, giving the factory an ample two weeks to meet the promised delivery date. Everything was going according to schedule.

That evening, Roland picked up Catarina from the Marble Arch home of a school friend where she was supposed to be staying. The girl's parents had gone away for the weekend to their country home in Sussex, leaving the apartment to their daughter, who had invited Catarina to keep her company. It was a fortuitous arrangement for both girls. Catarina's father thought she was in Sussex with the girlfriend and her family; and the girl's parents were relieved that their daughter wouldn't be home alone. Instead, Catarina planned to spend the entire weekend with Roland, while her girlfriend had planned a wild two-day party.

On Friday Catarina stayed the entire night with Roland for the first time. On the stroke of midnight, exhausted after making love three times, they fell asleep in each other's arms.

Early the following morning, while Roland bathed and shaved, Catarina set the table and made a simple breakfast of coffee, toast and marmalade. She had woken with a slight headache, but nothing like the pounding that had followed her first lovemaking with Roland. It disappeared completely as she moved around the kitchen. As she listened to Roland singing in the bathroom she wondered how she could have become so upset that first time. It must have been over losing her virginity, she decided. That was it – the emotional reaction of having passed from being a girl to being a woman. In that moment she had come face-to-face with the taboos drilled into her since childhood. She had struggled against them and had finally overcome them.

Finished with preparing breakfast, she looked around for something else to do. If Roland's cleaning woman hadn't left the apartment so tidy, Catarina would have been tempted to do the job herself. It was fun playing housewife, she suddenly thought. And there was a way to have even more fun . . . She raced into the bedroom, grabbed Roland's striped pajamas and threw them into the garbage. By the time Roland came out of the bath-room wearing a robe, breakfast was on the table, the bed had been made and the garbage emptied.

'Wonderful service, you should come here more often,' Roland said as he surveyed the table and accepted the newspaper Catarina had collected from the mailbox when emptying the garbage. 'A vast improvement on my normal routine.'

'What is your normal routine?' She sat down opposite him, chin resting on her hands as she gazed across the table.

'During the week it's a restaurant around the corner from the factory. Workman's café, actually.' Ignoring the front-page news he turned to the racing section, casting his eyes over the card for Leicester, where he and Catarina were going that day. 'Your friend's running again today.'

'Fat Fanny?' She stood and walked behind him, look-ing over his shoulder.

'In the one-thirty. Up a class this time, though. No hope.'

'What are the odds?'

Roland checked the betting forecast. 'Hundred-to-eight. That's twelve and a half to one, for the benefit of nonracing folks like you.'

'I know what a hundred-to-eight is.' Since the previous Saturday she had studied the racing pages of newspapers every day, determined to prove that she knew as much as Roland.

He handed her the newspaper and started to eat. 'Going to twist my arm to put some money on it?'

'You shouldn't need your arm twisted. You should be clever enough to learn from experience.'

After breakfast, Roland washed the dishes while Catarina got dressed. By nine o'clock they were ready to leave for St Pancras Station where they would take the train to Leicester. On the train, while Roland contented himself holding Catarina's hand and dreamily watching the countryside slip past, Catarina went through the Leicester race card, picking the names of horses she liked, discarding them as others took her fancy. By the time they reached Leicester, she had two more horses to go with Fat Fanny – two longshots with no winning record named Boring Dora and Jealous Nat. Roland had heard of neither of them.

'You must be joking!' he burst out when she showed him the circled names.

Catarina looked around the compartment at the other passengers, and Roland clamped a hand over her mouth. 'All right, all right! I'll put a bet on them for you. Just don't drag the entire world into it.'

Smiling triumphantly, Catarina stood up and prepared to leave the train.

At the track, they took their seats in the grandstand, huddling close to each other for protection against the damp chilling wind. 'What are you betting on?' Catarina asked. Roland pointed out the selections he had made for the seven races. 'What about Fat Fanny, Boring Dora and Jealous Nat?' she asked when she saw that the names of

130

her selections were missing from Roland's list.

Grimacing, Roland checked the card again. Then he noticed something he hadn't seen before. 'Your three crippled nags are running in the one-thirty, two-forty and three-fifty, the three races specified for the tote treble.'

'The what?' Catarina felt annoyed with herself for not understanding the term.

'Tote treble. It's a three-horse accumulator. Nearly all the money wagered goes into the pool which is shared by however many people hold the winning tickets.'

'How much are the tickets?'

'Couple of shillings each. Tell you what,' he said grandly, 'I'll treat you to ten tickets on that three-horse selection.'

'Last of the generous men. I'll tell you what – whatever my horses win will be my present to you.'

'Thanks, presents of nothing I can do without.'

'We shall see, Mr Know-it-all,' she said as he stood up. Catarina watched as he went to the tote window to place her bet, then thread his way down to the bookmakers' pitches in front of the grandstand to make his own bet on the first race. As he turned back towards her, still thirty yards away, she cupped her hands to her mouth and yelled above the crowd, 'Roland, I threw away your rotten candy-striped pajamas!'

Roland's face flushed crimson and he quickly looked the other way. When he turned toward Catarina again he saw, to his horror, that her hands were still at her mouth. 'They're in the garbage where they belong!'

Disregarding the people who were laughing at the incident, Roland rushed back to the seat and grabbed hold of Catarina's arm. 'One more word, and so help me I'll put you across my knee in front of this crowd.'

'You wouldn't dare.' She traced the contours of her lips with her tongue and grinned at him.

'Watch the race,' he said, turning away from her.

'Rollie . . . I am going to call you Rollie in the future

131

because you look so roly-poly in that coat,' she prattled on, hugging him. 'Rollie, I love you.'

'I love you, too. Now watch the race.'

Roland lost the first race and he accepted the result stoically. But he was shocked when his own selection in the six-furlong one-thirty, a strongly fancied mount named Nancy's Folly, lost by a nose to Fat Fanny. 'Ten to one,' Catarina crowed in his ear. 'How much have I won so far, Rollie?'

'Nothing.' Damn her – her luck was holding out better than his. 'Your other horses have to win as well.'

'They will,' she answered with a confidence that disturbed him.

In the two-forty, a mile-and-a-half race, Roland's selection – another favorite – avoided total humiliation by finishing one from last. To make matters worse, Catarina's Boring Dora put on a frenzied spurt in the final half furlong to win by a length, pulling away.

'What are you, a witch?' Despite the cold, Roland began to sweat uncomfortably inside the sheepskin coat. Boring Dora had paid twenty-five to one. Coupled with ten-to-one Fat Fanny in the first leg, the tote treble was already worth a small fortune. Roland knew that the track odds didn't reflect directly on the tote treble's value – that was determined by the number of winning tickets – but all the same he couldn't help wondering how many people were still left in the pool. Catarina's ten tickets and how many others? And who else, if anyone, had been foolish enough to couple the first two winners with such a dubious selection as Jealous Nat?

'Does two out of three count, Rollie?' She knew it didn't, but she couldn't resist needling Roland.

'Certainly, they let you take your tickets home as souvenirs.' He barely even noticed the name she had conjured up for him; all he could think of was the tote treble. What if Jealous Nat won? No . . . it couldn't. Damn it . . . it could! The longshots were having a field day out there.

He became so engrossed in possibilities that he barely followed the three-fifteen race. Catarina tapped him on the arm. 'Congratulations, you finally won. You had your ten pounds on an odds-on favorite. You won eight pounds.'

Rollie brightened up. 'Which is more than you'll do, my girl.' He went down to the bookmaker's stand to collect his winnings and place twenty pounds on the strong favorite in the three-fifty, Bonnie May. Catarina's Jealous Nat was shown at thirty-three to one. Some hopes, Roland thought as he returned to his seat.

When the horses for the three-fifty, a five-furlong sprint, entered the ring, Catarina walked down for a closer look. She returned, her eyes sparkling with excitement and confidence. 'Jealous Nat is beautiful, Rollie. He prances around like a ballet dancer, and his jockey wears a gorgeous emerald green shirt. I just know he's going to win, and then I'll give you the biggest present you've ever had.'

'Only if Bonnie May breaks a leg somewhere,' Roland replied, patting Catarina's hand. He watched the field of sixteen horses canter down to the start, his eyes riveted on the scarlet-and-white colors of Bonnie May's jockey. He felt a twinge of sadness that it was nearly impossible for Catarina's horse to win. Bonnie May had won the last three times out, all sprints, all won in the final hundred yards with a powerful finish.

The field came under starter's orders. Roland stood, clutching Catarina's hand as the race began. Immediately, the horses divided into two even groups, one on the stand side, the other on the rail. Both Bonnie May and Jealous Nat were close to the stand, lost in the middle of the pack. Then, as they entered the penultimate furlong, the emerald green of Jealous Nat's jockey moved up, into third, then second and, as the stand group passed the one-furlong marker, into first. The group of horses on the rail faded as Jealous Nat made its move. Right behind it, breaking from the pack and matching Jealous Nat step for step, was the scarlet and white of Bonnie May.

'Come on!' Catarina screamed. 'Come on!' She snatched her hand away from Roland, clenched both fists to her face in horror as she watched Jealous Nat falter. A hundred yards to go and the gap was closing. Fifty yards and there was nothing between the two horses. Mud flew from eight hooves as the favorite and longshot battled side by side. Only inches separated them. They seemed to collide and break apart again. Hunched over their mounts' necks the two jockeys flailed with their whips for that extra yard of speed. And as they passed the winning post in front of the grandstand, Roland closed his eyes and put his arm around Catarina.

'Sorry – the distance was fifty yards too much.'

She buried her face in his shoulder; the excitement had drained her, now only biting disappointment remained. 'But you won,' she managed to reply.

For the first time in his life, Roland fervently wished that he had lost. Not because of the money Catarina's treble would have paid – that was beside the point – but for Catarina herself and the lift it would have given her.

'How much did you win?' she asked quietly.

'Fifty pounds. Bonnie May started out at five to two.'

'Good.' She started to cheer up, managed a weak smile. 'You improved on your performance at Brighton last week. But what a thrill I had.'

'I shared every moment of it with you.' He felt in his coat pocket for his winning ticket and found Catarina's tickets, too. 'Here, two out of three – you get to take them home as souvenirs.'

'Thank you. I will have them mounted and framed.'

As Roland lifted his eyes toward the board announcing the winners he felt the hair on his neck begin to rise. Next to Bonnie May's number in the winner's slot was a large, ominous letter O. 'Objection,' he said to Catarina.

'Objection? What does that mean?'

'Maybe when the two horses seemed to collide.' He put a hand on her shoulder, too nervous even to speak. Thirty seconds dragged by . . . a minute . . . two . . .

At last, the public-address system crackled into life. There was a flurry of movement at the board as numbers were moved around. 'Following a steward's inquiry, the result of the three-fifty is now: first, Jealous Nat; second, Bonnie May; third . . .'

Roland did not even hear the third. He was too busy looking at Catarina. 'My god, you've won.'

With forced calmness they waited until the tote-treble dividend was announced. It was five hundred and thirty pounds for each of the ten winning tickets – and Catarina held all ten. Together they walked to the tote window and presented the tickets. The clerk gazed at them in amazement, then told Roland he would arrange for a check to be issued.

'We'll take cash.'

'Cash? Five thousand three hundred pounds comes to one thousand and sixty five-pound notes. And that's if we've got that many fivers, which I seriously doubt.'

'We've got big pockets.'

Half an hour later, when they left the track, Roland could appreciate the name Catarina had given him that afternoon. Rollie . . . roly poly. That was how he felt, big and bulky with bundles of money stuffed into every pocket. Even Catarina carried more than one thousand pounds stuffed into her handbag and coat pocket. They found a taxi to take them to the railroad station and sat in the back seat, laughing like schoolchildren as the enormity of their fortune became clearer.

'Presents of nothing you can do without, eh?' Catarina kidded.

'I can't take this money, be serious.'

'I can't take it either. What would my father say if I walked in with more than five thousand pounds? He would think I robbed a bank.'

'You could always tell him you've gone into your country's national business – taking in Nazi war criminals for a profit.'

She punched him playfully in the ribs.

As the taxi neared the railway station, Catarina let out a shriek. 'Stop! Stop at once!'

The driver jammed on his brakes. 'What's the matter?'

'Reverse. Go back to that car shop we just passed.'

'Car shop?' The driver looked behind him. A hundred yards away was a Jaguar showroom. He backed up.

'Thank you. This will be fine.' Catarina got out of the taxi, Roland followed, thrusting a large five-pound note at the driver and telling the amazed man to keep the change.

'Might I ask what we're doing here?' Roland said to Catarina as they stood in the street.

'I want you to spend some of your winnings. I dare not take any of the money, but you can buy something I will enjoy.' She raised her arm and pointed to a dark green convertible sports car standing alone in the showroom's parking lot.

Roland looked at the car and gulped. Low and long, the wings were swept back gracefully. In the front of the car a massive hood stretched forward until it ended in a narrow radiator grille, and the soft top made the car seem precariously unsafe. But Roland's initial reservations were balanced by his appreciation of the car's beauty. He had never thought of cars having personality, but this particular model was like a prize athlete, strong yet graceful, a balance of power and coordination. He walked around, looked inside, saw the short gearstick, the speedometer that showed a hundred and twenty miles an hour, the cluster of instruments he didn't even begin to understand.

'May I help you, sir?'

Roland turned around to see a young man in a tweed sportcoat and flannel trousers; just the sort one would

136

expect to drive something like this, he couldn't help thinking. Before he had a chance to say anything Catarina spoke up. 'We would like to buy this car. What is it, please?'

The young man smiled at the mixture of determination and naïvete. 'It's a Jaguar XK-120, miss. But I'm afraid it's not for sale.'

'Why not? You sell cars, don't you?'

'Yes, miss, we do. But this particular model hasn't been on the market long and we've got a backlist of orders that we can't fill until next year. This is my own car but I've agreed to let them use it as a showroom model.'

Roland looked inside the car again; five thousand miles showed on the odometer.

'How much is a car like this?' Catarina asked.

'New, nine hundred and ninety-eight pounds.'

'We will give you fifteen hundred pounds for it, right now.'

Roland spun around in shock as Catarina made the offer. He saw the young man blink in surprise, open his mouth to say something, then close it again.

'Isn't that enough? All right, sixteen hundred pounds.'

'Catarina!' Roland finally managed to blurt out. 'What in the blazes do you think you're doing?'

'I want you to have this car. For us.'

There was such determination in her voice that Roland knew when not to argue. He turned to the young man. 'Will you sell it to us for sixteen hundred pounds?'

The salesman nodded, amazed at the offer.

'Can you arrange insurance coverage as well? We want to drive it back to London.'

'Come inside.' Roland and Catarina followed the salesman into the office where he wrote out the sales contract. Then he telephoned a broker to arrange insurance.

'One other point,' Roland said. 'How about an hour's worth of driving lessons as well?'

'Do you *have* a driving license, sir?' The entire transaction was so unusual that the salesman wouldn't have been surprised to find out that neither of his customers could drive.

'Yes.' Roland produced it. 'But I haven't driven for a while. And certainly never anything quite like this.'

'Come on, I'll take you for a spin.' Leaving Catarina in the office, the salesman led Roland out to the car. He spent twenty minutes going over it, explaining the instruments, the engine. Terms like three-point-four-litres and double overhead camshafts were lost on Roland. He wasn't interested in the technical details. He just wanted to get his hands on the steering wheel. For the first time in his life he *wanted* to drive.

The salesman took the car slowly through Leicester, then out into the countryside. Before Roland realized what was happening they were doing ninety miles an hour. The wind whistled around the soft top, ballooning its shape, and Roland's stomach began to churn in almost childlike anticipation.

'Ready to try it now, sir?'

'You bet.' Roland changed seats, put the stick in first and let up on the clutch. The engine stalled. He tried again, this time with more success. Gently he eased the needle up to five thousand revs per minute and changed into second. Ahead of him, the massive hood seemed to stretch forever. The white lines in the road flew toward him, then merged into a single solid barrier as he pressed down on the accelerator.

'I think that should do it, sir.'

Roland dropped his eyes to the speedometer. The needle was flickering just below the hundred-and-ten mark. He eased off and let out his breath in one long, nervous sigh.

When they returned to the showroom, Catarina was waiting outside, worried because they had been gone so long. Roland climbed out of the car, a grin stretching across his face. He kissed her, then followed the salesman back into the office.

Ten minutes later the deal was complete. Roland handed over sixteen hundred pounds in five-pound notes and received the log book, bill of sale, keys and the insurance binder.

'Good luck with it,' the salesman said, still somewhat bemused by the rapid progression of events.

'Thanks.' Roland held open the passenger door for Catarina. As he slipped into the driver's seat he thought of Sally Roberts – wouldn't she be jealous; this was the car every owner of a prewar MG wanted!

He turned the key, pressed the starter button and listened to the engine burst into life. His elation quickly dimmed as he remembered one minor point. With a sheepish look on his face he climbed out of the car and walked back to the salesman. 'Which way is London?'

Having rarely driven Roland didn't know his way around the countryside by road. He figured it was about time he learned.

The hundred-mile drive back to London took more than three hours due mainly to Roland losing his way half a dozen times. They arrived at Regent's Park just after nine. In the bedroom, Catarina opened her handbag and turned out her pockers. Roland followed suit, tossing piles of money haphazardly onto the bed. Then they stood gazing in wonderment at the financial rainbow – white five-pound notes, green singles, red ten-shilling notes the racetrack officials had used to pay the bet.

'Looks like someone's made confetti out of an Italian flag,' Roland said. 'Want to count it?'

Catarina shook her head. 'I want to make love on it, not count it.' She threw herself backwards onto the bed, bouncing up and down, scattering the money with her hands while she giggled uncontrollably. Roland dropped down beside her, holding her tightly, trying to kiss her as the money fluttered between their faces.

'What are we going to do with all this?' Catarina asked.

'Spend it. Waste it. Every single penny on our own pleasure. You name it and we'll do it.'

'Why don't you do something sensible with it? Surely it would help your business?'

Roland thought about Bert Phillips – he could bribe the shop steward a hundred times with this money. But he'd be damned if he would with this or any money. 'Gambling winnings aren't real. They're to be spent and enjoyed. Money that you don't earn with the sweat of your brow doesn't mean a blasted thing.'

'I want fifty pounds to buy a gift for you.'

'Take a thousand – take two.' He scooped up a handful of notes and stuffed them down the front of Catarina's dress.

'Fifty is enough.'

'Is that all I'm worth?'

She laughed and bit his ear. Yelling in mock pain, he sat up and, before she could resist, dragged her across his knee. 'This is for throwing away my pajamas. One wallop for every candy stripe.' She pummeled his legs with her fists as the flat of his hand beat a gentle but steady tattoo on her flesh.

'You know what I'm going to do with all this money?' he said, refusing to let her up. 'I'm going to buy two thousand pairs of striped pajamas.'

'And I'll throw them away two thousand times!' Catarina said as she wriggled free and massaged her behind. 'With you inside them.'

At eleven o'clock they decided to get something to eat. They dressed and hurried down to the car, and Roland sped through the West End to an Italian restaurant in Soho where they gorged themselves on pasta and chianti.

140

When they finished, Catarina suggested they visit her girl-friend's house to see how the party was going.

Two young men were standing near the XK–120 when Roland and Catarina came out of the restaurant. Roland watched them with tolerant amusement. A day earlier he would have thought they were crazy, but now that he'd driven the Jaguar he could appreciate their interest. One man was admiring the car from a distance, taking in the graceful lines, while the other, with his back to Roland, was bending to look through the passenger window at the interior.

'Two thousand pounds and it's yours,' Roland called out.

'Profiteer,' Catarina whispered from behind him. 'How dare you try to sell my car?'

The man who had been admiring the Jaguar from a distance turned around. 'How fast have you had her up to?'

'Hundred and ten,' Roland replied nonchalantly. Even in the dim glow from the streetlamp he could see the envy in the man's eyes.

'Tell him where,' Catarina exhorted. 'Along Park Lane in the middle of the rush hour.'

At the sound of Catarina's voice, the second man straightened up and swung around. Slim and dark, he stood perfectly still for a moment, his eyes wide open in surprise. It was Juan Menendez, Catarina's brother. Suddenly he lunged forward, confronting her in a torrent of Spanish. 'What are you doing here? You were supposed to have gone away for the weekend! What are you doing with him?'

'It's none of your business what I do and with whom I do it!' Catarina shot back as Roland stepped in Juan's path. 'You mind your own business!'

'You are my business!' Juan tried to push his way past Roland. Because Juan was four inches shorter and fifty

141

pounds lighter, it was no contest. Roland held him easily, while the friend looked on, uncertain what to do.

'Are you going to calm down a bit?' Roland asked.

'Get your hands off me or I'll—'

'You'll what?' Roland smelled alcohol on Juan's breath and realized he was drunk; the liquor was giving him the courage to continue the struggle.

'You've kidnapped my sister!'

'Don't be so bloody stupid.' Roland opened his arms and Juan sprang free. Quivering with anger, he pointed a finger at his sister.

'Wait until father learns of this. Then see if he ever allows you to go away for the weekend again.'

'Please don't tell him.' There was fear in Catarina's voice.

'Of course I'll tell him. Even if you have no respect for yourself, I still care about our family name and reputation.'

'You're doing a lot for it yourself right now,' Roland couldn't resist saying.

None of them heard the steady measured tread of approaching footsteps. 'What's all this about, then?'

Roland turned around to face the middle-aged beat constable who had heard the raised voices. 'Nothing, officer. A discussion, that's all.'

'That your version, too, miss?' the policeman asked Catarina, who nodded. 'What about you, sir?' he asked Juan. 'You're the one doing all the yelling.'

'I am Juan Menendez, son of the Argentinian ambassador. And I am trying to rescue my sister from that man.'

'Are you his sister, miss?' The constable realized that he had to tread softly. Criminals were his meat, not diplomatic family fights where it wasn't even worth going after a drunk-and-disorderly charge.

'Yes, I am. And there is no need for rescuing, thank you. I'm with this man'– she slipped her arm through Roland's – 'by choice.'

'I reckon that's it then, sir,' the constable said to Juan. 'Now how about moving on? Go home and sleep it off.'

Juan fired a final, angry glare at Roland, then turned on his heel and stormed away, followed by his friend.

Catarina and Roland sat in the car for a few minutes, deciding what to do. They had no doubt that Juan would tell the ambassador. Menendez would be furious that his daughter had lied to him about spending the weekend in the country. But his anger would know no bounds if he ever learned that she'd spent the weekend at Roland's apartment. 'You'd better go to your friend's place,' Roland said at last. 'We'll pick up your clothes from my flat, then I'll run you over to Marble Arch. Maybe your father won't be too upset if he thinks you just wanted to have some fun with your friends.'

'I suppose so.' Catarina sat back, wiping tears from her eyes as Roland drove toward Regent's Park. The weekend had suddenly died and she felt a headache coming on. This one had nothing to do with guilt, though; it was from anger at her brother who she knew would betray her.

Roland dropped off Catarina at her friend's house and stayed at the party for a short while. When he returned to Regent's Park, he sat on the edge of the bed, surrounded by the money from Leicester and cursing both Juan Menendez and the Jaguar. If he hadn't bought the car they never would have bumped into Juan. And if Catarina hadn't won all the money he never would have bought the damned car to begin with.

He picked up a bundle of cash, crumpled it into a ball and threw it angrily at the wall.

Juan Menendez reached home just before one o'clock, too late to wake his father. He waited until morning, after his parents had returned from church. Then, in an embassy car, the ambassador and his son drove to Marble Arch. Half an hour later they returned with Catarina and her hastily packed suitcase.

The family quickly assembled in the drawing room for what Catarina felt was more of a trial than a discussion. As the defendant, she sat in the leather wing chair. Her father, prosecutor and judge, stood with his back to the fireplace beneath the painting of himself. Juan, the witness, sat on the sofa. Maria Menendez, the anxious spectator, sat on a straight-backed chair, nervously kneading a lace handkerchief between her plump fingers.

Ambassador Menendez wasted no time in leveling the accusation at Catarina. 'You lied to your mother and to me. Is this what your English education has taught you, to show no respect for your parents?'

'Father, I wanted to attend the party. What would you have said had I asked you?'

'I would have said no. I saw what kind of party it was – common music, bottles lying all over the place, boys and girls sleeping on the floor. No daughter of mine attends such parties.'

'What about Eagles?' Juan cut in. 'She wasn't at the party when I saw her. She was with Eagles.'

'Roland came to the party last night. We went out for something to eat,' Catarina lied.

'So, now you arrange to meet in secret, behind my back,' Menendez said.

'You left us no choice. It is the only way we can meet since you have virtually forbidden Roland to come here,' Catarina answered defiantly. She turned to her mother for support; surely she could remember how it felt to be young and in love. Or had it happened so long ago that such memories no longer existed?

'Nicanor, is there such harm in allowing Catarina to see this man?' his wife asked.

'I don't like him,' Menendez stated flatly. 'He's a gold-digger. He isn't interested in you, Catarina, he's interested only in this family's money. Believe me, if you were a poor girl he would not look twice at you. I know these things.'

144

'How dare you insult him like that? You only think you know about such things because *you* married into wealth, but you don't know anything about Roland!' It was the first time Catarina could ever remember raising her voice to her father, and she had picked a subject that was sure to wound – in fact, one his political opponents often used. The ambassador's own family had been comfortable when he had married Maria Menendez, but their wealth was paltry when compared to his wife's. Maria Menendez was an only child, and when her parents died control of the copper mine and the ranches had passed into Menendez's hands. From that base he had expanded his own family's single hotel in Buenos Aires into a small chain located in South American capitals.

Catarina saw the shocked expression on her father's face and for a moment she was too stunned by her own boldness to continue. Finally she broke the silence. 'He does not need our money', she said quietly. 'He has enough of his own.'

'He certainly has enough to buy an expensive sports car,' Juan cut in. 'You could be killed in a car like that. He even boasted that he's driven it at more than a hundred miles an hour.'

'I noticed *you* looking at it with envy dripping from your eyes.'

Juan fell silent, knowing his sister was right. He would give his right arm to own such a car, and his jealousy fostered hatred for this man his sister had grown so fond of.

'Were you with him when he drove that fast?' Menendez asked.

'No.' Catarina was not about to be trapped into admitting that she had gone to Leicester with Roland the previous day. 'And I don't think he ever drove that fast. He just said it for the benefit of Juan's friend.'

'Tell us about Roland, Catarina,' Señora Menendez said. Her husband's hard line approach was obviously solving nothing; it only served to increase Catarina's stubbornness. Surely a more sympathetic attitude would help . . .

'What is there to tell? He is a friend. I like him very much.'

'Catarina, your father and I are only concerned for your welfare. If we knew more about Roland, perhaps we wouldn't be so worried. What about his family? Have you ever met them – does he talk about them?'

'He has no family. His parents died in the war. His brother and sister, also. An air raid.'

'Tragic, tragic,' her mother said sympathetically. 'Is he a Catholic?'

Catarina lowered her eyes and stared at the carpet. 'His mother was.'

'And his father?'

'He was Jewish.' When she raised her eyes to look at he family, it was as if their expressions had been carved from stone.

'Do you love him?' Señora Menendez asked.

'No.' Catarina hated herself for the lie, but she had to assuage her parents' concern. 'I enjoy his company and he treats me well. What more could you ask from an escort?'

'Catarina, will you please excuse us?' Menendez said. 'You as well, Juan.'

Juan held open the door for his sister. As she passed, she returned his smirk with an angry glare.

Ambassador Menendez sat down wearily in the chair that Catarina had vacated. 'We must put a stop to this friendship immediately, Maria. Do we forbid her to see him again – or do we send her away?'

'Why do we have to stop it at all?' his wife replied. 'It is harmless.'

'It is anything *but* harmless. I don't care if this Eagles has money of his own, if he has his own business. As far as I'm concerned this man is only interested in increasing his wealth. We must protect her from someone like that.'

146

'Catarina is our only daughter. Would you really drive her from us by sending her away?'

'I know she is our only daughter and that is why we must act. Did we raise her to marry such a man?'

'Do you mean Jew – a half-Jew?'

'What does it matter what I mean?' Menendez said angrily. 'He is not fit for her. All right,' he admitted when he saw his wife's expectant look. 'Did we raise her to marry some half-Jew? What would our . . . our friends say?'

'Do we have to worry about such an eventuality?' Maria Menendez recalled the way Catarina had looked to her for support; now she felt she should side with her daughter, otherwise Catarina would feel she had no support and would run even faster into the arms of any man who showed affection. 'Catarina said herself that she is not in love with this Roland Eagles.'

'Of course she is in love with him. She is infatuated with him. Do you think she would defy us as she has for friendship?'

'Nicanor, take your time. Let this friendship, this romance, continue for a while. Perhaps he will grow tired of her.'

'Never. Such a man never tires of the company of money.'

'Then we must hope she will tire of him. Let it pass instead of sending her away or locking her up at home. If you stop them from seeing each other you will only drive her to him more. Give her a chance to come to her senses on her own. When she sees that it is wrong, she will thank us for our concern.'

Menendez raised his hand to his forehead. His wife was right . . . there was no point in driving a wedge between them now. His daughter had enough intelligence – enough Menendez blood – to know the difference between what was right for the family and what was wrong.

Or at least so he hoped.

CHAPTER FIVE

On Monday morning Bert Phillips found himself in a quandary over the fact that his employer refused to make a financial compromise to ensure a smooth production schedule. And it wasn't as if he couldn't afford to make such an offer, Phillips decided grudgingly as he thought about the new Jaguar he'd seen Roland drive to the factory that morning. Phillips had heard through the factory grapevine about the massive win on the horses over the weekend. Typical, he thought – money goes to money. We slave our guts out so the boss can treat himself to a car like that; then he's too bloody selfish to toss a few sheets my way.

By Monday evening, Phillips knew that negotiations between union and management at Carters had broken down. A strike was set for Wednesday morning, the same day that the delivery to Mar-Cross was scheduled. The delivery would be made since the drivers weren't on strike – but what was the point in ordering his workers to black Carters' merchandise if neither he nor they could profit by it? Oh, it would look fine to act on behalf of the Carters' people, but it was a principle Phillips couldn't afford – not when there was something to be gained by it.

It was a dilemma to tax the mind. Eagles had shown clearly that he wouldn't pay. Then who would? Certainly not Simon Aronson, even if he had floated the idea initially. He'd be sure to side with his partner. Then what about one of the customers who was expecting merchandise for the Christmas season? How desperate were they for their orders? Phillips stayed up thinking about it until long after his wife had gone to bed. Finally, he reached his decision. Most of the outstanding orders were small, with the exception of one large retail firm that would be caught up short if its order was late. Phillips decided to pay a call on Adler's.

The following morning he phoned the factory saying he was sick and would try to be in later. Then, wearing his one good suit, he traveled from his apartment in Burnt Oak to the West End. By ten o'clock he was at Adler's, asking to see the electrical goods buyer on an urgent matter. After ten minutes, Bruce Simpkins came out to see him. 'Mr Phillips, I'm a very busy man. You don't have an appointment. What can I do for you?'

'I think I might be able to help you.' Without waiting for an invitation, Phillips entered Simpkins' office and sat down. 'I don't know whether you've heard yet, but there's going to be a strike at the factory which supplies Mar-Cross with heat-resistant plastic components.'

'I was aware that a strike was possible, but I've been assured that our order will not be affected.'

'It won't. The parts for your order are being delivered tomorrow morning. The only problem is, the men are threatening to black Carters' goods once they arrive.'

'I see.' Simpkins bit his lower lip. 'Where do you come into this?'

'I'm shop steward at Mar-Cross.'

'Would your union members black Carters' merchandise completed before the strike began?' Phillips nodded. 'Why have you come to see me about it?' Simpkins asked.

'Because I'm disturbed by the stand our management is taking. They just don't seem to care. They're getting ready for a head-on clash with the workers and they don't give a damn about who gets hurt.'

'Like people waiting for orders, eh? What can *you* do about it, Mr Phillips? I assume you can do something, otherwise you wouldn't be here.'

'I can stop it. The men will listen to me.'

'I see.' Simpkins reached for the telephone. 'Blackmail, is it?'

'Calling Mar-Cross about my visit won't help you, Mr Simpkins. I'll catch hell and have to find another job, but your order will still be delayed indefinitely. Empty shelves at Christmas time won't do much for your store's profits."

'We could order elsewhere.'

'Not this late, you couldn't.'

Simpkins removed his hand from the telephone, aware that if the order went sour he might be held to blame. However, he was not about to bribe this crooked union official from his own pocket. It was time to shift responsibility onto those who could afford to carry it. 'Just a moment,' he told Phillips. He left the office and walked up the corridor toward the woman who sat in front of the executive offices. Monty Adler was busy, so Simpkins settled for Albert. He spent five minutes in the office, then returned to Phillips. 'Come with me.'

Albert Adler was standing by the window when Phillips entered the office. He waved for Simpkins to leave. 'Hardly the bearer of good tidings, are you?' he greeted Phillips in his high, reedy voice.

'I'm just doing my best to avoid a nasty situation, Mr Adler.' Phillips looked around the office and selected the most comfortable chair, confident that he held all the aces. He was perfectly at ease; Albert was just another member of management – another of the *thems*.

'And profit yourself at the same time, no doubt,' Albert said. 'Not that I've got anything against profit, let me hasten to add.'

Management never does, Phillips felt like saying. Instead, he remained quiet and waited for Albert to continue.

'How much did you have in mind to persuade your men not to interfere with our order?'

'I was thinking of a hundred pounds.' Phillips warmed

to the thin, bony man in the overly formal clothes; he understood the rules of the game exactly. All in all, a much better man to deal with than Roland Eagles.

'That's a lot of money.'

'You're expecting a big order.'

'True. But by ensuring the smooth passage of production you would also be helping other retailers. I don't see why we should pay a hundred pounds for their benefit.' Albert walked around the office, head bowed in thought. He knew he should throw this blackmailer out on his ear. His father would do just that. But who was to say that his father was always right? Perhaps Albert could use this situation to his advantage, and show his father just how shrewd a businessman he was. 'Will the strike at Carters be a lengthy affair?'

'It could go a month.'

'All right.' Albert had reached his decision. 'I'll give you a hundred pounds. But only if your men *refuse* to handle Carters.'

'What?' Phillips blinked in shock.

Albert smiled and Phillips couldn't help thinking that the pale man looked like a grinning corpse. 'You heard me. A hundred pounds to disrupt Mar-Cross. Make our order late.'

'But why would you want to do that?' Phillips started to flounder, realizing too late that he was hopelessly out of his depth.

'None of your business, Mr Phillips. Just do it. Otherwise I get right onto your factory and you're out of work. And even if we do have glaring gaps in our shelves come Christmas time, that won't be much consolation to you, will it?' Albert opened the door.

Phillips rose unsteadily to his feet, a sharp contrast to the self-assured wheeler dealer of a moment ago. As he passed Albert he said, 'Carters will be blacked. The shipment will be left to rot in the delivery area.'

'No, not to rot, Mr Phillips,' Albert corrected him.

151

'We'll want our order eventually. Good morning, you can find your own way out.'

Phillips returned home to change into his working clothes, understanding only that he had stumbled into something far beyond his own comprehension. He had come away with what he wanted, but he wasn't certain he knew why.

Tuesday evening, Roland drove apprehensively to Wilton Crescent to pick up Catarina for their dinner date. She had called him Sunday afternoon at home to tell him how her father and brother had collected her from the party, the meeting that had followed and her father's decision to allow her to continue seeing Roland, but under very rigid conditions. There would be no more afternoons and no more opportunities for stolen weekends. Only evenings, and then Catarina would have to be home by eleven o'clock.

It was better than nothing, Roland reasoned. In fact he was surprised that he could see her at all . . . why was Ambassador Menendez making this compromise? Because of his wife? Or because of Catarina? He knew that even the most powerful of men could be twisted around an only daughter's finger.

As he drove into Wilton Crescent Roland saw the stout figure of the ambassador standing in the drawing room window, a hand holding back the curtains. Roland reversed gently into a parking space, acting like a man driving a standard family car instead of an XK-120; he didn't want to give the man any further reason to restrict Catarina.

'Good evening, Mr Eagles, how are you?' the ambassador greeted Roland when he entered the house.

'Fine, thank you, sir. I must apologize for the other evening—'

Menendez held up his hand. 'I have discussed the matter with my daughter and now it is closed. Where are you going this evening?'

'Just out for dinner, sir.'

Memendez assumed his customary position in front of the fireplace. 'How is your business?'

'Doing excellently, I'm glad to say.' Roland wasn't about to tell him that there was the possibility of a strike the next day – that would be another mark against him – the inability to control his own work force. In fact, Roland was unsure what he would find when he went to the factory the following morning. Bert Phillips had told him that there was to be a union meeting that evening to discuss the situation, and Roland didn't have much hope.

Maria Menendez entered the drawing room to tell Roland that Catarina would be ready shortly. She joined her husband in front of the fireplace. 'My daughter mentioned that your family died during the war, Mr Eagles. I am so terribly sorry.'

'Thank you. A bomber jettisoned its load while trying to escape from a Spitfire. I watched it happen from a mile or two away.' He wondered why both the ambassador and his wife were keeping him company. Were they scared to leave him alone while he waited for Catarina?

'It must have been awful to live here during the war,' she continued.

'In the end it was far worse to live in Germany. Too bad that a lot of those responsible for the war escaped.'

'Escaped?'

'Escaped,' Roland repeated, looking pointedly at Menendez. The ambassador made his feelings clear to Roland; in turn Roland wanted to make his own feelings known to Menendez.

Menendez had no difficulty in catching the gist of Roland's comment, and he spread his hands sympathetically. 'In Argentina we are proud of our German colony just as we are proud of our Italian and Spanish influences.

153

It is impossible for my government to check thoroughly every German refugee who seeks to take advantage of our hospitality. If we know that a certain person is guilty of crimes against humanity we do not grant them sanctuary. But all too often, how are we to know?'

'Please – you don't have to explain anything. Besides, your government never gave sanctuary to the crew of the aircraft that wiped out my family. They crashed into the sea a mile from where they dropped their bombs.'

'I will see if Catarina is ready yet,' Señora Menendez cut in quickly. The war and the people responsible for it who now lived peacefully in Argentina were subjects best left alone. Too many Argentinian government officials, close friends of the ambassador, had made themselves wealthy by aiding such people.

Roland was relieved when Catarina appeared a minute later. The conversation between himself and Menendez was strained, artificial, and he knew he was there only under sufferance. The ambassador obviously was accepting him for his daughter's or his wife's sake, and hoped, in time, that Catarina would find another man. There was no way he could know that such optimism was completely baseless.

They dined at a French restaurant in Soho. Over dessert, Roland removed a small package from his jacket. 'I have something for you.'

'And I have something for you,' Catarina answered. She pulled a flat narrow box from her bag and set it on the table.

'Open mine first,' Roland said.

Catarina undid the package to find a gold charm bracelet with a single charm, a four-leaf clover with a minute inscription: the names of Fat Fanny, Boring Dora and Jealous Nat. She laughed delightedly and gestured for Roland to open her gift. Inside the box he found a gold watch; inscribed on the back were the same three names.

'And your father hopes to keep us apart?' Roland

asked. he removed his own watch and replaced it with the gift, while Catarina slipped the gold charm bracelet onto her wrist, jangling it merrily.

'Rollie, please give my father time. He is of a different generation.'

'I should have told him how drunk Juan was the other night, how he came within a shade of being arrested.'

'It would have made no difference. Juan can do whatever he pleases. He is a man,' she said, the anger in her voice rising. 'Oh how I hate him, you cannot believe how much I hate my brother for what he did.'

'He did what he thought was right for you,' Roland told her. 'You can't hate him for that. Just appreciate the fact that you've got a brother who's that concerned about you.' He didn't mean a word of it, but he refused to turn Catarina against anyone in her family. He had lost his, and he wouldn't rob Catarina of hers.

Roland's worst fears about the factory were confirmed the next morning. Five minutes after the Carters delivery was made, Bert Phillips knocked on the door of his office to announce that it was being blacked. Roland went out to the delivery area and saw for himself that the merchandise was untouched. He called a meeting of the men on the factory floor.

'None of you has any argument with Mar-Cross.' Roland stood on a workbench, looking down at the employees in their blue overalls. 'If you feel sympathy for the workers at Carters that's your privilege, but I won't allow it to interfere with the operation of this business. Now I'm asking you to get on with the work for which you're paid, bring in the Carters shipment and get it ready for assembly.' He looked around the circle of faces, finishing with Bert Phillips.

'Mr Eagles, if we touch that delivery we'll be stabbing our fellow workers in the back,' the shop steward replied, and there was a rumble of approval around him. 'Carters' management will think they can get away with grinding down their employees.'

'And if you don't handle that shipment you'll all be out of work by Christmas because there will be no business here to pay your wages!' Roland shot back. 'Can't any of you understand that?' He knew he was overstating the position, but a dramatic approach might get through some of the union-loyalty hogwash with which Phillips had been filling their heads. "What about you, Len?" Roland pointed to a young man with black hair and soft brown eyes. 'Your wife's just had a baby. Now what's more important to you – Carters' people or the money to support your family?'

The man shifted uncomfortably. Two weeks earlier, when his wife had given birth, Mar-Cross had sent a bunch of flowers to the hospital, a policy Roland had initiated to help the worker-management relationship. 'We took a vote on it, Mr Eagles,' the man answered lamely.

'A vote? Did you know you were all voting to put yourselves on the unemployment line?' Roland turned to another man. 'How are you going to keep up your mortgage payments on the house you just bought, Bill? Dole won't cover it.'

'We're solidly behind the Carters strikers,' Phillips butted in.

"Fine. You all stick by your principles and see what happens!" Roland snapped as he jumped down from the workbench. 'I'm not prepared to lose business. If you don't straighten this out by tonight, I'll get people in here who will.'

'Mr Eagles!' Phillips' voice rang out as Roland started to walk toward his office. 'If you did that we'd be forced to protect our jobs.'

Roland swung around. 'What jobs? You won't have any. I'll have gotten rid of you all.' He stormed back to his office and telephoned Simon Aronson to tell him that the blacking was official. Simon strongly advised caution. Mar-Cross might be able to weather a strike, but it would never outlast a dispute where blood was spilled when strikers and strikebreakers clashed.

Forcing down his anger, Roland returned to the delivery area. He picked up a crowbar and pried open one of the boxes from Carters. Inside was a layer of black plastic handles for electric kettles. He picked one up and turned to look into the factory. Marching toward him was Bert Phillips, face set in a grim mask.

'Mr Eagles, there's a very definite line between management's and employees' duties. You've just crossed it. Unpacking shipments is a job only for union members.'

Roland knew he had made a mistake and dropped the handle back into the box. 'I don't want the shipment left out here. It's going to rain soon.'

Phillips looked up at the darkening sky. 'I'll see that it's brought inside.'

'I thought your men were blacking it.'

'We are. But we don't want to see it ruined, do we?'

As he walked away, Roland shook his head in confusion.

By Friday afternoon sales meeting, the situation at Carters was still deadlocked, and the shipment lay just inside the factory door gathering dust. 'We're getting dangerously close to delivery dates,' Roland told Simon. 'If we get this thing sorted out soon we can squeak through. But it's got to be damned soon.'

'Have you tried going elsewhere for the parts?'

Roland handed Simon a sheet of paper. On it were the names of half a dozen suppliers he had contacted. 'They can give us all the stuff we want. But not when we want it, which is now.'

'What are you planning to do?'

'Wait until the end of next week, then I'm going to start trying to buy us some extra time.'

'When is the order for Adler's due?'

'Two weeks from Wednesday.'

'How long will it take to complete that order once you begin assembly?'

Roland turned to Alan Winters, the factory manager. 'With everyone working flat out, it'll take about a week.'

'All right, wait until the end of next week,' Simon agreed. 'I'll help you make up the excuses.'

The following Friday morning, the strike at Carters was still on. The plant was closed down completely. Pickets marched outside, and the Carters shipment gathered more dust.

Roland debated which of his customers to call first. They all knew about the strike but, like himself, they were hoping that it would be over in time for the completion of their Christmas orders. Now he had to disappoint them. He picked up the telephone and started to make the calls, beginning with the smallest. They were more likely to be sympathetic; their cooperation would give him confidence to tackle the bigger customers.

By lunchtime he had finished all but one – Adler's. Instead of simply telephoning Monty Adler with the news, Roland decided to give the old man the respect of telling him personally. He made an appointment to see Monty at two that afternoon, foregoing attendance at the weekly sales meeting. There was no point in even having a meeting; nothing was moving out of the factory, orders was stagnant. At least, Roland thought as he drove the Jaguar toward the West End, all this aggravation was taking his mind off Catarina's family; he was too angry and frustrated to even think about the Menendezes.

'Let me guess why you're here,' Monty Adler growled when Roland was shown into his office. 'Our order's late because you can't control your own staff, and now you've come to beg for more time. Am I right?'

'That's about the size of it.' Monty's gruffness didn't

surprise Roland; he accepted it as a reflection of the old man's no-nonsense manner.

'How long is this unpleasantness going to last?' Monty raised a handkerchief to his mouth and started to cough, then reached for a glass of water on the desk. 'Blasted cold I picked up somewhere,' he muttered.

Roland waited for the coughing spasm to pass. 'Difficult to say. It could be over today, and it might drag on into the new year.'

'What have your other customers said, or are we the first you've contacted?'

'You're the last. You top the bill.'

Monty coughed again, and his craggy face heightened in color. 'Don't try to flatter me, sonny. I've lived eighty years without ever seeing it work.'

'Everyone else promised to be elastic, leave it until the last minute. Then, if our problem isn't solved, they'll fill in their inventory from other suppliers.'

'Fair enough,' Monty said. 'We'll do the same. That deadline you've got for a week from Wednesday – keep as close to it as you can and we'll work with you.'

'Thank you.' Roland felt like hugging the old man. He left the office with a massive weight lifted from his shoulders. In the corridor leading toward the elevator he passed Albert Adler talking to Bruce Simpkins. Albert nodded a cool greeting but Simpkins turned his head away quickly. Roland didn't even notice; he was too full of the reprieve he'd just been given.

The blacking of the Carters shipment lasted another ten days, then Bert Phillips came to see Roland. 'We've just had a meeting, Mr Eagles, and the men have decided to handle Carters.'

'Why the change of mind? The strike at Carters is still on.'

'It doesn't matter anymore. Carters' management has

got the message. Their latest offer is a big jump from their original position.'

'Your men are prepared to resume work immediately?' Roland was already figuring out schedules. The Adler's order was due in two days. Maybe they could get it finished by the end of the week, then start on the others. He would call his customers, give them the good news, thank them again for being so considerate.

'The men are willing to work overtime, Mr Eagles.'

Yes, I bet they are, Roland thought. And they'll probably think Phillips is some kind of genius for getting them overtime to do work that should have been completed during regular hours. 'Whatever it takes, Mr Phillips, whatever it takes.' He would have to find a way to get rid of Phillips . . . Roland had little doubt that this entire affair could have been averted if he had let Simon have his way and bribe the man. But he refused to run a company on that basis. A day's pay for a day's work was the only fair rule.

Phillips returned to the factory floor to tell his members about the meeting. As he spoke he couldn't help thinking about a conversation he'd had the previous day. Albert Adler had telephoned him at home and told him to call off the strike . . . Phillips was still unable to make head or tails of what was going on.

In the office, Roland drew up a list of whom to call. He started with Monty Adler. The old man sounded terrible, wheezing and coughing over the telephone, complaining about how difficult it was to shake even a simple cold when you reached old age. Roland was sympathetic and asked Monty why he didn't stay at home until he felt better. The old man grumbled about refusing to let a cold keep him away from his business. As he hung up and checked the number of the next customer, Roland was grinning broadly.

By Wednesday afternoon, Roland was once again accustomed to the sound of the factory in full production.

160

The pile of completed appliances near the loading dock grew steadily larger, and he finally allowed himself to focus on a different source of anxiety – Catarina's family. Ambassador Menendez continued to watch Roland carefully; on his last two dates with Catarina, her brother and a friend – by sheer coincidence, they claimed – had turned up at the same restaurant.

That night he left the factory early to go home and change for his date with Catarina. As he was about to leave home the telephone rang; for a moment he considered ignoring it. Conscience got the better of him. The call was from Lawrence Chivers at the office.

'Albert Adler was just on, Roland. He wants to speak to you.'

Roland glanced at the gold watch Catarina had given him. He was late already and he didn't want to get stuck talking business now. 'Can't it wait until morning, Lawrence?'

'Albert said it's urgent. He wants you to call him at the store.'

'Damn', Roland muttered as he dialed the number.

'Mr Eagles, your company has caused our receiving department a tremendous amount of trouble,' Albert began.

'In what way?' Roland checked his watch again and wondered how long he would be stuck listening to whatever complaint Albert had.

'We've been waiting all day for our order to arrange for its distribution to our other stores. Our receiving department closed fifteen minutes ago and the order still hadn't arrived.' Before Roland could say anything, Albert continued: 'Don't bother to ship it at all now. This conversation is our notice of cancellation.'

Roland exploded. 'What in God's name are you talking about? Your father and I had an agreement about the delivery being a few days late. You'd better talk to him about it.'

161

'My father is away sick, Mr Eagles. I am running Adler's.'

'But we had an agreement!'

'Was it in writing, Mr Eagles?'

Roland was stunned by the question. 'Of course it wasn't in writing. I came up to see your father. We sealed it with a handshake.'

'If there is nothing in writing, then as far as I am concerned the original delivery date stands. Good evening, Mr Eagles.'

Roland slumped into a chair, still holding the receiver. He ran the conversation through in his mind, order canceled, nothing in writing, Monty Adler off sick. Something smelled. He called Catarina and told her he would be late, then ran downstairs to the Jaguar and headed for Adler's on Regent Street. Albert had already left when he arrived. Bruce Simpkins wasn't there. And yes, Roland was told, Monty Adler had been away all week. Roland considered driving to Albert's home in Maida Vale. He got as far as starting the car and changed his mind. Confronting Albert in front of his family would solve nothing. A cool head was needed now. He would wait until morning. Meanwhile, he would keep his date with Catarina. If he broke it he was sure her father would find some way to use it against him . . . That was all Roland needed!

The evening was a disaster. Roland couldn't shake thinking about his conversation with Albert and, hard as he tried not to, his conversation was mainly limited to the canceled order. So gloomy was his mood that even Catarina's mixture of sympathy and humor failed to lift him. Ambassador Menendez was glad his daughter returned home before ten o'clock; he was even more pleased when Roland didn't come in with her.

Roland spent most of the night sitting in his living room, but instead of thinking of a way to deal with Albert rationally, he only made himself angrier. By the time he arrived at Adler's early the next morning, he was spoiling for a fight.

'Your father told me to to do the best I could,' Roland said when he finally met with Albert. 'Ask him.'

'My father is a very sick man at the moment. I'm not about to pester him with problems I can resolve.'

'So any promises he made don't mean a thing now, is that it?'

'Mr Eagles, I was firmly against allowing your company any leeway with the delivery date. When you make a deadline you stick to it, otherwise you have no right to deal with us.'

'And what the hell am I supposed to do with almost a thousand appliances all bearing the name of Adler's on the casings and packaging?'

'I have no idea. But the problem isn't mine, is it?' Albert said staring at Roland, as if challenging him. 'Perhaps there is a solution that might accommodate both of us.'

'What's that?'

'We'll take the order from you after all – but at your cost.'

'What?' Roland's surprise at the suggestion soon passed when he realized that this was what Albert had been leading up to the whole time – canceling the order to leave him high and dry, then offering this as a means of partial salvation.

'For your cost, Mr Eagles,' Albert repeated. 'You're quite familiar with that practice, aren't you? I seem to recall that when you first took control of Mar-Cross you offered your products to selected shops at cost. Why is it so terrible to offer Adler's the same gracious terms? Besides,' he said, smirking, 'what are you going to do with almost a thousand appliances bearing Adler's logo?' Albert was obviously quite pleased with himself; the hundred-pound payment to Bert Phillips had certainly

163

brought handsome dividends, and his father being ill was an additional piece of fortuitous timing. Albert had argued strongly with his father against extending the delivery date, stressing that this was just the way that they could capitalize on Roland's misfortune – a misfortune that Albert himself had helped bring about. Given more time, Albert was sure he would have won his father over – just as he had won him over once before, many years earlier, on a far more important matter than this. But the problem had taken care of itself when Monty became sick. Now there was no one to block Albert's sharp moves that would save the store money. By the time the old man returned it would be signed, sealed and, most importantly, delivered. Monty would be forced to look up to his son, admit that he could carry his own weight. For as long as he could remember, Albert had felt that he was merely tolerated in the family business, and the experience was humbling, with every opportunity for responsibility taken out of his hands. He was nothing more than a man given a title and a position, then forced to react like a child to his father's mandates. Well, this episode would change all that. At last Albert would demonstrate his business acumen, and old Monty would have to recognize his worth. The only snag in Albert's scheme – the one he hadn't anticipated – was Roland's refusing to take him up on his offer.

'I wouldn't offer you the drippings off the end of my nose!' he said, turned abruptly and left. Driving back to the factory, his mind seethed with thoughts of Albert and Adler's. Roland wanted revenge; he would settle for nothing less. By the time he reached his office he thought he knew how he would have it.

Roland's first move was to call Lawrence Chivers into the office, then he telephoned Simon Aronson and Sally Roberts and asked each of them the same question: did they know anything about getting a permit for a street market? Specifically, the Berwick Street Market in the West End, less than half a mile from the Adler's store on Regent Street. Neither did. Sally, however, suggested that Roland contact Alf Goldstein. Cab drivers knew everything.

Sally's intuition proved correct. Goldstein told Roland who to contact and how much it would cost. The best booths would already have been allocated for the Christmas season, but bribery could work wonders. This time Roland had no qualms about paying off anyone. He wanted one of the top spots so he could sell off all the merchandise at his regular wholesale price and simultaneously cause considerable embarrassment to Adler's.

Once he had arranged for a booth for the week preceding Christmas, he called Albert Adler. 'I've thought over your proposition.'

'I'm very glad to hear it.' Albert's thin voice disguised the relief he felt. Roland's initial rejection of his offer had been a shock, forcing Albert to question his tactics. Sharp moves like his were only acceptable when they showed a reward, not when they resulted in a loss. And if Adler's came up with nothing – no reduced price, no delivery – how in God's name was he going to explain that to his father? 'When can we expect delivery?'

'You can't.' Roland wished he could see Albert's face as the conversation unfolded. 'My answer's still the same.'

'Then why did you bother calling me?' Confusion would be showing on Albert's face now, Roland thought.

'Because I want you to be the first to know what I'm planning to do.'

'What do you mean?' Concern now, as a yawning chasm began to open in front of Albert.

'I'm selling everything myself, from a stall in Berwick Street, right alongside all those stalls selling fruit and vegetables. And I'm going to advertise it as merchandise that would normally sell at Adler's for twice the price. It's even got your company's name on it, so people will know they're getting authentic bargains.'

'You can't do that! It's our merchandise!' Finally horror, as Albert began the long fall.

'Just watch me.' Roland hung up, immensely satisfied. At one time he'd thought that Albert was so thin because of the tension from being around his father. Now he was convinced that the man's anxiety was more likely due to his own blind incompetence.

Monty Adler returned to the store the following week. Within ten minutes he was on the telephone to Roland. Less than an hour later, Roland was at the store, riding the elevator to the executive offices.

'Just what the hell has been going on while I've been away?' Monty demanded. He looked pale, and the massive head seemed to have shrunk; but his voice was just as strong, his manner just as belligerent.

'Ask your son,' Roland said, nodding toward Albert who stood by Monty's desk.

'He's given me some cock-and-bull story about you holding on to the order because you want to try selling it yourself from some stall in Berwick Street Market. Listen, sonny, you can do whatever you want with your own goods but you'd better be damn careful what you do with goods that have my name on them.'

'I haven't been left with much choice. Your son called my factory at five-thirty on the date of the original delivery and informed me that the deal was off because we hadn't kept to the original date. Then he offered to take the stuff from me at my cost.'

Monty spun around to face Albert. 'Did you do that?' For a long moment, Albert remained perfectly still. Finally he nodded. 'Who the hell do you think you are to break my word? I gave Eagles a promise that we'd

166

accommodate any reasonable lateness on his part because of the strike. You knew that, you even tried to talk me out of it. So the moment my back's turned you do it anyway.'

As father and son squared off, they seemed to forget Roland's presence in the office. 'He gave small shops a break when he was getting started!' Albert retorted. 'What's wrong with trying to get the same terms for Adler's?'

'Because I gave him my word, that's what's wrong with it! What kind of business are you running when you don't honor your promises?'

Albert's face turned paler. He knew why his father was reacting this way. 'If it had been Meir who'd done it, you'd have approved wouldn't you?' he said, referring to his dead older brother. 'Even if it had cost Adler's money you'd still have patted him on the back and told him he was right for trying. But because it's my idea it's no good – right?'

'Meir, *olova sholom,* would never have done such a thing. He would have honored any word I'd given.'

'Epitome of virtue, wasn't he?' Albert sneered. 'We all know how virtuous he was.'

'Just keep his name out of this!' Monty yelled.

Roland began to feel uncomfortable. He remembered Lawrence Chivers' remarks about Monty Adler feeling the wrong son had died. Now, as he listened to Meir Adler's name being bandied about he realized that Albert was still paranoid about his brother, even if he had been gone for almost thirty years. Roland brought his hand to his mouth and coughed. Instantly Albert and Monty froze in embarrassment, then turned to face him.

'I regret that you are a witness to this disagreement, Mr Eagles,' Monty said slowly. 'I also regret that during my illness my son saw fit to go back on the word I had given you.' Roland glanced at Albert and saw that he was seething with anger and humiliation; the man clearly

167

wamted to leave but dared not. 'Our spoken bond still stands. Let me know when you'll be able to deliver and I'll have my people ready.'

Roland was in a fix. Was Monty's apology as sincere as it sounded? Certainly, the argument with Albert had been convincing, but Monty had been in business a long time. He was a canny old devil. He knew what damage it would do to Adler's reputation to have its merchandise sold in a street market; he couldn't afford to let that happen. Was his apology based on that fear? And what would have happened if Roland had accepted Albert's offer? Would Monty, quite happily, have accepted it too?

'I'm sorry, Mr Adler. I've already made my arrangements. Your former order goes on sale in Berwick Street Market the week before Christmas.'

Monty shook his head sadly. 'You're making a terrible mistake, Eagles. You're going to upset a lot of your regular customers by selling your own goods at retail level.'

'Not at all. Your name will be on the merchandise, not mine.'

'We'll never deal with you again.'

'I can't afford to deal with a company that doesn't keep its word.'

'That won't happen again, not while I'm around.'

'Fine, but how long will you be around, Mr Adler?' Roland could swear he saw the old man flinch at the question. Monty Adler wasn't frightened of dying – at his age he was resigned to it – but he was petrified at the thought of leaving the business to his remaining son. Roland couldn't help wondering if what Albert said was true and that the old man would be more at peace with himself if his older son were still here . . .

A green Mar-Cross delivery van inched its way carefully down Berwick Street with barely a foot to spare on either side. The driver leaned out of his window to judge the distance between the side of the van and the stalls that lined the road. Lawrence Chivers did the same on the passenger side. This was the easy part. Backing out was even tougher. On the previous three days that the van had brought merchandise from the factory in Wembley, reversing out of Berwick Street had left scratches on the paintwork. No one could blame the driver; he hadn't been hired to drive though the eye of the needle like this.

The van stopped in front of an empty stall where Roland stood. Chivers and the driver jumped out, then all three men unloaded the van. There wasn't much left to sell now. The first three days had cleared sixty percent of the Adler's order. Today, Saturday, would take care of the remainder. The advertisements Roland had placed in the *Mercury* had drawn the crowds, and Roland enlisted help from all quarters to meet the demands. Sally Roberts had worked for two afternoons while Alf Goldstein had put in a morning. Even Simon Aronson's wife, Nadine, had turned up. And Catarina had promised to do her best to be there today. Roland had never sold anything in a market before and didn't care if the people who helped him had never done so either. Just as long as they were strong in number and could shout loudly enough to drown out neighboring stall holders. Not that there was any direct competition . . . Roland's booth was flanked by stalls selling fruit and vegetables, toys and linens. No one else in the market was selling electric irons and kettles; certainly not with the Adler's logo.

'Going to rain,' Chivers remarked gloomily as he pulled his coat collar up around his neck.

'When doesn't it?' Roland tugged his sheepskin coat tighter. It was cold as well, that damp chill peculiar to London that drove right through to the bones. It was a wonder these regular stall holders didn't die of pneumonia or rheumatism by the time they were forty, Roland thought. Thank God today would be the end of it . . .

When they had finished unloading Chivers helped the driver back out of the narrow market place, then returned to help Roland set up the stall. A tarpaulin was spread across the top to keep off the rain. Enlargements of the advertisement from the *Mercury* were fixed to the frame. The green-and-white boxes, all marked prominently with the Adler's name, were piled high on the stall; those that wouldn't fit were placed under cover.

'Eagles' cheap-jack market, open for another day's business,' Roland laughed. He cupped his hands to his mouth. 'Kettles and irons – buy them at Adler's or buy them here for half the price! Buy now, they won't last forever!'

Chivers lit his pipe and watched. He had never seen anyone enjoy work this much before.

At ten-thirty Catarina arrived, dressed sensibly in a thick raincoat, heavy boots and a red wool hat. Wound around her neck was a long red-and-white wool scarf. 'Going to a football game?' Roland asked as he kissed her.

'Shopping for Christmas,' she answered. 'At least that's what I told my father.'

'Where's your escort?'

'Juan? I lost him in Oxford Street. I tried on some clothes in a store, and while he was looking at something else I slipped out the back way. Have you sold much so far?'

Roland nodded. 'Have you come to watch or help?'

'To help, of course. What do you want me to do?'

'See that cafe over there? Bring Lawrence and me some tea before we freeze to death.'

Catarina brought the tea in heavy, awkward cups, then stood behind the stall between Roland and Chivers. She watched them for a while, listening to their pitch. 'May I try?'

'Go right ahead.'

'Women!' Catarina's voice reached a volume Roland had never thought it possessed. 'Are you fed up with pressing your men's shirts? Tired of making them tea?

170

Make your life easier by getting your men to treat you to a new iron or electric teapot!'

'Not bad,' Chivers murmured around his pipe. 'Girl's got talent.'

Roland grinned as two middle-aged women approached the stall with their husbands. Catarina's approach had created new interest. Another man walked up, alone, but he was not interested in the merchandise on sale. 'Aren't you Ambassador Menendez's daughter?'

'Yes.' Catarina seemed mystified at being recognized. Belatedly, Roland recognized the man; he was one of the reporters who had been sitting at the press table on the night of the banquet at Claridge's.

'What are you doing working in Berwick Street Market?'

Roland was too slow to step in between Catarina and the reporter, and Catarina was too happy and too proud to even consider lying. 'Helping my boyfriend,' she answered brightly.

Roland felt his stomach sink. All he needed now was for this to appear in some newspaper. The ambassador would go through the roof. 'Do you want to buy something?' he asked the man roughly. 'If not, there are people behind you who do.'

'Sure, I'll take a kettle for my mother.' The man grinned as he handed over the money, took the package and walked away. Watching him leave Roland breathed a little easier. Maybe it was the reporter's day off and he wasn't interested in a story. Roland hoped so.

By four o'clock, as the sky began to darken, only six electric irons remained. Roland decided to wait half an hour, then he would give them away to the first people who walked past the stall. He was more than satisfied with his market venture. Lawrence Chivers had already left with the bulk of the money taken in to deposit it in a night safe. Just six more irons and they could pack it in. Impetuously, he grabbed hold of Catarina and kissed her.

As they broke apart, a bright flash of light seared his eyes. He heard Catarina scream something in Spanish. When his vision cleared Roland saw the reporter who had bought the kettle; standing next to him was a man in a raincoat and hat holding a press camera. Roland had no doubt what was on the film.

He leaped from behind the stall and threw himself at the photographer, but the reporter stepped in the way while his companion made his escape. Roland managed to push past the man but the photographer already had a thirty-yard lead, the camera swinging from his hand as he raced down the narrow alley leading to Brewer Street. Roland gave chase until someone's foot hooked around his ankle and he went flying onto the wet ground. The last thing he saw before his head hit the road was Catarina attacking the reporter, punching him in the head and kicking at his ankles until a group of shoppers surged forward to stop the melee.

Ambassador Menendez and his wife didn't attend church the next morning, too embarrassed to be seen in public. The cause of their embarrassment was the photograph on the front page of the *News of the World*. 'Ambassador's daughter turns street vendor,' read the headline. The picture was of Catarina and Roland embracing behind the stall. The reporter had even dug deeply enough to learn why Roland was selling his merchandise from a market stall; the strike at the factory and subsequent trouble with Adler's. Trouble with the unions was one thing, the story concluded humorously, but did British businessmen have to go to these lengths to find workers? Or were Argentinian diplomats so financially strapped that they had to send their daughters out to work in street markets?

'You have brought disgrace to this family!' Menendez thundered at his daughter. 'You will not see this man again, ever! Until I decide what further action to take you will not leave this house without your brother. How dare you do something like this, working like a common peasant?'

'I was not working! And even if I had been, it is nothing to be ashamed of!'

'You are too young to know what is shameful and what is not! It is for me to decide. But be assured that you will never be in a position to shame this family again. I will make certain of that!'

Catarina blinked back tears and ran from her father. In her room she locked the door and threw herself onto the bed. Then she wept, letting the tears flow freely. Through them, she noticed the telephone on the bedside table. Perhaps her father could stop her from seeing Roland but he couldn't stop her from talking to him. And she had to talk to him. Urgently. There was something he had to know, something she would have told him yesterday if only that blasted reporter hadn't shown up.

In the drawing room, Mendendez sat with his wife. 'No more chances,' he said. 'Yesterday . . . that photograph in the newspaper today . . . enough! Catarina will no longer leave this house by herself. And after Christmas I will make arrangements for her to go to Spain. She will stay with our friends there. They will keep people like this Eagles away.'

This time, Señora Menendez didn't argue. She knew her husband was right and that she – with her indulgent attitude toward her daughter – had been wrong. Catarina was hopelessly in love with the young Englishman. For her own welfare she had to be sent away, had to be given time to mend her emotions. Spain would be good for her. Their friends included government officials, men close to Franco. Catarina could mix in proper circles; there would be no opportunities for men like Roland Eagles to approach her.

'A pity,' the ambassador mused. 'I would like to have

seen Catarina meet someone from a noble English family.'

'Perhaps she will marry into a noble Spanish family instead,' Señora Menendez said, attempting to console her husband.

'Perhaps.' But it no longer mattered so much to Menendez, as long as Catarina was out of England away from the clutches of a man like Roland Eagles.

Roland was beset by troubles of his own that Sunday morning. His head throbbed where it had struck the road and his right eye was partially closed; a vivid blue-and-purple bruise discolored the skin. To make matters worse he had a furious Sally Roberts to contend with, who had been hammering on his door at nine-thirty, a copy of the *News of the World* in her hand.

'You louse!' she yelled at him when he opened the door dressed in his pajamas and robe, one hand caressing his injured eye. 'You promised me exclusive rights.'

'If you lower your voice I'll let you in.' He had not seen a newspaper yet, but he could guess why Sally was upset.

'Christ, what happened to you?' she gasped when he dropped his hand to close the door.

'One of your delightful press colleagues happened to me. He tripped me up as I was chasing the bastard who took that photograph,' he said, pointing to the newspaper. 'I'm assuming there's a photograph of Catarina and me in there, otherwise why would you be here so early in the morning screaming for my blood?'

Sally's anger quickly changed to compassion. 'Here, let me have a look.' She led Roland into the kitchen and pressed a cold, damp cloth against his head while he related the incident of the previous afternoon. Sally clucked sympathetically. 'Must make you like journalists even less.'

'Let's just say if I were Noah loading his ark I'd think twice before I'd let any member of the press on. Present company excluded, of course.'

174

'Thanks. You had breakfast yet?'

'No.'

'I'll make you something. Have you had that lump looked at?' she asked as she busied herself around the kitchen.

'Last night at Middlesex Hospital. The X-ray showed nothing. They wanted to keep me overnight for observation but I wasn't about to do that.'

'That's not very smart. What about Catarina?'

'God knows. When her father sees this, heaven help us all.'

The telephone rang. 'That's probably him now,' Sally said. 'Is it possible to shoot someone over the phone?'

'Very funny. You get it.'

Sally picked up the receiver, then held it out to Roland. 'For you. Catarina.'

He tried to forget the pain in his head. 'Have you seen the newspaper?' he said.

'Yes. So have my parents. Who was that who answered the telephone?'

Despite the blistering headache, Roland smiled at the hint of jealousy in her question. 'Sally Roberts.'

'Why is she with you?'

'For the same reason you're calling. That photograph. Now what about your parents?'

'I just had a terrible argument with my father. He's forbidden me to ever see you again.'

The pain in Roland's head increased. 'What about when you go back to school after Christmas? He can't keep you under guard forever.'

'My brother is having his work and play interrupted to keep me under control. And I'm certain that's only the beginning.' There was a long pause; he could tell that she was crying. 'Rollie, what are we going to do?'

Roland didn't have the answer. Holding his hand over the mouthpiece he looked at Sally. 'She wants to know what we're going to do.'

'Get a long ladder, take it to Wilton Crescent late at

175

night, prop it up against her window and run away together.'

'Thanks for nothing.'

'What do you expect me to say? I don't have any ideas.'

'Rollie, are you still there?' Catarina asked.

'I'm still here. Listen, why don't we just take each step at a time? Not see each other until your father's had a chance to calm down a bit.'

'He'll never calm down, not this time. He thinks I've made a fool of him, and that is unforgivable. And there is something else . . .'

'What?' What else could there be?'

Before Catarina could answer there was a click on the line as if someone had lifted an extension. Suddenly a man's voice cut into the conversation and Roland heard an explosion of angry Spanish. He only understood Catarina's name spoken before the line went dead.

'What happened?' Sally asked.

'Her father cut her off. Now what the hell do I do?' He propped his chin up with his hands and closed his eyes. What did Catarina mean by only the beginning? Sending her back to Argentina? And what was something else?

If Sally hadn't been there, Roland was certain he would have allowed himself the luxury of letting tears wash away the pain.

A taxi brought Monty Adler to the Mar-Cross factory early on Monday afternoon. He instructed the driver to wait, then walked into the reception area. Asked if he had an appointment to see Roland, Monty answered that he didn't need one. He was correct.

'I hear you did quite well with your market venture last week. Even got your picture in the paper.'

'We made our money back,' Roland answered, ignoring the reference to the photograph. Why had the old man come? To mend fences, or to damn him? Whatever the reason, Roland welcomed the visit. It took his mind

176

off Catarina and her family, even if only for a few minutes. She had not been out of his thoughts, and he felt helpless not being able to contact her. Not that he hadn't tried; he'd phoned her repeatedly that morning. The first two times Señora Menendez had told him quite firmly that Catarina was unavailable. When he rang the third time the maid had answered, informing him that there was no one who would talk to him and he wasn't to call again. Next he tried calling the embassy, where Menendez refused to speak to him. After repeated calls he'd been told by an aide that if he continued pestering embassy staff the matter would be referred to the police. Roland had slammed down the receiver, furious with the ambassador for his obstinacy, and even more furious with himself because he was powerless to do anything about it.

'You made Adler's look like dirt last week,' Monty said, 'running advertisements in the *Mercury* the way you did, bawling our name across a lousy street market. I don't forgive lightly for that.'

'I was left no choice.'

'Don't give me that rubbish about no choice! I offered you the full, agreed-upon price once I'd found out what Albert had done.'

'And maybe you offered me the full price because you didn't want to see the stuff going on sale in Berwick Street.'

'Is that what you really think, sonny? Oh, no. I made a deal with you, and Monty Adler's word is his bond. You ask anyone.'

'Pity Albert didn't inherit that trait.'

'Maybe, but at least Albert's got the brains not to pick a fight with someone a bloody sight tougher than he is.'

'What does that mean?'

Monty's mouth went tight. 'I'm going to grind you into the dust, sonny. By the time I'm finished with you, you're going to wish you'd stayed put in the army.'

'Don't forget David and Goliath – maybe I'll do to

177

Adler's what you're threatening to do to me.'

Monty snorted derisively. 'Over my dead body, sonny. Over my dead body.'

'I sincerely hope not!' Roland called after him as he left the office. Crusty old fellow that he was, Roland couldn't help feeling a sneaking admiration and affection.

Late that afternoon, Bruce Simpkins telephoned Roland to say he had resigned from Adler's. 'I've been thinking about quitting for some time, but when you've got a family to support and tenure at one place – even if it's a madhouse like Adler's – you tend to think twice. After this business, though, enough is enough. You did a favor for me by standing up to Albert and now I'd like to do you one in return.'

'Favors are always welcome, Mr Simpkins.'

'Your shop steward, Bert Phillips, was up here awhile back—'

'Phillips? What was he doing at Adler's?'

'Trying to get me to pay him off and avert that blacking of Carters. I didn't want anything to do with it, so I passed him off to Albert.'

'Obviously Albert didn't want anything to do with it either.'

'Oh, he did,' Simpkins corrected Roland. 'He paid Phillips a hundred pounds – but to have the men black Carters.'

'So we'd be late . . .'

'It all fell right into Albert's lap, Mr Eagles. He'd hoped to persuade Mr Monty to knock down your price. When Mr Monty went down sick, he didn't have to. I gave my notice this morning and Mr Monty wanted to know why I was leaving. I gave him the whole story, Bert Phillips coming up, everything.'

'Thank you very much for calling, Mr Simpkins.'

So, the old man hadn't been lying. It *had* been Albert working behind his back. Monty was probably just as horrified by his son's part in it as he was at having his name dragged through a street market. Poor devil, Roland couldn't help thinking. When you get to that age you're supposed to be sitting back, taking it easy – not trying to unravel a mess caused by a crook of a son.

Roland wondered how to tackle the problem of Bert Phillips. He had wanted to get rid of the shop steward, now he had the way . . .

Roland waited until the last working day before the Christmas break. In the afternoon he went onto the factory floor with a batch of white envelopes and Christmas boxes which he passed around. Some of the men were obviously surprised at receiving a gift after the action against the company. Roland told them he didn't hold grudges. Even with the strike it had been a good year; it was his custom to share it.

He held on to Bert Phillips' envelope until last and stayed around while the shop steward greedily ripped it open. Phillips expected to find money inside, as the other men had. Instead, he found his employment cards, all stamped up to date.

'What's this?' The shop steward looked around, bewildered. The other men stared at him, uncertain what was happening.

'A Christmas present to go with the hundred pounds you took to stir up trouble here. Maybe next time' – Roland turned to the other men – 'you'll elect a shop steward who works for your benefit, not his own.' Without another word he returned to his office, leaving Phillips to explain why he had been fired on Christmas Eve.

Roland spent his Christmas with the Aronson family in South Kensington. There was no turkey, no Christmas tree, no mistletoe, and the only presents were those Roland gave to Simon's daughters, identical gold pen-and-pencil sets; he had no idea what one gave to fifteen- and twelve-year-old girls.

Originally, Roland had planned to spend Christmas with Catarina. Since that was now out of the question, he didn't want to substitute alternate festivities. He'd even turned down Sally's late invitation to a Christmas in the country with her parents near Aldershot. But a quiet afternoon and evening with the Aronsons was perfect.

Before dinner, Sharon pestered him for a ride in the XK-120. Roland looked at Nadine, who nodded a cautious approval. They both bundled up in warm clothing before he took her for a half-hour spin with the roof down. He drove toward Victoria, past the back of Buckingham Palace, through Wilton Crescent. All the drapes in the Menendez home were drawn. The family might have gone away for Christmas, Roland reasoned, with Catarina in tow as a virtual prisoner.

'Want to play some backgammon after dinner?' Sharon asked when they returned to Kensington. Her cheeks were flushed from the wind and her eyes sparkled.

'I want to talk to your father first.'

'If you don't play I'll tell him you drove through two red lights and knocked down an old lady.'

'Did I?' Roland had been so preoccupied thinking about Catarina after he'd driven down Wilton Crescent that it seemed anything was possible.

'Of course not, silly.' She kissed him on the cheek and squeezed his arm. Roland remembered blushing when Sharon had kissed him on his first visit to the Aronson home. Then she had been a child. Now, at fifteen, she had grown into a young, self-assured woman. He felt uncomfortably warm at her closeness. Embarrassed, he pulled away quickly.

Later that evening, Roland sat with Simon in the book-lined room where they had once played a hand of poker for equal shares in the company. Now Roland had expansion on his mind. 'I think we should look seriously into retailing, Simon.'

'A few days in the market gave you that much confidence, eh?'

'Not confidence, an education. I learned a very simple but valuable lesson in Berwick Street which you, as a

180

banker should be able to appreciate. A manufacturer has to wait for his money for however long the billing period is. A retailer gets his money the instant the product changes hands. That makes a lot of sense to me.'

'What are you suggesting?'

'Come the new year, why don't we begin looking for small electrical shops? A chain if we can pick up one for the right price, otherwise single shops and we'll form our own chain.'

'Supply them from Mar-Cross?'

'Some of the lines, obviously. We'll keep both businesses separate so our customers won't get upset.'

Simon nodded. 'All right, let's look into it. But there is one thing we must clear up first. This business with the Menendez family, Roland. Sort it out. You've been distracted all day long, and I would hate for you to speculate with our money in the same frame of mind.'

'I'll do my best. This whole damned mess is Albert's fault, you know.'

'Do I? How did you reach that conclusion?'

'If Albert hadn't double-crossed us, there wouldn't have been any picture of me and Catarina in the paper. I'd still be seeing her, and I'd still be on good·terms with Monty Adler.'

'There are many other large stores we can sell to besides Adler's. Besides, you've just broached the possibility of our becoming retailers – someday we may not need Adler's or any of them.' Simon was suddenly perplexed. A cloud seemed to have fallen over Roland – even more so than what he was already feeling about Catarina – and he didn't understand it. 'Is being on good terms with the old man so important to you?'

'I suppose it is. It wasn't Monty who tried to put one over on us, it was his son. Yet Monty's carrying the full weight of it, and I can't help feeling sorry for him.'

'Sorry for him?' Simon burst out laughing. 'You're the first person I've ever heard express sympathy for Monty Adler. Congratulations.'

CHAPTER SIX

Unknown to most, Monty Adler's crusty exterior concealed one soft spot he reserved for his twenty-six-year-old grandson, Michael. Often the old man wondered how he could have produced a sly, spineless son like Albert who, in turn, had fathered a *mensch* like Michael. In fact, Monty decided, Michael could have been Meir's son. That was who he really took after. Good-natured, honest, unafraid of hard work; even in appearance he was as Monty remembered Meir to have been: tall and muscular, a young man who took pride in his body and reveled in the athletic enjoyment it brought him.

Monty felt badly that he didn't see much of his grandson these days, what with his living in Edinburgh where he worked at the branch store. Still, it was good for the young man to learn the business from the bottom up. He'd started as a porter before moving to the selling floor. By the time he was finished he would know every aspect of Adler's. Maybe, Monty often mused, he could hang on long enough to see Albert retire. Then Michael could take over the business, and Monty could go to his grave knowing the stores were in capable hands.

Over the Christmas holidays Michael was home for a few days, staying with his parents in Maida Vale. On the Monday morning after Christmas he called for his grandfather at his flat in the West End and took him for a leisurely drive before going to Maida Vale for lunch. Despite the tired feeling that lingered after his illness, Monty enjoyed the time with his grandson. He was anxious to learn how he was faring in Edinburgh. Michael, in turn, wanted to know about the trouble in

Berwick Street Market; the Edinburgh store had been rife with gossip.

'Your father, God bless him, stage-managed the whole thing.' Monty knew Michael wouldn't be offended at hearing blame placed on Albert's shoulders. Michael respected his father, but he wasn't blind to his shortcomings. 'Took matters into his own hands and concocted a few new rules. Bribed a union man to cause trouble at one of our suppliers so our order would be late.'

Michael nodded; he had heard that too. 'What about this chap Eagles?'

'Another lunatic.' Monty started to cough and told Michael to roll up his window; he could do without the draft. 'You'd probably get on well with him. He's just like you. Young, knows what he's about, stubborn as a mule and not afraid of anyone.'

'Not even of a cantankerous old warhorse like you?' Michael flashed his grandfather an affectionate smile.

'Not even of me. Hard to believe, isn't it?' Monty said with a laugh. 'Maybe that's why I came down so hard on him, because he refused to bend. Even after he'd sold our stuff in the market he had this holier-than-thou attitude, kept telling me that we'd left him with no choice. Never even showed one bit of regret. And on top of that, he had the damned nerve to suggest that I only offered him the full price because I didn't want to see Adler's merchandise go on sale in Berwick Street – not because it was our agreement.' Just thinking about it made Monty feel worse. Albert and his bloody stupid schemes. The man had no business in retail; with that kind of warped attitude he should have been a politician or a lawyer. And all because of him, Adler's had been made to look foolish and Monty had come down like a ton of bricks on a young man whom – he had to admit – he actually liked. Roland Eagles was hard-headed, bombastic, vengeful – just like Monty himself – but he was likable all the same. To compound matters, Simpkins had quit. Not that it

183

mattered all that much . . . if the buyer hadn't resigned Monty would have dismissed him for not bringing Albert's double-dealing to his attention. If Simpkins had said something instead of refusing to get involved, the whole mess would have been avoided.

By the time they reached Albert's home in Maida Vale, Monty had worked himself up into a quiet fury. 'Have a good Christmas?' he greeted Albert. 'If you did, you must be the only one around here who managed to.'

Albert's wife, Helen, a mousy woman with hair dyed jet black to hide the onset of gray, attempted to kiss Monty, who abruptly turned his head away. 'Michael . . .' His grandson was the only member of the family he could tolerate at the moment. 'Get me a drink, there's a good boy.'

'Now you know what the doctor said, Mr Monty,' Helen Adler chimed in. During her twenty-eight years of marriage to Albert she had never called her father-in-law by any name other than Mr Monty. 'You know it's bad for you.'

'A drink's good for me. It's your bloody husband that's bad for me.' Monty was past caring whom he upset now. He took a glass of Scotch from Michael and sat down, suddenly uncertain why he had even bothered to accept the lunch invitation. He cooked for himself at home a damned sight better than Helen did. She specialized in burned meat and raw vegetables – or was it the other way around? He couldn't remember. No wonder Albert and Helen looked like a couple of rakes. Thank God his grandson was there, he thought. At least his company compensated for the food.

Monty only picked at lunch, then debated how long family courtesy – if any remained within him – dictated he stay before asking Michael to drive him home.

'Christmas takings were up eighteen percent over last year,' Albert remarked conversationally after lunch.

'Of course they were. There's more money around,'

184

Monty replied. He turned to Michael. 'You like it up in Scotland?'

'I'd rather be in London.'

The answer was what Monty had been hoping to hear. 'Do you want Bruce Simpkins' job? It would give you a chance to get into the buying side of the business.'

'I'd love it.'

'Albert, make the arrangements. There's no point in keeping Michael in Edinburgh when we can use him down here.'

'But he's never done any buying.' Albert was horrified at the prospect, knowing why Monty was bringing his son into the London store. He was using Michael as he had once tried to use Meir, as an ally against him. But was it his fault that he'd never lived up to his father's expectations? That he hadn't been physically strong like Meir? If anyone was to blame for that it was Monty. But the old man had never been able to see it and blamed Albert for his shortcomings.

'So what if he's never done any buying? He's got to start somewhere. Anyway, we need a buyer in a hurry – a buyer who knows when to come to me and tell me what's going on.' Insulted, Albert got up and left the room.

'Michael,' Monty said, turning to his grandson, 'do me a favor and take me home. I feel tired.'

Michael drove his grandfather back to his apartment, then went inside with him. After Monty put on the kettle the two sat in the living room with tea. The apartment looked just the way Michael remembered it when his grandmother had been alive. In seven years, Monty hadn't had the heart to change anything; the sameness seemed to be a comfort to the old man.

'You're getting too old to live here alone.'

'What do you want me to do?' Monty asked. 'Move in with your parents? God forbid! Go into an old age home? I'm happy here, thank you. Walking distance to the store. What else do I need?'

'Company.'

'I'm past the stage of wanting company. Your grandmother, bless her, was the only company I ever needed.' Monty swung around in his chair to look at a framed photograph of his late wife. 'Tell you what, Michael, when you're back in London you can come in and see me a couple of nights a week.'

Michael grinned and leaned over to clasp his grandfather's hand. 'I promise.'

'Good. Now go out and enjoy yourself. Young fellow like you doesn't want to waste a day off with an old man like me.' He pushed Michael toward the door, wanting for the moment to be alone with the memories the apartment generated. From the window he watched his grandson drive away, then sat down in a chair next to a mahogany bureau. He opened one of the drawers and took out an old, frayed picture album. Faded black-and-white photographs of his wife when she was young stared out at him. As he leafed through the pages, the pictures became more modern. Monty with his wife, family shots. Then pictures with pieces missing as if some mischievous child had wielded a pair of scissors at random; blank spaces where pictures had been removed entirely.

Monty felt his eyes mist as he studied the pages. He replaced the book and fumbled among the other mementoes stored in the drawer. At the very bottom his fingers felt a wooden frame, then glass. He pulled it out and sat staring at a photograph taken of Meir Adler when he was eighteen.

Meir . . . Monty mouthed the name silently, looking at the photo until he was overcome by a coughing spasm. Before he could raise his hand, spots of saliva had spattered onto the glass covering the picture. Monty carefully wiped them away with his handkerchief, put the photograph back in the drawer and went to his bedroom to lie down. Contrary to his customary fastidiousness he didn't bother to undress. Instead, he fell back onto the bed and lay quietly as he stared at the ceiling.

Michael – how in God's name did Albert have a son like Michael? Meir would have had a son like Michael, but surely not Albert . . . It just didn't make any sense.

Monty raised his hand to his forehead. It felt cold and clammy, yet his cheeks were burning. He felt a sharp pain growing in his chest. Damned indigestion, he thought. Bloody Albert's wife had poisoned him again with her rotten cooking.

The room seemed to be getting dark. Couldn't be twilight already, he thought. Monty's hand fell away from his forehead, dropped listlessly onto the bed. It *was* getting darker. He could barely make out the pattern on the ceiling now. He shifted his focus. The outline of the wardrobe in the corner of the room was dim and fuzzy, too.

Monty's last thoughts before the black veil descended completely were of his older son. With his last bit of strength he forced the tears of agonizing sorrow from his eyes.

Simon Aronson telephoned Roland the following afternoon with news of Monty Adler's death. Details had made the early editions of the evening newspapers. When the old man hadn't turned up for work nor answered any phone calls, Albert and Michael had gone to the flat. The superintendent let them in and they found Monty lying on his bed, the victim of a heart attack.

'When's the funeral?' Roland asked.

'Tomorrow morning. Edmonton. Why?'

'I'm going.'

Simon was amazed. 'I can understand you wanting to attend if Adler's was a major client. But surely—"

'I'm going,' Roland repeated firmly.

'Do you think you had something to do with his death? Don't weigh yourself down with that kind of guilt, Roland.'

'Never mind my reasons.' Roland dabbed at his eyes, felt the moisture. Would the old man have still been alive if Roland hadn't caused him all that aggravation, especially when he was so sick? Stop it . . . Roland told himself. If anyone was to blame it was Albert. Albert had set the ball rolling, and once it was in motion there was nothing anyone could do until it halted of its own accord.

Roland recalled the last time he'd seen the old man, when he'd visited the factory threatening revenge. He hadn't looked well then, but he wasn't the kind of man to let something like a cold slow him down. Stubborn old bugger, Roland thought. Now he was dead, with his cheating son left to run the business.

'I'll see you at the cemetery,' Simon said resignedly.

'Why are *you* going?'

'We're equal partners, remember? If you turn up, so should I.'

Roland was about to protest that their reasons for attending couldn't possibly be the same, but Simon broke the connection.

Roland reached the cemetery in north London at ten the following morning, and parked next to Simon's black Daimler. The lot was packed and he could see a huge crowd streaming into the chapel. Monty Adler had known a lot of people. Roland found Simon standing just inside the chapel door, pressed back by the mass of people.

'Here, put this on.' Simon handed Roland a black silk skull cap. Roland peered across the heads of people to the coffin lying on a simple wooden trolley. Standing next to it was Albert, head bowed, a hand resting on the trolley handle. Behind him stood a young man of roughly Roland's age, tall and broad-shouldered, with black hair and blue eyes.

'Who's that with Albert?' Roland asked Simon.

Simon shrugged his shoulders and asked the man standing next to him. 'Albert's son, Michael,' came the reply.

Roland had no idea what the service was about. He

188

simply stared at the prayer book Simon was holding and tried to make sense out of the strange letters, the lines running from right to left. He'd only seen a large body of Hebrew lettering once before, when he had taken apart the *mezzuzah* his father had given him; had he stayed in the army and gone to Palestine, he thought, he might have become more familiar with it.

The praying stopped. There was a movement at the front of the chapel as Albert wheeled the trolley carrying Monty's coffin toward the door leading to the burial ground. Michael walked alongside his father, holding his arm. The crowd of mourners filed after them at a solemn pace as Albert led the procession toward a freshly dug grave. Roland stood at the back of the crowd, blinking back tears. Even when the mourners shoveled earth onto the coffin he didn't step forward. He couldn't bring himself to face Albert; at least, not yet.

After the interment Simon joined a line of men waiting to ritually rinse their hands at a small fountain. Roland waited for him. Back inside the chapel after the service Albert sat alone on a stone bench as people filed past to shake his hand and offer condolences. Roland fell in behind Simon, feeling awkward as he approached the stone bench. He saw Simon grasp Albert's hand, wish him a long life, and move on. Then Roland stood in front of Albert, shook his hand. Albert stared blankly until he heard Roland speak. 'I'm very sorry about your father.' Only then did Albert look up. As he finally recognized the voice, his mouth tightened, his eyes blazed.

'What the hell are you doing here?' He leaped up from the bench, throwing Roland's hand from him.

'I came to pay my respects.'

'I don't need *your* respects!'

·'My respects are for your father, not for you.'

Around the two men, the movement of people stopped. Everyone was watching the small drama which had suddenly unfolded in the chapel. 'My father doesn't need

189

your respects either! If it weren't for you, he'd still be alive!'

Roland felt himself slipping. He tried to hold back, but failed. 'Don't you mean if it weren't for you? You're the one who broke the deal, not me!' The moment the accusation was out he caught hold of himself. Damn! Why had he come? Out of sorrow and respect, or to get involved in a fight?

'You . . .!' Albert brought up his hands, clenched them angrily into fists. Simultaneously, two figures darted between the men. Simon grabbed hold of Roland's arm and dragged him away while Michael Adler stood in front of his father, gently pushing him back onto the bench.

'What's the matter with you?' Simon hissed as he escorted Roland out of the chapel, back toward the cars.

'All I said was that I was sorry about his father—'

'You should never have come here,' Simon muttered, still unable to understand why Roland had attended the funeral.

'Mr Eagles!' a voice called from the chapel doorway. 'Mr Eagles! Can you wait a minute?'

Simon and Roland turned around. Loping toward them was the tall figure of Michael Adler. Roland braced himself. Perhaps Michael was not as tall as Roland but he was far more muscular; he looked as if he enjoyed sports as much as Roland detested them.

Michael reached the two men. To Roland's surprise – and relief – he seemed contrite, even embarrassed. 'I must apologize for my father's behavior, Mr Eagles. He's under a tremendous strain at the moment, but that doesn't excuse what he did.'

'It's all right. I know what he's going through.'

'I'm sorry that he blames you for my grandfather's death. If anyone is responsible it's my father and myself.'

'You?'

'I was the last person to see him alive. I took him home

190

from my father's house. I could see he wasn't well but he wanted to be alone. Maybe I should have been more attentive, stayed with him a while longer.'

Roland managed to smile. 'Your grandfather wasn't the easiest person in the world to say no to, was he?' he said as he continued walking toward the parking lot.

Michael kept pace. 'It didn't take you very long to know him, did it? But he was a wonderful man.'

'I saw the size of the crowd, you don't have to tell me. Do you know my partner, Simon Aronson?'

'I'm familiar with the name.'

'Incidentally, how did you know *my* name?'

'Easy. Only one man could have gotten my father so worked up at the moment. You had to be him.'

'That wasn't the reason I came.'

'I know, and I appreciate your presence. My grand-father mentioned you to me the day he died. He spoke very highly of you.'

Roland was surprised and at the same time moved that, regardless of what had happened, old Monty had spoken of him fondly. 'The last time I saw your grandfather he threatened to grind me into dust.'

'That was his way. You'd got the better of him and he wasn't about to let it go at that. It didn't stop him think-ing a lot of you, though,' Michael said as they reached the cars.

'You had better get back inside and take care of your father,' Simon told Michael.

'I will. But I just wanted to set the record straight.' He shook hands with both Roland and Simon and jogged back toward the chapel.

'Would never have guessed he was Albert's son,' Simon remarked as he climbed into his Daimler.

'Neither would I. See you Friday at the sales meeting.' Roland started the Jaguar and drove slowly to the fac-tory, going over the incident once again and reaching the same conclusion that Monty Adler once had; the son had more character in his little finger than Albert had in his entire body. When Roland arrived at the factory, his secretary told him he had a visitor. Still wrapped in thoughts of the funeral he opened his office door, then came to an abrupt halt. Behind his desk sat Catarina.

'What are you doing here?' Roland said, amazed at the sight of her. He rushed across the room, lifted her from the chair and hugged her. 'How did you get away?'

She answered neither of his questions, just grateful to hold him, unwilling to let go even when he dropped his arms. Finally she said: 'I had to see you, Rollie. I just had to.'

'How did you get out of the house?'

'I ran. Straight through the front door before anyone could stop me and into a passing taxi.' As she clung to him he could feel her slender body trembling. 'Rollie, there is terrible trouble. A terrible thing has happened.'

'Tell me about it,' he said gently. After what he'd just been through at the funeral, what else could be so terrible?

'You know there is a certain time of the month for a woman?' Catarina looked into his eyes, found strength there. 'Rollie, I'm always punctual, like your Big Ben. Now I've missed my period twice. I'm already a week late for this month.'

'Are you telling me you're pregnant?'

'Yes. Are you angry with me?'

'Angry?' A burst of delighted laughter echoed through the office. 'I'm not angry – I'm ecstatic! That's wonderful news, the best possible news I could have heard!' He kissed her, held on to her until her nervous trembling subsided. Nature . . . a life for every death! Only an hour ago he'd mourned at Monty Adler's funeral, now Catarina had filled his heart with joy.

'What will we do?'

'We'll get married, of course. That's what we'll do. We'll confront your father together. When we tell him that we want to get married – that we're *going* to get married, we'll see how well his objections stand up to that!'

Catarina paled at the prospect. 'If my father ever learns I'm pregnant, he'll be like a madman.'

'He won't have to know.'

'But what will happen when the baby is born less than nine months after our wedding? My father can count.'

'He'll be so delighted to have a grandchild it'll never even enter his mind.' Roland gripped Catarina's hand and pulled her toward the door. A minute later they were sitting in the Jaguar, heading toward the center of London. Roland steered with his right hand, alternating his left between the gearshift and Catarina's belly. A baby! His baby! More than nine years had passed without a family, with nothing to cushion him but work . . . the army and now the factory. But a baby – and a wife – would be enough to make him forget about work. If he could once again enjoy that security and love, to give it as well as receive it, he would be perfectly happy with a job as a . . . as a bus driver, damn it!

Catarina sat pensively as he drove. She didn't have the heart to deflate Roland's happiness by arguing that her father would never allow such a marriage. And if the ambassador should ever guess· that she had slept with Roland, was pregnant by him . . . Roland was clearly convinced that her father's objections would be no defense against their love and determination to marry. She was afraid for both of them that he was badly mistaken . . .

Wilton Crescent was packed with parked cars. Roland double-parked the Jaguar, opened the passenger door and helped Catarina out. As they walked toward the house, the front door flew open and Juan Menendez came running out. He grabbed Catarina by the arm and tried to rip her from Roland's grasp. Catarina screamed. Roland let go of her hand, took hold of Juan by the lapels of his jacket and lifted him high off the ground, forcing him against the black, pointed railings that surrounded the house.

'If you ever lay a hand on your sister again, I'll impale you,' he whispered in Juan's ear.

'Let go of me!'

'Where is your father?'

'In the embassy.'

'Go get him. Bring him to your home.' Roland released his hold. Juan dropped to the ground, glared at his sister who stood in the middle of the road watching, then jogged toward the embassy. Roland turned back to Catarina, took her hand and led her toward the front door, whch had been left open. Maria Menendez, who had witnessed the incident with Juan, stood inside, her hands clasped nervously in front of her. When Catarina entered the house Señora Menendez threw her arms around her, asking her why she had run away. She didn't seem to notice Roland behind her.

Ambassador Menendez arrived out of breath less than two minutes later after excusing himself from a meeting with a delegation from the British War Ministry, arranging the sale of surplus war hardware to Argentina.

'Catarina! How dare you leave here without my permission? And you!' Menendez turned toward Roland. 'What insolence allows you to show your face in my home?'

Roland locked eyes with the ambassador, neither willing to yield. 'Sir, your daughter and I wish to be married. We have come to ask your blessing.'

Maria Menendez burst into a fit of crying. Juan stood rigidly at his father's side. 'Never,' Menendez said, his voice level and without emotion. 'You will never marry my daughter.'

'Sir, I regret to hear that because Catarina and I will be married whether you see fit to give your blessing or not.' In that moment, Roland knew that he'd done what he'd tried to avoid – driven a wedge between Catarina and her family. Menendez looked as if he would explode as Roland tried to retract some of the bitterness his announcement had caused. 'Would you stand in the way of your daughter's happiness, sir?'

'My daughter is far too young to know what will bring her happiness. And you – a gambler, an owner of a petty business that has to sell its merchandise in a street market – are certainly not it.'

'Father!' Catarina cried out. 'We are in love with each other. You cannot stop us.'

'I cannot? You are under the age of consent. That is all I need to stop this madness.' He turned back to Roland, studied the sheepskin coat that was showing signs of wear, the shoes that were still muddy from the morning's trip to the cemetery. 'Let me explain it very simply to you, Mr Eagles. The Menendez family is a very old and very proud family.' He paused to let the words sink in. 'A very old and very proud *Catholic* family.'

Roland felt his stomach tighten. He knew exactly where the ambassador was heading, and he was glad Menendez had chosen this route. Now the cards were on the table. He no longer felt compelled to show a respect he didn't feel.

'Then we're a fine match, sir. Because I also come from a very old and very proud family – a very old and very proud *Jewish* family.' There, he had said it, publicly and defiantly stated a heritage he had once never given a second thought to. Love had made his father deny it, now Roland was accepting it again – for love.

'Perhaps I should make myself even clearer to you, Mr Eagles. It is not the custom in my family to marry Jews.'

Roland glanced at Juan, saw the ambassador's son smirking. Suddenly he wished he'd impaled him on the railings when he had the chance . . . Not since the war had Roland felt such hatred. Bergen-Belsen and all the other camps hadn't meant a damned thing after all. Maybe the bigotry was veiled now, but it was still there. 'Nor is it the custom in my family, sir, to marry people from a nation

195

which grants refuge to Nazi war criminals who are willing to pay handsomely for their safety.' He watched Menendez's face turn crimson, his eyes bulge in shocked fury. 'But in your daughter's case, I am willing to make an exception.'

'Get out!' Menendez hissed. He motioned for Juan to escort Roland from the house. Juan hesitated, remembering only too well what had happened in the street.

'With or without your blessing, sir, Catarina and I will be wed.'

Refusing to grace such disrespect with a response, Menendez swung on his heel and walked away. No one had ever spoken to him in such a manner. At home, in Argentina, he could use his friends in high circles – yes, those friends who had made themselves even wealthier by assisting Nazi refugees – to pay back such impudence. But here, in Britain, he was ruled by other laws.

Juan finally made a move in his direction, but Roland held up his hand. 'I'm leaving. Save yourself the bother.' He turned to Catarina and managed to give her a reassuring smile. 'Try not to worry. In a month we'll be married and all this will have passed.' With that he turned and left.

Sitting in the Jaguar, listening to the purr of the engine, Roland calmed himself down enough to think lucidly. He would be damned before he would let Menendez – or Juan – stand in his way. Or any of them. He wanted to marry Catarina and she wanted to marry him. It was as simple as that. Nothing would stop them from having each other. And there *was* a way. Sally Roberts had unknowingly suggested it to him when she'd joked about putting a ladder against Catarina's window. They would elope. But first, Roland needed to learn the legal ramifications before he took on Menendez in a head-on clash.

Simon Aronson was in a meeting when Roland arrived at Aronson Freres, insistent on seeing his partner on an urgent legal matter. Five minutes later Simon emerged, wondering what the emergency could be. He did little to hide his astonishment when Roland explained that he wanted to elope with Catarina.

'You are incredible, Roland! First you cause a fight at a funeral this morning, now you drag me out of an important meeting to ask about eloping. I didn't bargain for any of these distractions when I became your partner.'

'Are you going to help me or not?'

'If I said no, would that be reason to dissolve our partnership? Of course I'll help you. Come into my office.' While Roland sat impatiently, Simon sorted through legal volumes. 'Scotland,' he said at last. 'Scottish marriage laws are different from those in England—'

'Gretna Green and the village blacksmith?'

Simon shook his head and smiled. 'Those days are gone. Nonetheless, there is a lower age of consent in Scotland. You'll have to establish residence there for two weeks and post formàl notice of your intention to marry. That's all. But you'd better make certain you stay one step ahead of Catarina's father. He isn't going to take this lying down.'

'Thanks for your help.' Roland got up and was heading toward the door when Simon called him back.

'Aren't you forgetting one minor detail, Roland? You just told me you took Catarina back to her family – now how do you plan to get her away again?'

'I'm working on it.' In fact, Roland didn't have the slightest idea. How would he even get in touch with Catarina to let her know his plan? If only he'd known about this before Catarina had turned up at the factory. They could have driven to Scotland that morning . . . Now that she was back in their grip, God only knew what they would do to thwart him.

Ambassador Menendez didn't return to the embassy after Roland had left; as far as he was concerned the delegation from the British War Ministry could cool their heels while he attended to more important matters.

He busied himself on the telephone, making an international call to Madrid. He should have acted earlier, he cursed himself, after that incident in the street market. Even before that . . . He should have sent Catarina away at the very first sign that she might be interested in this Roland Eagles.

Menendez's connection was finally made. After speaking at length he hung up the phone, satisfied. Perhaps he had moved late, but he had moved positively. After learning that Catarina was in her room he called for his wife and son.

'I've just made arrangements for Catarina to stay in Madrid. Juan, tomorrow morning you will escort her there. She will stay for as long as necessary – even until we leave London and return to Argentina. I do not want her to ever see that man again, nor do I want to hear his name spoken in my presence.'

'It will be my pleasure as well as my duty to protect our family honor,' Juan replied.

Menendez ran his hands through his thick hair, relieved. 'Just be sure she doesn't slip away from you.'

Juan waited until his father had returned to the embassy, then knocked on the door of Catarina's room. When he entered she was sitting on the edge of the bed, staring blankly at the wall. 'What do you want?' she asked tonelessly.

'Pack your cases.'

'Why?'

'You are going away tomorrow. To Spain.'

'No!' She swung around to face him, hoping that he was teasing her.

'Yes . . . not no. Say good-bye to London and to your Roland, your Jewish golddigger.' The anxiety he saw on her face made him smile.

'Laugh if you want to, Juan, but Roland and I will be together.'

198

'Forget him, Catarina. In a week he will have forgotten all about you. He'll have another little rich girl sitting in his fancy car, and she might not be as fortunate as you to have such a caring family.'

Catarina bit her lip and returned to staring at the wall. She refused to give Juan the satisfaction of seeing her cry, even if the headache she had was getting severe enough to force tears to her eyes.

Roland's telephone rang at ten o'clock that night. He grabbed it, hoping it would be Catarina. Instead, it was a woman named Anita Alvarez. Roland had never heard of her.

'You might remember me, Mr Eagles,' the woman said in broken English, 'if I told you that I wore a black dress and a white apron. I work as a maid at the home of Ambassador Menendez.'

'Catarina asked you to call me?' Roland asked excitedly. 'What did she say?'

'The family is planning to send her to Spain tomorrow,' the woman replied. Roland's heart plummetted as she continued talking. 'Did you write that down, Mr Eagles?' she asked.

'Sorry – did I write what down?'

'The flight number from London Airport. It leaves at ten minutes past eleven.'

Roland grabbed a pencil, found a piece of paper and asked the woman to repeat the flight number and time of departure. 'Tell Catarina I'll be waiting for her. We'll go to Scotland and be married there. Be sure to tell her that. In Scotland, she won't need her father's consent. And thank you for calling.'

He sat by the telephone after they hung up, running plans through his mind, growing more confident as each new one unfolded. The maid's call was an omen. By this time tomorrow he and Catarina would be well on their way to Scotland, together at last and forever.

He picked up the phone and first called Alf Goldstein, then dialed Sally's number. She had a right to know that the romance of the year had just sprouted wings.

An embassy car took Catarina and Juan from Wilton Crescent to London Airport the following morning. Throughout the ride Juan continued to taunt his sister, telling her that even now Roland was probably making plans to ingratiate himself with some other wealthy girl if he hadn't done so already while he was seeing Catarina – creating options for himself, laying off his bets. That was what any gambler would do, Juan told his sister. Roland was no different.

Catarina tried to close her ears to her brother's spiteful gibes. She knew her message had gotten through to him. Roland had promised to be waiting for her, ready to take her up to Scotland where they could be married. She knew nothing about the difference between English and Scottish law, but if Roland said it was so, then it must be. Still, even if he were waiting for her, how would she get away? And how could he have made plans at such short notice?

She kept looking out of the car window for the familiar lines and color of the Jaguar XK-120. Would he be at the airport already? Or had his message meant that he would be waiting for her in Madrid? No, it couldn't be. In Madrid, surrounded by her father's friends in Franco's government, escape would be even more difficult. Roland could end up in jail, or worse. He *had* to be waiting at the airport. Her heart quickened as a dark green sports car drew alongside, then slowed again when she realized it wasn't the Jaguar she wanted to see.

He had to be there! she kept repeating to herself. She couldn't even consider what would happen to her if he weren't.

Roland and Alf Goldstein drove to London Airport in a two-car convoy, the Jaguar leading the way at a steady thirty miles an hour. Roland wanted no possibility of being stopped for speeding, no chance of delay.

They reached the airport just after ten o'clock. Gold-stein left his cab at a taxi stand while Roland parked the Jaguar close to the terminal entrance, risking a ticket. They went into the terminal together. Goldstein carried a leather briefcase with the initials J.M. stamped in gold on the flap.

Away from the ticket counters, out of sight, they waited.

The embassy car reached the airport at ten-fifteen. The chauffeur helped Juan to carry his and Catarina's luggage into the terminal. At the counter, Juan told the man to return to the embassy. He produced two Argentinian passports and two sets of tickets for the flight to Paris where they would change for Madrid. As he handed over the documents he kept his eyes fixed firmly on his sister. He was taking no chances now. Not until they were sit-ting on the plane with their seatbelts on would he dare relax . . .

'There they are,' Roland said. 'Make it good.'

Goldstein nodded. He pulled a tweed cap low over his forehead and gripped the briefcase tightly while he waited for Juan and Catarina to finish at the counter. Their bag-gage disappeared toward the loading area and they turned to follow the sign pointing to passport control. Goldstein stepped out and walked briskly as he closed the distance between himself and his quarry.

'Excuse me, sir!' Goldstein's voice rang through the terminal. 'You, sir, in the blue coat!'

Half a dozen men stopped and turned but Goldstein looked only at Juan. 'That's right, you! You left this in my cab!' He waved the briefcase in the air.

'Me?' Juan pointed to himself, confused as the cab driver approached. 'I'm afraid there must be some mis-take. I didn't come by taxi.'

'What on earth are you talking about?' Goldstein

201

noticed that other passengers were taking an interest in the scene. Good, more confusion. 'You gave me a pound tip, sir, don't you remember?' He looked at Catarina, now wide-eyed as she recognized the man who had brought the roses to the embassy. Juan was holding her by the wrist. Goldstein *had* to make him let go.

'I tell you there is a mistake.'

'Are your initials J.M.?'

'Yes,' Juan said uncertainly. 'Juan Menendez.'

'Then this is your bag, sir.' He thrust the briefcase at Juan who, despite himself, reached out for it with both hands, letting go of Catarina. From the corner of his eye Goldstein saw Roland working his way toward her along the ticket counter.

'I didn't come here by taxi!' Juan repeated, angry now, wondering why he was holding this unfamiliar briefcase. How on earth could it have his initials on it? 'Here – you found it, you keep it!' He shoved the briefcase at Goldstein's chest.

Goldstein pushed it right back. 'What's the matter with it? Why don't you want it back? Why did you leave it in my cab?' Goldstein shouted the questions loudly enough so that a crowd began to press in, forming a circle around him and Juan. 'What's in the bag, a bomb?'

A shocked gasp erupted from the crowd at such a dramatic possibility. At the same time Roland's hand snaked out from the crowd, grabbed Catarina by the wrist and dragged her into the mass of people. 'We'll get to the bottom of this!' Goldstein yelled, red in the face. 'Let's find a policeman and get him to open it!'

'For the very last time, I did not come here in your taxi and this is not my bag!' Juan shouted back. 'I came with my sister in a limousine from the Argentinian Embassy! My father is the ambassador!'

Goldstein gazed over the heads of the crowd, spotted Roland and Catarina rushing through the terminal door toward the Jaguar. 'What sister?'

202

'Here!' Juan spun around and his mouth dropped open in shock. Catarina was nowhere in sight. All he could see were the people watching him. 'Where is she? Where is my sister?'

'The girl who was standing with you?' a stewardess asked.

'That's right! In the brown coat!'

'She left with a man while you were arguing with the cab driver.'

Juan swung back to confront Goldstein, but he was no longer there. He had slipped to the other side of the crowd and was walking quickly toward the taxi stand. Juan was left holding a leather briefcase with his initials stamped on it. Close to tears, he realized too late that he'd been outwitted. He opened the case and pulled out a single white envelope. He ripped it open to find a map of Madrid along with a greeting card.

'*Bon Voyage,*' it read.

'Police!' Juan screamed as he tore up the card and map and threw them to the floor. 'Police!'

Roland and Catarina ran the full distance to the Jaguar. He opened the passenger door, pushed her inside, jumped into the driver's seat and gunned the engine. With a squeal of tires he sped from the airport, heading back toward London. In the rearview mirror he could barely see Alf Goldstein running toward the taxi stand. Roland grinned.

'My baggage is on its way to Madrid and I am not,' Catarina said joyfully. 'You are marvelous, Rollie. You and your cab driver friend.' She leaned across the car and kissed Roland on the cheek. He responded by wrapping his arm around her and pulling her close to him.

'Shall we name our first child after him?' He ran his hand across her belly, certain he could feel life there.

'Not if it's a girl.'

'You're right. Alf's a funny name for a girl.' He

laughed and hugged her again, steering with one hand.

'Are we going to Scotland right now? I only have the clothes I'm wearing.'

'No, not for a few days.' After his conversation with the maid, Roland had changed his mind about going to Scotland right away. The abduction from Juan would create havoc; he wanted to let the heat die down before he acted. 'You're going to lie low for a while, Catarina, and I'm going to continue working just as usual.'

'Where will I stay? Not with you, surely? That's the first place my father will look.'

'Not with me, although I'd love you to.' That was another subject he'd considered carefully. He wanted Catarina with people he knew and trusted, but at the same time he didn't want her staying with anyone Menendez might suspect. That ruled out both Sally Roberts and Simon Aronson. So Roland had gone to Alf Goldstein.

By midday, Catarina was comfortably esconced on the top floor of Goldstein's rambling three-story house in the North London section of Stoke Newington. Goldstein's wife Sara, a plump, red-haired matronly woman, explained that the top floor was usually let out as a furnished apartment; now it was empty, and Catarina could use it for as long as she wanted. The Goldsteins and their two young sons shared three bedrooms on the second floor; on the ground floor were the living room, dining room and kitchen.

'Remember, you mustn't leave the house,' Roland reminded Catarina. 'I'm sure your picture's going to be in the newspapers, and someone on the street might recognize you. I'll get messages to you because I can't take a chance on calling you directly. Be patient.'

'I can't be patient for very long, Rollie. Please make it happen quickly.'

'I will.' He looked at his watch, the one Catarina had

given him. Juan would have returned to the embassy long ago; by now the search must have started. 'Catarina, telephone your father and tell him you're all right. It won't make him any less furious,' he added when he saw Catarina's surprise, 'but he has the right to know that you're safe. And maybe . . . just maybe . . . when he sees we're this determined he might soften.'

Catarina went to the telephone and dialed the number of the embassy. When she identified herself she was put straight through to her father. 'Papa, it's Catarina—'

'Where are you?' Menendez roared. 'Are you with that fortune hunter?'

'Papa, will you please listen to me?'

'I will listen to you only when you come home! When you have learned respect for your parents again!' With that, Menendez slammed down the receiver.

Catarina turned to Roland, white-faced and shaking. 'I heard him,' Roland said, holding her. 'He'll come around, don't worry. When he has time to think it over, he'll act more sensibly.' Roland only wished he could believe his own words.

'I hope so, Rollie, but I know my father better than you do. He sees this as an insult; it will take him a long time to recover from it.'

'But he will, that's all that matters.' He kissed her, thanked Goldstein's wife for her help and left the house.

Roland didn't bother returning to the factory since it was just a few days short of the new year and business was slack. Instead he went home to Regent's Park, stopping once to telephone Sally Roberts and bring her up to date.

Once in his apartment he settled down in an easy chair with a book and waited for the action to begin.

He didn't have to wait long. Five minutes after he'd arrived, the telephone rang. 'Where is my daughter?' Ambassador Menendez roared into the phone.

'I have no idea, sir.' Roland guessed the ambassador had been calling every few minutes.

'You were at the airport this morning! You took her from Juan!'

'I'm sorry, sir, but I don't know what you're talking about. If Catarina left Juan, it was her own doing.' He cut off the next explosion by gently replacing the receiver. Who would call next? Menendez again? Or would he bring in his big guns? Roland had no doubt that the ambassador would use every means at his disposal, every ounce of influence he had. Not only was the man concerned for his daughter but he had his own reputation to consider . . . he was being made to look like a fool, unable to control his own daughter.

Although there were no more phone calls that afternoon, there was a series of visitors. First the police came to question Roland about his knowledge of Catarina's disappearance. In answer to their queries he gave them a carefully worked out statement: 'Catarina has run away from her family of her own free will. We are very much in love and plan to be married. Ideally we will marry with the Menendez family's blessing, but if they see fit to withhold it, we will marry without it.' The police left, convinced that there was little they could do; this wasn't a case of kidnapping as Menendez insisted it was; it was a lovers' entanglement that he would have to work out with his daughter.

Next came government officials, who pressed Roland harder for answers in their attempt to placate the ambassador. Surely, they explained, Roland could see that he was harming Britain's relations with Argentina. There was a big arms deal in the balance, and the ambassador was using it for leverage. Why not return Catarina to her family, they suggested, then Roland could sort out his differences smoothly with the ambassador? Blank-faced, Roland repeated the statement he'd given the police. He had no interest in arms deals. 'Indeed,' he told one junior minister who arrived with bowler hat in hand, as unctuous as any civil servant could be, 'if I can thwart the supply of weapons to a nation which harbors Nazi war criminals, then my romance with Catarina will pay additional dividends!'

At this the junior minister's ingratiating manner was dropped suddenly; he became threatening, belligerent. 'Just because the police don't think a crime's been committed doesn't mean you're home scot-free, Eagles! We can still make life damned difficult for you and your snot-nosed little company.'

'Coming from a snot-nosed civil servant like you, I find that hardly surprising,' Roland replied. 'Would you care to repeat that statement for the *News of the World*? I'll get one of their reporters on the telephone for you. The Ministry won't even have to pay for the call.'

The junior minister jammed his bowler hat onto his head and stormed from the apartment as Roland, laughing, closed the door behind him.

The press was last to arrive. Flashbulbs popped in Roland's face each time he opened the door as anxious reporters fired questions at him. In the end he tired even of giving his prepared statement and simply answered, 'No comment.' By late that evening he thought – in fact hoped – the worst was over.

Only one journalist was destined for success. At nine-thirty that night Sally Roberts drove to Stoke Newington. Alf Goldstein opened the door and showed her into the living room where Catarina sat playing rummy with his wife while the children slept upstairs.

The Goldsteins left Sally and Catarina alone for the *Mercury's* exclusive interview with the eloping heiress. Sally felt that she had more than a professional interest in the story. Not only had she been a friend of Roland's for two years; it was she who had originally introduced the lovers.

'Have you considered that your father might disinherit you?'

'Yes, but I don't upset myself by worrying about it. If my father wishes to react in that manner, that is his privilege. As long as Roland and I are together nothing else matters. All the money in the world can't change that.'

Sally's pencil skipped across the page as she took notes. 'Did you really think he would rescue you the way he did?'

Catarina smiled as she recalled the events of that morning. 'I was surprised myself how he did it, but I knew he would. Roland is my knight in shining armor. What else can I say?'

'Catarina, are you prepared, if necessary, to go through life without ever seeing your family again?'

Catarina's dark eyes went soft as she considered the question. 'I pray that it never comes to that. I pray my father will change. But if that is my father's wish I will have to accept it. My father feels that I have an obligation to marry a man of whom he approves. I believe it is wrong for any father to feel that way. The only obligation I have is to my own happiness. If any obligation exists at all, it is that of a father to his child. I am grateful to my father for everything he has given me, but as I've said, the obligation is of him to me.'

Sally snapped her notebook shut. She would use one of the photographs taken at the ambassador's ball at Claridge's. Run the story on the front page of the *Mercury*. All the other newspapers would have the story, sure; but she would be the only one to run an interview with Catarina.

'Sally, I have to ask you something now.' Catarina's question cut abruptly into Sally's thoughts. 'Were you in love with Roland?'

'Me?' Sally laughed. 'I was in *like* with him.'

'I'm sorry, I don't understand.'

'If I was in love with him, I'd have never put the two of you together. Does that make it any clearer?'

Catarina got up from the chair and kissed Sally on the cheek. 'Thank you for everything.'

Roland was listening to a play on the radio when the telephone rang. It was Sally calling from Fleet Street to say she'd just finished her interview with Catarina. 'God alone knows what she sees in you, Eagles. She's prepared to lose her inheritance, everything for you. I'm damned sure I wouldn't, if it were me.'

'How did she seem?'

'Calm and confident. Just waiting for you to spirit her up to Scotland to tie the knot. What on earth are you waiting for?'

'I want to let the heat die down first.' He looked around as he heard the doorbell. 'Hang on a moment, Sally – there's another one of your colleagues trying to bash the front door in.'

'Don't tell him anything.'

'Relax, you've got it all.' He placed the receiver on the table and took the stairs two at a time. There were no journalists outside when he opened the front door, only the solitary figure of Juan Menendez, wearing the same blue coat he'd worn at the airport that morning.

'Bastard!' Juan spat out. His wildly swung fist missed Roland's face completely and smashed into the door-frame. He doubled over in pain, clutching his bloodied hand.

Roland grabbed hold of Juan's coat lapels and dragged him close. When he smelled the alcohol on his breath he let go and Juan collapsed in a sobbing heap on the ground. Roland dragged him inside, closed the door and raced upstairs. 'Sally, that was Catarina's brother. He's downstairs, drunk, with a broken hand where he clobbered the door instead of me.'

'What are you going to do?'

'Call Menendez to pick up his son.'

'Can I use it in my story?'

209

'I can't believe you're even asking.' He hung up and dialed the Menendez home. The ambassador answered.

'Ambassador Menendez, your son is at my home.'

'I don't want my son! Where is my daughter?'

'You'd better pick up your son first. He's drunk and he just assaulted me. Are you going to collect him or should I call the police to do the job?'

'I'll be there.'

Roland waited downstairs until an embassy limousine pulled up quietly. Menendez and the chauffeur got out; between them they carried Juan into the car. 'You'll pay for this, Eagles. I'm going to ruin you. By the time I'm finished Catarina will hate the sight of you after everything you've put her through.'

'Good night, sir,' Roland said politely and closed the door.

On the way to the factory the next day, Roland stopped to buy all the morning newspapers. The lead story on the front pages of all the tabloids was the disappearance of the Argentinian heiress. Pictures of her and Roland were everywhere.

When he reached the factory the staff gave him a standing ovation. Gruffly, but unable to resist a grin, he told them to return to work.

At ten o'clock the first edition of the *Mercury* came out. Pictures of Roland and Catarina were on the front page, along with Sally's bylined interview, plus a sidebar on Juan Menendez assaulting Roland. After reading the story, Roland decided that Sally had got her money's worth.

At lunchtime, Roland drove into town to meet with Simon Aronson and discuss future plans. They agreed that Roland and Catarina should leave for Scotland in two days, on New Year's. 'You might be better off if you didn't use your own car,' Simon pointed out. 'It is rather distinctive. Believe me, aside from Menendez, every reporter worth his salt will be turning the country upside down to find you two, and that green Jaguar will only make their job easier.'

'I've already found that out,' Roland replied. 'I'm sure I picked a shadow when I left home this morning. A black Vauxhall followed me almost to the factory. And when I came here I'm sure I spotted the same car.' He knew he shouldn't be surprised that Menendez had ordered a tail on him . . . obviously if they were going to elope, they'd have to meet sooner or later.

'Then be very cautious,' Simon advised. 'You've already gotten through the most difficult part. Getting to Scotland and establishing your residence should be nothing compared with what you've managed so far. Just be certain you aren't careless.'

'We won't be.'

The moment the story appeared in the papers, Ambassador Menendez found his well-ordered life in total disarray. Hounded by journalists, he was unable to cope with his official duties and delegated minor matters to his staff.

His wife and son offered little comfort, between Juan's drunken attack on Roland and Maria Menendez begging her husband to reconsider his opposition to their marriage. The woman clearly was more concerned with losing a daughter than gaining a thoroughly unprepossessing son-in-law.

But as head of his family and a top official of his government, Menendez wasn't about to bow to anyone. He resolved to retaliate, hitting back at Roland through the same medium that was pillorying him. He held a press conference at the embassy and threatened to cut his daughter off without a single penny. That was what they wanted to hear, these journalists who reveled in a high-ranking official's personal crisis. He would not disappoint them.

'When my daughter is penniless we shall see how much

211

this fortune hunter loves her. We will learn exactly how much he cares for her when she can't afford to cater to *his* expensive tastes.'

From the many journalists who clamored for attention, Menendez selected an auburn-haired woman in a dark green coat to speak. 'Aren't you being just a trifle unfair, Ambassador Menendez? Roland Eagles is not exactly a pauper.'

'How would *you* know?'

Before his question could be answered, the other journalists turned toward her. 'Come on, Sally!' one of her colleagues yelled. 'Tell us where she's hiding!'

Menendez felt his face flush with anger when he realized who the woman was. He pushed his way through the crowd until he was face-to-face with Sally. 'You know where my daughter is! I demand that you tell me immediately!' Some of the other journalists encouraged the ambassador for confronting her, but Sally stood her ground. 'I'm not at liberty to give you that information.'

'At this moment you are standing on Argentinian ground. You have no liberties or rights here!'

Sally calmly regarded her fellow journalists. She understood why they were mad at her; she had the scoop that they did not. Still, there was a kinship between them; if one was injured, they would all suffer. 'I'm not prepared to reveal my source.'

At that the mood in the room changed abruptly – they had all been reminded how vulnerable they were. 'That's right, Sally!' yelled the same man who, moments earlier, had demanded that she share her information. 'You tell him.'

Menendez sensed the change and was wise enough not to fight it. 'We shall see,' he said before he turned and left.

The group of journalists left the embassy satisfied. Even though they hadn't been able to interview Catarina and were subsequently forced to rehash the *Mercury*'s story, Menendez's fury was excellent copy. Every newspaper in town was cashing in on the public interest aroused by Catarina's rebellion against her family. It was a classic battle between the young and the old, and overnight Roland and Catarina had been unwittingly transformed into the leaders of a new generation, two young people from different backgrounds determined to bridge the gap, come what may, for love.

Sally left knowing that her exclusive connection to the story was in danger. She had little doubt that her fellow journalists – those same people who had just supported her – wouldn't think twice about tailing her every move, just as Menendez would. They all wanted to know her secret. Roland had already told her that he suspected the ambassador was having him followed; it wouldn't take much for Menendez to extend the action to Sally as well.

No, she couldn't risk visiting Catarina again, but that wouldn't put an end to her exclusive connection – there was more than one way to skin a cat.

When Roland read the interview with Menendez in the next day's papers he ripped them up in disgust. How dare he suggest that he was only interested in Catarina for her family's money? What galled him even more was Menendez's threat to disinherit his daughter. Not from the family wealth – he knew he could always provide for her – but from the family itself. Roland understood too well what that meant, and no matter what Catarina had said in her interview with Sally, the reality of it, he knew, would destroy her. Roland's own father had been cut off from his family for precisely the same reason, and it had turned one corner of his personality into a breeding ground of hatred. He couldn't bear to see that happen to Catarina as well.

Roland called a press conference of his own in retaliation to Menendez's accusations. 'Ambassador Menendez believes I want to marry his daughter for his money. He is one hundred percent wrong. I wouldn't touch a single penny of his money, even if he got down on his hands and knees and begged me to take it. Like all Argentinian money it is stained with blood, and I have no desire to soil my hands with it. All I ask of the ambassador is that he think of his daughter, to relent for her sake. He is entitled to think whatever he likes of me, but if his attitude harms Catarina he will have to carry that on his conscience for the rest of his life.'

After the reporters rushed away to file their reports of this latest round Roland once again went over his plans for their escape. Regardless of what the ambassador said or thought, soon they would be together.

CHAPTER SEVEN

Long before dawn on New Year's day, Roland sat in the living room of his apartment. Beside his chair was a picnic hamper and two suitcases; one suitcase was packed full, the other empty.

At four-thirty he heard a surreptitious rapping on the front door. He went downstairs and quickly let Lawrence Chivers in. The sales manager looked as if he'd come straight from a party: his eyes were red-rimmed, beneath his heavy coat Roland could see that his tie was askew, his shirt collar undone. Going up the stairs he noticed that Chivers was limping, as if he couldn't bend his right leg.

'Happy New Year,' Roland greeted him. 'Sorry to drag you out so early.'

'My pleasure. Elopements don't happen that often to people I know. Even my wife didn't complain when I started roaming around the house at three-thirty.' He unbuttoned his coat, opened the top of his trousers and drew out a twenty-two caliber air rifle which he set down on the floor. 'That's better, now I can walk.'

'Where did you leave your car?'

'Two streets away, like you told me to. I had it serviced last week – oil changed, plugs, points, the works. Should get you to Scotland with no trouble. Pity you're going up there a day too late for New Year's Eve.'

'I'll make my own celebrations,' Roland answered, glancing down at the air rifle; he just hoped that Chivers was as good a shot as he claimed to be. He picked up the hamper and full suitcase and passed them over to Chivers. 'Stick these in your car, then come back up.'

'Where's the fellow who's watching you?'

Roland turned out the light and led Chivers to the window. He pulled back the drape and pointed down the street. The Jaguar was parked twenty yards away; fifty yards further was the familiar shape of the black Vauxhall. Even as they watched, a tiny glow flickered inside the Vauxhall, as if its driver were lighting a cigarette to keep himself awake.

'Just the one lamp?' Chivers asked, looking at the gas streetlight near the Jaguar.

'Just the one. Figure you can hit it?'

'It's harder to miss.' Carrying the hamper and suitcase he went downstairs. Roland watched through the window as Chivers left through the delivery entrance on the side of the building and walked toward his car, opposite in direction to the Jaguar and the man in the Vauxhall. Five minutes later he was back, stumbling around in the darkened living room.

'Now you're sure you know how to get to Jack Johnston's place in Peebles?' Chivers asked as he raised the window and slid the air rifle out.

'I've got the directions you gave me.'

'Jack's a good lad,' Chivers said, sighting in on the solitary gas light. He pulled the rifle back in, broke the barrel to compress the powerful spring, inserted a waisted lead pellet and took aim again. 'Old Jack'll see you all right. Slip him a little something and he'll keep his mouth shut tight.'

'He'd better,' Roland said. Jack Johnston lived in the town of Peebles, near Edinburgh, where he rented rooms above his pub to traveling salesmen. Chivers knew Johnston from his days as a vacuum cleaner salesman, and vouched that – for a price – the publican would keep secret the fact that Roland and Catarina would be establishing residency there. Roland felt it was a risk, but Chivers had convinced him of the publican's integrity.

'I hope city council forgives me for this,' Chivers muttered as he concentrated on his aim. 'Some smart aleck teenager will probably get blamed for it.'

'Get on with it, for Christ's sake,' Roland said. The man was making him nervous.

Chivers squeezed the trigger, the report barely audible. At the same time there was the faintest sound of splintering glass as the lead pellet passed through the light, throwing the street into darkness. Chivers opened his trousers, jammed the rifle down his right leg and picked up the second, empty case.

'Keys,' Roland said.

'Oh, of course.' Chivers fished the keys to his Austin from his coat pocket, exchanged them for the Jaguar's keys. 'Good luck,' he said, shaking Roland's hand. 'Next time I hear from you, it had better be Mr and Mrs Eagles.'

'It will be.' Roland returned to the window and watched Chivers walk slowly along the street. Even at twenty yards it was impossible to identify him, and he knew the problem would be even more difficult for the man sitting in the Vauxhall. Chivers went to the trunk of the Jaguar and threw in the case. Then he opened the driver's door, fiddled with his clothing for a minute – Roland assumed he was removing the air rifle – and climbed in. Moments later the Jaguar's engine roared into life. Chivers turned the headlights on, lighting up the entire street, then tore the sports car away from the curb with a squeal of tires, accelerating hard toward the end of the street. Roland knew none of his neighbors would appreciate the noise, but he couldn't be concerned about that; he was too busy watching as the Vauxhall's lights came on, its engine started and the driver prepared for pursuit.

Laughing to himself, Roland closed the window. He waited for ten minutes, long enough to be certain that Chivers was giving the Vauxhall's driver a good run-around, then locked up the flat and walked quickly to Chivers' Austin.

While most of London slept off celebrations of the previous night, Roland sped through the dark streets toward the northwestern edge of the city. By a deserted stretch of road close to the highway leading north, he pulled over and waited. Fifteen minutes dragged by before the familiar square shape of a taxi cruised to a halt behind the Austin. Alf Goldstein clambered out and held open the passenger door for Catarina. It was the first time Roland had seen her since their escape at the airport. They kissed and clung to each other until Goldstein coughed pointedly into his hand.

'It'll be getting light before long. You two are like a pair of sitting ducks out here. Better be on your way.'

Roland helped Catarina into the Austin and turned to Goldstein. 'Thanks for everything. If I can ever repay you, just let me know how.'

'Get to Scotland and get married before her old man catches up with you, that's all you have to do.' As Roland moved away, Goldstein caught him by the arm. He removed a flat, oblong package from his coat. 'I know you never read this, so take it along with you. A little gift, in case you want to do any bedtime reading.' He winked broadly and walked back to his cab, made a U-turn and headed back toward the center of London.

'What's that?' Catarina asked as Roland got into the Austin.

'Alf gave it to me. A wedding present.' He tore open the package to find a signed copy of Goldstein's book on Bergen-Belsen. Turning to the index he found his own name and looked up the page. 'You read it,' he told Catarina as he started the car.

'He thinks a lot of you,' she said after reading aloud Goldstein's account of Roland's work in the camp. 'He's a very kind man.'

'What does he say about Heinrich Kassler?' Roland asked, spelling the German's name for her.

Catarina checked the index. Goldstein had written a few lines about the German, relating how he was captured and how the camp survivors corroborated his testimony. Roland nodded, satisfied that Goldstein thought Kassler's efforts worth mentioning.

'Did Alf and his wife give you everything you needed?'

'Everything except clothes.'

Roland glanced at her and saw that she was wearing the same outfit she'd worn when he'd snatched her from Juan at the airport – a brown wool coat, with a beige dress.

'I washed out my . . . my . . .' She smiled coyly, embarrassed. 'You know what I mean, Rollie. I washed them out every night and left them to dry in front of the electric heater.'

'Don't worry about clothes, that's all been taken care of. Sally went out and picked some things out for you. They're in my case. Not exactly a trousseau, but . . .'

'God bless Sally.'

'Oh, He undoubtedly will,' Roland chuckled. 'She'll probably find a way to use it in her story somewhere.'

They drove throughout the day, a young couple attracting no attention in a nondescript family car, stopping to eat from the hamper Roland had brought. As night fell, they crossed the Scottish border into Gretna. Roland stopped the car and gazed around curiously. He had taken a slightly circuitous route, going too far west, but he had wanted to visit Gretna first, a well-known spot for runaway lovers.

'We're here a few years too late,' he explained to Catarina. 'There was a time when you could get married here by the village blacksmith or the tollgate keeper or whoever. All you had to do was declare your vows.'

'That was all?' Catarina opened the door and swung her feet out. 'I declare—!'

She got no further. Roland pulled her back in and slammed the door shut. 'For Christ's sake – that's the last thing we need right now! Your father will know soon enough where we are once we give notice of our intention to marry. Don't make it any easier for him.'

'I'm following a tradition, that's all.'

'Let's save it for the wedding ceremony. I want to make sure we have one.' Roland drove in silence for a while, then he asked. 'Did the things I told the newspapers about your father upset you?'

'They should have, but somehow they didn't. I told Sally things that were just as bad. I hope my father can forgive me for them.'

'Do you think he'll ever come around?'

'If he does it will only be because of my mother.'

'Then I hope she's working damned hard on him.'

'So do I, Rollie.' She clutched his hand as it gripped the wheel. 'I want you more than anything in the entire world, but I also want my family – even my brother.'

'Believe me, Catarina,' Roland said, the pain of his own memories flooding to the surface, 'I want you to have them too.'

When they reached Peebles, they found that Jack Johnston's place, the Bonnie Prince, was located in the center of town. Roland left Catarina in the car and went inside to ask for him. The barmaid called out his name, and moments later a robust, red-faced man in his sixties came up from the cellar, dusting himself off.

'Mr Johnston? I'm—'

'Ssh . . .' Johnston admonished him, nodding toward the few customers in the bar. 'I know who you are. You're the friend Lawrence Chivers called me about. Where's your lass?'

'Outside in the car. I didn't want to bring her in.'

'Good thinking. Her face is a bit too well-known. So is yours, for that matter, but how many men remember another man's face?' He followed Roland outside to the

car. 'So you're the young lass who's got the country looking for her. Never fear, you'll be safe in the Bonnie
Prince.'

'Lawrence said you've given us both your bedrooms,'
Roland mentioned as he grabbed the case with one hand
and took Catarina's with the other. They followed Jack
Johnston through a back entrance into the public house,
up a winding flight of stairs.

'Aye, they're yours until you're ready to leave. I've put
off all my regular reservations. Bit of trouble that . . .'

'I'll pay you for your trouble.' Best to get the financial
matters out of the way first, Roland decided. 'How
much?'

'I normally get ten shillings a night for each room.'

'That's twenty-one pounds for the three weeks then.''
Roland handed the publican fifty. 'Will that ensure your
confidence?'

'Aye.' Johnston opened the door to the first bedroom. It
was sparsely furnished and cold, but the sheets were clean
and the double bed was covered by a huge, puffy comforter.
'The lass can sleep in here. Yours is next door.'

Roland left the suitcase with Catarina and followed
Johnston to an exact replica of the room they'd just left.
'Toilet's down the hall, but if you want to take a bath
you've got to turn the heater on first. Takes a wee bit of
time to warm up and it might run a bit rusty to begin
with, but it works.'

'Thank you, Mr Johnston. You've been very helpful.'
Roland waited until the man went downstairs, then
joined Catarina in her room. He found her sitting on the
bed, looking lost and forlorn. When he told her about the
bathing arrangements, she burst out laughing.

'Does that mean we shall be married smelling?'

'It doesn't matter,' he answered, sitting beside her. 'If
everyone else smells, I'm sure no one will notice.'

For the next two weeks, Roland and Catarina's lives

221

followed a set pattern. Jack Johnston's wife brought them breakfast in their rooms, then they left by the back way to spend the day touring the locale in the Austin, lunching at small inns where they felt they were safe. Catarina never went anywhere without dark glasses and a wide hat that shadowed her face, and Roland allowed himself the luxury of growing a beard. In the evening they kept to their rooms, reading, listening to a radio Johnston gave them, or playing cards. Any other time it would have been a tedious existence, but because it was part of a conspiracy, the couple found it easier to endure.

One evening Roland received a phone call from Simon who told him that Ambassador Menendez had hired an entire regiment of private detectives to canvas hotels and guest houses throughout the country with photographs of Catarina; he was leaving no stone unturned in his search for his daughter.

The story of the two lovers continued to dominate the front pages of the newspapers. Although a number of sightings in places as far apart as Aberdeen and Plymouth had proven false, the press refused to lose interest. Their readers wanted to know the latest, and the papers were milking it for all it was worth; one was even offering a prize to the reader who located Roland and Catarina. The two read all the stories and laughed. As long as they stayed at the little-known public house they felt they were safe; from newspaper accounts, it didn't seem the detectives were anywhere near picking up their trail.

Only once did their pattern change. After ten days in the house Catarina complained of a migraine and blurred vision. More concerned about her health than continuing the secrecy, Roland asked Johnston for the name of a doctor. Johnston arranged for one to come to the house, explaining that one of his guests had taken ill. The doctor prescribed medication and suggested Catarina have her eyes checked as the headaches were obviously linked to a vision problem. He left not knowing that he had just examined the most sought-after woman in the country.

Roland gave Johnston another twenty pounds for his help.

After two weeks, Roland and Catarina drove into Edinburgh to post formal notice at the Chief Registrar's Office of their intention to marry. At last they were coming out into the open . . . After today there would be no more rumors of their whereabouts, the entire country would know where they were.

Before entering the office they decided to make the most of their day in Edinburgh by walking along Princes Street, window-shopping, certain that no one would recognize them.

'Look, Rollie!' Catarina suddenly cried out, pointing across the street to a department store. 'Let's go in and see if they have any of your merchandise.'

The sight of the Adler's store on Princes Street jerked Roland back to the previous month. Since Catarina had appeared in his office on the day of Monty Adler's funeral, he hadn't had time to think of anything but his own predicament. Hand in hand the pair ran across the busy street and entered the store. Smaller than its London counterpart, the Edinburgh Adler's was in the middle of its January sale. Bargain hunters thronged the aisles and crowded the counters, tossing clothing aside as they searched for a certain size, burrowing through china, pestering the harried salesclerks. Roland and Catarina joined in happily, losing themselves in the bustle. After two weeks of secrecy, the mayhem in Adler's was like oxygen to a drowning man.

Then Roland froze as a hand fell on his shoulder and a voice said quietly, 'I could make a fortune by calling up a few newspapers right now.'

Cursing himself for their impulsiveness, Roland swung around to look into the grinning face of Michael Adler. He should have known how exposed they would be . . . why hadn't they just gone to the Registrar's Office, done what they had to do and left?

Michael's grin faded as he recognized the panic in

Roland's eyes. 'Don't worry. I'm enjoying the chase as much as everyone else. The beard threw me for a minute, but your height's a giveaway for anyone who knows you.' He turned to Catarina. 'And this, I take it, is the young lady the entire world's dying to find.'

Roland made the introductions, and Michael invited them to an office in the back of the store where he locked the door. Away from the sales floor he asked what they were doing in Edinburgh, and Roland explained they were on their way to the Registrar's Office. 'Ten minutes after you leave every newspaper in the country will have a reporter on his way here,' Michael warned.

'We know. And we'll be on our way out of Edinburgh in an anonymous black car.'

'Anything I can do to help?'

'Sure – don't breathe a word about seeing us.'

'I promise I won't. Say, while you're in the store did you look through our bridal department?' he said, kidding them. 'My last few days here before I get transferred back to London, so I'm trying to increase the sales figures.'

'How's your father?' Roland asked, more out of courtesy than genuine interest.

'He's getting over my grandfather's death but he's going to need a lot of help with the stores. A few key people left after that business with you. Can't say I blame them,' he added quickly, in case Roland should feel he was being reproached. 'It could be rough sailing for a while and I want to give him whatever help I can.'

'Does he mention me at all?'

'Not in a very generous manner, I'm afraid. He still believes my grandfather's death was all your fault; he can't see – or refuses to see – that what he did started it. He's hoping you'll get your just desserts over this business with Catarina's father.'

'Of course he would,' Roland said in a tone that neither Catarina nor Michael understood. 'What about yourself?'

'Me? I only wish the best for the two of you. In fact, if I

had a bottle of champagne here I'd open it right now and drink to your health.'

'Thanks. I believe you would.' Roland checked his watch; it was time to be going. 'Let's keep in touch when you get back to London. Maybe between us we'll be able to change your father's opinion.'

Roland and Catarina left Adler's for the short trip back to the Registrar's Office. They parked the Austin as close as possible to the entrance, feeling like a couple of bank robbers preparing for fast escape. Inside, they followed directions until they found themselves in front of a young, red-haired clerk.

'We want to post notice of intention to marry,' Roland told him. He felt Catarina squeeze his hand as he spoke; now it was official.

The clerk gave them no more than a passing glance before searching for the necessary forms. 'Names?'

Roland took a deep breath to steady his nerves. 'Roland Jeremy Eagles.'

'I never knew your middle name was Jeremy,' Catarina whispered.

Roland hardly heard her. He was too busy watching the clerk whose apparent boredom was suddenly replaced by a keen interest. 'And Catarina Luisa Maria Menendez.'

The clerk's pen splattered black ink across the forms as he pressed too hard. He couldn't believe his good fortune. The couple who were the subject of an intense hunt were standing right in front of him! How could he keep them there? The question nagged as he completed the forms . . . if he could only keep them there for just a few minutes. 'Could you wait a moment, please, sir? I just have to check that these are made out correctly. New regulations came into effect in the New Year.'

Roland gave the man a tight-lipped smile and nodded. He waited . . . but only until the clerk had left his position. Then he grabbed hold of Catarina and they raced from the office. By the time the clerk returned, having

225

made phone calls to three newspapers, they were in their car heading back towards Peebles.

'By now your father's going to know that we've surfaced,' Roland said as they reached the outskirts of Peebles. 'That army of detectives he's hired will converge on Edinburgh, followed by about a hundred newspeople. How does it feel to be wanted?'

'Just as long as you still want me, that's all I care about.'

'How are the headaches?'

'Gone. Those pills worked. But when we return to London I'll make an appointment to see an optician. How will I look with glasses?'

'Like a schoolteacher,' Roland joked. 'A very desirable schoolteacher.' He stared through the windshield. Off to the side of the road was a car and Roland could swear the man standing next to it, looking anxiously down the road to Edinburgh, was Jack Johnston. He slowed down as he neared and the man began to wave frantically. Roland pulled over.

'What's the matter?'

'You can't go back to the Bonnie Prince. I left there five minutes ago and the place was crawling with reporters.'

'What? How?'

'Don't ask me. I just came out to try to warn you. They turned up about fifteen minutes ago . . . with pictures of you and your girlfriend. I ran up to your rooms, stuffed your clothes in your case and brought it with me.'

Roland saw the panic in Catarina's face and tried to think. The clerk at the Registrar's Office! He had expected him to contact the press, but how had they reached the Bonnie Prince? Wait – he forced his mind to be calm . . . Menendez's people and the press had tried all the hotels and guest houses across the country. Hotel owners would have been too willing to tip them off for a reward. But they hadn't tried public houses, with those one or two rooms reserved for travelers. That's what they

226

must be doing now, checking all the public houses, showing photographs. Someone would be sure to mention the strange couple seen around the Bonnie Prince. Damn! They had to find somewhere else to stay.

'Thanks for warning me.'

'Where will you go?'

'Back to Edinburgh.'

'They'll be as thick as mud on the ground there. You'll never get away.'

'I think I will.' Roland threw the suitcase into the Austin, turned the car around and headed back to Edinburgh. Michael Adler had said he was all for Roland and Catarina . . . Well, now he was going to get the chance to show how much he supported them.

Roland telephoned Adler's from the first public phone booth he spotted once they reached Edinburgh. Michael Adler was surprised to hear from Roland again so soon, but when Roland explained what had happened he immediately offered to help. 'You and Catarina can use my apartment. Just stay put there for as long as necessary.'

'Where will you stay?'

'I can get a room at a hotel . . . the North British or something. Meet me at the service entrance to the store and I'll get you to the apartment. It's not far.'

Half an hour later they were in Michael Adler's apartment, off Princes Street, watching Michael pack some clothes to take with him.

'I'll bring you food, whatever you need. Just don't stick your heads outside the door.'

'We won't. Not until we're able to get married.'

'Are you going to need a best man?'

'If you're offering, the answer's yes. And if you're not offering, we'll conscript you.'

'Good enough. I'll be in touch.'

In London, Ambassador Menendez received the news

of the marriage application from a *Daily Mirror* reporter. 'I have nothing to say!' he yelled at the reporter before slamming down the receiver.

'What was that about?' Maria Menendez asked, concerned about the flushed appearance of her husband's face.

'Catarina and Eagles are in Edinburgh. They've applied for a marriage license. I'm putting a stop to this immediately.' He told his wife to prepare for the overnight train ride to the Scottish city. While she packed a case, Menendez instructed an aide to locate the best lawyer in Edinburgh and arrange to retain him.

The following day, settled in Edinburgh's North British Hotel, Menendez met with the lawyer and sought an injunction to prevent a marriage certificate being issued to Roland and Catarina. After leaving the lawyer, the ambassador and his wife went downstairs to eat. They were immediately mobbed by a group of reporters anxious for them to comment on their daughter's elopement and what plans the ambassador had. Menendez and his wife responded by leaving the restaurant, grateful for the courtesy of a tall, well-built young man who held open the restaurant door for them, then delayed the reporters long enough for the Menendezes to make their escape.

Back in his suite, Menendez locked the doors and leaned against them, breathing heavily. He wished now that he had never been given the position of Ambassador to the Court of St James. But in his most grotesque nightmares could he have ever imagined the appointment turning out like this?

And downstairs, Michael Adler left the restaurant with a broad smile on his face. Surely, he thought, relating this episode would brighten Roland and Catarina's temporary confinement.

Ambassador Menendez's legal maneuver came as no

surprise to Roland. He had been expecting it, an obvious move, and he had Simon Aronson all ready to leave London and travel up to Edinburgh to act on Roland's behalf and give notice of an appeal.

Before Simon could leave for Edinburgh, however, Catarina offered a proposal of her own. Her father, her entire family, had suffered enough already. Dragging the case through the courts – although she was as certain as Roland that they would win and be allowed to marry – would only drive an even greater wedge between herself and her parents. She wanted to try one last personal approach.

Roland encouraged her. Regardless of some of the remarks Catarina had made about her father, Roland knew she needed her family's support, and hoped this last effort would somehow salvage their relationship.

That afternoon, while Menendez and his wife sat in their hotel suite besieged by reporters, the telephone rang. The ambassador regarded it suspiciously. Another journalist? More aggravation? Finally, and against his better judgment, he answered it.

'Papa, it is Catarina.'

'Where are you?' Menendez saw his wife staring at him, wide-eyed with hope.

'I'm with Roland. Are you and Mama well?' She held tightly onto Roland's hand as they sat in the living room of Michael Adler's flat, less than four hundred yards from the North British Hotel.

'We're both worried sick about you.'

'There is no need to worry, Papa. I am perfectly all right. May I speak to Mama?'

Menendez passed the receiver to his wife. 'Catarina, why are you doing this to us?'

'Mama, I want to marry Roland. I am going to marry him. We will appeal against what Papa has done and we will win. But I don't want it to be like this, our family set against each other.'

229

'It is your father, Catarina. You know how he feels.'

'Mama, I have something to tell you. Inside of me, right now, is your grandchild.' A gasp came from the other end of the line, and Catarina fought back tears as she pictured her mother's shock and dismay. If only she could have avoided this, but there was no other way. Only by admitting everything could she hope to make her parents understand. She glanced at Roland and found support in his eyes. 'My child will have no grandparents on my husband's side, Mama; they are dead. Do you wish for my child to have no grandparents on my side as well?'

'I will talk to your father again.'

'You will talk to me again about what?' Menendez shouted at his wife. 'My answer is well known already. There is no need for further talk.'

Maria Menendez clamped a hand over the mouthpiece. Be blunt, she told herself. 'Catarina is pregnant.'

Menendez felt behind him for a chair, dropped into it, deflated. 'I knew it . . . I knew it all the time. I just didn't want to believe it could be so.'

'Are you going to speak to her?'

'What should I speak to her about? Should I congratulate her because she has become pregnant without getting married first?'

'Nicanor, you can't stop them from marrying. This legal procedure is only a delaying tactic. Make your peace with Catarina while you can. Even if you are too proud to bend, I want a grandchild to hold.'

'Even one with Jewish blood running through his veins?'

'What difference does it make? Can any of us look back four centuries and say positively we have only Catholic blood in ours?'

Menendez stared sullenly at the carpet. He was tired, despondent. This trouble with his daughter had drained him completely. She was his favorite child and she had disappointed him. Yet, if he didn't accept this peace offering he knew he would lose her forever. She was as proud, as stubborn as he was. 'Give me the telephone.'

Señora Menendez couldn't hide her faint smile of relief as she handed the receiver to her husband. 'Catarina, your mother and I are deeply shocked by your news, but you leave us with no choice. You have our blessing.' Without another word he handed the phone back to his wife.

'When will the wedding be?' Maria Menendez asked.

'Not for another week. Oh, Mama, I am so happy!'

'So am I, Catarina, so am I. Where will you be married?'

'Roland and I haven't made up our minds yet. We'll decide at the last minute, to avoid all the reporters.'

'Will you tell us?'

'No, Mama. It will just be Roland and me.'

'I see.' Maria Menendez struggled to keep her voice even as she felt the tears in her eyes. Although she would miss her only daughter's wedding she consoled herself by thinking of the child Catarina was carrying. A grandchild would make up for so much. 'Good luck, Catarina. To you and to Roland.'

'Thank you, Mama.' Catarina hung up and turned to Roland. Tears spilled down her cheeks as she clung to him. Her heart ached for the pain she knew her mother must be feeling; her father, too. Their daughter pregnant before marriage. But there was no other way her father would have consented – she had to tell them.

'They'll come around,' Roland whispered. 'Once your parents bounce their grandchild on their knees, they'll come around.'

Roland and Catarina were married a week later in a simple civil ceremony. Aside from the registrar, only three other people were present: Michael Adler, Sally Roberts, who had traveled up from London after Roland had given her the date, and a local freelance photographer Sally had hired.

Roland wore a dark gray suit with a white carnation in the buttonhole; his beard was gone, the disguise no longer necessary. Catarina's dress was the same one she'd worn the day they had run away. Sally had managed to get a bouquet for the bride, and now the couple stood nervously in front of the registrar as he read the words that would make them man and wife.

'The ring . . .?'

Roland gazed blankly into the man's face, then turned to Michael. Ring? In all the pandemonium of the past few weeks neither Roland nor Catarina had given it a thought. Michael looked just as bemused.

'The ring, please,' the registrar repeated, unable to understand the dazed expressions on the faces of the wedding party.

Suddenly Roland's blankness changed to a smile. He slipped his mother's wedding ring from the small finger of his right hand and held it up; a finer, more deserving use he could never find for this particular memento. From his middle finger he took his father's wedding ring and passed it to Catarina. Under the registrar's watchful eye, they exchanged them.

'Congratulations.'

The bride and groom kissed before they signed the register and prepared to leave. On the steps of the office Sally took over, arranging Roland and Catarina in various poses, instructing the photographer about the shots she wanted.

'How could you forget the ring, you idiot?' she whispered in Roland's ear as she kissed him on the cheek. 'And how could you let him forget?' she asked Catarina.

'Who had time to worry about a ring?' Catarina said, hugging Roland's arm happily.

Sally's final act was to supervise the photographer as he unloaded his camera. Like a hawk she had watched him take eight shots with the bulky press camera and she wanted to make damned certain that he handed over eight pieces of exposed film. She was taking no chances on even one picture getting into the hands of another newspaper. The *Mercury*, and Sally, had worked too hard on this assignment to share the results.

'Good luck to both of you!' she shouted before she dove into the taxi that was waiting to take her to the airport for the flight back to London.

'When are you returning to London?' Roland asked Michael.

'In a few days.'

'Catarina and I will be putting on an official wedding reception. You're getting your invitation as a guest of honor now.'

Michael laughed. 'I'll be there. And don't forget the ring next time.'

'It was *your* responsibility.'

'Then *you* should have told me.'

Roland and Catarina drove back to London the following day. News of their wedding was carried in all the newspapers, although the *Mercury* was the only one to carry exclusive photographs. Some of the papers substituted with pictures of Ambassador Menendez and his wife, running with them the ambassador's statement that ultimately it was his daughter's happiness that he was concerned about; that was why he had relented and given the couple his blessing.

For Catarina's sake Roland pretended to forgive her father. Deep inside, though, he nursed a steady anger at the ambassador. Menendez had inferred that Roland was drawn to Catarina only for her money; he couldn't forgive him for that, just as he couldn't forgive him for his sneers at Roland's background. Nor could he forget that some reporters had gleefully accepted the ambassador's allegations as truth, if only to add spice to their stories.

233

Roland and Catarina's first stop in London was at Wilton Crescent to collect Catarina's remaining clothes. The cases she was supposed to have taken to Madrid were still in Spain, and as far as bride and groom were concerned they could stay there; they were only a reminder of tragedy that had been narrowly averted. The ambassador was in the embassy when they arrived and Maria Menendez went with Catarina to her room, tearfully watching her daughter clear out the closets and drawers. Roland sat patiently in the drawing room, content to allow Catarina as much time as she wanted with her mother.

'Mr Eagles, may I offer you my congratulations?'

Roland swung around to see a uniformed maid standing in the doorway. 'Would you be Anita Alvarez?'

'Yes, sir.' The middle-aged woman closed the door and came closer. 'I am so happy that everything worked out so well for you and Señorita Menendez . . . Mrs Eagles.'

'Bless you.' Roland felt in his pocket and pulled out all the money he had with him. He knew it was in excess of two hundred pounds, probably more than this woman would see in a year, but she deserved every penny of it. 'Here, our wedding gift to you.'

'Sir, I cannot.'

'If you don't take it, I'll tell Ambassador Menendez it was you who tipped me off about Catarina going to Spain,' Roland threatened with a mischievous twinkle in his eyes.

'Thank you, sir.'

'Thank *you*, Miss Alvarez. You don't know how much joy you've brought.'

'I think I do, sir. I have been with the family ever since Catarina was a child. All I have to do is look into her eyes and I can see the happiness.'

When Catarina had finished packing she had filled three large suitcases. Roland loaded them into the car and they set off for Regent's Park. While she unpacked Roland went through the stack of mail that had accumulated. Most of it was cards wishing him and Catarina well. There was also a framed photograph of himself and Catarina standing on the steps of the Registrar's Office. Attached to the picture was a card from Sally containing the cryptic message that she was giving it to him before he called her up in the middle of the night to demand it; as a postscript, she mentioned that *Mercury* sales had increased by ten percent following the newspaper's exclusive coverage of the elopement. Roland laughed and showed the card to Catarina.

'Rollie, when I first saw you at Claridge's I wondered why you wore two rings on your right hand,' Catarina said as they lay in bed that night. 'Now I know – they were for us.'

'I knew it, too, the moment I saw you in the receiving line.' He reached out to turn off the bedside lamp. 'We have to make plans for a proper wedding party.'

'Where? Here?'

'Good Lord, no. We haven't got the space. I was thinking of Eldridge's in Knightsbridge, where I bought that picnic hamper that first day in the park.'

'Would you invite my family?'

'Of course. They'd get the first invitation.' He placed the flat of his hand on her stomach, convincing himself that he could already feel the baby kick. She held his hand there, breathing evenly, wondering how she would look when her belly swelled.

'Happy?' she asked.

'You'll never know how happy. It's been a long time since I've had a family.'

'Would your family have approved of me?'

Roland thought about his parents; they, more than anyone, would have appreciated what he and Catarina had been through. 'Not only would they have approved of you . . .' He moved his hand higher, cupped one of her breasts. 'They'd have sanctified you.'

'Santa Catarina!' She laughed with delight at the

notion. 'First you call me a witch because I can pick better horses than you, now you say I'm a saint. How can that be?'

'Schizophrenia,' Roland answered easily. 'One side of you is close to the devil, the other side's close to God.'

'Rollie, do you believe in God?'

'I started believing in Him one evening last autumn. Why do you ask?'

'Because of our child. I would like our child to be raised as a Catholic.'

Roland had no feelings either way, but if that was what Catarina wanted she would have it. 'Certainly.'

'Even if I'm no longer here, I want you to promise me that.'

Roland stirred uneasily at the words. 'Where are you going?'

'Please, I'm serious.' Catarina remembered how she'd considered suicide when her father arranged for her to go to Spain. Now, lying in bed with Roland, discussing the child growing inside her, she was beset by the idea of death again; as if she would be punished for defying her father, for breaking the rules of the church by making love to a man outside of marriage. 'Will you make me that promise?'

'I promise.' Roland's hand fell away from her breast and he held her tightly, disturbed by her words. For Catarina to even harbor such thoughts seemed so out of place. She was eighteen, pregnant, in love. A new, wonderful phase of her life was just beginning. Why would she even think such a thing?

By the time the Friday sales meeting came around, Roland had brought himself completely up to date with what had happened at the factory during the three weeks he'd been gone. Orders were strong, spurred by the trouble with Adler's. Other large stores were showing their admiration for his stand in the only way they knew how – with business.

'Nice to see you back again,' Simon said. 'Perhaps we can all get down to some work now.'

'You're making it sound like I've been on holiday,' Roland protested. 'Scotland in the middle of winter isn't exactly the same as a luxury cruise in the Caribbean, you know.'

'Nonetheless, while you were gallivanting around Scotland, I did some work. Your idea of starting a retail side is now more than just an idea.' He pushed a large envelope across the desk to Roland. 'The details are in there. I'd like to know if you see it the same way I do.'

Roland opened the envelope and pulled out the contents. The name of the company Simon was interested in was P.D. Jameson, a sprawling, old established firm that included two factories that manufactured an assortment of products, from hair dryers for beauty parlors to battery chargers, and a group of fifteen electrical shops. 'We keep the shops and sell the factories?'

'Precisely. The same way, basically, that we took over Mar-Cross.'

Roland returned to studying the papers. The shops were losing money; the factories were barely breaking even. 'What about capital?'

'I don't anticipate any problems. One of the advantages of success, Roland, is that it tends to breed further success.'

Two weeks after their return from Scotland, Roland and Catarina hosted a party at Eldridge's. Their guests included a cross-section of people in their lives, Roland's friends and customers, Catarina's parents and brother, Argentinians living in London who were friendly with the Menendez family. It was the newlyweds' way of both thanking everyone and mending fences.

For Catarina's sake Roland spent as much time as possible with her parents. Despite his own feelings toward the ambassador, he wanted to demonstrate to everyone that the wounds had healed. When he gave a short, after-dinner speech, Roland pointedly referred to his father-in-law: 'Now that our differences are history, I look forward to nothing but the finest possible relationship between us.'

Ambassador Menendez responded just as graciously, followed by a sustained round of applause. But later in the evening he quietly cornered Roland. 'I want to leave you in no doubt that what I did was for my wife's sake and for the sake of our family name. I still do not approve of you, and if it were at all possible to turn back the clock, I would make certain that my daughter never got the opportunity to meet you.'

A brief spark of anger flashed in Roland's eyes. 'So you still believe I am only interested in your wealth.'

Menendez nodded slowly. 'But you will never see one penny of it.'

'How much are you worth, sir? Just a quick, conservative estimate.'

Menendez blinked at the directness of the question. 'Perhaps fifty million pounds.'

'Sir, by the time I am your age I will be worth at least twice that much. And I will not have inherited a single penny of it from you. I will have made it all myself. Neither Catarina nor our child will ever want for anything. And if we did, we certainly wouldn't come to *you* for assistance.'

Roland bathed the ambassador with a smile like a January wind, his blue eyes dark with scorn. 'Enjoy the party, sir. Enjoy it in the knowledge that we don't expect you to pay for any of it.' With that, he walked away to find Catarina, and together they mingled happily with their other guests.

CHAPTER EIGHT

Catarina stood naked in the bedroom, inspecting herself in the mirror, running her hands lightly across her distended belly. 'Rollie!' she called toward the open door. 'Do you want to feel the baby kick?'

Roland came in from the hallway, fully dressed in a charcoal gray suit and a wine colored tie. 'Come on, Catarina, you should have been dressed already. It's past two o'clock.'

'Feel our baby kick first.' She took Roland's hand and placed it against her stomach. 'Can you feel it? Like a football player.'

Despite his mild irritation at being ready to go out while Catarina stood admiring herself, Roland felt a thrill as her belly seemed to jump of its own accord. A tiny jab hit the palm of his hand as if the child were throwing a very weak punch. 'I think he wants to come out but he hasn't found the way yet.'

'Not for another four weeks. And I wish you would stop calling our daughter a *he*.' Catarina flounced away to put on the clothes spread across the bed. 'We're going to have a little girl.'

'Good . . . we'll have a little girl. Now that we've agreed on that will you please hurry up? We can't keep my girlfriend waiting.'

'Your girlfriend?' Catarina laughed at Roland's description of Sharon Aronson, whose sixteenth birthday party they were going to. 'Just because I'm fat at the moment doesn't mean you can look elsewhere. Besides, what makes you think a beautiful sixteen-year-old girl like Sharon would ever look at you?'

'I know a beautiful eighteen-year-old girl who did.'

'She was too young and inexperienced to know any better.'

Roland left Catarina alone, certain that she would dress quicker if he weren't there to talk to her. While waiting for her he walked aimlessly around the new apartment they had leased four months earlier. It was also in Regent's Park but far more spacious, with four bedrooms. He went into the smallest bedroom, which had been transformed into a nursery. Papered and carpeted in pale blue, the nursery overlooked the park and shared a balcony with the master bedroom. A white crib was in the center of the floor with a table and chair beside it – for when Roland diapered the baby, Catarina had pointed out. Above the crib, hanging from strings pinned to the ceiling, was a cluster of cartoon characters which moved in the gentle breeze blowing in from the balcony. On top of a white dressing table, already filled with clothes, was the model racing car Catarina had given to Roland during the early days of their romance.

'Are you ready yet?' he called as he came out of the nursery into the hallway.

'Another minute.'

Roland glanced at his watch. He and Catarina were supposed to have been at Simon's South Kensington home ten minutes ago. He considered returning to the master bedroom to see how far along Catarina was, then decided against it. His presence would only distract. Instead he went into the second bedroom which, as in his last apartment, he had converted into an office. He picked up the agenda for the previous week's sales meeting and leafed through it, noting the figures for the string of Jameson shops. Since they had taken them over at the beginning of the year the two factories had been sold off to slash the purchase price. He and Simon then expanded the inventory of the shops to include luxury items such as radios, black-and-white television sets and phonographs. Two of the shops which seemed to have no future were sold, but the remaining thirteen were well above their projected budgets. Jameson had been a sound buy.

'I'm ready!' Catarina announced triumphantly, standing in the hall. Roland dropped the folder and turned to her. Pregnancy had done nothing to tame Catarina's impish spirit and gypsy looks. If anything, her black hair was even more lustrous and her dark eyes shone with an increased vivacity. 'Do you have the gift, Rollie?'

'In my pocket.' Roland said, patting the small box containing a gold pendant.

'We'd better hurry, then . . . we're late.'

'Late? And who made us late?' He pretended to give her a swat across the rear as she walked past him, then caught her arm and pulled her close, feeling the baby between them. 'I'm not so sure you're even going to fit into the car.'

'I'll manage. Or are you thinking of trading in *my* beautiful Jaguar for something old-fashioned and conservative like yourself?'

Downstairs, he opened the passenger door and helped Catarina into the car. It was a tight squeeze but she made it; another week or so and Roland wouldn't want to put any money on her repeating the feat. He was about to get into the driver's seat when he heard the tapping sound of wood on stone. He looked around and saw the elderly blind widow who lived in their building.

'Everything all right, Mrs Peters?' Roland called out. The blind widow was a familiar sight in the neighborhood tapping her way around with as much dexterity as if she had full sight.

'Is that you, Mr Eagles?' she asked, recognizing his voice. 'Beautiful day, isn't it? Going out for a ride with your roof down.'

'Wouldn't miss a day like this, Mrs Peters.' He grinned

as he climbed into the car and started the engine. The blind woman knew more about the neighborhood than any sighted person; she paid more attention to her surroundings with her other senses.

The garden of Simon's home had been transformed into a park-like setting. Tables with gaily colored umbrellas dotted the lawn, and an artificial fountain in the center sent a stream of water soaring into the air. From a bar and kitchen set up inside a brightly striped marquee, smartly dressed waitresses kept up a steady supply of food and drink for the hundred guests.

Simon and Nadine were the first to greet Roland and Catarina. As Nadine showed Catarina to an empty table and made the expected joke that she hoped the baby didn't arrive during the party, Simon took Roland over to Sharon, who was holding court among her friends.

'Happy sweet sixteen,' Roland said and handed her the box containing the pendant.

Sharon opened the box, saw the gift and threw her arms around Roland's neck, kissing him. He backed away, aware that he was blushing. Damn . . . Sharon always seemed to do that to him. 'You're going to make someone very upset,' he whispered.

Sharon looked past Roland to where Catarina sat, talking to Nadine. 'I think Catarina's too sure of you to ever worry. Pity,' she said with a playful grin. 'If you were really set on capturing an eighteen-year-old, couldn't you have waited a couple of years?'

'For you?' Roland was amused by the suggestion. 'I don't think your father would have approved of me.'

'What difference would that have made? Catarina's father didn't approve of you either.' She gave him another kiss, slipped the pendant around her neck and went back to her friends. Roland joined Catarina and Nadine, who were discussing names for the baby.

'If it's a girl we're going to name her Elizabeth, after Roland's mother,' Catarina said. Listening, Roland felt relieved that she never used his pet name in front of other people. What would they have made of Rollie?

'And if it is a boy?' Nadine asked.

'It won't be. But, in that unlikely event, we've decided on Henry Nicholas. Henry for Roland's father, Nicholas for my father – an anglicized version of Nicanor.'

'Personally, I prefer naming the child something original,' Roland couldn't resist interrupting. 'Like Bald or Golden.'

Nadine gazed at him, not comprehending. 'Pardon . . .?'

'Don't listen to him,' Catarina advised. 'His English sense of humor – Bald Eagles or Golden Eagles.' Nadine burst out laughing and went off to tell Simon.

The party broke up just after seven. Roland drove home slowly, the Jaguar's roof folded down, asking Catarina every few minutes if she was comfortable. Finally she told him to stop it; he was beginning to sound like her mother who telephoned every morning and night to check that her daughter was well and following the doctor's advice. Roland appreciated his mother-in-law's concern. Since the wedding he had become genuinely fond of Maria Menendez, and once a week he and Catarina visited the Menendez home for dinner. His father-in-law, though, remained a different matter altogether. Roland's relationship with the man was strictly formal, a mutual respect given grudgingly; no small amount of affection had developed between the men. Menendez continued to distrust his son-in-law, waiting for the moment when Roland would come to him for money, demand it as his due – then, too late, the ambassador's worst fears would be proven. Roland, in turn, could never bring himself to forget what the ambassador really thought of him and his background.

As they neared home, Catarina asked Roland to drive around the park. It was such a beautiful evening, the finale of one of those golden days that occur all too rarely during an English summer. Lovers strolled hand in hand along the park's paths or lay together on the grass; children chased balls; boats filled the lake. The scene was idyllic, and Catarina asked Roland to stop so they could sit and watch.

'Rollie, don't you sometimes feel that the entire world is in love?'

'June always does that . . .' His hand found hers and caressed it gently. 'See over there?' He pointed to a woman pushing a baby carriage; behind her cavorted three small children. 'That's going to be you in four or five years.'

'Are you going to keep me that occupied?'

'You're the one who wanted a mountain of dirty nappies.'

'Diapers,' she corrected him, and they both laughed. She opened the car door and got out, walking a few yards to stand under a towering oak tree. For a minute Roland watched, enjoying the sight of her. Then he, too, got out of the car and joined her. She pointed to the bark of the tree, at the dozens of initials that had been carved there over the years. 'Do you have a knife, Rollie? I want you to carve our initials.'

'I'm sure it's illegal. What would your father say if we were arrested for defacing a tree?'

'He would blame you, of course.'

Roland pulled out his keys. Attached to them was a tiny penknife with a one-inch blade. He scratched away at the bark of the oak tree, scraping his fingers as he formed two sets of initials – R.E. and C.E. – and enclosed them with a ragged heart. As he tried to carve the shaft of an arrow piercing the heart, the blade snapped, leaving the point stuck deeply in the tree.

'Let it stay there,' Catarina said when Roland tried to

dig it out. 'Whenever we pass this tree we will see it still embedded in the bark, just as our souls are embedded in each other.'

'You're an incurable romantic.' Roland snapped the broken blade shut and put the keys back in his pocket.

'Take me home now, please, Rollie. I feel tired.'

He led her back to the car and helped her into the passenger seat. Even before he got behind the wheel she had closed her eyes. He couldn't help smiling as he turned the car around and started the short ride back to the apartment. Catarina would go to bed and then, perhaps, he would sit up in the office and go through the sales reports. Or maybe he would sit in the nursery – at the table Catarina had told him was expressly for when he changed the baby – and daydream about how his life would change in just a few weeks. After ten years he would have a family again, be surrounded with the warmth and love that had been so painfully absent.

Roland found himself reflecting on memories of the past ten years – an indulgence he rarely allowed himself – what had he accomplished? Half of the time he'd spent seeking revenge against the country responsible for his family's tragedy. Then there was that hellhole Bergen-Belsen, where he'd been forced to come to terms with his father's heritage. After that it was two years in limbo, playing soldier while he tried to decide what to do with his life, until another confrontation over his heritage had forced his decision to leave the army. Really, he thought, the question he should be asking himself was what had he accomplished in the three years since he left the army? That was when his life had really begun again. The seven years before that were just a gap, a wilderness he had successfully managed to cross.

Yes, in the last three years he had achieved everything, had turned his life from an emotional wasteland into a fertile oasis . . . meeting Sally Roberts on the very day he'd left the army, the business, Simon, and now Catarina and

245

their child. If he had any regrets they were over Monty Adler. Poor devil, cold in the ground these past six months because he'd overtaxed his heart over a business argument ... Even with Michael Adler's absolution Roland couldn't help feeling he was still somehow responsible for bringing on the old man's death. If he'd accepted Monty's offer to set things right, sent the consignment to Adler's, would Monty still be alive?

Roland tried to push the disquieting thoughts from his mind, told himself that his own actions had made little difference. Nonetheless, he couldn't rid himself completely of his guilt.

He felt Catarina stir as he swung the Jaguar onto their street. The she screamed: 'Rollie, watch out! Mrs Peters!'

Roland snapped his eyes at her, saw her hand pointing wildly ahead, then looked through the windshield again. Ten yards ahead, appearing suddenly from behind a van, was the elderly blind woman. She stopped and waited, and Roland touched the brake pedal ... just in case.

Then, as Mrs Peters abruptly stepped forward into the road Roland gripped the steering wheel in a sudden panic. The memories he'd been reliving jarred him back to another day ten years ago ... that damned old blind woman outside the school in Margate ... watching her walk into the railings ... her indignant screams that he'd taken her to the wrong corner ... Old Spotty and the gambling winnings ... then the threat of expulsion hanging over his head as he pedaled home ... All of it came surging back, overwhelming him. The car continued to move forward as Roland's feet fumbled with the pedals. Why wasn't the car stopping?

'Rollie!' Catarina screamed again as the Jaguar closed the gap.

His left foot aimed for the clutch, his right foot for the brake pedal, but he only caught it with the tip of his shoe and suddenly his right foot was jammed down on the accelerator. The engine roared and the rear wheels spun frenziedly. Mrs Peters swung toward the threatening sound, her sightless eyes searching the street as she tried frantically to regain the safety of the sidewalk.

The rear wheels gripped the road surface, then the Jaguar shot forward. Roland jerked the steering wheel to the right to avoid hitting the woman, slammed his foot down on the brake pedal again. The heavy sports car swung sideways, skidded as the back wheels broke traction, then spun around completely. Roland held the steering wheel with one hand, fighting to regain control; he threw his other arm in front of Catarina, pressing her back into the seat as he saw the red shape of a mailbox on the opposite sidewalk looming closer. The back end of the Jaguar bounced over the curb with a sickening jolt. Catarina's side of the car smashed into the mailbox, shearing it off at the ground. Letters spilled out as the mailbox rolled off the curb into the street to rest against the Jaguar's front bumper.

Despite his protective arm Catarina had been hurled forward by the impact. 'Are you all right?' he said anxiously.

Slowly, she straightened up to look at him. Across her forehead was a thin red line where her head had banged into the top of the dashboard. Her eyes were open, glassy with shock.

'Are you all right?' Roland held her, pressing her body to his.

Finally she nodded. 'I think so. Go and see about Mrs Peters.' Roland was reluctant to let go . . . all he could think of was Catarina's earlier thoughts of death, how she'd alarmed him . . . and now this. 'I'm all right, Rollie. See about that poor woman,' she repeated. 'You must have taken ten years from her life.'

Roland set Catarina back against the seat, climbed out of the car and ran across the street to where the blind widow still stood by the van. Attracted by the noise of the collision, people were coming out of their homes. Some joined Roland, others went to the Jaguar.

'Mrs Peters, are you all right?' Roland said, grasping the blind woman by the shoulder.

'Is that you, Mr Eagles? I'm sorry . . . so sorry.'

'Why did you step out like that?'

'I waited a long time. No one came. I know my way around here. I didn't hear a car coming. Was it your car?'

'Yes. I was just turning into the street.'

'Was anyone hurt?'

'No, thank God.'

'Was your lovely car damaged?'

Roland hadn't even looked. 'It doesn't matter.' He turned to a woman who stood next to him. 'Please call a doctor. I don't think my wife's injured but she's pregnant. She should be examined.' The woman ran back to her home to make the call. Roland placed Mrs Peters in the care of another neighbor, then turned to go back to the car. As he did a man came running toward him. 'What's the matter?' Roland called out.

'It's your wife. I think she's fainted.'

Roland raced past the man and leaned into the Jaguar. Catarina was lying back in the seat like a broken doll. Her face was white, the mark on her forehead was even more livid now, an ugly line etched across her pale skin. Her breathing was irregular, a series of shallow gasps. Roland had no idea what was wrong, he just knew this wasn't a fainting spell. He frantically looked up at the crowd gathered around the car.

'Will someone see what's holding up the doctor? Tell him to hurry!'

Like a man possessed, Roland paced the floor outside Catarina's private room in the Middlesex Hospital. He strode up and down the corridor, his tall frame stooped over, hands clasped tightly behind his back. He stopped only long enough to grab the arms of doctors whenever they came out of the room and ask about his wife. When they shook their heads, he resumed his relentless pacing.

Following the accident, Catarina had been taken to Middlesex Hospital on Mortimer Street. It hadn't taken doctors long to diagnose that she was suffering from an enormous cerebral hemorrhage. Roland calmed down just long enough to telephone his father-in-law. Then he resumed his frantic pacing.

Ambassador and Señora Menendez arrived at the hospital within half an hour. The ambassador was wearing white tie and tails, his wife a long evening dress; they had been ready to go to a diplomatic affair. 'What's happened to my daughter?' Menendez demanded the moment he spotted Roland in the corridor. 'What have you done to her?'

'I didn't do anything to her!' Roland's anguish momentarily turned to anger at the ambassador's question. 'We had a minor accident!'

'In that sports car of yours? How fast were you driving?'

'Ten miles an hour. We were just outside our building. A blind woman stepped out in front . . .' Roland quickly related what had happened.

'When can we see Catarina?' Maria Menendez asked. She wanted to break up this confrontation before it had a chance to grow. There should be no blaming done now; their only concern should be with Catarina.

'I don't know. She's unconscious. They're deciding when to operate to relieve the pressure on the brain.'

'And the baby? What about the baby?'

A doctor swept out of Catarina's room. Roland grabbed him, introduced the Menendezes and asked him to explain exactly what was going on. 'We believe your daughter was suffering from a berry aneurysm—'

'A what?' Menendez asked.

'It's a bulge that forms in the wall of an artery at a weak spot, like the bulge an inner tube makes when it sticks out through a worn tire. In this case, the artery was at the base of her brain. It could have been congenital, with her from birth.'

'And this accident caused it to rupture?'

'Yes, just as any knock to the head might have. Tell me, has Mrs Eagles ever complained of double vision?'

Roland pursed his lips in thought. 'Yes. Coupled with headaches.'

'When would this have been?'

'January, when we were . . .' He glanced at the ambassador and his wife. '. . . when we were in Scotland.'

'Hiding from me,' Menendez said. 'Would the double vision and headaches have been a symptom?'

'Quite possibly. Such an aneurysm at the base of the brain could produce double vision by interfering with the nerves that supply the external muscles of the eyes.'

Menendez turned to Roland. 'Didn't you see a doctor when she was ill?'

'Yes, in Scotland.'

'Some country idiot who is accustomed to dealing with cattle, I suppose. What did he say?'

'He examined Catarina and recommended she see an optician. We saw one when we returned to London and he could find nothing wrong.'

'So you didn't bother to check further?'

'Nicanor . . .' Señora Menendez clutched her husband's arm. 'When she was younger, long before we ever came to London, Catarina had attacks like that. Headaches that we thought were caused by nervous tension. Even the doctors *we* took her to told us that.'

Menendez fell silent, stared at the floor. 'I remember,' he said softly. and reached out to place his hand on Roland's shoulder. 'I'm sorry.'

'What are Catarina's chances?' Señora Menendez asked the doctor.

'We don't know yet. At the moment your daughter is in a coma. Her heart and lungs are functioning normally which means that the baby's growth is assured. If your daughter's condition deteriorates, though, that will be another matter. Then we would have to consider a Caesarian section.'

'Could pregnancy have made the aneurysm worse?' Roland asked the question, dreading the answer.

'It's a possibility.'

'I'm going to call in other opinions, other specialists,' Menendez announced.

'That is your privilege, sir,' the doctor said. 'If you wish to use a telephone, please come to my office.' The ambassador strode after the doctor. Roland followed, holding Maria Menendez by the arm.

Menendez called the embassy, instructed his staff to contact the best brain surgeons in France and Switzerland; no matter what the trip to England would cost, he would pay for it.

Roland listened, then waited for his father-in-law to replace the receiver. 'Sir, I am perfectly capable of paying for my wife's medical treatment.'

Menendez eyed Roland incredulously. 'Do you actually believe that I would exploit this tragedy for my own personal satisfaction in exposing you as a money-motivated playboy? At this moment I don't even think of you – only of my daughter lying in there.' He jerked a finger in the direction of Catarina's room.

'I apologize, sir. And I appreciate any assistance you can offer.'

Menendez's face softened a fraction. For a second time he rested his hand on Roland's shoulder and gazed into the younger man's eyes. 'You know, at this moment I can believe that you really do love my daughter. It is a great pity that all too often it takes something like this to bring us to our senses.'

For the first time, as Maria Menendez smiled tearfully,

251

Roland felt the briefest spark of fondness for his father-in-law.

Ambassador Menendez and his wife left the hospital shortly after eleven that night, convinced there was nothing to be gained by staying. Roland lingered, sitting on a chair in the corridor, chain-smoking, waiting to hear something. Just before midnight he was joined by Simon Aronson and Sally Roberts. News of the accident had reached the *Mercury*. Roland had no doubt that all of Fleet Street would be carrying the story in the morning editions, the latest chapter in the elopement saga ... Roland just prayed it wouldn't be the final chapter ...

'Roland, if you need money ... I can pay for the finest brain surgeons,' Simon began.

'Thanks. My father-in-law's already got his staff calling all over the world. But the people here—'

'They're as good as anyone,' Sally broke in.

'I know. They say they're going to have to operate to relieve pressure on the brain. That's only the start. They won't know until then what the real damage is.'

'Are you going to sit out here all night?' Simon asked.

'What else can I do?'

'You should get some rest,' Sally answered. 'I'll run you home and bring you back first thing in the morning.'

'I don't want to go home.' Roland dreaded being alone in the apartment. He would only think of Catarina being there, standing in front of the mirror, running her hands over her swollen belly. He would sit in the nursery and wonder forlornly if his child would ever sleep there.

'Then stay with me.'

Both Simon and Roland looked at Sally. 'Oh, for Christ's sake, the two of you! Just like two bloody men to think the worst of anything a woman says!'

Despite his own bleak feelings, Roland managed a smile. 'Just get me back here first thing in the morning.' He left Sally's telephone number with the night nurse.

When he climbed into Sally's red MG he thought about his own car. It was still drivable, nothing a body shop couldn't repair easily enough. But as far as Roland was concerned he never wanted to see the damned car again. A car bought on impulse with money won at gambling . . . some pleasure it had brought!

In Hampstead, Sally fussed over him. She made him a cup of hot chocolate, which he normally detested but drank obediently. Then she found pillows and a blanket, made up a rough bed on the couch in the living room and set the alarm for six in the morning.

Sleep refused to come to Roland. He lay on the couch, staring at the ceiling, unable to stop his mind from replaying the events of the day. He touched his scraped fingers and thought of the broken blade embedded in the oak tree. Tears came to his eyes, thinking of it. Would the bark eventually grow back to cover the piece of blade, disfigure the initials and heart he'd carved for Catarina? Would even that small memory of her be gone? What would be left?

No . . . there would be more. The baby. A Caesarian delivery. Suddenly he sat up, bathed in sweat. Why was he even allowing himself to think along these lines, assuming that Catarina would die? That's what he was doing, wasn't he? Of course she wouldn't die. The surgeons would operate successfully – they were the best, weren't they?

He got up from the couch and walked to the window, looking down into the empty street. He heard footsteps behind him and turned to see Sally wrapped in an over-sized robe. 'I heard you walking around,' she said.

'I can't sleep. I should have stayed in the hospital. What time is it?'

'Just after four. Do you need anything?'

'A miracle.'

The stillness of the night was shattered by the ringing of the telephone. Roland grabbed it before Sally could.

He listened intently, his only words an occasional yes. Then he hung up. 'They're going to operate in an hour.'

Sally was already hurrying back to her room. 'I'll drive you there,' she said, unable to hide the tension in her voice.

By the time the operation began, Ambassador Menendez and his wife were also at the hospital. Juan would be coming later. Two eminent brain surgeons from Paris were also on their way. The family was closing ranks – ranks that for the first time included Roland.

It seemed like an eternity to him, sitting with his in-laws while they waited for news. Juan arrived at the end of the lengthy operation, and together they listened to the surgeons explain that it would be some time before the operation's success could be measured. Catarina was still in a coma, lying in an oxygen tent, being fed intravenously.

Roland only vaguely heard the information. He knew already. He was fated to lose Catarina just as he had lost his family once before.

Juan left, but Ambassador Menendez and his wife stayed with Roland. That evening, after a further examination, the combined group of specialists from England and France voiced extreme pessimism. It was time, they advised, to think of saving the child. Menendez and his wife turned to Roland, recognizing that though they were her parents, Roland was her husband. The decision was his.

Exhausted, managing only to stay awake by sheer determination, Roland struggled with the decision. If the doctors concentrated solely on Catarina they might lose both mother and child. If they performed a Caesarian section to deliver the premature child, they would almost certainly lose the mother. The equations rocked around inside his head like boulders. He looked to his in-laws for guidance, but they could only stare back at him, helpless in the midst of their sorrow.

Finally, Roland sat back in the chair, closed his eyes in agonizing defeat and told the surgeons to go ahead with the operation.

Just before midnight Catarina was delivered of a five-and-one-quarter-pound girl. Roland and the Menendez family, masks covering their faces, got one brief look at the red-faced, wrinkled baby before she was placed in an incubator. Then they returned to their seats to wait.

At twenty-eight minutes after midnight, as if accepting that her life's work was complete, Catarina died.

Three days later in London's Westminster Cathedral – the Roman Catholic equivalent of Westminster Abbey – Roland stood with his head bowed, hands clasped, as Catarina's funeral service was read.

His mind failed to register even one word of the service, nor did he recognize a single face in the congregation that packed the country's leading Catholic house of worship. All he could see was the catafalque, the casket on top that held Catarina's body. He could only think of the bitter injustice that determined that an eighteen-year-old girl should lie inside.

After the service, with head still bowed, his body rigid, Roland stood by the catafalque to receive condolences. Diplomats from a dozen countries filed past, all attending out of respect to Ambassador Menendez. Roland shook their hands automatically before they moved on to the ambassador, his wife and son. Roland's friends, those who had shared in the joy and excitement of the whirl-wind romance formed a protective circle around him as members of the press, who had been kept outside the cathedral during the services, now tried to push their way inside for photographs and interviews.

'Hold on to me,' a man's voice said. 'I'll get you to the car.'

Roland looked up to see Alf Goldstein, ill at ease as

ever in a dark blue suit. Next to him was Michael Adler, the Aronsons, Sally Roberts and Lawrence Chivers. Together, they formed a wedge, forcing open a passage for Roland to reach the car that would take him to the cemetery.

One of the few things he could remember of the actual interment was the sun blazing down unmercifully; it was another one of those golden days, just like the one when he and Catarina had stood in Regent's Park beneath the oak tree. He shook his head to clear the memory – he couldn't bear to live with it just now.

Afterwards, Sally drove him to Middlesex Hospital to see his daughter. His mood wasn't lightened when doctors informed him the premature child was pitifully weak. They were optimistic that she would recover fully, but there was still room for concern. Roland took that disquieting knowledge back with him to his apartment in Regent's Park. Sally offered to stay, but he told her to leave. He was no longer frightened to be left in the flat. He had overcome that fear in the three nights since Catarina's death. Now he welcomed solitude. This night, after the final, irrevocable separation from his beloved Catarina, Roland sat in the darkened nursery angry at the fate – at the God – that had sought him out twice. Sleep finally came to relieve him of his grief, and as he felt himself drifting into that welcome state the same question he'd asked himself ten years before continued to burn in his mind – why?

Roland returned to Middlesex Hospital the following morning to learn that his daughter's condition had stabilized. She was expected to remain in an incubator, but the doctors were now more confident. Feeling slightly more at ease, Roland decided to take a taxi to the factory. The only thing to do now was immerse himself in work; it was the only way he knew to cope with his sorrow. He wasn't at his desk for ten minutes before a reporter telephoned.

Roland slammed the receiver down, left the factory and returned home.

He remained in the apartment the entire day, dividing his time between sitting in the nursery and taking Catarina's clothes out of the wardrobes and drawers, setting them on the bed, on the backs of chairs and wondering what to do with them. He went through her jewelry box and sat staring at the charm bracelet he'd given her, the four-leaf clover with the names of three horses inscribed on the back. Then he spent the next half hour putting everything back as he'd found it.

As dusk settled Roland left the flat and walked toward the park. Beneath the oak tree he stopped, felt with his fingertips for the broken piece of blade. He pressed against it until the sharp, jagged steel pierced his skin, drawing blood. Roland welcomed the pain of that cut; it gave him something else to think about. He sat under the oak tree until it was completely dark, wishing the pain was even sharper.

As he walked back to his apartment he heard the familiar tapping sound of a stick on concrete. Ahead of him, beneath a gas streetlamp, Roland saw the lonely figure of Mrs Peters, waiting at the curb for someone to help her. He wondered if she would ever try to cross a street by herself again. It didn't appear so – she stood a long while at the curb, obviously waiting for someone to come along. Roland crossed to the other side of the street, strode past, hoping she wouldn't hear him. His footsteps carried on the crisp night air and the woman called after him. Roland closed his ears to her pleas and hurried on.

Outside his building he found Sally sitting in her car. 'We've been calling you all day long, ever since you left the factory. We've been worried crazy about you.'

'I put the phone in a drawer so I couldn't hear it.'

'Simon wants to see you. I've come to take you over there.' She opened the passenger door and started the engine. Roland climbed in.

'What does he want?'

'He wants to speak to you – before you kill yourself.' She noticed him sucking on his finger and asked what had happened. He told her he'd caught it on a splinter.

Simon and Nadine were waiting for them in the drawing room. Simon sat Roland down, poured him a large drink and got to the point. 'Before this week the closest person to you was Catarina. Now the closest people to you are right in this room, with the exception of your daughter who is in no position to offer you any advice. Quite frankly we're worried sick about you.'

Roland stared at the glass in his hand, wondering how it had got there, not fully understanding what Simon was trying to say.

'Go away, Roland. Do yourself a favor and go away for a few weeks, a month, two . . . it doesn't matter. Just give yourself a chance to recover from this tragedy.'

'What about my daughter? When she comes out of the hospital?'

'What about her, Roland?' The question came from Nadine. 'What arrangements have you made for her?'

'Arrangements?'

'Yes, arrangements. Or are you planning to look after her all by yourself? You'll need a nurse, a housekeeper. You can't bring up a child on your own, especially one who's a month premature to begin with.'

'I'll get a nurse and a housekeeper.'

'Forget about that, Roland,' Sally interrupted. 'Just do as Simon suggests and take a holiday. There are others here who can look after your daughter.'

'Who?'

'What about your in-laws?' Simon asked. 'Maria Menendez telephoned here earlier to ask if we'd seen you. Have you spoken to them since the funeral yesterday?'

'Last night. I telephoned them.'

'And you didn't call them today? They are Catarina's

family as well, just as much as you are. Go see them – explain to them that you need to go away for a while. I'm sure if you asked them to care for the baby while you get your bearings they would – in fact they'd probably be delighted to do so.'

Roland recalled the weight of the ambassador's hand on his shoulder, the way Catarina's death had drawn them together. 'Where would I go?'

'Anywhere. It doesn't matter. Take a boat trip to South Africa, to New York. Just get away from all the familiar sights.'

New York . . . Roland toyed with the idea. A place he had always wanted to visit; perhaps he could even look up some of the survivors of Bergen-Belsen whom he'd helped to put in contact with relatives over there. His mood lifted momentarily as he considered the idea . . . He could visit stores there, see how the Americans did things, maybe learn something from it. 'New York,' he said, seeming to confirm it.

'Good. Now telephone your in-laws.'

Half an hour later, Roland was at Wilton Crescent. Sally waited in the car as Roland walked up to the ambassador's house. The front door opened and Juan came out, wearing a tuxedo, a light raincoat slung over his arm. He walked past Roland as if he didn't exist and waved for a passing taxi. Roland watched Catarina's brother climb into the cab and muttered under his breath; his sister was only buried yesterday and the little bastard's going out.

'We tried to telephone you today,' Menendez said when Roland entered the house. 'We wanted to see how you were.'

'Thank you. I disconnected the telephone. I just wanted to be alone.'

'We understand.'

Roland really thought he did. Menendez had certainly undergone a dramatic change; he seemed genuinely sympathetic, as if all the anger he had towards Roland was drained by Catarina's death. 'I just passed Juan,' Roland said, looking from the ambassador to his wife.

'He had an appointment,' Señora Menendez answered softly, and Roland wished he hadn't brought it up. Juan's period of mourning must have lasted for as long as it took him to arrange his next date.

'Sir, with Catarina gone I have no one except my daughter,' Roland said. 'But before she comes home I feel I must get away, at least for a while. I would be grateful if you and your wife would care for my daughter while I'm away.'

'But of course!' Maria Menendez exclaimed. 'How long will she be in the hospital?'

'Possibly four or five weeks.'

'We're more than happy to care for her. Go away for as long as you wish. Let us know where you'll be and we'll keep you informed of her progress.'

'Have you decided on a name yet for the baby?' Menendez asked.

'Catarina and I were going to call her Elizabeth, for my mother,' Roland replied. 'Now I would like to name her Katherine Elizabeth. For Catarina.'

Señora Menendez dabbed tears from her eyes. 'We will be delighted to care for Katherine for as long as you wish. She is as precious to us as she is to you.'

'Thank you.' As Roland left the house he, too, felt tears brimming in his eyes. He had misjudged the Menendez family as badly as they had misjudged him.

CHAPTER NINE

Roland left for New York a week later from South-ampton on the *Queen Mary*. He forced himself to mix with his fellow first-class passengers, enduring the condo-lences they seemed duty-bound to offer him. Understand-ing that he was still somewhat of a celebrity, he resigned himself to a lack of privacy during the voyage.

Roland occupied himself by playing bridge and poker all day long and far into the night, seeking out the high-stakes games and playing with a cold ruthlessness that swept all before it. By the second night he had won enough money to pay the steamship fare.

Every evening at seven o'clock he used the ship's radiotelephone to call the Menendez home to inquire about his daughter. And every night, when he finally went to bed because he had run out of card partners or people to talk to, he lay very still, trying to remember every moment he had ever spent with Catarina.

He stayed in the United States for two months, splitting the time between New York, Chicago and the West Coast, filling every minute with visiting stores, comparing the workmanship of American products with those of his own country, and sightseeing. The daily telephone calls continued, and by the time he reached Chicago the first photograph arrived, taken the day after Katherine had been released from the hospital. Roland stayed in his hotel room for half an hour, just gazing at the picture. In a month, the weak, underweight baby had become a chubby china doll with eyes that were as blue as his own and a wisp of curly blonde hair that rose from her head like a question mark.

A second photograph reached Roland at the Sir Francis Drake Hotel in San Francisco. Taken only a week after the previous one, it showed a totally different child – she had filled out more, with ringlets of fat on her arms and legs, tiny fists clenched, bright eyes wide open. Holding the photograph in one hand, Roland picked up the telephone and asked for the local Cunard office. He canceled his homeward-bound reservations on the *Queen Mary* from New York that was still two weeks away and booked a plane flight instead. He didn't want to play any more cards, speak to any more people, watch the wake spill out from the majestic liner's stern any longer. He just wanted to be home. The period of intense mourning for his young wife was over; now it was time to resume life with his daughter.

Simon Aronson was waiting at the airport. 'Roland, you look wonderful! America must agree with you!' the banker exclaimed when Roland emerged from customs carrying two leather suitcases.

'The pictures of my daughter agree with me.' Roland knew he had gained almost ten pounds. His face shone with a healthy copper glow and his eyes sparkled. He was raring to pick up the pieces of his life – a life that would center around his baby daughter.

'Where do you want to go first? Regent's Park or your in-laws?'

'Where do you think?' He threw the suitcases into the trunk of Simon's Daimler and climbed into the passenger seat. 'Tell me all about her.'

'I wish I could,' Simon answered. 'But none of us has been to the Menendez home to see her.'

Roland was mystified by the reply. 'Why haven't you been there? Or Sally? You're my friends. Surely you kept in touch with them while I was away.'

'We telephoned, yes, but we were never invited.

Besides, there was trouble with Juan. Shortly after you left he was involved in a drunken driving incident, almost killed a man when his car went out of control.' Simon took a press clipping from his picket and passed it to Roland. 'The family packed him off to Argentina to avoid scandal.'

'I see.' Roland barely glanced at the story. He had no time at all for Catarina's brother. 'Well, you can come with me now. We'll see my daughter together.' He sat back, though he couldn't relax. Damn! . . . he wanted to see Katherine. Wanted it so badly it was almost a physical ache. He couldn't wait until he held her in his arms, bounced her on his knee. And yes, even sat at the table in the nursery and changed her, just as Catarina had said he would.

Simon went with Roland into the Menendez home. Maria Menendez led them right through to what had been Catarina's room. A crib stood where once Catarina's bed had been. Next to it sat a stern-faced, gray-haired woman in a crisp white uniform whom Maria Menendez introduced as Queenie Blackwood, a nurse sent by an agency.

Roland leaned over the crib. Katherine stared up at him, big round blue eyes looking like two small lagoons, the blonde hair much thicker than in the photographs. 'May I pick her up?' he asked the nurse. She nodded and instructed him to be gentle.

Roland reached down and lifted Katherine into the air, held her close, supporting the back of her head with his arm. He made a face at her, funny sounds. 'Look, she's smiling.'

'Gas,' Nurse Blackwood said in a manner designed to dampen paternal overindulgence. 'She's just been fed.'

Roland refused to be cowed by the nurse's manner. 'To you it might be gas, but to me it's the biggest, brightest smile in all the world.' He returned to Maria Menendez.

263

'Thank you for everything you've done, especially the photographs. They're what made me come back in such a hurry.'

'It was the least my husband and I could do.'

'Where is the ambassador?'

'In a meeting. He asked to be notified when you arrived.'

Roland sat down with Katherine in his arms to wait for the ambassador. 'And Juan, where is he?' he asked, curious to hear what the woman would have to say about her wayward son. Roland had to feel sorry for her – daughter dead, son never up to any good. What wonderful hopes the Menendezes must have held for their children, and this was how it all turned out.

'Juan has returned to Argentina to work in our hotels,' Señora Menendez replied flatly.

The ambassador arrived fifteen minutes later to find Roland still holding Katherine. 'I trust your vacation was agreeable.'

'Thank you, sir, it was just what I needed. Now I'm ready to take care of Katherine myself.'

'Have you arranged for a nurse yet?'

'No, sir. I'll get onto it right away. Perhaps Nurse Blackwood would be so kind as to offer me her services.'

'My agency refers me to clients,' the nurse said primly.

'Fine. I'll contact your agency.'

'You're not taking Katherine right now, are you?' There was a tremor of fear in Señora Menendez's voice.

'No. That would be unfair to her, and to you. I'll make the necessary arrangements first. Would you be amenable to keeping Katherine here until I'm ready?'

'Of course. It will be our pleasure.'

With affected gentleness, Roland kissed his daughter on the forehead and laid her back in the crib. As he let go she started to cry, to Roland's delight. 'She misses me already. Come on,' he said to Simon, who hadn't spoken a word since entering the house, 'drive me home and I'll get on with what I've got to do.'

That evening, Roland reserved a table at Eldridge's to celebrate both his return to London and his reunion with his daughter. The Aronsons, the Goldsteins and Sally were his guests; as an afterthought he also invited Michael Adler. On this night Roland didn't have time to be lost in memories of the wedding party he had held there. Too many other matters occupied his mind, and he wasn't above asking his friends for advice about hiring a nurse and housekeeper. All three women – Sally, Nadine and Sara Goldstein – were quick to offer suggestions. 'Fine,' Roland laughed. 'You're all appointed to a special committee to sort everything out for me.' Then he turned to Michael Adler and asked how he was faring at the Adler's store on Regent Street.

'It's a battle,' Michael answered bluntly, 'between my father and everyone else.'

'In what way?'

'He's alienating our suppliers by demanding ridiculous deals, and at the same time he's upsetting our buyers because they think he's overriding their responsibilities.'

'More of what he did to us?' Simon cut in.

'Not quite so underhanded. He's just determined to show everyone that he can run the stores as profitably as my grandfather did.'

'Your grandfather was interested in more than profit,' Simon pointed out. 'His reputation came first – and once that was established the profit followed.'

'I know, but my father doesn't understand that. Or maybe he doesn't want to understand it. The way I see it, he was kept under my grandfather's thumb for so long that now all he wants is to show what he can do. He feels the stores can only be judged by the profit they make, and the only way he knows how to make a profit is by shaving suppliers' prices. We've already lost one big supplier, and customers are complaining that we no longer stock their favorite products. So we're losing customers as well.'

'Can't anyone make him see sense?' Roland asked.

Michael shook his head. 'Apparently not. He's convinced that we're more important than suppliers. If one supplier drops out, he claims, another will take its place.'

'I get the picture – megalomania. Anything I can do to help?' Roland wondered why he had made the offer. Not for Albert's sake, that was for certain.

'Sure, buy us out,' Michael answered to laughter from Roland and Simon.

As dinner broke up and the guests prepared to go home, Roland pulled Alf Goldstein aside. 'Do you want a job?'

'Me?' Goldstein seemed surprised by the question. He had been very quiet all through the dinner, feeling out of his depth surrounded by a banker, a journalist and people who were worth more than he could ever hope to be. This abrupt proposition set him back even further. 'I've got one.'

'I want you to work for me. I need a full-time driver . . . chauffeur, personal assistant.'

'Why?'

'Because I'm never going to get behind the steering wheel of a car again, that's why. Can you understand that?'

Goldstein nodded. 'I guess I can. Let me think about it for a while.'

Roland split the next week between working in the office and searching for a nurse and housekeeper. He hired the housekeeper first, an elderly Scottish widow named Elsie Partridge who was looking for a change from her current position in a home with four young children. 'One, even two, I can handle, Mr Eagles,' she told Roland during the interview. 'Four's a wee bit much.'

Roland laughed and assured her that he had no intention of adding to his own family in the immediate future.

He hired a nurse the following day, an attractive, well-educated young woman named Janet Taylor, the daughter of a naval officer who was killed during the war. The additions to his household caused Roland to rearrange the apartment. He transferred his business paraphernalia to his bedroom, making room for the housekeeper, while the nurse installed herself in the third bedroom. Finally, with more than a touch of sadness for the parting the Menendez family would certainly feel with their grandchild, Roland telephoned them to say he was prepared to move Katherine home with him.

Roland and Janet Taylor traveled in Alf Goldstein's taxi to Wilton Crescent the following morning. Despite Roland's persistent ringing of the bell, the front door remained closed. His feelings of sympathy quickly turned to confusion as he walked from the house to the embassy, with Janet Taylor following behind. He got no further than the front steps of the embassy when he was stopped by two men in military uniform.

'I demand to speak to Ambassador Menendez!' Roland snapped at the two soldiers who stood in front of him.

Behind the soldiers, the embassy door opened. Menendez appeared on the top step. 'What is it you want?'

'What do I want? I want my daughter! I arranged to collect her this morning and I can't get into your home.'

Menendez shook his head; the bushy eyebrows drew together in a determined line. 'Nor will you ever be allowed into my home again.'

'What the devil do you mean?'

'My granddaughter will remain with us. A man such as yourself is totally unfit to care for a child. When she was in the hospital, lying in an incubator, what did you do? Did you stay beside her, as any responsible father would do? No! You took off, left her in our care. And that is where she is staying!'

The ambassador felt a surge of relief as he stared down at Roland. Finally, he could stop the charade that had been forced on him since his daughter's death. How could he have felt sympathy for Roland in those black days? Felt pity for the man who had caused them? But no more! The ambassador's pain at losing Catarina had been heightened by the pretense of drawing close to Roland until he could find a way to steal the daughter of the man who had stolen his own daughter. And Roland had played right into his hands, asking Menendez and his wife to care for Katherine while he went away. Catarina was dead because she had loved this man. If Menendez was denied his daughter, then this man would be denied his own. Even his wife could see it now. She had been soft, begged him to allow Catarina to marry this half-Jewish adventurer. But now her heart was as hard, her resolve as firm, as his own.

'We'll see about that!' Roland tried to push his way past the soldiers. They shoved him back, down the steps to the sidewalk where the nurse waited, shocked by the unexpected drama.

'Mr Eagles, I would advise you not to try to force entry into my home. I am sure the police would not look kindly upon such an action.'

'You mean the way they looked unkindly on Juan?' Roland fired back, unable to resist retaliating with anything that might wound the ambassador.

A frozen smile was etched on Menendez's face. 'It would be a different matter completely. In this country my family enjoys diplomatic immunity – you do not.' He swung around and walked back into the embassy, slammed the door shut. Roland grabbed Janet by the arm and hustled her back to Goldstein's waiting taxi.

'Take me to St Swithins' Lane, Aronson Freres!' Anger boiled through Roland's veins. He had been robbed of Catarina and he'd be damned if he would let Menendez rob him of Katherine as well . . .

'What's all the fuss about?' Simon Aronson wanted to know when Roland burst into his office; the nurse remained outside in Goldstein's taxi. Roland explained

268

the situation and Simon sighed. 'Now it all becomes too clear why none of us was ever invited while you were away. They were planning this all the time. They comforted you with the photographs, put your mind at ease, wanting you to stay away for as long as possible. At the same time they kept us at a distance in case we should suspect anything.'

'Never mind all that! What can I do to get Katherine back?'

'Legally? I think a lawsuit would be a waste of time. Menendez might just take Katherine out of the country.'

'Not without this he won't,' Roland waved his daughter's birth certificate.

'Perhaps that's the reason he hasn't done so already, although I doubt it. I would imagine it would be difficult for him to just pack up and leave as he pleases. He is serving a post, remember. Now he's counting on winning any court case you might choose to bring against him. And, to be quite honest, your case has been gravely jeopardized by your going away.'

'For Christ's sake, Simon! You're the one who suggested I go away!'

'I know. For your own sake I wanted you to take a break. But whoever thought something like this would happen? The Menendezes fooled us with their show of sympathy for you.'

'Can we use the *Mercury* to bring pressure in some way?'

'No, I don't think that would be wise at this stage.' Simon stood up and started to walk around the office. 'In this situation, the old adage seems to apply—'

'What old adage?'

'Possession being nine-tenths of the law. At the moment, Ambassador Menendez is in the right because *he* has Katherine. If you, however, should reverse that situation, he would be forced to sue you—'

'For what – kidnapping?'

'Roland, you can't be charged with kidnapping your own child when there is no court order that stipulates the child should be in the charge of another party. He could only sue you as an unfit father on the basis that the child's well-being would be better served if she were in his care.'

'He'd bring up my going away for more than two months.'

'Most certainly he would, otherwise his legal representation would be worthless. But you, on the other hand, would have Katherine, and you could counter that by demonstrating that she's in a proper, loving home. You have a housekeeper and nurse already. Your defense will hinge on showing how much you love your daughter, and how much you are willing to sacrifice to bring her up properly.'

Over the next two weeks Goldstein and three fellow cab drivers hired by Roland took turns keeping Wilton Crescent under observation. Cruising black cabs were so common in that section of London that there was little chance of the family's suspicions being aroused.

Ten days passed before any of the drivers saw the gray-haired nurse bring a baby carriage out of the embassy home. She wheeled it a short distance down the road, then back again, never going more than a hundred yards. The brief outings became more frequent until, by the fourteenth day, Nurse Blackwood was taking Katherine out three or four times daily.

Goldstein reported all this information back to Roland and Simon. 'They're obviously worried about your taking Katherine by force,' Simon concluded. 'Otherwise what kind of nurse would let a young baby stay inside for ten days without fresh air?' he paused briefly, only to answer his own question. 'I'll tell you – a nurse who has been instructed by her employer that she is to do so. Now, either this woman is very conscientious and has told Menendez that she'll quit if she isn't allowed to properly care for Katherine – or else the ambassador is feeling more confident that you won't fight for your daughter. Either way, he's now allowed these very short walks, always within sight of the embassy. I believe it's time to use the *Mercury*.' Simon said the last sentence almost regretfully; he was about to harm the integrity of his newspaper by inserting a deliberately false story. But there was no other way . . .

As a matter of procedure, the Argentinian mbassy received copies of every British newspaper. The ambassador read only the *Times*, leaving his subordinates to scan through lesser publications for anything of interest to the Argentinian government.

It was the military attache who brought to the ambassador's attention an item so small that it was almost lost in the *Mercury's* gossip column. 'The Eagle Flies' . . . ran the bold-type headline. A ten-line story told of Roland deciding to sell his business interests in England and leaving for the United States. A brief quote blamed the decision on the tragedy he had suffered, the need to get away and start again where the memories were not so poignant. His daughter, Katherine, would be left in the custody of her grandparents.

Menendez studied the story carefully, pleased that his son-in-law had yielded the battle, and satisfied in a vengeful way that after all the headline-grabbing Roland had achieved he was now relegated to such a minor spot in the newspaper. But Menendez had to be certain. He placed a call to Roland's flat in Regent's Park. The telephone rang, then a woman's clipped voice informed him that the number was no longer in service. Menendez smiled and made another call, to the factory in Wembley. There he was told that Mr Eagles was no longer with the company; he had left the country and gone to America, and could anyone else help? The ambassador didn't even bother answering before he hung up. Clutching the copy of the *Mercury* like

271

a trophy, he left the embassy to show the story to his wife.

'The child is ours and rightfully so! This alone, running away again because he lacks the strength of character to accept responsibility, shows exactly what kind of man he is. May he never find peace for what he did to Catarina.'

Señora Menendez read the short story, then went into the nursery. Katherine slept peacefully, her tiny fist close to her mouth, thumb planted firmly between her lips. 'You will grow up in Argentina,' Maria Menendez whispered. 'You will bring your grandfather and me joy as Catarina should have brought us joy.'

Janet Taylor hung up the receiver and dusted her hands symbolically. 'And that,' she said, 'takes care of that.'

'Are you sure it was Menendez?' Roland asked the nurse who had been answering the telephone all day, giving the same impersonation of a GPO operator.

'Either him or one of his staff. The voice had a definite accent. None of the other calls sounded anything like it.'

Roland didn't care about other calls. Those people close to him knew enough not to call the apartment, just as they knew that if they tried to reach him at the factory they would be told by the switchboard operator that he was no longer there. Anyone else who called didn't matter; if their business was important enough they would try to reach him again after they learned he was still in London.

'Did you ever expect to be carrying on like this when I hired you?' he asked Janet.

The young nurse shook her head, smiling. 'No. But did you ever expect to ask me to behave this way? Or is everything always so hectic around you?' When she had accepted the job Janet had been uncertain what to expect from her employer – all she knew was that she would be working for a man whose private life had become a source of great public interest. None of the positions she had held before could have prepared her for this, though, and she found she was actually enjoying the excitement. She was a nurse because she loved children, but there was nothing in the job description that stipulated she couldn't have fun as well. And this *was* fun, the thrill of conspiracy and adventure.

The front door opened and Elsie Partridge entered, carrying two loaded shopping bags. 'We're all set now, Mr Eagles. Enough food to last a fortnight.'

'Good. I appreciate how you're both pitching in like this. Being stuck here isn't going to be much fun but we can't take a chance on the ambassador finding out that the apartment is still occupied.' Roland had even drawn the building's management into the conspiracy, instructing them to give the same story should anyone call about his whereabouts. With almost all bases covered, Roland knew that the only way the ambassador could learn the truth was if he contacted airlines or immigration officials, who would have no record of his having left the country. But Roland didn't think Menendez would check that closely. He and his wife would *want* to believe that Roland had left; it would fit in with their view of him.

'Don't you go worrying about Nurse Taylor and me,' the housekeeper said as she sorted through the shopping. 'We're not about to let any blasted foreigner bring up a British child.'

Roland couldn't help smiling as Janet nodded her vigorous assent to the patriotic motive. Both women had taken sides. They were as committed as he was.

Katharine's outings in the baby carriage lengthened the moment Ambassador Menendez confirmed to his own satisfaction that Roland had really left the country. Within a day, Queenie Blackwood was parading the baby carriage around Hyde Park with the other nannies, enjoying her role as the center of attention because of the controversy which surrounded her charge.

The nurse's movements were reported back to Roland

273

by Alf Goldstein who, with his posse of fellow cab driv-ers, continued to keep the Menendez's home under sur-veillance. Roland let four days slip by to ensure that the nurse's walks to the park were regular. Then he decided to act, knowing that in doing so he would cata-pult himself back onto the front pages of Britain's newspapers. The *final* chapter – he hoped – of his doomed romance with Catarina. The final *triumphant* chapter . . .

At ten o'clock in the morning, Goldstein picked up Roland and Janet Taylor to take them to Hyde Park. Elsie Partridge stayed in the apartment, giving it a final inspec-tion before the arrival of its tiny new occupant.

'The nurse usually takes the baby out at eleven o'clock, spends an hour or so in the park if the weather's decent, then returns home around one,' Goldstein reported.

Roland looked out the cab window. The only clouds to be seen were high, streaky tufts of cirrus, and he felt confident the nurse wouldn't change her habits today.

'What if we get stopped by the police?' Janet asked. 'The woman is certain to scream blue murder. I know I would.'

'We'll worry about that when it happens.' Roland pat-ted her hand reassuringly. He was excited, nervous, emo-tions he hadn't felt since going to London Airport to rescue Catarina from her brother and banishment to Spain. History was repeating itself a generation later, yet only a few months had passed.

Goldstein stopped the taxi near the park entrance which Queenie Blackwood used. Nannies pushing baby carriages seemed to be everywhere, dressed primly in dark gray or navy blue uniforms, an entire tribe of them caring for the children of the privileged classes. 'Here she comes, bang on time,' the cab driver murmured.

On the other side of the street, waiting for the light to change, stood Nurse Blackwood. Even from twenty yards away Roland could see her stern features, the no-

nonsense approach she took to her job. The Menendez family had hired the stereotypical British nanny, a woman who ruled not by love but by fear. Roland was grateful he had looked for someone as warm and loving as Janet Taylor. Katherine would respond far better to the younger woman's care.

Traffic stopped as the light changed. Like a sentry marching, Nurse Blackwood stepped into the road, back rigid, the baby carriage pushed at arm's length, looking neither left nor right. She pressed down on the handle to lift the front wheels as she reached the curb, then continued toward the park entrance. Roland opened the taxi door and stepped out, helped Janet down, and together they walked toward a spot that would intercept Nurse Blackwood just inside the entrance.

The gray-haired nurse looked up as Roland and Janet approached. The precise step faltered as she recognized the tall man with the round face and piercing blue eyes. She stopped and stared, unable to believe it was Roland. He was in America ... that was what Ambassador Menendez and his wife had told her; that was the reason she was being allowed to take Katherine as far as the park.

Before Nurse Blackwood could recover her composure Roland was at her side, his hand gripping the baby carriage. 'What are you doing?' the nurse demanded. 'What do you want? Get away before I call the police!'

Roland didn't say a word as he reached into the baby carriage and lifted out his daughter. Katherine began to cry as Roland passed her quickly to Janet, like a hand off in a football game. Janet clutched the baby to her chest and ran toward Goldstein's cab.

Nurse Blackwood's angry scream pierced the air. She let go of the baby carriage and tried to run after the younger woman, but Roland blocked her way, holding her arms with just enough force to stop her. 'You can tell the ambassador that I am prepared to meet him in court.' He jogged over to the cab which was already rolling forward, jumped in and ordered Goldstein to put his foot down. When he looked back, he saw Nurse Blackwood with her arms raised in the air as she screamed for help. People ran toward her. One, dressed in a navy blue uniform, was blowing frantically on a whistle.

'May I?' Roland held out his hands for the baby.

Janet passed Katherine across, watching Roland carefully. The adventure was over. Now she had a job to do, and she intended to do it well, even if it meant taming the overenthusiastic affection of the father.

'Don't hold her quite so tightly, Mr Eagles.'

'Sorry.' Roland eased his grip. 'Is this all right?'

Janet smiled. 'That's better. Rock her gently and she'll stop crying. Even a baby knows when it's loved.'

Sitting back, Roland moved his arms from side to side, grinning hugely when Katherine's cries gradually changed to satisfied gurgles He forgot all about Nurse Blackwood and the hell Ambassader Menendez would create. He could think only of his daughter – a part of him, and a part of Catarina.

Goldstein shattered the bliss when he turned the cab into Roland's street. 'You've got visitors . . . didn't waste any time, did they?'

Roland looked ahead and passed Katherine back to Janet as he recognized the two black Wolseley sedans parked in the street. There was no need to question why they were there.

'Mr Eagles?' An inspector stepped in front of Roland as he got out of the cab. 'We'd appreciate it if you'd come with us to the station, sir, to answer some questions.'

'About what?'

'About the abduction of the granddaughter of Ambassador Nicanor Menendez, sir.' The inspector peered into the cab. 'The young lady and the driver as well. We'll have someone at the station take proper care of the baby until it's returned to the Menendez family.'

'Not so fast, inspector.' Roland was enjoying the confrontation. After the excitement of the successful abduction this was the icing on the cake. Another opportunity to deflate Menendez and the establishment which he felt had been set against him from the moment he met Catarina. He reached into his jacket pocket. 'This, inspector, is the birth certificate for Katherine Elizabeth Eagles, the child in the taxi. You will notice, where it reads father, that the name is mine. As is the address. There has never been any legal ruling that I am not to have charge of my own daughter, therefore there cannot be any question of my having taken the child from her temporary guardians. Now, if you'll kindly excuse me, I have to attend to my daughter.'

Roland returned to the taxi, helped Janet out and escorted her into the building. He left behind a perplexed police inspector who had been ordered to recover the infant and arrest the abductors, but who now found that he had no legal grounds to do either.

Ambassador Menendez's fury was like none he'd ever known. First he'd been tricked, now he'd been robbed. The story in the *Mercury* had been a skillfully plotted ruse, supported by liars who had answered his telephone calls; because he'd fallen for it his granddaughter had been taken from him. All he had left was Roland's brazen challenge to meet in a court of law.

Well, damn it, that was just what they would do. He would pick up the gauntlet and pass it to the finest lawyers his money could buy. The welfare of the child no longer concerned the ambassador – his priority was personal vengeance. He would do anything, pay any price, to ensure that Roland Eagles did not keep his daughter. Menendez would use the courts to wrench the child away, and demonstrate to the entire world that his son-in-law was nothing more than a cheap, conniving, irresponsible scoundrel.

Menendez filed suit that Roland Eagles was unfit to be a father and that Katherine Eagles should be brought up in the care of her maternal grandparents, people of great wealth and influence who would ensure that the child was raised in the finest possible surroundings.

After hearing his lawyers express the utmost confidence in his case, the ambassador sat back, smugly satisfied. Let the playboy wriggle out of that.

Simon Aronson represented Roland in court. Regardless of his earlier advice to Roland that possession in this instance was nine-tenths of the law, Simon was still worried. There would be some very tricky moments, especially when the ambassador's counsel tried to smear Roland's character to show how unfit he was to care for the child.

Simon briefed Roland carefully. There would be enormous sympathy for both parties – one had lost a daughter, the other a wife, and now they were struggling over the child who was the sole link to the dead woman. Additionally, the case would, for all intents and purposes, be tried on two levels: in the court itself, and in the entire nation – if not the world – through saturation press coverage. No matter how hard the judge tried to remain impartial he would have to be affected to some degree by the public opinion the case would generate.

Custody of Katherine would be decided, Simon told Roland, by whichever side demonstrated it could care best for the child . . .

'Is it true that you introduced your late wife, before you were married, to the sport of horse racing, Mr Eagles?' Menendez's counsel asked when Roland took the witness stand. 'You taught her how to gamble on horses?'

'I took her once. After that she wanted to go.'

'But you introduced her to horse racing. I believe you like to gamble.'

'I enjoy testing my skill.'

278

'I see. You even *tested your skill* – quite heavily, I am given to understand – on board the *Queen Mary* when you went away for more than two months shortly after your wife died. Is that true?' The lawyer, a thin ferret-faced man with a bristling red moustache, spun around to fix Roland with an accusing glare.

Damn . . . how in God's name had they found that out? Menendez must have really paid them to dig up some dirt! 'At the time I was trying to find a way to cushion myself against my wife's death.'

'But you went away all the same. Gambled heavily. Did you feel no responsibility at all toward your daughter who was lying in an incubator in Middlesex Hospital?'

'I felt *every* responsibility for her. That was why I asked my in-laws, Ambassador Menendez and his wife, to care for Katherine until I had recovered from the tragedy.'

'Are you implying that Ambassador Menendez and his wife had no tragedy from which to recover? That they could care for Katherine because they did not feel as grief-stricken as you were?'

'Of course they were grief-stricken!' Roland snapped back. 'But they had each other. I had only Catarina.'

The lawyer allowed himself a slight smile. He had rocked the witness's composure . . . Now to shake it further, and let Roland show what kind of a man he really was. 'I would suggest, Mr Eagles, that you were only concerned with yourself at the time, certainly not with your daughter. After all, your late wife was obviously pregnant when you married her – simple arith-metic can deduce that – and you looked upon the child not, I would further suggest, as your daughter but as a hindrance which had forced you into marriage.'

Roland gripped the rail of the witness box and forced himself to say nothing in response to this distortion of the truth. He knew that if he opened his mouth now he would scream.

'And did you not manipulate a prestigious London

279

newspaper, the *Mercury* – of which, incidentally, your learned counsel is part owner—'

Simon, who had been listening to the questioning with growing dismay, leaped to his feet to object. The judge upheld him, instructing Menendez's lawyer to stick with relevant facts.

'Did you not manipulate a prestigious London newspaper, the *Mercury*, so that Ambassador Menendez would believe you had left this country, sold your business interests?'

'I did. I deliberately fed the newspaper false information so that Ambassador Menendez would allow my daughter to be placed in a position where I would be better able to rescue her.' Roland knew he was lying under oath but he refused to implicate anyone else. The press would probably crucify him for the planted story but he could take it. He could take anything as long as he kept custody of his daughter.

'*Rescue her?* What an unusual choice of words.' Menendez's counsel sat down, pleased with himself. Roland left the witness stand in a black rage. His eyes flashed across the packed press box, then to the public gallery; it was jammed with both the curious and the concerned. The familiar faces of his friends were there but he avoided eye contact. The anger he felt was not for them.

Simon tried the same discrediting tactics on Ambassador Menendez. He accused the diplomat of trickery, of encouraging Roland to go away so that he could steal the infant. He dragged out the entire story of the elopement, accused Menendez of being primarily interested in revenge because his wishes regarding Catarina had been thwarted. Then Simon brought up the character of the ambassador's son and the drunk driving incident which had resulted in Menendez sending him back to Argentina. What kind of family environment was that for a child to grow up in? Simon demanded. The opposing counsel

280

objected immediately. Juan wouldn't be responsible for raising the child; an uncle's disquieting habits were of no concern to the court. The judge upheld the objection.

When Simon sat down he felt utterly dejected. The complacent smile he saw on Ambassador Menendez's face was there for a good reason. 'We are losing it,' he told Roland during a recess. Even the popular press – with the exception of the *Mercury* – was siding with the ambassador, coloring coverage of the case by rehashing Menendez's old claims about Roland being nothing more than a fortune-hunting playboy.

'Then do something before we lose it completely!' Roland urged him.

'I have an idea, and I think it's the only chance we have left. I am going to propose a motion that the only way to judge this case is not by character assassination but by inspecting the home where you will bring up Katherine . . . if you win the right to her custody.'

'I don't like your *if*.'

'Neither do I.'

Despite objections from Menendez's counsel, Simon's motion was approved. The following morning the scene moved to Regent's Park. Hundreds of curiosity seekers gathered outside while the judge and everyone connected with the case entered. Instructing Roland to stay back, Simon introduced Janet Taylor and Elsie Partridge to the judge, who allowed the two women to show him around the apartment. In the nursery, Katherine was lying in her crib, eyes wide open, totally unfazed by the procession of strange faces that peered down at her. The judge stepped out onto the balcony that overlooked the park, took in the fine view for several seconds. He toured the rest of the apartment, inspected the well-stocked linen closet, the two sparkling bathrooms, the kitchen; he even tasted the lamb stew the housekeeper was preparing and declared it to be delicious. Then he returned to court, stating that he would give his judgment after the luncheon recess.

'How do we stand?' Roland asked Simon nervously as they waited for the court to reconvene.

'Look at them' – Simon nodded to the Menendez family and their counsel – 'and then you tell me how we stand.'

Roland gazed across the courtroom. The satisfied smile that Menendez had worn all through the trial was no longer evident, but had been replaced by an expression of anxiety.

A hush settled over the court as the judge took his seat.

'In biblical days, when King Solomon was asked to pass judgment on a matter that bears an astonishing similarity to this case, he suggested cutting the disputed baby in two and each of the women claiming to be the real mother would receive half. King Solomon's reasoning was that the real mother would rather see her child given away than killed. I believe the wise monarch of the Israelites would face a more difficult task if he were in this court today.'

Roland closed his eyes and wished the judge would get on with it instead of playing to the gallery.

'Ambassador Menendez and his wife have suffered the tragic loss of their only daughter following a well-publicized elopement, and now they only want the opportunity to bring up their daughter's child. A splendid ambition, one we must all applaud and have sympathy for . . .'

Roland clenched his fists and felt his stomach wrench into a tight, painful knot. Simon's gamble had not paid off after all!

'But the father, despite aspersions which have been quite liberally cast against his character, has also suffered a loss, perhaps even greater because it was his wife of only a few months who died. By his own admission, the father is a gambler. There is nothing wrong with that as long as gambling is not the overriding passion in his life. And again, by his own admission, he lied to a newspaper because he thought such a lie would help him to regain his daughter. Again, that is nothing terribly wrong. If every man who lied to the press was held accountable, our prisons would be overflowing.'

The judge paused long enough to allow the expected ripple of laughter to fade away. 'Most important to us is that the father is a successful businessman who lives in a style of comfort not enjoyed by many men of his age; certainly not by those young men who have carved their own way in the world as he has. He is also, as seems quite obvious to me, a very doting father who will spare nothing for his daughter's sake . . .'

Roland didn't need to hear any more. When he looked across the court the ambassador's face was set in a grim mask. Maria Menendez had her face buried in her hands and was sobbing quietly. Roland turned away, not wanting to gloat in this moment of triumph. He had won, that was all that mattered; triumph had swept aside all personal animosity. He looked back to the bench just in time to hear the judge say: 'To take Katherine away from her father and place her in the care of her grandparents who would, in all probability, bring her up in Argentina, would be compounding the tragedy Mr Eagles has suffered. This court therefore rules that Roland Eagles shall retain custody of his child.'

The court was in an uproar. Roland grasped Simon's hand, hugged him. He looked at the public gallery, held his hands above his head, like a victorious boxer. He felt like a champion. A king. And why shouldn't he?

Outside the court, standing with Simon, Roland waited for the ambassador to emerge. In victory, Roland wished to be magnanimous. Now that Katherine was legally his he had no desire to continue the war. If the Menendez family wanted to see their granddaughter, he would happily extend them that privilege.

'Sir . . .' Roland began when Menendez came out.

The ambassador brushed past, staring ahead, refusing to acknowledge him. Maria Menendez followed suit, her eyes red from crying. Roland turned to gaze after them, even now managing to feel a degree of sympathy.

'Don't waste your pity,' Sally Roberts said as she joined him. 'If the roles had been reversed, they wouldn't have felt a damned thing for you.'

'Thank God we'll never know.'

'There's a rumor going around that Menendez has asked to be recalled, wants to resign,' Sally said.

'I can't blame him for that when you consider the hopes he first came to London with – now look what he's got.'

Two reporters planted themselves in front of Roland, bombarded him with questions. He ignored them completely, instead turned away to look for Alf Goldstein. He finally located him in the crowd and waved him over.

'Alf, drive me home, please. I'd like to be with my daughter.'

'I'll bring the cab around.'

Roland waited, one arm around Sally, the other on Simon's shoulder. An important part of his life had just ended.

1970

After playing for more than an hour, the orchestra at Claridge's took a break, setting down their instruments as two waiters wheeled a massive, multi-tiered wedding cake into the center of the dance floor.

Roland stood next to Heinrich Kassler, two middle-aged men alone with their thoughts while they watched Katherine and Franz clasp the silver handle of the cake knife and slice into the bottom tier. Cameras flashed around them, recording the moment.

'If you still have any doubts about whether or not they're married, this should surely clear them,' Heinrich Kassler murmured. 'Come . . .' He grasped Roland's elbow gently and guided him toward one of the tables that were set for tea. 'We can watch from a sitting position just as well as from a standing position.'

'In a moment,' Roland answered as he pulled a check-book from his jacket pocket. 'I have to see someone first.'

'Time to pay the piper?'

Roland smiled. 'The privilege of the bride's father, and in this instance, Heinrich, it is truly a privilege.' He left Kassler and walked toward the banquet manager who stood just inside the ballroom entrance. The two men entered an office where Roland wrote out a check to cover the evening's festivities. By the time he'd returned to the ballroom, the guests were seated. Waiters glided from table to table, passing around pieces of the wedding cake. Roland surveyed the scene from the entrance, then walked slowly across the dance floor toward the cake stand. Only a section of the bottom tier remained, with

285

the sculpted figures of the bride and groom set inside. Roland picked up the figures, held them gently. For a moment he forgot his surroundings as memories came flooding back. He could find them everywhere, even in something as common as a piece of wedding cake. He picked up a piece of the white icing and tasted it thoughtfully. The sweet flavor was also a memory, reminding him of another cake – one smaller and less ornate than this, with candles decorating it instead of the figures of a bride and groom. Katherine had been smaller, too, the party itself on a much more modest scale.

Yet it had been just as important to Roland as this one because it marked yet another milestone in his life – not only had it been the first celebration of any kind since Catarina's death and the dramatic custody battle, it marked the time when he finally faced the fact that even without Catarina, life had to continue on a normal basis . . . if only for his daughter's sake.

1957–1970

CHAPTER ONE

Roland's lifestyle took an abrupt turn with the arrival of his young daughter. As the infant grew into a toddler, then a little girl, Roland divided his time between developing his business and raising his child, using every free moment to play with her, reading books, reveling in nearly every passing stage.

The business he had built with Simon continued to thrive, and the small group of electrical shops with which they had started expanded to a chain of over forty. In 1954 they opened a second factory in Leicester to handle the demand for their kitchen appliances. During the times Roland was away either at the office in Wembley or on the road managing the stores, Katherine remained at home, cared for by Elsie Partridge, who had become a permanent member of the Eagles household. Life resumed a sense of normalcy for Roland and Katherine in all respects but one – despite assurance to the contrary from specialists he'd taken Katherine to, Roland could not shake the fear that Katherine may have inherited her mother's physical deficiency, and that she, too, would be fated for a short life.

When she reached school age, Roland enrolled her in an exclusive private school with the understanding that the staff was not to allow her to participate in any strenuous activity. She played under the strictest supervision, and during competitive games was forced to remain on the sidelines, a frustrated spectator. When the other children were given riding lessons, Katherine could only watch, hearing what fun it was through her friends. Roland had seen too many jockeys unseated, and he refused to risk having his daughter fall – how could he forget that it was only a mild bump on the head that had led to Catarina's death? For Katherine, being refused permission to ride was the final disappointment, and Roland quickly learned that the only trait his daughter had inherited from Catarina was the same fiery temper. In childish fury she screamed that her father didn't want her to have any fun, she wanted a new father – one who would allow her to ride ponies and play like the other children.

But her protests fell on deaf ears. Roland had weighed her momentary unhappiness against the possible tragedy he was trying to prevent, and decided the risk wasn't worth it. She'll understand when she gets a little older, Roland thought . . . or at least he hoped she would.

At the start of school Katherine's new routine was set: each morning she was dropped off by Alf Goldstein, who had decided, following the custody battle, to work for Roland. Each afternoon he would pick her up, often taking her to the park when Roland was away. He became like a favorite uncle to Katherine, and the relationship was even more strongly cemented when he risked – but only after making her solemnly promise not to tell her father – treating her to pony rides at Regent's Park Zoo.

Roland's overly protective attitude toward his daughter was not unnoticed by his friends. Like Alf Goldstein, Sally Roberts had also taken a special interest in Katherine, and only hoped that Roland would come to his senses and see that the wall he'd built could only hurt her. Neither Alf nor Sally could convince him of it. Simon and Michael Adler joined in, trying to make him see that his attitude wasn't based on reality, but the tragic loss of his wife. Again, neither man could make an impression and Roland continued with his obsessive overprotection of her. It wasn't until the late spring of 1957 that Roland's rigid attitude was finally jarred loose. The unlikely occasion was the wedding of Simon's older daughter, Sharon.

It was a wedding match made to order for the city's

gossip columnists: the beautiful daughter of a wealthy banker marrying Graham Sharp, the twenty-five-year old owner of *the* most fashionable hairdressing salon in London. Models and actresses flocked to him and news of their patronage drew more customers than Graham and his seven stylists could handle.

Sharon had met Graham when he worked at another West End salon. They dated for three months before she accepted his marriage proposal. At that time – as Graham had anticipated – Simon stepped in, offering to finance a salon for his future son-in-law. Since he had no savings to speak of – most of his money went to clothes and flashy cars – he accepted readily, taking his own faithful clientele with him.

Before the wedding Roland had only met Graham a few times, but it was often enough for him to form a strong opinion – from what Roland could see, Graham was noothcmgmmorehthjn a harp-witted opportunist trying to make the most of his current popularity. Roland wondered whether Simon felt the same, or was he blinded by his concern for his daughter's happiness? What particularly annoyed Roland was the way Graham acted whenever they met. Aware of the schoolgirl infatuation Sharon once had for Roland, Graham seemed to go out of his way to gloat, as if Sharon had chosen him over Roland. Even on the night before the wedding during dinner at Simon's house, Graham couldn't resist the opportunity to make a cutting remark. 'Guess the best man won, eh?' Roland used all the self-control he had to resist punching him in the mouth.

The next day, with thoughts of Graham pushed aside, Roland decided he would enjoy the wedding, and it was then that he took a long overdue look at himself.

Not because of the wedding itself, but the fact that six-year-old Katherine was a bridesmaid in the ceremony. Demurely dressed in a long white dress – and missing one front tooth – she nearly upset the decorum of the procession when, coming down the aisle, she bathed the entire congregation with a mischievous, snaggled-toothed grin. It was then that Roland realized that his young daughter was reveling in the attention she received from the charmed guests, enjoying the sensation of playing to an audience. Sharon, strikingly elegant in her bridal dress, looked stunning as she stood beneath the wedding canopy with her new husband and both sets of parents. So did Miriam, her younger sister, who was matron of honor. Married six months earlier and living in Paris with her French husband, Miriam had shed the pudginess Roland had always associated with her; she took after Nadine, small and vibrantly energetic. But all through the service the guests kept turning their heads to steal a quick peek at the adorable towhead with the lopsided grin. Roland couldn't remember ever seeing Katherine so happy, and he finally realized what all his friends had known all along: Katherine needed room to blossom.

Before the service had finished he decided to make it all up to Katherine. In a few weeks it would be her seventh birthday. He would give her a party that she would remember for the rest of her life. Katherine's previous birthdays had been simple affairs – an outing to the park, a movie perhaps, presents. Birthdays had always been occasions shared solely between father and daughter. Roland couldn't bring himself to arrange for a bigger celebration; the child's birthday was also the anniversary of Catarina's death. It was time, Roland decided as he watched Graham Sharp break the traditional glass beneath his foot, to change all that.

Katherine was thrilled by the prospect of a big birthday party. She sat down with her father and reeled off a list of schoolfriends she wanted to invite. Roland added the names of his closest friends plus one other – Janet Taylor, the young nurse who had taken care of Katherine for the first two years until she moved on to another position. Janet had always stayed in touch, never forgetting to send a card on Katherine's birthday or a small gift, stopping at the apartment whenever she happened to be in the neighborhood. This would be a party, Roland decided, not only for Katherine, but for everyone . . .

Roland couldn't tell who enjoyed the party more – Katherine's friends or his own guests. Seated on folding chairs around the spacious living room, children and adults watched with equal fascination as a magician popped rabbits out of hats, made white doves appear and disappear. Only once did Roland find himself retreating with thoughts of Catarina, and as he did he glanced quickly at the framed photograph of her that hung above the fireplace. But the sound of laughter quickly snapped him back to the present and he looked from one happy face to another, finally stopping at his own daughter. As he took in the wide smile that split her face, her hands clapped together with delight, he realized that this was what he should have done years ago . . . Catarina would have wanted him to, he understood that now; but it wasn't too late to change.

As Elsie Partridge carried in a pink and white frosted birthday cake, complete with seven pink candles, Roland sat down next to Janet Taylor, Sally Roberts and Christopher Mellish, the man whom Sally had been dating for almost a year.

'What time does the *pièce de résistance* arrive?' Roland asked.

Mellish – tall, sandy-haired, in his early forties – glanced at his watch. 'Another ten minutes or so. I told the driver to be here no later than four o'clock.'

'You'll look a prize idiot if Katherine doesn't ask for a pony,' Janet said, teasing him.

'She will. She couldn't possibly want anything else after the way she carried on when I wouldn't let her take riding lessons. *And,* I'm damned sure that Alf Goldstein's been taking her for pony rides after school. I guess everyone knew how to bring up Katherine but me.'

'Don't be too critical of yourself,' Sally said, patting Roland on the knee. 'You only did what you thought was best, and no one can fault for that.'

'I suppose so. Still, the pony should make everything right.'

'Only if she asks for a pony when she makes her birth-day wish,' Janet reminded him.

'She'd better,' Roland said. All the adults were in on the secret, and he knew that they, too, would be dis-appointed if she made a wish for something else. He'd bought the pony through Christopher Mellish, who owned a farm and a small but successful racing stable in the West Country, as well as a very profitable cloth mill in Yorkshire. He'd inherited both from his late father.

Roland could never make up his mind about Sally's relationship with Mellish, whom she'd met while writing an article on the outrageous hats worn each year by attention-seeking women at Royal Ascot. It wasn't that he disliked the man, in fact the opposite was true. But somehow the racehorse owner seemed a little too slick for Sally. Never married, Mellish was a man who spent most of his time partying and gambling, either on his own horses or on the tables at Monte Carlo, where he traveled frequently. These were perfectly acceptable characteristics in a man Roland might have chosen for his own friend – although since Catarina's death he hadn't been racing at all – but he was uncertain that Mellish was suitable for Sally. Mellish's life revolved *too* much around pleasure, and Roland felt Sally would be better off with someone who worked more and played less. It was a chauvinistic attitude, he knew, but where Sally was concerned Roland felt he was entitled . . . he cared for her too much to simply ignore the possibility of her being hurt by a man like that. Unable to leave well enough alone, Roland had even tried to arrange a match between Sally and Michael Adler, an idea Sally had rejected immediately. Michael reminded her too much of him, she'd said, a man driven by his work – and she wasn't certain she wanted to play second fiddle to a job.

At the sound of a loud engine drifting up from the street Roland stood up and walked to the window. A horse box had drawn up outside the building and a man in red hunting coat, white breeches and top hat was leading a chestnut pony down the ramp. Roland turned back and caught Elsie Partridge's eye. The housekeeper took the cue and picked up a box of matches, lighting the seven candles on the birthday cake.

'A good hard blow now, Katherine,' the housekeeper said. 'All at once, otherwise your wish will never come true.'

Katherine, her long blonde hair tied in braids that fell onto her pale blue dress, sucked in a lungful of air, then blew out the candles in a noisy blast.

'Make a wish!' Roland yelled, and the guests joined in encouraging her.

'I bet she asks for a rag doll instead of a horse,' Janet whispered to Roland.

'I bet you dinner tomorrow night she doesn't. I know my daughter too well.'

'You're on.' Janet grinned at Roland, amazed at the spontaneous challenge but quick enough to take him up on it. She remembered the excitement.they'd shared the day they'd gone to get Katherine, running to the cab with the baby pressed tightly against her chest, the police waiting for them when they returned, the arrogance in Roland's tone as he dealt with them. To a girl of twenty, Roland had seemed an heroic if tragic figure, rescuing his daughter while fighting his own grief. Janet allowed herself to be swept into a world of fantasy where she consoled him, replaced the love he had lost, always yearning for him to approach her for the comfort she knew she could give. But during the two years she'd spent with Katherine and the years that followed, Roland had never shown more than a passing interest, wanting to know how Janet was faring but giving no indication that he wanted to be any closer. Now, Janet could swear to it, everything had changed. It was as if this birthday party somehow represented a break with the past for Roland, removing an entire mountain of barriers.

In the center of the living room, standing by the cake, Katherine closed her eyes. 'I want a . . .'

'Rag doll,' Janet whispered, and Roland laughed.

'I want a horse,' Katherine opened her eyes and looked hopefully at her father.

'Will a chestnut pony do?'

Katherine nodded happily.

'Look outside.'

Followed by the other children, Katherine ran to the window, shrieking with delight when she saw the pony and its smartly attired groom. 'Buttercup!' she cried. 'I'm going to call her Buttercup!' She threw her arms around her father, then raced to the door. A minute later she was downstairs, while in the living room Roland basked in the glory of a well-chosen gift.

'You, madam, owe me dinner tomorrow night,' he said to Janet.

'Do you expect me to take you out, sir, or do you prefer a home-cooked meal?'

While he considered the question, Roland studied the young woman. He had invited Janet to the party for Katherine's sake, yet now he realized that he wanted her to come for his own benefit as well. Roland had considered asking Janet out during the times she'd come to visit Katherine, but something had always stopped him. Only now did he fully understand what had held him back – the feeling that he would be betraying Catarina's memory by trying to build a relationship with another woman. But he knew that wasn't what Catarina would have wanted, for him to go through life like a hermit – just as she wouldn't have wanted him to smother their

296

daughter because of an obsessive fear that she might be harmed in some way . . .

'How come no one's grabbed you yet, Janet?' he asked impetuously.

'Do you mean why am I not married? Maybe being a children's nurse has made me too motherly. That scares some men.'

'Does it? Or are they scared that all children's nurses end up looking like Queenie Blackwood?'

'Heaven forbid! Do you think I could ever look like that shrew?'

'I doubt it.' Roland recalled the comparison he'd once made – Janet's warm and loving manner against the strict, no-nonsense approach of the Menendez nurse. That warmth was even more apparent now. The intervening years had softened Janet's face, filled her eyes with patience and understanding.

'You haven't answered my question,' Janet reminded him.

'We'll go out. And you'll be my guest. Would you mind a foursome?' He indicated Sally and Christopher Mellish.

'Are you afraid to be alone with me?'

'No.' Roland wasn't sure whether he was telling the truth. 'I just feel like a celebration on a larger scale.'

Roland took Janet, Sally and Christopher Mellish to Eldridge's in Knightsbridge. The restaurant was almost strange territory to Roland now; he hadn't been there more than half a dozen times in the past seven years, and as he followed the maître d' to the reserved table he couldn't help thinking of the times he'd spent there with Catarina. Maybe that was why he'd avoided it . . . But that was all in the past now. Katherine's birthday party had convinced him that he could enjoy life again. Catarina would always remain with him, her memory tantalizing his mind, forcing him to compare every other woman with her; but he had to, in a sense, release her memory and go on.

'Here's to the new Roland Eagles,' Sally made the toast, lifting a wineglass into the air as they finished dinner.

Roland felt his cheeks burn. 'Does it show?'

'The only thing the same about you is your face,' Christopher said. 'Your personality seems to have undergone a complete transformation.'

Janet, seated on Roland's right, squeezed his arm. 'You look like a man who's suddenly remembered how to live. What's come over you?'

Roland recounted his feelings at Sharon's wedding, how he had noticed Katherine's enjoyment from being with other people, basking in their attention. 'I was so frightened of something terrible happening that I smothered her. Her life would have been a misery if I'd carried on like that.'

'You were right, by the way,' Sally said. 'Alf did take her for pony rides at the zoo.'

'I know. I saw the way she handled Buttercup. That was no novice sitting in the saddle.'

'Are you angry at Alf?'

'Of course not. I'm grateful to him. What Alf did was probably the closest thing to normality the poor kid ever had.' He looked around the restaurant, noting how different it now seemed. 'I can't believe how seldom I've been here in the past few years. This used to be my favorite restaurant.'

'With Catarina?' Sally offered, guessing down which avenue Roland's memory was wandering.

'And even afterwards, for a while.' He picked up his wineglass and studied the pattern. 'Catarina once asked me if I owned a restaurant, on our first date in the back of Alf's cab. I picked up a hamper from here for a romantic picnic lunch.' He put down the wineglass and summoned the waiter. 'Is the owner of the restaurant available? I would like to speak with him, please.'

'Is there anything wrong, sir?'

'Everything is fine. Now may I please see the owner?'

Less than a minute later the owner of Eldridge's was standing beside Roland's chair, a man in his sixties who rubbed his hands nervously as if expecting a complaint. Instead, Roland simply told him, 'I would like to buy this restaurant. How much do you want for it?' He smiled at the surprised expression on the man's face, then realized it mirrored the astonishment of his own companions.

'The wine is very good, eh, sir?' the owner replied indulgently.

'The wine is excellent. I haven't drunk enough of it, however, to dull my senses. I would like to buy this restaurant.'

'Roland . . .' Sally hissed at him. 'What in God's name do you think you're doing?'

'Remembering Catarina, for one thing. Also, I used to spend a lot of money in this place. I've just made up my mind to start doing so again, so wouldn't it make sense if I owned it?' He looked optimistically at Christopher; the racing man was enough of a madcap to appreciate the gesture.

'It makes a lot of sense to me, old sport. I'll always have somewhere to eat for nothing when my luck's out.'

'Hadn't you better consult your partner first?' Sally suggested. 'You do have one, and he might not be as willing to diversify as you apparently are. He also happens to be my employer, and he won't look kindly on me if I let you give away his money.'

'I'll call him now.'

'It's past eleven o'clock!'

'He'll speak to me,' Roland said confidently before turning back to the owner. 'Are you interested in selling? I'm very serious.'

The older man's eyes twinkled as he finally recognized how sincere Roland was. 'If the price were right, I would consider it.'

'Good.' Roland walked quickly to a telephone and dialed Simon's number. Nadine answered, told Roland that Simon was in bed and asked if it could wait until morning. Roland said no; he had urgent business to discuss.

'What is it, Roland?' Simon said sleepily; he still remembered the time Roland had burst into his office to ask about eloping. Nothing his young partner did would surprise him anymore.

'I'm at Eldridge's in Knightsbridge.'

'So?'

'I want us to buy this restaurant.'

Simon could think of nothing better to say than, 'Do we need a restaurant?'

'I believe so. Why pay out money on business lunches when we can keep it in the family? Look, can we meet at your office at four o'clock tomorrow afternoon?'

'Are you serious, Roland?'

'Of course I am. I've got the owner here. He's perfectly willing to sell if we can agree on a price.'

'Four o'clock tomorrow afternoon.' Simon replaced the receiver and wondered what a restaurant had in common with electrical appliances.

Roland returned to his table, not at all surprised to find that two waiters were now on hand.

'Well?' Sally asked. 'Did Simon dissolve the partnership?'

'Not at all. We're on our way to becoming restaurateurs. How about that?' He leaned back in his chair and smiled broadly; he hadn't felt this good, this vital in years.

'News like that calls for a celebration,' Mellish said.

Roland turned toward one of the waiters but Mellish cut him off. 'I wasn't thinking about a drink. I've got a horse running at Goodwood this coming Saturday. Why don't the four of us go down there to watch the race, and if we win we'll spend Saturday night in Monte Carlo!'

'And if we don't win?'

'We have to!' Mellish looked horrified at the thought.

'But if we don't, we'll still spend Saturday night in Monte Carlo; then we'll really deserve a night out.'

'I'm game,' Sally agreed.

'All right with you?' Roland asked Janet.

The offer of a trip to Monte Carlo was as unexpected as the previous day's invitation to dinner, and Janet was just as quick to accept. 'I'm between assignments right now. Monte Carlo sounds terrific.'

Just before midnight, Sally left the restaurant with Mellish. Roland had little doubt that they would be spending the night together at Mellish's apartment on Curzon street. Again, he questioned his feelings about their relationship. Maybe he was concerning himself too much with Sally's affair. She could look after herself. Besides, didn't opposites attract – Sally's common-sense approach to life against Mellish's somewhat rash love of its pleasures? Roland decided he was worrying over nothing.

'Are you going to see me home,' Janet asked, 'before they close up *your* restaurant around *our* ears?'

'Sure.'

Janet lived in a two-bedroom mews house in Chelsea which she had bought with money left to her by her father. They took a taxi from the restaurant, and Roland told the driver to wait while he saw her to the door.

'Coming in?' she asked.

'I should get back.'

'Why? Katherine's asleep and the fearless Mrs Partridge is standing guard. What's your hurry?'

'I don't have one.'

'Then come in.'

'Five minutes!' Roland called out to the taxi driver, then followed Janet into the house.

'Thank you for a lovely dinner,' Janet said as she led Roland into the living room, 'although I feel I've taken advantage of you.'

301

'How's that?'

'You won the bet – I was supposed to take you to dinner.'

Roland feigned offense. 'Would I let *you* pay for a meal in *my* restaurant?' He walked across to a table and picked up a photograph of a man in oyal Navy uniform. 'Your father?'

'Yes.'

'What would he have said about his Roedean-educated daughter becoming a children's nurse?'

'He would have said that if that was what I wanted to do, it was fine with him. He was a wonderful man.'

'How long has he been gone?'

'Thirteen years, and I still miss him terribly.'

'Where did he die?'

'His destroyer went down on escort duty in the North Atlantic. Torpedo.'

Roland replaced the photograph and sat down on a couch. 'My family's been gone seventeen years . . . I miss them as well. They died in an air raid.'

'I guess we all love the Germans, don't we?'

'I met a decent one once, fellow named Kassler. An SS captain at Bergen-Belsen who doubled as a kind of Scarlet Pimpernel.'

'You were lucky then,' Janet said quickly, eager to change the subject; talk of the war was too painful. 'Want a drink? Cup of coffee?'

'Nothing, thanks.'

She ran the tip of her tongue across her lips. 'Want to make love instead?'

The directness of the question stunned Roland. 'Is that what you ask every man who takes you to dinner?'

'Not at all. It's just something I've given great thought to ever since I met you. I lived in your house for two years and every night I waited for a knock at my bedroom door.'

'I'm sorry if I disappointed you.'

302

'Didn't the idea ever cross your mind?'

'Well . . .' Roland felt embarrassed by both her forwardness and his own increasing awkwardness. 'But what would Mrs Partridge have said?'

'Nothing probably. She's a very loyal lady who thinks the world of you and Katherine. She's also a bit deaf. I don't think Elsie Partridge was the problem, though.' She sat down next to Roland and he felt enveloped by a sudden warmth. 'You were the problem. Was Catarina the last woman you ever made love to?'

Roland nodded, unashamed to admit it.

'And since she died you've used your business as a substitute, is that it?' She gazed deeply into his eyes, as if expecting to find the answer there. 'Roland, you're not the kind of man to throw yourself away on a business. No matter how successful you are you'll never be satisfied with just that.'

'It's taken me a long time to realize it.' He was aware of her arms sliding around his neck. He'd never been seduced before and wondered whether he would like it. Even more important, would he be able to handle it?

'What kind of person do you think I am?' he said, trying to slow things down.

'You're a wonderful if sometimes misguided father. And I don't think you'll be happy until you have many more children to make up for the families you've lost.'

'Are you trying to ensure yourself of more nursing work in the future? Is that how Roedean teaches business classes?' Her hand was tugging at his tie now, and he was only slightly conscious of his own hands gently caressing the back of her neck. Suddenly there was a loud, rapid knocking on the front door. 'The cab . . .!' Roland suddenly remembered. The knocking came again and he fumbled in his pocket for money, falling over his own feet as he stood up and raced toward the door.

'Hurry back!' Janet called after him.

Roland shoved a five-pound note in the cab driver's

hand and closed the door without waiting for the four pounds change. Then he ran back to the living room.

Early on Saturday evening Roland, Janet, Christopher and Sally were flying to Nice in the south of France. Mellish's horse had lost, finishing a poor eighth in a field of ten, and he swore that he would strangle both the jockey and the trainer; but that disappointment failed to dampen the group's spirits.

Roland, especially, was jubilant. The week had marked a distinct turning point in his life: Katherine's birthday party, the beginning of his first relationship with a woman since Catarina, and the agreement the previous day between himself, Simon and the owner of Eldridge's for the sale of the restaurant.

'How much did you lose?' Roland asked Mellish when they arrived in Nice and boarded the train for the short trip to Monte Carlo.

'A thousand. How about yourself?'

'Couple of hundred.'

'Better raise the prices in your new restaurant, old sport. Recoup your losses that way.'

'Today wasn't a loss, it was my initiation fee back into the world of racing. I'd forgotten how much fun it could be.' He looked past Mellish to Sally and Janet, who were engaged in conversation. 'Christopher, how serious are you about Sally?'

'Is that a run-of-the-mill question to pass the time, or do I detect a note of envy?'

'Envy? Not in the least. Sally's like a sister to me. I just want to make sure she gets the best.'

Mellish laughed, a high-pitched guffaw which always grated on Roland's ears; it seemed so out of place in the man. 'Sister? That's not the way I heard it. Sally seems to think it went a lot deeper than that.'

Roland felt himself tighten. 'I fail to see why something

that happened ten years ago is any concern of yours. Or why she would even tell you.'

Mellish pulled a small, velvet-covered box from his jacket pocket. Inside was a sparkling two-carat diamond ring. 'I'm popping the question, old man. In Monte Carlo tonight. That was the idea of the trip. Now do you understand why it's my concern?'

'Sorry . . .' Roland immediately forgot any offense he might have taken. 'Congratulations.'

'Sssh,' Mellish warned as Sally turned around. 'I want her to hear it from me, not from you.'

In Monte Carlo they checked into separate rooms at the Hotel de Paris. After refreshing themselves they met in the restaurant for a late dinner. Afterwards, they walked up the marble staircase to the casino entrance. Massive red carpets stretched ahead; statues, paintings and tapestries surrounded them. Janet gasped at the opulence.

'Just like Las Vegas, eh?' Mellish joked.

'I've never been there,' Roland replied.

'Don't. It's a meat market. Here, at least, you can still enjoy some old-fashioned decadence and grandeur. What's your game?'

Roland looked to Janet. 'Roulette,' she said, and Roland nodded.

'*Bon chance*. Sally and I are going to take our chances at baccarat. Meet back here in a couple of hours.'

Roland took Janet to a roulette table, gave her a pile of chips and let her play. He was content to watch. And think. Sally getting married? If she said yes, of course. She would, he had little doubt about that. She and Mellish had been going together for too long for there to be any other answer. And he felt happy for her. If anyone deserved some personal joy in her life it was Sally; often she reminded him of himself – a young war widow who had sought professional advancement as a means of happiness. And she'd achieved it, now controlling the women's magazine the *Mercury* had launched. Roland knew that Sally wanted to be appointed to the *Mercury's* board of directors, and he had no doubt that she someday would be. But there was more to life than just satisfying a drive for success. Hadn't he only realized that himself?

He jerked back to the present as Janet let out a happy shout.

'What happened?'

'My number came up.' She gazed in wonderment as the croupier pushed a small mountain of chips toward her.

'Sally's did, too.'

'How do you mean?'

'Christopher's proposing to her. He's carting the ring around in his pocket.'

'Good for Sally. A little late to start a family, though. How old are they?'

'Christopher's in his early forties. Sally must be close to thirty-five.'

'Shame. A marriage without a family isn't much of a marriage.'

Roland stepped back and allowed Janet to continue playing. A marriage without a family was no marriage at all. Perhaps Sally didn't see it that way, though. Mellish either. He could well imagine the two of them going on with their own lives, simply providing companionship for each other. A marriage of convenience. Perhaps it would be suitable for them, but Roland knew he could never be happy in such an arrangement. Marriage *was* children; that was the whole idea behind it – a bunch of kids running around, getting into all the trouble they normally got into, but always the warmth and joy of being together.

'All gone,' Janet said, brushing one hand against the other. It was a habit of hers Roland had first noticed on the day she'd pretended to be a telephone operator, waiting for Ambassador Menendez to phone his apartment.

'All of it? I thought you were winning a fortune.'

'I was. Then I felt extremely lucky and put everything on one go.'

'And the house suddenly became luckier than you?'

'I suppose so.' She linked arms wwith Roland and led him away from the tables. 'Anyway, i've had enogh. Let's go for a walk before we turn in. We'll tell Sally and Christopher that we're going out and we'll see them at breakfast.'

All Roland could think of was that Janet didn't have Catarina's luck at gambling. But the price Catarina had paid for that one burst of good fortune was far too high a premium for anyone to pay.

Sally and Christoper were married at London's Caxton Hall three months later. Again Katherine was in the wedding as a bridesmaid. Early on the morning of the wedding she went with Sally and Janet to Graham Sharp's salon to prepare for the occasion. As Roland was driven to the salon to pick up Janet and Katherine he couldn't help thinking of the irony of the situation. He'd made love to both Sally and Janet, yet Katherine was the offspring of the only woman he'd really loved. And, despite the relationship he'd built with Janet during the past three months, spending two or three nights a week at her Chelsea home while Elsie Partridge handled Katherine's inquisitive comments, Roland remained convinced that he would never love anyone as he had Catarina.

'Like my hair, Daddy? Like my hair?' Katherine bubbled as she climbed into the car.

'Beautiful.' Roland kissed her on the forehead, amused by the way she pulled back to avoid disturbing the soft pageboy style. 'But most important, will Buttercup like it?'

'Buttercup won't see it because I'll be wearing a hat when I go riding. But if she could, she'd love it too,' Katherine answered with childish logic.

Roland marveled at how his daughter, even at seven, had suddenly become ladylike, even vain. Twice during the ride she asked Janet for a mirror so she could inspect her new hairstyle, and when she thought no one was watching she touched and patted the ends to make certain everything was still in place. Charmed by his young daughter's vanity, Roland impulsively reached out and hugged her.

Goldstein first dropped Janet off at her house, arranging to pick her up later, then he and Katherine returned to Regent's Park to dress. While Roland put on a morning-suit with a gray top hat, Elsie helped Katherine into a long, pale yellow dress which had been especially made for the occasion. Just before noon they were back at Chelsea to pick up Janet. While Katherine waited in the car with Goldstein, Roland pressed the buzzer. After a third time he became mildly annoyed that she wasn't ready yet. He used the key she'd given him, entered the house and called her name.

'Upstairs, Roland.'

Something seemed wrong with her voice. Worried, Roland took the stairs two at a time, running into the front bedroom. Janet was lying on the bed, still in the dress she'd worn to the beauty parlor. Her face was pale and sweaty, the new hairstyle ruined. 'What's the matter?'

'What do you think?' she asked weakly. 'I guess I'm not as good a nurse to myself as I am to others.'

Roland had no idea what she meant, but when she leaned over the bed he smelled the sourness of her breath. 'Have you been sick?'

'Clever man,' she said. She struggled to sit up, her back againt the headboard. 'This looks like it's going to be a lousy pregnancy.'

'What?' Roland's mind began to spin. He hadn't even considered that she might be pregnant. 'How long have you known?'

'I found out a couple of weeks ago.'

'Why didn't you say anything?'

'I didn't want to steal Sally's thunder. Pat me on the

308

back for being so considerate.'

'Never mind Sally's thunder.' All of a sudden Sally's marriage was of no importance to Roland. 'Do you want to call off today?'

Janet shook her head. 'I'll be all right in a few minutes. I just felt dizzy when I got back from Graham's. Maybe sitting under the hair dryer had something to do with it. Why don't you and Katherine go on ahead? I'll catch a cab and follow later.'

'Do you think I'd leave you here by yourself?' He started toward the bedroom door. 'Stay right where you are.'

'Where would you expect me to go?' she called after him, touched by his concern. But she was upset with herself that she hadn't managed to keep her condition a secret for just another day. She knew how much Roland had looked forward to Sally's wedding, how much he cared for his friend. Now she felt she'd spoiled the day for him.

Roland ran down the stairs and told Goldstein to take Katherine to the wedding. At least Sally would have a full wedding party. When he returned he found Janet struggling to her feet.

'I'll make you a strong cup of tea, then we'll get you cleaned up and ready in no time,' he said.

'I'm supposed to be the nurse, not you,' she answered, trying to fight off his efforts to help her.

'When I'm sick you can nurse me.'

Janet recovered under the shower, a cap protecting what remained of her hairdo. She even managed a joke as she hurriedly dressed. 'You seem to make a habit of this, getting nice, respectable girls in the family way. At least I haven't got a father who's going to give you hell.'

'When did it happen?'

'Monte Carlo, I think.'

'So . . . we did win after all, even if not at the tables. Lucky at cards, unlucky at love and vice-versa . . . is that it?'

'Stop talking about it and let's go,' Janet said. 'We

309

don't want to miss what's left. Sally and Christopher will never forgive us.'

'Are you certain you're all right?'

'I promise I won't pass out again. Not until tomorrow anyway.'

Roland stayed in Chelsea that night after sending Katherine back to Regent's Park with Alf Goldstein. This time Janet allowed him to dote over her, watching with tender amusement as he walked around the house checking windows for drafts. 'You remind me of my father,' she said. 'He used to fuss over my mother like this whenever he was on shore leave. He'd bring her up tea in bed in the morning, make breakfast, do the shopping. I think he would have approved of you.'

'I'm glad to hear that because it's a damned sight more than my last father-in-law ever did.'

'Father-in-law?' Janet put down the cup and gave Roland a sharp look. 'Hold on just a minute. Aren't we jumping the gun a little?'

'What do you mean?' Roland turned from the window he'd just closed.

'Roland, please don't think you're obligated to marry me because of this. It doesn't work like that for me.'

'Then how does it work?' For the first time since he'd met Janet he felt like she was a virtual stranger. Here he was, closer to her than he'd been to any woman since Catarina, only to find he didn't know her at all.

'Roland of all the men I've ever been with – and I can count them on one hand – you're the one I would want to father my children. You obviously love childen and you're successful enough that I know they would never want for anything.'

Roland was barely listening. He felt confused. When Catarina had announced that she was pregnant it was the most natural thing in the world to plan marriage. Janet was the exact opposite.

'Remember what you said in Monte Carlo? That a marriage without a family isn't much of a marriage? Then what about a family without a marriage? Is that much of a family?'

'It's hardly the same thing, Roland. I want children of my own. You want more children. Fine. But that doesn't mean we're bound to get married, unless you've got some notion that children born outside wedlock are inferior to those born within it.' She saw him open his mouth to say something but carried right on. 'You're not ready for marriage, Roland. You might be trying to convince yourself you are, but you're not.'

'What makes you such an expert?'

'I've worked with enough families to become something of one. I've nursed the children of young couples who never had any business getting married, and those kids received more love from me than they'll ever get from their parents. Marriage needs a certain psychological commitment. You need to be ready for it, and I don't think you are right now.'

'Have you quite finished?'

'I'm not even halfway through yet. Roland, you just think you want to get married because you want more children, and it happens to be me you got pregnant because we made love—'

'Too impetuously?'

'And too well, but enjoyable nonetheless. Roland, I love you, I really do—'

'Then marry me.'

She smiled softly to take the sting out of her next words. 'If I knew it would be forever, I'd say yes – but it won't be forever.'

'How can you be so sure?'

'Because we'd never be equal partners. I'd never be as important to you as you'd be to me. You're a man who divides his life into little sections, compartments; call them whatever you like. In one compartment you put

311

your family obligations. In another you put your business, and that's probably the most important compartment of all. I've seen you do it with Katherine. When you were with her, she was the most precious thing in your life, but how often did you think of her when you were working? When you were running around the country buying up stores? You shut her out of your mind, knowing you'd arranged to have her looked after like royalty until you came home and had the time to be a full-time father again. Things don't overlap for you. You work at one thing at a time to the virtual exclusion of everything else. Any woman you marry will have to learn to put up with that kind of a life, and I'm not prepared to.'

Roland sat down, hands on his knees, unable to think of any argument. Janet understood him too well . . . in fact, he thought, she may be right, though he'd never considered it in those terms – he *did* live like that, able to cut himself off from one part of his life while he concentrated on another. Hadn't he shielded himself from the pain of Catarina's death by throwing himself into his work?

'So where do we go from here?' he asked, completely dependent now on Janet's judgment. Whatever she wanted would be all right with him.

'I'll stay here and you continue to live at Regent's Park. That way we'll both know what compartment you've placed me into.'

'But no marriage?'

'Not for the time being. We'll both be happier that way.'

'How do you figure that?'

'It'll save us the bother and bitterness of getting a divorce.'

The comment brought a smile to Roland's face. 'Aren't you going to brush one hand against the other now?'

At first, Janet didn't understand. Then she burst out laughing. 'You know me as well as I know you. I'm saving that for when we call it a day.'

Roland's new concern was the effect his unconventional lifestyle might have on Katherine. His staying with Janet in Chelsea two or three nights a week was one matter, but fathering a child by a woman whom he was neither married to nor living with was another problem entirely. Surely that would confuse the girl, and she'd already been through more than her fair share of confusion for one so young.

His worries, though, proved unfounded. Katherine accepted her father's explanation that she would soon have a baby brother or sister quite readily, just as she'd always accepted the fact that she had a father but no mother. It was as if she had become quite accustomed to having a family life totally different from that of her friends, full of people whom she thought of as aunts and uncles. Never having known what it would be like to have a mother, Katherine saw nothing odd about her father spending time away from home with the young woman who would give birth to her baby brother, Richard, named for Janet's father. Janet was kinder to her than any mother could have been, and that was all that mattered.

Within three years, Janet and Roland were expecting again, this time a girl whom they named Carol, after Janet's mother. Katherine naturally accepted them as her full brother and sister, even if she did only see them on weekends when Roland made a point of bringing the entire family together.

For Janet, her days of nursing other people's children were over. She was now a full-time mother to her own. At the same time she became even closer to Katherine, often taking care of her when Roland was away. It would only be a matter of time, Roland realized, before Elsie Partridge would retire; it was just as well that Janet and Katherine had become so close.

Even without the binding ties of marriage they could still be one family, Roland realized. He was learning to be satisfied with that.

CHAPTER TWO

A taxi took Roland from Regent's Park to Simon Aronson's home in South Kensington. Because of pressure at the bank Simon had been unable to attend that day's weekly meeting and Roland wanted to bring him up to date. Knowing that Graham and Sharon would be there for the traditional Friday-night dinner, Roland had waited until ten o'clock before arriving, hoping they would have left already. He was disappointed. When the taxi drew up outside Simon's house, Graham's new red Maserati was parked in the drive.

Walking up to the front door, Roland recalled nostalgically how simple the business had been when he and Simon had started twelve years ago. Then, there had been only one factory to worry about, uncomplicated figures to go through. Now there were two factories, fifty-three shops dotted around the country . . . and a restaurant! There were reports to be read from each of the small chains they had acquired; reports from regional managers; snags to be ironed out. It was a wonder to Roland that Simon ever found time for his work at Aronson Freres.

The maid opened the door and showed Roland through to the dining room where Simon, Nadine, Sharon and Graham were just finishing dinner. Roland kissed the two women, shook Simon's hand and nodded politely to Graham. That young man had certainly lucked out the day Sharon had walked into the salon where he was working, Roland thought. Aside from the salon Simon had opened for him on Regent Street, Graham now owned another at the top of Park Lane that was as successful as the first.

To Roland's surprise, as he waited for Simon to leave the table and go over the reports in the drawing room, Graham spoke to him. 'You're a businessman, Roland. I'd like your opinion on something if you've got a couple of minutes.'

Roland glanced at Simon, saw the banker sitting very tensely. He guessed that whatever Graham wanted to bring up had already been discussed. 'If it's anything to do with electrical shops I can probably help you,' he answered, not wanting to get involved in what he sensed was a family matter.

Graham stood up and dusted crumbs from the trousers of his navy blue suit onto the carpet. 'I'm famous, right?'

'Are you?' Roland couldn't resist the question, despite the times he'd seen Graham's picture on the fashion pages of various newspapers; his popularity hadn't waned at all in the past three years.

'Look, I own the top hairdressing salons in this country. I'm established. Surely I should take advantage of that by using my name to promote a line of my own beauty products?'

'I'm afraid that I don't know very much about that field.'

'Roland!' Sharon said, admonishing him. 'Look what you've done all by yourself, what you've created—'

'With your father, Sharon.'

'All right, but you're able to recognize opportunities. That's your strength. Just think what an opportunity this would be for Graham.'

Roland hated to disappoint the look of expectancy in Sharon's eyes, but he could raise no enthusiasm for either Graham or his business idea. Also, he wanted to get to Janet's house soon; he didn't have time to get embroiled in this. 'It's out of my bailiwick, Sharon. Sorry.' He moved his gaze to Simon, who sat at the head of the table. 'Have you got time for me now?'

Simon stood up and followed Roland into the drawing room. 'What was all that about?' Roland asked.

'Graham's thinking about diversifying, capitalizing on his success.'

'Nothing wrong with that.' Was that what had made Simon so tense? Why? And why had Graham tried to drag Roland into it? 'I was thinking about the same thing for us, but I won't bore you with it right now. These are more important.' He pulled out the weekly reports from the briefcase he'd brought.

They sat together for forty-five minutes, going over the decisions that had been made at the meeting. As they finished, Sharon and Graham came in to say good night. Sharon kissed Roland and her father, Graham offered Roland his hand. 'Thank you for your advice earlier,' he said sarcastically. 'Pity, because I'd heard a rumor that you were quite smart.'

'I'm not too good on anything that has to do with combing hair for money. Drive carefully.' He turned to Simon. 'I'd better be off as well, otherwise a certain young lady's going to wonder what's happened to me.'

'Can we give you a lift?' Sharon asked.

'No thanks.' Roland could swear he saw a look of relief in Graham's dark eyes. 'I'll catch a cab. See you next Friday at Wembley, Simon.' He left the house and started walking toward the main road to get a cab. Graham's Maserati roared past and Sharon waved. As Roland waved back, he wondered what in God's name she could have ever seen in Graham.

Simon was present at the following Friday's meeting. Roland went through the normal business quickly, then leaned back in his chair before addressing the group. 'The question we should all be asking ourselves is: Where do we go from here?'

Lawrence Chivers, who had in time been promoted from sales manager of the original manufacturing plant to operations manager for the complete retail side, stared thoughtfully at his pipe. 'Into another field?'

'Exactly. What else can we do but diversify? I think we've just about gone the limit as far as electrical shops are concerned. With the exception of the factories and Eldridge's, we're retailers. That's our main thrust, where our expertise lies, so let's look at other areas of retailing. Simon?' Roland regarded his partner curiously. Simon had appeared distracted throughout the meeting, offering little comment on any of the reports. 'Are you feeling all right?'

'Something on my mind, that's all.'

'Will it cost us money?' Roland glanced at his watch, concerned about the time. He wanted to be away soon. The long August Bank Holiday weekend was starting that evening and he had arranged to take Janet and the three children to Christopher Mellish's farm and stables in Somerset. Katherine, especially, was looking forward to seeing the racehorses Mellish owned, even if she would have to be content with riding something less exotic during the weekend. Roland, too, was looking forward to the trip. Business had been so brisk that he'd been unable to take a proper vacation that summer – he'd sent Janet and the children away once already, and he had the nagging suspicion that Janet was critical of him for it. Never mind – he'd make it up to all of them this weekend.

'It might cost *me* money,' Simon replied mysteriously, 'but it will be money well spent. Can I speak with you afterwards?'

'Certainly. Is there any other business?' No one responded and Roland closed the meeting. 'Let's go for a walk outside,' Roland suggested to Simon.

The two men walked around the perimeter of the factory grounds, Roland swinging his arms in the carefree manner of a man ready to go on vacation, Simon with his hands buried in his trouser pockets, his shoulders sagging. 'How does one go about getting rid of a son-in-law?' the banker finally asked.

Roland turned to stare at his partner, the scene at the

317

table the previous Friday night vivid in his mind.

'Trouble in paradise?' He told himself he shouldn't be surprised, but a trace of amazement still managed to creep into his voice. What was really incredible was that it had taken so long. Graham Sharp had been sponging off Simon from the start. Only Simon had reacted in a manner that was totally out of character – he seemed willing to ignore his son-in-law's shortcomings just to keep Sharon happy.

'There always was, but Sharon wanted to marry Graham so I refused to stand in her way. Her happiness always came first, as I'm sure you can understand. Now Graham is using our love for her against us, always with the implied threat that he'll leave Sharon if we don't give him what he wants. I've already loaned him' – Simon laughed abruptly – 'given him is more like it, the money to open that second salon—'

'And now he's trying to tap you for money to start this line of beauty products, is that it?' When Simon nodded, Roland asked: 'What about the profits from those two salons? Surely he has something to invest there? They're the two most popular salons in London if what I read in the gossip columns is true.'

'According to his books, he's barely breaking even.'

'That's ridiculous! Those two salons are always packed. Or has he got his hand in the till?'

'I think so.'

'Where does the money go?'

'Certainly not to Sharon. Most evenings she sits alone in the house I bought them while he goes out. He has a wardrobe with enough suits for an entire army, a new Jaguar *and* a new Maserati.'

'He certainly lives well, better than you or I do.' A really slimy devil, Roland thought, trying to get me to side with him against Simon. And Sharon as well – where are her brains?

'He lives well off *my* money while he makes my

318

daughter miserable. The thing is, I wouldn't even mind financing him for this new venture – this licensing idea – if only he would *leave* Sharon, promise to make a complete break with her.'

'Is he playing the away game?' The words slipped out and Roland hated himself for the unintentional vulgarity.

'I'm certain he is.'

'Then why does Sharon stand for it?'

'She won't let herself believe he's cheating on her. She only wants to believe what Graham tells her – that he goes out almost every night looking for the chance to promote himself. His name is in the newspapers often enough for her to believe it.'

'Can't you do anything?'

'I'm afraid to try. Even if I told Sharon that Graham was seeing other women – that he was stealing from the shops – she'd hate me, not Graham. Nadine and I have talked it over many times. We've wanted to tell her, to show her some proof, but we don't think it would do any good. Graham would defend himself with some lie, and she's still so much in love with him that she would believe his lies – or want to believe them – rather than anything we told her, even if it is the truth.'

Finally, Roland saw where the conversation was leading. 'But if someone else brought it to her attention . . .?'

'Nadine and I were hoping that you could see your way clear to help. You are . . .' Simon struggled to find the words he wanted to convey his thoughts without causing offense. 'Roland, Sharon might pay more attention to you than she will to us. She always liked you . . . a young girl's crush . . .'

Roland gritted his teeth. He owed Simon and Nadine, owed them more than he could ever repay . . . For the help in starting the business, the faith they'd shown in him, the sympathy and support after Catarina's death. But here he had to draw the line. 'I'm sorry, Simon. I can't interfere.'

'Why not?'

'I can't butt into someone else's marriage.' He stared at the banker, torn with pity. 'Look, you said it yourself – Sharon had a crush on me. If I cut in like you're suggesting I do, it might throw her from the frying pan into the fire. If I showed her what Graham was really like –and if she listened to me – she might rebound right onto me. What good will that do her? Or me?'

Simon walked a few paces, forcing himself to recognize the logic in Roland's words. 'Then what do I do?'

'Be cruel to be kind, Simon. Don't give Graham another penny. If he's going to leave Sharon, that will make him leave.'

'What will she do?'

'Let her find out for herself. In the long run it's the kindest thing you can do. And when it happens, you and Nadine will be there to catch her.' Roland turned back toward the factory, feeling angry with himself that he'd been unable to offer further help to his friend. But short of taking Sharon away from Graham – making a play for her himself, using that old crush – what else could he do?

That evening, Roland, Janet and the children had the first-class compartment of the train to Bath to themselves. While Katherine and Janet sat reading a book together and Richard and Carol slept, Roland thought again of his talk with Simon. He felt like he'd betrayed his friend, but to go between Sharon and Graham would only be playing with her emotions. She would be torn up, forced to face the reality of the man she had married and desperate for support – support Roland couldn't give her. Not now, not with Janet and the children. At another time, perhaps . . . no, there was no point in even thinking about it. The support she would need would have to come from her parents – they were the ones who had to tell her.

At Bath, they were met by Christopher Mellish, who drove them to his farm. Katherine sat up front while

320

Roland and Janet sat in the back of the car, each holding a sleeping child.

'Smell that fresh country air, eh?' Mellish enthused. 'Nothing quite like it, is there?'

Roland laughed. 'You spend most of your time in London. What would you know about fresh country air?' He decided that Mellish looked the part of a gentleman farmer in a rough tweed jacket and twill trousers tucked into a pair of gumboots. The mud on his boots was fresh and Roland wondered whether he'd brought the right clothes – all he'd packed were clothes made by his tailor on Savile Row; they were finely made and good to look at, but he wasn't certain how well they would stand up to the rigors of farm life.

'Living in London is what makes me appreciate fresh air,' Mellish answered. 'I should spend more time down here.'

'Why don't you?'

'I like to watch my horses run, old man, not train. The same goes for my mill. I like to wear the cloth in suits, not watch it being woven before my very eyes.'

When they reached the farm, Sally had a snack ready. Afterwards, Janet put the two younger children to bed while Mellish took Katherine out to see the mare she would be riding for the weekend. Roland stayed in the kitchen with Sally.

'How's married life, Mrs Mellish?' He always teased her about her double identity; on the magazine she was known as Sally Roberts, while in private life she used her husband's name.

'Pretty good. I guess I could ask you the same question, even if it isn't literally correct.'

'I'm not complaining.'

'One marriage isn't going too well, though, is it?' Sally remarked as she dried plates and put them away in a cupboard above the sink.

321

'Sharon? Simon asked me to help.'

'I thought he might. He talked to me about her a few days ago. He mentioned you and I tried to discourage him. What did you say?'

'I told him to cut Graham off. If he decided to leave Sharon, so much the better. He'd be doing her a favor.'

Mellish returned with Katherine who kissed Roland good night, then went upstairs to bed. Later, the four adults sat around the kitchen table, playing bridge and talking. At eleven-thirty, after both Janet and Sally excused themselves, Mellish leaned forward conspiratorially, telling Roland he had some news for him . . . 'news that will make you as happy as a pig wallowing around in a ton of muck.'

'Put you on a farm for five minutes and you sound like a farmer,' Roland said, laughing. 'All that's missing is the straw between your teeth. What is it?'

'Adler's . . . your old nemesis. They're about to go belly-up.'

'That isn't news,' Roland said, 'I've been hearing that rumor ever since old Monty died and Albert got his hands on the rudder. Somehow they manage to keep stumbling along. It's always the same with these family firms,' he added, sounding as if he were angry at the injustice of it all. 'Even if profits and dividends are way down, the shareholders let them get away with murder. A family name carries a lot of weight.'

Mellish waited for Roland to finish, then shook his head, eyes twinkling. 'This time it's different. I heard a whisper about the two branch stores in Edinburgh and Manchester. There's been an offer on them.'

Roland lit a cigarette and gave himself time to think. That *was* news, and it shocked him. He saw Michael Adler once a month or so, a lunch or dinner date, and he'd never mentioned any difficulties that could result in the two branch stores being put up for sale. 'Where did you pick this up? How fresh is it?'

322

'Very fresh.' Mellish's eyes stayed bright at Roland's interest. 'I heard this week. One of my mill customers deals with them.'

'How reliable is this customer?'

'I haven't got the faintest idea. I just thought you'd want to know.'

'Thanks. May I use your phone? Long distance?'

'Be my guest.'

Roland got through to the operator and asked her to reach Michael Adler's home in London. When Michael came on the line, Roland said he wanted to see him. Right away.

'What about?' Michael said, mystified by the call. 'I was just going to bed.'

'I picked up some information that your Edinburgh and Manchester stores have had an offer made on them. What's going on, Michael?'

There was a long moment of silence. 'Perhaps I'd better see you,' he finally said.

Roland turned to Mellish. 'Is there a late train to London?'

'Not this time of night. I'll be glad to lend you my car, though.'

'I haven't driven in ten years.' He turned back to the telephone. 'Michael, I know this is asking a hell of a lot but can you get out to Somerset tonight? I'm staying at a farm for the weekend.' He waved at Mellish, asked for directions.

'It'll take me at least three hours.'

'I'll be up.' He passed on the directions, waited for Michael to repeat them, then hung up.

'I'll wait up with you,' Mellish offered. 'Fancy some backgammon or chess?'

'Make it backgammon. Chess might put me right to sleep, and I want to be wide awake when Michael arrives.'

'Funny,' Mellish mused as he set out the board. 'I thought my news would make you happy – Adler's being

323

in such dire straits. I never thought it would give you a sleepless night.'

'Oh, it does make me happy.' Roland grinned across the table and shook the dice savagely. 'Just as long as *I'm* the one who gets to buy those stores.'

Michael arrived at the farm after three o'clock, looking like a man who had driven half the night. His hair was awry, face lined; dark shadows were under his eyes. Mellish stayed up just long enough to say hello, then went to bed. Roland searched round the unfamiliar kitchen, found a kettle and made Michael tea.

'If you'll pardon my saying so, you look absolutely terrible,' Roland remarked, setting the cup down in front of Michael.

'I'm entitled to with what's been going on. Thanks.' He picked up the cup and took a long swallow. 'I don't even know where to begin.'

'Take your time, we've got all night.'

'It's my father. Everything my grandfather ever said about him has come true, and I don't think there's a damned thing I can do about it.'

'Can *I* do anything about it?' Roland asked. He didn't want to push Michael by asking him straight out what was wrong – the man looked so distraught that Roland didn't want to add to his pressures.

'Sure, if you can work miracles.' Michael closed his eyes and shook his head slowly. 'My father hasn't got the feel for the business, not like the old man had – not like I know I have. But he's in charge. He's the oldest Adler, so the shareholders are satisfied to see him there.'

Roland remembered expressing a similar view to Mellish. 'What about this offer?'

'Manchester and Edinburgh. They were that far away from being closed down' – he held his finger and thumb half an inch apart – 'and then someone stepped in. Made an offer which I feel is way below market value, but my

324

father's desperate. He sees it as the only way to raise capital to keep the Regent Street store running. But even that won't last if he carries on the way he is now. And – damn me for saying it! – I think he's doing it on purpose.'

'What? How can you make an accusation like that?'

Michael stared gloomily into the cup. 'My father had a brother—'

'I know. Meir.'

'Who told you?'

'I was in Monty's office one day when he and your father had an argument over the shady deal your father tried to pull on me. Your father threw in Meir's name, claiming that if Meir had done the same thing to me old Monty wouldn't have been so furious. Claimed that because it was your father who did it, your grandfather was trying to belittle him, make him out to be a crook.' It had happened eleven years ago but Roland could still remember every word of the argument.

'That's the cause of the problem right there,' Michael said. 'There was always friction between my father and his brother. Meir was a year older, and from what I can gather a damned sight more businesslike than my father. My father was jealous of him, always had been, ever since they were young. Meir could always do everything better – school, sports, work, the lot. Even when he went off to America and was killed in a car accident, his ghost came back to haunt my father. No matter what my father did – what he tried to do – my grandfather would always say that Meir would have done it better. Don't forget, my grandfather retired once, then came back and carried on working until he dropped dead.'

'I thought he came back because his wife died,' Roland interrupted. 'He got lonely rattling around the house by himself . . .'

'Like hell,' Michael countered. 'He came back because he didn't trust my father. And he was right.'

'But running the business down deliberately? That's a hell of a claim.'

'Roland, I've given it a lot of thought. Even if my father's doing it subconsciously, I think that's what he's doing. I believe he's always had it in his mind – since he was our age, even before – that Adler's had always been intended for his favorite son . . . Meir. Whether my father realizes it or not, I think he hates it with a passion.'

Roland began to feel a trace of sympathy for Albert Adler. If what Michael was saying was true, then Albert's life, too, had been ruined by hatred. 'How far along is this offer for the two branch stores?'

'It's tentative at the moment. Why?'

'I might be interested. But I'd have to talk to my partner first.'

'For the two branch stores?'

'No. For the whole thing. Adler's itself, lock, stock and barrel. I once asked you if I could help in any way, and you said only if I bought the business.'

Michael flinched as he remembered the conversation. 'I was joking at the time. I never thought it would come to this.'

'Your father would fight me for obvious reasons. How about you?'

Michael chewed his lip uneasily. He had the choice of watching the company his grandfather built up be destroyed, or turning against his father. 'No, I don't think I'll fight you. You've got a sound record.'

Roland breathed out a barely audible sigh of relief. 'What's the share disposition of Adler's?'

'My father holds twenty-five percent. I hold ten. The other directors hold twenty-five percent between them, and forty percent's out there.' He waved a hand at the window before stifling a yawn. 'Excuse me.'

'How many other directors?'

'Five, each with five percent.'

'How loyal are they?'

'To my father? They're very loyal. They're not family, but it's a family firm – my father's the figurehead and they reckon they owe him their positions. They're all living quite nicely—'

'Even if it's only for a short time.'

Michael nodded. 'They're too shortsighted to even see that far ahead. They're yes-men. They all think that their positions are secure just as long as they agree with my father.'

'So your ten and the forty that's out there make fifty percent.'

'You'd be equal with my father and the other directors. You'd be unable to do very much.'

'Unless I got the other directors to rally around me. Their shares would give me a seventy-five percent holding.'

'It's unlikely that they'd do that. Once you had seventy-five percent and the power to change the board you might get rid of them all. None of them would risk that.'

'Is there anyone worth seeking out as an ally?'

'No. They're all old and on the board by reason of longevity. If I controlled the firm I'd do exactly what you're planning to do – get rid of the lot, appoint a new board and start from scratch.' Michael smothered another yawn. 'But there's one thing I want to get clear before we even start, Roland. I want to know exactly why you're doing this. Is it for revenge against my father? If it is, I don't want any part of it. I'm not blind to my father's shortcomings, but I won't help you run him down for your own personal satisfaction.'

'Any revenge I wanted against your father I took when I sold that consignment in Berwick Street. Rest assured I wouldn't try to turn you against him over something like that. The truth is' – Roland paused long enough to light a cigarette – 'that right now I've got a jumble of a company, chains of small shops, a couple of factories, even a restaurant. It's time to head those companies up with something big and respectable. I can't think of anything more respectable than Adler's, even if it is on its last legs right now.'

Michael relaxed. 'I did notice some writer in the financial press referring to you as a rag-tag of companies with, I believe he said, little apparent cohesion or direction.'

'But we make money, and you can't argue with that. Coincidentally, at our last weekly meeting we were discussing where to go next. Basically, we're retailers, and now we're thinking of branching out into other retail areas. This couldn't have come at a better time.'

'Don't count your chickens just yet,' Michael cautioned. 'My father's still very keen on the offer for the two stores. He'll do anything to keep Regent Street operating – until bad management decisions fritter away that money as well.'

'Who's making the offer? And how hard will they fight to get those two stores?'

'Difficult to say. It's a German conglomerate – into everything from engineering to retail – that wants to get its first foothold in Britain.'

'German?' Roland's brow creased. 'Your grandfather must be spinning in his grave at the thought of your father selling two of the stores to a German company.'

'The offer came right out of the blue, and my father's naturally grabbing at it. I can't say I'm too keen on the idea myself, selling to Germans, especially for what I consider to be a low price, but Kassler, the president of the company, is pushing my father hard.'

'Kassler?' Roland felt his stomach give a sudden, uncomfortable lurch.

'Heinrich Kassler.' Michael went right on talking, unaware of Roland's confusion. 'Took over his father's engineering business in Stuttgart after the war. Got a reputation as a good German so he got all the breaks from the occupying forces. Now he's richer than we are.'

Could it be? At first, Roland refused to believe it.

Surely there must be a hundred . . . a thousand . . . Germans with the same name of Heinrich Kassler. But from Stuttgart? A *good* German who took over his father's engineering business?

The kitchen door swung open suddenly and Janet stood there, a dressing gown covering her flimsy nightdress. She stared at Michael and Roland, the dirty cups, the ashtray full of crushed-out cigarettes. 'What's going on? It's five o'clock and I wondered where the hell you were.'

'You know Michael, don't you?'

'Of course I know Michael. What's he doing here?'

'He's about to run me back to London.'

'Now?' The surprised question came simultaneously from both of them. 'Let me get a couple of hours' sleep first,' Michael said. 'Unless you want to end up a Bank Holiday traffic statistic.'

'Use the couch in the living room.'

'What's this all about?' Janet asked after Michael walked sleepily out of the kitchen.

'I've got to see Simon.'

'Today? Right this instant? Why can't you telephone him?'

'It's too important to discuss over the phone. I want us to go for Adler's.'

The importance of it went right by Janet; all she could think of was the immediate weekend. 'Roland you haven't had a holiday yet this year. These three days are it! The only time you'll have with us . . .'

'I'm sorry,' he said, interrupting her. He kissed her, held her tightly. The warmth of the bed still surrounded her and he almost changed his mind. He couldn't do anything until Tuesday when the banks and the Stock Exchange reopened, so why should he rush back to London now, on Saturday morning? Why see Simon when a telephone call would surely suffice? He knew the answer: to share the news and get his partner's approval to move

329

on the deal . . . and to see the expression on Simon's face when he learned what that deal included.

'Nothing's open until Tuesday,' Janet said, as if reading Roland's mind. 'How bloody urgent can it be?'

'This particular deal is urgent enough to warrant my seeing Simon.'

She fought her way out of his arms and stepped back a pace. 'Are you putting me into a compartment already?'

'What's that supposed to mean?'

'Three days in the entire year is all you've given me and your children. Three days in one lump. And now you're even backing out of that.'

'I'll be back this evening, I promise you.'

'But your mind will still be in London. We don't want just your physical presence, Roland. We want you.'

Roland decided to kill the argument. Another minute or two of raised voices and the entire household would be awake. 'I'm going to do the same as Michael, grab a couple of hours' sleep. Coming?'

'No. Once I'm up I stay up.' She turned away from him, arms folded resolutely across her chest. Roland just shook his head in exasperation and went to bed.

He was unable to sleep, though. Instead he lay tossing and turning, his mind concentrating on Adler's – and Heinrich Kassler. Could it be the same man he'd come so close to shooting at Bergen-Belsen? The *good* German? That's what Michael Adler had called him . . . How many *good* Germans were there with the name of Heinrich Kassler, whose fathers had owned engineering factories in Stuttgart? And hadn't Alf Goldstein once mentioned that Kassler was one of the leading lights in trying to rebuild Germany? Damn – it had to be the same man. Just wait until Goldstein heard about it! He would want to meet Kassler again as much as Roland did.

But *did* Roland want to meet him? Now, when he wanted to steal Adler's from underneath his nose? Perhaps . . . perhaps it would be better to meet him afterwards, once the deed was accomplished. On that sweet note of anticipated triumph, Roland finally drifted off to sleep.

Christopher Mellish banged on the bedroom door at eight-fifteen. Roland rose quickly, dressed while cursing himself for oversleeping. He had wanted to be well on the way to London by now, but when he came out of the bedroom he saw that Michael Adler still slept soundly on the living room couch. Without ceremony, Roland woke him. 'Time to get going. If you want a job as my chauffeur you're going to have to keep better hours than this.'

Sally made the two men breakfast and Roland asked where Janet and the children were. Sally pointed outside. Through the window Roland could see Katherine riding a docile mare. Dressed in jodhpurs, tweed jacket and hard black hat, Katherine sat comfortably erect, her hands gripping the reins with the authority of a rider years older. Beyond her was Janet in a pair of slacks and an old sweater, keeping a watchful eye on Richard and Carol as they chased each other.

'I'll see you outside,' Roland told Michael. He went through the kitchen door and approached Janet. 'I'm sorry about before. I'll get back as soon as I can.'

Janet said nothing as she watched him pick up Richard and Carol, bouncing them in his arms and closing his eyes as they ran their hands across his face. 'Are you still mad at me?' he asked.

'Ask your children. They also wanted to spend some time with you this weekend.'

Gently, he placed the two younger children on the ground and turned toward Katherine. 'I have to go away for the day,' he said, 'but I'll be back tonight. All right?'

'Everyone else is on holiday this weekend,' Katherine replied primly, looking down at her father from the mare, her blue eyes like chips of glittering ice. 'Why can't you stay here?'

Roland tried to make light of her cold anger. 'You know, for a ten-year-old you're very adult. I've never been snubbed more effectively by a grown woman.'

Katherine dug her heels into the mare and cantered away, leaving Roland standing alone, feeling foolish. Finally he turned back to Janet. 'I guess I'm at the bottom of the popularity poll.'

'You could be right. What time will you be back?'

'Before dinner.'

'Make sure Michael takes it easy – all the lunatics are on the road this weekend.'

He smiled at the truce contained in Janet's word of caution. 'I'll probably be coming back by train. I'll ring through and Christopher can pick me up at the station.' After kissing Janet, he followed Michael to the car.

They arrived at Simon Aronson's home shortly after one o'clock. Nadine let them in, surprised at the unexpected visit, and took them through to the drawing room where Simon was going over some papers from the bank.

'I thought you were going away for the weekend,' he said.

'I did. I came back.'

'So I see. And you brought Michael with you. What's up?'

Roland let Michael speak. Simon listened attentively while he described the offer that had been made for the branch stores, the way the business had been run down and how it was only a matter of time before the Regent Street store went the same way.

'I think we should step in immediately, Simon,' Roland said the moment Michael had finished. 'This Tuesday, as the market opens, mount a raid. We'll have Michael's ten percent of the equity and we'll work on the forty percent that the public holds. That'll give us half. Then we'll work on the other directors.'

To Roland's surprise, Simon shook his head. 'No, Roland. I don't think it's in our best interests to go after

332

Adler's. Let this German have the two stores. Let him take the gamble – and the loss if it doesn't pay off.'

'What?' Roland could hardly believe what he was hearing. Simon had never gone against him before. 'It's there for the taking. You might be satisfied with the profits we've got coming in at the moment, but a company like Adler's will give us legitimacy.'

'Roland, I already have legitimacy. I'm the director of a bank and a reputable newspaper. Besides, I don't think it's legitimacy you're after. I think you're more interested in revenge.'

'Against Albert Adler?' Roland glanced at Michael, recalling his questions. 'That has nothing to do with it. I'm only interested in what's best for us.'

'Are you? Interested in what's best for *us*? Then why didn't you offer to help me yesterday, when I begged you for help with Sharon?'

'Michael, wait outside, will you?' Roland said quietly. He waited until Michael had left the room. 'What was that last comment supposed to mean?'

'You wouldn't intercede with Sharon for me. You, the one person she would listen to, refused to step in and tell her the truth. Instead you gave me advice. So I tried your way. Sharon and Graham were here for dinner last night, as they are every Friday night. Graham mentioned twenty thousand pounds as the sum he needed to launch his licensing venture. I turned him down, just like you suggested. We argued, and when he stormed out of the house, Sharon went with him. He has Sharon so twisted around his little finger that he used my refusal to turn her against us. Do you know what she said? She told us she hated us because we had rejected her husband, refused to help him when we could so easily afford to. This morning Graham telephoned me, threatening to leave Sharon if I didn't change my mind.'

Roland was amazed. 'What the devil is wrong with that? It's the only way to make Sharon see the rotten

333

truth of the situation. Graham will leave, and she'll be well rid of him. No matter how much she's in love with him, even she will understand the truth eventually.'

'Eventually . . .' Simon repeated the word softly. 'And what will happen until *eventually* comes?'

'Simon, I never thought you were a coward. Stand up and face the problem. Use this opportunity to get that leech out of Sharon's life. Everyone will be better off. Or' – like a chess player, Roland's mind moved around to explore all the options – 'are you waiting for me to speak to Sharon before you'll agree to this Adler's deal?'

'Would you?' A flicker of hope shone in Simon's eyes.

'No, Simon. Not even if this Adler's deal hinges on it.'

The telephone rang. Simon cocked his head and waited to see if Nadine would answer it. When she did he turned back to Roland. 'No matter what you've told Michael, I still believe you want Adler's for one reason and one reason only . . . to get back at Albert Adler. To show him – and the world – that you never forget a slight. That's not the way to run a business, Roland.'

'Simon, you'll never understand—' Roland broke off as the drawing room door opened and Nadine rushed in, her face white, eyes brimming with tears.

'That was Sharon on the phone!' she burst out. 'Graham's left. Took a suitcase and walked out.'

Roland watched Simon intently; now he had to decide how he would handle his son-in-law. 'It's a ploy,' Simon answered. 'He'll return if he gets the money he wants.'

'Do you mean you're going to give in to him?' Roland asked. 'Because if you do, it'll happen again and again and again. He's a blackmailer, and a blackmailer never stops taking. And Sharon will go through this hell every single time.'

'What do you care? All you're interested in is revenge against Albert Adler.' Simon turned back to Nadine. 'Did she say anything else?'

'Yes. She blamed us for it.'

'Let me speak to her,' Simon said resignedly. 'I'll make everything right.'

'What about Adler's?' Roland asked.

'What about them? Can't you see I have no time to discuss it with you now?'

'Simon . . .' Roland didn't know how sincere Simon was in blaming him, but it was obvious that the argument with Sharon had temporarily unbalanced his thinking. He was caught up completely with this one problem, and while Roland sympathized he couldn't afford to wait until this family matter was sorted out. Adler's wouldn't be there forever. If he were to act at all he had to act now. He took a deep breath and forced himself to be firm. 'I want Adler's. If you aren't interested in this move, then I think it's time we took a good, objective look at our partnership.'

'You mean, dissolve it?' Simon said flatly, as if he couldn't care less.

'Perhaps. Isn't that what happens when two equal partners can't agree on a course of action?' Roland was sure that the ultimatum would snap Simon's back to reality.

He was wrong. 'Then dissolve it,' Simon said abruptly. 'I have more important things to worry about.'

Roland had intended to take the train back to Somerset. Instead, Michael offered to drive him back to the farm, feeling in some way responsible for the argument with Simon. Roland accepted the offer, then changed his mind. He wanted to go to Wembley and spend the weekend going through the company's accounts.

He telephoned Janet from his office. 'I won't be able to get back today,' he said.

'Why not?'

Briefly, he told her of the meeting with Simon, the question that had been raised about their continuing partnership. To his surprise she wasn't interested in hearing any of it. All she seemed to understand was that Roland

335

was reneging on his promise to spend the weekend with her and the children. 'I'll try to get back tomorrow. Just give me a chance to go over all the figures so I'll have some idea of a settlement.'

'Roland, I don't care about your figures. I'm not the slightest bit interested in your damned business! You have a responsibility to be with your family. Even if Richard and Carol are too young to understand that you're not here, Katherine's going to be even more hurt than she is already. Not to mention me!'

He recalled the glint of icy steel in Katherine's eyes as she had wheeled the horse away from him that morning.

'Katherine wants a father, Roland – someone she can rely on. The last thing she needs is a man who drifts in and out of her life whenever he feels his business commitments permit him to. She's finally able to lead somewhat of a normal life. Don't dangle her on a string now.'

Roland cast his eyes frantically around the office. Papers were scattered all over the desk where he had hurriedly pulled them from files. Michael sat expectantly in a chair. 'I'll be there in three hours, but I'm bringing work with me.'

'Bring all you want with you. But do it at night when the children are in bed.'

He hung up, sorted through the files and jammed everything he needed into a briefcase. 'Is that offer still open? For the ride?'

'Let me get some clothes from my apartment. I'll spend the weekend at the farm with you.'

'Fine. They've got a spare bedroom you can use. Otherwise you can sleep in the barn – probably with me.'

The weekend was ruined, not only for Roland but for everyone. Despite being there he shut everything from his mind, leaving Janet and the children to themselves while he spent hours poring over the company figures. Michael, feeling embarrassed at what was obviously an

336

awkward situation, did his best to relieve it by offering to go riding with Katherine. She considered the invitation for a moment, then climbed down from her mare and walked away. She didn't want a substitute; if her own father didn't care enough to spend time with her, she wasn't interested in a friend who was trying to cover for him.

On Sunday afternoon, having divorced himself from the coldness of everyone around him, Roland telephoned Simon. He skirted around the real purpose of the call by first asking about Sharon, and was relieved when Simon mentioned that she was at the house, having succumbed to her parents' pleas to talk it over. If only Simon would stick to his guns, Roland thought, then this could be the start for Sharon to escape the trap her marriage had become.

'Look, Simon . . . I'm sorry about yesterday but I've got to talk to you.'

'About Adler's? I'm still not interested in your scheme. I won't help you seek revenge against a man who you've felt for years has slighted you.'

'That's not why I'm doing it, can't you understand that? I want us to have Adler's because I feel it can give us something important.' He didn't want to use the word legitimacy again – Simon had bluntly told him how legitimate he already was. That bothered Roland, as if Simon were looking down his nose at him. Head of a bank and a newspaper . . . what did he think his partnership with Roland was? A hobby? 'Were you serious about what you said yesterday?'

'About dissolving our partnership? Yes, I am. Roland, I can't give the time or commitment to the business that you seem able to. I have other responsibilities. I have a family, which at the moment is my main concern. They need me more than you do.'

His remarks hit Roland like a punch in the stomach. Everyone seemed to be reminding him that a family came first. But wasn't he doing this for his family? To give them comfort – to ensure that they would never want? And wasn't that one of the reasons Janet had given for wanting him to father her children in the first place?

'Simon, I've worked out some figures. Would you be willing to take both factories and a cash settlement while I keep hold of the shops and Eldridge's?' Roland hoped he didn't sound too callous. He felt sorry for Simon, all this trouble with Sharon, but surely the banker knew he had made a rod for his own back? If Simon had stood up to Graham Sharp – even before Sharon married him; especially before she married him – it would never have come to this. Now Simon had to live with the consequences. Suddenly Roland wondered if Simon really blamed *him* – first for refusing to intervene, then suggesting the course of action that led to Graham's leaving.

'I'll sell the factories anyway,' was Simon's reply. 'I have no more interest in them.'

'That's your privilege. Does the offer sound all right?'

'Come into my office on Tuesday, Roland. We'll arrange a settlement then.' He hung up, leaving Roland holding a dead receiver. Roland replaced it gently, scarcely able to believe that his partnership with Simon – after twelve years – could end like this, so quietly, a man torn by personal trouble just turning over and dying.

He walked into the kitchen where he found Sally preparing dinner. 'Simon and I just called it a day,' he said quietly, still finding it difficult to accept it. 'He's taking the factories and cash. I'll take everything else.'

Sally wiped her hands on the apron tied around her waist. 'It's because of Sharon. Maybe you could learn a lesson.'

Roland regarded her blankly. 'Do you mean about putting my family first?'

'Precisely.'

'But this is such an opportunity.' He was about to say that he could steal Adler's from underneath Heinrich

Kassler's nose, but then he remembered that Sally didn't know who Kassler was. Neither did Michael, for that matter.

'You'll get a lot more opportunities. Go outside and make it up with Janet and Katherine.'

'You're right.' He kissed Sally on the forehead and went outside, where Christopher Mellish was trying to entertain Katherine with card tricks, while Michael played with the two younger children. Janet stood off to one side, watching.

'Have you finished your business?' she asked.

'Simon and I are splitting up.'

'Is that the way you wanted it?'

Roland was glad Janet had thawed. The break with Simon was so sharp that he needed to talk to someone – someone close, whom he could trust, and Janet filled that space in his life. 'Not really. I'd rather Simon stayed with me but he feels he can't give the same commitment I can. I can't afford to buy him out so he'll take the factories and we'll figure out a cash settlement as well. From now on I'll be solely retail.'

'And now do we have *all* of you for the rest of today and tomorrow? Your mind as well as your body?'

'I promise. I think I've worked everything out. It's just a matter of seeing Simon on Tuesday and making it official.'

'Are you still friends with him?'

'I hope to God I am,' was all Roland could say as they walked over to Katherine and Mellish. 'Is that how you always manage to win at cards? By trickery?' He saw Katherine's face turn toward him as he took the cards from Mellish.

'Here, Kathy. Pick a card . . . any card you like.' He held them out in a fan and was gratified when she accepted the challenge.

On Tuesday morning, Roland met with Simon in his

339

office at Aronson Freres. Simon dictated a simple agreement based on Roland's offer to terminate their partnership. Simon would retain the name of R.E. Electrics – and the Mar-Cross name – for the factories, which he intended to put on the market immediately; and Roland would call his new company, including the shops and the restaurant, the Eagles Group.

'I wish you every success in your venture, Roland, although I still think you're making a mistake.'

'Do you still see it as an act of vengeance?'

Simon nodded. 'How else can I view it? This thing with Albert Adler – the way he tried to cheat you that time — has worked on you like a cancer, worming its way into your system. Now you have the opportunity to strike back by taking his company and pushing him out into the cold. And you're using his son to do it.'

The accusation hurt. 'You're wrong, Simon. So wrong. I wish I could show you how mistaken you are.' Roland took the agreement and signed his name, gave it to Simon's secretary to witness. 'Is Sharon still with you and Nadine?'

'Yes.' Simon looked at Roland's signature on the agreement. 'Perhaps your method was right after all. We had a long talk yesterday. Sharon apologized for the way she left on Friday night. We hope that by being away from him – away from his influence – she'll begin to see it in a different light. It'll take time, of course. Nadine and I think the best thing to do is send her to Paris to be with Miriam and Claude. We think a change of environment would help.'

'I agree. But what about all the money you gave Graham for the salons?'

'He's welcome to it. Eventually we'll have Sharon file for divorce on the grounds of mental cruelty, and if we say nothing about the money I've given him he may not fight any action.'

Another capitulation, Roland thought. An improve-

340

ment, but a capitulation all the same. If any man treated Katherine the way Graham had treated Sharon, Roland would sue until he had bled him dry.

'Roland, during these past few days . . . any harsh words . . . I am truly sorry.'

'It's all right, Simon. You were under stress, I can appreciate that. Do you' – Roland paused, glancing at the signed agreement – 'want to reconsider your decision?'

'No. We had twelve good, profitable years together. Everything has to end eventually.' Simon held out his hand. 'Good luck.'

'Thank you.'

Six days later, Roland was ready. He had switched his partnership with Simon for an alliance with Michael Adler which, he hoped, would bring him control of Adler's. Everything depended on the reaction of Albert Adler's fellow directors when they recognized the raid that had been mounted against the company. Would they stand by Albert, even if they lost in the long run? Or would they sell to the new bidder?

Roland instructed a large stockbroking house to act for him. On Monday morning they stepped into the market, offering considerably above the previous Friday's closing price for Adler's shares, contacting the big institutional shareholders, mounting an all-out blitz. By the close of business that day, the share price had started to creep up at the sudden interest.

The following day, the buying and subsequent rise in the share price continued. The sudden upward movement in a normally sluggish stock attracted attention in the financial pages of newspapers. And Albert Adler, whose initial reaction had been one of confusion, experienced his first taste of anxiety.

By Friday, Albert's worry had turned to panic because it was obvious to him that some company – or some individual – was making a concerted assault on the publicly owned Alder's stock . . .

Just when Albert had relaxed in the knowledge that the deal was set to sell the two branch stores, a raid was being made on Adler's shares. Whoever was behind it, though, wouldn't get control. The most the raiders could finish up with would be forty percent. He, Michael and the other five directors would still retain sixty percent – enough control to fight off any takeover. But one shareholder with the remaining forty percent could still cause difficulties, he thought – could even serve an injunction against selling the two stores. And while that legal problem was being sorted out, the two branch stores would continue to be a drain and the entire company could go under.

Albert called an urgent board meeting. Five of the directors came immediately to the office overlooking Regent Street which Monty Adler had once occupied. Although these men weren't family they were all eminently reliable, Albert decided as he watched them file into the office and sit down; between them they had more than one hundred and fifty years of service to the company, and they would do whatever Albert said. The family name still counted for a lot.

Only Michael, who now occupied Albert's old office, hadn't yet arrived. Albert impatiently went to the door between the offices and looked in. Michael was on the telephone.

'There's a meeting. You're supposed to be there.'

Michael clamped a hand over the mouthpiece. 'In a moment.'

Albert had to be satisfied with that. He returned to his desk, leaving Michael to finish his conversation. A minute later Michael joined the other directors. The telephone call had been from Roland, and now Michael waited with a mixture of confidence and trepidation.

Albert stood up, nervously pacing in front of the window, glancing every so often at the Friday night traffic. 'Someone is making a raid on us. But all they can do is increase the value of our company. Our shares have risen

342

from last Friday's close of fourteen shillings to just over nineteen shillings. Fortunately, we in this room still control sixty percent. However—' He was about to bring up the legal problems that might arise if the raider tried to block the sale of the two branch stores when Michael interrupted.

'The raid is just about over. Most of the shares on the market have been bought up.'

Albert's face creased in puzzlement. 'How do you know?' He didn't give Michael the opportunity to reply before he continued. 'And if you know so much perhaps you'll be kind enough to tell us who the hell has been buying up all the shares.'

'Roland Eagles.'

Albert turned white with rage and shock. 'Eagles? That jumped-up bastard! What does he think he's doing?'

'Stopping the sale of those two stores, for a start.'

'Is he? Then someone had better tell him that before he can do that he needs more than the forty percent he can get his hands on out there. He needs another ten percent plus one share.'

'He understands that. And you're wrong about those of us here controlling sixty percent. *You* control fifty. *My* ten percent is with Eagles.' Michael looked from one bewildered face to the next, starting with his father and ending with the gray-haired financial director who had started with Adler's forty years earlier as a bookkeeper. Not even the sound of breathing, the squeak of a chair, broke the sudden quiet.

'You . . .?' Albert finally managed to blurt out. 'Your ten percent . . .?'

'My ten percent.'

'Who the hell do you think you are, siding against this company, against your own father? Allying yourself with this bloody upstart?'

The cold ruthlessness in Michael's voice as he answered was surprising even to himself. 'I would rather side with

343

an upstart, as you call him, to a man who's prepared to sell two-thirds of the company my grandfather built up so that he can ruin the remainder of it.'

'Is that so? Well let me remind you of something. Maybe you are siding with Eagles, but *we* still control fifty percent of this company and there isn't a damned thing you or Eagles can do about it. We're still selling those two branch stores. In fact, you and Eagles might have done us a favor with this raid.' Albert smiled thinly. 'We might get more from Kassler Industries for the two branch stores.'

'You'll have to fight a court case first. We're taking out an injunction against you to stop any sale.'

'Take out an injunction,' Albert dared his son. 'This company will still go the way I want it to go.'

'We'll see.' Michael turned to the other directors. 'Gentlemen, I would advise you to weigh your options very carefully. You can ally yourselves with my father and watch your interests in Adler's become quite worthless as the company continues to deteriorate. Or you can sell your shares at the present advantageous prices to Mr Eagles and myself.'

Albert's face twisted into an ugly mask. Now even his own son was turning against him, just like his father had. He watched his fellow directors carefully. Which one, if any, would break? That was all that was needed to tip the balance drastically. Just one to throw his five percent into this outrageous alliance which Michael had formed with Roland Eagles, then they would have control. It wouldn't be enough to start changing the board around, but enough to thwart his plans to sell off the two branch stores. Then where would he get the money to continue running the Regent Street store? Not from Eagles, that was certain! Albert was positive that Roland's first priority would be to get rid of him. That was the reason he wanted to buy the company. The little bastard had money now and he wanted to flaunt it, use it for revenge against

Albert. Even after all these years he still wanted his pound of flesh.

None of the directors responded to Michael's offer. Slowly, Albert began to relax; they were on his side. The ingrained loyalty to the family name had paid off when it really counted. While Michael and Roland started whatever delaying tactics they had in mind, Albert would contact the German to explain the situation. At the same time – the idea flashed into his mind like a beacon – he would hire someone to take a hard look at Roland's background. Maybe there was something in his past – not the ridiculous affair with the Argentinian heiress, but something unholy, a lapse which Albert could really capitalize on – to make him loosen his grip.

Something that might make Roland Eagles susceptible to a little friendly persuasion . . .

CHAPTER THREE

Albert could do little over the weekend but think about his son. A traitor, allying himself with someone who was determined to destroy his father. It was small consolation to Albert that even a businessman as successful as Roland would be able to save Adler's and the money he had invested in the shares would be lost; only the sale of the Edinburgh and Manchester stores would enable the London flagship to survive. No, Albert didn't care whether Roland lost money on the deal or how much he lost. All he understood was that Roland had suborned his son. Eleven years earlier he'd turned old Monty against him, now he'd done it again by turning Michael against him as well.

All through the weekend Albert moped around the house, barely speaking to his wife, Helen. She was of little comfort anyway, he decided. Didn't understand a damned thing about the business. Never had. All she knew was that the share prices had risen dramatically, and surely that must be good.

'They've risen because Eagles is trying to buy us out,' he said, trying to explain to Helen.

'Then why don't you sell, Albert? Retire. You're sixty-three. Are you going to keep working until you drop dead, just like Mr Monty did?'

'Retire? And let Eagles win? Let my own son stab me in the back?' No, Albert would never do that. He'd see Eagles burn in hell first. And Michael with him. Yes, damn it, even his own son. All his life Albert's own family had turned against him. His father . . . his brother . . . and now his son. But this one time, Albert would win. He would make sure of that.

The first thing Monday morning Albert hired a private investigator named Derek Hawkins, a retired police detective who had worked for the law firm Adler's used.

Hawkins, middle-aged with a puffy red face and thin gray moustache, sat across the desk from Albert, pen in one hand, notebook in the other as he listened to the Adler's chairman explain exactly what he wanted.

'I don't care how you do it, Mr Hawkins, but I want you to dig up filth about Roland Eagles. Some evidence of wrongdoing, either in business or his personal life – and there should be plenty of that the way he's carried on – that I can use to fight this takeover.'

'Where's he from originally? London?'

'No.' Albert recalled that first meeting between himself, Roland and Monty, when Roland had demonstrated the electric kettles and irons. 'Margate. But he's been away from there for some time.'

'Have you got anything particular in mind?'

Albert flashed the investigator a scathing look. 'If I did, I wouldn't need your services, would I?'

Hawkins snapped the notebook shut, slipped the pen into his pocket. 'Leave it with me, Mr Adler. If it's there, I'll sniff it out.'

'And if you don't sniff it out, invent it. And make it good enough to stick.' He waited for Hawkins to leave, then told his secretary to place a call to the headquarters of Kassler Industries in Stuttgart. Best to get this particular encounter out of the way immediately, before his prospective buyer learned of the raid from another source.

'Mr Adler, what a pleasant surprise.' Heinrich Kassler's voice was as clear as if he were speaking from the next room. 'Do you have some good news regarding my offer?'

'There's been a raid on our shares. The forty percent on the market has been bought at well above market price.'

'How does that affect our negotiations?' Kassler's tone remained polite, though there was a trace of suspicion in it, as if he suspected Albert was trying to drive his selling price up.

'I don't know. The problem is that my son Michael, who holds ten percent of the shares, has thrown in his lot with the man who has bought up the forty percent.'

'Why would he do that?'

'Because he doesn't want to see those two branch stores sold. He's got this family loyalty idea, doesn't want them to—'

'To go to a German, is that it?' Kassler's laugh echoed in the earpiece and Albert was grateful for the reason Kassler had offered. It sounded so much better than admitting – or even thinking – that Michael didn't trust his own father's business decisions. 'Who is this man who has taken such a sudden interest in Adler's?'

'His name's Eagles.' Just speaking the name was distasteful to Albert. 'Roland Eagles. He owns a string of electrical shops and a restaurant in Knightsbridge. We dealt with him years ago. Just once, though. That was all we needed to learn what an unscrupulous rogue he was. We've never dealt with him since.'

'Eagles?' The same bewilderment that hit Roland when Michael had mentioned Kassler's name now assailed the German. During a lifetime one met many people, forgot their names as quickly as they were out of sight. But some names, possibly because of the role that person played in one's life, refused to disappear. Roland Eagles was such a name. 'How old is this Eagles? Would he be in his middle to late thirties?'

'Something like that,' Albert answered without thinking. What importance was his age?

'Very tall, with a round face?' Kassler stared at the wall of his office in Stuttgart, picturing a man in a British Army captain's uniform, a Webley revolver held in a shaking hand. 'Blue eyes?'

'That's him . . . why?' The question crept out as Albert

abruptly realized the significance of Kassler's questions. Did the German know him? And then a bizarre thought: was Kassler in this thing with Roland and Michael, delaying the sale of the two branch stores until the company finally went into liquidation? No, that was ridiculous. All the shares that Roland had bought would collapse. He would take a beating.

'If it's the same man I'm thinking of, we met a long time ago. At Bergen-Belsen.' Kassler ran his eyes over the calendar on his desk, then rang for his secretary. 'Mr Adler I will fly to London this afternoon. I'll be staying at the Connaught. Please be kind enough to telephone me there after dinner and let me know how I can contact this Roland Eagles. Perhaps between us we can arrive at a solution to this puzzle.' Kassler hung up and instructed his secretary to make the necessary arrangements.

That evening, Kassler was settled at the Connaught. He had eaten and now waited for Albert's phone call. During the flight to London he'd been considering his options. Of course he was apprehensive that this unforeseen event might interfere with his planned takeover of the two branch stores. But it seemed there was also a chance for him to meet again with Roland Eagles. Surely there could be only one Roland Eagles, with features matching those he had described to Albert. Sharp as well – he had even managed to persuade Albert's son to join forces with him. Yes, Kassler looked forward to meeting Roland again.

The telephone rang. Kassler jotted down the information Albert gave him, then called Roland's home in Regent's Park. A woman answered, the heavy Scottish brogue difficult for Kassler to understand at first. 'May I speak to Mr Eagles, please?'

'Not at the moment,' Elsie Partridge answered. 'May I take a message?'

'This concerns a rather urgent matter. Perhaps you could tell me where I might reach him.'

349

The housekeeper was uncertain whether to give Janet's number in Chelsea. 'If you tell me where you're staying, sir, I'll have Mr Eagles contact you.'

Kassler smiled to himself; this woman, whoever she was, knew her job. 'Please tell him it is Heinrich Kassler and I am staying at the Connaught.'

'I'll do that, sir.' The housekeeper immediately phoned Janet's house; Roland answered. 'Mr Eagles, there was a gentleman asking for you a couple of minutes ago. A Mr Heinrich Kassler.' She managed to mispronounce both names but Roland knew, with a flush of excitement, who it was.

'Where's he staying?'

'At the Connaught.'

Roland put down the receiver and turned to Janet, his face alight. 'Things are happening.'

'About Adler's?'

'The man they were going to sell the two stores to just called my apartment. He's come over from Germany and is staying at the Connaught.'

'Are you going to see him now?'

'If he'll see me, and I think that's what he wants.' Roland's fingers were already spinning the dial.

Janet reached out quickly and pressed down the receiver rest. 'My God, Roland! Can't it wait until morning? Do you have to phone him right now?'

'I wasn't calling him. I was calling Alf Goldstein.'

'Are you going to drag him away from his family as well? You haven't got an ounce of consideration in your body for other people, have you?'

Roland removed her hand gently from the receiver rest. 'If I didn't call Alf right now, he'd never forgive me. This man Heinrich Kassler, who's trying to buy those two branch stores . . .' While he dialed Goldstein's number and waited for the telphone to be answered, he explained about Bergen-Belsen and their first meeting with Kassler. 'Alf, can you pick me up from Janet's house and run me to the Connaught? I'm going to see Heinrich Kassler. That's right, Kassler. He's the one who's trying to buy the two Adler's stores. My mounting a raid on the shares has brought him out into the open.'

Goldstein said he would be at the house in thirty minutes; he wanted to see the German again as much as Roland did. Then Roland phoned Kassler at the Connaught.

'This is Roland Eagles. It seems our paths are destined to cross again.'

'Indeed,' Kassler replied. 'I had quite a shock when your name entered into my conversation with Albert Adler.'

'It was nothing to the shock I received when your name came up when I was talking to Albert's son, Michael.'

'We have split a family in our quest for allies.'

'It would seem that way. But I have a feeling that you're quite willing to discuss it; wasn't that why you called me?'

'Of course. And I also wanted to meet you again. I believe we ended our last encounter on that note.'

'We did indeed. I'll be at the Connaught in half an hour or so.'

'I look forward to seeing you.'

'What will you do?' Janet wanted to know after Roland had hung up. 'Swap war stories? Reminisce a little?'

Some of the excitement drained out of Roland in the face of Janet's coolness. 'I just want him to back off from buying those two stores, that's all. If I can do it nicely, play on an old tie, I will. Otherwise I'll tell him straight out that we'll block his purchase with an injunction.'

'But you can't tell him that tomorrow, can you? It has to be now. What do I do about that?' Janet pointed to the dining room table, set for a late dinner. 'I suppose I should be grateful that you said good night to the children before you rushed off.'

'Janet, please don't start. Not now. You know how important this is to me. I've taken an enormous chance by buying all these shares. I could lose everything if we don't get control of Adler's.'

'You know something, Roland? You're a very strange man. You're convinced that family life is the be-all and end-all, yet you shun it whenever an important deal comes up. After three years of almost living with you, I'm still not sure I understand you.'

He wondered how much truth was in her words . . . If Catarina were still alive, if he were still married to her, would he be rushing out like this? Or would he leave whatever business he had until the following day so that he could share dinner with her, spend a quiet evening with her? Even begrudge a man like Kassler – with all the importance this meeting held – the time away from Catarina? No, there was more to it than that. Much more. He recalled the promise he had once made to Nicanor Menendez, that when he was the ambassador's age he would be worth twice the fifty million pounds the Argentinian was worth. And he recalled another promise, made much earlier to himself: to meet his father's family as an equal. Tonight was all part of realizing those promises.

When Goldstein rang the bell, Roland kissed Janet and promised he would be home as soon as possible. Then he climbed into Goldstein's car for the trip to the Connaught.

Kassler was waiting just inside the lobby when Roland entered the hotel. For a moment the two men stood facing each other, as if unable to believe that fate had brought them together again. Then the German stepped forward and clasped Roland around the shoulders. 'Anywhere, anytime, I would have recognized you.'

'You as well,' Roland said. It was a lie, though. He would have walked straight past Kassler on the street without the faintest hint of recognition. The blond hair had become stringy, the blue eyes had lost their luster, the once erect frame was now stooped over. Somwhere between Bergen-Belsen and the Connaught, Heinrich Kassler had aged tremendously. 'You remember Alf Goldstein, don't you?'

Kassler's eyes turned to Goldstein, who stood next to Roland. 'Of course, your interpreter – after you refused to permit me to speak English.' Momentarily the blue eyes sparkled. 'I don't want to hear my language coming out of your bloody filthy Nazi mouth.'

Roland blushed at the memory. 'The heat of the moment, you understand.'

'Of course.' Kassler shook Goldstein's hand before leading the two men into the lounge. 'Now we are on opposite sides again, eh?'

'But with the same result. My side will be victorious.'

Kassler shrugged his shoulders. 'Perhaps. But after a separation of fifteen years must we talk business first? What has happened to you in all that time?' Kassler signaled for a waiter, ordered drinks. 'You own a chain of electrical stores and a reputable restaurant, I'm told.'

'Who gave you that information – Albert Adler?'

Kassler nodded. 'He was helping me to size up my opposition. You've done very well for yourself.'

'Not as well as you, apparently. A company with a grandiose name like Kassler Industries sounds almost forbidding.'

'I've been most fortunate. I had help from the Americans. My father's factory somehow escaped the bombs and it was in the Americans' interest to assist me in putting it back into operation. Engineering, though, never interested me as it did my father. He was a man who could create anything with his hands, while I prefer to use my brain. I expanded into retail, small shops at first that sold anything you could possibly think of. Then, when I was strong enough, I enlarged the operation into department stores. There are Kassler stores now in Bonn, Cologne, Stuttgart, Frankfurt and Munich.'

'And soon you intend to have them in Manchester and Edinburgh?'

'I hope so . . . just as I intend to be represented in other European cities.'

'And who said Germany lost the war?' Goldstein muttered as the waiter returned with the drinks. Roland glanced sharply at him, but Kassler hadn't heard the remark.

'Are you married, Roland?' the German asked.

'I was. My wife died.' He reached into his wallet and produced photographs of Katherine, Richard and Carol.

'Beautiful children,' Kassler said looking at the photo. 'To your children.' He raised his glass in the air and drank a toast, then brought out a photograph of his own. 'I have only one child, a boy named Franz. I married shortly after the end of the war.'

Roland took the photograph and studied it with Goldstein. A tall, thin blond boy of about fourteen posing very formally in short trousers and hiking boots. 'And your wife?'

'We are divorced. Franz lives with her just outside Stuttgart. He spends one weekend a month with me, when my work schedule permits.'

'Is success that important to you, to forego seeing your son?'

'Success, Roland, is *all* that matters. Seeing what you have done since we last met, I would think you would appreciate that.' Kassler returned the photograph to his wallet and finished his drink. 'What about Adler's? I'm positive we can work this out quite amicably.'

'Of course we can,' Roland agreed pleasantly. 'Drop out of the fight.'

'I didn't come over here to do that. Albert Adler tells

me you and his son now control fifty percent of the equity.'

'Only for the time being. Once we start on the other directors we'll control even more.'

Kassler considered Roland's confident statement. Albert seemed quite certain that none of his fellow directors would throw in with Roland and Michael Adler. That left a stalemate, which was of little use to anyone. Kassler thought what a pity it was that the company's articles of incorporation didn't stipulate that a director couldn't sell his shares without the approval of the board. That would have taken care of the son's ten percent and Roland would now only hold forty. But it was a family company, formed in the days when the founder must have acted like a tin god; such practices that were normal today were never even considered then. 'Roland, perhaps you and I could come to an arrangement of our own?'

'What do you have in mind?'

'You and me, join forces. We'll take those two stores. Expanding into Britain is one thing for Kassler Industries. Finding the management to make them profitable is another entirely. And there, you have the expertise.'

Roland didn't even need time to think over the proposition before rejecting it. 'Sorry, Heinrich. I want all or nothing, and I intend to have all.'

Kassler's eyes hardened. He had flown to London to meet with Roland. To renew a sentimental tie, yes – but the overriding reason was to evaluate his opponent, learn how tough he was. The offer to work together was a final gambit on Kassler's part, an admission that he respected the Englishman and would rather join forces than fight him head-on. But Roland had turned down the offer out of hand; he hadn't even given Kassler the courtesy of considering it.

Kassler's life was ruled by his business. Its success was the yardstick he used to measure his own worth as a man.

And, like Roland, he hated to lose. 'Do you believe your alliance with the son is as powerful as my alliance with the father, Roland?'

'At the very least.'

'Then may the best man win.'

Early the following morning, Derek Hawkins stepped off the train in Margate and considered where to begin his investigation in Roland's home town. Hawkins had spent the previous day in London, telephoning Roland's stockbroker, his bank, visiting anyone he thought might offer a lead that he could take back to Albert. At times Hawkins pretended to be working for a bank, other times for a newspaper. Occasionally he pretended nothing at all, just letting his gruff, officious manner fool people into believing he was a police officer.

So far he had learned nothing that he felt Albert could use. He knew that Roland having had two children by a woman he wasn't married to wasn't the kind of dirt Albert was looking for . . . he would have to dig deeper. Hence Margate.

A look through the town records gave Hawkins his start. He visited the school which Roland had attended. Spott-Mandray had retired, and the teachers who remained remembered Roland only vaguely from twenty years earlier. He was a chess champion, excelled in all subjects. School records indicated that he'd left quite suddenly. That tied in with what Hawkins knew already about Roland's family being killed in an air raid; following that he'd run off to join the army.

He returned to the town records, painstakingly copied down everything he could find. If he couldn't satisfy Albert with any genuine smears, at least he could impress him with the amount of ground he'd covered.

While Hawkins was digging in Margate, Roland was at his old office in Wembley which Simon allowed him to use until the Adler's business was sorted out. After that he would either move into the store's executive offices or find a new headquarters for the Eagles Group.

Michael Adler was with Roland, listening attentively, as he was briefed on the previous night's meeting with Heinrich Kassler.

'I thought coincidences like this only happened in books,' Michael said when told of the past relationship between the two men. 'Think of the favor you could have done us all if you'd just shot him when you first met him. We wouldn't have this mess now.'

'There is no mess. We'll start legal proceedings immediately to block any sale of the stores. Then we'll persuade the directors to sell their share of the equity. It's all cut and dried.'

'Easier said than done. Not one of them is budging. They're sticking to my father come hell or high water.' Michael had approached each of the directors, only to receive a series of rebuffs. The damned fools were so shortsighted they couldn't see that holding onto their shares would only harm them. They were too frightened of being kicked out once Roland had the power to change the board. But at least they would be kicked out with a fair price for the shares they held.

Roland's secretary rang through. 'Mr Aronson's on the line for you.'

'Thank you. Simon, what can I do for you?' For a dreadful moment Roland feared something might be wrong with Sharon. An emotional relapse, a breakdown; he couldn't even begin to think what it might be.

'Someone is poking their noses into your business, Roland. I thought you should know.'

'Tell me more.'

'I had a telephone call yesterday. At the time I thought nothing of it, but now I realize it could be very serious. A man named Jenkins who claimed to be from the business page of the *Evening News*. He wanted to know why we

357

had split up, was there any problem? Strange questions. I've checked with the *News*; they have no reporter by that name.'

'Thanks for letting me know, Simon. I appreciate it.' He put down the receiver and looked at Michael. 'I think your father's getting worried. He's trying to see what I've got to hide. Let's check and see if questions have been asked elsewhere.' Roland telephoned his bank. Yes, there had been inquiries about him there, from a man named Johnson purporting to represent another bank. His brokerage house; yes, again, from the same Mr Johnson. Even his tailor, from a police officer named Jarvis. Roland debated how far back this investigator would go. How deeply would he dig? All the way back to Margate?

'Let's go have some lunch,' he suggested to Michael. 'We can continue talking at Eldridge's.'

'Are you paying?'

'Of course I am.' Roland clapped Michael on the shoulder. 'I'm taking the money from one pocket and putting it in another.'

As Michael and Roland lunched at Eldridge's, Derek Hawkins stood jammed uncomfortably in a telephone booth in Margate, talking with Albert. He thumbed through his notebook, reading out facts and figures as he had once done in court, pausing between sentences to let the information sink in, letting the jury reach its own conclusions.

'Apparently Roland Eagles left school under rather abrupt circumstances, Mr Adler. The day his parents, sister and brother were killed in an air raid was his last day at school. He never returned. Two days later, on his sixteenth birthday, he lied about his age to enlist in the army.'

Lied about his age to enlist in the army . . . that was worse than useless, Albert thought. Nothing like the kind of information he needed for a smear campaign. That was the act of a hero, not of a man who couldn't be trusted. Joined the army at sixteen. And five years later he'd met Kassler at Bergen-Belsen, of all places. Came within a second of killing him, according to what the German had told Albert.

Albert had met with Kassler that morning, assured him that nothing would be allowed to interfere with their negotiations for the two branch stores. Now Kassler was on his way back to Germany and Albert was not at all certain he could keep his promise. Roland's threatened legal proceedings would tie up the future of the stores indefinitely. In the meantime, Michael – his own son, for God's sake – was working on the other directors.

'Isn't there anything else you can tell me, Mr Hawkins?' Albert asked the investigator. 'I could have found that out myself by telephoning around.'

Hawkins refused to be rushed. Judges resplendent in wigs and robes had never made him quicken his pace when testifying on the witness stand, and he wasn't about to let this nervous department store owner change a lifetime habit. 'He does, of course, have these two children out of wedlock by a Miss Janet Taylor of Twelve—'

'Yes, I know all about that. Give me something I can use against him, not a load of drivel fit for a gossip columnist.'

Hawkins looked through the notebook again. 'You might be interested in this, then, Mr Adler. While I was in Margate, going through birth records, I came across this piece of information . . .'

As Albert listened, he felt his heart give a savage jump. 'Thank you, Mr Hawkins, you've been very helpful.' He put down the receiver, wiped away the sheen of sweat from across his forehead and called for his secretary to come in.

'Will you please locate Mr Michael for me?'

'He . . . Are you all right, Mr Albert?'

'Yes, I'm fine.'

359

'You look very pale.'

'I'm fine. Will you please find my son?'

'He went out a couple of hours ago, a lunch appointment.'

With Roland Eagles, of course – hatching up more dirty tricks. 'Have him come in the moment he returns.'

'Of course. Are you sure you feel all right?'

'I'm positive.' He stood up from his desk and walked over to the window. The door closed softly as the secretary left and Albert stared down at Regent Street.

All his life he had dreamed of having this office, and all his life his family had conspired to keep him from it. Now they had achieved their ultimate goal – driving him from the building completely.

Roland parted company with Michael at Eldridge's just after two-thirty. Instead of having Goldstein take him back to Wembley he returned to Regent's Park. This was Katherine's last day of summer vacation and he wanted to spend some of it with her. He still hadn't recovered from the way she had glared at him from the horse at Christopher Mellish's farm, and God alone knew how much time he would have to be with her in the next few weeks, once the battle for Adler's really got under way.

'Wannt to go to the cartoon theater on Baker Street for an houR?' he aske her. The idea had come to him in a flash, and Katherine accepted instantly. Roland couldn't even remember the last time he'd taken his daughter to a film, and they sat through the hour-long show of Bugs Bunny, Mickey Mouse, and Tom and Jerry holding hands and laughing.

'Why didn't we do this before?' Katherine asked as they were driven back to the apartment. 'It was fun.'

'I just had the time and I was in the neighborhood. Besides, I haven't seen cartoons since I was your age. I'd forgotten how much fun they are.'

'Maybe you should see them more often, then you'll be happier more often.'

'I am happy. Why shouldn't I be happy when I've got you and Richard and Carol?'

'Then why don't you spend more time with us?'

Roland felt too deflated by the question to even think of an answer. After dropping Katherine off he went on to Wembley. When he arrived at the office, he found a message waiting from Michael to call him immediately.

'Michael, what's the matter?'

'It's my father.'

Roland went numb. Was something wrong with Albert . . . a heart attack brought on by the excitement, the pressure? That was all Roland needed . . . 'What about him?' he asked fearfully.

'I don't understand it. He called me into his office right after I got back and told me he would sell me his twenty-five percent at today's closing price.'

If Michael thought the news would startle Roland, he was doomed to disappointment. 'Did he give you any reason why?' Roland asked calmly.

'Just that he's been thinking about retiring, and perhaps right now is a good time. He's sixty-three, you know.'

'What about the other directors?'

'I haven't spoken to them yet, but with us having seventy-five percent it makes it kind of obvious what they'll do now. They'll sell their shares as well and get out. But, Christ, Roland, what a turnaround!' Michael's exuberance got the better of him. He and Roland had achieved their objective without the aggravation of a drawn-out family battle. 'My father met with Kassler this morning – do you think that could have had something to do with it? Maybe Kassler told him to back off – you know, in return for what you did for him?'

'Anything's possible.' Like hell it is, Roland thought. Kassler would never have backed off so willingly. The

German was made of steel, and he wanted those two stores badly. Maybe he figured Albert wasn't strong enough to battle his own son. But that wasn't it. Roland knew the real reason, and he couldn't resist a smile . . . a smile that reflected his feeling of triumph, satisfaction and justice finally being done. 'I'll get together with you tomorrow, Michael. We've got a ton of things to do. We have to select a new board for one thing, and I'll arrange to sell the electrical shops and Eldridge's into Adler's so I can recoup the money for the shares. Before this year's out, I want Adler's well on the way to regaining the reputation it had when old Monty ran it.'

'I'm looking forward to it.'

'Michael . . .' A thought registered in Roland's mind, a trace of sympathy for the vanquished. 'Should I meet with your father, give bygones a chance to be bygones?'

'I already thought of that, mentioned it to him.'

'What did he say?'

Michael took a deep, audible breath. 'He never wants to hear your name again, let alone see you.'

Roland was not the least bit surprised.

Heinrich Kassler telephoned Roland the following day after he learned of Albert's sudden stepping-down. 'To the victor go the spoils, eh, Roland?'

'And the problems.' Roland was glad for the call. He'd been debating whether to contact Kassler, but didn't want to seem like he was gloating. The German had solved the dilemma.

'If you ever find you want to sell those two stores, please give me first refusal,' Kassler said.

'Thanks, but I doubt that we'll ever come to that. No hard feelings, I trust?'

Kassler's laugh boomed in Roland's ear. 'None at all, Roland. Your ally was well chosen. And who knows – we may meet on another battlefield at another time. Perhaps I will be the fortunate contestant the next time.'

'Perhaps you will be,' Roland said, not meaning a word of it. He'd enjoyed taking this round from Kassler and he would do the same if they were to meet again. 'Have you any other plans for expanding into this country?'

'None at the moment. I was rather counting on picking up the Adler's stores.'

'If it means anything, I'll apologize for thwarting you.'

'Ah, don't be ridiculous. Business is like war, Roland. There has to be a winner and a loser. Besides, my defeat in this particular instance is tempered by having met you again.'

'Thank you. I feel the same way.'

'*Auf Wiederhören*, Roland. Until the next time.'

During the drive home that evening, Roland mentioned to Alf Goldstein that Kassler had phoned to offer his congratulations.

'He must have choked on them,' Goldstein muttered.

'What's that supposed to mean? And what about that crack you made at the Connaught . . . you know, who said Germany lost the war?'

Goldstein's eyes left the road for an instant, just long enough to fix Roland with a bleak stare. 'Believe me, I really wanted to meet Kassler again. He was the one good thing we found in that god-awful place. But when I saw him at the Connaught, the first thing that hit me was he looked just like a typical Nazi – the bloated face, pale blue eyes stuck there like a pig's, bleached straw hair. And on top of that he's rolling in it.'

'Was that why you hardly said a word that night?' Roland laughed. 'Come on, Alf. You're thinking in terms of stereotypes. Don't you feel embarrassed talking like this? Especially after the way you mentioned him in your book?'

'Of course. Don't forget, I helped make him into a hero of sorts, a knight in shining armor coming to the rescue. Now I come face-to-face with him fifteen years later and

I'm having second thoughts.'

'Alf, you know what he did at the camp. Forget what he looks like, just accept him for what he really is.'

'I know. But remember what I told you fifteen years ago – that your feelings couldn't possibly be the same as mine. No matter what Kassler did – how many people he saved – he looks like a bloody Nazi to me.'

'You've seen too many war movies, Alf. I told you you're reacting to a stereotype.'

'Maybe,' Goldstein agreed as he stopped outside Roland's building. 'And then again maybe not.'

From that day, Roland and Michael were together almost constantly, working until late every night, trying to set Adler's on the road to recovery. Within the first week, all trace of Albert Adler and the established directors was gone. Roland named Michael managing director and appointed Lawrence Chivers to the board as director of store operations. Feelers were sent out to former buyers who'd left under Albert's leadership. Management personnel and department heads from each store were brought to London and interviewed at length. And those who Roland and Michael felt weren't up to par were let go immediately with a month's pay in lieu of notice. Under the Eagles Group, the three department stores were starting with a clean slate. And Roland settled comfortably into the office where he had once removed his trousers to have them pressed by Monty Adler.

Within two months, much of the ill feeling that Albert had generated among supplierrs had disappeared. Roland's credit among the chain of electrical shops had always been good; as a one-timemanufacturer himself he understood the value of paying bills on time. Now he brought those same attitudes into Adler's. Outstanding accounts were cleared, and manufacturers who had refused to deal with Albert's management returned, knowing they would be treated fairly.

But in the middle of all this change Roland's relationship with Janet deteriorated drastically. He'd done exactly what she feared he would do when he threw himself into the new venture – it would be to the total exclusion of everything else. One evening, when he turned up three hours late for dinner for the second time that week, claiming he'd been unavoidably detained, she decided to settle the issue.

'Did you and Michael make any important decisions today?'

'We hired a china buyer. Why do you ask?' Janet usually avoided discussing business because she hated the hold it had on him.

'Because it's high time you made a decision about yourself. About where I and the children fit into your life.'

Roland set down his soup spoon. 'I take it you've already got a suggestion on the tip of your tongue.'

'You know me too well. I refused to marry you in the first place because I had the notion it would never last—'

'That was a negative attitude to begin with.'

'Not really. If this arrangement had worked out I would have seriously considered marriage.'

'What's wrong with it? It's working fine.'

'Maybe it's working on your terms, Roland, but it's not working on mine. You spend most of your life in the office, and when you've finished – and you feel like seeing me and the children — you come on over. But do you really think it's fair for me to spend all my time just sitting around, waiting to hear from you . . . wondering if I'm going to? You had a choice to make between your work and me and the children. You seem to have chosen your work.'

'You're the one who mentioned compartments.'

'Yes, I did, because I knew it would happen this way.' She ran her hands through her hair, suddenly flustered. 'Don't get the idea I'm angry, Roland. I'm not. I've just resigned myself to us splitting up, that's all.'

'What about the children?'

'They'll stay with me, of course. It's about time to think of Katherine's future. She can't stay with Elsie Partridge forever in that huge apartment – she's literally a prisoner in luxury.'

Roland considered how Katherine would react if he broke up with Janet. No *if* about it – Janet was breaking up with him, and he couldn't blame her. He couldn't expect to leave her dangling on a string all the time. She had her own life, was entitled to lead it any way she wanted if he couldn't be involved with her in any meaningful way. But what would Katherine do? She was so close to Janet that they could almost be mother and daughter. 'Do you want to look after her?'

'I think I should. It's the only chance she's got at living a normal life. And once all that's cleared up, you can arrange a pension for Elsie. Let her go back to Scotland with her last days all paid for.'

'I wasn't aware she wanted to return to Scotland.'

'Poor Roland . . .' Janet gave him a smile that was filled with tenderness and sympathy. 'Once you get wrapped up in one of your schemes, you're not very aware of anything that's going on, are you? It's lucky that Michael's single, otherwise you'd have his family on your conscience as well. As it is, he's gone through girlfriends like anyone else goes through pairs of socks; they probably can't compete with your demands on the poor fellow.' She reached across the table and grasped Roland's hand. 'I do love you, Roland. I just can't bear to be so dependent on you when your heart's someplace else. Does that make any kind of sense?'

'I suppose I could always change my habits—' He broke off, feeling lost. A support was being removed and he was frightened he might fall . . . Janet had always been there when he needed her . . . who would he turn to now?

'Don't even think of changing,' Janet told him. 'You're the way you are for whatever reasons, and nothing's

366

going to make you any different. Your children are still your children – you'll always have them. It's just that I want something a little more now.'

'Marriage?'

'If the right man came along I'd think about it. But what about marriage, Roland? How would you feel about your children being brought up in a home with a man who wasn't their father?'

Roland knew the question was only theoretical at the moment. Nonetheless, he had to give it some thought. 'Would I get to approve of him first?'

Janet shook her head. 'Only I would have to approve of him.'

'Marry someone decent, that's all I ask. He doesn't have to be wealthy. I'll make sure you and the children never want for anything. Just make sure he's decent.'

'Of course he would be, Roland. You should know me better than that. I'll use you as a yardstick and remember to change a couple of things – like having him with me every evening, sharing holidays with him, knowing that I'm the most important thing in the world to him.'

'You shouldn't make comparisons, they can be very misleading.' To his surprise, Roland found he was enjoying the conversation. Janet's feelings, her decisions on what she wanted, were out in the open now. He could afford to be more relaxed.

'You should know about comparisons, Roland. Tell me the truth: have you ever stopped comparing me – comparing any women you've ever met – with Catarina?'

'No, I guess I haven't.' Even as she spoke he couldn't help thinking of the difference between Janet and Catarina. Catarina would never have stood for him being away all the time, just seeing her when work permitted – she would have greeted him one day with a saucepan aimed at his head! The thought made him smile, and brought an uncomfortable lump to his throat. Ten years – he couldn't believe she'd been dead that long. It seemed

like only yesterday, an entire collection of wistful yester-
days . . .

When Roland returned to Regent's Park later that
night, the flat was dark and silent. He had wanted to
speak to Elsie Partridge, tell her about the pension he
would give her so that she could retire comfortably in
Scotland, but the housekeeper was asleep, her door
closed. Roland settled instead for opening the door of
Katherine's bedroom. Light from the hall spilled softly
into the room, gently illuminating the bed. Roland stood
in the doorway for a full minute, taking in the sleeping
form of his daughter, the books on horses that were
stacked high on the bedside table, the prints of thorough-
breds and steeplechasers that covered almost every inch
of wall space.

Katherine's blond hair was spread across the pillow
and Roland wondered whether Alf Goldstein would be
offended by this blondness — by these blue eyes – as well.
Did Katherine, too, remind Goldstein of the typical Nazi,
the children with whom Hitler had wanted to populate
his new, racially pure Germany? Damn Goldstein,
Roland suddenly thought. Why the hell did he have to say
something like that? It was true that his feelings went a
lot deeper than Roland's; they extended to the depths of
fanatical bigotry, which Roland had never known.

Roland suddenly caught himself, ashamed for even
considering such a thing. It was he . . . Roland . . . who
was making the comparison between Katherine and
Heinrich Kassler, not Goldstein. No, it wasn't the blond
hair and blue eyes that disturbed the former sergeant. It
was just Germans of Kassler's generation.

Roland entered the room quietly, bent over the bed and
kissed Katherine on the forehead. She stirred and he
feared he'd woken her, until she rolled over, still asleep.
Roland pulled a chair up to her bed and sat down, content to watch his daughter while she slept. He had so

many things to consider . . . would she be better off living with Janet and the other two children? Even if Janet eventually married? Perhaps had more children by another man? He knew that Katherine would never refer to another man as her father; he didn't have to worry about anyone usurping his role. He would see her regularly, probably as frequently as he saw her now – which he knew wasn't all that often, especially since the Adler's deal.

Janet was right, he decided as he stood up, replaced the chair and started toward the door.

'Daddy, is that you?'

He turned around. Katherine was sitting up in bed, woken by the noise of his movements. She rubbed sleep from her eyes, squinted at the form silhouetted in the light from the hall.

'I just came in to check on you.' Roland walked back to the bed and sat down on the edge. 'Feel like talking?'

'What about?'

'Kathy, would you like to live with Janet and your brother and sister? All the time?'

'Will I still see you?'

'Of course. Nothing will really change. You'll still go to the same school, have the same friends.' The two-bedroom house in Chelsea would be cramped with three children, he decided. He'd buy Janet something larger, closer to where he lived.

'Why can't I stay here with you?'

'I'm going to be very busy all the time now. And Elsie wants to go home to Scotland.'

'Why don't you hire another housekeeper?'

'I probably will,' Roland answered, thinking that his daughter's reasoning was all too frequently mature beyond her years. She considered all the angles, the same way he did until he was satisfied. She was his daughter, all right; there was no getting away from that. 'But you don't want to stay in such a large apartment with just a housekeeper, do you? I'm going to be away a lot.'

'Do you *have* to be away so often?'

'Yes. I do. You've seen my picture in the newspaper,' he said, referring to the stories of the Adler's takeover. 'I have a big company to run now.'

'Why don't you get other people to help you, so you can spend more time with us?'

He tried to come up with a reply, a gentle lie he could tell her that would salve his own painful conscience. But he was unable to. The truth eclipsed anything he thought to tell her: that he was only really happy when he was pushing himself to the limit with a project.

Instead of trying to explain himself to his daughter, he kissed her a second time and left the room. Once in the hallway, an idea flashed in his mind. He strode to the telephone and dialed Michael Adler's number.

'Michael's something's just hit me. Why don't we close the three stores for two days – a Monday and Tuesday, which are usually our slowest days anyway – and then have a grand reopening, special sales, the works? Show the public that the *new* Adler's really means business?'

Lying in bed, Michael looked at his watch; it was two minutes before midnight. But he was used to calls from Roland at strange hours. When Roland was involved in something hot he worked almost non-stop and expected those around him to do likewise.

'I'll arrange a meeting with our advertising people for tomorrow, Roland. Let's get their thoughts on it.'

'Good enough. See you first thing in the morning.' Roland hung up and walked into the living room. He lit a cigarette and sat down, thinking the idea over, expanding on it, trying to decide on the slowest-moving merchandise to include in the sale.

Already the conversation with Katherine had been pushed far to the back of his mind.

The takeover of Adler's was destined to give Roland a dubious kind of fame – and an enemy. As a rule he

370

took little interest in newspaper stories about the acquisition, regarding the press as something of a necessary evil. Always fresh in his memory was the cheap way newspapers had treated him during the elopement with Catarina and the subsequent custody case, but with regard to Adler's the reporters behaved as Roland believed they should, focusing on the facts and refraining from embellishing their stories with personal background.

Except for one – a weekly, antiestablishment, satirical magazine called *Probe*. If Michael hadn't brought the article to his attention, Roland would have missed it altogether. *Probe* wasn't on his required reading list. At least he never placed it on the same level of importance as the *Financial Times* and *Investor's Chronicle*. Until now . . .

'Read this when you get the opportunity.' Michael tossed the magazine onto Roland's desk. 'Page eight, I marked it for you. The "Rushes" column.'

'*Probe*?' Roland's eyes lifted. 'What are you, of all people, doing reading this garbage?'

'My secretary gave it to me, says she's a regular subscriber.'

'Is that so? Maybe we'd better choose our secretaries more carefully,' he said, laughing. He turned to page eight and skimmed his eyes across the column Michael had circled in red. 'Vulture?'

'Obviously a play on your name.' Michael smiled as if he found it amusing. 'By their lights you're a businessman who gobbles up dying companies.'

'Thank you, I can see that.' Roland went through the article more carefully. 'Sarcastic bunch of bastards . . . "The Vulture, an old-fashioned St George-like figure who took on the German dragon to preserve the virtue of a fair British maiden . . ." I bet no one ever referred to Adler's as a fair British maiden before. What's the editor's name?'

'Daniel Rushden. He writes the "Rushes" column every week.'

Roland rifled through the pages until he found the masthead. Daniel Rushden was editor and publisher. 'I wonder if there's anything here on which I can base a libel suit.'

The indulgent smile on Michael's face dropped away. 'Don't even bother with them, Roland. *Probe's* the kind of bully that will pack up and go away if you ignore them.' He reeled off a string of names – all public figures politicians, industrialists, entertainers – who had taken *Probe* to court during the magazine's five-year existence. 'Each time they're in court, their damned circulation goes up. So does their advertising.'

'Who would advertise in this kind of thing?' Roland glanced through the magazine again; the advertising was obviously directed at a young audience – popular records, movies, clubs. 'I'm going to call Simon, see what he thinks.'

While Michael waited, Roland phoned Simon at Aronson Freres. He read the article over the telephone and waited for Simon's opinion. It was the same as Michael's . . . leave it alone. Roland considered what he'd said after they hung up, but he wasn't in the mood for accepting such advice. When newspapers had taken shots at him in the past he'd been unable to retaliate; he'd been either too busy to bother himself, or he felt it was below him. Well, now he had the time. And, more importantly, he had the power. A magazine was sniping at him, and he was going to respond. He grinned at Michael as he reached his decision.

'No libel suit. I'm just going to offer to take a journalist out to lunch. What do you think about that?'

'I think you're risking a hell of a lot for personal satisfaction. Give a publication like *Probe* the chance to sink their teeth into you, let them know they're getting to you, and they'll never let go.'

Roland telephoned Daniel Rushden that afternoon, introduced himself and invited him to lunch the following day. Rushden accepted warily. His targets didn't usually respond this cordially to an attack, and he was puzzled.

Roland met the tall, angular editor at Eldridge's, secure in the knowledge that he was on home territory. There was nothing Rushden could do to him here. In this place, Roland was all-powerful. He wanted Rushden to be aware of that – too powerful to tangle with.

The only son of an eminent Harley Street doctor, Rushden had received a public school education before turning against the establishment, mocking it for what he considered its false values and pompous attitudes. The magazine he had launched five years earlier – after spending six years as a political journalist on a leftist newspaper – had succeeded beyond Rushden's wildest expectations. The more *Probe* attacked establishment figures in stories that reputable publications considered too risky to print – and the more these figures responded angrily – the larger his magazine's circulation grew. Rushden's anti-establishment viewpoint had very quickly achieved cult status for *Probe*.

'What made you buy a restaurant?' Rushden asked Roland after they had ordered.

'I like to eat well, so why should I pay someone else for the privilege of feeding me?'

'Bravo! The decisive action that so befits a hero who beat back the German hordes from our shores once again,' Rushden responded, filing Roland's comment away in his memory. 'You make quite a habit of this, don't you – clobbering Germans for the Union Jack? Military Cross *and* Military Medal . . .'

'And you seem to make quite a habit of upsetting people.' Roland was surprised by the magazine owner's comments; he had done his homework thoroughly and quickly, the sign of a man to be watched.

'Only those who need upsetting.'

'What made you decide I was one of them?'

'Well, your little escapade with Adler's and this Kassler fellow did have all the melodramatics one could wish for. World War Two revisited, playing on nationalistic pride. Just like your final confrontation with your former father-in-law . . . a British baby being brought up in Argentina. Perish the thought!'

'You seem to know quite a lot about me.'

'I make it my business to learn about those men in positions of power. One way or another, they influence the way the rest of us have to live.' Rushden still was uncertain what to make of Roland. He seemed such an odd mixture. At first glance, the perfect gentleman, dressed immaculately and expensively, courteous; but just below the surface lurked a ruthless business mind that would stop at nothing for success. A decade earlier Rushden had admired Roland for the way he'd run off with Catarina, evading her powerful father. Then he'd been somewhat of a rebel, like Rushden himself. Now he was a pillar of respectability, chairman of a public company, a man who flaunted his wealth by inviting critics to lunch in a restaurant he'd once bought on a whim.

'It appears to me that you exert some considerable influence yourself, Mr Rushden.'

'Thank you.' Rushden's face brightened for an instant. 'But not as much as you. A vulture's—'

'I'm not particularly fond of that nickname.'

Rushden ignored the interruption. 'A vulture's so easily recognizable. Such a good source of copy.'

Roland sat back as a waiter placed a dish in front of him, remained silent until the waiter left. Then his expression hardened. 'A vulture could also prove to be a very expensive source of copy.'

Rushden's brown eyes sparkled at this. 'Finally – to the meat of the meeting! A threat! Can I assume that a libel action will follow? If so, I'll instruct *Probe's* counsel to be prepared.'

Roland began to eat, giving himself time to think. Had it been a mistake, reacting like this? Everyone had warned him against locking horns with *Probe*, but he'd be damned if he would. He had never backed off from a fight yet, and this magazine publisher who had found a comfortable niche pandering borderline stories wasn't going to change his ways unless he was forced to.

Roland didn't respond to the comment, decided to stay on more neutral territory – at least for now.

'Thank you for an excellent lunch,' Rushden said as they prepared to leave. 'Such a civilized way to waste half the day.'

'I'm glad you enjoyed it.' Roland knew he should end it there, but some perversity urged him on, forced him to show the *Probe* publisher just how powerful he was. 'I can be very civilized when I'm not annoyed. This vulture wouldn't harm a fly.'

'Probably not,' Rushden agreed as he shook Roland's hand. 'Too bad that I'm a masochist, though. I have this odd reaction to people who suggest they can hurt me. I always want to see if they can.'

Roland watched sourly as Rushden waved for a taxi. And he wondered how this lunchtime meeting would be covered in the next 'Rushes' column. He had little doubt that it would be covered. Instead of dissuading Rushden from further stories, Roland's meeting had merely whetted his appetite.

The following week Rushden sent Roland a note thanking him for lunch, including a complimentary copy of the latest issue. Roland turned to the 'Rushes' column. 'Fine Fare at The Vulture's Nest,' read the headline, and Roland knew he had made an enemy – an enemy who would undoubtedly make him as notorious as some of the other personalities he had chosen to ridicule.

CHAPTER FOUR

Daniel Rushden and *Probe* dogged Roland's steps during the next three years as he set about consolidating and then expanding Adler's stores. Roland knew he was exaggerating the situation out of all proportion, but it seemed to him that barely an issue of *Probe* passed without some mention of 'the Vulture.' When he sold forty percent of the electrical shops to raise capital to acquire a floundering department store in Birmingham, Rushden wrote that the Vulture had found the carcass in the Midlands quite to his taste. When Katherine turned twelve and won the junior class of a show-jumping championship, Rushden put together a speculative story stating that Roland's entire family was driven to succeed, no matter what the cost. He even suggested that this passion for winning was fostered by the lack of a conventional family structure. His reasearch had brought to his attention the two children Roland had with Janet Taylor – a certain indication, in Rushden's reasoning, that Roland was a man who felt he was unbridled by the rules of society.

Gradually, as Roland had feared, he was being transformed into a public figure. Despite the fact that his fame was only among readers of *Probe,* it was a recognition he'd never cared to have. Publicity always reminded him of his time with Catarina, the way the press had jumped on the story with no regard for the feelings of those involved, simply to boost their circulation through sensationalism. He suspected Rushden was doing it for a similar reason – creating a dubious fame for Roland, if only to benefit from it himself.

Roland's increasingly frequent visits with Michael Adler and Christopher Mellish to gambling clubs in the West End of London titillated Rushden's interest even more. Such clubs smelled of decadence, the successors to the gambling houses of Victorian England where fortunes – and even daughters – were staked on the turn of a card. And when, in the company of Mellish and Michael Adler, Roland won a backgammon tournament in Monte Carlo in the summer of 1962, Rushden launched a new section to honor the event – the Vulture Chronicles, the story of a flamboyant playboy intent on proving that he is not the fortune hunter (Roland recognized Menendez's words . . . Rushden must have checked back carefully) he was once accused of being.

After the first appearance of the Vulture Chronicles, Roland seriously considered a libel action. Then he dismissed the idea in favor of retaliating the way he knew best – by trying to take over *Probe* and then put it out of business. After making discreet inquiries into Rushden's personal life – a wife, three children, a large mortgage and the cost of operating the magazine – he made an offer through an intermediary which he felt the journalist would be unable to reject. Everyone else had a price, so why not Daniel Rushden?

At best, the idea was ill-conceived; at worst, it was the most pitiful scheme Roland ever had, because it was a decision based not on sound financial judgment but on personal anger. Not only did Rushden turn down the offer, he managed to learn on whose behalf the intermediary was acting. The next issue of *Probe* contained a damning indictment of Roland as a powerful businessman who thought his money could silence all critics. And there was nothing Roland could do – no action he could take – in his own defense. He had handed Rushden the sword and bared his own neck.

Roland was finally given a respite from the attacks in 1963 when the Christine Keeler affair broke. Rushden jumped on it – a prostitute sharing her favors with the British War Minister *and* a Soviet spy – and Roland hoped that the Vulture would finally be allowed to slip away into the night. He needed the break not only from the attacks, but from the anger they stirred in him at his inability to fight back. At the time he was negotiating to buy a small chain of department stores in France. Even if DeGaulle had refused Britain's entry into the Common Market, that didn't stop Roland and Michael Adler from trying to expand across the English Channel. But, as negotiations reached the final stage, Roland's move was delayed by the death of Helen Adler – Michael's mother and Albert's wife – who died suddenly from a heart attack.

Roland put all business affairs on the back burner as funeral arrangements were made. He did everything he could to help Michael . . . everything short of visiting his father's house. Meeting Albert would come soon enough at the funeral. Roland remembered too well what Albert had told Michael following the takeover of Adler's . . . nor could he forget the last time he had seen Albert at a funeral and the confrontation that nearly turned into an all-out brawl. He didn't relish meeting his former adversary again under such similar circumstances. Yet out of his respect and friendship for Michael he felt he should attend the funeral.

Standing in the chapel at Edmonton, he felt there was something disconcertingly familiar about the day as he looked over the mass of people there. Simon wasn't with him this time, nor had Roland driven himself; he had been chauffeured from the Regent Street store by Alf Goldstein, who now waited outside. But the sight of Albert with Michael at his side couldn't help but remind him of Monty Adler's funeral. Later that day he'd found Catarina waiting in his office with the news that she was pregnant.

Roland made the same slow journey out to the burial

plot, only this time there were two people with their hands on the cart that carried the coffin – Albert and Michael. He waited at the rear of the crowd while the coffin was lowered, prayers were said and the first spadefuls of earth were shoveled. It wasn't until after they returned to the chapel that Roland approached Albert, joining the line of friends and family who waited to offer their condolences. Roland reached Michael first, shook his hand, asked if there was anything else he could do. Michael managed a wan smile and shook his head. Then Roland stood in front of Albert, his hand offered. Albert looked up, and for the first time Roland noticed he was wearing glasses. Behind them, the eyes were red-rimmed, glazed. In recognizing Roland the eyes sharpened and suddenly Roland tensed; just as quickly they became dull again.

'I'm sorry about your wife.' Roland noticed that Michael was watching closely, as if ready to act should there be another scene.

Very slowly, Albert extended his hand, grasped Roland's. 'Thank you. Thank you for coming. I appreciate it.' The eyes sharpened again, bored into Roland with an intensity he found uncomfortable. Roland understood the sudden fire, even if it was obvious that Michael did not. Michael looked from one man to the other, but Roland wasn't about to answer the questioning look in his eyes.

'Thank you,' Albert repeated, before dropping Roland's hand and turning to the next person in line. Roland nodded to Michael and walked out of the chapel to where Goldstein waited.

'Did he say two civil words to you?' Goldstein asked as they drove away from the cemetery.

'Yes, he thanked me for coming. Said he appreciated it.'

Goldstein whistled in shock. 'Must be getting a bit soft in his old age.'

'I doubt it,' was all Roland said before he fell silent for the rest of the journey back to Regent Street.

That evening he roamed around his apartment unable to settle down. It seemed so large and empty now, with Elsie Partridge having returned to Scotland and Katherine living with Janet in the four-bedroom house he'd bought for them in St. John's Wood, a mile away. Normally the emptiness didn't bother him; he didn't spend enough time alone there for it to have any effect. Tonight, though, after seeing Michael and his father at the cemetery, he wanted company.

He left the apartment and caught a taxi to St John's Wood. He stood in front of the large house for a minute, wondering whether he should have telephoned first. He normally visited Janet and the children on the weekends; maybe this surprise call wasn't such a wonderful idea after all. But the downstairs lights were on, and their brightness lured him toward the front door.

Janet opened it and her face fell in shock. 'Roland . . . what . . . ?'

'I thought I'd drop by. Nothing to do.'

'For God's sake, why didn't you phone first?'

Standing in the hall behind Janet, half in and half out of the living room, was a tall man with thinning brown hair and a full, friendly face. Roland felt his skin begin to burn. 'Maybe I'd better leave.'

'Maybe you'd better come in now. At least you can say hello.' She tugged him by the arm and introduced him to the man, who came forward hesitantly. Though he was standing in a house he had bought, in the company of a woman who had given him two children and mothered a third as if she were her own, Roland felt like a complete stranger.

'Is Kathy asleep?' he managed to ask, trying to regain his composure.

'I don't think so,' Janet replied. 'Go up and take a look. Just don't wake Richard and Carol.'

Roland went up the stairs quietly. First he peeked into the rooms of Carol and Richard; they were both asleep and he kissed them fondly. Then he knocked on the door of Katherine's room, opened it. She was lying in bed, reading by the light on her bedside table while a small radio softly played a Beatles song.

'Hello . . .' She opened her arms to embrace her father. 'I thought I heard your voice. What are you doing here in the middle of the week?'

'Just dropped by on the off-chance of getting a hug and kiss from you.'

Katherine kissed him on the cheek. 'Did you meet Uncle Ralph?'

'Who?' then he remembered the man Janet had introduced. Ralph . . . Ralph Morrison. 'I saw him downstairs.'

'Did you like him? Janet's been seeing him for almost two months now.'

Two months, and she hadn't mentioned a word. Or maybe she had, and Roland – wrapped up in the French deal – had let it slip completely by. 'Kathy, it doesn't matter whether I like him, do *you* like him?'

'He's all right, I suppose.'

'What does he do?'

'Sells insurance, I think. Or something boring like that. He's not anything like you.'

Roland laughed delightedly. His own sentiments exactly, and he was so pleased that his daughter shared them with him. Insurance was respectable enough, no doubt. Profitable, too. But hardly the same as owning your own business.

'How do you get on with him?' Ever since he had broken up with Janet he'd never spoken about her men friends with Katherine. When they saw each other on weekends or on special occasions such as birthdays, or when she had won the show-jumping trophy, they spoke only about themselves.

'All right. He buys me lots of presents' – she indicated a row of costumed dolls on the dressing table – 'as if he thinks being friendly with me is very important. See that Household Cavalry officer? He brought me that tonight.'

'Being friendly with you *is* very important.'

'I just wish he wouldn't keep calling me Kathy,' Katherine complained. 'That's your name for me.'

Roland reached out and hugged her. Only he was allowed to call her Kathy; everyone else had to abide by the more formal 'Katherine.' He was relieved to be assured that no matter what else happened, he would always be the number one man in his older daughter's life.

When he went back downstairs, Janet and Ralph Morrison were sitting in the living room, listening to a Chopin recital on the radio. 'Join us for a cup of tea?' Janet asked.

'No thanks, I'd better be going.'

'I'll see you out.'

Roland noticed the look of relief that his refusal brought to Ralph Morrison's face, and he felt flattered. The man was obviously nervous about filling his shoes.

'Kathy says you've been seeing Ralph for a couple of months,' Roland said to Janet as he stood on the doorstep. 'Is anything going to come of it?'

'He's thinking about asking me to marry him.'

'How do you know?' Roland was amazed by the statement; did women really possess such uncanny intuition?

'He's started looking at houses this weekend.'

'What's wrong with this one?' Roland felt offended that anyone would even consider moving them somewhere else, to a place he hadn't approved of and paid for.

'Roland, Ralph and I have talked about you a lot, what you and I meant to each other, the children, the way you still keep in touch. He's a little bit scared of being permanently in your shadow. You have that effect on people, you tend to overwhelm them.'

'When he gets around to asking you, what will your answer be?'

'I'll consider it.'

382

'Does Ralph break his life into tidy little compartments?'

Janet shook her head. 'No. Basically he's a very simple man.' She followed the words with a quick grin. 'Which makes one hell of a change from you.'

'No matter what you decide to do, *I* still want to look after the well-being of my children. That's my responsibility and my privilege.'

'You will. We've talked about that as well. Ralph's comfortable with the children – he likes kids – and he understands the situation. You know, Richard and Carol being ours, Katherine being Catarina's but living with me.'

'And I want to see the house he's thinking of buying—'

'Shut up, Roland.' She placed a finger against his lips. 'Give him room to breathe. Give us all room to breathe. Good night.' She removed her finger, gave him the most fleeting of kisses and closed the door softly. Roland walked out to the street and turned back to gaze at the house. A twinge of envy coursed through him as he pictured two people secure in each other's company. Sharing. He began to feel sorry for himself until he remembered this was the way he had wanted it. He could have been in there with Janet now, with the children, but he had chosen to follow another course.

He looked at his watch. It wasn't even ten o'clock yet. He had no desire to return to Regent's Park, to sit alone in the apartment. He wanted company, needed it. There were other people he could call on, and he began to look for a cab. He spotted a telephone booth before he found a cab and dialed Sally's number. He would be welcome there. She and Christopher Mellish were past the stage of wanting to spend a romantic evening alone; in fact they would probably welcome company. Mellish answered, delighted that Roland had called. Sally was away in Paris, covering the new fashions for the magazine and wouldn't be back until the following day.

'How about I meet you at Kendall's in half an hour, Roland? I probably would have drifted over there anyway.'

'Sounds good to me.' Roland stepped out of the booth and searched for a taxi again. He finally spotted one and gave the driver directions to the casino.

Of all the clubs in the West End, Kendall's was Roland's favorite. Introduced to it by Mellish, Roland found the club – which took up the lower two floors of a massive Regency house on Mount Street – to be a throwback to an earlier, more elegant age. Ornate chandeliers hung gracefully from high vaulted ceilings. Luxurious carpets covered the floors. Even the voices of the croupiers – the hum of conversation around the tables – were muted, as if the people were attending a service instead of gambling. Often, Roland went just to sit and watch, finding a kind of peace within the club – the gentility of it soothed his nerves, allowed him time to think. And when he played, that same low-key decorum distilled his senses, made planning a pleasure instead of a chore.

He sat for a short time, watching players at a roulette table. As Simon had once claimed to judge people by the way they played backgammon, so Roland was able to form opinions by the way the club members gambled. There were stock types to be found at every table: the nervous ones, those whose fortunes were reflected in their faces; the American visitors whom the club welcomed only for their money, always so emotional about their luck; and then those who carried on expressionless as they either won or lost and walked away without batting an eye. Roland placed himself in the last category; when taking a risk, either on a table or on a company, he never let his thoughts show.

It was a page out of Simon's book – taken to extreme proportions – but Roland thought that if he could, he would bring all of his prospective management candidates to Kendall's, give them a handful of chips and assess their potential from the way they handled themselves at the tables. Roland liked the way Michael played – almost like himself, with a firm belief in the power of his own luck. He played with confidence and always set himself a limit. When he began to lose he quit. And if he were winning, he ran the streak right through until he sensed his luck had changed. Christopher Mellish, though, was another matter entirely. He played haphazardly, as if winning or losing was of little importance. Admittedly, he had the money to lose – as did Roland and Michael – but he often played as though he were simply passing the time before moving on to more pressing matters. Roland liked Mellish as a friend – but he certainly wouldn't want him working in the Eagles Group.

'Hello, old man, thinking about playing, or just playing at thinking?'

Roland looked up to see Mellish standing over him. 'Waiting for you, actually. What do you fancy – the big tables or just a private bout?'

'Private bout sounds good. Give me a chance to test the reflexes.' While Roland set out a backgammon board, Mellish asked about Helen Adler's funeral. 'Go down well, did it?'

Roland winced. 'Save those jokes for Sally, will you?'

'If I told her jokes like that, she'd kick me out of the house.'

'Good girl. I always did think she had sense.'

'Must put the kibosh on your Paris business, though. Michael was supposed to be going with you, wasn't he?'

'I'll have to do without him for a week. I'll probably go the day after tomorrow. Nothing I can't handle myself.'

They talked and played for a couple of hours, during which time Roland won a little more than three hundred pounds. 'Have to raise my cloth prices again, make up for this embarrassment,' Mellish muttered as he wrote out a check.

'How about having a horse that wins occasionally? The

385

fastest piece of horseflesh you ever had was Buttercup, that pony you gave to Katherine six years ago.'

'And Katherine's probably a better jockey than most of the cripples who ride for my stable,' Mellish retorted.

On the way out of the club they passed a roulette table. Roland took ten pounds from his pocket and placed it on evens. Eleven came up and he shrugged; it wasn't his money anyway, it was Mellish's.

'Run you back to Regent's Park?'

'Please.'

'You ought to try to get over this fear of driving, old man. From everything I've heard, what happened to Catarina wasn't your fault.'

'It's been thirteen years since I sat behind the wheel of a car. The way traffic's getting these days I don't think I'd have the nerve to try it again.' Roland followed Mellish to the new Aston Martin he owned; the three hundred pounds he'd lost would hardly affect his lifestyle.

'I see your pal Rushden's giving you a break these days,' Mellish said as they sped through the dark streets toward Regent's Park.

'God bless Christine Keeler and Mandy Rice-Davies. Rushden's got his plate full picking up all the little bits the other papers won't print.'

Mellish burst out laughing. 'Maybe he'll forget all about you, just as long as you keep your head out of sight.'

'I try to.'

'Oh, no, not you. You attract publicity like honey attracts bees. You're built that way.'

And though Roland didn't like to admit it, he knew it was true.

Roland stayed up until four o'clock in the morning, reading, thinking about the funeral – the way Albert had thanked him for attending – the meeting with Janet's boyfriend, and, finally, the work he had to complete in

Paris. He would go the next day. Check that Michael was all right, then make arrangements to fly to Paris and close the deal. The sooner he got those French stores operating as part of the Eagles Group, the more he'd like it.

Undressing for bed he turned out his jacket pockets and came across the check Mellish had given him, crumpled up, forgotten. As he straightened it out, he noticed something he hadn't seen before. Cheeky bugger had forgotten to sign it. Grinning, Roland lifted the bedside telephone and dialed Mellish's number. Too bad if he woke him up; an unsigned check for more than three hundred pounds was damned good reason.

The telephone rang three times and then, to Roland's surprise, Sally answered. 'Sally . . .? What are you doing home?'

'I got in a couple of hours ago, didn't want to bother waiting until morning. Why are you calling at this ungodly hour?'

'I wanted to speak to Christopher. We went to Kendall's before. He gave me a check for three hundred pounds and forgot to sign it.'

'He's not here.'

'What? He dropped me off at home—'

'When?'

'Half an hour ago.' The lie slipped out in a flash. Two hours was more like it.

'He should be home by now then.'

'Maybe he went back to the club – tried to recoup the money he didn't pay me.'

'Maybe. I'll get him to call you when he gets in.'

'Don't bother. Just tell him to send me another check, signed this time.' Roland hung up quickly, with the disconcerting feeling that not only had he put his foot in it, but he had lied to Sally as well.

The group of French department stores that Roland was acquiring was named Girard et Fils. Although the

387

company had been forced to close its Paris store on the Boulevard Haussman, it still had branches open in Lille, Nantes and Orleans. The buying offices, at least, were still in Paris, and Roland could still use the prestigious address.

Roland had learned about the store's difficulties through a habit which he'd picked up in the past couple of years – looking through not only the London Stock Exchange but the European ones to see if there was anything he could use. At one time Britain had seemed to him as vast and limitless as the solar system itself; now, having tasted success and power in his own backyard, he yearned for an international arena. First Europe and then, if it weren't beyond his scope, the United States. The trip Roland had taken to America following Catarina's death had remained an indelible memory. Almost untouched by the wars that had ravaged Europe, it was a country of consumers – real consumers with money to spend. Soon, he knew, European retailers with imagination to match his own would be heading west in droves to invest in America. But before he joined them he wanted as secure a base as possible in Europe.

Roland's attention to the European stock markets had also allowed him to follow the fortunes of Kassler Industries. The German group was expanding at a rate Roland would have been happy to follow, acquiring stores in Belgium and Holland. Roland had little doubt that Kassler would be one of the first retailers to take the plunge across the Atlantic – just as he had little doubt their paths would cross again.

Late the next day Roland finished putting the final touches on the Girard deal. The papers were signed, and he was in the mood to celebrate. Not knowing much about Paris and knowing even less about the language, he decided to find a knowledgeable taxi driver to help him out.

'Take me to the finest restaurant in Paris,' he instructed

a taxi driver. 'Not the Tour d'Argent, though.' He had lunched there that very day with the bankers who'd helped close the deal.

The Frenchman gave Roland a long stare, taking in the well-cut suit, the silk tie, the arrogance in the clear blue eyes. 'Does *monsieur* wish to go to Le Grand Vefour?'

'Where's that?' Roland felt ridiculous having to ask.

'Rue Beaujolais in the first *arrondissement*. The best.'

'We'll go there.'

'Perhaps a reservation would be advisable, *monsieur*.'

Roland instructed the driver to stop at a telephone and make the reservation for him. There were no tables for at least two hours, so Roland told the driver to take him on a sightseeing tour of the city. Halfway through he had him stop at a souvenir shop where he bought modelss of the eiffel tower for richard and carol, and for katherine a pennant from longchamps; any gift for his oldr daughter had to be somehow associated with horses.

Roland eventually arrived at Le Grand Vefour at ten-fifteen, car-weary and ravenously hungry, ready to throttle the taxi driver if the restaurant failed to live up to his recommendation. Entering the eighteenth-century ambience set his mind at rest immediately. A restaurant owner himself — even if only for sentimental reasons — Roland could always appreciate well-prepared food, and the atmosphere of Le Grand Vefour assured him he was in for a treat. As he was shown to his table for one he took in the room, identifying familiar faces. He thought he spotted Charles Aznavour and Alain Delon; later he would ask the waiter to get their autographs for Katherine.

But he barely had time to sit down, appreciate the menu and extensive wine list, before he felt a hand drop gently onto his shoulder. 'Roland? It is Roland, isn't it? What on earth are you doing here?'

He turned around in his chair and looked up into a pair of deep brown eyes, dark hair that fell softly onto delicate shoulders. 'God almighty! Sharon! What are you—'

'I asked first.'

Roland was speechless, so overcome by the coincidence of seeing Sharon. She looked so wonderful, vibrant, alive. Paris must have worked wonders, cleansed her spirit of the ordeal she'd been through. 'I just bought some stores. Now I'm trying to celebrate the acquisition, but I've got no one to celebrate with.'

'Why not join us?' She indicated a table on the far side of the restaurant, and Roland saw Miriam sitting with her French husband, a slim, dark man.

'What's your brother-in-law's name?' As he asked the question he noticed the familiar gold pendant Sharon wore around her neck.

'Claude . . . Claude Lazarus. Will you eat with us? We're just starting.'

'I'd be delighted. What a wonderful surprise.' He got up from the table, followed Sharon over to her sister and brother-in-law. He barely remembered Claude from the last time he'd seen him at Sharon's wedding.

'Are you still playing backgammon with our father?' Miriam asked.

'I regret to say that I rarely see your father these days. Not since we split up.' Roland's meetings with Simon had grown fewer and fewer, as if the business they had shared had been their only true link. Roland knew the lapse was his own fault and he regretted it, but it seemed he had been so busy these past years . . . All of his relationships had suffered, except those with people whose lives were as uncluttered as his was, like Michael, Sally and Mellish. 'Our paths only seem to cross when I need unofficial legal advice.'

'Oh, that's a shame. You two were so close at one time.'

'I see you've been busy over here,' Claude said. Roland remembered he was a banker, just like his father-in-law;

Simon must have approved wholeheartedly of his marriage to Miriam. 'The English invasion, the press calls it.'

'I feel flattered.'

All through dinner, Sharon and Miriam peppered Roland with questions about London. He did his best to answer, and at the same time respond to Claude's business queries. When the check came, Roland reached for it before Claude could make a move. 'I told you, I'm celebrating. Before I was by myself – luckily I met you three and we made it into a party.' He stood up and helped Sharon from her chair. 'Where do you live?'

'Off Rue La Fayette. I have a small apartment close to Miriam and Claude.'

'May I see you home?'

'I'd like that very much. It would seem a shame to bump into you so unexpectedly after all this time and then have to say goodbye so soon.'

They said goodnight to Miriam and Claude, then Roland helped Sharon into a taxi. 'That pendant around your neck—'

'You gave it to me on my sixteenth birthday. Remember?'

'Of course I remember. How often do you wear it?'

'All the time. Does it bother you?' she asked, toying with the pendant, running her fingers along the slim chain as she recalled the day which had turned into such a tragedy for Roland.

'No. It just reminds me of when you were sixteen,' he lied.

'That was a long time ago. Remember what I asked you that day?'

'No.' Another lie. He remembered everything that had happened that day, but he wanted to hear it from Sharon.

She clutched his arm. 'I asked you whether you couldn't have waited a couple of years if you were so keen on marrying an eighteen-year-old girl.'

391

'And what answer did I give?' He still couldn't get over the way she looked, so fresh and young.

'You said my father wouldn't have approved of you, and I asked what difference that would have made. Catarina's father hated you. My God, Roland! It's been a lifetime . . . an absolute lifetime.'

They reached Sharon's building and she led the way up to an apartment on the second floor. A long hallway, with doors running from it to the bedroom and bathroom, led into a spacious living room. Roland sat down on a couch, content to watch as Sharon got cups and saucers, made coffee. 'Do you ever hear from Graham?' he asked.

'Graham who?' She made a face. 'No, thank God. Good riddance to bad rubbish, I say.'

'That wasn't what you were saying at the time.'

'I know. When you convince yourself you're in love, your powers of reasoning really get messed up, don't they?'

'I suppose so.'

She sat down next to him. 'It was your idea, wasn't it? Getting Daddy to cut Graham off.'

Roland debated how to answer. Finally he decided on the truth. 'Yes. I didn't see any other way of getting rid of him. Did you know at the time?'

'I guessed. I knew Daddy was going to ask you. You know, because of the way I felt about you before . . .'

'Before you met Graham. Your father wanted me to step in, but I knew it wasn't my place.'

'To whisper words of advice in my ear?' She laughed and drew even closer to Roland. He felt a familiar warmth steal over him. Sharon still had that effect, just like the day he had taken her for a ride in the Jaguar, whipping along Wilton Crescent to see what the Menendez family was up to. That day – it was Christmas – her closeness had embarrassed him. How old had she been? Fifteen? Now, it was a totally different situation. He was alone in a strange city. Even more lonely after seeing Janet and his children in a house with another man. 'Why didn't you?' Sharon asked. 'I'd have listened to you.'

'I was worried that you might rebound onto me.'

'I still might.' She gave him a conspiratorial smile, a slow half-wink. 'How are your children?'

'Fine. Katherine gets bigger and more beautiful each time I see her, and the others get more mischievous.'

'Do you ever feel favoritism? You know – do you look on Katherine differently than you do Richard or Carol?'

Roland had often asked himself the same question. 'I suppose I do.'

'Because she's Catarina's daughter?'

'That's part of it. And I know her better than I know Richard and Carol. Katherine's thirteen, the others are still infants. Besides, Katherine lived with me until Janet and I split up. Richard and Carol have never lived with me. They're my children, but it's almost as if they're niece and nephew. Does that make any sense?' Roland wasn't certain it made much sense to him; all three were his, yet he always felt closer, more attached to Katherine.

'I still remember when she was my bridesmaid,' Sharon mused. 'We'd spent a fortune on my dress and every eye in the synagogue was on her. I could have strangled her. The truth is' – her voice turned cold and brittle – 'I'd have been a lot better off if someone had strangled Graham that day.'

'How much did he cost your father in the end?'

'Who knows exactly? The shops, other money he'd given him. He cost me plenty as well. Emotionally. But I guess that was my fault as much as anyone else's. It was a long time before I could look at myself in the mirror, remembering how I'd turned against my own parents. And all because I'd let myself get wound around that leech's finger.'

'He's still riding high.'

'I know. I read about him in the English newspapers I buy over here. Only the *Mercury* never mentions him. He could get a knighthood and marry into the Royal Family on the same day and the *Mercury* still wouldn't mention it.'

'That's a publisher exerting editorial privilege.' Roland finished the coffee and leaned back on the couch. 'Graham did precisely what Ambassador Menendez feared I would do.'

Sharon looked shocked at the comparison. 'Don't you ever put yourself into the same category as Graham. He was a louse, an out-and-out money grabber. I was available, and I suppose I was susceptible to his charm. He had that, all right, could turn it on and off like a switch. You *had* money. Graham had nothing and wanted to be supported . . . while he played around.'

Roland glanced at the clock on the mantelpiece. It showed twelve-thirty and he knew he should be getting back to his hotel. He was booked on a flight at nine the next morning and didn't want to miss it. Next to the clock he noticed a backgammon game. He got up and set the board on a table. 'Do you still play, or is this just for show?'

'I still play sometimes. But you said—'

'I said I rarely saw your father. I play, though. Championship level these days. For pocket money.'

'You always were a gambler.' As she picked up a set of dice, her hand touched Roland's in the center of the board. 'How often will you be coming over to Paris, now that you have business here?'

'I hadn't really thought about it.' He let his hand rest on the board, unwilling to move it from Sharon's. Unwilling now to even play . . . or return to the hotel.

'I do hope you'll make it a regular trip, Roland. You're the only familiar sight I really miss from home. Other than my parents, of course.'

'Why don't you go back then?'

'Too embarrassed to, I suppose.'

'Because of Graham? Don't be silly.' He lifted her hand

394

to his lips, kissed it gently. The hell with the hotel and the flight to London. He could always make up for missing it by working late. He had little to do in England anyway, except work.

Sharon shared a taxi with Roland the next morning, first to the Meurice Hotel to settle his bill and get his luggage, then to the airport to catch the London plane. He had missed the nine o'clock flight and had to make do with a ten-thirty, which would mean he wouldn't get into the office on Regent Street before one o'clock.

'When are you coming back?' Sharon asked as she waited with Roland in the departure lounge; on the table in front of them were coffee and croissants.

'How does next week sound?' He hadn't planned to, but he was certain he could rearrange his schedule. Paris was no longer such a strange city. He had business here. And now Sharon . . . 'Ever hear of *kismet*?'

'I was thinking the very same thing.' She lifted Roland's hand from the coffee cup and held it to her lips. 'It was fated to happen, Roland . . . fated that you and I should bump into each other in Le Grand Vefour. Fated from the very first moment we met.'

Comparisons flashed through Roland's mind as he felt his hand caressed by Sharon's lips. Janet's no-nonsense approach to their relationship, almost cynical, he now decided, not wanting marriage because she wasn't one hundred and ten percent certain it would last. Now here was Sharon, a throwback to an earlier, more romantic time, with an ardor that had made him lose his head, surrender his senses completely. That last night in her apartment . . . Roland's brain reeled as he recaptured the slow, sensuous embraces, lifting her up, carrying her to the bedroom. Drifting off to sleep in each other's arms, gentle breathing set against the hum of nighttime Paris. Paris – that was it. The entire city spread a blanket of romance – how could he not have been affected by its charms?

'Did you ever do something and just know it was right, Roland? Just from a feeling, down here?' She took his hand and pressed it against her stomach. 'It's what the Americans call a gut feeling – your own body telling you that something's right.'

He could feel her stomach trembling as he touched it, and he marveled at how she had summed up his own feelings as well. Lying in bed that morning, awake while Sharon continued to slumber, he had studied her face, unable to believe what had come over him . . . And when she'd woken, her brown eyes like two wide, clear pools, he'd recognized something he'd once seen in Catarina – but somehow never in Janet – a warmth, a glow of adoration. A love that was all-powerful, totally irresistible. Sharon knew it was right, and because of that, Roland, also, knew it was right.

'Will you see my father when you return to London?'

'I hadn't planned to. Why?'

'About us.'

Roland considered the question carefully. He had no reason to see Simon, and he certainly didn't intend to drop by his office just to say that he'd bumped into Sharon in Paris and had slept with her. Had made the sweetest love with her that he'd experienced since Catarina. 'I'm not certain it would be a very good idea right now.'

'Perhaps you're right.' Her eyes fastened on the gold watch that barely showed beneath the cuff of Roland's shirt. 'Is that the watch Catarina gave you? With the names of the three horses?'

'Boring Dora, Fat Fanny and Jealous Nat.' He took off the watch and showed Sharon the back. 'The most unlikely trio of horses ever to win a tote treble.'

'Why do you still wear it?'

He was about to say because it was a constant reminder of Catarina which he treasured, but something made him stop. 'Because it keeps excellent time.'

'So do a thousand other watches. I will buy you a Longines for your birthday. It's soon, isn't it?'

'A couple of weeks.'

The announcement was made for the London flight. Roland gulped down what was left of his coffee, picked up his briefcase and, arm in arm with Sharon, walked toward the gate. 'Call me when you get home,' she said.

'I will. The minute I get to the office. And tell Miriam and Claude that I'll see them again next week.'

'No,' Sharon replied firmly. 'I don't want to share you. I want you for myself.' She clung to him, pressed her lips against his own. Finally, and regretfully, he had to break free. He gave her a last kiss and walked toward passport control. As he passed through and looked back, Sharon was still watching and waving. He waved back and joined the line for the London flight.

Michael Adler returned to work after the customary week of mourning for his mother, just in time to be told by Roland that he was in charge of the Adler's operation. Roland was returning to Paris for further meetings with the French bank which had financed the acquisition of Girard et Fils. When Michael asked Roland if he would be staying at the Meurice, Roland just smiled, then gave him the number for the apartment off the Rue La Fayette.

'Someone you met?' Michael asked.

'Someone I met. How's your father getting along?'

'He's a bit lost right now without my mother. Funny thing is, he's almost like my grandfather.'

Roland pictured Monty Adler and Albert together in the office, one thin and reedy, the other white-haired, short and dynamic. He failed to see any similarity between the two men.

'With my mother gone he's just left to wander around the house by himself. He doesn't seem to have any other interests.'

'I see.' Despite any dislike he may have held for Albert,

Roland felt pity for the man. He could never take the bull by the horns and make his mark on the company again. 'What's he going to do?'

Michael shrugged. 'Get a housekeeper and find something to take up his time, I suppose. There's only so much I can do for him. I know the wound's still fresh, but I talked to him about joining one of these clubs. You know the kind of thing, for widows, widowers. Maybe he'll find someone else, but I doubt it. Not the best way of life, is it? I'm worried about him. His sight's going—'

'I noticed he was wearing glasses at the funeral.'

'Been wearing them for a year or so now, not that they help very much. And something seems to be bothering him. He becomes very quiet and pensive. No, depressed is a better word for it. Even when my mother was alive he had these bouts. She couldn't get through to him. He'd just sit there, all alone, staring into space as if he could see something that we couldn't. Acts a bit strangely sometimes, like with you at the funeral. I still can't figure out that look he gave you.'

'What look?' Roland remembered the intense gaze, the firm grip of Albert's hand.

'Maybe it was just my imagination – I've got so used to him acting strangely.' Michael shook his head, dismissing the thought. 'When will you be back from Paris?'

'A couple of days. I might stretch it into the weekend, though, and come back on Monday.' That would mean he'd miss seeing his children this weekend, but he knew they wouldn't mind this one time.

'You lucky devil.' Michael grinned and punched Roland playfully on the shoulder. 'This mademoiselle must be something really special.'

Roland just smiled back.

CHAPTER FIVE

During the next four months, Roland managed to find an excuse to spend at least one night a week in the French capital. With the exception of that first time, Roland found weekend trips to Paris impossible. That was his only time to be with his children, and the only way around the situation would be to take them with him. That, of course, was out of the question. Richard and Carol were still too young, and Katherine, as mature as she might be at thirteen, couldn't be relied on to keep such an important secret . . . which was the way Roland wanted his relationship with Sharon, at least for the moment. Even Miriam and Claude Lazarus were unaware of Sharon's trysts with Roland.

For his thirty-ninth birday, Sharon gave him a gold Longines watch, as promised. He wore it whenever he traveled to Paris, but when he returned to London he always replaced it with what he called his three-horse watch which Catarina had given him. And when close friends remarked on the change that had come over him – the ten pounds he'd gained, the more contented demeanor – Roland simply smiled. Only Michael Adler knew the reason for the change, but he had no idea who the woman was.

In the early part of 1964, Roland attended Janet's wedding to Ralph Morrison. He even offered to give away the bride, since both of her parents were dead. Janet took him up on it, and Roland walked her down the aisle of the Presbyterian church in Hampstead where Morrison attended regularly. Understanding the position Roland had in Janet's life, Morrison spoke at length with him before the wedding. He and Janet had decided to continue living in the house Roland had bought in St John's Wood, but Morrison wanted it understood that he alone would be responsible for supporting the family. Roland agreed . . . in part. If Morrison felt duty-bound to support Richard and Carol, Roland wouldn't stand in his way; they were Janet's children as much as his own. But Roland drew the line where Katherine was concerned. She lived with Janet only so she would have a semblance of normal family life. And though she would remain a member of the family – subject to the same rules as the other children – Roland wouldn't allow her to be supported by Morrison. That was Roland's responsibility, his privilege alone.

At about the same time as the wedding, Roland decided to move from the Regent's Park apartment he'd lived in for fourteen years. With all the memories the apartment held for him, moving would be a dramatic wrench, but he felt it was time . . . Since he'd been a child growing up in Margate, he'd never lived in a house with a garden, a staircase leading up to bedrooms instead of having everything on one level. He also felt ready to leave the bustle of central London, wanting to be somewhere more convenient to the airport for the regular trips to Paris.

After much searching, Roland settled on Stanmore, a small but affluent northwest London suburb which still prided itself – snobbishly, so Roland thought – on being a village. In truth, it was little more, a compact shopping area where even the big names hadn't yet managed to penetrate, then a long hill leading up to Stanmore Common. Roland chose a sprawling, old-fashioned five-bedroom house located opposite the common at the very top of the hill. Soon after, he hired a firm of builders to gut the house from the inside out and renovate it completely.

Even with the builders working around the clock seven days a week, the renovation process took two months, during which Roland maintained his regular routine of weekly trips to Paris to be with Sharon. Each time he returned to London, though, he had Alf Goldstein drive him back to Regent Street through Stanmore so he could view the progress. He was becoming impatient to move in, the same way he felt about any project once it was started. He hated hanging around, especially this time because he intended to bring Sharon to London, marry her and raise another family – one that wouldn't be destroyed by a freak accident or by the unwillingness of a woman to compromise.

By mid-April Roland was ready to leave the Regent's Park apartment and begin living in Stanmore. While the movers cleared his furniture out, he wandered idly through the park, appreciating a rare warm spring day. He stopped beneath an oak tree and fingered the bark. The initials he had cut out fourteen years earlier were no longer visible. Bark had grown back to cover them, just as it hid the broken blade of the small penknife he had used. It was just as well; now was not the time to be hindered by awkward, tearful memories.

The first weekend in his new home, with the help of a butler and maid he'd hired, Roland threw a housewarming party. Seventy people crowded the house, sitting down to lunch in the huge living space that had been created by knocking down the wall that joined the living room to the dining room. Under the supervision of the butler, waitresses tripped down t the wine cellar that had been constructed in the basement. Roland barely had time to eat, wandering from one table to the next, mingling with his guests.

'When do you spring the big surprise?' Sally Roberts asked when he stopped by her table.

'Surprise? What surprise?'

'You always use parties to spring surprises, Roland Eagles. Why should today be any different?'

He looked from Sally to Christopher Mellish and wondered, as he often had, what happened that night they'd gone to Kendall's together and Roland found out hours later that Mellish hadn't yet arrived home. Mellish had never mentioned it, but Roland knew from his own subtle inquiries that he hadn't returned to the club. Was he, too playing the away game, as Roland had once asked Simon about Graham Sharp? If so, what did Roland owe Sally? Was it his business to tell her?

'You'll see the surprise later on,' he promised Sally before walking to the table where Simon Aronson sat with Nadine, Michael Adler, and an attractive brunette Michael had brought to the party.

'A beautiful house, Roland. May you enjoy many happy years in it,' Simon said.

'Thank you. I'm glad you and Nadine could be here today.'

'We've been looking forward to it ever since you sent out the invitation. We don't see enough of each other anymore.'

'I think that will be changing soon enough.' Roland glanced at Michael and saw a sharp glimmer of understanding in his friend's eyes.

As dessert was served, Roland walked past Alf Goldstein, who was sitting with his wife, and tapped him on the shoulder. Goldstein dabbed at his mouth with a linen napkin, stood up and excused himself.

'I just called the airport and the flight's due in twenty minutes.'

'I'll bring her right back.' Goldstein left the house and climbed into Roland's Bentley. Traffic was light and he reached the airport fifteen minutes after the estimated time of arrival of the Air France flight bringing Sharon from Paris. He hurried into the terminal, checked the arrivals board and stood by the gate, holding a small placard with her name printed on it.

Sharon came through ten minutes after, wearing the

full-length sable coat Roland had given her the previous week and carrying one small valise. Her eyes shone when she saw the sign with her name on it. Goldstein took the valise and led her out to the Bentley, trying to remember the last time he'd seen her. At her wedding, probably, and then only fleetingly. He hadn't been an invited guest, just a driver for Roland and Katherine.

'Are my parents at Roland's new house?' Sharon asked, as the Bentley glided through the town of Hayes, next to the airport.

'They were enjoying dessert when I last saw them. I had to leave mine in the middle,' Goldstein added with a trace of regret.

Sharon feigned sympathy. 'Oh, you poor man. But your sacrifice is for a worthy cause.' She thought Roland's idea for springing the news on her parents was wonderful. A new house . . . a party already in progress . . . and then the announcement of their marriage.

Goldstein laughed. 'I know, my waistline.' He patted the bulge which spread above his belt.

'Who else is there?'

'Pick a name. Everyone Roland knows, does that help you?'

'Janet?'

Goldstein nodded. 'With her husband and the three children.'

'How is Katherine?'

Goldstein's face softened. 'Beautiful.' Goldstein continued to carry an extra soft spot for Katherine; he supposed it was the same for everyone who'd shared with Roland the experiences of the romance with Catarina and all that had followed.

'Does she get on well with Janet's new husband?'

'*He'd* better get on well with *her*. Otherwise he'll have me to answer to . . . after Roland finishes with him.'

'Roland is fortunate to have such friends.'

They reached the house and Goldstein pulled the

Bentley into the circular driveway, grateful that no one else had turned up and stolen his place. Cars lined the hill; there wasn't a spare spot within fifty yards. God only knew what the neighbors thought. 'Stay here, Roland's orders,' he told Sharon. He got out of the car and walked quickly into the house to find Roland. 'Your delivery's waiting outside.'

'Thanks.' Roland went searching for Simon and Nadine. He found them talking to Sally and Mellish. 'May I interrupt, please? Simon, Nadine . . . there's something I'd like you to see.'

'Where?'

'Outside.'

'It *is* a surprise!' Sally called out. 'Can we all come?'

'Not now. Later.' He took Simon and Nadine by the arm, guided them to the front. 'In the Bentley.'

Simon started forward as the passenger door swung open. 'Sharon, I thought—'

'You thought I was still in Paris! I know!' She ran forward and hugged her parents. 'But you didn't know I had also been invited to this party, did you?' She stood in front of Roland, threw her arms around his neck and kissed him. 'Pleased to see me, darling?'

'What do you think?' Roland returned the kiss and embraced her warmly.

Simon turned to watch them, confused, fingers stroking the short beard that was now liberally sprinkled with gray. 'I don't understand. You haven't seen—'

Roland released Sharon and turned to face Simon and Nadine. 'We *have* been seeing each other, Simon. Very frequently. In Paris. And we've decided to get married.' Even as he said the words, Roland was struck by the novelty of the situation. Sharon was the first woman he'd ever considered marrying who was *not* pregnant. And Simon and Nadine would be the first parents who would bless the union. Or so he thought . . .

404

Simon's face collapsed. 'You can't be serious, of course.'

Roland's whole demeanor changed as he felt his anger spring to the surface. 'Of course we're serious! Why do you think I bought this house, Simon? For your grandchildren!'

'No, Roland.' Simon shook his head very slowly. 'This can never be. Never!'

'For God's sake, why not?' Roland held out his hand to stop Sharon from rushing to her father; he didn't want tearful recriminations right now, he wanted reason. 'What's wrong with it?'

'Come with me.' Simon began to walk toward the road, turned right and started down the long hill leading toward the village. Roland went after him, brain seething with confusion.

'Just what the hell is wrong with me marrying your daughter, Simon? Are you against it because of religious grounds?' After all these years was he destined to learn that Simon was a bigot too? Was he on the same despicable level as Roland's own father's family? He turned back and looked toward the house. Sharon and Nadine were in each other's arms; he couldn't be certain but he could swear that Sharon was crying. Some party this was turning out to be! Some joyful announcement!

'Don't be stupid, please.' Simon stopped and turned to face Roland. 'I don't care about religious differences — they are too minor to even concern me. I only care about Sharon. Do you realize what you would do to her? Do you understand the agony you would put her through?'

'Agony? What are you talking about?'

'I took your advice once to help her out of a terrible marriage. Sharon was distraught for what seemed like ages, and Nadine and I feared for her. Thank God she's recovered. Being in Paris with Miriam and Claude — away from London and the memories it holds — has helped. But have you considered the relapse she would be bound to have if she had to put up with the way you live?'

'The way I live? Would you please explain to me how I live?'

'Why did you and Janet break up? Why didn't you marry her?'

'Because she wasn't ready for marriage.'

'Not to you, perhaps. But she was ready to marry someone else, wasn't she? It's *you* who are not ready for marriage.' He cut off Roland's denial with a swift wave of the hand. 'You aren't prepared to fully give yourself to a relationship. There will always be a barrier between you and a family, Roland, no matter how much you love them. There will be your business – this ambition of yours to rival the greatest captains of industry the world has ever seen. I've witnessed it the whole time I've known you. When I first had you at my house, I spent a long time wondering about this ambition. I thought at first it was because of the way you'd lost your family so suddenly, that you needed to substitute power and success for family love. But over the years I've seen that it goes even deeper than that—'

'Do you think it interfered with my relationship with Catarina?'

'No, but my daughter is not Catarina. Sharon is far more sensitive than Catarina ever was.' Simon recognized the hostility that blazed in Roland's blue eyes and sought to change the harshness of his words. He wiped a hand across his eyes; he needed time to think, time to find the right words before he caused offense that could never be repaired. 'I don't mean that ... forgive me, please. Sharon is not as strong as Catarina was. Catarina was resilient. She could bounce back from adversity, you know that. I don't think Sharon has that same capacity, especially after that terrible experience with Graham.'

'Simon ...' Roland grasped the banker by the shoulders, gazed into his eyes. 'I'm in love with Sharon, can't you understand that? Just the way I was with Catarina. Please accept it. Don't do an Ambassador Menendez on us.'

Simon smiled weakly. 'I'm afraid I wouldn't be able to stop you. An elopement wouldn't be necessary this time, you are both well past the age of consent.'

Roland tried to think of something to say, something that would assuage Simon's concern. He understood his anxiety . . . He would be worried sick as well about a daughter who had barely survived one bad marriage. But such worries in this instance were groundless.

'Simon, don't you understand how much I delegate work these days? If I were working full-steam-ahead like you claim, I would never have managed to spend so much time in Paris with Sharon during the past few months.'

'You were in Paris because you had business there.' Simon wondered what had gone on between his daughter and Roland in Paris, then he struck the thought from his mind – he didn't want to know.

'Girard et Fils doesn't need me fouling up the works. We appointed management to run the company. My reason for visiting Paris wasn't work – it was to see Sharon. I have plenty of time to myself now, and I want to share it with Sharon and the family we'll have together.'

'Roland, I want to believe you. God knows how much I do. But always there is this feeling that you—'

'Divide my life up into tidy little sections?'

Simon looked at him, amazed. 'You took the words right out of my mouth. Did someone . . . did someone else describe you that way?'

'Janet did. But that was six years ago when you and I were still building our business. You know how hard I was working then. How hard we were both working, breaking our backs to cut corners so we could stay afloat.'

'Roland, you were working much harder than I was. In

407

fact, you seemed to take a fiendish enjoyment in stretching yourself to the limit.'

'Maybe I did, but those days are past. I have nothing to prove now, except that I can settle down and raise a family. A conventional family.' He sensed a softening in Simon's attitude, sought to capitalize on it. 'Shall we go back to the house?' he asked, taking him by the elbow. 'Before they wonder what's happened to us?'

'Roland, promise me you will never relegate Sharon to second place,' Simon said as they walked back to the house.

'I promise.'

Simon stared straight ahead and willed himself to believe Roland. It had to be so, because if Roland hurt Sharon – hurt her as she had been hurt before – then Simon would never forgive him, nor would he ever lift a finger to help him again. No matter how much he had liked Roland as both a friend and a business partner, where Sharon was concerned he had to draw the line.

The two women were still waiting in front of the house. Sharon dabbed her eyes with a lace handkerchief while her mother tried to comfort her. Simon, eager to smooth over the troubled moment, took his daughter in his arms, kissed her. 'A little misunderstanding,' he whispered. 'Roland and I have straightened it out.'

Roland kissed Nadine . . . 'Just don't expect me to call you mother,' he said to the petite blonde woman. 'Put your happy face on, we're going to tell everyone the good news.' Roland put his arm around Sharon and together the group returned to the house.

After the announcement Roland had the butler bring out bottles of Dom Perignon from the wine cellar; then boxes of Davidoff cigars were passed around. Roland took one, lit it; normally he preferred cigarettes, but this was an occasion for a cigar, wasn't it? He walked grandly around the house, accepting the congratulations of his friends. This was how the day was supposed to turn out –

408

the confrontation with Simon had been forgotten already. But when Roland reached Sally, she pulled him off to one side.

'Do you know what the hell you're doing, Roland?'

'I beg your pardon?' he removed the cigar from his mouth, set it down in a crystal ashtray.

'I asked you if you know what you're getting into? You're taking a wounded bird under your wing, and believe me you're not much of a therapist for that kind of injury.'

'Oh, for Christ's sake!' he snapped, momentarily losing his good humor. 'Not you as well!'

'As well as whom?'

'Simon. It took me fifteen minutes to convince him that it was the right thing do.'

'That's because it might not be.'

'Of course it is. Sharon loves me . . . and I love her. It's as simple as that. What else do you need for a marriage?' He looked past Sally at Mellish, who was busily pouring himself another glass of champagne. And what about you, Sally? he felt like asking. Is your marriage so sweet and rosy that you don't even know where your husband wanders off to in the middle of the night when he thinks you're not there?

'Roland, you need more than love in a marriage. You need commitment, understanding.'

Roland's eyes sought out Janet. She had told him the same thing. Only this time it *was* different. Sharon wasn't pregnant; Roland didn't feel compelled to marry her. He just *wanted* to – was that such a crime?

'We'll see, Sally,' he said, picking up the cigar and moving on to other people. 'We'll see.' He needed to hear congratulations again, not warnings of doom. He spotted Katherine standing at the rear bay window, gazing at the garden.

'What do you think, Kathy?'

'About you getting married? I love the idea.'

'You do? Bless you!' He picked her up and whirled her around in his arms. This was the kind of reaction he wanted to hear. When Katherine agreed with him, he knew it was right. A gut feeling, just as Sharon had said at the airport in Paris. A gut feeling – so descriptive of when you just knew that something was right. Or wrong . . . 'Do you want to live with us, Kathy? There are some wonderful schools around here. Stables. You'll be able to ride to your heart's content.'

'What about Richard and Carol?'

'They're Janet's children as well as mine. It would be wrong to think of taking them away from their mother. But you . . . you're different. You're all mine.'

Katherine let her eyes roam around the room, taking in the guests, the waitresses, the uniformed butler. It all seemed such a contrast to the home she knew with Janet and Ralph Morrison. Although Janet and Morrison shared no blood ties with her they were good, kind people, and Katherine loved them as dearly as if they were family. But how could they compare with her own father?

'Will I see you often? Or will you always be away, running off somewhere at a moment's notice?'

'Oh, my little grown-up Kathy . . .' Roland laughed and hugged his daughter fondly. 'Of course you'll see me often. I'll be living here with you.'

'This is an awfully large house to feel alone in.'

'How can you possibly feel lonely with so many people?'

'You can feel lonely in a crowded room.'

Roland understood exactly what his daughter meant – that holiday weekend at Christopher Mellish's farm in Somerset, when Roland was caught up in the Adler's deal – and the icy gaze she'd given him as she sat on the horse. 'I promise you, Kathy, this time it's for good.' He called Sharon over to tell her the news. 'We'll have a family even before we start . . . Katherine's going to live with us.'

'Isn't she happy with Janet and Ralph? Is something wrong there?'

Roland glanced oddly at Sharon, unable to understand the reason behind such a comment. 'It's nothing to do with being happy there. She'll be happier here, with me, her father.'

'That's fine, Roland. I just thought that it might be unwise to break up a good situation.'

Roland relaxed, comprehending now. Everyone was so damned concerned about Katherine's welfare, seeing her shifted from one place to another. 'It's only unwise to leave a good situation for a bad one; it's never unwise to exchange a good situation for an even better one. Now let's get on with the celebration.'

Following a sit-down dinner, the party eventually broke up just after ten o'clock that night. Katherine left with Janet and Ralph Morrison, then Roland saw Sharon and her parents to Simon's car. He couldn't hope to have Sharon stay the night with him, not when Simon and Nadine knew she was in London. He would have to be patient . . . a few more trips to Paris while all the details were ironed out, then Sharon would be with him permanently.

Simon helped Nadine into the car, then climbed into the driver's seat while Roland held the rear door open for Sharon.

'This has been a very special day for us, hasn't it?'

She responded by kissing him, then looked deeply into his eyes.

'Will I see you tomorrow?' she asked before getting into the car.

'Just try and keep me away. I'll phone you first thing in the morning. We can have lunch in town. I'll cancel whatever appointments I've got.' He bent down to kiss her again, half in and half out of the car. She held his left hand, her fingers feeling for his jacket sleeve. Only when

411

he realized what she was doing did he allow himself an indulgent smile. 'I'm wearing your Longines, see?' He pulled back his sleeve to show the watch she'd given him.

'I just wanted to make sure,' she said, laughing.

He kissed her a final time, closed the door and slapped his hand on the roof of the car as a signal to Simon. The car moved off and Roland stood on the curb, watching the red lights disappear down the hill. As he walked back into the house, he laughed to himself about the watch. Sharon really was keeping tabs on him. A touch of jealousy, perhaps? Or was it the insecurity Simon had mentioned? Roland couldn't blame her, not after what she'd been through with Graham. But surely she couldn't feel threatened by a memory . . .

Inside the house he found the waitresses busily cleaning up while the butler stood to the side, hands clasped behind his back, supervising. The only remaining guests were Sally and Christopher Mellish. Roland joined them, noticing the one remaining bottle of Dom Perignon that Mellish had managed to find.

'Join me?' Mellish invited.

'Why not? I'm still celebrating.'

Mellish poured for himself, Sally and Roland, then lifted his own glass high into the air. 'To marriage, old man . . . may it never erode friendships.'

'Strange toast,' Roland replied, but he drank to it all the same. 'What's it supposed to mean?'

'Well, I doubt if we'll be seeing much of you down at Kendall's anymore. You've got that crazy look in your eyes . . . babies, dirty nappies . . .'

'Diapers,' Roland responded automatically, feeling a twinge of sentimentality when he remembered hearing the word Catarina had used.

'Whatever . . . it's all there in your baby blues. All the comforts of home and family.'

'Some of us are meant to be that way, right, Sally?'

'And some of us aren't.' She brushed her long auburn

412

hair back and as she did so Roland noticed for the first time the gray at the roots. He'd never realized that she had gray to cover, never realized that she should even be getting older. 'Just remember what I said earlier, Roland. About Sharon.'

'I will. I'll tie a knot in my handkerchief to remind me.'

'Coming to Kendall's later on, old sport?' Mellish asked. 'One of your last flings before you tie the other kind of knot?' He burst out with his high-pitched laugh at his own joke.

'Not tonight, Christopher. I've got a few things I want to do around here.'

'Shame. I was looking forward to winning some money from you.'

'Anytime you want an unsigned, useless check, I'll be glad to oblige.'

Mellish groaned and took Sally's arm. 'That's it, old sport, kick the poor man when he's down. I guess I'll just have to find another sucker then.'

Roland saw them out, watched them drive away, then closed the door and rested his back against it. The party was over, and suddenly the house seemed totally empty.

'Was everything to your satisfaction, sir?' the butler asked, appearing next to Roland's side.

'Fine, thanks. You all did an excellent job.'

'Thank you, sir. If it's convenient now, I have to arrange for some purchases tomorrow morning.'

Roland went to a bureau, pulled out a checkbook and signed three blank checks. 'Will that be sufficient?'

'More than adequate, sir. Good night.'

'Good night.'

By midnight the house was quiet. Roland sat in an armchair by the front window, looking across the road at the darkened square. Every so often a car's lights flashed past and his vision dimmed momentarily. He sat thinking, imagined Katherine cantering across the square – if the cricket club would let her! – trotting down one of the

413

village's side roads, her back straight, reins held gently but firmly . . . while Sharon busied herself in the kitchen, around the house, creating a proper family environment. For Roland it was a vision that bred pure contentment. That's what had been missing in Regent's Park, he thought. Luxury by itself meant nothing. You had to have people with whom to share it; people you felt for, people you loved. Soon, Roland thought, he would have such a life.

An hour passed and he continued to sit by the window. The cars went by less frequently now. He knew he should feel sleepy. It had been a hectic day, but his mind was alert, his body tense. He stood up and walked around, noticed the box of cigars still sitting on the table. He lit one and sat down again, surrounded by the aromatic smoke. Perhaps Mellish was right, he should go out, make the most of one of his last days as a bachelor, of being . . . uncluttered . . . the word popped into his mind, the same word he had used to describe these people with whom he had remained close.

He picked up the telephone, dialed the number of the local taxi service. A taxi arrived fifteen minutes later to take him to the West End. He entered the foyer of Kendall's, looking forward to seeing Mellish. This was better than sitting alone at home, gazing out at the square. How many times could he imagine Katherine sitting astride a horse before the novelty wore off such an image? As he signed the register he checked through the preceding names. There was Mellish's, on the previous page. Anticipating a battle over the backgammon board, Roland entered the club.

Mellish was nowhere to be seen, though. Roland asked around and learned that Sally's husband had been in for no more than ten minutes. He had played a few hands of blackjack, lost, then left. Roland was undecided what to do. Should he stay and play now that he was here? Or try and find out where Mellish had gone? Again he told himself it was none of his business, but some persistent inner force prodded him to find out. He left Kendall's and began walking the short distance to Curzon Street where Mellish and Sally lived. Once there, he saw no sign of Mellish's Aston Martin which was normally parked in the street, but there was a light on in the front room of the apartment. Feeling oddly foolish, Roland went up the steps and knocked on the door.

Sally opened it immediately and Roland was vaguely disturbed that she hadn't even bothered to find out who it was first.

'Sleepwalking?' Sally asked, showing no surprise at seeing Roland.

'I just got fed up with my own company at home. I took a taxi here thinking I'd go to Kendall's. Did Christopher go?'

Sally nodded. 'He's probably passing off some unsigned checks right now. Are you coming in, or are you going down to join him?'

Roland was in a quandary. Should he tell Sally the truth, that he'd already been to Kendall's and hadn't seen hide nor hair of her husband? Or should he continue playing it the way he was now? For God's sake, he thought, isn't there anyone with a sound marriage – a normal, civilized relationship?'

'You won't be keeping me up if you come in,' Sally said. 'I was going over some figures for our next budget meeting.'

'I'll let you get on with it. This is one of my last opportunities to lose some money without having someone telling me what I'm doing wrong.'

'That's a fine attitude to take into a marriage with someone as delicate as Sharon. I hope you're joking.'

'Of course I am.' He kissed Sally goodnight and retraced his steps to the street. A taxi was passing and Roland hailed it. He would return to Stanmore, force himself to go to sleep. God only knew what Mellish was up to. A woman, probably, while Sally obliviously carried on with life. He wondered what story Mellish would dream up when Sally mentioned that Roland had stopped at the apartment on his way to Kendall's. Would Mellish lie, claim he'd seen Roland? And then what would Roland say? Should he back him up? Or destroy his cover by telling the truth?

To Roland's surprise, lights were on when he reached home. Concerned, he let himself in and saw the butler waiting in the open hall, almost unrecognizable in pajamas and robe – Roland was convinced he never removed his uniform, not even for bed. 'Mrs Mellish telephoned for you a short while ago, sir.'

Sally? 'Thanks,' he said, then picked up the receiver and dialed. 'Sally . . . what's the matter?'

'I think I've caught you out, Roland. I knew you didn't have any intention of going to Kendall's after you left me.'

He tried to think of an excuse why he had returned home, why he hadn't gone to the club. 'I just changed my mind, that's all—'

'Roland, do me and yourself a favor. Stop worrying about Christopher.'

'Pardon?'

'You heard me. You came here *after* you went to the club, didn't you? After you found that Christopher wasn't there.'

'How—"

'I was looking out the window when you walked up the street. What were you doing, looking to see if Christopher's car was there? And then you decided to knock on the door to see if I knew where he was?'

No wonder Sally had opened the door so quickly. She'd watched him coming. 'I was curious, that's all. You know, after that last time, when I called you up and Christopher hadn't got home.'

'There have been plenty of other times since then, Roland.'

'Aren't you concerned?'

'No, although I suppose I should be grateful that you are. If you really must know, Christopher and I haven't even slept in the same room for a couple of years.'

'What kind of a marriage is that?'

'One of convenience, and don't sound so horrified. Christopher's great company. I like him a lot, we get along well. We're satisfied with that kind of an arrangement, even if it is only a friendship. Like I said, it's convenient. If I ever need an escort, I have Christopher. And vice-versa.'

'Your choice. But don't you even know where he goes?'

'No, and I'm not sure I want to. That's his business. He puts on a little show for me, like asking if you wanted to go to Kendall's with him tonight. Once he'd found out that you didn't, he was free to do as he pleased.'

'He was there for a few minutes, signed the register.'

'That's part of the show. He's considerate enough to believe he's fooling me, even if he isn't. Now will you do me a favor and stop worrying about it?'

'If that's the way you want it, Sally.' He hung up and flopped into a chair. He would stop worrying about it for Sally's sake, all right, but he would concern himself with it for his own. Maybe Sally claimed she wasn't interested in what Christopher was up to, but Roland certainly was. Whatever it was might hurt Sally, and he wasn't about to stand by idly while that happened.

His mind leaped forward as he made plans ... He would get Alf Goldstein to do the work for him. He could follow him, just as he'd spied on the Menendez family. Goldstein was good at that; and if he still had the contacts to organize a proper tailing system, he could do as efficient a job as any detective agency.

Sally was very wrong about it being none of his

business, he thought as he climbed the stairs to his bedroom. What she didn't know just *might* hurt her – and he was going to be prepared for whatever shock he felt was bound to strike . . .

Daniel Rushden and *Probe* magazine reentered Roland's life with a vengeance a month later. After milking the Christine Keeler-Profumo affair and the fall of the Macmillan government for all it was worth, Rushden sought more familiar targets, and the announcement of Roland's wedding to Sharon Aronson renewed his interest in his old adversary.

Since the last time Rushden had written an episode of the Vulture Chronicles, Roland had branched out into France – an interesting development, to Rushden's way of thinking. His new father-in-law and former partner was French, a banker; his brother-in-law, Claude Lazarus, was also French, another banker. Was Eagles setting the groundwork for creating a banking and business dynasty – alliances that could be translated into an oligarchy? He used the notion to write another chapter in the Vulture Chronicles, exposing what he considered were the possible ramifications of the marriage . . .

The article reached Roland when he and Sharon were having breakfast in Jamaica, one of the stopover points on the Caribbean cruise they'd chosen for their honeymoon. Roland ripped open the envelope, read the story and passed it to Sharon. He refused to be angry about it; he was on his honeymoon and he wasn't going to allow anything to interfere with his happiness. Or anyone – even a muckraking journalist like Daniel Rushden.

'Why don't you telephone my father?' Sharon asked after Roland told her about the earlier episodes with *Probe* and Rushden. 'This article maligns him as much as it maligns you. Let him take the magazine to court and put an end to it once and for all.'

'I don't think it would help, and your father agrees with

me. We've talked about it before. That's just what Rushden wants, an ugly libel suit that would only win him sympathy and increase his circulation. Actually, he hasn't stated anything as fact . . . I even would have found some of those points interesting if they didn't damn well center on me,' Roland paused. 'No, Sharon, I won't give him the satisfaction of suing him.' Roland picked up the article, read through it again. 'Besides, it's partly my own stupid fault. If I'd listened to your father the first time and just ignored Rushden, he would have lost interest in me; someone who doesn't hit back is of no use to him. As it was, I tried to drown him with money – buy him out, pay him off – so he got the needle to me.' That much was clear. Roland's attempt to try to shut down *Probe* by taking it over had been a gross error. Now Rushden would never drop his interest in him . . .

The next day, as they were about to reboard the ship and continue on to the next port of call, Roland received another jolt – this time one he couldn't ignore. He received a letter from Alf Goldstein with the details of his investigation into Christopher Mellish's nocturnal wanderings. Those nights didn't involve women – they involved a man. For three nights Goldstein had followed Mellish to an apartment in Marble Arch which was rented in the name of Charles Marsden. Inquiries revealed that Charles Marsden was a twenty-three-year-old actor who, Goldstein added cryptically, didn't make enough money acting to buy food, let alone pay the rent of a luxury flat. Roland didn't need any help from Goldstein to figure out what the relationship was: Mellish was paying for the young actor's friendship.

Roland thought it over for a long time before deciding he didn't feel strongly enough one way or another to do anything about it. He considered himself liberal enough to accept such a relationship, could even appreciate Mellish's attempt at discretion. Roland wondered about

Sally, though. Did she know what her husband was up to, and simply didn't want to tell Roland? Or did she just assume he was chasing after other women?

Roland decided it was Sally's problem – if she ever saw it as a problem – and she could handle it herself. She would be happier that way, far happier than she would be if Roland stuck his nose in and told her what he knew about Mellish. If he did that he would be sure to lose a friend. Perhaps even two friends, he thought ruefully. Goldstein's revelations about Mellish didn't make him like the man any less. He was still good company – even if he did prefer to spend time with a young actor instead of losing money to Roland that he never paid.

The thought of it made Roland laugh, and when Sharon asked to share the joke, he just shook his head and tossed the crumpled letter into a wastepaper basket. It never occurred to him that Sharon's curiosity might get the best of her and she would pick it up later and read it.

CHAPTER SIX

During the next six months, Roland's life settled into a comfortable routine in which each weekday morning Alf Goldstein picked him up from the house to take him to his office at Adler's on Regent Street, from which he controlled the Eagles Group. At six every night Goldstein drove him home except for the few nights when Roland worked late. He made a point of keeping foreign trips to a minimum, and Roland was content to let his management team — mostly Michael Adler — handle overseas business. Roland was learning to delegate.

Most evenings he had dinner at home with Sharon and Katherine. Sharon had taken after her mother in one respect — the kitchen was her domain and no one else dared set foot in it. She even had a large sign hung on one wall: 'Sharon's kitchen . . . trespassers will be forced to wash dishes for a week!' Although the meals were always served formally, Sharon insisted on preparing them herself.

Every Friday night, Roland, Sharon and Katherine went to South Kensington for dinner at Simon's home. Despite the fact that Roland had neglected any and all religious tradition, and Katherine had essentially been raised Catholic, they both felt at ease taking part in a traditional Jewish sabbath meal; Roland had once thought it was because of his own father's Jewish roots that they both felt comfortable . . . Still, he welcomed the opportunity to become familiar with Jewish tradition, knowing that any children he had with Sharon would be raised in her faith. He would be doing his share for religious understanding and tolerance, he'd once joked to Simon — fathering children who were Presbyterian, Catholic and Jewish.

Weekends, though, were the time Roland enjoyed the most, when the whole family was together. The butler might have raised an eyebrow at the pandemonium which swept through the house with the arrival of Carol and Richard, but Roland never noticed. While Katherine was out riding, he would play in the garden or on the common with his two youngest children, merrily chasing a ball or rolling in the grass with them. And they would return to the house, red-faced and sweaty, demanding to know where tea was. Katherine tried to interest her young half-sister and half-brother in horses, wanting to share her love of animals, but soon found it wasn't a trait that ran in the family. On one weekend that Roland especially remembered, Katherine had resolved to acquaint them with her favorite horse. Held securely by her older sister, Carol sat on the animal like someone settling into an electric chair, white and rigid with fear. And Richard, when his turn came, managed to break free of Katherine's grasp even before she lifted him off the ground; he ran screaming in the opposite direction, only to slip and fall into a pile of horse manure. As Katherine cleaned him off at a nearby pond before they returned to the house, Roland sat on the grass, lovingly watching his children's antics, thinking that there had never been a happier time in his life.

Early in 1965, Sharon learned she was pregnant. It would be his fourth child, but it would be the first time a birth had been planned, with a large, warm family ready to welcome the baby into its midst. Under Sharon's watchful eye, builders converted one of the bedrooms into a nursery. She began exercising regularly and going to prenatal classes. She would be thirty-one when her first child was born, and she was determined to make sure nothing went wrong.

Roland and Sharon broke the news to her parents over

Friday night dinner. Simon set down his knife and fork and stood up from his place at one end of the table. First, he kissed Sharon. Then, to Roland's mild embarrassment, Simon kissed him as well – a tight bear hug and the Gallic kiss on both cheeks. When Simon stepped back, Roland could see tears in his eyes. 'This is marvelous . . . marvelous . . .' he kept repeating. 'A grandchild. At last a grandchild.'

Roland understood the depth of Simon's feeling. The marriage to Graham Sharp had produced only heartbreak, followed by Simon's obvious misgivings about his daughter's marriage to Roland. Now, the wheel had turned. Any doubts that Simon still had had been swept away by this news. He felt joy not only at the prospect of becoming a grandfather, but because his daughter's second marriage was working out as well.

'Is there anything we . . . Nadine and I . . . can do to help? Anything you need, just name it,' Simon said, standing by his chair, the dinner now forgotten.

'You can relax for a start,' Roland answered with a smile. 'You're acting the way I'm supposed to act a few months down the road.'

Simon waved a hand at his son-in-law. 'That can come later,' he said, then looked down the length of the table at Katherine. 'How about you? How do you feel about having a new sister or brother?'

'Katherine would rather have a horse any day,' Sharon said before the girl could answer.

'Oh, come on,' Roland chided lightly. 'Kathy does accept that people are also entitled to a place on earth.' He recalled a conversation he'd had with her many years earlier, when she was ten or eleven; he couldn't remember exactly. Horses, she had told him in her uniquely grownup manner, were to be trusted far more than people. They didn't kill each other for a start, and didn't cause each other sadness. Roland had replied that he could name at least a dozen horses which had caused him untold misery

423

– all because they'd finished out of the money. Before flouncing off in a tight-lipped rage, Katherine had curtly replied that God didn't put horses on earth for men to bet on! Roland still smiled when he thought about it. Katherine's view of horses and Christopher Mellish's view didn't match up at all. Roland doubted that Mellish had ever once stopped to consider a horse as something other than an object to place a bet on. The only beauty he knew . . . Roland caught himself just in time.

'I'd love a new brother or sister,' Katherine finally replied. 'The house is too big, we need more people in it.'

'Shall we turn one of the rooms into a stable?' Sharon asked. 'Then you can keep a horse there as well.'

'That's not what I meant!' Katherine's face turned scarlet as she realized how rude she had sounded. She mumbled an apology and lowered her head, staring at her plate.

After dinner, Simon and Roland sat in the drawing room, sipping brandy. Conversation drifted from the Eagles Group to Aronson Freres, then Simon set down his snifter. 'Roland, I think there's something else on your mind. What is it?'

Roland grinned. 'Right as usual, you read me very well.' He stood up and started to walk around the small room, stopping occasionally to look at one of the titles on the bookshelves. 'We've got an opportunity to step into a new field, Simon, and I want your advice. And a favor.'

'My advice? I'm flattered. Why?'

'Because it's a business you know a lot about.'

'Banking?'

'No. I'm not ready for that . . . yet. Publishing.'

'Publishing? Newspapers?' When Roland nodded, Simon started to laugh. 'You of all people! Why would you even consider newspapers? You hate journalists; you'd like to see them all hanged, drawn and quartered.'

'I'll agree that image holds some appeal,' Roland answered, smiling, 'but I hate only the irresponsible ones.

And once I expand into publishing I can do my part to put irresponsible journalists out of work.' When he realized that Simon might feel he was only thinking in terms of revenge, as when the Adler deal had come up, Roland quickly disabused him of the notion. 'Actually, it's Michael's idea, not mine. He's been handling a lot more recently, and I can see the sense of his proposal. Ever hear of Burnham Press?'

'Certainly. Local newspapers around the country. Six . . .?'

'Seven. Plus a group of specialists' trade magazines. They've run into some trouble, short of capital, and we're negotiating for seventy-five percent of their stock.'

'What would you do then?'

'I've always been jealous of one of your successes, Simon – the *Mercury*. I'd like to own a morning paper.'

'You want to try to open in London? Do you realize what that would entail, Roland? To make profits from newspapers in the provinces is one matter, but London is the biggest rat race of all. Sometimes I wonder why we even bother keeping the *Mercury*. I've often said it should be sold—'

'To me?' Roland asked hopefully.

'No, not to you. You don't really want the aggravation of owning a London newspaper, Roland. You know nothing about newspapers or publishing. Where would you even begin?'

'The same place we began with the factory in 1948,' Roland answered evenly. 'By hiring management people who *do* know what they're about. Remember when I told you then, about the bottom line? That it was the only thing I really understood? All right, I've improved since then, but I still believe my original approach can work again.'

'Where would you find the management to run the newspapers and magazines as they already stand? Let alone the new venture you propose in London?'

425

'As far as Michael can see, the management in Burnham Press is fairly adequate – they're just short on capital for some needed improvements. But the London project, that's the favor I need, Simon. I'd like your permission to approach Sally and offer her a job.'

'Sally?' Simon was dumbstruck. 'Sally works for me. She's worked for me for twenty years.'

'Certainly she has, but would you ever give her the position I'm thinking of offering her: editorial director of the entire group, a seat on the board with the responsibility for planning the London venture?'

'No. She's happy as editor of the magazine—'

'Is she, Simon? I wouldn't bet on that. She has respect there, a well-paying, responsible position. But I have the feeling she wants to do a lot more. I'm asking you because you're my friend—'

'And your father-in-law,' Simon pointed out, and both men laughed as they realized the absurdity of the remark.

'Forget that. Because you're my friend I'm asking your permission to approach Sally. Obviously if we didn't have the relationship we've had I'd approach her on the sly, try to lure her away the way anyone would.'

'Do you think your proposition would appeal to her?'

'I'm certain it would.'

'You haven't mentioned anything to her yet?'

'No. Out of respect to you.'

'Why Sally, Roland? What's so special about her?'

'I know her, that's all. I know what she can do, how she handles situations. She knows the newspaper business and she's ambitious.'

Simon stroked his beard thoughtfully. 'Roland, I want you to be honest with me. Was there once something between you and Sally?'

The question came out of the blue and startled Roland. He took his time answering, needing to compose himself. 'A long time ago, Simon. When I got out of the army, when I first met you. Since then we've remained close friends, that's all.' Roland couldn't help wondering why he would ask such an indiscreet question? Was he thinking not of losing Sally, but of Sharon? Roland fought to clear his mind, to understand the reason for the question. Was Simon still so concerned for his daughter – even after he could see how well the marriage was working – that he viewed every friendship Roland had as a possible threat to Sharon's security? 'Simon, it was Sally who helped introduce me to Catarina, helped us to elope. Does that satisfy you that whatever we once had fizzled out a lifetime ago?'

'Yes, yes, of course it does,' Simon agreed hurriedly. 'Please forgive me for even mentioning it.' He pointed to the telephone. 'Call Sally now. Offer her the job. If she wants to leave the *Mercury* for your new venture, I won't try to stop her.'

As Roland dialed Sally's number, he wondered whether Christopher would be home. Probably not. Friday was one of the nights when he usually wandered off to the casinos, then to Charles Marsden's apartment. If Sally worked for him – the thought suddenly came to Roland – how would he be able to keep such a secret when they would be so close? Assuming she didn't know already . . .

'Sally, it's Roland. I'm at Simon's—'

'Do you need a ride home?' she said.

'No, Sharon's driving. Not for much longer, though. One piece of news is that she's expecting.'

'Fantastic! Congratulations!'

'Thanks. The other piece of news, which is the main reason I'm calling, is that the Eagles Group is negotiating for seventy-five percent of Burnham Press, and I've asked Simon for permission to approach you for the position of editorial director. Among your responsibilities' – he paused for effect, anticipating her reaction – 'will be overseeing a new London morning newspaper we intend to launch.'

'You – a press baron!' Sally burst out laughing and

427

Roland felt slightly foolish; everyone seemed to have this opinion about him and newspapers. 'What did Simon say?'

'After much hesitation, he agreed.'

'Roland, before we discuss anything, there's one thing I would like to know. How much will *you* be involved?'

'What do you mean?'

'How often would you be sticking your nose in? Because I wouldn't even dream of working for a man who tries to influence me. Being involved in the stores – well, that's one thing – retail is your field. But if you tried to exert pressure on a newspaper, it would be death.'

'That's the reason I want you, Sally. I make it a custom to hire people who know more than I do.'

'Thanks for the compliment. Give me a week to think about it.'

'Christopher there?' Roland didn't know why he asked the question. Curiosity, he supposed, to see if Sally would volunteer any information . . .

'He went out about half an hour ago.'

'Give him my regards.'

'I'll do that.'

Roland hung up and turned back to Simon. 'She'll think about it.'

'What did she ask that got you so hot under the collar?'

'Whether or not I'd be sticking my nose into the running of the newspaper.'

'I hope you won't, Roland. Journalists are quite unlike any other profession. They respond strangely to incursions into their odd little world,' he paused, finished his brandy. 'Let's go back inside with the others before they wonder what's happened to us.'

Later that night, when Sharon drove the family back to Stanmore, Katherine sat in the back of the car unusually quiet. At first, Roland took little notice, his mind too busy with the conversation with Sally. How did Simon really feel about having his people poached . . . even by his son-in-law? Then noticing how quiet Katherine was he wondered if it had anything to do with the way she'd snapped at Sharon. What could that have been about? He said nothing, but later when he thought Katherine was in bed, he knocked softly on her door and entered.

'Everything all right, Kathy?'

'Why shouldn't it be?' She sat upright, resting her chin on her tucked-up knees.

'I don't know.' Roland sat down on the edge of the bed and looked around the room. The photograph of himself and Catarina that had been over the fireplace at the Regent's Park apartment was now on Katherine's window sill. Funny . . . he could have sworn it had been downstairs on a coffee table. 'You just seemed a bit off tonight, that's all. Didn't you feel well?'

'I felt fine. I just . . . I just don't like being made fun of.'

'About the horses? Kathy, darling, we've made fun of you for years and you never complained. You said you thought the jokes went with the boots and saddle.'

'I don't mind jokes from *you*.'

'Oh?' He began to understand. 'Don't you like hearing the same jokes from Sharon?'

'She makes them all the time. When you're not here she asks me what I'm going to do when I leave school. Am I going to be a mounted policewoman?' Katherine's voice cracked, as though she were on the verge of tears. 'Or will I work in an abattoir because I know so much about animals?'

'Kathy, she's only teasing you.'

'I don't like being teased by *her*' Finally the tears came, spilling down Katherine's face. Roland held her close while her shoulders shook from sobbing, and he wondered about the odd inflection placed on the word *her*. It was always *her* and *she* – never Sharon. Was it simple jealousy on Katherine's part? After being the favorite girl – no, woman – in Roland's life for so many years, was she frightened of having to share him? Of taking second place

429

to Sharon? Or was there more to it than that? Had he become so comfortable in his new environment, that he'd missed all the danger signs?

'Would you like me to speak to her . . . to Sharon?' he added quickly, afraid he was falling into Katherine's habit. 'Tell her to pick on someone else?'

Katherine didn't respond. After a while Roland gently eased her head back onto the pillow, stood up and left the room. Katherine barely heard the door close as she lay with her eyes fixed wide open, watching the shadows of trees outside the window dance across the ceiling. She had wanted to say more, much more. But she'd held it all in, not wanting to hurt her father. He'd been hurt enough, and Katherine loved him too much to ever want to see him hurt again.

If she didn't love him so deeply she would have asked why the picture of him and her mother had suddenly appeared in her room, placed out of sight from everyone else? She would have asked Roland why he no longer wore the watch with the names of three horses engraved on the back? Katherine loved the story of that watch, the win on the horses, the romantic exchange of gifts over dinner . . . with each gift having the same inscription. She had the charm bracelet now, hidden away in a box. But she never wore it – not since Roland had married Sharon. Just like her father never wore the watch.

Katherine turned over and buried her face in the pillow, muffling the sound of her crying. Everything had seemed so wonderful only a few months ago, when her father had bought the house and told her of his plans to marry Sharon. Katherine remembered Sharon from when she was young, most of all being the bridesmaid at her first wedding. She'd anticipated Sharon's return from Paris so eagerly, looking forward to renewing their friendship. But Sharon was nothing like the young woman Katherine remembered from her childhood. She'd changed drastically, become possessive – not of objects, but of Roland. Katherine swore that Sharon was trying to cut him off from the family he already had. She wanted him solely for herself. She even wanted to separate him from his memories – the watch, the photograph; and that, Katherine felt, was the cruelest of all.

The pillow became damp as the tears continued to fall, but Katherine made no attempt to move or dry her eyes. She knew that Sharon wished she still lived in St John's Wood with Janet and Ralph Morrison, so she wouldn't be around to interfere with Sharon's marriage . . . just by being there. Katherine wished it, too. She'd been happier in St John's Wood.

But most of all she wished that Sharon's first marriage had succeeded. If Sharon were still married to Graham Sharp, she wouldn't be here, in this house, trying to force Roland away from his daughter.

Sally's decision was to leave the *Mercury* and begin working for Roland at Burnham Press. The publishing group's headquarters were off Fleet Street, in the heart of the city's newspaper industry. Sally's first move was to have her office painted in pastel colors. She hated the drab atmosphere of so many newspaper offices, and was determined to show that a woman had arrived on the board – a woman who wasn't content to sit in the corner and pretend she was a man.

Her next move was more difficult – that of reassuring almost every journalist on the staff of the Burnham Press newspapers and the trade magazines that they hadn't been acquired by a man who had no regard for journalists. Their fears weren't helped by a new chapter in the Vulture Chronicles, in which Daniel Rushden hinted that Roland had bought the publishing group so that he could control what was written about him. Rushden even compared Roland with Citizen Kane, painting an interesting picture of the Vulture living in a fantasy world created by the movie, prodded on by an Orson Welles figure –

Roland couldn't help wondering who that was supposed to be . . .

Roland's response to the latest attack was to consider banning *Probe* magazine from the premises of Burnham Press, threatening to put on notice any employee found reading it during working hours. Sally stood her ground firmly, winning the admiration of the long-established directors and staff by taking the opposite stand. Instead she encouraged employees to read *Probe*, and privately told Roland that the best way to fight back against Rushden was to show that he didn't care. Roland backed off, remembering he'd offered Sally the position with the understanding he wouldn't get involved in the group's affairs.

Feeling duly humbled, he returned to the world he knew and enjoyed the most. His interest in Europe began to pick up again as he spotted companies he believed were ripe for acquisition by the Eagles Group. Instead of taking on the bulk of the work as he had before – no matter how much he reveled in it – he passed it on to Michael. Roland wanted to spend as much time at home as he could, especially with Sharon growing large with child. He felt content with life, as if he were being paid back handsomely for the two families he'd lost.

But Katherine, he couldn't help noticing, was becoming quite the opposite. His daughter seemed to be spending more and more time at the stables taking care of her horse, and less time at home and at her studies. She'd dropped from being a straight-A student at her previous school to midway in the class, bringing inquisitive comments from her teachers. Early one evening, while Katherine was at the stables and Sharon was at home preparing dinner, Roland went to a parent-teacher meeting. He learned that her behaviour at school, as well as her grades, had also taken a turn for the worse. She frequently didn't complete homework assignments, and showed little respect for her teachers. When asked if she was experiencing any problems at home, Roland just shook his head numbly.

When he returned home, though, he resolved to find out for himself what was causing the problem; it could only be the friction between Katherine and Sharon, and he wanted to know who was causing it – his wife or his daughter. Tonight would be the perfect time. Both the butler and the maid were off, and Katherine was going from the stables to a friend's house for dinner, after which they would do homework together. It occurred to Roland that Katherine had been doing that more frequently as well. Whatever the cause of the problem, he was convinced it went far deeper than simple jealousy.

After telling Sharon that he was going to change for dinner, Roland went to the bedroom and changed from the plain gray suit he'd worn for the school meeting to a sportcoat and a pair of gabardine slacks. He sat down on the edge of the bed, still not ready to approach his wife, debating how to bring up the subject. Too much was beginning to seem coincidental. That question from Sharon on the very day they'd announced their wedding plans – about Katherine leaving Janet and moving in with her father. The picture of himself and Catarina that was now in Katherine's room. Perhaps that wasn't so strange, though, he thought; the new wife not wanting pictures of a predecessor on display. But what about the watch? The three-horse watch? The way Sharon had pushed up his sleeve that day she'd come back from Paris, just to see which one he was wearing? All that, coupled with the way Katherine was acting lately, was very peculiar. He stood up and went to his jewelry box. He wasn't quite dressed for dinner yet . . .

When Roland went downstairs, Sharon was preparing to serve dinner. He waited for her to finish, helped her into a chair and took his own, thinking how empty the huge room looked with just two people sitting at the long table. He began to eat, trying to think of a tactful way of

433

broaching the subject. Sharon saved him the bother when she said, 'With all this trouble Katherine's having at her new school, I'm beginning to think she was far happier when she lived with Janet and Ralph.'

'Oh, what makes you say that?' Roland set his left arm on the table, the cuff of his jacket slightly raised. He saw Sharon's eyes flicker towards his wrist.

'Well, her schoolwork was much better, there wasn't any trouble with the teachers. I think she spends too much time at the stables now. It's interfering with her—' Sharon stopped talking as Roland moved his hand a fraction. 'Why are you wearing that awful watch?'

'I thought it would make a change. Is there something wrong with it?'

'Roland, you know how I hate that watch. It's so . . . so crass.'

'Was the photograph of Catarina and me at Claridge's also crass?'

Sharon's eyes went blank for a moment. 'Oh, that. I thought it should be in Katherine's room. After all, Catarina was her mother.'

'Catarina was also my wife.'

'Roland . . .' Sharon leaned as close to the table as her swollen belly would allow. '*I* am your wife now. And I'm expecting your child. Are you showing me as much consideration as you showed Catarina when she was pregnant? Or Janet?'

'What kind of a question is that?'

She didn't answer. Instead she fired back another question. 'Will you love our child as much you love Katherine? When we met in Paris I asked if you had a favorite among your children. You admitted that you did. You admitted that you felt closer to Katherine because she'd lived with you, while Richard and Carol had always lived with Janet. How will you regard our child? As your own, or just another niece or nephew?'

'That's ridiculous, Sharon. It'll be our child, of course. Living with us in this house—'

'With Catarina's shadow always coming in between?'

'No, not in between. Her memory will always live with me, just as Graham's will live with you—'

'Don't mention him!'

Roland held up a hand, intent on finishing what he had to say. 'My memory of Catarina is a beautiful one, unlike your memory of Graham. But no matter what the memory is, you can't wipe it away; it always remains a part of you.' Well, he had wanted to find the crux of the problem, and now he had it. It wasn't Katherine – it was Sharon. Her jealousy, her insecurity, was driving a wedge between him and his daughter. But could he really blame her? In truth he found it difficult. Sharon had already been through one stretch of hell, and because of that she was doubly sensitive. The scars of her marriage to Graham were carved too deeply to ever disappear, and Sharon was obviously petrified of anything that might come between them. Roland knew he had to live with it, to help her over the rough patch. He loved her, just as he knew she loved him. And he *didn't* want anything to come between them – but he wouldn't turn his back on Katherine.

'Sharon, believe me . . . you, the child you're carrying, are the most important things in the world to me. Just as important to me as Katherine, can't you understand that?'

'Roland, I try to. But each time I see Katherine, I . . .' Her mouth opened and closed as she struggled for words. 'I feel like Catarina is living in this house with us.'

'That's crazy, Sharon, and you know it. Catarina has been gone for fifteen years, since the week of your sixteenth birthday party.'

'When you gave me this.' She touched the gold pendant around her neck. 'I always wear it. Why don't you always wear the Longines I gave you?'

'I usually do. I just wore this watch tonight – put it on especially – because I thought it might help me get to the root of this problem. I was honestly believing something

435

was wrong with Katherine. But it isn't her, Sharon. It's you.'

Sharon's voice rose as she became defensive. 'She doesn't give me a chance, Roland. She's always there, a constant reminder of how much Catarina meant to you. Tell me, do you love me as much as you loved her?'

'Of course I do!' he shouted back. And then he wondered. Could subsequent love ever equal that first romance for its passion and intensity? For the excitement – and the ripping, agonizing grief that accompanied it?

'Then prove it to me, Roland. Send Katherine back to Janet—'

'What?' He started to get up from the table, unable to believe what he had heard.

'Just for a while. For eight weeks, until I have the baby in July.'

'I won't hear of such a thing. Katherine belongs in this house. Please accept that. She belongs here . . . and she's staying here.' Why was it that he could control a virtual empire yet he couldn't manage his own family? At work he was the consummate professional; here at home, he felt like a clumsy amateur. Was there some gross deficiency in him that continually tripped him up?

A tear spilled from Sharon's right eye, then another. Soon she was crying uncontrollably, tears spilling down her cheeks. Roland felt helpless, hated himself for being the cause of her misery. He walked around the table, knelt beside Sharon and hugged her. 'Come on, don't cry. It's a waste of energy and you've got to save all that for the baby. We want a big, bouncing baby, don't we?'

She turned her face into his chest. 'Roland, I know everything will be all right once the baby is here. But just eight weeks, is that too much to ask?'

The tears had worked. Roland felt his resolve soften, then disintegrate completely. He'd come down to dinner, prepared to search out the core of the trouble, settle it there and then. Be cruel to be kind – just as he'd told

Simon to do at one time. Then it had been easy to give such advice, when he didn't have to face the effects of it. Now it was a different matter altogether. He had no defense against a woman's tears.

'I'll talk to her,' he promised. 'I'll talk it over with Katherine, explain the situation to her. I'm sure she'll understand.' He helped Sharon from the chair, put his arm around her as they walked toward the door leading to the downstairs hall. He would help Sharon to bed, then wait up for Katherine. She wouldn't be home that late from her friend's house. He would sit down with her and they'd discuss the problem as two adults. She knew the trauma Sharon had been through already, knew how much the birth of this child – the success of this marriage – mattered to Roland. Katherine was his own blood; he knew she'd understand.

By the door Sharon stopped, lifted her head and gazed tearfully into Roland's eyes. He felt the bulge of her belly between them, swore that he could feel the pulse of life within her. His mind flashed back fifteen years, to Catarina standing naked while she admired herself in the mirror before dressing for Sharon's birthday party. Standing in front of the mirror, then blaming him for making them late! Of all the memories, perhaps that was the sharpest, the most poignant. But it was only a memory now, something to be treasured but not permitted to interfere.

'Do you really think Katherine will understand?' Sharon asked.

'I'm certain of it.' He opened the door to the hall and his stomach lurched, twisted into a tight, painful knot. Standing there, her face white and stretched, blue eyes like glass, was Katherine.

'Katherine . . .' Roland couldn't remember calling her by her full name for years, but the immediate moment seemed inappropriate to use the nickname. 'How long have you—'

'Been listening?'

'Eavesdropping, that's what you were doing,' Sharon accused her. 'You listen openly. Only sneaks eavesdrop.'

Katherine ignored Sharon as she answered her father's question. 'I came back five minutes ago, to get some schoolbooks. Then I heard you both talking. I was going to come in—'

'Why didn't you?' Roland asked.

'Because I heard my name being mentioned. And I thought for one marvelous moment' – her face grew even whiter, her eyes like blazing sapphires – 'that you were going to stand up to *her*. That you were going to tell *her* that the entire universe does not revolve around *her*. You almost did, do you know that?' she added, lifting her chin defiantly. 'But then she started crying, and you drowned in her tears . . . just like she knew you would.'

'Katherine! Go to your room!'

'What? Before you sit down with me and explain the situation? I'll understand. Understand why I'm being shoved around like some piece of driftwood, bumped onto this shore, thrown onto that.'

'Katherine!'

'I'm going! Good night!' She swung away and ran up the stairs. Moments later her bedroom door slammed with enough force to shake the entire house.

'Now do you see what I mean?' Sharon asked.

Roland clutched his head. 'All I can see is that I'm caught up in a fight between two women. And whoever wins, the loser's going to be me.' He started toward the stairway but Sharon pulled him back.

'Roland, you have to make a decision. Who is more important to you? Katherine or me? Make your mind up about that right now.'

'That isn't a question to ask your husband!'

'I know it isn't. Because it should never have to be asked.'

Roland breathed out a deep, anguished sigh. If he went up the stairs to Katherine's room, would he lose Sharon?

And if he stayed down here, with Sharon, what would happen to Katherine?

He couldn't bring himself to face the predicament, and he cursed himself for being a coward.

Sharon went up to bed soon afterwards, while Roland remained sitting in the front room with the lights out, smoking a cigar, staring out the window. He was hoping that Katherine would come down, that she would make the move. He wasn't brave enough to go up to her room and face the accusation in those clear blue eyes. But the only sounds he heard were when the home help returned from their evening off; first the maid, at eleven-thirty, and then, fifteen minutes later, the butler. The maid went straight to her downstairs room. The butler, however, made a conscientious inspection of the house before retiring.

'Is there something the matter, sir?' he asked Roland when he found him sitting in the darkened front room.

'No. Doing some thinking, that's all.'

'Perhaps I can fetch something for you?'

Sure, some family togetherness, Roland felt like replying. He shook his head and told the butler to go to bed.

He stayed in the front room for another hour, wondering what to do. Whatever he decided seemed wrong, whether he sided with Katherine or with Sharon. Finally he dragged himself up the stairs, undressed and sank into bed beside Sharon. He didn't know whether she was asleep or just pretending, but he had no desire to find out. To wake her might lead to another confrontation, and he didn't have the strength for that now.

He lay staring at the ceiling, listening to Sharon breathing evenly beside him, feeling the bed move as she turned restlessly. What would have happened if Mrs Peters hadn't stepped out into the street that summer afternoon? If there had been no accident? No . . . that was wrong. He should be wondering what would have happened had Catarina not been born with a defect, had her body been whole. Would he be experiencing the same problems? No, of course not, there never would have been any enmity between Catarina and her daughter. There would have been a bond of love – what there should be between Katherine and Sharon.

He turned the question over and over in his mind. Somewhere in the distance a door closed, a car engine started up then died, started again, died, started a third time, roared for a few seconds before descending raggedly down the hill toward the village. Someone who couldn't drive too well . . . or someone who'd drunk too well, Roland decided. He hoped the police caught the driver, glad even for a moment to think of something other than his own problems. He remembered the first time he'd driven the XK–120, when Catarina had ordered the taxi driver to stop in the middle of Leicester. 'We would like to buy that car . . . what is it, please?' she'd asked the salesman. Roland chuckled silently, warmed by the memory, then drifted off to sleep.

Sharon woke him up, tugging at his shoulder. 'The phone, Roland! The phone!'

He sat up in bed, looking at the luminous hands of the clock. Four-fifteen. Very faintly he could hear the telephone ringing downstairs. Who the hell would be calling at this hour? The insistent ringing stopped as the butler took the call. Moments later came the sound of footsteps on the stairs, stopping outside the bedroom door, then a hesitant knock.

'Sir, there's a telephone call for you. Mrs Morrison.'

Mrs Morrison? Janet! Roland climbed out of bed, walked barefoot across the carpet into the upstairs hall where there was an extension with the bell removed. 'Janet . . . what's the matter?' It had to be one of the children, he thought; why else would she call in the middle of the night?

'Roland, I'm at New End Hospital in Hampstead—'

'What's wrong? Is it Richard? Carol?'

'Neither, Roland. It's Katherine.'

Roland felt his grip on the receiver tighten. 'What are you talking about? Kathy's here, sleeping.' He looked toward her closed bedroom door, recalled how she'd slammed it the night before.

'No, she's not, Roland. She's in New End Hospital, badly injured in a car accident. The police say she was driving.'

'That's crazy. She can't drive, doesn't even have a license.' He heard Sharon come into the hall and told her to look in Katherine's room. She came back; the room was empty. 'But why . . . why didn't anyone call me?' Roland asked Janet. 'Why did they contact you?'

'Katherine had no identification on her. When the police asked her name, she told them she was Katherine Morrison and gave my address and telephone number.'

The name Katherine had given – the reason for giving it – went right by Roland. He was too confused, unable to believe that his daughter had been behind the wheel of a car. She wasn't even fifteen yet! 'What kind of a car?'

'A blue Ford.'

Sharon's car . . . Wait a minute! That noise of a door closing . . . the garage! The continuous stalling . . . the engine racing . . . then the sound of a car going down the hill toward the village . . . That had been Katherine, taking Sharon's car, using the keys that were always left in the downstairs hall closet. The car had an automatic transmission; Katherine must have known just enough to get it started, manage to reverse it out of the garage. But heading where?

'The accident, where did it happen?' Roland asked Janet. Another accident . . . just like the one that had brought about Catarina's death? God no . . .

'On the Edgware Road going through Cricklewood.'

Cricklewood? What was she doing down there? Roland immediately knew the answer – driving toward St John's Wood, to Janet's.

'I'll be at the hospital as soon as I can.'

441

'I'll take you in my car, sir,' offered the butler, who had stood by Roland's side throughout the conversation.

'Thanks. Janet, stay with Katherine. I'll see you in fifteen minutes.'

'Of course I'll stay here,' Janet said as Roland hung up the phone. He strode back to the bedroom, dressed hurriedly. Sharon followed, watching.

'Do you want me to come with you?'

'I don't think so. You stay here. Go back to bed, you've got to look after yourself.'

Sharon walked around the bedroom, sat down on the chair in front of the dressing table. 'Katherine doesn't have a license to drive.'

'That's the last of my concerns right now.'

Sharon seemed not to hear him. 'She can get into an awful lot of trouble. Not just the accident, but driving without a license, driving under age, without insurance. Taking *my* car without *my* permission.'

'What . . . did . . . you . . . say?'

'Oh, nothing,' Sharon said quickly as she glimpsed the fire in Roland's eyes. 'I was just thinking aloud.'

'That last part. What . . . did . . . you . . . say?'

'I said she could get into trouble for taking my car without my permission.'

'Are you *hoping* she'll get into trouble, Sharon? Is that it? For Christ's sake, what the hell is the matter with you?' He swung around as a knock sounded on the bedroom door. 'Come in!'

The butler entered, aloof from the tension in the room. 'I'm ready, sir.'

'So am I.' Roland flashed a final, furious look at Sharon before following the butler downstairs to his small car, sitting cramped in the passenger seat as they sped through the empty streets.

They reached the hospital twenty minutes later. Roland found Janet sitting in the emergency room. She pointed to a small room; Roland looked inside. Katherine lay sedated in the bed closest to the door, her head bandaged, a cast on her right arm. A doctor stood by the bed, checking a chart.

'I'm Roland Eagles, this girl's father. What's the extent of her injuries?'

'Broken arm plus cuts and lacerations to her face and scalp where she went through the windshield.' The doctor saw Roland blanch at the news and placed a comforting hand on his shoulder. 'It might have been a lot worse, if that's any consolation. She's young, healthy. She'll bounce right back.'

'Thanks for the encouragement.'

'I'm afraid you're going to need all you can get, Mr Eagles. There's a police officer waiting outside who'd like some details.'

'He's not the only one.' Roland stood by the bed, fingers gently stroking Katherine's shoulder. Had they shaved her head? Was all that beautiful blonde hair gone? It didn't matter, he told himself. Hair always grew back. Just as long as she recovered, it didn't matter at all.

'Want some company when you talk to the police?'

Roland turned around, surprised to see Janet standing next to him; he hadn't heard her enter the room. 'I think so. Where's Ralph?'

'At home. Someone has to stay with Richard and Carol.'

Roland walked out to the emergency reception desk, holding Janet's hand. First he told the butler to return home, then went to where a police officer sat waiting, pad and pencil in hand. Roland sized up the young man, the eager look, and decided that he hadn't even turned twenty – too young to even understand the meaning of sympathy, of compassion.

'I'm Roland Eagles, the father of the accident victim. Can you tell me what happened, officer?' He sat down and Janet took the seat beside him, still holding his hand.

'I was hoping you could tell me, sir.' The voice went with the face – young and officious.

'About the circumstances of the accident, I mean.'

443

'According to witnesses, sir, the car was traveling at between forty and fifty miles an hour along the Edgware Road in a southbound direction. The speed limit there is thirty miles an hour.'

Get on with it, Roland prayed.

'As the car approached the junction with Willesden Lane, the lights changed. The driver attempted to brake – the rear lights came on – then the car went out of control, mounted the curb and ploughed into a lamp post. We've identified the car as belonging to Sharon Eagles of Stanmore—'

'My wife,' Roland interrupted, wondering what Sharon was doing right now. He still found it impossible to believe that she had mentioned the possible charge of driving *her* car without *her* permission.

'Your wife, sir?' The constable looked curiously at Janet, the holding of hands.

'I'm Janet Morrison, a friend of Mr Eagles.'

'Is Mrs Eagles the mother of the girl?'

'No,' Roland answered. 'Katherine's mother is dead.' He waited for some hint of recognition in the officer's eyes. None came, and Roland realized that Catarina – the elopement, the custody case – had all been before his time.

'What is your daughter's full name, sir?'

'Katherine Elizabeth Eagles.'

The constable consulted his notebook. 'When police officers removed her from the car and asked for identification, she claimed she was Katherine Morrison.'

This time, the use of the name stuck in Roland's mind like a barb. Katherine had fled the house in Stanmore – when she felt unwanted and neglected – and had been heading for St John's Wood and Janet. She'd even taken Janet's name for herself – had abandoned Eagles, cast it out as she wished to cast out her own father. Just like Roland's father had done so many years before – changed his name in an act of defiance, to show his bigoted family exactly what he thought of them.

444

'That is against the law, sir.'

'What is?'

'Giving a false name to police officers.'

'Maybe she was confused. Maybe she was trying to tell you the name of the people she was trying to reach. How would *you* react with a broken arm and *your* head cut open?' Roland snapped.

The officer looked up from his notepad, as if the question were a direct threat. 'Mr Eagles, what can you tell me about this? Why was your daughter – how old is she, anyway?'

'She'll be fifteen in June.' It sounded slightly better than saying fourteen; fifteen was only two years short of legally applying for a driver's license.

'Do you know why your daughter was driving the car?'

Roland nodded slowly. He felt Janet's hand squeeze his own as he started to answer. 'There was an argument at home last night, between my daughter and my wife. I sided with my wife, and my daughter felt she'd been betrayed. I heard a car start during the night, but I never imagined it was Katherine. I didn't even realize she knew how to start the engine.'

'She knew enough to get as far as Cricklewood.'

'It's almost a straight run from Stanmore – down London Road and turn right at Canon's Corner,' Roland said automatically. 'No traffic in the middle of the night, so maybe she felt she could make it all the way to St John's Wood.'

'Why St John's Wood, sir?'

'That's where I live,' Janet answered. 'Katherine used to live with my husband and myself, until Mr Eagles remarried and decided she should live with him.' The officer was clearly confused.

'Will there be any charges?' Roland asked, concerned more with Katherine than explaining his personal situation.

'I would imagine so, sir. Exceeding the speed limit, reckless driving, driving without a license and insurance,

445

driving while under age. By the way sir, did your wife give your daughter permission to use the car? If she did, she could also be in hot water.'

Roland shook his head. 'No.'

'Then there'll also probably be a charge of taking and driving a car without the owner's permission.'

Roland's eyes closed, his head dropped to his chest. He felt totally defeated. He didn't care about the charges Katherine might face, only about Katherine. He felt that he'd forced her into doing this – forced her to flee the house in the middle of the night because she felt she was living in enemy territory. He blamed no one but himself. Not even Sharon. If he'd put his foot down, established control in his own house, within his own family, none of this would have happened . . .

Roland and Janet stayed at the hospital until eight o'clock in the morning. He called Sharon and told her the extent of Katherine's injuries – she sounded sympathetic although Roland hardly noticed – then waited for Katherine to waken from her sedated sleep. A different doctor was on duty, and he allowed Roland five minutes with her, after which she would be transferred to the main hospital.

Roland went into the room and sat down next to the bed. Despite the bandages, Katherine's eyes were as sharp and clear as they had ever been, and seemed to burn right through her father. Roland laid a hand on her uninjured arm, flinched as she tried to withdraw.

'Kathy, I'm sorry. I'm not angry . . . I'm just sorry. Don't worry about the car, don't worry about the police. Just get better.' He could see she wasn't going to reply, so he continued talking in a soft, soothing tone. 'Kathy, I'm not going to ask you to go away until Sharon has the baby. I wouldn't dream of it. It's as much your house as it is hers. No, it's more your house, your home . . . will you believe me?'

The blue eyes just stared, offering no answer, no comfort of forgiveness. At last the doctor tapped Roland on the shoulder, said the five minutes were up. Roland left the room reluctantly and joined Janet outside.

'Do you want me to drive you home?' Janet offered.

'Let's get a cup of tea somewhere first. I'm parched.'

They went to a small restaurant in Hampstead that was serving breakfast, sat in a corner away from the crowd. 'Shall I talk to Katherine?' Janet asked. 'Will that do any good?'

'Probably more good than me talking to her,' Roland said dismally. 'I think she's blotted me out completely.'

'I'll ask her if she wants to come back to St John's wood, live with Ralph and me. She was happier with us, Roland.'

'That's not the whole story. The truth is she was happier when she didn't have anyone competing with her for me.'

'Are you telling me *that's* the whole story? Just because there's another woman in your life now?'

'No.' Roland fingered the handle of the teacup. 'She feels I've let her down, betrayed her.'

'So she headed back to our house. Maybe that's where she really belongs, Roland. Let me talk to her later on. I think I can get closer to her than you can, especially after this.'

Three days later, Katherine was picked up from the hospital by Ralph Morrison and driven to St John's Wood. Her clothes, which had been brought from Stanmore, were all hanging neatly in her old room. The cast would be on her arm for at least four weeks, and she was required to return to the hospital in a week to have the stitches removed from her scalp and forehead. Despite doctors' assurances that any scars would be barely noticeable, Roland worried. For some reason he doubted that Katherine would even consider plastic surgery to remove any unsightly scars. No, the bitterness she felt would make her wear them proudly, like a banner, reminding her of the night she'd stood up to her father.

Even when the cast was removed, Katherine didn't return to school and Roland immediately knew why – vanity. Her blonde hair was barely half an inch long, covering her scalp like a pale fuzz, not even hiding the three scars that would take years to fade. Only one scar showed on her forehead, a razor-thin, red line about an inch long that ran above her right eyebrow.

Roland visited her every night after work, driven by Alf Goldstein on the way back to Stanmore. She always greeted him formally, never forgetting to ask for Sharon. Roland always replied with the same uncomfortable formality – that Sharon was inching toward her final weeks of pregnancy and apologized for not coming to see Katherine, but she was feeling unfit to travel any long distance. Roland wondered if that was really the truth. He suspected otherwise . . . that Sharon didn't even *want* to see Katherine; that she just wanted to erase any thought of Roland's eldest daughter from her mind.

A week after Katherine had the cast removed, Roland received the piece of mail he'd been dreading . . . summons to appear with Katherine at juvenile court to answer a handful of charges stemming from the accident. Instead of going to Regent Street that morning, he had Alf take him to Aronson Freres. Simon knew all about the accident, although he was unaware of the reasons behind Katherine's dramatic nighttime drive. Roland had thought it better not to tell him; and Sharon, as Roland had guessed, had never made any mention of it.

'What do I do about this?' Roland asked Simon, showing him the summons.

'Quite a collection, I must say.' He glanced through the charges, lips moving as he read silently. 'I am grateful, Roland, that you didn't press Sharon to say she'd given Katherine permission to use the car. It might have saved one charge for Katherine, but in Sharon's present state

448

the trouble it might have caused would have been catastrophic.'

Simon's calmness, his concern for his own daughter,
irked Roland. 'It was all because of Sharon that Katherine
ran away that night.'

'Ran away?'

'That wasn't some spoiled brat taking the family car
for a joyride, Simon. That was my daughter running
away—' He stopped suddenly, aware of what he was
saying. 'Maybe I should have mentioned this to you earlier, but there's been hell going on between Sharon and
Katherine. Ever since Katherine came to live with us.'

'What kind of hell? Sharon never said a word—'

'They've been fighting with each other.'

'With you as the prize?' Simon guessed. 'Is that why
Katherine has gone back to the Morrisons'?'

'That's where she was trying to get to that night.'

'I see,' Simon was surprised; he'd been given no inkling
of any trouble with his daughter. 'What will happen after
this?' He waved the summons. 'After Katherine recovers?
After Sharon has the baby? Wait a minute . . .' He studied
the summons again. 'Surely this is for the week Sharon is
expecting?'

'That's right.'

'Do you plan to go to court that week? I can get a
postponement.'

'I'll go.' Roland didn't want the trial postponed, he
wanted it over and done with. If he put it off, Katherine
would see it as another capitulation to Sharon, and
Roland couldn't afford that. He'd never win her back.

'You will? But your wife—' Simon sat up straight in his
chair, fixed Roland with a steady gaze. 'Roland I have to
ask you a very pointed question – who are you placing
first here? Your daughter or your wife?'

'Don't you mean *your* daughter or *my* daughter?'

'If you wish. Who do you place first?'

Ever since the accident . . . no, even before that, when

449

he'd first sensed that something was wrong between Sharon and Katherine, Roland had asked himself the same question. And he kept running away from the answer, fearing that one day he would have to make a cutting choice: Sharon's possessiveness that threatened to cut him off from everyone he loved? Or a freer life where he could enjoy those people he loved, all of them?

Simon waited patiently for an answer, sensing Roland's turmoil. Finally he spoke. 'Roland, soon you will have to make a choice, and you will have to choose Sharon above all else. I warned you about the responsibilities of marrying her. You accepted them.'

'Can we concern ourselves with more immediate matters right now? Like that summons.'

Simon continued to gaze steadily at Roland, undecided whether to continue the conversation about Sharon. Finally he looked down at the sheet of paper. 'We will have Katherine plead guilty, with mitigating circumstances.'

'And have all that trouble at home brought out into the open?'

'Perhaps it should be brought more into the open. We might all be better off.'

'We?'

'Yes, we. I'm just as concerned about this unfortunate business with Katherine as you are, although I think our reasons differ. My main concern above all else is Sharon. I won't stand by and see her hurt again.'

'I'm not hurting her.'

'If you ignore her in favor of Katherine you surely will be.'

'She's not being hurt because she's being ignored. She *thinks* she's being hurt because I want to have a normal relationship with the rest of my family!' Roland shot back.

'Then you must compromise.'

'Why can't Sharon compromise?'

'Because she's been through enough already.'

'And I haven't? Is that what you're saying?'

Simon handed the summons back to Roland. 'Under these rather trying circumstances, I think it might be better if you seek legal advice from another quarter. I can refer you to some very good lawyers who specialize in juvenile crime.'

Roland snatched the summons from Simon's hand, senses stinging from the last two words. Juvenile crime! Before they'd been talking about Katherine, trying to decide whatever was best for her. Now Simon had relegated her to the level of a juvenile delinquent!

Roland went to the lawyers he used for corporate work, a firm located in the city. He knew it was like using a power hammer to crack open a peanut, but maybe it was better this way. Simon was obviously more interested in how the whole affair would affect his daughter, so his representing Katherine was definitely out. Instead, Roland would respond to the charges with what he considered the most impressive display of legal talent ever to grace a juvenile court.

The firm's senior partner, Alan Martin, a fleshy, bulbous-nosed man with graying hair who normally handled Roland's business affairs, seemed surprised at being asked to take such a case. Nonetheless, he agreed to handle it. Roland put him in the picture as clearly as possible, and Martin suggested he could – if not lie outright – at least bend the truth a little. As Simon had suggested, he would have Katherine plead guilty; but, in mitigation, he would explain that she'd been emotionally disturbed by the move to the new house, the new school and her inability to settle. Rather than face up to her father, who had been called to the school regarding her deteriorating performance, she'd sought flight in the middle of the night, wanting to be back in the house where she used to live.

'The only problem is,' Martin mused, 'considering the feeling between you and your daughter, will she go along with this defense?'

'It's almost the truth. It just leaves out the trouble she's had with my wife . . . and with me. I'll talk to her about it,' he added, and wondered how effective that would be.

'In that case, I can quite safely say that she'll get nothing worse than probation and a fine, not to mention being banned from driving for a few years.'

'She doesn't have a driving license now.'

'The ban will take effect when she comes of age to have a driver's license.'

Roland left the lawyer's office feeling relieved – until he thought of Simon. Once before, when Roland had wanted to acquire Adler's and Simon was caught up in trouble between Sharon and Graham, the two men had come close to breaking apart. Then, they had settled for ending their business association. This time, however, it was far more serious. Simon was now his father-in-law. Would this be when the final, irrevocable break would occur?

As Sharon entered the final week of her pregnancy, Roland breathed a sigh of relief. The preceding weeks had been impossible; from now on, things could only improve. Sharon had called in the doctor almost every day with some complaint – her back, her head, her legs. Roland knew the reason, and it wasn't hypochondria. She wanted to keep Roland in the house, frightened that at this ultimate moment she might lose him. To whom? To Katherine, who was still icily remote from her father, although she had agreed to use the story devised by his lawyer? Or was Sharon even now frightened that she might lose her husband to his work?

Much of the time, Roland was forced to run the business from home, permanently on the telephone to Michael Adler at Regent Street. And it seemed to Roland

452

that whenever he sat down, receiver in hand, he could hear Sharon's voice calling to him. She didn't want the butler or the maid; she always wanted Roland. He would tell Michael to hold on while he saw to her, and each time he returned Michael would have hung up, moved on to more pressing matters.

With a chilling certainty, Roland knew exactly what was going to happen: Sharon would go into labor right before Katherine's appearance at juvenile court. It could be no other way, as if Sharon were consciously trying to coincide the two events. And she would beg him not to leave her. Plead with him – and then accuse him of favoring Katherine over her ...

When the time came, Roland wished he could be as uncannily prophetic when he picked horses. He was due in court with Katherine at ten o'clock, and Sharon woke him at five-thirty that morning to say that the baby was on its way. He dressed quickly, picked up the suitcase that had lain packed for almost a week and had the butler telephone for an ambulance.

They reached the hospital at six-fifteen. Sharon clung to Roland's hand, begging him not to leave her, to stay the entire day. As gently as he could, he explained there was nothing he could do. Nadine would be coming over from South Kensington later on, although there was nothing she could do either.

'I have a very important appointment at ten o'clock, Sharon. I dare not miss it.'

'Katherine has the lawyer there. Why do you have to be there as well?'

'Because I'm her father.'

'And you're my husband, the father of this child.' She pointed to her belly.

It sounded like an old broken record Roland had heard for the past weeks ... or was it months? He no longer remembered, time meant nothing anymore. 'Sharon, the only people you need right now are the doctors and the

453

nurses. I'll come by and see you tonight.' He attempted to remove his hand from hers, but she only clung more stubbornly. To Roland's relief a West Indian nurse approached, her face breaking into a warm smile as she understood what was happening.

'Come on now, Mrs Eagles, there's no need to drag your husband into the labor ward.' She took both their hands and gently separated them. 'There now, your husband can come back later when you're all pretty and you've got something to show him.'

Roland kissed Sharon quickly on the cheek and backed away. She turned her head toward him, brown eyes beseeching, calling his name. He forced himself to close his ears, and quickly left the hospital.

At nine-thirty he was at the court, talking to Alan Martin about the case. It was listed sixth on the court sheet and they estimated they wouldn't be heard until the afternoon. Katherine sat a few feet away, next to Alf Goldstein, who had driven her from Janet's home. They were talking softly and Roland wondered what she was telling him.

'I took Sharon to the hospital early this morning, Kathy,' Roland said, sliding closer. 'She'll probably have the baby while we're here.' At first, when Katherine made no response, Roland thought she hadn't heard. Then Goldstein tapped her gently on the shoulder and pointed to her father. Roland repeated the words when Katherine turned toward him, his eyes fixed on the thin scar that sliced across the skin above her eyebrow. She was wearing a scarf to hide the newly growing hair, and Martin had suggested she remove it for the trial – if the court clerk didn't order her to do so – to win sympathy from the magistrate.

'Didn't she want you there, with her?' Katherine asked.

'Yes, she did.' Roland refused to take offense at the implication contained in the question. He needed Katherine to be calm now, ready to face the trial. 'I told her I

454

was needed here instead. She'd have the baby no matter what.'

Katherine looked away, her role in the conversation finished. 'What do you want – boy or girl?' Goldstein broke in with forced cheerfulness as he tried to bridge the awkward silence.

'What does it matter as long as it's healthy?'

'True, that's what I always say. Michael'll be glad to see you back, though. Poor devil's lost ten pounds.'

Assuming I'm allowed to go back once Sharon comes home, Roland thought. He could see her carrying on the act forever, fearing to be alone, needing him, needing him, needing him . . . until she turned him into someone as insecure and neurotic as herself.

'I'll be bloody glad to get back.'

The morning passed as they sat outside the court, not interested in following the earlier cases. When they went out for lunch, Goldstein locked himself away in a telephone booth for several minutes and Roland surmised he was calling the office to check on things. Roland appreciated the gesture. They returned to the court building and took the same seats, wondering how much longer they would have to wait. Finally, at two-thirty, Alan Martin tapped Roland on the knee.

'Our turn,' the lawyer said before collecting his papers and leading the way into court.

Roland watched the case dispassionately, feeling there was little he could do to influence the outcome. He stood next to Katherine as the guilty plea was given, listened to evidence from the police, to Alan Martin's description of the mitigating circumstances.

'Mr Eagles . . .'

Hearing his own name spoken by the magistrate jerked Roland awake.

He looked across the court to the bench. 'Yes, sir.'

'Have the unfortunate circumstances which affected your daughter so badly been straightened out?'

'Yes, sir. My daughter is now living with Mr and Mrs Ralph Morrison in St John's Wood.'

'Have her school marks improved since the move?'

'She hasn't returned to school yet, sir, because of the accident.'

'I see.' The magistrate turned his attention to Katherine. 'Young lady, you're an extremely fortunate individual. Firstly, because you were not killed in your mad little escapade; nor did you kill anyone else. Secondly, because you are surrounded by a family that obviously cares for you very deeply . . .'

Roland swore he saw Katherine flinch at those words, and he felt more pain than he could ever remember.

'The court also takes into consideration your previous good character,' the magistrate continued, 'and sentences you to a fine of one hundred pounds, one year's probation, and a three-year suspension of your driving license to take effect from the day you first apply for a license.'

Roland took Katherine's hand and led her, unresistingly away from the dock. The decision to use Alan Martin had paid off, the penalty nowhere as severe as it might have been had not Martin so eloquently pleaded Katherine's case. At least Roland was given scant comfort knowing that, as a juvenile, his daughter wouldn't be in the newspapers. The case would be reported – if it received any coverage at all – as a fourteen-year-old being fined one hundred pounds. And when Katherine turned seventeen, she would start out with a clean slate. If not a valid driver's license . . .!

He looked around for Alf Goldstein, but he was nowhere to be seen. Was he that upset that he had to leave the court? Roland knew how much the man doted on Katherine, almost as much as on his own children. Had seeing her in the dock, the shaven head, the scars, disturbed him that badly? Then Roland spotted him, bustling his way through a crowd of people, pushing and excusing himself to those who didn't get out of his way soon enough.

'Congratulations! You're a father again. A boy . . . seven pounds, nine ounces. Half an hour ago.'

'How—?'

'I reckoned your mind was somewhere else,' Goldstein said, pumping Roland's hand up and down, 'so I've been calling the hospital regularly.'

'Did you hear that?' Roland asked Katherine, hoping to elicit some response from her. 'You've got another brother.'

Katherine stood perfectly still, her face composed as if her father's words had been meant for someone else. Then a tear appeared, a single drop that slowly dribbled down her right cheek. Roland felt a hard lump forming in his throat and started to move toward his daughter. He got no closer than a step when Katherine suddenly flung her arms around his neck and buried her face in his shoulder, crying. Goldstein and Martin turned away, walked off to let them share a private moment.

'It's all over, Kathy. All you've got to do is see some man or woman once a week or so, and that's it. Just for a year. You can manage that.'

'That's not why I'm crying.' She tried to hold back the tears and only succeeded in choking, coughing wetly onto Roland's jacket. 'I'm happy . . . for you. You've got what you wanted.'

'Do you really mean that?' He felt tears form in his own eyes, a warm wetness that blurred his vision.

'Of course I mean it. I'm happy for you.'

Roland took the silk handkerchief from his top pocket, dabbed at Katherine's face, ran his fingers through the fuzz of blonde hair and felt the scars. 'You should have used those tears before, Kathy. Maybe you'd have got away with a fifty-pound fine. Maybe the magistrate would have even paid you . . .'

A smile appeared on Katherine's face, and to Roland it

457

was a bright, colorful rainbow in the middle of a storm. 'Do you think it would have worked?'

'Communication always works.'

'I tried to communicate with you.'

'I know.' He started to walk after Goldstein and Martin, arm held protectively around her. 'I just wasn't tuned to the right wavelength. Do you want to forgive me . . . live with us again?' There, he had made the decision, the choice he'd been avoiding all this time. When Sharon came home from the hospital, he would tell her as tenderly as possible that he couldn't continue living the way he'd been, centering his life around her to the exclusion of everyone else. It was time for her to accept that there were others in his life, or risk losing him altogether . . .

Roland visited the hospital that evening armed with two dozen red roses which he gave to the nurse to place in a vase beside Sharon's bed. Sharon was sitting up, looking drawn but happy as she talked to her parents who had arrived five minutes earlier.

'Congratulations.' Simon shook Roland's hand and Nadine stood on tiptoe to kiss him.

'Thanks, but I think Sharon deserves some of the credit.' He bent over the bed to kiss her. 'How are you feeling?'

'Worn out, and fed up to my back teeth with hospitals.'

'That's a good sign. You'll be home in a couple of days. Is the baby asleep?'

'He should be, he dined well enough.'

'Roland,' Simon cut in. 'What happened this morning? At court, with Katherine?'

Roland wondered whether he should be surprised that Simon had remembered. 'A fine. Probation—'

'*Must* we talk about Katherine now?' Sharon said sharply. 'You came here to see me.' She looked to her parents for support. 'Isn't it bad enough that you left me

458

alone this morning? Do you have to talk about Katherine's court appearance now?'

'She was also banned from driving for three years,' Roland continued with deliberate slowness. 'But that doesn't come into effect until she's old enough to apply for a license.'

'Roland . . . I do not wish to hear about Katherine,' Sharon said.

'You'd better get used to it, because she'll be coming back to stay with us.'

'What?' Sharon fought to sit up higher, her face aflame. 'After what she did?'

'After what we forced her to do.'

'She has no right—'

Roland ignored the anxious stares of Simon and Nadine. What he had seen that morning in court had hardened his resolve. 'She has every right to live in our house with us. She's my daughter, Sharon. And unlike my other children, she doesn't have a mother she can live with. So she's going to live with us.'

'Roland, is this really the time for such a sensitive discussion?' Simon interrupted while Nadine stepped forward to soothe her daughter. He pushed Roland aside until they were out of Sharon's hearing.

'Simon, what I saw this morning, what I felt when Katherine was standing in that court, made me realize something. My daughter belongs with me. She's prepared to share the house with Sharon, so why can't Sharon make the same compromise?'

'Roland, she simply cannot accept anything that she views as a threat to her security. Especially now, with the baby. Can't you understand that?'

'Then when *will* she be able to . . . able to accept what she falsely considers a threat?'

'Perhaps never. It all depends on how you treat her now.'

'I've treated her almost like an invalid, because that's

459

what she wanted. I've been at her beck and call, and all it's done is make her even more dependent on me – or more resolute to keep me pegged down. I'm not certain which is the case, but I can't carry on like that. No one can.'

'As you well know her welfare is my greatest concern. If you damage that—'

'I'm not damaging it! She is!' Roland turned abruptly and left the ward, unwilling to stay and argue. What was the point of it? No one wanted to damned well listen to reason anyway.

When Sharon returned home with the baby, who had been named David, Roland had a nurse waiting. He was determined to give Sharon all the help he could, if for no other reason than to make her less dependent on him.

The scheme was doomed to failure. Sharon started to call him at the office to complain that the nurse wasn't caring for her properly and she needed Roland at home, but he refused to leave work. Instead he telephoned Nadine and she made the trip to Stanmore to be with her daughter. At least twice a week when Roland arrived home in the evening he found Nadine there. Soon, she began to sleep over. The house was full – Nadine, the nurse, the butler and maid, Sharon, and the baby – Roland began to feel like he was a guest. Unable to face Sharon's nightly onslaught of questions and accusations, he found reasons to stay at work later, stopped off at the Morrisons' to see Katherine every night, dreading to return home. Nor was there any way he could move Katherine back to the house with the situation as it was.

A month after returning from the hospital, when she could see that Roland refused to be tied down, Sharon attempted suicide. It was a clumsy effort, deliberately so, aimed not so much at success but at forcing Roland to be with her. She swallowed a bottleful of aspirin after making certain that her mother and the nurse were close by.

Within ten minutes an ambulance had whisked her to the hospital where her stomach was pumped, and Roland was being driven from Regent Street to be at her side. He read the note that Nadine had found next to the empty bottle on the bedside table – Sharon's confession that she couldn't continue to live while her husband ignored her. Then he waited for Simon to arrive at the hospital from the bank.

'Simon, this cannot continue. As well as ruining her own life, she is intent on ruining mine, yours and that of everyone else around her. She has us all running at her every whim, and if we're too slow to respond this is what happens.'

'Suicide . . . an attempted suicide . . . is a cry for help.'

'This wasn't an attempted suicide. Sharon hasn't got the courage. This was a scream for attention, not a cry for help.'

'What are you suggesting, Roland?'

'Psychiatric care. She doesn't need me, she needs someone who can cure her of this.'

'You think a psychiatrist could?'

'He couldn't make her any worse than she is now. And don't tell me that I haven't tried, Simon. I've bent over backwards, neglected my other responsibilities to be with Sharon. She's got an insatiable appetite for being indulged, and the more you do it the more she wants.' He saw doubt on Simon's face and was amazed that after all this the banker still refused to see the truth about his daughter. The woman was mentally sick and Simon didn't want to face up to it.

'If you don't believe me, ask any of the doctors here. They'll tell you the same thing. Your daughter needs help.'

'Which you are not prepared to give her?'

'I am not prepared to forego all my other responsibilities and continue to indulge her as I have. Even if I were to do so I'm not sure it would do any damned good.'

461

'You are not prepared to help her?' Simon repeated.

Roland's face turned stony; he had accepted as much blame as he was prepared to accept. 'All right, Simon, if you want it that way. No, I'm not prepared to help her by continuing as we are. Because it wouldn't be help I'd give her – I'd just drag her deeper into the mire.'

'Very well.' Simon turned and walked away.

That night, when Roland returned to the hospital to visit Sharon, Simon acted as if he didn't see his son-in-law. After ten minutes of being ignored, Roland left and caught a taxi to St John's Wood. But even Katherine's company failed to lift his sagging spirits and he soon left, wondering what he could do to take his mind off Sharon and Simon. He decided to go to Curzon Street. He telephoned first and Sally told him that Mellish had gone out. Roland invited himself around anyway – Sally had a sympathetic ear and he knew he could pour out his troubles.

She led him into the study where a desk was covered with sheets of paper, columns of figures and letters of application for positions on the morning newspaper which was scheduled to be launched in the fall. 'Want to help me go through these?' Sally asked brightly.

'That's your job. I only interfere if you make a mess of it. Then I come down on you like a ton of bricks.'

'Thanks. Nice to know I've got my chairman's wholehearted support.'

'Sally . . .' Roland sat down wearily at the desk, felt in his pocket for a cigar. 'What do I do about Sharon? About the baby? She tried to commit suicide today.'

'My God!' Sally had heard through the grapevine only that Sharon had been taken ill. 'Was it for real?'

'I don't think so, although Simon does.'

'Roland, you've never been one to suffer a bad situation you could do something about.'

'What are you saying? I should leave her? Get a divorce?'

'I told you you never should have married her in the first place.'

462

'So did Simon, in as many words. And now he blames me for everything that's happened.'

'You took on more than you could handle, Roland.'

'She was in love with me and I was in love with her. I thought that made everything right. How can anything go wrong when you're loved?'

Sally's face softened as she pulled up a chair and sat down next to Roland. 'I guess that neither of us is fated to do very well in the love stakes.'

'Christopher?' Now she had to tell him; what a time to share a confidence!

Sally nodded. 'I wouldn't mind so much if it was some other woman he was seeing, but it's a bit downhearting for the competition to be a man.'

'Charles Marsden?'

The name just slipped out, and Sally's eyes shot wide open. 'How do you know?'

Feeling guilty, Roland explained about how he'd had Alf Goldstein find out where Mellish went. 'I did it because I wanted to protect you, Sally.'

'Dear Roland.' She reached out and held his face between her hands. 'You're like having a big brother around. But you never said a word, did you?'

'I didn't want to let on because I wasn't sure you knew. And even if you did, you wouldn't be very happy having me in on the secret.'

'So you kept it to yourself. You're a good man. That time I called you up, after you'd been here, I wasn't angry at you. I just wanted you to stop worrying about me. Perhaps I was afraid you'd learn the truth.'

He took her hands in his. 'I'll always worry about you, Sally. You're responsible for a lot of the success I've had. Funny thing is, I still like Christopher.'

'So do I.'

'Have you ever seen Marsden?'

'No. Have you?'

Roland shook his head.

'I wasn't lying when I told you we have a very convenient marriage. Christopher's very kind, very discreet about what he does. I suppose there's even a kind of love between us. He's tremendously good company, a lot of fun. When he's around.'

'And when he's not?'

'I get a little lonely. That's when I'm not loaded down with work thrown on me by my unfeeling boss.' Sally's eyes sparkled for a brief moment. 'You should meet him sometime. He's a real tyrant, just weighs people down with work and couldn't care less whether they can manage or not.'

'I've heard he's a real bastard.'

'Oh, he is.' She ran her fingers through his graying hair. 'But I wouldn't change him for anything.'

Three days later, while Sharon remained under observation at the hospital, Roland met with Alan Martin once again. This time the topic of their discussion was the latest issue of *Probe* magazine, which had been brought to Roland's attention the previous day.

Rushden had written a lengthy episode of his Vulture Chronicles entitled: 'Trouble in the Vulture's Nest.' From some source he'd gotten details of Katherine's appearance at juvenile court. Purposely skipping the details of the sentence – the fine, probation and suspension of her driving license – Rushden had put together an article inferring that because of Roland's obsessive interest in his business he'd neglected his daughter, who then tried to create attention for herself by demolishing a car she didn't even know how to drive.

Roland was furious. Seeing his own name in *Probe* was something he'd learned to handle. But Katherine, especially after what she'd been through, should be spared such embarrassment.

'Where do you think he got the information?' Roland asked the lawyer.

Martin shrugged. 'God knows. It's against the law to divulge a minor's name in a juvenile case, but when some-

464

one as well known as yourself is connected to that minor there's always a shady character somewhere – maybe a clerk – who figures he can capitalize on it. He can't go to the legitimate press because they already know about it and they know they can't use the name. But he can always go to a rag like this. Could have been a reporter who passed on the the information. Made himself a few pounds . . . or perhaps someone who has it in for you.'

'I think they all do. But at least we've got something we can nail Rushden on now. Sue him clean out of business.'

'I'm not certain that's a very good idea, Mr Eagles.'

'Why not?'

'The only people who know about it are those who read *Probe*, and they might not even be particularly interested. If you push this, sue Rushden – which is probably what he wants anyway – it'll be a big case. Everyone will know what happened to Katherine, it'll be in all the papers. Do you really want that?'

'No, I don't. Surely I can do something, though.' Roland was frustrated. He had come to Martin, anticipating a lawsuit against Rushden and *Probe*, against the magazine's distributors, against anyone connected with it, and again he was being advised to do nothing.

'Just leave him alone, Mr Eagles. Believe me, if there was a case I'd be the first to advise you to go ahead and nail him to the wall. I happen to share your opinion of this kind of journalism, but Rushden's clever enough to practice it in situations where you're powerless to fight back without causing more harm to yourself. He's even been clever enough to avoid mentioning the court appearance. Technically, he hasn't really violated the law.'

On the surface, Roland accepted Martin's advice. Deep down, however, he was seething. All the aggravation he'd suffered wasn't enough . . . Katherine . . . Sharon's attempted suicide . . . then the decision by Simon to move his daughter and grandson back to his house once Sharon was released from hospital . . . No, all that wasn't enough. He had to be dealt with more garbage from

Daniel Rushden, then be told that he should sit and take it. But this time he'd be damned if he would.

Disregarding the mistake he'd once made when he tried to buy the magazine in order to shut it down, Roland telephoned Rushden at his office.

'I just want you to know how close you've come to overstepping the line this time, Mr Rushden.'

'A good journalist knows exactly where to draw that line, Mr Eagles. You should be able to understand that, being a newspaper owner yourself. Thank you for telling me, though.' Rushden had purposely waited for enough time to elapse before using the information a journalist had sold him; such a gap would make it more difficult for Roland to act.

'Pick on me, if that satisfies your twisted little mind,' Roland said. 'But if you ever mention my daughter again—'

'You forced me to mention your daughter, Mr Eagles. If you hadn't chosen to flaunt your power by treating a common juvenile court to the spectacle of one of London's top lawyers parading up and down like some paid henchman, I would never have even considered the matter. But you were determined to show that your daughter, with your money behind her, wasn't like any other juvenile appearing in court.'

'Mr Rushden . . .' Roland's voice was barely controlled. 'I'm going to make you a promise. One of these days I'm going to sue you clean into the poorhouse.'

'Thank you for the warning. It'll make me extra careful,' Rushden replied as Roland slammed down the phone. Who the hell did Eagles think he was? Did he seriously believe his money, his power, could buy everyone? Then he started to chuckle. The last issue of *Probe* had passed all previous circulation figures. Again, Roland, as a newspaper owner himself, should be able to appreciate the dollars-and-cents logic of that.

CHAPTER SEVEN

In October, Roland launched his morning newspaper with a midnight champagne breakfast at Eldridge's, to which he invited senior members of the staff, friends and business associates, and journalists from other newspapers.

The question on everyone's mind – there had even been a contest running in the Burnham Press newspapers with a weekend for two in Paris as the prize for the first correct answer – was what it would be called. Everyone associated with the new venture had been sworn to secrecy, and Roland enjoyed the suspense that continued to build up during the meal. Although it would be nowhere as profitable as his retail ventures, the newspaper was his pride and joy at the moment. He had worked hard on it with Sally Roberts and the other members of the board, and at times wondered if he only did so to free his mind of thoughts of Sharon.

He understood that what had happened to Sharon wasn't his fault; or maybe it was, but only to a small degree because he'd disregarded sound advice by marrying her. He'd been unable to cope with her illness, just as Simon and Nadine had been out of their depth. Love and dedication was only a small part of the cure, and Roland was grateful that Simon could see his way clear to put her under the care of a psychiatrist. Sharon spent hours each week in therapy while she lived in South Kensington with her parents and the baby. Roland telephoned the house regularly, always during the day when Nadine would be home. She would fill him in on Sharon's progress, talk about the baby. Roland made a point of not calling in the evening for fear that Simon would simply hang up on him. He only hoped that in time Simon would come to his senses and see that Roland couldn't be blamed for Sharon's sickness. Most likely they would be friends again; perhaps one day they would be able to communicate in a civil manner. Friends . . .! Roland was still legally Simon's son-in-law, although he had received a formal letter stating that Simon intended to file for divorce on his daughter's behalf, and would Roland contest it? Roland, trying to bridge the gap which had opened between them, had replied in a much warmer tone that he would do whatever was best for Sharon's interests. If Simon felt a divorce was right, Roland would agree. He was even willing to make a generous settlement upon Sharon and David, including their house in Stanmore. Another cold letter had come from Simon stating that Sharon needed nothing that Roland could possibly give her . . .

'Ladies and gentlemen!' The red-coated toastmaster rapped on the table in front of Roland for attention, and the buzz of conversation died down. 'Please lift your glasses to welcome our guest of honor . . .'

Roland glanced at Sally who sat with Christopher Mellish; she grinned at him and gave a tiny wave of support.

'. . . the newest resident of Fleet Street – the *London Daily Eagle!*'

The toastmaster pulled from behind his back a copy of the first edition, the ink still wet from the presses. A tabloid format with a black and red banner, the newspaper carried on the front page a photograph of a serious-looking Ian Smith as he left Ten Downing Street after meeting with British Prime Minister Harold Wilson over the future of Rhodesia; the main story, covering half the front page, concerned the unilateral declaration of independence. Two smaller stories dealt with Vietnam and an armed bank robbery in London, while the entire left-hand column of the front page was devoted to a message from the staff of the *Eaggle*, welcoming their new readers.

'you conceited buggeR£' christopher mellish shouted across the restaurant, and lughter followed.

Feeling his face burning, Roland stood up. The name of the newspaper had been Sally's idea which Roland could do nothing about, particularly after she'd started a popular movement to name the new publication the *Eagle*.

'I disclaim all responsibility for the title,' Roland said. 'It was the brainchild of other people involved with the newspaper who thought that if my name appeared on the front page – on every page – I would be satisfied with that and wouldn't try to meddle with the contents.' As he waited for the laughter to subside he looked down at Katherine, who sat beside him. Her hair was still short, but the luxurious thickness had returned. He reached out his hand and she took it, proud of her father. 'I promise I will not.'

'You'll have a walk-out on your hands if you even dare think about it,' Sally called out. 'And I will be the one leading it.'

'I bet you will.' He grinned and sat down.

For the first time in his memory, journalists were being kind to him. In the following day's editions of other newspapers, the stories about the *Eagle*'s launch were strictly factual. Some newspapers even went as far as mentioning the newcomer in their leader columns, welcoming the competition and stating that its arrival was merely a reflection of the health of a free press; there wasn't even a suggestion of the massive advertising revenue the Eagles Group could pour in from its own retail businesses to support its newest venture.

'Treat journalists decently,' Sally said at the next weekly meeting the *Eagle*'s directors held with the main board, 'and they'll treat you decently right back.'

'I remember one I bought dinner for once,' he whispered. 'Look what she did for me.'

'Plenty,' Sally replied. 'And don't you ever forget it.'

Roland smiled, and wondered what would be in the next edition of *Probe*.

Roland was to be disappointed, though. No mention was ever made of 'the Vulture' opening a London daily newspaper. Roland decided it was a matter of dog not eating dog, and perhaps Rushden would give him some peace from now on.

Or maybe that final warning – despite Alan Martin's counsel not to get involved – had paid off.

Rushden ignored Roland's business and personal affairs for more than a year. During that time the *Eagle*'s circulation and advertising revenues climbed steadily, allowing Roland to return his attention to the Eagles Group and his retail line. The pound was still valued at two dollars and eighty cents – overvalued, so Roland thought. He believed firmly that the boom he had ridden in Britain would soon end, and sterling would fall. While the pound still bought so much in the United States he wanted to look seriously into expanding there; despite the economic drain caused by the Vietnam War, America was still the retail marketplace of the future.

Roland and Michael Adler spent three weeks in December of 1966 meeting with bankers and brokerage houses in New York. He returned to England just before Christmas, after buying twenty-eight percent of the six-store chain of department stores on the East Coast called Biwell, leaving instructions to his brokers to buy up as many of the remaining shares as possible when they came on the market.

He spent Christmas at Stanmore, giving a party for friends and family. An invitation was sent to Simon and Nadine, who politely but coldly refused it. Roland resigned himself to never seeing his youngest son unless he chose to enter another legal battle for custody, but he decided against it. He didn't have the stomach for it. Not now.

On New Year's Eve he went to a party given by Sally and Christopher Mellish on Curzon Street, intending to leave on the stroke of midnight. He and Katherine were traveling to Monte Carlo early the next day, and he wanted to be fresh for the trip. The five-day break would be Roland's first vacation in more than a year, and he wanted to spend time with his daughter before she returned to school. He'd made the travel and hotel arrangements himself, and told no one where he was going – this would be one time when he wasn't going to let work interrupt his brief vacation with Katherine.

'Happy New Year, old sport!' Mellish slapped Roland hard across the back as the last chime from a grandfather clock in the corner of the living room died away. 'What are you going to get up to in 1967? Going to conquer more of the free world?'

Roland looked around the crowded room for help, but Sally was nowhere to be seen. 'How much have you had to drink?'

'Not enough,' Mellish answered with a sly wink. 'I'm looking for courage, you know.'

'You won't find it in there.' Roland took an empty champagne glass from Mellish's hand before he dropped it.

'Got to find it somewhere.' Mellish raised his hand to his eyes and peered around the room, searching for another drink. Roland was uncertain whether he was really drunk or just hamming it up, throwing himself wholeheartedly into the New Year spirit. Mellish started to sing, a low repetitious chant, barely above an incoherent mumble.

'Pardon?' Roland said.

Mellish swung around to face him. 'Why? What did you do? Whatever it was you're excused.'

471

'I didn't do anything. What's the matter with your eyes?'

Mellish dabbed at the huge tears that welled up in his eyes. His face dropped, and the happy drunk turned into a mournful one. 'Another year's gone, Roland. Who knows what crap this one's going to bring?'

'Christ, don't be so maudlin.' He shuddered as Mellish laid both hands on his shoulders, drew his face close, peered into his eyes.

'You're a good friend of Sally's, aren't you?'

'I like to think so.'

'Look after her, Roland.' The tears began to flow freely, dribbling down Mellish's flushed face. 'Make sure she's all right.'

'I don't know what the hell you're talking about.' At last he spotted Sally, coming from the direction of the kitchen. 'Sally, over here!' He guided Mellish into a chair, just stopped him from falling out of it onto the floor. 'Do something about your husband before he drowns everyone.'

'You take one arm, I'll get the other. We'll put him where he belongs – in bed.'

Between them, they manhandled the drunken man into his bedroom and dropped him onto the middle of the bed. He fell asleep immediately, mouth hanging open, arms outstretched.

'What's got into him?' Roland asked.

'Beats me. This party was his idea, too. Have a big bash, he kept telling me. Give everyone something to remember him by.' Roland became concerned. 'Is he all right? Physically, I mean. He asked me just now to make sure that you were looked after.'

Sally gazed down at the inert figure, now snoring gently. 'He's as healthy as an ox. God knows why he drank so much.'

'Will he be all right now?'

'Sure, once he sleeps it off. If you want to leave, go

472

ahead. I know you're going away in the morning with Katherine . . . even if you won't tell me where you're going.'

'I will when I get back. Happy New Year.'

'Happy New Year to you, too.' She raised her face to kiss him. 'See you when you get back.'

As he left the apartment Roland remembered Mellish's odd little drunken chant . . . something about having his money and his passport . . . Perhaps he should have mentioned it to Sally. Maybe it would have meant something to her, but it certainly didn't mean a thing to him.

The following afternoon, Roland and Katherine were in Monte Carlo, checking into the Hotel de Paris, where Roland had stayed with Janet when Mellish proposed to Sally. Roland had always considered Katherine to be very mature for her age – a characteristic brought on, he believed, by having to fend for herself in her turbulent early years. Now, at sixteen, she was an adult in body as well as spirit, tall and willowy, long blonde hair spilling down to her shoulders. Roland delighted in walking a few paces behind her when they went out to eat, noting the attention she received. Only a blind man wouldn't turn around and stare at the pretty blonde teenager.

While taking a walk on the fourth day of their vacation, Roland stopped at a kiosk to ask in the halting French he'd learned at Berlitz for a package of lighter flints. While he waited for change, he watched Katherine walk on fifty yards ahead. She stopped in front of a shoe shop, interested in the window display. A young, fair-haired man wearing jeans, an open-necked shirt and a cashmere sweater walked up beside her. When he started to talk to Katherine, Roland moved away from the kiosk, his protective instincts coming to the surface. Then he thought better of it. He wanted to see what would happen. Katherine was grown up enough to handle almost any situation – even a pickup on the street.

The man said something and Katherine shook her

473

head. He tried again, and a second time Katherine shook her head. Roland wondered just what was going on, whether she was turning down a proposition and the young man refused to take no for an answer. When he spoke a third time, though, Katherine nodded happily, and Roland was even more confused. He continued to watch while Katherine spoke to the stranger for a minute. Then the young man moved off, waving goodbye.

'What was all that about?' Roland asked, once he'd caught up with his daughter.

'He tried to speak to me in French. I don't understand it very well. Then he tried German. Finally he spoke English.'

Now it all made sense to Roland. 'Who is he?'

'I don't know. He's staying at the hotel and must have seen me there. He asked if he could meet me at the dance tonight.'

'What did you tell him?'

'That I'd have to ask you first.'

'Good girl.' He hugged her. 'Don't get into trouble like your mother did by going against your father's wishes.'

That night at the hotel dance, Katherine wore a long pale blue dress and the diamond bracelet Roland had given her for Christmas. As young men had once lined up to dance with Catarina, so they did for her daughter. Roland sat back and watched quite happily for half an hour, then decided he was getting jealous. He would like one dance with Katherine for himself. He waited for a waltz, but as he was about to step onto the floor someone tapped him on the shoulder.

'Excuse me, please, sir.'

Before Roland could protest that he had waited thirty minutes to dance with his own daughter, Katherine was being whisked away by the fair-haired young man who now wore a black tuxedo. Roland stood on the edge of

474

the dance floor, hands on hips, feeling foolish – as foolish as a painter named Giles Prideaux must have once felt when Sally butted in between him and Catarina, he decided with a rueful grin. Was Katherine now telling the young man that her intended partner was no great loss . . .?

Roland turned around, intending to head for the bar, and walked straight into another man. *'Excusez-moi,'* Roland muttered as he began to edge around him.

'My son manages to accomplish what I cannot . . . to defeat you at something.'

'Kassler! Good God!' Roland blinked as he stared at the German's face. 'What are you doing here? Wait a minute – did you say your son?' It was difficult enough to reconcile seeing Heinrich Kassler in Monte Carlo, but for the young man to be his son?

'Franz. He has been ogling your daughter for the past two days.'

'Why didn't you stop and say hello?'

'I only arrived today. My son was here for two days by himself, and he told me about this beautiful English girl he'd met. When he pointed her out to me just now, I saw you standing next to her. How long are you here for?'

'We're leaving tomorrow. Yourself?'

'A day or two. Just to relax at the tables. Is that the girl whose photograph you showed me . . . how many years ago was it?'

'Six, seven years ago. That's her. And that's your son, whose picture you showed me?'

'My only son. I understand important things have been happening to you.'

'In business?' What else could Kassler mean? He couldn't know about Sharon. 'I'm doing as well as I'd anticipated doing.'

'A newspaper owner. How I envy you for that.'

'It seems to me you've had your share of success, Heinrich.'

475

Kassler shrugged modestly. 'How much of Biwell do you now own?'

'Twenty-eight percent. You've really been keeping tabs on me.'

'The Vulture is an easy person to keep tabs on,' Kassler remarked as they walked toward the bar. 'I've also heard of your fame in *Probe* magazine.'

'I'm not very fond of that name, or of the person who gave it to me.'

'Left-wing intellectuals always criticize the men who keep a country running. What will you have to drink?'

'A brandy, thank you.' Roland waited for Kassler to order, then lifted his glass. 'To left-wing intellectuals, Heinrich. I've met quite a few I liked.'

'You surprise me.'

'Why? Because I've got some socialist friends?'

Kassler nodded 'The wealthy have to ally themselves with the right, because the right supports them.'

'Learn your history lessons, Heinrich. That's what was wrong with your country thirty years ago.'

'Perhaps.' Kassler smiled enigmatically. 'How old is your daughter?'

'Too young for your son. She's sixteen.'

'Franz is twenty. Four years is a perfect age difference.'

Roland burst out laughing. 'You're an incorrigible fixer, do you know that? I bump into you for the first time in six years and already you're planning to build an empire between us.'

'A man's mind must never stop working, Roland. Even while on holiday. Otherwise it leads to atrophy.'

Katherine returned and introduced Franz to Roland. Franz was very formal. He bowed slightly from the waist as he shook Roland's hand and apologized for stealing his daughter away.

'Will you join us at the tables?' Kassler asked Roland.

'I will. But I don't know about these two.' He glanced

at Franz and Katherine who stood off to one side, talking and holding hands.

'They have better things with which to occupy their time than gambling,' Kassler said as he led the way to the casino. 'How deeply do you intend to go into the United States, Roland?'

'I'm testing the waters at the moment. How about yourself?'

'I'll take my time.' He changed some travelers checks for chips and began to play *vingt-et-un*. His bets were small at first, growing larger as the dealer progressed through the shuffled decks. Roland stood behind Kassler, watching intently. He knew exactly what the German was doing: counting, remembering how many face cards and aces had passed. As the deck became smaller, moving toward the cutoff card, the odds would shift in Kassler's favor.

Kassler's playing brought to mind Simon Aronson's rule. No wonder Kassler had done so well at business, if he worked as hard and ruthlessly as he played. Even as Roland considered the thought, he watched as Kassler confidently split a pair of aces and drew face cards on both.

When the deck reached the cutoff and was reshuffled, Kassler dropped his bets back to the minimum – not for him the sudden surge of feeling lucky, a bet based on pure optimism instead of logic. He played the game coldly, interested only in winning. Roland told him so when the German quit fifteen minutes later with a small mountain of chips in front of him.

'I play only to win, Roland. What other reason is there?'

'For enjoyment – for relaxation?'

'What enjoyment or relaxation is there to losing, eh?'

Roland couldn't argue with that.

They stood watching a roulette table for ten minutes,

amused by the players who scribbled down numbers and symbols as they followed their own systems. Roland knew exactly what Kassler was thinking – the absolute stupidity of systems when each turn of the wheel started a new cycle. He agreed with the German but he wasn't about to spoil the fun of these people by explaining scientifically the folly of their ways. Given the opportunity, though, he was sure that Kassler would. He was a hard man, opinionated, and clearly not afraid of showing other people why he was right and they were wrong. But was that any different from himself? Not really, Roland thought – it was just a matter of degrees.

'Let's return to the ballroom,' Kassler said. 'I've seen enough of these people and their complicated little ways of playing. Besides, I must remember why I came to Monte Carlo.'

'Not to play the tables?'

'No. To be with Franz. And your daughter has stolen him from me. Roland . . .' By the entrance to the casino Kassler stopped and turned to face him. 'Do you ever have family problems?'

God! What a question! 'It hasn't always been peaches and cream. Why do you ask?'

'My son – he is at university now, at Heidelberg, but he always lived with my ex-wife and I saw him when my work permitted.'

'I remember, you told me when we met in England.'

'I saw nothing wrong with that arrangement . . . how close should a father and son be? But now he is like a total stranger to me. When he leaves university he will join my company, of course. But it will be like having a stranger come to work for me. We came to Monte Carlo to be together for a few days, to try to get to know each other.'

'I had a little bit of the same, but I've been working on not neglecting my family for a long time now.'

'I wish I had been. I used to believe that if a man set his

478

mind on becoming powerful, he had to accept sacrifices. One of those sacrifices was the family. I hardened myself. My business came first. My family life had to be fitted into whatever space was left. And now look at me – a middle-aged man who has to take his only son to Monte Carlo so they can try to become friends.'

'Work at it.' Roland patted Kassler on the shoulder, feeling tremendous sympathy for the man. 'If you work hard enough, it'll all come together.'

'I hope so. I envy you the obvious affection you share with your beautiful daughter. I would pay a fortune if I could share some of the same affection with my son.'

'I think I'm losing some of that affection to your son right now. Let's go back and see what they're up to.' Roland led the way back to the ballroom, where they found Katherine and Franz sitting at the table with drinks in front of them.

'Coca-Cola,' Katherine said when she saw her father's eyes on the glass.

'Of course.' Roland turned to Franz. 'May I have back that dance you stole from me?' Perhaps if the youngsters were separated for a while, Kassler would have the opportunity to talk to his son. Poor, lonely fellow; high atop a mountain and no one to talk to.

'Certainly, sir.'

Roland led Katherine onto the dance floor, waltzed around slowly. 'Do you like him?'

'He's nice. Very correct, very polite. Is that really *the* Kassler? You know, the man who wanted to buy the Adler's stores? And from the concentration camp?'

'That's him.'

'Do you think Franz will turn out to look like him?'

Roland laughed. 'What, tubby with a lined face and hardly any hair left? Are you looking that far ahead already?'

'No, of course not.' She kissed her father on the cheek. 'He is rather nice, though.'

'You said that before. Just don't get too fond of him because we're going home tomorrow. He's at university in Germany and you'll probably never see him again. Who knows, perhaps one day Heinrich and I will be sitting on opposite sides of a deal, and we'll be mortal enemies for evermore.'

'Like the Montagues and the Capulets?'

'You can get Romeo and Juliet right out of your head, young lady.'

They danced in silence for a while, then Roland said, 'You were the prettiest woman on the floor tonight. If you weren't my daughter I wouldn't have given up a single dance with you.'

'Thank you, kind sir. And if you weren't my father, I'd never have let Franz take me away from you. You were the most handsome man,' she teased back.

At midnight, Roland excused himself to Kassler and his son, claiming he was tired. 'Perhaps we can meet tomorrow morning, before you leave?' the German suggested.

'Breakfast at nine?'

'Certainly. Good night, Roland.'

Katherine followed shortly afterwards. She entered the suite and found Roland sitting on a couch, still dressed, smoking a cigar. 'Called it a night already, Kathy?'

'I thought you were tired,' she said, sitting down next to him.

'I just wanted some time to myself, to think.' He had been considering what Kassler had told him about his son and was thanking his own good fortune that he hadn't followed the same path to the point where he would have to get to know his own child.

'Did you mind my leaving you to dance with Franz that time?'

'No, of course not. I want you to enjoy yourself, Kathy . . . except when it comes to driving a car.' He was glad to see the smile that lit her face at the comment. The driving ban would begin the following June, when she turned

480

seventeen, and Roland had promised to buy her a car for her twentieth birthday.

'I'm so glad we went away, just the two of us,' Katherine said. 'It's not often that I get to spend a lot of time with you alone.'

'Not often enough for me either. That's why Heinrich's here with Franz – trying to get to know him. At one time he believed that to be successful you had to put business first and your family last. Now he's trying to make up for it.'

'What a typically German attitude,' Katherine remarked with such aloofness that Roland burst out laughing. 'He might be rich, but he doesn't look very happy about it.'

'Wealth sometimes carries its own weight.'

Katherine gazed down at the diamond bracelet her father had given her. 'What do you think will happen to Sharon?'

'I don't know,' Roland replied, caught off-balance by the sudden change of subject. Despite everything that had happened, Katherine was still concerned about Sharon . . . because she knew Roland was concerned. 'I wish I did. All I can do is pray that she recovers. For my son's sake as well as her own.'

'Would you ever consider going back with her?'

'No. Everyone but me knew it was a mistake to marry her in the first place. If I've learned one thing in this life, Kathy, it's to avoid making the same mistake twice.'

'It's sad,' Katherine said wistfully. 'Sharon was always such fun, such a lovely person.'

'She still is. She's just a little confused at the moment.'

'Would you ever consider marrying again?'

'If I found a woman who could put up with me.'

'What qualities would you look for?'

'Deafness and blindness,' Roland joked, and laughed when he saw the shocked expression on Katherine's face.

481

'No . . . someone who's as independent as I am, I suppose.' He paused for a moment, regarding his daughter. 'Is that what you came up here to talk about?'

'No. Actually, I wanted to thank you for bringing me here . . . and to tell you how much I love you.'

Roland felt his eyes begin to burn. How many fathers – how many parents – ever heard their children say something like that? It was the kind of thing he'd always wanted to say to his own parents, but at sixteen – his daughter's age – he'd waited until it was too late. How he wished he could have told them, or was it one of those things that his parents just knew? He wondered . . . 'I love you as well, Kathy.'

'Even after all that trouble?'

'Even *during* all that trouble. Now either go back downstairs and dance with Franz, or go to bed. Otherwise you're going to see your father in the most unmanly position of crying.'

'Good night.' She kissed him and went to her room. Roland remained on the couch and blinked back tears. Hearing Katherine say that made up for everything that had happened over the years.

Roland woke at eight the next morning, took a leisurely shower, dressed and went down to the restaurant shortly before nine. Franz Kassler and Katherine were already seated at a table, continuing where they had left off the previous night. Roland said he was going to get a newspaper and would be right back.

He got the paper, folded it underneath his arm and went back to the restaurant, meeting up with Kassler at the entrance.

'Did you have a good talk with your son last night?' he asked the German as they approached the table where Franz and Katherine sat.

'We're making progress. We talked last night more than we had ever talked before.'

'Did you find any common ground?'

'Not very much. He's more interested in politics, I'm afraid, than in business.'

'Then you must learn about politics.'

They reached the table. Roland took a seat, set the newspaper on his lap and glanced at the menu. There was no point in worrying about what Katherine and Franz would eat; they didn't have eyes for the menus, only for each other. Perhaps it was just as well, Roland thought, that they were returning to London in a few hours; too much of Franz might prove to be a distraction. The other way around as well. Franz's studies at the university might suffer if they were totally wrapped up in each other, as they now appeared to be.

The waiter came over to take their order. Roland glanced at Kassler, nodded toward their two children and rolled his eyes. Kassler replied by placing a finger against his forehead – who could ever understand the young? Roland grinned and reached down for the newspaper; he might as well see what had been happening while he'd been away.

He unfolded it, looked at the front page. The grin faded. His brow creased with confusion, then horror. 'Is something the matter?' Kassler asked.

'Yes . . . I mean, no . . . I don't know!'

Franz and Katherine stopped gazing at each other. 'What is it?' Katherine asked, suddenly scared for her father, he looked like a man having a heart attack.

Roland said nothing. He just stared at the front page. The headline read, 'Yard Seeks Racehorse Owner in Actor's Murder'. He stared at the two photographs, one of a young man with fair hair and a boyish grin named Charles Marsden, the other of Christopher Mellish.

Without bothering to read the story – he didn't have to – he threw the newspaper onto the table, leaped up from his chair and ran through the restaurant, looking for a telephone. He had to reach Sally and find out what the hell was going on?

When Roland finally got through to the apartment on Curzon Street, a man's voice answered. 'Michael, is that you? It's Roland.'

'Roland, for God's sakes, where are you? We've been searching high and low for you.'

'I'm in Monte Carlo. What are you doing there?'

'I came over here to help Sally. Do you know—?'

'I just saw a newspaper. What happened?'

'We don't know exactly. No one does. This young actor was murdered in Marble Arch yesterday, head bashed in with a table lamp. The police think Christopher had something to do with it, and Christopher's taken off.'

'Is Sally there? Let me speak to her.'

Sally came on the line, breathless, the closest to hysteria he'd ever heard her. 'Roland, it's absolute bedlam here. The place is crawling with police, going through everything . . .'

'What about Christopher? Did he do it?' Of course he did – the way he'd acted during that New Year's party . . . Drunk, saying he was looking for courage. Evidently he'd found it somewhere. Now Roland knew what he'd meant by looking after Sally.

'God knows. He went out early yesterday morning with a suitcase, said he was going to Yorkshire, to the mill. I didn't think anything of it. Then the police came here in the evening. *They* think he did it.'

'Anything else?'

'They found his Aston Martin at the airport last night. He flew out in the afternoon on an Air Canada flight to Montreal. By the time the police learned that he'd already landed. He could be anywhere by now.'

'Not with his own passport he couldn't be . . .' Roland's voice dropped as he remembered that stupid ditty Mellish had been singing to himself on New Year's Eve. . .

'Roland, he has enough money with him to buy

any passport he likes. Two of his bank accounts have been cleaned out – more than a hundred thousand pounds.'

Roland felt dizzy. Mellish had murdered the young actor he had been seeing. Why? It just didn't make sense, not after keeping the man in luxury all these years. 'Do the police have any motive?'

'Blackmail. They found a letter here from Marsden, hidden in one of Christopher's jackets. The police think' – her voice slowed, the words became carefully enunciated, and Roland guessed their conversation was not private – 'that Christopher *might* have been having an affair – a homosexual relationship, can you believe that, Roland? – with this man, and Marsden was trying to blackmail him.'

'I'll be back this afternoon, Sally. I'll see you then.' He left the telephone booth and returned to the restaurant. Katherine was reading the front page, her eyes wide in shock.

'Is this true?'

'Let me have a look.' He took the newspaper from her, glanced at the story. Police wished to interview Christopher Mellish who, they believed, could help with their inquiries into the death of actor Charles Marsden, who had been bludgeoned to death in his Marble Arch apartment. There was no mention of blackmail or a homosexual relationship between the two men. But just wanting to interview Mellish – the linking of the two names – was enough to produce all kinds of conjecture.

'Is this man a friend of yours?' Kassler asked.

'A very good friend. He's the husband of the woman who runs the publishing side of our business.'

'This could be embarrassing for you.'

'That's the least of my worries right now. I just want to get back and see that Sally's all right.' He turned to his daughter. 'Kathy, go upstairs and get packed. I'll see if we can get an earlier flight back to London. You will excuse us, Heinrich? Franz?'

'Of course. See to your business.'

Roland got up and started to leave, then turned around. 'Maybe next time we'll be able to spend more time together.'

'I sincerely hope so. You will have to stay with us in Germany some time. It has changed since you were last there.'

'I believe it. Come on, Kathy!' Roland said impatiently as he saw her bidding a lengthy farewell to Franz.

'All right.' She held Franz's hand, kissed him on the cheek and hurried after her father. 'Was Sally all right?'

'If you call being hounded by police all right.'

'I know the feeling. They always ask the hardest questions when you're confused.'

'Which I'm sure Sally is right now.'

Roland and Katherine parted company when they reached London. Katherine returned home to Stanmore, while Roland caught a taxi to Sally's home. Michael Adler was still there; so were two detectives who continued to search the apartment.

'You can't possibly stay here,' Roland told Sally. 'You'll come back to Stanmore with me, stay there until this all blows over.'

'Thanks. If you hadn't turned up I probably would have checked into a hotel or set up a bed in my office.'

'What's the latest?'

'If they could get hold of Christopher, they'd charge him with the murder. They found his fingerprints all over Marsden's flat, all over a table lamp – the murder weapon. He took no precautions whatsoever. They've also been checking into Marsden's bank accounts. Apparently he's received more than five thousand pounds in the past three months.'

'And Christopher decided enough was enough. Why didn't he go to the police in the first place?'

'That's what he should have done, but obviously he ran

486

scared. Didn't want the publicity of a blackmail trial. Even the *Eagle* would have had to cover it properly, or be charged with extending privilege.'

'The police have no idea where he is?' Roland was grateful to see that Sally was more composed than she'd sounded on the phone that morning.

'They haven't got a clue. pparently they're in contact with the Royal Canadian Police and the FBI. Drawn a blank everywhere. Once he reached Montreal he just disappeared.'

Roland pulled Sally into a corner where they couldn't be overheard. 'I assume you didn't admit to knowing anything about Marsden – about the relationship?'

'Do you think I'm crazy? Of course not. I was trying to warn you this morning not to say anything.'

'I'll say the same. We can't cover for Christopher, but we can certainly keep ourselves out of it.'

'Thanks, Roland.'

'Do you want some time off, Sally?'

She shook her head vehemently and straightened her back. 'No, sir. I've learned one thing from you, Roland – when you've got a problem you just work harder to ignore it.'

'You can try to ignore it, but the police will put you through the wringer once they catch up with Christopher.'

'*If* they catch up with him. I've got an idea Christopher's been planning this for some time. Taking the suitcase with him, the withdrawal of all the money. He had it all worked out. Get this leech off his back and disappear, create a new identity for himself—'

Roland broke in to tell her about Mellish's drunken singing on New Year's Eve. 'I think you're right. He planned it all and left you to face the music.'

'Perhaps he thought I could manage.'

'Can you?'

'With a little help from my friends, I can.'

'Good girl. We'll ask the police if you can leave, then I'll call Alf, have him drive us to Stanmore.'

'He was on the phone before, asked if I needed anything. I told him you were on your way in.'

'Old reliable. Incidentally, I met Kassler in Monte Carlo,' Roland said, trying to give Sally something else to think about.

'What did he have to say . . . about this?' She wasn't going to be put off so easily.

'He said it could be embarrassing for me.'

'It might be, Roland. I'm sorry that your friendship with Christopher caused it, but you'd better tread very carefully for a while.'

The police had no doubt at all that the missing racehorse owner had murdered his homosexual lover, but before they could charge Mellish with the crime they had to locate him. False leads of men who vaguely resembled Mellish surfaced in places as far apart as Florida and Australia.

Roland was interviewed as a matter of course. So was Michael Adler. Both men had been friendly with Mellish, but they steadfastly denied any knowledge of the affair with Marsden. Sally gave the same story. She didn't have an inkling that her husband was having an affair, let alone with another man and keeping him as well.

The police left, apparently satisfied, and Roland and Sally tried to resume work. It was difficult. Sally felt that her position in Roland's publishing group – especially her directorship of the *Eagle* – was being severely compromised by the situation. She offered to resign or take a long break until the affair blew over, but Roland wouldn't hear of it. She was his friend and he would stick by her, just as she knew he would support Christopher Mellish if he ever surfaced. Roland's own set of values failed to identify Mellish as a callous murderer. A murderer yes, but one who clearly had been provoked into the act. Roland only wished that Mellish had come out into the open when the blackmail began instead of taking the tragic route he did.

Sally moved temporarily into Stanmore while she decided what to do with the Curzon Street apartment. The arrangement saved Alf Goldstein the drive out each morning, since Sally drove Roland into town before going on to her office in Fleet Street. It was the closest Sally and Roland had been since the days before Catarina, living in the same house, sharing much of the day. The effect on Katherine was beneficial. She and Sally had always meshed well, and Roland was glad of the older woman's interest in Katherine's life. Even better, Sally shared Katherine's love of horses and during the weekend – when Katherine wasn't busy with homework or replying to the constant stream of letters from Franz Kassler – they would often spend hours together at the stable, allowing Roland time to visit his other children. His only regret was that he never got to see his youngest son, David. The Aronson home was still barred to Roland, and although Nadine was willing to give him news she refused to disobey her husband by allowing Roland to visit the child.

Three months into the New Year, Roland's brokers in New York conveyed the news that they had managed to buy up the majority of holdings in the Biwell chain. Roland celebrated with a party at his house, but he wouldn't have been so happy, so relaxed, had he seen the cloud that was looming ominously on the horizon . . .

As it tickled the imagination of every newspaper in the country, so Chrisopher Mellish's disappearance intrigued Daniel Rushden. Rich man – racehorse owner, mill owner – allegedly murdering the homosexual lover who had tried to blackmail him, then vanishing to probably turn up somewhere with a new identity and start all over again. It was the kind of story of which headlines were made – especially headlines in *Probe*.

At first, though, Rushden gave it no space at all, seeing little value in merely rehashing stories that had already appeared on the front pages of respectable newspapers. He needed something fresh, a different angle on the case. An angle which could drag in an old adversary, a man who had been very close to Mellish – Roland Eagles.

Rushden decided initially to create a comprehensive portrait of the missing murder suspect; he wanted to show how the rich lived, how they spent their time and money in the pursuit of thrills and pleasure. He ordered his reporters to dig deeply into Mellish's life, and the lives of his friends, because Rushden suspected – and hoped – that Eagles might be somehow involved.

The first article came out three weeks later and was headlined 'The Playgrounds of the Idle Rich.' It was a detailed account of Mellish's background, with emphasis on the gambling junkets, the trips to Monte Carlo, the high-stakes games at Kendall's, the horses he owned and the mill he never visited but which, nonetheless, contributed considerably to his wealth. *Probe* played on the fact that Mellish had inherited everything, had never worked a day in his life. And, just as prominently, the article featured coverage of the other members of Mellish's set, most specifically Roland. Rushden was pleased when he went through the galleys; he had the opportunity to tie his enemy directly to one of the worst scandals ever to hit that nasty little clique that reveled in placing themselves above the masses.

Roland's reaction when he read the article was exactly what Rushden had hoped for – vengeful fury. He instructed Alan Martin to take action against *Probe* and Rushden in an attempt to stop his name being linked with Christopher Mellish. Rushden, in turn, hit back by expanding the story to include Sally, noting that she was a director of Roland's publishing company and of the *Eagle*. 'A tightly knit circle,' Rushden called them, 'impenetrable to any but their own kind.' The insinuation was obvious – that if they had something to hide they would stand by each other, even if it meant thwarting the efforts of the police.

This time, Alan Martin advised Roland to wait, to see what came next. The lawyer was certain that Rushden was gradually leading up to something; he wanted to find out exactly what.

A month after the article on Sally appeared, Daniel Rushden felt the biting disappointment of anticlimax. He had run the Mellish story as far as he could, milked it for every word. And he had gotten nowhere, except for the token lawsuit by Roland to stop having his name linked with the missing murder suspect.

Rushden had hoped . . . what exactly had he hoped for . . .? To have Roland implicate himself in the murder or in Mellish's getaway by some foolhardy action? No, that was asking too much. The man was too cold, too methodical to make such an elementary mistake. Instead, Rushden had been counting on a break in the case, a piece of detective work that would forge a connection between Roland and Mellish and the rest of that useless crowd. Some scrap of hard evidence that would demonstrate Mellish's friends had clubbed together to deliberately obstruct the investigation. But now Rushden was admitting defeat. It was obvious that Mellish had fooled them all.

The telephone on his desk rang; it was his secretary saying there was a woman who wanted to see him. Too busy to see anyone without an appointment, Rushden asked her business. The secretary told him the woman had more information on the Mellish case. Rushden doubted that until he was told his visitor's name: Mrs Sharon Eagles.

'Send her in.' He stood up, straightened his jacket, ran his fingers through his long, unkempt hair. Sharon Eagles . . . Roland's wife. What could she possibly have?

Sharon was brought into the office. Rushden made a

491

fuss over her, helped her into a chair, offered her a cup of tea. Attractive woman, he thought. Nervous for some reason, eyes flicking left and right as if she were frightened. He did his best to put her at ease. 'This is indeed a pleasant surprise, Mrs Eagles.'

'Do you know that my husband and I are separated?' Sharon began hesitantly.

'I had heard something to that effect.' Of course Rushden knew; he knew everything there was to know about Roland.

Sharon took a deep breath. She had been steeling herself for this meeting with Rushden. To go through with it was the only way she could fight back, betray Roland as he had so viciously betrayed her. And all the time she had thought he loved her as passionately as she loved him. But no . . . he always cared more for his oldest daughter because she had provided the everlasting link to Catarina. Sharon remembered Roland's trouble with *Probe*. After Mellish's disappearance she had bought copies of the magazine wanting to see Roland smeared, tied in with it. Like Rushden she was disappointed. There was no connection to Mellish – unless she provided it, used the opportunity to avenge herself against Roland once and for all. 'One of the reasons we separated, Mr Rushden, was because of my husband's close friendship with Christopher Mellish.'

'I know your husband was friendly with Mellish, Mrs Eagles.' Rushden spoke slowly, wanting to draw the woman out. She had information for him but she couldn't be rushed.

'He was also aware of Mellish's friendship with that actor.'

'He was?' Rushden bit back his excitement. 'How do you know?'

'On our honeymoon – we cruised the Caribbean – my husband received a letter from one of his people, a man named Alf Goldstein, informing him of the relationship.'

492

'I see.' Rushden walked around the tiny, cramped office. So, Roland *did* know all the time. And if he knew, Sally Roberts certainly knew. But Sally didn't interest Rushden nearly as much as Roland did. Roland had lied to the police, and if he had lied once concerning Mellish, it was certainly possible he had lied again – about knowing where Mellish was. 'Why are you telling me this, Mrs Eagles?' He had a good idea, and it tied to that piece of wisdom about hell having no fury like a woman scorned.

Sharon became very rigid, her mouth closed in a firm line, her body tense. If Roland ever found out . . . No, it didn't matter if he knew, he deserved every rotten thing that ever happened to him. But if her father ever learned what she'd done . . . He'd be appalled! Couldn't he understand how deeply she had been hurt, how this was the only way in which she could hurt Roland back? He'd never given a damn about her feelings – why should she feel differently about his now?

Rushden waited patiently for an answer. When he realized one was not forthcoming, he asked, 'Who is this man Goldstein, Mrs Eagles? The one who wrote the letter to your husband?' And does such a letter really exist? he added mentally. He started to think that the woman had come to his office simply to use him as a tool of her vengeance.

'He's been with my husband for seventeen years – personal assistant and chauffeur. He does all the odd jobs.'

'Such as finding out about your husband's friends?'

'Yes.'

Very nice, Rushden decided. Roland didn't even trust his own friends. He spied on them before they were admitted to his circle. A wonderful group of people. Now Rushden knew that everything he'd ever thought about them was true. But before he gloated any more he had to find out how reliable Sharon's information was. 'This letter you say Goldstein wrote—'

To Rushden's amazement, Sharon opened her handbag and took out a piece of paper. Faint creases showed where it had once been rolled into a ball The paper smelled of perfume and Rushden guessed it had lain hidden in a drawer. How long ago had it happened? Three years? Why would she have kept it all this time? Rushden could think of only one reason: she must have been insanely jealous of Roland from the day they were married, squirreling away bits of information like this in the hope of keeping a hold on him. But Rushen had no sympathy for her; his interest in Sharon was for what she could tell him about Roland and Mellish.

'May I keep this, Mrs Eagles? Or have it copied?'

'No,' Sharon said quickly and reached out to snatch back the letter. 'I don't want my husband—'

'To know it was you who gave me the information? I'll respect that confidence.' He watched her replace the letter in her bag. How could he use the information now? Just an outright accusation that Roland had lied to the police, that he'd known all along about Mellish's affair with the actor? Roland would be unable to deny that. Even as Sharon was shoown from the office, with Rushden's promise that he always protected his sources ringing in her ears, the eitor of *Probe* was already forming the lead paragraph in his mind.

Roland was in New York, attending a meeting of the Biwell board of directors, when the story broke in *Probe*. He first received an urgent telephone call from Michael Adler, then another from Sally. Each read the story to him . . . that for three years, Roland had known about Mellish's friendship with the actor and had lied to the police, claiming ignorance of it. The story also played on Roland so conveniently being away at the time of the murder, gambling in Monte Carlo with his daughter, then rushing back the day after the murder, moving Sally into his house as if he were nothing more than a concerned friend. The question that had to be answered, Rushden stated at the end of the article, was whether Roland knew what Mellish intended to do, and was his role in the unsavory episode to hamper police investigation until Mellish had the time to create a new identity for himself?

Roland immediately telephoned Alan Martin in London. 'I'll be back from New York in a couple of days. I want you to start preparing libel writs against Rushden, against *Probe*, against the magazine's distributors.'

'I'm no not certain how effective that will be,' Martin replied. 'He's covered by libel insurance. You'll hurt the insurance companies and *Probe* will get the publicity.'

'Then find some other way. I want that man out of my hair, out of my business and out of my life!' Roland slammed down the receiver and returned to the Biwell board meeting, forcing himself to concentrate on the matters at hand.

When he arrived in London two days later, red-eyed from lack of sleep on the overnight flight, Alf Goldstein was waiting with the Bentley. Roland told him to drive to the lawyer's office; any business with the Eagles Group could wait.

'What have you come up with so far?' Roland demanded of Martin.

'I'm working on the libel suits. And . . .' He pushed an open law book across the desk for Roland to see.

'Criminal libel?'

'Criminal libel. I don't think there's been a big criminal libel case for twenty years or so. You'll have to apply to the High Court for permission to proceed with it, of course. They'll decide whether you've got the grounds for such action. If you're really set on going through with this, I believe the High Court will approve your application.'

'Thank you.' Roland didn't attempt to conceal the vindictive smile on his face. Criminal libel – that would knock Rushden for six.

Roland was correct. When Rushden received notification of the civil libel suits against himself, the magazine and its distributors, he wasn't particularly perturbed. That was why he carried libel insurance. The publicity such a suit would generate in the national press would more than compensate for any increased deductible or higher premiums he would have to pay in the future. What appealed to him even more was the prospect of watching Roland writhe in embarrassment while he tried to explain why he'd lied to the police about knowing of Mellish's relationship with Marsden. So what if he hadn't actively hampered the investigation . . .?

When he received notification that Roland was applying to the High Court for permission to bring a criminal libel action, Rushden's mood changed drastically. Rushden's own lawyer went back through the books and found there had only been a handful of criminal libel cases during the entire century, including the famous suit evolving from Lord Alfred Douglas' accusation in 1920 that Winston Churchill had purposely lost the Battle of Jutland so that he could make money in the American stock market. Douglas had been sentenced to six months in jail for his libelous accusation.

Rushden now found himself facing a similar situation, and he could only hope the High Court wouldn't approve Roland's application. Insurance companies only picked up the costs of the civil libel suits; they didn't serve jail sentences for their policy holders.

To Rushden's complete dismay, the vendetta he'd been waging against Roland had taken a dangerous, unforeseen twist.

While Roland waited for the decision regarding the suit he tried to concentrate on work. He wanted to reorganize the Biwell chain in the United States, find other companies he could buy into. But his first move in striking back at *Probe* disrupted his life completely, not allowing him the peace of mind he needed to concentrate on business affairs.

Although he found a certain delight in scanning through the piles of mail he received from people – famous and otherwise – who applauded his stand, he also sensed a cool aloofness from the employees of the publishing group, especially the staff of the *Eagle*. It was a coldness he even perceived in Sally.

'Roland, back out of this while you still can,' she told him one morning as they traveled into town.

'While *I* still can?' He laughed at what he thought was her concern for his welfare. 'I've finally got that bastard Rushden over a barrel, and I'm going to roll him all the way to the nearest prison.'

'You're also going to make an enemy of every journalist in this country. Including me.'

'You?'

'A publisher does *not* sue for criminal libel. The civil libel suits, go through with those by all means—'

'They won't mean a damned thing. Rushden carries insurance.'

'So what? But don't send the man to prison without first learning on what he based his story.'

'We'll find that out in court, won't we? Do you think he's going to name his source if I simply ask him?'

As she stopped outside the Adler's store to let Roland out, Sally tried one final time, 'Somehow or other, Rushden knows that you were aware of Christopher's friendship with Charles Marsden—'

'He may have guessed, what does it matter?'

'A lot. If you insist on dragging this thing through court, you're going to besmirch your own character. You're also going to cause embarrassment to me, Michael . . . to everyone you know.'

'Sally, don't you understand what this man has done to me over the years? He's stood at a safe distance and mocked everything I've ever done. What can the police do to me because I lied about Christopher? Knowing he was seeing Marsden is hardly damning evidence of a conspiracy. But Rushden's insinuated that I helped to thwart a police investigation—'

'He just posed the question. Unethical, perhaps, but not worthy of a criminal action.'

'Sally, I want revenge.'

'Sure you do, against a journalist. You're a newspaper owner, you run a group of magazines. How the hell do you think your people are going to react if you send Daniel Rushden to jail? You might get a kind of respect from him – sitting behind bars – but you'll be finished in publishing.'

'Why would decent journalists care about slime like Rushden?'

'You really don't understand a thing about this game, do you? Decent journalists, as you call them, use publications like *Probe* when they've got a story – a good scandal – that their own papers won't touch. That's right, Roland, even gutter journalists like Daniel Rushden have their place in the overall scheme of things.' She drove away as Roland slammed the door.

He stared after the car and thought about what she'd said. Was she right? Surely not. He was going to go through with it. This time Rushden had overstepped his bounds for the last time – Roland was going to stop him once and for all.

Roland was formally correct when he next saw Daniel Rushden, giving him a curt nod when they faced each other at the hearing before a High Court judge who would decide whether there were grounds for criminal proceedings.

Rushden's legal counsel stated there was no case to answer, that Roland's action in applying for criminal libel was blowing a possible error on the magazine's part all out of proportion. Roland's counsel, though, claimed his client had been the target of a long-standing smear campaign by *Probe*. His character had been besmirched, his friendships ridiculed, his entire life poked apart and vilified . . . and all for the sin of being a prominent, successful businessman. *Probe*'s last attack – the question of whether Roland knew of Mellish's intentions to commit murder, and that he'd deliberately tried to thwart a police investigation – showed a flagrant disregard for journalistic ethics *and* the truth.

The judge considered the matter carefully before siding with Roland's counsel; there *were* grounds for criminal charges. Roland couldn't resist a brief smile as he watched Rushden's face sag. The man who had made his life a public misery since the takeover of Adler's was looking at a prison sentence; and he understandably didn't like what he saw.

Roland was driven home to Stanmore that night in an expansive frame of mind. The hearing had made front page news in every paper; even if some writers had castigated him for being a vengeful tyrant he couldn't have cared less. Revenge was the greatest motivation; its taste was sweet. But he had known that all along. He had the muscle and this was one time he was able to use it.

As Goldstein pulled the car into the circular drive, Katherine came running out of the house. Roland climbed out of the car and she rushed straight into his arms. 'What's the matter? I thought you'd be at the stables by now.' When she looked up he could see she'd been crying.

'Read this!' She pulled a sheet of paper from her pocket. Roland read it and some of his elation immediately dimmed.

'What's the matter?' Goldstein asked.

'Sally. She's gone back to Curzon Street. Doesn't want to share a house with someone as pig-headed, stubborn and vindictive as me.' He crushed the note into a ball and shoved it into his pocket. 'What do you think, Kathy?'

He knew she'd been following the case; her opinion was more valuable to him than anyone's.

She followed him into the house where he dropped his briefcase. The butler appeared and wordlessly carried it into the room Roland used as an office. 'Is it worth losing Sally as a friend?' Katherine asked.

'I never thought it would come to that.'

'Didn't you? She warned you all along not to proceed with this. She told you to give that terrible man and his slimy magazine the chance to crawl out, apologize and call it even.'

Now even Katherine was lined up against him, and that hadn't happened since Sharon's days. 'I'll speak to her.'

'I wish you luck. She was fit to be tied when she left here.'

Roland rang through to Curzon Street. 'Why do you think I left?' Sally demanded. 'I warned you that you'd lose any respect you had with the press if you proceeded, and that included myself.'

'You're not a journalist,' he tried to argue. 'You're the director of a publishing group.'

'I'm still a journalist first and foremost. Rushden may be the worst possible kind of reporter who ever sat behind a typewriter, but he's still a journalist. Just like me. When you take an unfair punch at one of us, you hit us all.'

Faced with Sally's anger, Roland became sarcastic. 'You're really putting me in my place, Sally, moving out of the house. If nothing else could do it, that really showed me the error of my ways.'

'Don't be such a stupid ass, Roland. It doesn't become you.'

'Will you be in the office tomorrow?'

'For part of the time.' She hung up, leaving him to wonder what she meant.

The next morning, while he was in a meeting with

Michael Adler, Roland found out. Sally phoned to say the entire union membership of the publishing group – including all the provincial newspapers and the *Eagle* – had walked out in protest of Roland's action against Daniel Rushden.

'Couldn't you do anything to stop them?'

'Stop them?' She laughed harshly. 'Who the hell do you think organized the whole thing?'

Roland knew he should have guessed. 'What conditions do you want to return to work.'

Sally's voice softened. 'Sort this thing out, Roland. You've got permission to press criminal charges but you can still back out of it.'

'Sally, I won't be blackmailed. Not by you or anyone else.'

'Then do it for the sake of your friends, if you value their friendship. Remember that no matter how strongly you feel about it, we're all going to be dragged through the muck if this thing goes the full distance. Just forget your foolish wounded pride for one minute and consider this: Christopher was my husband as well as your friend. Have some consideration for my feelings as well.'

Roland put down the receiver and looked helplessly at Michael. 'They've all walked out. Sally led them.'

'I know. She told me she was going to.'

'Oh, fine. Another friend.'

'I've tried to be but you were too irate to listen to anything rational. All you had to do in the first place with this chap Rushden was ignore him. You were told he thrived on controversy and you provided him with it. Now you're both in a position where neither of you can be seen to give way. You're going to fight it out in a criminal court, and believe me, Roland, you've got plenty more to lose than he has.'

'Six months in jail, he'll lose.'

'He'll do that standing on his head. And when he gets

out, the entire country will look on him as the victim of a rich, ruthless man who uses the law to send his critics to prison.'

Roland sighed in defeat. He didn't have the strength to fight Rushden *and* his own friends. 'What do you suggest I do?'

'Call him. You might find him a lot more amenable now. You've done what you wanted to do, proved how strong you are. Now show him you can be a human being as well.'

Daniel Rushden received Roland's phone call with trepidation. Roland was the last person from whom he expected to hear; the man hired expensive lawyers to do his talking for him.

'Mr Rushden, I would like to meet with you as soon as possible.'

'What about?' To gloat over an impending jail sentence? Once Rushden had considered the entire episode a bizarre joke. Criminal libel . . .! A throwback to an earlier era, an era to which Roland clearly belonged. But since the High Court judge believed Roland had adequate cause to pursue criminal proceedings, it was a reasonable assumption that a jury in a criminal trial would think the same way.

'I believe it's about time we discussed our situation like reasonable men, Mr Rushden.'

Reasonable? Rushden's mind went blank as he repeated the word to himself. Who was Eagles to suddenly claim he was a reasonable man? 'What do you have in mind?'

'Can we talk over dinner tonight?'

'At your restaurant, Eldridge's?'

'The Vulture's Nest, as you once referred to it.'

'I feel a little out of my depth there, Mr Eagles.'

'Enemy territory? Then why don't you suggest a place?'

Rushden tried to think but Roland's call – the invita-

502

tion to dinner – had blown all logic from his mind. Finally he mentioned an Italian restaurant near the law courts. 'Just to remind ourselves that it's not a social call.'

'I seriously doubt either of us will need much reminding. I'll see you there at seven o'clock.'

When Roland arrived at the restaurant, Rushden was already seated at a table in the back, anxiously dividing his attention between his watch and the door. 'Sorry if I kept you waiting,' Roland said, as he sat down and looked around. It wasn't the kind of place he would have chosen for himself – checkered plastic tablecloths, cheap cutlery, thick heavy plates. But then this was not really dining for pleasure . . .

'Do you smoke?' Rushden pulled out a pack of Embassy cigarettes, offered one to Roland as if the gesture would break the ice.

'No, thank you.' Roland extended his gold lighter, watched while Rushden lit the cigarette, inhaled deeply. Poor devil was scared out of his wits over what the evening might hold – asked to dinner by the very man who seemed intent on putting him behind bars. 'You seem very tense, Mr Rushden.'

'I'm just confused by your invitation, Mr Eagles. Or would it have something to do with the walkout at Burnham Press and the *Eagle*?'

Roland smiled thinly; there was no way he could have kept that from Rushden. There would be no copies of the *Eagle* on the street the following morning, and the story had already been carried in late editions of other newspapers, all covering the union problems faced by one of their own. So much for dog not eating dog. The staff who worked for Roland might side with a fellow journalist they felt was being persecuted, but there was no such camaraderie among publishers.

'Not really, Mr Rushden, Do you seriously think I'm a man who can be influenced by blackmail?'

Rushden gazed across the table into Roland's clear blue

eyes. The answer lay there, just as it lay in the expensively tailored suit, silk tie and crisp cotton shirt. This was a man who made his own laws and bowed to no one.

'We are both in an awkward situation, Mr Rushden—'

'For which you are responsible.'

'Please be courteous enough to allow me to finish.' Roland stopped speaking while the waiter took their orders; he decided to play it safe in this strange restaurant and settle for a salad. 'The awkwardness of this situation dictates that neither of us can win – we can only lose. You, because you will probably spend time in jail should I pursue this criminal libel action now that the High Court have given me permission. And me' – again that thin smile – 'because whatever happens I'm going to be regarded as a tyrant. I have conferred with my lawyers, and they agree that a settlement is possible before I institute proceedings.'

'What kind of settlement?'

'*Probe* will take advertisements in all national newspapers retracting the insinuation it made concerning me. This will take the form of a letter which my lawyers will dictate. You will also agree not to ever mention my name again—'

'Never?'

'Never.'

Rushden considered the choice. A few hours ago he might have said no, but now, sitting opposite the man who had been his enemy for so long, he wasn't sure. The image that Rushden had built up – the playboy intent on carving his name across the world – no longer seemed quite so true. The man sitting opposite him was human, and just as worried about what could happen as Rushden was. 'I'll need to take advice on your offer.'

'Please feel free to.' Roland inspected the salad the waiter placed in front of him, picked at it, and decided he didn't like it; too many years of eating only the finest had spoiled him. 'There is one other thing.'

'Of course. There would be.'

'I would like to know on what evidence you based your assumption that I knew of Christopher Mellish's relationship with Charles Marsden.'

'Is it true?'

Roland smiled faintly and ignored the question. 'On what did you base your claim?'

Rushden looked down at a steaming dish of lasagna and couldn't even remember ordering it. 'Do you know where Mellish is?'

'I haven't the faintest idea. And even if I did, I wouldn't say. He was a friend, and I don't run out on friends.'

'But you did know about the friendship with Marsden.' It was no longer a question.

'Yes, I did. If you had stuck to that fact, this meeting wouldn't have been necessary. You had to be that extra bit clever, though, didn't you, and suggest that I'd known about everything.'

'I never dreamed you'd react the way you did.'

'Why not? Criminal libel is a legal weapon, and the High Court in its infinite wisdom offered me its use.'

Whatever else he might have been — muckraker, satirist — Daniel Rushden was still a journalist. His greatest loyalty was to his sources, and he would rather go to jail than divulge them. This moment was different, though, because he had the opportunity to hurt this man more than he ever could in a *Probe* article. Just once, one final barb before they settled their differences. 'Your wife told me about your knowing of Mellish and Marsden.'

'My wife? Sharon?'

'Mrs Sharon Eagles,' To the day he died Rushden knew he would treasure the look of pure shock that passed over Eagles' face. 'She came to my office and showed me a letter you once received from the man who does your dirty work, Alf Goldstein.'

Roland closed his eyes for a moment, pictured in every

detail the letter Goldstein had sent him while he was on honeymoon with Sharon. He had screwed it up into a ball, dropped it into a trash can. Had Sharon . . . ? Of course she had! How else could she have known? How else could she have shown Rushden the letter? She'd kept it all these years. But why . . . for God's sake why?

In that moment, Rushden knew regret. He had wanted this one chance to hurt Roland, but the pain he saw in the man's face made the journalist wince. The articles he wrote – sniping at public figures – were like fighting a battle from a rear position; you never saw the enemy's eyes when the bullet hit. This, however, was close combat. He had a firsthand look at every trace of pain that registered on the enemy's face, and Rushden found he had no stomach for it. 'I'm sorry,' he said.

'So am I,' Roland answered, recovering quickly. 'When can I expect your reply to my conditions for not pursuing this matter further?'

'Tomorrow evening.' Rushden answered. 'I'll see my lawyers first thing in the morning to discuss your offer.'

'Would you hazard a guess at their advice?'

Rushden took a forkful of lasagna, chewed thoughtfully. 'I think they'll agree that your terms are most generous.'

'Good. I'll be glad when this unpleasantness is over. I think we've both had quite enough.'

Instead of going straight home, Roland went to Curzon Street to see Sally. She allowed him only as far as the hallway, then stood with her arms folded across her chest, waiting to hear what he had to say.

'You can call off your strike. I've made peace with Rushden.'

'How did you leave it?'

'I offered him settlement terms which he thinks his lawyers will find satisfactory. No criminal proceedings.' He saw Sally relax a fraction. 'It was Sharon who gave

506

Probe the information that I knew about Christopher and Marsden.'

'Why would she do a thing like that?' Sally was so shocked at the news that she didn't even think to ask how Sharon had known.

Roland shrugged. 'To lash out against me? Who knows?'

'What are you going to do about it?'

'I don't know. If it were just Sharon, I'd leave it and walk away. But I can't walk away from Simon. Having him against me still—'

'He's not against you.'

'He's not damned well speaking to me, what do you call that? He was my friend for years, and it hurts.'

'Are you thinking of telling him what Sharon did?'

'I think it's the only way to make him see what I was going through while Sharon and I were together. Simon believes I neglected her, but she was so insecure – so jealous of anyone I even spoke to – that it was impossible for the marriage to work.'

'Shall we see him now? I'll come with you.'

'I was hoping you'd offer.'

Sally drove to South Kensington. While Roland waited in the car Sally rang the bell of Simon's house. The maid answered, then Nadine appeared. Roland couldn't hear what was being said, but he saw Nadine look toward the car, then back into the house. Finally, Simon came to the door. Moments later, Sally beckoned for Roland.

'Hello, Simon.' Roland thought the banker looked much older than when he'd last seen him. His eyes were sunk deeply, lines crisscrossed his face like deep scars, the beard had more gray than before. Even his shoulders seemed stooped.

'Come in, please,' he said. 'I think it's time we sat down and talked, something we should have done a long time ago.' A little of the sprightliness returned as he led Roland into the drawing room.

507

'Where's Sharon? And David?'

'They're in Paris, with Miriam and Claude. She left a few days ago, before your court hearing. Now I understand why. She sowed the seeds but didn't wish to see the harvest reaped.'

'Is she any better?'

'We thought she was improving, but obviously the trouble is still there. Roland . . .' Simon spread his arms beseechingly. 'What can I say? None of us had any idea how serious her problem was.'

'I didn't want to believe it myself, when we were married. I always remembered Sharon as she was when she was young. Bright, alive, beautiful. She's still beautiful, but somewhere . . .'

'Something happened. I try to tell myself it was that terrible time she had with Graham, but even then I'm not certain. Now I'm more inclined to think that Graham simply acted as a catalyst, made Sharon's condition worse – and to think that I blamed you.'

'I blamed myself as well, Simon. For a while – God forgive me – I even blamed Katherine. I thought she was trying to come between Sharon and me, that it was *her* jealousy that was causing the trouble.'

Simon looked at the floor, unwilling to meet Roland's eyes. 'For Sharon to have done such a thing . . . To see this man Rushden and show him a letter that had been written to you. Hate runs so deep, it's so inexplicable.'

Roland shifted uncomfortably in the chair, uncertain now why he had even come to the house. Perhaps he would have been better off just leaving the past alone. No . . . friendships weren't like old clothes, meant to be thrown away when you no longer wanted them; they were meant to be kept forever, no matter what. 'Simon, the most painful part of this whole unhappy affair was losing you and Nadine as friends.'

Simon looked up, as if recognizing reconciliation in

Roland's words. 'Do you think friendship can ever mend such a rift?'

'Only if we try,' Roland answered. It was all he could say.'

Sally drove Roland back to Stanmore from South Kensington, a trip during which neither said much. Roland thought over the meeting with Simon and decided nothing had been resolved at all . . . Even if Simon now saw the situation in its true light, Roland felt no closer to him. The split between the two men over Sharon had been too deep to bridge with just one meeting, a few words of apologetic conversation. Damn . . . ! If only he'd listened to the advice everyone had given him about marrying Sharon, so much of this could have been avoided. Even the final clash with Daniel Rushden never would have occurred if he'd occasionally listened to the advice of his friends.

'Home, sweet home,' Sally said as she pulled into the driveway. 'For God's sake, try to put a smile on your face before Katherine sees you.'

'Thanks for the advice.' He turned to face Sally as she switched off the engine. 'What about you? You've sorted out my life, now what about your own? Are you staying at the apartment, or do you want to move back here? I've gotten used to having you around.'

'I'll stay put now. I did myself a favor when I went back there last night. I found out that ghosts don't exist. The police have finished with me and there's really no reason for me not to stay there. Besides, I like living in town. I might have been brought up on a farm, but I'm not a country bumpkin like you.'

'What about Christopher? What are you going to do about him?'

'He won't turn up again. Maybe one day I'll receive some cryptic letter postmarked Pango Pango or somewhere to tell me he's all right, but that's all. I guess I'll just wait a year or so and then file for divorce. I imagine it'll be uncontested.'

'Coming in?'

Sally shook her head. 'I've got a lot of work to do. When a newspaper's closed down for a day there's plenty to do before you put out the next issue. As a publisher, I thought you would have understood that.' She grinned in the darkness. 'Besides, I think you've got something to say to Katherine.'

'Yes, I do. You know something, Sally . . . when I bumped into Kassler in Monte Carlo that time, we talked a lot about how our family lives had suffered because of our commitment to work – his far more than mine, I'm glad to say. But I wonder how much easier my own life might have been if I'd put a limit on what I felt I had to achieve.'

'What kind of limit?' Sally started to feel uncomfortable as she sensed Roland becoming maudlin.

'Maybe just a couple of companies. Eldridge's, because of its tie to Catarina. And Adler's, because it was my first major acquisition.'

'That's it?'

'I suppose the *Eagle* as well. It has my name, after all. And it did show me the error of my ways.'

'Thanks. Nice to know I'm appreciated. Now stop being so damned introspective; it doesn't suit you. What's done is done, so get out of my car and tell your daughter everything's straightened out.'

'That's what I needed . . . sympathy and encouragement,' Roland said, determined to shake off the dark mood. 'Thanks for the ride and for coming with me to see Simon.' He kissed Sally on the cheek, climbed out of the car and let himself into the house. 'Kathy!'

'In the kitchen.'

Roland walked through the house and found Katherine leaning over the kitchen counter, drinking a glass of milk while she read a letter.

'From Franz?'

510

'Of course.' She smiled brightly and kissed him. 'Who else ever writes to me?'

'*Horse and Hound* to say your subscription's overdue.'

'Did you see that terrible man?'

'I had dinner with him.' Roland was amused by the way Katherine always referred to Rushden. He was even more amused by the manner in which she swiftly scooped up the letter and jammed it into the pocket of her robe. Love letters needed privacy. 'I also saw Simon.' He told her about Sharon keeping the letter from Alf Goldstein.

'That must have shocked him.'

'I think Simon's past that stage, Kathy. He looks old, tired. A man who had everything and now finds that life's left him with very little.'

Katherine moved closer to her father, wrapped her arms around his neck; he could smell the freshness of her skin, straight out of the shower. 'I prefer you this way, do you know that?'

'What way?'

'Being sympathetic toward other people. Before, when you were plotting your revenge against that terrible man, you were like a stranger. Cold, nasty, vindictive. I'm glad you sorted it all out.'

Roland looked at his daughter . . . her smooth, unblemished skin, eyes like two pools of clear blue. No wonder Franz Kassler wrote to her so regularly. 'Can you cook?'

'Of course I can cook.'

'Dinner was lousy, a limp salad at a greasy Italian restaurant. Make me an omelet, there's a good girl.'

Katherine set to work enthusiastically. Pots and pans clattered as she put together the ingredients for a mushroom omelet. Ten minutes later when she served it to her father at the table in the breakfast room, he saw that the edges were burned while the inside was still half raw.

He didn't complain. He didn't say a word.

He ate it, every single scrap.

And to him it was the finest meal he'd ever eaten.

CHAPTER EIGHT

Katherine graduated from high school in the summer of 1968, at the age of eighteen. Instead of going to college, though, she insisted on beginning work immediately in her father's business. Roland remembered the omelet and prayed she didn't intend to make her career at Eldridge's; he breathed a sigh of relief when she opted for the *Eagle*. She decided she wanted to learn the newspaper business. Roland understood why: apart from himself, the person to whom Katherine had always been closest was Sally Roberts – even closer than she'd been with Janet, who raised her like her own daughter. In Sally, Katherine recognized what a woman with her own mind could achieve – success, respect and power. Built in her father's image, Katherine wanted to taste that same success.

At the *Eagle*, Katherine started as she expected to – by running errands, acting as a messenger for the newspaper reporters. At first having the chairman's daughter as a copyboy brought indulgent smiles from the more cynical of the journalists, and they treated her with kid gloves. To Roland's delight, Katherine would have none of it, insisting that she be treated like anyone else. She wanted to learn the business from the bottom up, starting the way Sally had begun, taking training courses, serving her apprenticeship. By the time her first year was finished, she was following doggedly in Sally's footsteps by working on the women's page as a junior reporter. After a lifetime of squabbling with journalists, Roland realized he had one in the family – a journalist who was just as argumentative as any he had met . . .

They sat up together late at night – the first time

512

Roland could remember making a point of watching television. This was a special occasion, though, history in the making – the landing of the moon module from Apollo Eleven. When Neil Armstrong placed his foot on the surface of the moon and said the words that a team of public relations experts had labored over for months, Katherine's sarcastic comment was, 'You do realize that this entire episode is being filmed on some Hollywood set, don't you?'

'What?' Roland looked from the television to his daughter, expecting to see her laughing. She was dead serious.

'That's what millions of people in the United States are saying, that Apollo Eleven – the whole moon landing – is just a hoax to divert attention from what's happening in Vietnam.'

'And you seriously believe that? That this is a hoax?'

'No.' Katherine smiled at her father. 'But just think how timely it is – what a coup for Nixon when he's fighting all that unrest over Vietnam.'

'That just happens to be the way it worked out.'

'How can you be so naive? Nothing ever works out that fortuitously. Remember the old saying of when you've got trouble at home you stage a diversion abroad to unite the people? Nixon's just went one better and staged a diversion on the moon.'

'So he's a clever man.' Had Katherine always been so interested in international affairs? 'Since when have you been so involved in politics?'

'I've had my eyes opened for me at the *Eagle*.'

Roland could believe that. The *Eagle* enjoyed a moderate platform but that didn't stop many of the staff from criticising American involvement in Southeast Asia. The reporters voiced a position with which he didn't necessarily agree, but he wasn't about to try to sway their views; that was a certain way to bring the house down, and he'd learned that lesson already.

'Franz also writes to me of demonstrations in Germany,' Katherine said.

'That's a fine country to demonstrate against war.'

'That was not Franz's generation. It was his father's – your friend, remember?'

Roland questioned how serious the relationship with Franz was becoming. Katherine and Roland had spent a few days at Kassler's winter home in the mountains the previous year, taking Richard and Carol with them. While Katherine had spent most of her time skiing with Franz, Roland had played with the two younger children, romping in the snow, pelting each other with snowballs and sledding down the gentler slopes. Franz had also visited London the following Easter, staying at Roland's house for three days. The correspondence between Franz and Katherine was as regular as ever. They even had common ground now. Katherine at the *Eagle*, and Franz, having graduated from the university, was working for his father in the Kassler Industries head office in Stuttgart.

Katherine turned her attention back to the television. 'This could be straight out of a science fiction movie.'

'I wouldn't know – I never saw one.' Roland decided he'd seen enough and went to bed.

When he reached the office the following morning, he wasn't surprised to find that the main topic of the conversation was the American lunar landing. Just for effect, he repeated Katherine's opinion, only to learn that she wasn't alone in her conviction that the landing had been timed to take people's minds off domestic problems. Even Michael Adler agreed, saying it stood to reason. Roland felt saddened that no one could take historical events at face value anymore – was he the only romantic left in a world full of cynics?

Like all the other newspapers, the *Eagle* gave full coverage to the moon landing, and he couldn't help noticing that one of the side stories was a wire service report

514

that many Americans did regard the event as a hoax. No doubt Katherine would brandish that in his face . . . if it was in the *Eagle*, surely it must be the truth!

'Believe half of what you see, a quarter of what you hear, and absolutely nothing of what you read,' he told her that night after she challenged him on the story.

'Can I quote you on that?' she asked mischievously. 'That's an interesting statement for a publisher to make.'

'I believe you probably would.'

'Sorry, but no favoritism in the press.' She kissed him and ran upstairs to read the latest letter from Franz which had come in the afternoon mail. Roland lit a cigar and wondered whether he was beginning to worry about Katherine as Ambassador Menendez had once worried about his daughter.

At least there was no possibility of Franz Kassler being a fortune hunter. He had a family fortune already.

In the spring of 1970, Roland repaid a favor Michael Adler had done for him twenty years earlier. He acted as best man at Michael's wedding to Lisa Sorensen, a red-haired, Swedish-born doctor he'd been dating for the past two years, since meeting her at the hospital where he'd had his appendix removed.

'I thought you were a confirmed bachelor,' Roland remarked when Michael asked him.

'I was just biding my time. I'm forty-six now; leave getting married until late enough in life and there's not enough time for it to go sour.'

'Some of those marriages you saw go bad didn't get that way because the bride and groom were too young,' Roland reminded him.

'I was joking. It's just that I seem to be surrounded by people whose marriages have broken up for one reason or another. But if Catarina had lived I think you'd still be married to her.'

'So do I. What does your father have to say about it? Does he approve?'

515

'Why shouldn't he?' Michael was puzzled by the question.

'Well, you know . . .'

Sensing what he was trying to say, Michael helped him. 'About Lisa not being Jewish? I don't think it bothers him particularly. Why should you even think of it?'

'It's just that I thought it would have been important to him. Only son and all that.'

Michael laughed and shook his head. 'No, I don't believe so. My grandfather might have been upset, but he was a member of the old school. Besides, Lisa and I aren't thinking in terms of a family, so what's the problem?'

'Nothing. I guess I just read your father wrong.' Really wrong, Roland decided. He would have sworn that Albert would have screamed to high heaven about it. Or was he getting too old to even care? Roland only knew about Albert through Michael, living with a full-time nurse who took care of him. He was almost legally blind now, barely able to identify someone standing right in front of him. 'Will he be at the wedding?'

'Of course.'

'What does he say about me being best man?'

'He just accepted it, pretty well like he seems to accept everything these days – a kind of resignation that comes with age, I guess.'

'How old is he?'

'Seventy-two.'

'If your grandfather's anything to go by, then your father's got a few years left to him.'

'I wonder. My grandfather was an active man, that's what kept him going. My father just sits around, listens to the radio, eats when he's told to, goes to bed when he's told to.'

Even though he'd introduced the subject, Roland now wanted to change it; hearing of Albert's worsening health made him depressed. 'Where are you and Lisa going to have your reception?'

'Where else? Eldridge's, of course. I learned one thing

from you, Roland . . . keep the business in the family.'

'Have this one on the house – you deserve it.'

While Michael Adler went ahead with his wedding plans, the Eagles Group main office acquired another employee – Franz Kassler.

Heinrich Kassler contacted Roland to ask if he could find a trainee management position for Franz. 'Working for another company, especially in another country, will be more broadening for my son,' Kassler explained over the telephone to Roland. 'Here Franz feels he has to fight to get out of my shadow, and if I did anything to smooth the path for him there would be charges of nepotism.'

Roland understood Kassler's position all too well . . . hadn't Katherine fought the same way at the *Eagle*, wanting to be treated on her own merits, not because of her family connection? 'You're not trying to plant an inside man on me, are you, Heinrich?'

Kassler's laugh boomed in Roland's ear. 'You shouldn't give me ideas like that. Besides, if that were my idea I wouldn't use Franz. He's too fond of your daughter to ever work against her father.'

'Yes, Katherine,' Roland murmured. How much did she have to do with this unexpected request to find Franz a job in the Eagles Group? 'How are you and Franz getting along? Are you on friendlier terms?'

'A little. Unfortunately we . . . no, I . . . let too much time elapse before making the effort. I fear that I'll never be as close to Franz as you are to your daughter.'

Roland told himself he should be grateful he had one child to whom he was really close. Richard and Carol were still pretty distant from him, despite their visits, and he never saw David, who was now four and living in France with his mother. All in all one daughter – Catarina's daughter – made up for the relationships he lacked with his other children.

When he saw Katherine at home that night, he mentioned Kassler's call. 'What do you think I should do,

Kathy? Should I bring him over here?'

'Of course! It would be a wonderful opportunity for Franz.'

'That's what I thought you'd say. Now tell me something – did you have anything to do with him wanting to come over here?'

Katherine turned coy, looked away from her father. 'I *might* have mentioned the possibility of his working in London. Franz *might* have mentioned it as well.'

'I see. The pair of you have been busy hatching up a plot in your interminable correspondence.'

'It's better for Franz to get out of Germany. He and his father don't get along that well, you know.'

'No, I didn't know,' Kassler hadn't made it sound like they weren't communicating at all, Roland thought, but why should that interest him?

'They argue a lot.'

'We've also argued.'

'Not the way they do. Franz and his father don't see eye-to-eye on many things—'

'How do you know all this?'

'Franz tells me everything in his letters. Three months ago he was arrested during a demonstration outside the Rhein/Main Air Force Base in Frankfurt. It was an anti-Vietnam protest. When Franz was fined in court, it was very embarrassing for his father.'

'I see.' Roland was no longer so sure of the wisdom in helping Heinrich Kassler, no matter how much the German wanted his son out of his hair. If Franz was in London there would be plenty of anti-American demonstrations he could join; Grosvenor Square, outside the American Embassy, was filled each week. The question was – did Roland want Katherine to be with Franz. 'Kathy, if Franz comes over here and demonstrates he would stand a good chance of being deported.'

'He knows that.'

'I'm going to say yes. But the moment he arrives I'm going to tell him straight out that I won't tolerate any shenanigans from him. And I want you to promise me that even if Franz does get involved in political demonstrations over here, you won't join him. I don't want any phone calls in the middle of the night.'

'I promise.'

'All right then. I'll offer him a position in store operations, that's what he's doing for Heinrich now.'

'Thank you!' Katherine threw her arms around Roland's neck and kissed him.

But he knew that even if she hadn't made the promise he wouldn't have been able to refuse her anyway.

Roland and Katherine were driven to the airport by Alf Goldstein to meet the Lufthansa flight bringing Franz Kassler from Stuttgart. Goldstein had been surprised at Franz's appointment to the Eagles Group, and curious to meet the son of the man whose path he had crossed in Bergen-Belsen. When Roland described Franz's appearance as they waited for the flight, Goldstein just nodded.

'Another of your stereotypical Nazi specimens, eh?' Roland asked.

'They all look the same to me.'

'Change your mind about this one, Alf. He's already been in hot water for demonstrating against the right. Katherine says he and his father get on like cat and dog, and Kassler's no Nazi to begin with.'

'I'll take your word for it, but please excuse me if I click my heels and start goose-stepping when I see him.'

Roland heard Katherine's excited shout and looked toward the arrival gate. Franz Kassler was even taller than he remembered, blonder still. After a quick embrace they walked over to where Roland and Alf waited, arm in arm.

'How are you, sir? I am delighted to see you again.' Franz set down his two cases, shook Roland's hand formally, waited to be introduced to Goldstein.

'This is Alf Goldstein, you'll be seeing him around the office.'

'I am pleased to meet you, sir.'

519

'Likewise,' Goldstein muttered and stooped to pick up one of the cases.

'Thank you, but I can manage perfectly.' Franz hoisted the two heavy cases and began walking toward the terminal exit with Katherine beside him.

During the drive back to Stanmore Roland asked Franz about his father, tried to elicit some information about the arguments Katherine had mentioned. All Kassler had ever admitted was regretting that he would never be as close to his son as Roland was to Katherine.

Franz was quite open about his relationship with his father. 'He believes that I should agree with him about everything. I don't, which is why we fight. I see in my father the generation that led us into a catastrophic war—'

'Wait a minute, young man,' Roland grabbed hold of Franz's arm. 'Your father was one of those who did their best to stop it. I can vouch for that. So can Alf.'

'Their best was not good enough. Tell me something, sir, does Katherine agree with everything you say, with every position you support?'

'You must be joking,' Roland murmured. He glanced into the rear-view mirror and saw Goldstein looking at him, face beaming in a wide smile. Despite the rigid formality, this young man reminded Roland uncannily of himself; stiff-necked, determined to speak his mind. How could he accept such qualities in himself and question them in Kassler's son? 'There are plenty of demonstrations in London against the American presence in Vietnam, Franz. If you join those and get arrested, the odds are you'll get deported. And if you drag Katherine along with you to a protest, you won't even have to wait to get deported. I'll do the job myself.'

'There's no need for concern, sir. When I protested in Germany I wasn't demonstrating so much against the Americans – no matter how unjust their involvement in Vietnam – but against the government of my father's generation. They took us into a war and they still govern our country. I was protesting what my father's generation left as a legacy: a divided country, and the reputation of being the birthplace of some of the most horrendous acts known to man.'

'I see.' Roland was no match for the young man's intensity. No wonder Katherine was so taken with him; those countless letters must have read straight from the heart. He turned to look at her but she was hunched forward, gazing raptly at Franz. 'Would you like to bring Franz to Michael's wedding?'

'I'd love to.' The question indicated to Katherine that her father had accepted Franz completely.

Throughout Michael Adler's entire wedding party, Albert Adler sat at a table formally dressed in a tuxedo, thick glasses hiding his eyes. Sometimes the nurse who had accompanied him to Eldridge's sat with him, talking, patting his hand. Other times he was joined by one of his relatives, a niece or nephew from his late wife's family. Roland went up to Albert only once, to ask if there was anything he could get for him. Albert shook his head and, quite courteously, replied that he needed nothing. For a moment it seemed to Roland that he wanted to say more. He waited expectantly, but Albert only looked away. Roland walked off, wondering what confused thoughts were going through Albert's mind . . . his son working for the man who had taken over what should have been his birthright. When he reached the other side of the restaurant, Roland looked back. He pitied Albert, had wanted to speak to him, but couldn't bring himself to do so. Roland knew there were words that had to be said, words that might bridge the differences – the hatreds – of the past. But he couldn't find them, at least not now.

He looked around the small dance floor that had been set up in the middle of the restaurant. Michael was dancing with Lisa, completely oblivious to anyone else. And Katherine with Franz. Since he'd started working for the Eagles Group three weeks before, Franz and Katherine had been inseparable – evenings together, lunch hours when they could arrange them to coincide. Franz had stayed at the house in Stanmore for four days, the amount of time it took him to find a furnished apartment in town. Money didn't present a problem. What he lacked from the salary he earned at the Eagles Group was compensated for with money sent by his father. Roland found the gesture both touching and amusing – though the only point Franz and his father could apparently agree on was that they should live in separate countries, Kassler continued to be a father to Franz – the kind of father he believed he should be, making up with money what they lacked in closeness. And Franz accepted it, as if he understood that this was his father's way of showing love, the only way he knew how. Roland mused that it *was* a kind of father-son relationship after all . . .

'Doesn't watching all these people make you want to dance?'

Roland turned to find Sally standing next to him. 'Is that an invitation?' He took her in his arms and began to circle the floor slowly.

'Whom do you want me to bump into this time?'

'No one.'

'I was watching you just now, when you were staring at Franz and Katherine. You reminded me of Ambassador Menendez keeping an eye on Catarina that time at Claridge's.'

'Funny you should say that. It's a comparison I've been making myself lately.'

'Why don't you get in touch with the old bastard? He's still alive and kicking.'

Roland nodded. He had seen a story in a business magazine only a couple of months earlier about his former father-in-law. One of his hotels had been sold to the Hilton chain. 'Maybe I will one day. Do a good deed by

522

giving him the opportunity to see his granddaughter.'

'You were looking worried, though. Is it Katherine and Franz?'

'No. If anything I was thinking about Michael's father. He seems like such a deflated man. Sometimes I wonder if I could have used a softer touch when I was trying to acquire Adler's.'

'You're in a pensive mood.'

'I know. I was thinking about Simon as well. I've seen him twice since that business with Rushden. It seems that everywhere I go I have a negative effect.'

'Don't be so stupid. Just look out there at Katherine. You had an effect on Franz's father as well. You certainly did something very positive there.'

'Yes, I did.' Roland cheered up at the thought. Katherine's face reflected sheer happiness as she danced with Franz; a joy she might never have known had another British officer interrogated Kassler.

When the party ended, Sally offered to drive Roland back to Stanmore. He looked for Katherine, who told him that Franz would see her home; they wanted to go to a nightclub first. Roland glanced at Sally and saw she was fighting to keep a smile from her face; history had an uncomfortable knack of repeating itself.

On the way out, Roland stopped to wish Michael and his wife good luck. They were standing next to Albert, and at the sound of Roland's voice some life flickered in the old man's eyes.

'Mr Eagles, I want you to know that I hold no ill feelings for what happened between us.'

'I'm glad to hear that, Mr Adler.'

'You and I . . . I think we have to sit down and talk one day. Despite our own differences, my son has become very close to you.'

Roland waited for more, for an opening he could use to say what he wanted but Albert looked away, spoke to a member of his late wife's family. Roland realized the man's concentration span was limited; the moment Albert's attention left Roland he forgot about him completely.

'Albert seems to have softened,' Sally said as she and Roland left the restaurant.

'Maybe he figures his time's coming, he wants to make amends.'

'For what? The way he treated you?'

Roland didn't answer; he felt he had said enough already.

They reached Stanmore just before midnight, and Roland asked Sally in. She made coffee, then they sat in the front room with one dim light on, looking through the window at the darkened common. 'You're worried about Katherine, aren't you?' Sally said.

'I wouldn't be much of a father if I weren't, would I?'

'Then why did you agree to take Franz into the Eagles Group?'

'Katherine wanted it.'

'Roland, she's almost twenty. She can take care of herself.'

'No father ever admits that about his own daughter, Sally. You know that.'

'Don't you mean that no middle-aged, insecure father ever admits that about his daughter?' She tweaked him playfully on the chin and he grinned. 'So that's why you invited me in – so you'd have company while you wait up for her?'

'How did you guess?'

'It doesn't require much guesswork to know the way your mind operates, Roland. I've known you for far too long. But I'm not going to be a party to any confrontation. Katherine works for me and I intend to keep our relationship strictly professional. Good night.' She took the cups into the kitchen and left them on the counter. Roland saw her to the door, then returned to the front

524

room, turned out the light and sat down by the window, smoking and thinking.

It was almost five o'clock when a red MGB sports car pulled into the driveway, its tiny sidelights the only illumination. The doors remained closed as Katherine and Franz shared a final, passionate embrace, then the interior light flickered on as Katherine climbed out. She waved, blew a kiss and stood watching as the MGB roared off down the hill toward the village. Roland set the cigar down in an ashtray when he heard the front door open and softly close.

'Kathy!'

She stopped in the hall, startled at hearing her name called.

'In the front room.' He turned on the light. 'Where did you go with Franz?'

'To a jazz club.'

'Until this late?' There was no anger, no reproach in his voice even when he noticed how disheveled she looked; her hair mussed, her makeup smeared.

'We went for a walk along the Embankment afterwards.'

Roland glanced through the window; it couldn't be any warmer than forty degrees out there. Katherine wore nothing heavier than a narrow sable stole over a long, flimsy dress. He knew she was lying but he played the game her way. 'You must have frozen half to death.'

'Franz had his arm around me.'

'I should hope so. You'd better get some sleep, you've got work in the morning.' He wished now that he hadn't waited up, hadn't known what time she got home. He had asked her questions that had forced her to lie.

Katherine began to climb the stairs. Halfway up, she turned around and returned to the front room. 'Will you promise you won't scream?'

'About what?'

'I can't lie to you. We didn't go to a jazz club — we didn't even go for a walk. We went up to Franz's apartment.'

'All right, Kathy. Go on up to bed.' He felt an odd mixture of emotions. Relief because she had told him the truth; and shock because he knew now what that truth meant.

'Are you going to see Franz tomorrow?' she asked.

'Undoubtedly.' He saw a worried expression on her face and added, 'We do work in the same building after all.'

'That isn't what I meant.'

'I know exactly what you meant. Do you love him?'

'I think so.'

'That's not good enough, Kathy. I *knew* I loved your mother when I was with her the first time. She *knew* she loved me. We didn't make love just for the exercise.'

'How about Sally then, when you first met her?'

'Sally? Has she been talking to you?'

Katherine nodded. 'I ask her for advice sometimes.'

'Did she tell you it was all right for you and Franz to . . . ?' He couldn't even finish the sentence; he couldn't believe that Sally would give Katherine such advice. So much for keeping their relationship on a purely professional level . . .

'She told me to do whatever I thought was right.'

'Katherine . . . ' Without realizing it, Roland had used her formal name. 'Was this the first time?'

'Yes.'

He found himself wishing that Sally had stayed. She would know how to handle this situation better than he could — but God only knew how he'd managed to let himself be trapped into this conversation in the first place . . . Because he had wanted to find out what time his daughter came in, that was why. 'Did you take precautions?' he asked, and realized he was blushing.

'Franz did.'

Feeling his face burn even more, Roland tried to think

526

of something witty to dispel the tension. 'Did the earth move?' he said, smiling slightly.

'I think so. No . . .' Katherine said, her eyes shining, 'I *know* so.'

'Good. That's all that matters.' He waited for her to go upstairs, then let himself out of the house, cigar glowing in his mouth as he walked across the common. What kind of a conversation was that to have witth his daughteR? He had no business askingabout her private life. He'd never had parents to answer to, so why should he expect his daughter to answer to him?

She had, though. So truthfully and guilelessly that he had turned crimson. Was he really getting that old?

Roland saw Franz in the office the following day but he never mentioned waiting up for Katherine. If Katherine had said anything, the young man didn't show it. He simply carried on his work as normal, helping to ensure that the stores ran smoothly.

Roland wondered what to do. The last thing he wanted was to project himself into the kind of situation he'd suffered with Ambassador Menendez, where he stood like a forbidding figure between two young people in love. But wasn't that the position in which he continued to see himself, ever since Katherine's interest in Franz had become so serious? And who was to say that Menendez's position had been so terribly wrong? Misguided, perhaps, but his main concern had still been the welfare of his daughter.

A week later, Katherine resolved the dilemma for her father by telling him she wanted to live on her own.

'In some dingy apartment?' Roland asked, horrified. 'That's all you'll be able to afford on the rate the *Eagle* pays you.'

'Well . . . not exactly on my own.'

'With Franz? Move in with him?' That did it for Roland. 'I'm going to invite him here for dinner tomorrow night, Kathy. I think it's time I spoke to the two of you.'

Dinner was a formal affair, with Roland seated at the head of the table, Katherine on his right, Franz to his left. He waited until the meal had been served, the wine poured.

'What's this about Katherine wanting to move in with you, Franz?' Roland said once the meal was under way.

'We want to live together, sir,' Franz replied candidly.

Roland gazed down the length of the table at the crisp linen table cloth, the sparkling crystal, gleaming silverware. He wished fervently he had someone here to help him through this. Even Sally. Especially Sally, since she'd been the one to advise Katherine to do whatever she felt was right. 'Living together is not something you just decide to do on the spur of the moment.' He hoped he didn't sound too pompous — too much like a company chairman giving his annual report. 'It's a proper commitment.'

'We understand that,' Katherine replied.

'On the contrary, Kathy. I don't believe you do. Either of you. You don't set up house together and then tear it all down a few weeks or a few months later because your arrangement hasn't worked out. Planning to live together is like a business deal — you weigh each factor very carefully, assess everything —'

'Sir,' Franz broke into Roland's speech. 'I love your daughter very much. She loves me. Is that a strong enough basis for such a commitment?'

'She *thinks* she loves you. That's what she told me.'

Franz gazed across the table at Katherine. 'I do love him,' she said. 'Does that satisfy you, or are you going to stand in our way as my grandfather did to you and my mother?'

Again that comparison . . . Roland could see him now, standing in front of his own portrait . . . 'It's not the custom in my family to marry . . .' Well, never mind what

528

was or wasn't the custom in Menendez's family. Roland looked at Franz, then at Katherine. 'Please don't place me in the same category as Nicanor Menendez. He objected to me because of my background, not because we had decided frivolously to marry, let alone live together.'

Katherine and Franz stared blankly at Roland, and he realized that neither had caught the gist of his words.

'Kathy, you know it's not Franz I object to, otherwise I never would have agreed to find a job for him over here. If you two are that certain that living together is right, then you might as well go the whole damned route and get married!'

Franz looked startled at the suggestion. 'We . . . we had never thought of that, sir.'

'Well start thinking about it now. If you two are so serious about each other you should do what's proper and right, the same as your mother and I did, Kathy. Besides, if I'm to be blessed with grandchildren, I would like it to be while I'm still fit enough to push a carriage. And I would like to have a son-in-law as well!'

Heinrich Kassler flew to London the moment his son telephoned him with the news. He wanted the wedding to be in Germany. Roland argued it should take place in London. They then sat and laughed when they realized how like typical in-laws they were acting already.

'According to protocol, the bride's family pays for the wedding. Therefore, it is the privilege of the bride to choose the location,' Roland said. 'Besides, Franz is working in London now. He'll stay with the Eagles Group, or do you have other ideas?'

'No, that's fine. If you wish him to continue in your company, that's perfectly acceptable to me. How is he faring?'

'Very well. He'll be a valuable asset to the operations side. He's got the German mind for detail, figures at his fingertips.'

'Good. I'm pleased that he learned something at university, other than how to demonstrate.'

'Katherine did mention there had been some trouble.'

Kassler's face softened and he shook his head. 'Youth was the trouble. He was young and wanted to change the world; political ideals got the better of him. I hope that marriage and a career will mature him.'

'Didn't such ideals get the better of us when we were young?' Roland asked, feeling Kassler was being unjustly hard on his son. 'Me at sixteen, running off to single-handedly fight an entire nation. You, who could have had anyone believe you were a fanatical Nazi.'

'That was different, Roland; that was in a time of war. We weren't students trying to put ourselves on the front pages of newspapers while our parents paid for that privilege. We were earnest in doing what we thought best for our countries.'

'Thank God we were,' Roland added. 'There'll never be another generation like us, will there?'

Kassler sighed sadly. 'We were the very last. Ah, what a time that was.' He leaned back in the chair and stared at the ceiling, stubby fingers drumming against the tabletop. Roland could swear he was playing a march.

He thought of Goldstein and found himself agreeing with his old friend. There was never any getting away from it with the Germans. He hoped that Katherine had caught Franz in time.

Roland booked Claridge's for the wedding, wanting to be reminded of Catarina on this one occasion. His first wife might have been dead for twenty years but at Claridge's – at her daughter's wedding – her spirit would be alive.

Next, Roland worked on his guest list. He included Simon and Nadine Aronson, hoping they would come. And at the very bottom of the list, like a postscript, he wrote the name of Nicanor Menendez. Twenty years had a way of healing all rifts. Despite the fact that the ambassador had brushed past Roland the last time they had met, Roland still felt pity for him as he did on the day of the custody trial. To Roland, Menendez was like a loose thread in his life and he wanted to make it up – just as he wanted to put things right with Albert Adler. Roland wrote down the old man's name, then stared at it while he considered everything the name meant to him. Finally he crossed it out; he wasn't yet ready for that particular reconciliation.

By return mail, Simon and Nadine accepted the invitation to Katherine's wedding. Roland took that as an omen and waited eagerly for the weeks to pass, for Menendez's response to arrive. When it did, he could feel only disappointment. The former ambassador had simply crossed out the 'will-be-able-to-attend' section of the reply card, a brusque stroke with a thick black pen. No message of regret, no words of congratulations for his granddaughter.

Twenty years made no difference at all to him, Roland concluded sadly. He was still as bitter as he'd been on that day outside the court. Katherine was fated to never know her grandparents. But she would have a husband who loved her. The closer Roland became to Franz Kassler, the more he liked and respected the young man. Never mind the blue-eyed blondness that Goldstein read so much into, Roland was genuinely fond of his future son-in-law. He was intelligent, respectful, ambitious. Most importantly, it was obvious that he loved Katherine as much as Roland had loved her mother.

That was all Roland needed to know.

1970-1974

CHAPTER ONE

The only guests to leave the wedding celebration early were Ralph Morrison and Janet. Both of Roland's younger children, Richard, now twelve, and ten-year-old Carol – who had acted as pageboy and bridesmaid for their older half-sister – were practically asleep on their feet. Carol was being carried in Morrison's arms while Richard trailed behind Janet, barely keeping up. Roland kissed each of them tenderly, regretful that he'd been unable to play a more direct role in their lives. Still, he was happy that Janet had married a decent man who treated the children as kindly as if they were his own. How had Katherine once described Ralph Morrison? Roland tried to recall as he watched Janet say good-bye to his daughter, a long, affectionate hug and kiss between the bride and the woman who had been her nurse and friend. Oh, yes ... an insurance salesman, something boring like that. Boring, perhaps; but more importantly, kind.

'I still feel as though she's part of me,' Janet told Roland as she wiped away a tear.

'You shared a lot with her, the good and the bad.'

'From now on it will only be good.' Janet kissed Roland, who then shook hands with Morrison and kissed his children a final time.

After they left Roland looked around for Heinrich Kassler and saw the German sitting alone at a table, a drink in front of him as he watched the dancers on the floor. Roland considered joining him, easing his loneliness. Aside from Roland, Goldstein and his own son, of course, Kassler had hardly spoken to anyone during the entire evening, as if he'd been too occupied with his own thoughts. Business, probably, Roland decided in an uncharitable moment; he'd never known a man who seemed to find so little enjoyment in life, except when it came to business – to coming out ahead of the game. Even then Roland wasn't certain what pleasure Kassler found in winning; it was more like feeding an obsession.

He allowed his gaze to wander around the room until he spotted the table shared by Simon and Nadine Aronson and Michael Adler with his wife. Of all Roland's friends, of all the people he knew, Michael was probably the most stable, the hardest to ruffle. He was the calming influence on the board of the Eagles Group. Even his decision to marry only a few months earlier had been made logically. Roland smiled as he recalled Michael's words – that by leaving it so late, there was little chance of it having time to go sour. Michael was also the most considerate of Roland's friends; even tonight he'd gone out of his way to spend time with Simon and Nadine, so that Roland would be free to circulate with his other guests.

Roland decided to balance that lapse now. He walked over to their table, pulled out a chair and sat down. 'Can you believe it?' he asked Simon and Nadine. 'Little Katherine getting married.'

'Children grow up far too quickly, Roland,' Simon said, nodding. 'They have no respect for their parents, they push us toward old age.'

Roland debated whether Simon was thinking of Sharon when he made the remark. It was her problems that had aged the man so. She hadn't returned to London even once since she and David settled in Paris. When Roland asked about her Simon expressed doubt that she would ever marry again; he was just grateful that she seemed to be living a normal existence.

'You're not that old, Simon. Nadine's certainly not.'

'I'm old enough to consider resigning from the bank.'

536

'Are you serious?'

'Nadine and I would like to return to Paris. Our family is there. And Sharon needs us. Miriam and Claude are near her, but they have their own lives to lead. We can give Sharon the time and attention she needs. Isn't it ironic?' he asked Roland, with a sad smile. 'More than thirty years ago we came to London from Paris, and now we're making plans to return.'

A waiter appeared at Roland's elbow, coughed discreetly into his hand to get his attention. 'Mr Eagles, there's a gentleman who wishes to speak with you.'

'Where?' Roland looked around the busy ballroom, glad for the interruption. He found it impossible to reach Simon anymore – and to think they'd been so close . . . Communication was now painfully difficult.

'Outside, sir. He's not a guest.'

'Excuse me, will you?' Roland asked Simon and Nadine. He stood up and followed the waiter into the lobby outside the hall. There was only one figure sitting out there, an elderly man with bushy gray eyebrows, a dark raincoat buttoned all the way to his throat. Roland, who prided himself on a memory for faces, couldn't place him at all.

'May I help you, sir?'

The elderly man rose and looked into Roland's face. 'Are you worth one hundred million pounds yet, Mr Eagles?'

The question, so completely out of context, threw Roland's mind back down the labyrinth of memories he'd been experiencing that night. 'Mr Ambassador! This is indeed an unexpected pleasure! Where is Señora Menendez?'

'She was unable to accompany me. She is not well, her heart.'

'I'm sorry. Would you like to meet your granddaughter, sir?'

'I most certainly would.' Menendez was clearly moved

537

at the prospect. 'You know, that invitation you sent me —'

'I received your reply that you wouldn't be able to attend. I understood.'

'My first impulse was to tear it up, to not even reply,' Menendez continued, as if Roland hadn't said a word, 'I thought you were . . . you were making fun of me, mocking me by sending an invitation to my granddaughter's wedding. I thought you were using it to gloat again about your victory in court over me.'

'That was never my intention, sir. If you recall, after the trial I offered you the opportunity of seeing Katherine whenever you wished—'

'I know, I know. An old man's stupid, stubborn pride. I could never accept you, and therefore I could never allow myself to believe you would find it in your heart to forgive me.'

Roland could see that the meeting was going to be an emotional one. It looked like the former ambassador was going to be moved to tears at any moment, and Roland felt he might follow.

'I never intended to come here, never intended to give you the satisfaction of seeing me travel eight thousand miles just because *you* invited me. And then I began to think about it. My wife told me I should come. Katherine is our only granddaughter—'

Roland broke into the old man's rambling speech by helping him to sit down. He told the waiter to stay with him while he returned to the ballroom. Katherine and Franz were standing together just inside the entrance, posing for a photograph. Roland broke in just as the flash went off. 'Come outside, quickly.'

'What's the matter?'

'Just come outside. There's someone I want you both to meet.'

Half-dragged, half-walking, lifting her long dress with one hand, Katherine followed her father into the foyer,

538

with Franz a step behind. She saw an elderly man sitting on a chair, a waiter hovering beside him. 'Who's that?' she whispered.

'Kathy, I'd like to introduce you to your grandfather.'

'Menendez?' Katherine gasped. She held out her hand to the Argentinian.

'Your grandfather's come all the way from Argentina just to see you.' Roland asked the waiter to bring chairs for Katherine and Franz. Then he nodded politely and returned to the party, looking for Sally; she was entitled to share in this precious piece of news.

'You'll never guess who's sitting outside, talking to Katherine and Franz,' Roland said excitedly. 'Menendez.'

'He came?'

'Just arrived. Wanted to see Katherine. I didn't want to drag him in here, with all these people, so I left them outside to say whatever they've got to say to each other.'

'That's wonderful,' Sally said, and Roland was certain he saw tears begin to well in her eyes. 'Funny how forgiving you get as you grow older, isn't it? How's his son?'

'Juan? I never thought to ask.'

'Better that way. Give me a dance.'

It was a waltz, and Roland held Sally tightly. All the memories had come home to roost that night, especially with the former ambassador sitting outside the very ballroom where Roland had first met him, had first danced with Catarina . . .

'You're going to miss Katherine, aren't you?' Sally asked.

'I never got to see that much of her during these past few months. She spent all her time with Franz.'

'Doesn't that big house get lonely, even with the help?'

'I try not to stay in it too long by myself.'

Sally looked over Roland's shoulder at Heinrich Kassler, still sitting alone at a table. 'Just don't get like him. There's a man with a problem that's just eating him up.'

'No problem – just his business.'

The waltz ended and Roland walked outside to find Katherine and Franz still talking to Menendez. Tears were falling freely down the old man's face now, and Roland wondered just how deeply he was regretting the pride that had kept him away for the past twenty years.

'Where are you staying in London, sir?'

'Here, at Claridge's'

'But your coat?'

Through the tears Menendez gave a wistful smile. 'I had to take a walk first, to pluck up the courage to see you. Even then, I couldn't simply walk into the ballroom. I had to send a waiter.'

'I understand. How long will you be staying?'

'A few days. This will be my last trip to England, and I'm grateful that the good Lord has given me time to make it. I haven't been here since my ambassadorship. I always loved this country, and now I would like to take a final look.'

'If there is anything I can do for you while you're here, sir, please don't hesitate to call.'

'Thank you. You're very kind.'

Through the door to the ballroom, Roland heard the bandleader tell the guests to take their partners for the final waltz. He pulled Katherine aside, whispered in her ear. She smiled and nodded happily.

'Grandfather, will you have the last waltz with me?'

Menendez seemed startled at the invitation. His face shone, happiness pushed aside his tears. 'I would be delighted to do so, my child.' He took off his coat, handed it to Roland and escorted Katherine back to the ballroom. Roland followed and stood watching from the entrance as Katherine and her grandfather started to circle the floor. She was taller than Menendez, a striking comparison between the young woman and her grandfather. Roland saw heads turn, imagined that questions were being asked and he smiled to himself. Who among the guests could possibly guess who Katherine's partner was for this final waltz?

'Sorry to steal her away from you,' Roland said to Franz, who stood next to him.

'That's not theft, its kindness.'

'Thanks for seeing it that way.' Roland patted his son-in-law on the shoulder. 'Tell you what, how about doing a kind act for your father? He's sitting over there like a lost soul.'

Franz looked across the ballroom at Heinrich Kassler, who had still not moved from the table. 'Why is it, sir, that I feel closer to you than to my own father?'

'You shouldn't, because your father and I are very much alike. The only difference is that when we had to choose between work and family, your father made a more extreme choice than I did. I think your father's wishing he had the opportunity to make that choice again. Why don't you help him do it?'

Franz walked slowly toward his father, pulled out a chair and sat down. Roland saw that they began to talk. He had no idea what was being said; he just hoped the bridge was being crossed.

As the final strains of music died away, Roland looked back at the dance floor. Katherine and Nicanor Menendez stood quite still, holding their waltz position. Then Katherine leaned forward and kissed Menendez on the cheek. Roland captured the picture, filed it away in his mind with other treasured memories – another loose thread tucked neatly into place.

As the guests left, Katherine, Franz, Roland and Kassler stood by the door to wish everyone goodnight. The bridal couple were in no hurry to leave; they were booked into Claridge's for the night, and the following morning were scheduled to fly to Portugal to begin their honeymoon.

Nicanor Menendez was one of the very last to leave, standing alone for the longest time by the edge of the dance floor. He was in the same position Roland remembered him from the night of the ambassador's ball when he'd regarded Roland with that confused expression, uncertain if the tall, young Englishman had been one of those men included on Catarina's dance card. Roland walked over to him, waited for the old man to speak.

'Do you worry, as I did, about your daughter, Mr Eagles?'

'Never an hour passes without my thinking about her, sir. I have three other children as well, much younger. Two of them were here earlier.'

'You are a very fortunate man. I had two children. One died, the other uses the power I've given him and spares no thought for me.'

'Juan?'

Menendez nodded sadly. 'Because of me he is a very wealthy man. But he cares little for me or his mother. That is the gratitude a father receives. I hope your children don't treat you in the same shabby fashion.'

Roland almost answered that he doubted very much that they would. He'd never pushed his children, had never dreamed of trying to arrange an advantageous marriage for Katherine, had never tried to live his life through her, as Menendez had done. Instead he said, 'So do I, sir. When you're ready, may I see you to your room?'

'Thank you, but I think I'll go for a walk first.'

'It was a pleasure to meet you again.'

'I believe you really mean that.'

'I do. Should you need anything at all while you're in London, please contact me.' He shook his hand and watched him walk slowly toward the door where Franz, Katherine and Heinrich Kassler stood. He saw a white envelope passed as Menendez kissed his granddaughter before he left.

'He didn't have to give me this,' Katherine said, showing Roland the white envelope as he joined her. 'His coming was enough of a gift.'

'Open it.'

'Oh, I feel so mercenary doing this.' Nonetheless, Katherine slit the envelope with her fingernail, pulled out a blue check. Roland guessed the amount would be large as Menendez attempted to make up for the twenty years during which he'd ignored his only grandchild.

Katherine's eyes shot wide open and she gave a most unladylike whistle of surprise.

'How much?' Roland asked, pleased that he'd been correct. 'Fifty thousand pounds?'

'One . . .' Katherine gulped and looked again at the check as if she couldn't believe what was written there. 'One million dollars.'

'What?' Amazed, Roland looked for himself. He had seen larger checks, signed them, received them for business deals. But the sight of seven figures – the single one followed by six zeroes – on a check that was a wedding gift was too much for any of them to comprehend.

'Franz and I can't possibly accept this,' Katherine said.

Roland glanced at Kassler; the German was also stunned by Menendez's generosity. 'You most certainly can accept it,' he told his daughter firmly. 'Menendez is trying desperately to clear his conscience, so have the goodness to allow him to do so the only way he can see fit.'

Katherine understood the wisdom of her father's advice. She folded the check and passed it to Franz, who placed it in his pocket. 'Thank you for the most wonderful day of my life,' she told her father again.

'You're more than welcome.' Roland kissed her, shook hands with Franz. 'You'll call me at the office before you leave tomorrow?'

'Of course, and we'll write to you twice every day.' She threw her arms around Roland's neck and kissed him. 'Will you please stop worrying about me? Your little girl's all grown up now.'

'I know. It makes me worry all the more.' He stepped back to allow Heinrich Kassler to say farewell to the

543

bridal couple. The German kissed Katherine, then faced his son. For a moment, Roland thought a handshake was going to suffice between the two men until he saw each man reach out to hug the other; whatever Franz had said to his father while Katherine had danced with Menendez had removed a wall of reserve.

'Do we just go home to bed now?' Kassler asked Roland when they stood alone at last.

'Do you want to go out? To a casino?' Although he'd kept his membership current, Roland hadn't been to Kendall's in ages, as if the club reminded him of Christopher Mellish . . . wherever he was now . . . The riffle of cards, the sound of dice, the spin of the wheel might make a pleasant change.

'Why not?'

They walked the short distance to Kendall's, conspicuous in their tuxedoes as they enjoyed the cool night air. Roland offered Kassler a cigar, which he refused, then lit one for himself, chewing the end happily. If he won at Kendall's, it would be the perfect ending to a perfect day.

'Enjoy the party?' Roland asked. 'You seemed to do an awful lot of sitting by yourself.'

'I was thinking. Weren't you doing the same – reminiscing?'

'Of course. What were you and Franz talking about near the end while the band played the last waltz?'

'Franz was telling me about Katherine's grandfather suddenly appearing, how you two had made amends. And then . . .' Kassler paused for an instant, as though he still couldn't believe what he'd heard. 'Then he told me he loved me . . . he just said it, out of the blue. It's a strange sensation, Roland, to hear one's son say that for the first time in twenty-four years.'

'Maybe he never had the opportunity to say it before.'

'True,' Kassler answered. 'Or has it something to do with him now being part of a family where love is more important than success?'

544

'It took me a long time to learn that lesson, Heinrich. Don't be too hard on yourself.'

Kassler walked on in silence for a while. 'That was quite a sentimental moment when Katherine's grandfather put in an appearance, coming all the way from Argentina. How long was it since he'd last seen her?'

'Twenty years. We fell out when I married Katherine's mother. He only saw Katherine when she was a baby.'

'Why was there a split?'

Why indeed? Roland asked himself. It all seemed so trivial now, so damned stupid. Lives wasted because of misplaced pride. 'I wasn't good enough to marry his daughter, that's what he thought at the time. Fortunately, his daughter didn't see it in quite the same light.'

Kassler's face expressed surprise. 'What did he have against you?'

'He thought I was after his money. I guess I don't need to go into how wrong he was about that. He also had his family name to think about, told me it wasn't his family's custom to marry Jews.'

'You?' As they turned into Mount Street, Kassler stopped and stared at Roland.

'My father.'

In that moment, Kassler seemed aloof to Roland, a plane removed. Then the German burst into a roar of laughter. 'Now I understand!'

'Understand what?'

'Why you were so furious when we first met.'

'I don't follow you.' Roland didn't know what to make of the German, the abrupt switches in emotion – the aloofness, the laughter, and now this claim to understand. Understand what, for God's sake?

'All this time I thought it was your British sense of justice, the British loathing at what the dirty Huns had done. I thought that was why you reacted the way you did that day, came so close to killing me. It wasn't that at all, Roland. It was your righteousness, your Jewish lust for vengeance, that same vengeance that sent hundreds to the gallows at Nürnberg. That man who still works for you – Goldstein. Him I could always understand; even now, twenty-five years later, he still hates Germans. But I never really understood the reason for your fury – until now. Why did you hide it all this time?'

'I never hid it. I never promoted it either.'

'Is your father still alive? No, he couldn't be, otherwise he would've been at Claridge's tonight.'

'Both my parents are dead; my younger sister and brother too. They died two days before I joined the army in 1940. An air raid.'

'A *German* air raid,' Kassler said understandingly. 'I'm sorry.'

'That was the other reason I went mad that day,' Roland explained as they entered Kendall's. 'When you were captured wearing that corporal's uniform – and we knew you were a member of the SS – you picked the worst British officer in the world to be interrogated by.'

'I see. And, ironically, he turned out to be the fairest.' Kassler watched Roland sign him into the guest book. 'It was a strange time. The men of the *Schutzstaffel*, even down to the lowliest cooks and mechanics, were either being shot out of hand or placed into special detention centers because they were all branded murderers. That was why I wore that corporal's uniform.'

'Where did you get that uniform? I never did ask you.'

'From a dead soldier. At the time I wasn't too fussy about removing clothes from a corpse. My life was worth more than any distaste I might have felt.'

'I'll bet it was.' Roland followed Kassler to a blackjack table, watched him begin playing. The German used the same system he'd followed in Monte Carlo, remembering the high cards, narrowing the odds in his own favor as the four decks the dealer used became smaller. No hint of enjoyment whatsoever showed on Kassler's face as the pile of chips in front of him steadily grew, but Roland

546

knew he was delighting in his success. He was winning, and that was still the most important thing of all to Kassler.

After a few minutes Roland walked away and began to play roulette. He studied the people playing their systems while he stuck with red, doubling up until he reached the house limit. For ten minutes he broke even, then a run of seven blacks left him losing five hundred pounds. Deciding to cut his losses, he returned to the blackjack table where Kassler had won about the same amount.

'Can we talk?' Roland asked.

'Certainly. Just allow me to play this hand.' Sitting in the last spot before the dealer, Kassler eyed his open card, a nine against the dealer's six. The German drew a seven. 'Give me another,' he told the dealer, and the three players before him who had already stood – one with eighteen, two with nineteen – muttered angrily. The dealer flipped over a five to give Kassler twenty-one. Roland knew it wasn't blind luck. The deck was close to the bottom and Kassler had merely been following the cards; he knew there were plenty of low cards left. Roland watched the dealer turn himself another six and an eight – twenty. Kassler, using the house limit of five hundred pounds, was the only winner. He collected his chips, returned the scowls of the other players with a courteous if cold smile, and left the table.

'You didn't make any friends just then, Heinrich. If you hadn't drawn that final card the dealer would have been forced to stand on seventeen and they would have all won.'

'But I, with sixteen, would have lost. That's not the way the game is played, Roland.' Kassler took the chips to the cashier's cage, pocketing the wad of money he received in exchange. 'What do you wish to talk about?'

Roland led the way to two plush armchairs placed in a corner of the club, well away from any noise – or any inquisitive ears. 'We formed a union today, Heinrich.

Franz and Katherine. How about discussing a second one?'

'Kassler Industries and the Eagles Group?'

Roland nodded. 'The idea's been popping in and out of my mind ever since that night I sat Katherine and Franz down in my dining room and told them I expected them to get married.'

'I must admit that it's also crossed my mind.'

'I know – the very moment we bumped into each other in Monte Carlo. When you realized the girl your son was ogling was my daughter, the possibility of a merger was the first thing you thought about.' He laid a hand fondly on Kassler's arm. 'I'm not criticizing your sense of priorities, Heinrich. In this instance, you had far more foresight than I did.'

'Is it because of the wedding that you're broaching the subject now or is there another reason?'

Roland gave Kassler a thin smile. 'You read me as well as you read a deck of cards. How familiar are you with the Ganz operation in the States?'

Kassler glanced up at the ceiling while he ran the name through his mind. 'A supermarket chain headquartered in White Plains, New York. Approximately four hundred and fifty branches located throughout New England, the East Coast and part of the South . . . also a chain of some sixty discount stores launched six years ago . . .' The facts flew from the German's mouth like a computer printout. 'The company began shortly before the first war as a chain of small grocery shops, switching to the supermarket concept in the 1930s. A year ago it was taken over —'

'Enough!' Roland said, laughing and raising his hand for Kassler to stop. 'You've already touched on what I wanted to discuss, the discount store operation.'

'BarGanz?' Kassler shook his head, grimacing as he mentioned the name of the supermarket chain's discount store operation. 'A terrible pun, BarGanz.'

'I know. It goes in the garbage can the moment we get control of it.'

'You . . .? The Eagles Group acquiring BarGanz?'

'One of the consequences of the company being taken over was to see who was interested in buying BarGanz – using the assets to pay in part for the acquisition of Ganz itself. Michael Adler has been over to White Plains to discuss a deal—'

'You don't have the money?'

'We can raise a loan for the acquisition, that's no problem. I'm just whetting your appetite to buy into the Eagles Group, let you know how extensive we'll be shortly in the United States.' Roland thought back to the conversation he'd had with Sally the night he'd made his peace with Daniel Rushden, when he'd pointed out the three companies within the Eagles Group which meant the most to him. 'I hold forty percent of the Eagles Group, Heinrich, and I'm willing to sell some of my holdings to you so that I can pull three companies out and own them privately.'

'Which three companies?'

'The *Eagle* – not the entire publishing group, just the newspaper, Eldridge's and Adler's.'

'Which would leave the group with what?'

Roland ticked off the companies on his fingers. 'Girard et Fils in France, the companies we own in Scandinavia, the remainder of Burnham Press, Biwell in the States, along with the BarGanz stores once we finalize that, and the electrical appliance shops we still own over here. Not to mention the cash I'd pay for Eldridge's, the *Eagle* and Adler's.'

Kassler thought it over. 'Why those three companies?'

'Sentimental reasons. They all mean something very special to me.'

'In what way?'

'Eldridge's has a strong link with Katherine's mother, my first wife. The *Eagle*' – he paused, not wanting to go into detail about how the newspaper walkout had made

549

him rethink his attitude toward the press – 'let's just say it bears my name.'

'And Adler's?' Kassler asked. Before Roland could give the same reason he'd given Sally – his first major acquisition – the German said, 'Because it also bears your name. I've thought of that coincidence often, Roland, the reason you fought so strongly for that particular group. *Adler* is German for *Eagle*. You were astute enough to buy a group that already bore your name.'

Roland laughed. 'I think you're the first person who ever caught that, Heinrich.'

'If I can remember my way perfectly through four decks of cards, how hard is it translating a single word of German to English?'

'Are you interested in a deal?'

Kassler waved down a waiter who was passing, took a stack of paper napkins from the surprised man. 'Figures . . . let us work on figures, Roland. Exactly how much of your holdings are you prepared to sell to Kassler Industries, and at what price?'

Roland sat back and watched Kassler busily scribbling figures. Maybe he hadn't won at roulette as he thought he might, but this was even better . . . the opportunity to own privately the three companies which meant the most to him.

'Roland . . .' Kassler finally finished writing; four napkins were crammed full of figures, and Roland's eyes caught the European crossed seven, just to make sure it wasn't mistaken for a one. 'I think we might have a deal here.'

'Good. What better way to celebrate a marriage than to join two companies such as our own?'

'What better way indeed?' Kassler said, nodding in happy agreement. 'That cigar you offered me during the walk here? I think I'll have it now.'

Three months later, Roland and Michael Adler flew to

New York to finalize the acquisition of the BarGanz discount store chain. Their first move on gaining control was to drop the BarGanz name and tie the chain in with the Biwell group; almost overnight, the Biwell name appeared in suburban shopping malls throughout New England, the East Coast and in the South, as BarGanz disappeared.

Michael's wife, Lisa, and Sally accompanied the two men on the trip. While Michael and Roland worked, the two women shopped and planned for dinners and shows during the evening, turning what was ostensibly a business trip into a mini-vacation. During the preceding months, Roland had grown closer to Sally; whenever he wanted a dinner companion, someone to talk to, it was always Sally he seemed to turn to. Once he'd tried to rationalize the increasing nearness by telling himself he was merely using her as a substitute for Michael, who had been Roland's constant companion before his marriage. Of all Roland's friends, with the exception of Alf Goldstein, Sally went back the furthest.

During dinner on their final night in New York, Roland and Michael discussed the management team that would be needed to run the large discount store chain. Michael nominated himself to head the team; and Lisa, eager to try living in the United States, was quick to support him.

'Sorry . . .' Roland said regretfully, 'you're not coming over here on a permanent basis, Michael.'

'Why not?' Michael and Lisa asked together.

'For the same reason I gave my son-in-law when he asked to move over here.' Franz and Katherine had peppered Roland with requests to be involved with the expanded American side of the business. 'You're family, Michael.'

'Close friend, yes – family's a little strong.'

'You know what I mean, friends are often closer. Let's just say I'm too selfish to let you go.' He needed Michael full-time at the Eagles Group main office. Since Kassler's purchase of stock and the separation of the *Eagle*, Adler's and Eldridge's from the main group, Roland was spending more time on the restructuring of his privately owned empire. 'You and Lisa can make all the trips you like over here for the board meetings, but I want you to stay based in London.' He saw Michael open his mouth to protest again but stopped him. 'Besides, who's going to keep an eye on your father if you relocate over here, Michael? Think about that.'

Michael pursed his lips. Why Roland should even think of such a thing was beyond him; his consideration for a former adversary went far beyond the bounds of anything Michael might have expected.

'Your father's in his seventies, Michael, and you're all he's got. Make the most of each other while you can.'

The last comment brought an instant flush to Michael's cheeks. He saw Albert once or twice a week, dreaded the visits but made them out of a sense of duty. If the weather was nice when Michael called, Albert would insist on his son taking him out for a short walk, clutching his arm tightly while he asked about the business, anxious to hear any details Michael could supply. Michael never understood why his father should be so interested in the business, but he realized he was Albert's only real contact with the outside world, except for the nurse who only coddled him.

'Who do you have in mind to head this team?' Michael asked.

'I was thinking of Lawrence Chivers.'

'Lawrence? He's pushing sixty.'

'That's right, but he wants to keep on at it. He's enjoyed what we've accomplished as much as any of us. Besides, since his wife died four years ago, he hasn't got any really strong ties to keep him in England.' Roland thought fondly of the pipe-smoking Yorkshireman, another who had been with him for many years. Chivers

552

had already retired once on his fifty-fifth birthday, but his wife had died shortly afterwards. Not having any children and with nothing else to keep him busy, he asked Roland if he could return. Roland had already appointed a new director in his place; nonetheless, he created a position for Chivers at his former salary with the promise that he could stay with the firm for as long as he wanted. When the possibility of heading an American management team had cropped up, Chivers had jumped at the challenge – a new area where he felt he could use his experience and expertise.

'With his accent and that blasted pipe stuck permanently in his mouth, no one will be able to understand a blasted word he says,' Michael joked.

'Be that as it may,' Roland said, 'but he'll do an excellent job for us during the transition period. After that, he can stay here for as long as he likes.'

'Who'll help him?'

'I was thinking of putting Vincent Generoso in as Lawrence's number two.'

Michael chewed his lower lip thoughtfully as he considered Roland's answer. Generoso, a tall, elegant, gray-haired man in his late forties, had been a vice-president of the BarGanz operation, having worked himself up through the Ganz parent company. Although his future with the parent company was assured, even if not at immediate board level, Roland had approached him during the negotiations to see if he were amenable to joining the Biwell group as it absorbed the much larger BarGanz discount chain. 'He knows his way around, that's for sure. Could be a big help to Lawrence,' Michael said.

Roland nodded. 'He was with BarGanz when it started, slotted in from the parent company and given board position. It seems stupid to me not to use him. We'll have to make up his pension rights and meet a few other conditions, but that seems a small price to pay for someone who already has the situation at his fingertips.'

'How do you think he'll get on with Lawrence?'

'We'll have to find that out, although I've got a suspicion that Generoso might have been thinking company president when I brought up the matter of his staying with us. I'm meeting with him tomorrow before we catch the London flight.'

'Are you two going to carry on talking business all night long?' Sally asked. 'We have tickets for a show, so make up your minds whether or not you want to see it with us. Otherwise Lisa and I will find two other men to take.'

Roland gave her an admonishing glance. 'Last time I bring you along for the ride. You nag me enough in London, so why do I have to listen to it here as well?'

'Look where you'd be if I didn't nag you from time to time,' Sally retorted. 'And, come to think of it, make sure you call the London office before we leave tomorrow, otherwise we won't be met at the airport.'

'Does Lisa nag you?' Roland asked Michael as they left the restaurant and searched for a taxi. 'No, of course not,' he said, answering his own question. 'You left getting married too late for there to be any time for nagging.'

Roland met with Vincent Generoso the following morning at the Biwell Group's head office above its Lexington Avenue store. He could see immediately that Generoso wasn't very happy at the idea of occupying a number two position and he tried to put the former Bar-Ganz vice president at ease.

'It's essential for us to have one of our own people here at the beginning, Vince. Any foreign company that acquires a large American concern would act the same way. But I'm counting on you, on your experience with this particular market, to back up Lawrence.'

'How long will this arrangement last?' Generoso wanted to join Roland, to be part of what he considered a fast-expanding company. Yet he didn't relish the prospect of playing second fiddle to an import. He had put in six years of hard work with BarGanz and felt vaguely betrayed at how the discount store operation had been sold off once Ganz had taken over. Roland's offer to join Biwell was more palatable than the prospect of returning to the Ganz organization, washing his hands of the time and effort he'd spent building up BarGanz, but Generoso expected more. Surely those six years were worth the presidency?

'I'm going to have to ask you to be patient with me. Lawrence is going to be here to knock the company into the shape that conforms with Eagles Group standards. Once he's satisfied that he's accomplished that, and once he decides he wants to call it a day, the top spot is yours. And with the presidency goes an appointment to the main board of the Eagles Group. Are you prepared to bear with me?'

'I think so.' The appointment to the main board was like a beacon. 'You can tell Lawrence Chivers that he'll be able to count on me for any support.'

Roland smiled and shook the New Yorker's hand, sealing the bargain. 'You can tell him that yourself, Vince. He'll be over next week to look for a place to live. Maybe you can help him out there.'

CHAPTER TWO

The next three years were among the happiest Roland could remember, one of the main reasons being the two grandchildren Katherine and Franz gave him – a boy named Henry, after Roland's father and a girl named Joanne.

With some of the money from Nicanor Menendez's generous wedding gift, Katherine and Franz bought a sprawling six-bedroom house overlooking Hampstead Heath, which they renovated completely. It seemed to Roland that he spent more time there than at his own home, playing with his grandchildren – both of whom had inherited the blue-eyed blondness of their parents – taking them for walks in the baby carriage, playing the role of doting grandfather, albeit a very youthful one, to the fullest extent. He was especially glad when Katherine always remembered to send copies of any photographs of the children to Menendez in Argentina. He regretted never having done the same with photographs of Katherine when she was growing up, but he'd never thought of it. Perhaps had he done so he could have healed that particular rift years earlier . . .

The two businesses he was now involved with – the Eagles Group with its major foothold in the United States under Lawrence Chivers' supervision, and the companies he'd separated and now owned privately – were prospering; Roland had even looked into the possibility of opening an Eldridge's restaurant in New York. Michael Adler was on the board of the smaller group, as was Franz Kassler, who was no longer involved with the main Eagles Group. Roland often wondered if the young man was glad not to be associated in business with his father, although the two seemed much closer now than they had ever been. The grandchildren had done that, Roland decided. Kassler now visited London regularly. Although he had business there as a large shareholder and a director of the Eagles Group, he spent as many hours with his son and his family as he did in the Eagles Group offices. The gifts he brought each time for the children left them with little space in their rooms for their beds. Roland, too, had become closer to Kassler, now that they were linked by family and business. He always looked forward to Kassler's visits to London; they would even argue good-naturedly over whose turn it was to take the children out, whose turn it was to push the baby carriage, then they would laugh at the sight of two middle-aged executives fighting over such an issue. Kassler's visits also gave Roland an excuse to frequent the casinos and rekindle his love of gambling.

Roland's greatest pleasure of all, though, was to be surrounded by what he called his extended family which included the Kasslers and Sally, Michael and Lisa Adler, the Morrisons and Richard and Carol. Then he was truly in his element, the leader of a thriving tribe, a throwback to the old lords of the manor who cared for everyone on their land. For his forty-eighth birthday in September of 1972 he took everyone on a five-day trip to the Bahamas, playing on the beach with the children during the day, and amusing himself in Kassler's company in the casinos at night. After two visits to the casino, however, Kassler was politely but firmly banned from the blackjack table. The card counting he had employed in London and Monte Carlo was not welcomed by the American dealers and supervisors in the Bahamas. When Roland suggested he try a different game, the German refused. Blackjack was the only game where he could eventually work the cards in his favor; he was interested in nothing at which he couldn't be reasonably certain of winning.

Aside from the contentment he received from family and business, Roland had one other happy event to anticipate . . . a knighthood for services to industry. He had been approached by the government to see whether he would be amenable to being included in the 1974 New Year's Honours List. He had replied with a touch of vanity — feeling that he deserved it — that not only would he be amenable, he would be absolutely delighted . . .

'You!' Sally exploded with laughter when Roland told her the news, during dinner at her apartment the next night. 'Sir Roland Eagles?'

'What's wrong with it?' He didn't consider it a laughing matter; neither did anyone else to whom he'd mentioned it confidentially. Katherine, especially had been thrilled by the notion.

Sally wielded an imaginary sword, laid it gently across Roland's shoulders. 'I dub thee Sir Roland Eagles. Oh, God . . .!' She burst into laughter again. 'Half the people who've ever been knighted will return theirs to Buckingham Palace once they find out you've been made a knight, just like those pompous idiots who sent back their OBEs after the Beatles were honored. I never thought I'd live to see the day when you'd not only accept such a thing but actually be proud of it. Whatever happened to Roland "the-establishment-can't-bribe-me" Eagles?'

'Don't criticize it, Sally.'

'Criticize it, hell! I expect you'll want me to call you *sir* in the future.'

Sally's remark made Roland think of all the people he'd ever called *sir* — superior officers in the army, Spott-Mandray, even Nicanor Menendez. How many of those people had ever done anything worthy of the respect? Certainly not Old Spotty! 'I think I'll fire anyone who calls me sir.'

'Ha!' Sally cried triumphantly. 'You don't really want the title, do you?'

'Actually, now that it's been offered to me, I think I do.

I didn't inherit a massive fortune or a company running very nicely, thank you very much. Whatever I've got I achieved myself. That deserves some recognition.'

'You've got all the recognition you ever wanted, Roland Eagles. Family, friends, people who respect and admire you. Some of them, although God alone knows why, even love you. And they'll probably still feel the same way even if you are knighted.'

'I should hope so. A knighthood will go well' – he winked at Sally – 'with my Military Cross *and* my Military Medal.'

'Oh, you conceited bugger!' She wielded the imaginary sword again and lopped his head clean off.

In mid-December, two weeks before his name was due to appear in the New Year's Honours List, Roland flew with Michael Adler to New York for a board meeting of the Biwell Group. Heinrich Kassler accompanied them as well not only to lend his weight as a member of the Eagles Group main board, but because he was interested in a takeover Roland was trying to arrange of an ailing group of eight discount stores named Brady, located in the New York-New Jersey area. Only one other company was bidding for the Brady stock, and Roland hoped that a heavy presence from the main board might swing the decision in his favor.

Vincent Generoso met the early afternoon flight from London. After shaking hands with Roland, Michael and Kassler, Generoso led the visitors out of the terminal to a Cadillac limousine with darkened windows. The chauffeur, a heavy-set square man with a neck that bulged over his shirt collar, dropped the car into gear and sped away from the airport, heading for Manhattan.

'Stuffy in here,' Roland remarked. Outside it was forty-five degrees, and the limousine's heating seemed to be on full blast. He reached to open a window.

'Please don't do that,' Generoso said. 'I'll turn down

the heating if you prefer.'

'What's wrong with having a window open?'

'Lawrence Chivers' orders.' Generoso fiddled with a dial and the temperature dropped quickly. 'You'd better take one of these as well.' Generoso handed out plastic identification tags to Roland, Michael and Kassler, instructed them to wear the cards on their jacket lapels.

'What in God's name is the reason for this?' Roland demanded. 'We've never done this before.'

Generoso sighed. 'New policy. Lawrence asked me to put you in the picture during the drive from the airport. We've had a problem develop in the past couple of weeks and we've had to tighten up on security.'

Kassler looked around the inside of the limousine, rapped his knuckles against the windows; now he understood why they were darkened. 'Is this a bulletproof car?'

'Yes, it is. Enjoying the ride?'

'Beautiful,' the German grunted sarcastically.

'What kind of a problem?' Michael asked. He was starting to feel nervous. Installing scanners in company mail rooms to check for bombs was one thing; every large company in Britain was doing that now. But not being allowed to open a window, being driven around in an armored car . . . what kind of business operation was that? All of a sudden he was glad Roland had rejected his request to work in the United States.

'It began two weeks ago with something quite minor,' Generoso replied. 'A large box of cockroaches was let loose in our Rego Park store. I was there when it happened and you can imagine the pandemonium.'

Roland nodded and he heard Michael suck in his breath.

'That closed the store for three days,' Generoso continued. 'The exterminators had to come in, inventory was moved out, everything checked carefully. Then last week we had a small fire in the children's wear department of our Lexington Avenue store, below the executive offices.

Police say an incendiary device was concealed in the clothing. On the following night, one of our transportation depots was broken into. The tires on twenty trucks were slashed, windshields and headlights smashed. Also, one of our store managers had his home broken into, absolutely destroyed. He and his family were on vacation at the time, thank God. That was when we began to take these security measures.'

'What's behind it all?' Roland asked.

'Lawrence seems to think it might have something to do with our trying to buy up those eight Brady stores.'

'I see.' Roland stared at the back of the chauffeur's head and wondered whether the man was armed. 'How do you know the break-in at the manager's home wasn't just an ordinary burglary?'

'The detectives who investigated it told us they'd never seen such systematic destruction. Besides, nothing was actually taken.'

At the Lexington Avenue headquarters of Biwell two uniformed men stood at the main entrance – not the usual company guards who watched for shoplifters and directed people to different departments, but two armed security guards. On the top floor, before Roland, Michael and Kassler were allowed to enter the office area, the passes Generoso had given them were scrutinized by another armed guard. Roland felt like he was visiting a prisoner in a top-security ward.

'Lawrence, just what the hell is going on?' Roland demanded the moment he saw Chivers. 'When I was over here six weeks ago you were running a chain of stores; now you're running an armed camp.'

'What did Vince tell you?'

'He mentioned the troubles you've been having, but aren't you overreacting just a little bit? Are all these melodramatics really necessary?'

'Our own security people seem to think so.'

'Was that chauffeur armed?'

'Yes. Bernie's a former police officer.' Chivers smiled and picked up the pipe which lay on his desk, lit it to surround himself with a familiar cloud of gray, pungent smoke. 'He was, to use the local vernacular, packing a rod. I trust you all feel immensely safer.'

The attempted humor fell flat. 'Vince said this whole thing's to do with those eight Brady stores we want.'

'I think so, although the police have nothing to go on, no proof that these incidents are even related. My own belief is that the firm competing with us for the Brady acquisition, a New Jersey company called Milano, they own four stores—'

'I know of them.'

'I don't think they believe in a free and open market.'

'Mafia?' The question came from Michael.

'That's an all-encompassing term that covers a multitude of evils. A very slick bunch of thugs is more like it,' Chivers explained. 'Either the company is a Mafia business, a legitimate – and I use that word loosely – front for the Mafia money, or else it's hiring these thugs to keep us from buying Brady.'

'How much is the Milano offer?' Kassler asked.

'Two million dollars below our own.'

'I see,' Kassler said. 'And who is behind Milano?'

'Joe Milano's the man who owns it. He started out twenty years ago in the garbage collection business in New Jersey, servicing a few towns. Since then he's become more respectable.'

'Have the police tried to establish a link between these incidents and Milano?' Michael asked.

'They have to catch someone first.'

'How often does this kind of thing happen?'

Before Chivers could answer, Generoso cut in. 'There was quite an infamous case a few years back, in 1964 I think it was. The Mafia did fifty-million dollars worth of property damage to the A & P and murdered two of its managers to try and persuade the company to stock a

562

detergent in which the Mafia had a considerable financial interest. If this is what's behind these incidents, I think it would be to our advantage to remember that these people play tough. And they play for keeps.'

Roland felt a chill run down his back; he wished Generoso hadn't brought that up, especially with such lurid attention to detail. 'Do you want to come home?' he asked Chivers.

'You must be joking.' Chivers took the pipe from his mouth and tapped it in the ashtray. 'You and me, Roland, we've been through a bloody war—'

'I went through the same war,' Kassler pointed out.

'So you did, and you can appreciate what I'm going to say as much as anyone else. After surviving a war like that are we now going to let a bunch of gangsters make us turn tail and run?'

'That's all right for you to say,' Generoso interrupted. 'Your families don't live here. Mine does.'

Roland knew the vice president was right. The concerns of the people living in the area had to be taken into account. 'Have there been any personal assaults, threats of any kind?'

Chivers shook his head. 'Just property damage.'

'We should be thankful for that then. I suggest we take a vote at the board meeting tomorrow whether we see this Brady deal through or not.'

Roland, Michael and Kassler stayed at the Sherry Netherland that night, eating an early dinner and then retiring. Roland was up at four-thirty the next morning, unable to adjust easily to the time difference. He placed a call to Katherine in London and spent ten minutes chatting with her without mentioning the trouble in New York; there was no point in upsetting her. Then he called Sally at the *Eagle* offices. At five o'clock he went downstairs to go for a walk. In the lobby, he found Heinrich Kassler staring out at the dark, empty street.

563

'Couldn't sleep either?'

'I was awake all night,' he answered, 'wondering what business is coming to. Seems the gangsters have taken over from the legitimate businessmen.'

Roland nodded in agreement. 'I remember reading somewhere how the established Mafia families have their money all tied up in seemingly legitimate business now. But they still run them in the old way, using force to achieve what they can't get honestly.'

'Are those eight Brady stores worth all this trouble?'

'I've been asking myself that same question. Vince does have a family here and we should be as concerned about him as we are about ourselves.' Roland walked out onto the street, bracing himself against the cold air. Kassler followed, and the two men began to walk north along Fifth Avenue. A sanitation truck passed and they stepped back quickly as a spray of water hit the gutter and part of the sidewalk.

'Can you go for a cup of coffee?' Roland asked as they turned east and passed a restaurant that was full of people eating an early breakfast or a very late-night snack; he was never sure in New York, it seemed to run twenty-four hours a day. He held open the door for Kassler and they sat down at a booth in the far corner.

A couple of minutes after they went in a florid-faced man wearing an overcoat and a hat pulled over his forehead followed. Roland watched as he took a seat at the counter. 'Wasn't he standing outside the Sherry Netherland when we came out?'

Kassler swiveled in the seat to look at the man who had removed his hat. He had dark brown hair streaked with gray, aged about fifty. He was reading a newspaper, seemingly oblivious to anyone else in the restaurant. 'I don't remember,' Kassler said. 'Are you seeing things in shadows?'

'Maybe, but this series of incidents has got me worried. What if this mob decided to go higher than Biwell? What

564

if they started to exert pressure on the Eagles Group? I've got a family.'

'We both do, Roland. I would hate to see anything happen to them just as much as you would.'

Probably more so, Roland thought, and wished he hadn't taken such a selfish attitude. The German had come to know the love of a family so late in life that he was probably more anxious than Roland about the possibility of anything happening to them.

They finished their coffee in silence and left. Fifteen yards down the street, Kassler tugged at Roland's arm and motioned toward the doorway of a furrier's shop. They ducked inside and waited. A minute later, the man who had followed them into the coffee shop hurried past, newspaper tucked under his arm.

'Looking for us?' Roland asked quietly, stepping out from the doorway and tapping the man on the shoulder.

The man spun around, startled by the sudden confrontation. 'I beg your pardon?' The accent was definitely not that of New York; if anything, it bore a strong resemblance to Franz Kassler's accent, clipped and formal.

'Why are you following us?' Roland gripped the man's arm as he asked the question.

'I have no idea what you're talking about. Let go of me!'

Kassler stepped forward, his blue eyes fierce. 'You were waiting outside our hotel, you followed us into the coffee shop. Why?' He grabbed hold of the man by his coat lapels, dragged him away from Roland.

'Let go of me! I am a German citizen! You have no right—'

'Why were you following us?' Kassler asked, switching to German.

Hearing German spoken and watching as Kassler pinned the man against a building, Roland realized how foolish they were, jumping to conclusions as they had.

Accusing a complete stranger – a German probably, a tourist or just another businessman in New York for a meeting – and he and Kassler were accusing the man of being a mobster. The whole idea was so preposterous that Roland felt like laughing; and he would have if the situation hadn't become so serious. 'Let go of him, Heinrich.'

Kassler ignored Roland's softly spoken command. 'You *were* following us. I'm going to summon a police officer.'

'For Christ's sake, leave him alone!' Roland shouted abruptly and pushed Kassler back. The man in the overcoat took the opportunity to escape. He broke into a run heading south, glancing back over his shoulder just once to be certain he wasn't being chased. 'We're both imagining things now,' Roland said as he held out an arm to stop Kassler giving chase.

'He was following us,' Kassler insisted, though he didn't sound as convinced anymore.

'No, he wasn't. And why should a bunch of New York crooks use a German to follow us?' He took Kassler by the arm and guided him slowly back to the hotel.

Over breakfast with Michael Adler, Roland repeated the story, expecting Michael to laugh. Only Michael failed to find anything amusing in it; he would have done the same thing, he admitted, and all three men realized just how deeply Lawrence Chivers' warnings had alarmed them.

They arrived at the Biwell office on Lexington Avenue at eight-thirty. Chivers was on the telephone. He waved at them to sit down while he finished the call. 'That was the police,' he finally said, replacing the receiver. 'There's a fire at our New York-New Jersey distribution center over in Rutherford. Started about an hour ago. They've got it under control now, but damage could be in the millions. All the stock we were shipping for the final pre-Christmas week.'

'Can we make up the shortfall?'

'I suppose so, but is it really worth it?'

'What happened to you?' Roland asked, surprised by the change in Chivers' attitude. 'Just yesterday you were talking about fighting to the last man.'

'That was yesterday, Roland. Last night I had a telephone call, a threat on my life.'

'Did you call the police?'

'Of course. The apartment where I live is now guarded.'

'Did the man speak with an accent?' Kassler asked. 'A German accent?'

'God, no!' Chivers said. 'Broad New York, definitely a New Yorker.'

'See?' Roland said to Kassler. 'We assaulted an innocent man.' He explained to Chivers what had happened, and the Yorkshireman nodded understandingly.

'I suppose we're all suffering from a siege mentality until this is sorted out. There isn't much we can do sitting around here, so let's get the meeting started. Maybe we'll be able to come up with an idea.' He called his secretary to assemble the board members, then led Roland, Kassler and Michael through to the conference room which joined his office. They took their seats around a long mahogany table, scanning through the stacks of paper set in front of each place. The other board members filed in and sat down. Vincent Generoso settled himself in the seat next to Roland.

'By now you've all heard what happened at Rutherford this morning,' Chivers began. 'We've got to assume that every piece of merchandise in that center is worthless now, either damaged by fire, smoke or water, and we've got to start arranging for fill-in shipments immediately. Otherwise, we'll be in for our worst Christmas ever.' He pointed a finger at the merchandise manager. 'Get your people onto that straight away, duplicate whatever was stored there. Yes, Vincent?' he said to Generoso who had a hand half-raised.

'Shouldn't we discuss the wisdom of proceeding with the Brady acquisition first? We spoke yesterday, just us,' he indicated the members of the main Eagles Group board, 'of the possibility of personal threats. Last night Lawrence received a threatening phone call. So did I.'

'You as well?' Roland cut in. 'What did the man say?'

'That I shouldn't forget how vulnerable my wife and two daughters are.'

'Have you arranged anything with the police where you live?' Chivers asked.

'I telephoned them the moment I had the call, about four-thirty. Two detectives came around to the house. I explained the situation here, the acts of vandalism. Now a patrol car is making regular sweeps.'

'Biwell will pay for full-time guards on your house.'

'Is it worth all that, Lawrence?' Generoso asked. 'Is this one acquisition worth having our families threatened . . . possibly harmed?'

'This business with Brady should be over by Friday, two days from now. Whether they sell to us or not – and they'd be crazy not to, with our offer being two million more than Milano – the entire situation will be over by then.'

'You hope!' Generoso interrupted, his voice rising. 'And what do you expect us to do for the next two days? You haven't got a family here to worry about, Lawrence . . . None of your people from the Eagles Group has to worry about that.'

'There's no point in turning this into a shouting match,' Chivers said, trying to control his own voice. He was just as worried as Generoso, but shouting wouldn't serve any purpose in helping to resolve the problem.

'Can we first carry on with the business at hand?' Michael suggested, picking up the stack of papers in front of him. 'We can get together again this afternoon to discuss it further.'

Generoso had to be satisfied with that although,

Roland noted, he was clearly the most agitated by the recent threats. Thinking of Katherine, safe at home in London, he couldn't blame him.

Chivers took his three visitors from Europe to lunch at La Coupole on Park Avenue. The moment they were seated he turned to his guests and, making certain they couldn't be overheard, said, 'Did any of you catch what I caught?'

They all looked at him blankly.

'It might just be a coincidence but Vince and I both received threatening calls last night. What makes it especially coincidental is that we broached the possibility of personal threats only yesterday. Also, my number is unlisted. Vince's as well.' Chivers paused to let those facts sink in, then added, 'And there is one other point that seems to have escaped your attention . . .'

Kassler was the first to speak. 'While Roland and I were making fools of ourselves by assaulting innocent tourists we would have done better to keep a closer eye on members of our own group?'

'Wait a minute,' Roland cut in. 'Vince was at Rego Park the day the cockroaches were let loose, right? He told us so.'

Chivers nodded. 'And it wouldn't have taken much for him to plant that fire in the Lexington Avenue store. He even could have been in on those other attacks – today's fire and the break-in at the transportation depot. Even the trashing of the store manager's home, because he knew when the family would be away.'

'Why would he do such things?' Michael asked.

'Your guess is as good as mine. Money? Fear? Who knows? The question is now – what do we do about it?'

'Where does Generoso live?' Roland asked.

'Mamaroneck, Westchester County.'

'How good is your chauffeur . . . Bernie, whatever his name is?'

'At tailing people?' Chivers guessed. 'Probably better than Alf Goldstein, and certainly a lot more willing to use brute force.'

'I forgot – a former policeman. Why don't we drop a hint this afternoon that we're pulling out of the Brady deal? See what Generoso does then?'

They met again that afternoon and, in well-rehearsed lines, argued the pros and cons of proceeding with the Brady acquisition. Finally, Roland rapped on the mahogany table, his mind apparently made up. 'It isn't worth all this aggravation,' he said wearily. 'I went to lunch in a bulletproof car. I was brought back here in a bulletproof car. My identity is checked by an armed guard whose salary I pay. I don't want to work in that kind of an atmosphere. If we're being pressured to drop Brady, then let's do it and get it over with before someone really gets hurt. There are plenty of other stores we can buy up.'

To Roland's right, Generoso nodded in agreement. 'I'm glad someone finally agrees with me. I'd like to stop living like a scared rabbit, having a police car go past my house every half hour or so. God knows what the neighbors think.'

'They're probably grateful to you,' Chivers said in a forced jest. 'No one in your street will get robbed for a while.'

'We'll get in touch with Brady,' Roland continued as if there had been no interruption. 'Tell them our offer is withdrawn.'

On that note the meeting ended. Roland returned to Chivers' office while Kassler and Michael walked around the store, watching shoppers loading up for Christmas. 'Think he fell for it?' Roland asked.

'We'll know soon enough. Bernie's following him.' Chivers picked up the telephone and rang through to Generoso's office. Generoso's secretary answered; her boss had just stepped out.

'Maybe he's gone to the men's room?' Roland suggested.

'Why not? There's a public phone in there. I just hope he washes his hands before he uses it.'

Vincent Generoso had just deposited a dime in the public telephone located in the men's room when he heard the door open. He dropped the receiver and turned away as Bernie, Chivers' chauffeur, ambled in. Bernie nodded and went straight to a urinal, unzipping his fly and breathing a loud sigh of relief. He looked behind him as the noise of the dime dropping into the return box of the telephone attracted his attention.

'Ma Bell paying out money these days instead of stealing it?'

'Probably belongs to someone who tried making a call earlier on,' Generoso replied as he stood at a basin washing his hands. His face was flushed and he realized it must be obvious to the chauffeur that it was he who had tried making the call. What business was it of his anyway? It probably wouldn't even connect. Or would it? Bernie was an ex-cop, suspicious of everything. He'd probably wonder why Generoso hadn't used his own telephone to make a call, why he'd want to use the public phone in the men's room.

His stomach tense, Generoso dried his hands and left, hurrying back to his office. He wouldn't try to telephone Joe Milano again from here – that was stupid. He'd call him later on from outside, arrange to meet him somewhere so he could tell him the deal between Biwell and Brady was off. The well-planned vandalism, the personal threat to Chivers, the alleged threat to himself, had paid off. Biwell was backing off. Brady would have to accept the lower offer from Milano. And Generoso would be a hundred thousand dollars richer.

It had been the most natural thing in the world for Joe Milano to contact Generoso when Biwell had first

571

expressed interest in acquiring the stumbling Brady chain. Milano also wanted it, but he wasn't prepared to top the price Biwell was offering. Nor did he believe he had to – not with Generoso, the husband of his wife's distant cousin, sitting on the Biwell board. And it was such a far-off, confused connection that it would never be traced. Milano knew how disgruntled Generoso was after having some Limey brought in over his head as company president. That resentment had grown as it became obvious that Lawrence Chivers wasn't about to retire after a year, or two, or even three. Only death would remove the Englishman from the president's chair.

Milano knew exactly how to use Generoso's resentment. The help he'd given with the little accidents – the cockroaches, the fire in the children's wear department, access to the transportation depot and the distribution center, even information about staff vacations so that a house could be safely vandalized. At the same time, Generoso had argued against the Brady deal, pointing out the folly of risking so much for a chain that was in trouble anyway; he had told, with great relish, of the war between the Mafia and the A & P in the sixties. And as a final touch – after Roland Eagles himself had pointed the way – the personal threats Milano himself made after Generoso supplied him with Chivers' number.

Generoso stayed in the office until five-thirty, forcing himself to concentrate on work. When he finally left, he walked quickly to the parking lot where he left his Lincoln Continental, climbed in and headed for the FDR Drive, the route he normally took home to Mamaroneck. Instead of crossing over to the Major Deegan Parkway, though, he took the crowded Harlem River Drive toward the George Washington Bridge and New Jersey.

As soon as he cleared the bridge, Generoso pulled into a shopping mall, located a phone booth – situated, ironically, right outside a Biwell store – and called Milano's home in Alpine, on the Palisades Parkway. A gruff voice answered. 'Joe, it's Vince. Can I meet you somewhere?'

'You got news for me?'

'The very best news.'

'Make it the Forum on Route 4 in half an hour.'

Generoso hung up and returned to his car. He pulled out of the shopping mall and headed toward the west-bound ramp for Route 4. He was so excited – and relieved that his role in the necessary unpleasantness was over – that in the dark he never noticed the Cadillac limousine which took the ramp one hundred yards behind him.

In the Cadillac, Roland occupied the front seat with Bernie while Chivers, Michael and Kassler sat in the back. 'Where do you think he's heading?' Roland asked Bernie.

'Okay, he made a phone call. We assume it was to Milano for a meet. Milano's suggested someplace west of here. I'd guess the Forum Diner. Busy this time of night, good place for a meet.'

'Do any of us know what Milano looks like?' Kassler asked. 'Or are we just assuming that any man Generoso meets will be this Milano?'

'Here.' Bernie dug into his breast pocket, pulled out a black-and-white mug shot of a square-faced man with a belligerent expression; beneath his chin was a number. 'Courtesy of the New York City Police Department. Milano was arrested once for assault, beat the hell out of a tow-truck driver who was pulling his car away from a no parking zone. He got off because the tow-truck driver suddenly lost his memory. My guess is Milano either paid him to shut up or used other persuasive means.'

Ahead of them Generoso swung the Lincoln off Route 4 into the parking lot of the Forum Diner. Bernie went right by, took the next exit and returned to the diner by a back road. By the time he entered the parking lot Gener-oso was inside. Bernie cut the engine and lights, and they settled down to wait.

Ten minutes later a chauffeur-driven black Cadillac

pulled into the lot. The uniformed chauffeur climbed out and opened the rear door. A heavy-set man, hunched up in a camel hair coat, walked quickly toward the restaurant door. As he passed under a light, Bernie said: 'That's him. That's Joe Milano.'

'Now what do we do?' Chivers asked.

'Stay right here. Unless you want to go inside and break up their little meeting?'

'No, thank you. We'll follow your advice in this matter.'

Generoso was seated in a booth by a window which overlooked the parking lot, sipping a cup of coffee and picking at a wedge of cheesecake when Milano dropped heavily into the seat opposite him.

'Biwell's pulling out of the Brady deal,' Generoso said. 'Last night was the finishing touch, the fire and then the phone calls. Eagles is scared of having any of his people hurt.' And Chivers didn't look too happy either, Generoso thought; maybe this will be enough to send him packing and I'll get the position that's rightfully mine.

'Good. A man with sense,' Milano said. 'When will it be official?'

'Tomorrow, I believe. They'll inform Brady tomorrow.' Generoso glanced out of the window toward his car; he'd only had the Lincoln four weeks, and New Jersey always made him nervous.

'Nice work, Vince. You can always count on family to get the job done.' Milano pulled a bulky envelope from his pocket. 'Just a small token of my appreciation.'

Generoso opened it just wide enough to see the edges of hundred and thousand dollar bills. 'Thanks.'

'Thank *you*. You'll get the other fifty thousand after it's official.' Ignoring the cup of coffee the waiter had placed in front of him, Milano rose to leave. Generoso didn't even look up as he left the diner.

'Here comes Milano,' Bernie said softly. He started the Cadillac's engine and pulled out of the parking lot, back

574

onto westbound Route 4, as Milano walked toward his own car.

'Where to now?' Roland asked.

'How about we try Generoso's home?' Chivers suggested. 'We'll wait for him to get back. Before I speak to the police, I'd like to talk to him first, find out why he did it.'

Bernie took the first exit ramp, came back down on the eastbound ramp and headed back toward the bridge. He wished all crooks were as stupid as Generoso, sitting in the window of a diner with Joe Milano.

Generoso left the Forum Diner fifteen minutes after Milano, the fat envelope full of money feeling comfortable in his breast pocket. He even managed to convince himself that even if it had been a crime, it was victimless. Who had been hurt? No one. Any damage to Biwell over the vandalism would be made good by the insurance companies: those thieves charged too much for their premiums anyway.

He took his time driving home to Mamaroneck, thinking about what he'd do with the first fifty thousand dollars. He would spend it quietly on his wife and daughters, use it as he would have used the extra money that would have come with the top position at Biwell and a seat on the main board – the position that should have rightfully been his. Generoso didn't mind a British company taking over an American chain; that was all part of business. He didn't even mind them bringing in the Englishman during the transition period. But he'd never bargained on Chivers staying this long, and he wasn't going to sit on his hands any longer, especially when this opportunity had come up.

Driving easily, he reached home an hour later, swung the car into the driveway and pressed the button to open the garage door. A figure materialized from the shadows at the front of the house, then four more, standing in a line across the open garage. Generoso panicked as the lights of the Lincoln shone on terrifyingly familiar faces. He braked suddenly, considered throwing the transmission into reverse. Before he could act, though, the driver's door was pulled open and Bernie had a hand in the car to remove the key.

The other men were quickly gathered around his side of the car.

'Why did you do it, Vince?' Roland asked.

'Why did I do what?' Generoso had no doubt why the men were there, but he'd be damned if he'd help them.

'We saw you meet with Milano at the Forum Diner. There's no point in trying to hide anything. What did he do? Pay you off to keep us out of the Brady deal so he could pick it up for a song?'

The front door of the house opened and Generoso's wife looked out, attracted by voices. She started to step back and Roland called out to her. 'If you're thinking of phoning for the police, please do. We'll need them here shortly.'

'May I be allowed to resign?' Generoso asked.

Roland would have preferred it that way, without the breath of scandal that would taint the company, force share prices down, if only temporarily. 'I'm afraid not, Vince. The police want your friend Milano out of the way just as much as we do.'

Generoso looked from one face to another, not for sympathy but for an answer. Finally he stared at Chivers. It had to be him. He'd managed to foul up the rest of his life, his plans.

'What tipped you off? What made you follow me to the Forum?'

'You did. If it's any consolation, Vince, you're not cut out to be a crook. I never told anyone but Michael, Roland and Heinrich that I had a threatening phone call last night. Funny you seemed to know about it.'

Bernie drove Roland, Michael and Kassler to the air-

576

port on Friday evening to catch the TWA flight to London; Kassler would be staying with his son's family for the weekend before returning to Germany since he wouldn't be able to spend Christmas with them.

This time, the trip to the airport was made in a Cadillac limousine with clear windows and normal gauge steel; the terror over and the Brady deal signed, the men were feeling jubilant while, no doubt, Vincent Generoso and Joe Milano were trying to explain their actions to the police.

'Bernie, thanks for all your help,' Roland said to the chauffeur as porters carried their baggage into the TWA terminal.

'Ah, it was nothing, Mr Eagles. All in a day's work.' Nonetheless, he swiftly accepted the five one-hundred-dollar bills that Roland passed as they shook hands.

Inside the terminal, the three men studied a bookshop display, looking for reading material for the flight to London. Suddenly, Roland touched Kassler's arm. 'Up there.' He motioned toward the terminal restaurant. 'Is that him again?'

Kassler stared up at the man who had followed him and Roland into the coffee shop that morning. Now he was sitting with a cup of coffee and a sandwich, looking aimlessly across the terminal from his elevated vantage point. 'I think we owe him an apology,' Kassler said. He took the stairs to the restaurant two at a time, with Roland and Michael following. 'It seems our paths are destined to cross again,' Kassler said, reaching the man's table. Glancing down he saw a passport wallet resting next to the coffee and sandwich; flight tickets protruded from the top.

This time, the man seemed neither surprised nor frightened, as if he'd already spotted Roland and Kassler in the terminal and had resigned himself to another confrontation. 'What do you want?'

Roland stepped in quickly. 'We came over to apologize

for the other morning. We'd been through some trouble and were a bit nervous, that's all. Have a good flight.'

The man regarded Roland stonily before returning to his coffee.

'Come on,' Michael said, steering his two colleagues away. 'Let's have a drink, and forget this madness before we all wind up in a padded cell.'

By Sunday, as Roland and Kassler walked across Hampstead Heath with their grandchildren, they were able to joke about the experience. Surrounded by the serene safety of London, the trip to New York didn't seem as threatening anymore.

'The look on that man's face when you stepped out and touched his shoulder,' Kassler said. 'Such shock – it was priceless.'

'It was nothing compared with the expression on your face when you grabbed him. He must have thought he was being mugged – and by a fellow German to boot. Heinrich, you looked really vicious. I certainly wouldn't have wanted to meet you down a dark alley just then.'

'How did you expect me to look? You thought he was following us, too.'

'And he's probably back home now, telling his family that the biggest thugs in New York are Germans and Englishmen.'

Kassler walked on in silence for a while, then turned to Roland, his tone serious. 'I owe you a lot, Roland, more than I can ever hope to repay. Because of you, I've found what it means to have a family – to have a son who . . . who loves me.'

Roland felt embarrassed at the German's gratitude, and he considered a flippant reply to dilute the intensity of the moment. Instead he said nothing, letting Kassler continue.

'I can't believe I let all those years pass without acknowledging Franz . . . no, that's the wrong word. I mean without sharing his growing up, being a proper father to him, like you were to Katherine.'

'I had my lapses as well,' Roland reminded him.

'Lapses. Short ones. I just had one long lapse.'

'Stop punishing yourself, you've more than made up for it in the past few years.'

Kassler's face barely brightened at the words. 'I think,' he said slowly, 'that if I ever lost Franz now, I would kill myself. Life would be so empty, such a vast vacuum, it just wouldn't be worth continuing.'

Roland clapped the German on the shoulder. 'Let's get back to the house before Kathy starts worrying that we've abducted her children.' The cheerfulness in his voice was forced. Kassler's soulful admission had moved Roland so, making him realize just how fortunate his own life – especially with his children – had been. 'We'll have something to eat, then Franz and I will take you to the airport. Are you sure,' he said as they started toward the house, 'that you can't arrange to be here over Christmas?'

Kassler shook his head. 'I have too much work to do in Stuttgart. The office will be quiet then, I'll be able to complete it. But my thoughts will be with you all.'

'You'll be in our thoughts as well.'

CHAPTER THREE

At ten-thirty on Christmas morning, Sally picked up Roland to drive him to Katherine's for the day. After loading a pile of gifts in the trunk, Roland got into the car. Sally pointed to the glove compartment.

'In there, something for you.'

Grinning, Roland opened the compartment and took out a gaily wrapped box the size of a book.

'Merry Christmas,' Sally said. 'Open it and see what Santa Claus brought you for being a good boy all year.'

Roland undid the wrapping carefully, opened the box and found a painted stone figure of an armor-clad man astride a horse. 'I give up. What's it supposed to be?'

'That's a knight of the Round Table,' Sally answered, one hand on the wheel as she took the small statue from Roland. 'And I expect you to go around dressed like that after you receive your knighthood.'

'Do you now? And what am I supposed to do when it rains?'

'Turn rusty probably. Take a good look at the face.'

Roland took back the statue and studied it. The carefully painted face was his own – the features, the blue eyes, the hair a dark silver.

'I gave the artist a photograph of you,' Sally admitted.

'I like it. Merry Christmas.' He leaned across the car and kissed Sally on the cheek. 'I was saving this for later, but you may as well have it now.' He took a slender box from his coat pocket and gave it to her. She opened it and held out a gold and diamond pin in the shape of a letter S.

'Just in case you ever forget who you are.'

'It's very pretty,' Sally said, sticking the pin on her coat. 'Where did you get it?'

'New York, in between lowering the crime rate over there.'

'Oh, that reminds me.' Sally fumbled in her handbag. 'Read this.'

Roland looked at the envelope which bore an American airmail stamp and a New York postmark. Inside was a Christmas card – he supposed it was a Christmas card anyway ; it had 'Season's Greetings' embossed on the front with a picture of a group of young women in bikinis sunning themselves on a crowded beach.

'Came yesterday,' she said.

Roland read the message, written in fountain pen in a scrawly hand . . . 'The horses run better upside down, but then I always did prefer life that way. Sorry for any trouble, old girl. Fondly, C.'

'Christopher?' Roland asked, staring at the bikini-clad girls again.

'I guess. That card was printed in Australia – that's what it says on the back – and he had it mailed in New York. He could be anywhere.'

'Australia sounds reasonable. And you thought you'd get a note from Pango Pango.'

'What do you think I should do about it?'

'Do you mean turn it over to the police?' When Sally nodded, Roland said, 'You don't *know* it's from Christopher. That C could stand for anything, you must know a hundred people with that initial.' He tapped the card against his fingernails; what would he do in Sally's place? 'I'd let sleeping dogs lie, Sally,' he said at last.

She took the card back from him and backed out of the driveway, heading for Katherine's house. As they stopped at a traffic light she looked at it one more time, rolled down the window and let the card fall onto the wet road. 'Sleeping dogs and other assorted animals have been officially allowed to lie. At least, he apologized . . . eventually.'

Roland and Sally were the first to arrive at Katherine's.

581

While Franz took their coats and offered them drinks, Roland piled presents under the Christmas tree which was alight in the huge hallway. 'Too bad your father couldn't be here today,' he said, when Franz finally dragged him away from the tree and handed him a glass of scotch and water.

'What, so the two of you could bore us all day long with tall tales of how you trapped this crook?' Franz joked.

'Got a date to see the Queen yet?' Katherine asked. She held a huge box in her hands which she shoved at her father. 'Merry Christmas.'

'I'm scared to open it. What's inside?'

'Something you'll wear when you go to the Palace.'

Roland glanced at Sally, who was having a difficult time keeping a straight face. Whatever was inside the box – and it seemed every gift today would be somehow connected with his knighthood – Sally already knew about it. He undid the wrapping and opened the box, surprised to see a pearl gray top hat. 'God almighty! A sensible gift! It'll go perfectly with my morning suit, bless you.' He kissed Katherine, then tried on the hat. It slid straight over his eyes and bent his ears double before it stopped.

'It's a size nine,' Katherine said, between bursts of laughter. 'We had it made especially because we figured your head would swell that much when you received your knighthood.'

'Very funny.' He struggled to remove the hat and jammed it over Katherine's head. It covered her completely, right down to her chin. Roland rapped with his knuckles on the crown. 'That'll teach you to make fun of your father.'

Within half an hour the other guests arrived – Ralph and Janet Morrison with Carol and Richard, and Michael and Lisa. More presents were exchanged. Roland was grateful that there were no more jokes about his impending knighthood or the business in New York. Finally, everyone sat down to lunch. Roland caught Sally's eye and he debated whether she was thinking about the card she'd received from Christopher. He didn't even understand why she'd asked him what to do. Mellish was in the past, gone — surely she wasn't feeling sentimental about him now . . .

But Roland couldn't be sure. With that thought in mind, he raised his glass. 'Before we start, how about a toast to absent friends?' He looked squarely at Sally as he suggested it.

'An excellent idea,' Franz agreed, thinking of his father.

'To absent friends,' Sally joined in. 'And may some of them stay absent . . . for all our sakes.'

Halfway through the main course, the telephone rang. Franz answered it, then motioned to Roland. 'It's Alf Goldstein, he was told you were here.'

Puzzled by the call, Roland left the table. 'Merry Christmas, Alf.'

'Not anymore it isn't. I have to see you right away.'

'What about? Can't it wait?'

'I can't tell you what about until I see you. And no — it can't wait. I'll come by Katherine's house in half an hour. There's someone you have to meet.'

Roland didn't protest; the agitation in Goldstein's voice was too strong for the matter to be of little importance. He returned to the table and told Franz and Katherine he would have to go out shortly. 'Alf's got a problem and he needs to see me.'

'Oh, what a shame,' Katherine said. But she made no attempt to dissuade her father from leaving. Roland had a strong sense of loyalty to his friends and she refused to question that.

Goldstein arrived exactly thirty minutes later, left the Bentley's engine running and banged on the front door. When Katherine answered he declined going in and remained standing in the doorway, waiting for Roland.

'All right, where's this person you want me to meet?' Roland demanded when he came to the door and saw Goldstein standing alone.

583

'He's waiting for us at Hampstead Station.'

'What in God's name is he doing there?' Roland lost the edge of his seasonal good will. He didn't spend half as much time as he would like with the entire family together, and now he had Goldstein trying to drag him out in the pouring rain on some wild goose chase. Perhaps Christmas didn't mean anything to Goldstein, but it meant a hell of a lot to him when the family was gathered.

'He's waiting for us there because I can't bring him here. Will you come with me, please?'

'Why can't you bring him here?'

'Because of Franz, that's why.' Without another word of explanation, he took Roland by the arm and led him toward the Bentley.

'This had better be a real emergency, Alf,' Roland complained as he climbed into the back seat.

'Oh, it is. A real, bona fide emergency.' Goldstein swung the car out of the driveway and headed toward Hampstead Station. When Roland tried to find out more of what it was about Goldstein remained stubbornly quiet, lips stretched in a thin line, his jaw set.

Outside Hampstead Station, Goldstein braked sharply and jumped out, disregarding the no stopping signs. Moments later he was back. He opened the rear door of the Bentley and half shoved a man inside. Roland, who had been unable to see clearly through the rain-spattered window, was shocked when he recognized the face as the man climbed into the car.

'You! From New York!'

'That's right, Mr Eagles. The man you and your friend Kassler assaulted and later spoke to in the TWA terminal.'

'Alf, what in blazes is going on? What are you doing with this man?'

'I'll tell you in a minute.' Goldstein rolled the Bentley into a parking space fifty yards from the station, cut the engine and turned around. 'Roland, this is Peter Hoffbein. Mr Hoffbein works for the public prosecutor's office in Stuttgart, and was under the impression that you're a Nazi sympathizer who deliberately falsified records at the end of the war to save Heinrich Kassler from facing charges as a war criminal. And he thought I helped you to do it.'

'What?' Roland slumped back in shock against the Bentley's leather upholstery. Now he understood why Goldstein had refused to bring the man to Katherine's home. Franz would have a fit hearing such a ludicrous allegation. 'Is this a joke, Alf? Surely it's a mistake.'

'That's what I thought. Mr Hoffbein's made me see it quite differently.'

Slowly, Roland recovered from the double jolt of seeing the German again and hearing that Kassler was a suspected Nazi sympathizer. 'Perhaps you'd better tell me what's going on, Mr Hoffbein. And very slowly.'

'Certainly, Mr Eagles. For the past nine months my office has been investigating Heinrich Kassler. Certain allegations have been made against him regarding his conduct during the war and we've been checking these out very thoroughly. Discreetly, but thoroughly.'

'You weren't too damned discreet about it in New York.'

Hoffbein acknowledged the rebuff with a slight inclination of the head. 'That was clumsy and I regret it, but I was trying to learn whom Kassler – and you – were meeting over there. Fortunately, as I understand it from Mr Goldstein, you and Kassler mistook my presence for something else.'

'Never mind that. What are these allegations against Heinrich?'

'A short time ago, Mr Eagles, I wouldn't have considered even telling you. I wouldn't have consented to even meeting with you because I had reason to suspect that you, as Kassler's initial interrogating officer, had concocted a deal with him, that you'd helped him to escape justice and then remained in mutually profitable contact ever since, leading to your daughter marrying his son, and your business partnership.'

'That's preposterous!' Roland burst out. 'I was ready to shoot him on the spot in Bergen-Belsen!'

'I have only become aware of that recently, Mr Eagles when I interviewed Mr Goldstein—'

'He turned up at my house this morning of all days,' Goldstein interrupted.

'At one time during this investigation, Mr Goldstein was also a suspect in the conspiracy which I believed had taken place – after I learned of that book he wrote, show- ing Kassler in a positive light. But when I inquired into Mr Goldstein's background, I learned of his work for the camp survivors' association, the fact that he is a Jew. I realized I'd been wrong about him, that he could be trusted. Additionally, he was only the interpreter at that initial meeting with Kassler, and at his rank wouldn't have had the power to make any kind of a deal. But I figured he could tell me something about you. And, of course, he has.'

'What are these allegations against Heinrich?' Roland repeated. 'Who made them?'

Hoffbein remained very calm in the face of Roland's obvious impatience. 'Nine months ago we were interro- gating another man, an entirely different case – a sergeant in the *Schutzstaffel* suspected of war crimes. He sought to bargain with us by implicating a much bigger fish . . . Kassler. This man claimed that Kassler lined his pockets with jewelry and money stolen from inmates who passed through the camps. Before Bergen-Belsen Kassler was at Dachau, you know. My original suspicion was that Kas- sler had bribed you – paid you well – to help him—'

'Wait a minute. We got affidavits from inmates at Bergen-Belsen. What about those? Don't they mean a damned thing?'

'They mean a lot. My office has managed to locate some of those people. What they swore to in those affidavits was true, perfectly true. Kassler did help the inmates

. . .' Hoffbein's voice turned very brittle. 'But only after he realized which way the war was going. He was prudent enough to understand from the fall of 1944 that the Nazis would lose. So he began to prepare alibis. He made friends with those who would stand him in good stead. You were one of the last of those alibis.'

Roland sat speechless. He listened to the rain drumming on the roof of the Bentley, and thought about what the German government official was saying. Kassler had fooled them all. He had played both sides and walked out ahead. But mostly Roland thought about Katherine, married to Kassler's only son. The mother of Kassler's grandchildren.

'There's more, Roland,' Goldstein said gently from the front seat of the car.

What else could there be – what could possibly eclipse this? Roland wondered. Nonetheless, he returned his gaze to Hoffbein.

'Did Kassler ever mention that his father died in Buchenwald?' Hoffbein asked. Roland nodded. 'Why did Kassler claim his father was sent to Buchenwald?'

'Because he refused to manufacture tank components for the Nazis, I think.' Roland looked to Goldstein for confirmation.

'Our investigation, by interviewing people who worked for the senior Kassler, has revealed that father and son argued continually about whether the company should comply with the Nazi work orders. Heinrich Kassler, your friend—'

'Will you stop referring to him as my friend?'

'What is he then?'

Roland couldn't think of an answer.

'Heinrich Kassler was in favor of working with the Nazis. According to those who knew him then, he was certain that the Nazis would be in power for a long time. He wanted very much to be on their side, to be a favored member of the winning side.'

'And he made no attempt to stop his father being sent

away,' Goldstein interrupted. 'Kassler's rotten right through, Roland. Do you still think I've been seeing too many Hollywood Nazis?' he added disgustedly.

'With his father out of the way, Heinrich Kassler stood to inherit everything,' Hoffbein explained. 'He joined the SS to gain further acceptance within the party, to ensure his position of power within the new order. And he exploited that power for all it was worth, including, as I said, helping himself to whatever gold or jewels the camp inmates had brought with them.'

'And then in 1944 he switched boats in midstream,' Roland murmured. He closed his eyes and pictured Kassler playing blackjack, counting the cards, gradually working the odds into his own favor. The pieces were beginning to fit – he *had* to be on the winning side, no matter what the game, no matter what the cost . . .

'And when the war was over?' Roland asked.

'Those affidavits you collected helped to clear him; they were the final touch. He practically became a hero overnight, was trusted implicitly by the occupying forces. He returned to Stuttgart and persuaded the Americans to assist him in setting up the engineering factory again. He used the valuables he'd stolen to restart his life as an upstanding German who'd fought against the Nazis and saved lives.'

'Christ Almighty,' Roland muttered. 'How do I tell this to Kathy? To Franz?' He caught himself immediately, turned back to Hoffbein. 'What is your office going to do now? Do you have enough evidence to prosecute?'

'We believe so. Your relationship with Kassler was the last thing to be checked. If we had reached the conclusion that you had actively consorted with Kassler to pervert the course of justice for personal gain, we would have forwarded such evidence to your government for appropriate action. When I mentioned that possibility to your friend here—'

'I told him in no uncertain terms he was bloody mad,' Goldstein finished.

'This entire episode seems mad,' Roland said. 'I can't believe I could have been fooled so completely. That we all could have been fooled so completely,' he added quickly, looking at Goldstein.

'Believe it,' Goldstein answered, 'because it's damned well true. Don't you wish you could turn back the clock? Give me that Webley like I asked you to?'

For a brief instant the idea loomed appealingly in Roland's mind. Give the gun to Goldstein or use it himself. Point it at Kassler as he stood between the two British soldiers and pull the trigger. But he quickly dismissed the image from his mind. 'No, I don't, Alf. Because I just left Kathy, and she's so damned happy with Franz and the two children.'

A song he had learned when he was a boy in school sprang into Roland's mind, a ditty entitled 'The Bishop of Bray,' about a politically adept clergyman who had weathered the changing times in England by supporting whichever monarch or government was in power. After all these years, the first lines of the song came back to Roland: 'In Good King Charles' golden day when loyalty no harm meant, a zealous High Church man was I and so I got preferment . . .' Kassler was another Bishop of Bray. More sinister, perhaps, but just as skillfull at reading the changing times – and profiting by them.

'Was there ever any evidence pointing to Kassler being involved in the atrocities that took place at the camps?' Roland asked Hoffbein, dreading the answer.

The German shook his head. 'Not actively, if that's any consolation to you. He just stood by and watched what went on, but in so doing gave his silent approval, knowing he was ensuring his own future by cooperating. We will, of course, require testimony from you, Mr Eagles. Whenever it is convenient I would like to meet with you again. Your testimony will help to clear any shadows from you own reputation.'

'Damn my reputation!' Roland snapped. That was the least of his problems; he was far more concerned about the effect this news would have on Katherine and Franz — on their marriage, on his daughter's happiness. 'When do you make everything official?'

'That's the problem.' Quite suddenly, Hoffbein's attitude changed. From being a calm narrator of fact he seemed to become coy about the matter, nervously shifting on the seat as though he were uncomfortable. 'Quite a problem, in fact,' he added, and Roland abruptly sensed that all that had gone before was just window dressing. Only now was the German official getting down to the real reason for the meeting.

'What kind of a problem?'

'All these years after the end of the war, my government finds it inconvenient to have old wounds reopened. I'm sure you can understand that.'

'Perfectly.'

'Although,' Hoffbein added swiftly, 'the government which sanctioned the atrocities of that war and my own government are two totally different entities.'

'What about the SS sergeant you were questioning, the one who dropped Heinrich's name? You went ahead and prosecuted him, didn't you?'

'Yes, but he was a small man. A plumber, I believe. Who cares about a little tradesman suddenly appearing in a newspaper? But for a man of Kassler's importance and stature . . .' He let the insinuation hang.

'Your government would find it embarrassing, is that it?'

'Quite embarrassing,' Hoffbein concurred. 'Heinrich Kassler is a pillar of the reconstructed German society, the epitome of respectablity. My government would find it almost as embarrassing as your Eagles Group would find it having a Nazi war criminal on its board of directors . . . as your family would find it . . .' He smiled faintly when he saw the gloomy understanding register on Roland's face. 'Am I right in assuming that your family is at the forefront of your mind, Mr Eagles?'

Roland just nodded.

'I'm quite certain that we would all like to avoid any embarrassment, Mr Eagles.' Hoffbein spoke with certainty now, no longer reserved. 'My government . . . your company . . . your family. Just imagine how much easier it would be if Heinrich Kassler's memory was that of a fine upstanding German. Suicide – or ideally, a regrettable accident – before my office was forced to take this to court would be so much more appealing.'

'Are you suggesting that I could arrange such an event?'

The trace of a smile appeared again on Hoffbein's ruddy face. 'You're probably closer to Kassler than any man has ever been—'

'His son is closer.' At least he is now, Roland thought. And I helped to make it that way; helped to set him up for this knockout punch.

'But we would all like to see his son – and your daughter – spared from this tragedy, would we not?'

'You smarmy bureaucratic bastard.'

The insult registered nothing on Hoffbein's face. 'As you are so close to Kassler, Mr Eagles, you could persuade him to do the proper thing. He has enjoyed the lie of a hero's life. Surely you, as his friend – as a member of his family – would not like to see that image tarnished.'

'If I went near him with what you've just told me, he'd be on the first plane out of Germany. Heading for Argentina or Paraguay.'

'Impossible. Kassler's every move is being monitored. If he tried to run, he would be picked up immediately and charged. Then all of our embarrassments would begin, Mr Eagles.'

Roland looked to Goldstein for help. He was being asked to help murder a man, force him into suicide, which amounted to the same thing. Goldstein just stared back, as numb as Roland himself; when he'd arranged this meeting between Roland and Hoffbein he'd had no idea this was the motive behind it.

'Alf, drive Mr Hoffbein back to his hotel. I don't think

591

there's anything more to discuss,' Roland said. He moved into the corner of the seat and turned away, signaling that the meeting was over. When Hoffbein first told the story of Kassler's wartime activities, Roland had regarded him as a civil servant simply doing his job, no matter how unpleasant it turned out to be. But now Roland saw him in a totally different light – as a dirty little man doing a dirty little job, fashioning the bullets for someone else to fire so his own embarrassment could be avoided. Neither he nor the German government cared two bits for how it would affect Roland's family, but he recognized it as something he could appeal to.

Goldstein drove the Bentley toward Bayswater, where Hoffbein was staying at a moderately priced hotel. 'I will be in touch again only if we *need* your testimony, Mr Eagles,' Hoffbein said as he stepped from the car. The implication was obvious: if Roland didn't follow up on Hoffbein's suggestion, Kassler's true past would be exposed and all his affairs, both personal and business, would be affected. Roland responded with a courteous if cold nod of the head.

'I'm sorry,' Goldstein muttered as he headed the car back toward Hampstead. 'I had no idea . . .'

'Forget it, if he hadn't got to me through you, he'd have found some other way. I don't believe for an instant that garbage about his thinking I helped Kassler hide his past. That bastard was using it as a lever. Maybe he thought he could blackmail me to do his dirty work, show me how miserable he could make my life just through insinuation.'

'If they're so intent on avoiding all this embarrassment, why don't they bump Kassler off themselves?'

Roland wondered about that too. 'Perfect crimes are few and far between. Maybe the Germans don't want something else to cover up.'

'What are you going to do?'

'For one thing keep Katherine and Franz out of it, but

how? Hoffbein thinks I can persuade Kassler to take an overdose. That's murder.'

'Roland, take yourself back to Bergen-Belsen. You were prepared to murder him then, shoot him out of hand for what you'd seen at the camp. What's so different about this? And let me ask you something else: what's more important to you, the people in the camp or Katherine's happiness?'

'Katherine, of course,' Roland responded instantly. Damn it! He had to try it Hoffbein's way. It was the only way he could keep Katherine and Franz ignorant of the truth. If he could find a way to stop Kassler coming to a trial that would wreck all their lives, he'd do it – even if it meant murdering his daughter's father-in-law. Some way he'd keep the lid on it. Katherine's well-being was more important than any personal feelings.

'You're going to see him, aren't you?'

'Yes. I think there is one way, the only way.'

'Do you want me to come with you?'

The offer came as no surprise to Roland. He knew that Goldstein would walk through fire for him.

'Thanks, Alf, but the answer's no,' he said, appreciating his friend's loyalty. 'This is something I've got to do for myself.'

'I wish you luck,' Goldstein said as he swung the Bentley into the driveway of Katherine's home. 'Tell everyone that I apologize for messing up their Christmas by dragging you away.'

'I will.' Roland watched the Bentley glide away. He rang the doorbell, forcing a smile onto his face. Even though his own Christmas was a wreck he wasn't about to ruin everyone else's.

'What was that all about?' Katherine asked when she opened the door.

'There was an attempted break-in at Eldridge's last night.' Roland was amazed at how easily the lie sprang to his lips, but lying was simple now, especially when he'd agreed to commit what was virtually murder. 'The police couldn't get hold of the manager but they had Alf listed as one of the keyholders. He thought I should know about it.'

'Anything stolen?'

'Only my time with you,' Roland answered as he wrapped an arm around Katherine's shoulder and walked with her into the house. 'No, it was a storm in a teacup; they never even managed to get in before the burglar alarm went off. Now where's the rest of my lunch? I'm famished.' As he walked into the dining room, his eyes met Franz's, held them for an instant and then broke away. Tomorrow he would try to talk the young man's father into committing suicide; how could he look him in the eyes now? Searching for something to concentrate on – to mask his fear, the self-loathing he felt for allowing himself to be forced into such a situation – Roland skipped his gaze around the room until it rested on the outsized, gray top hat Katherine had given him for his trip to the Palace. His knighthood! How could he go to the Palace, be dubbed a knight by the Queen, when he'd helped a Nazi war criminal escape justice . . . and when he now planned to push the same man over the brink?

The knighthood was unthinkable now. He couldn't accept it and live with himself.

Early the next morning Roland took a taxi to Heathrow Airport and booked the first flight to Stuttgart. The moment he cleared the landing formalities in Germany, he called Kassler's private number at his office, the line that bypassed the switchboard.

'Heinrich, it's Roland.'

'*Fröhlich Weihnachten*, Roland. How was your party at Katherine and Franz's? I tried to telephone you twice yesterday but all the circuits were busy,' Kassler said, believing Roland was calling from London.

'Very enjoyable. Heinrich, I'm in Stuttgart, at the airport, and it's imperative that I see you immediately.'

The urgency in Roland's voice was so clear that Kassler

didn't question the reason for the summons. Without telling anyone where he was going he left the office, climbed into his Mercedes 300 SEL and drove toward the airport at Echterdingen.

Roland was waiting by the terminal, under cover from the heavy rain, when Kassler drew up in the steel gray Mercedes. After Roland was settled in the front seat Kassler asked the nature of the emergency.

'Drive somewhere quiet where we can talk. I'll tell you then.' As he gave the instruction, Roland forced himself to look at Kassler, to stare at the heavy face and pale blue eyes, the thin gray blond hair, and to superimpose over those features the face of the man he'd interrogated at Bergen-Belsen. An angel of mercy, he'd called himself. Like hell – a thief! A conscienceless villain whose lies had backed Roland into this corner.

Suspecting nothing, Kassler left the airport and drove two miles toward Stuttgart before pulling off the road. 'Now will you tell me?'

'Sure I will. Do you remember that man we accosted on Fifth Avenue? The man who was in the coffee shop when we were there?'

Kassler nodded. 'The one we saw again at the airport. Of course I remember him.'

'He *was* following us, Heinrich. More specifically, he was following you. His name is Peter Hoffbein and he works for the public prosecutor's office, right here in Stuttgart.'

Kassler's pale face turned a shade whiter as the first traces of a terrifying realization touched his consciousness.

'Do you know why he was following you, Heinrich? Because you've been the subject of an intensive investigation for the past nine months. One of your former *Kameraden* threw you to the wolves, told the truth that you'd managed to hide all these years.' Like a snake striking, Roland reached out and grabbed hold of the lapels of Kassler's coat, dragging the German close. 'You despicable bastard! You had me believing all that garbage about how you saved people! How you were working within the system to destroy it. And because I believed you, I helped you get off when you should have been rotting in jail all these years or squirming at the end of a rope!

'How much did you steal, Heinrich?' Roland's shouted question stunned the German in the confines of the car. 'How much of your success is due to those poor bastards you robbed on their way to the ovens?'

'I stole nothing!' At last Kassler found his voice, found strength to fight against Roland's savage grip. 'I tell you the truth—'

'Shut up!' Roland gripped Kassler's lapels even tighter, dug his thumbs into the German's throat so viciously that he threatened to cut off the air supply. 'Hoffbein's got proof of what you did. People have spoken out against you. And because of you, I'm tainted. Because I believed you, helped to make you into a hero. Because I befriended you. Because I used your money. And because' – the thumbs dug even more painfully into Kassler's throat and Roland's voice became a harsh growl – 'I let my daughter marry your son!'

'My son had nothing to do with any of it!' Kassler's screamed denial tailed away under the pressure of Roland's hands.

'How the hell do I know that? How do I know that's not a lie, like every other damned thing you ever told me?'

'You know my son better than I do, Roland. You know what he's like. Do you believe he would even consider such things as you accuse me of?'

Roland released his grip on Kassler's lapels and the German sank back against the door of the Mercedes, gasping for breath. Roland, too, slumped back, physically drained by his own fury. But his mind was racing. He knew Kassler was telling the truth about Franz. The son wasn't tainted by the father; in this particular case the apple had fallen far from the tree. But Franz was the weapon that Roland had to use against Kassler – the only weapon he had that would ensure Kassler's destruction.

Roland was certain that Franz – in his father's wartime situation – would have done exactly what his father had claimed to do: try to destroy the system from within. But that had never been Kassler's intention when he had joined that system; he had only been interested in what benefits he could reap. Even turning against his own father to ensure his future!

'What about your father, Heinrich? The Nazis put him in Buchenwald, didn't they? What did you do to stop that happening? Or did you even try?'

'I could do nothing to stop it,' Kassler answered slowly. 'Nothing that would have made any difference, except to send me and the rest of our family with him. Roland . . .' Kassler leaned forward, the terror on his face yielding to earnest cunning. 'You understand these things. You are like me. You know that if you are to succeed you must swim with the current. If you swim against it, you will drown.'

'Not if you swim hard enough against the current, you won't.' Roland glanced down and saw that his knee was touching Kassler's. He pulled back sharply; even such slight contact was offensive now. What he wanted to do more than anything else was get out of this car, get away from Kassler, wash the bastard from his mind. But Katherine . . . ? What would happen to Katherine then? To Franz? To the entire family? What would be left of the family Roland loved so dearly when Kassler was tried and convicted, led away to jail?

That thought alone hardened Roland's resolve, reminded him why he had made this hurried trip to Stuttgart. He hadn't come just to listen to Kassler's confession, hear his excuses.

'Heinrich, you're going to spend the rest of your life in jail. Think about that. Your picture's going to be in all the newspapers, flashed across every television screen. Those friends you've made, all those rich industrialists, aren't going to want to know you in a month or so. Even your former colleagues – your fanatical *Kameraden* in the SS – will despise you. You weren't a supporter of the Nazis because you believed in them; you were just a sly opportunist siding with whichever ideology you thought would pay the most. And worst of all, your son's going to see you for what you really are – a greedy, soulless crook. Think how proud Franz is going to be of you.'

'No . . .' Kassler shook his head wildly and Roland experienced a fierce elation that he'd judged the German's weak spot perfectly. 'Not my son, not Franz.'

'Your son, Heinrich. Franz. Remember when you asked me in Monte Carlo how you got close to your children? You wanted that desperately, didn't you, to be close to Franz? Well, in the past three years you achieved that. You worked hard at it, and you realized what a joy a family could be. And all the time you were setting Franz up for the most bitter disappointment in his entire life.'

Kassler continued shaking his head, now bewildered, frightened. Tears began to form in his eyes. 'He will not believe it—'

'Oh, he'll believe it, all right, Heinrich. A parade of unshakable prosecution witnesses will force him to believe it. His own life will be ruined, just because he's your son.'

'No . . . not Franz.' Kassler's voice broke into choking sobs as he visualized Franz learning the truth. Franz would hate him, would never visit him in jail.

In jail! Kassler's mind sharpened as he realized the capitulation he had just made, admitting to himself that he would go to jail. The switch from a life of luxury to the penury of prison meant nothing when compared with what his son would think and feel. Franz would despise him. And even after he died . . . in jail . . . Franz would loathe his very memory. There would be no moments of regret on the anniversary of his death. Only Franz's hatred of what his father had been, of what he'd hidden all these years.

'Roland, I could leave. I could run away. I could . . .' A

598

crafty gleam shone in Kassler's eyes as he considered methods of escape, ruses that would mean his son never having to know the truth about his father. 'I could do what your friend did after he murdered that man. None of this would have to come out.'

'Do you really think you could run away, Heinrich?' Roland turned around in the seat, stared through the rain-spattered rear window. 'Do you see that black car?' He gestured toward a BMW that was parked two hundred yards behind the Mercedes. Roland had no idea who owned the BMW. At this distance he couldn't even see if anyone was in it; all the same the car would serve his purpose. 'Police, Heinrich. They're not letting you out of their sight until they're ready to charge you.'

As Kassler stared at the black car, his eyes dimmed and he trembled.

'There's nowhere to run, Heinrich. No place to go except to a courtroom that will be so full of reporters there'll barely be room for you.'

Roland watched Kassler carefully for the moment of the final, irrevocable breakdown. Franz was the key, the fact that Kassler and his son had finally drawn together. Above all else – even above Kassler's business, his drive to win – was the joy of this closeness which had come so late in life. To have that destroyed would be worse than death itself. 'Imagine what Franz is going to think about you then, Heinrich. When you die he'll visit your grave only to spit on it. Is that how you want Franz to remember you? Do you really want him to know the evil you performed?'

'Enough!' Kassler screamed. 'Enough! I understand you!'

'Do you? Do you *really* understand me, Heinrich?'

Kassler breathed in deeply, fought against the fear of what must be done. 'You leave little room for *mis*understanding,' he said coldly. 'Roland, is this your idea? Or does it come from those fools in government who wish to avoid the embarrassment of such a publicized trial?'

599

'Does it matter?'

Kassler shook his head. 'All that matters to me, as you know, is my son. You have used him against me well, Roland. But what guarantees do I have that he will never know?'

'You have my word.'

'And what is your word based on? The word of some bureaucrat in the German government . . . this Hoffbein fellow? Can you trust him?'

'If he breaks his word to me, I'll kill him,' Roland answered simply.

Kassler turned the ignition key and drove through the rain toward the airport. The black BMW remained where it was but Kassler never noticed. Now that he'd decided his course of action – his only course of action if his son wasn't to detest his very memory – he had no fear of the police, no fear of exposure. He felt quite calm, able to think rationally, to act in the civilized fashion he'd always enjoyed before Roland had torn the facade apart. 'What time is your return flight to London?'

'I have an open ticket.'

'Please have the decency to be on the first flight,' Kassler said; there was even the hint of an order in the request as the German regained full control of himself.

'I will be.'

The two men didn't speak another word until Kassler pulled up in front of the terminal. Roland opened the door stepped out, then stooped down to look at Kassler a final time. 'Remember Franz, Heinrich, and what this will do to him.'

'Goodbye, Roland. At our first encounter I recall expressing the desire that we should meet again. I don't believe that sentiment is appropriate any longer.'

'Goodbye, Heinrich.' Roland closed the passenger door softly and walked toward the terminal entrance; he never looked back.

Kassler sat with his hands on the steering wheel as he watched Roland disappear into the terminal building. If the Englishman had come to Stuttgart with a loaded pistol, placed it against Kassler's temple and pressed the trigger, he couldn't have accomplished more destruction than he had done with those carefully chosen words about Franz.

For ten minutes Kassler remained in the same position, running through his mind every moment he'd ever spent with Roland. That first meeting, Roland's threat to kill him, and the group of camp survivors who had spoken out on his behalf. Of course they'd spoken out for him. He *had* done good in the camp . . . ever since the autumn of 1944, once he realized that Hitler would lose the war.

Kassler had always prided himself on his ability to read the future, to understand which way it would swing, to play the turns and make his plans work. And they *had* worked. For almost thirty years they worked, allowing him to build himself up into one of the most successful industrialists in postwar Germany, a pillar of respectability. Indeed, a *good* German. But no more . . . somewhere, an anonymous little man who had been caught in some fervent Nazi hunter's web had dropped Kassler's name in order to ease his own way through the courts. Because of that, Kassler's dream empire had crumbled.

Slowly, he drove away from the airport. Before reaching the autobahn he pulled into a gas station and had the gas tank filled. Then, with an increasingly mechanical certainty about his actions, he continued on toward the autobahn.

Would Roland still be at the airport, waiting for his plane? Did he intend leaving Germany before learning whether his visit had achieved the desired result? Kassler understood perfectly the reason for the visit. Roland didn't want personal vengeance or the opportunity to confront Kassler with the accusations. He had come to persuade Kassler that for his son's sake — as well as Roland's own daughter's sake — there could be only one solution. One honorable way out, as they might have said during the war, Kassler thought grimly.

He reached the autobahn and headed toward Ulm, watching the speedometer needle creep up to one hundred and twenty kilometers an hour as he kept the car in the inside lane. He wasn't ready yet. He still needed time to think, to remember; time to consider whether he could have changed anything.

The wipers swished monotonously across the Mercedes' windshield, clearing a path through the water that streamed down from leaden skies as Kassler drove steadily onward. He passed Ulm, saw signs for Augsburg and Munich. His foot pressed down harder on the accelerator as he switched to the outside lane. The speed increased . . . one hundred and fifty kilometers an hour, with the powerful 6.3-liter engine not even straining. Cars swept by as Kassler maintained his position in the outside lane, almost motionless as they struggled on in the rain. In the mirror, far back, he saw a blue light flashing. Was it meant for him? It didn't matter. There was small chance of the police car catching up with him, unless its driver placed as little value on his life as Kassler did on his own at that moment.

He wondered if the Mercedes was aquaplaning now, the tires no longer in contact with the road surface but riding only on the water that covered the autobahn like a giant oil slick . . . Kassler knew he would find out soon enough, when the road swung left; then he would see how much traction the tires gave him on the wet road.

The bend came in sight and he pressed down even harder, waiting for the speedometer needle to hover just over the two-hundred-and-ten mark, the top end of this powerful car, the fastest he'd ever driven since buying it four years earlier. Were those drivers he passed watching his progress with envy? Ashamed of their own fear for not driving as shamelessly? God . . . he hoped so! In death, he wanted the same respect and admiration he had enjoyed in life.

The bend loomed close and Kassler moved the wheel. The Mercedes continued in a perfectly straight line, tires contacting only water. Centrifugal force had overcome friction. Foot still pressed to the floor, Kassler removed his hands from the wheel and closed his eyes.

The Mercedes flashed over lane markings, across the soft shoulder and ripped through the safety barrier. Like a clumsy, wingless aircraft it soared into space as it left the raised autobahn, still in excess of two hundred kilometers an hour. Then it plummeted downward to smash nose first into a plowed field. A plume of mud soared into the air, and moments later a gigantic, booming explosion ripped through the Mercedes, blowing doors open, shattering glass.

Heinrich Kassler felt no pain at all. He had died at the moment of impact, with the steering column embedded in his chest.

Roland reached home in the early afternoon, taking a taxi from Heathrow Airport to Stanmore. He entered the house, told the butler that he would accept only telephone calls from his family, and sat by the front window, staring out at the rain-soaked common, smoking and waiting.

Six hours later, when the butler knocked on the door, Roland was still sitting by the window.

'Sir, a telephone call from Mrs Kassler.' When Roland turned around, face blank, the butler added, 'Your daughter, sir.'

'Thank you.' Roland walked to the telephone. 'Yes, Kathy.'

'We've just had some terrible news from Franz's mother.' Katherine's voice sounded choked, as if she were crying. 'Franz's father was killed in a car accident a few hours ago.'

Even knowing it would happen, knowing he'd pushed Kassler into a corner from which there was no escape, failed to shield Roland from the shock. Anticipating the news and then receiving it were two different things. In spite of everything Roland felt shattered. 'What happened?'

'Somewhere on the autobahn. He went through a barrier at over a hundred miles an hour. The car blew up.'

'How's Franz taking it?'

'He's here. Do you want to speak to him?' Without waiting for an answer Katherine put Franz on the line.

'Franz, I'm terribly sorry to hear about your father. Is there anything I can do?'

'Thank you. Will you travel to Stuttgart for the funeral?'

'Of course. We'll all go. Your father had a lot of friends over here.'

'I know. I am grateful to them.'

Roland returned to staring out of the front window. Regardless of the unthinkable consequences if he'd done nothing, Roland had pushed a man to suicide, and from the depths of his being he felt disgusted with himself. Yet if he hadn't done so surely Franz would have been destroyed by the very hatred of his father's memory that Roland had stressed to Kassler . . . and wouldn't the pain that Katherine now felt on Franz's behalf be of a different, more destructive nature had she learned the truth?

When midnight came, and he continued to sit by the front window, he had convinced himself he had followed the only acceptable course. Kassler was dead, and his memory would remain sacred to those who cared.

Among the group that flew from England, to attend Heinrich Kassler's funeral three days later were Roland, Michael and Alf Goldstein. Franz had flown to Germany immediately on hearing of his father's death to be with his mother. Katherine, with two young children to care for, had decided not to go.

Once during the flight, Goldstein caught Roland's eye and a silent communication passed between the two men. Goldstein was the only one who knew the truth, knew that Roland had been to Stuttgart, of the final meeting with Kassler. Goldstein would have to figure out for himself what was said, because he instinctively knew

Roland would never divulge it.

A large crowd attended the interment, business associates of Kassler, people who had worked for him. And one other man who kept to the rear of the crowd, bundled up in a heavy coat and a hat that partially obscured his face. Peter Hoffbein.

Hoffbein refrained from approaching Roland while he was in Michael's company. Michael might remember him from New York, that brief meeting at the TWA terminal. After the service, however, when Michael was already in one of the cars that would return the British party to the airport, the German managed to get Roland alone.

'We have both achieved our ambitions, eh, Mr Eagles? Your family and business are saved embarrassment, as is my country.'

'Your country can go to hell in a goddamned handcart! You with it!' Roland snapped, pushing his way roughly past the German.

Hoffbein turned to gaze after Roland, a faint smile on his face. '*Auf wiedersehen*, Mr Eagles. Have a safe flight back to London.'

Roland sat with Michael Adler for the return flight to London while Alf Goldstein occupied a seat across the aisle. No one seemed prepared to say anything after the mournful solemnity of the funeral. It was Michael, as the aircraft circled over London, who eventually broke the dreary silence.

'At the risk of sounding like a vulture—'

'That's a bad pun,' Roland said.

'Sorry. *Probe*'s the furthest thing from my mind right now. But I was just thinking . . . what happens to Kassler's holdings in the group? Hadn't we better consider that?'

'They'll all go to Franz, I imagine. Unless Kassler's ex-wife wants something.' The funeral had been the first time Roland had ever met the woman, a simple, down-to-earth soul who probably would never have considered that her ex-husband could have hidden such a past. Roland could understand why she and Kassler hadn't stayed together. She shunned the limelight; at the funeral it was obvious she felt uncomfortable when photographers turned their cameras on her. She hadn't even attended Franz's wedding to Katherine, Roland recalled. Evidently had no desire at all to be a part of life's big events. 'Franz has suddenly become a very wealthy and very powerful young man.'

'I'll remember to tip my hat next time I see him,' Michael said.

'I don't think you'll have to.' Roland turned in his seat to face Michael and lowered his voice. 'I'm going to push for you to be the next chairman of the Eagles Group.'

'What?' Beneath Michael's amazement at the sudden prospect of his own immediate advancement was concern for Roland. 'What are you planning to do?'

'Today put the lid on it for me, Michael. Seeing Kassler lowered into the ground was like the end of an era.' He gave no hint of what that era had contained, however. 'I don't want the chairmanship anymore. I'm offering you my shares.'

'I haven't that kind of money. I wish I had. I'd grab them in a flash.'

'We can come to an arrangement, Michael. All I really want are those three companies I'm running on the side. They mean more to me than anything else.'

The intercom crackled into life to inform passengers the final approach to Heathrow had begun. Roland glanced through the window, saw the Thames snaking its way through London. He tugged at the seat belt to ensure it was fastened, straightened the seat back.

'It'll be novel, I've got to admit that,' Michael said. 'An Eagle in control of Adler's, and an Adler in control of the Eagles Group.'

'Not novel. Your name's already on the group,' he added, remembering what Heinrich Kassler had told him that night they had agreed on the share deal at Kendall's.

'My name?'

'Don't you speak any German?'

'Only the obscenities.'

'*Adler* means *Eagle*. Your father would probably understand.' The aircraft shuddered slightly as the undercarriage lowered and locked, and Roland made up his mind that if one chapter in his life had ended today, it was also time to close another. 'Michael, I'd like to see your father. I want to speak to him, before it's too late. I've had plenty of opportunities but I never took them, even when he told me he held no ill feelings toward me. Now I know I've got to see him, before I miss my chance forever.'

Roland's words came spilling out in an uneven flood, leaving Michael confused and worried. Was Roland's emotionalism because of Kassler's funeral? A total breakdown of his self-control? An abrupt realization of his own mortality and the feeling of having to make peace with everyone he felt he'd wronged? Or did it have something to do with his peculiar action the previous day when he'd thrown the New Year's Honours List into turmoil by requesting that his name be withdrawn? Michael couldn't understand that either, the last-minute rejection of the knighthood after he'd been looking forward to it so . . . and without a word of explanation!

'We'll go to my father's house right after we land,' Michael said, eager to soothe his friend. 'He'll probably be very pleased to see you, he doesn't get many visitors these days.'

The aircraft passed low over the perimeter fence and touched down. Roland stared up at the light above his seat; the time had finally come for him to repair any damage he'd done to the people whose lives he'd touched.

When they cleared customs and immigration, Alf Goldstein drove home alone while Michael took Roland to Albert Adler's home in Maida Vale. The nurse answered Michael's knock and showed the two men into the living room where Albert sat in an armchair, a skeletal, grayhaired, sightless figure listening to a play on the radio.

'You have two visitors, Mr Albert. Your son and his friend.'

Slowly, Albert turned his face toward them. Roland looked first at the useless eyes, then at the white stick that rested against Albert's chair. That damned white stick! He struggled to shove away the powerful memories it brought back . . . the incident in the schoolyard, and later the accident which led to Catarina's death.

'Michael? Where are you?' Albert struggled to stand and Michael stepped forward to help him. Fingers felt for Michael's arm, his shoulder, touched his face. 'This isn't one of your regular nights for seeing me.'

'Do I have to come only on a special night? Roland wanted to see you, too.'

'How are you feeling, Mr Adler?' Roland took Albert's right hand in his own, remembering all too well the first time he'd shaken it, his feelings then.

'I feel fine.' Animation showed in Albert's voice as he addressed Roland. He stood a fraction straighter. 'How about yourself? How's that big company you've created? I always ask Michael about the company whenever he comes to visit me.' Albert's right hand remained in Roland's, while his left hand moved to Roland's shoulder, steadying himself against the young man. 'I'd like to hear you tell me all about it.'

'I'm considering resigning as chairman, selling my shares to your son and recommending to the board and shareholders that he succeed me.'

'Really?' Albert's head swung toward Michael. 'You'll be chairman then?'

'It looks that way.'

'I know that Michael wanted to work in the United States,' Albert said, turning back to Roland. 'He told me you wouldn't let him. That you needed him here and . . .' The voice trailed off and Roland wondered whether the old man was overcome by emotion or had his attention lapsed?

Michael took over for his father. 'I told him what you

said, Roland. About staying here because of my father.'

'That was a very kind gesture,' Albert said. 'Thank you for thinking of me. If Michael had gone, I don't know what I would have done.'

Roland felt his face beginning to burn. 'I've been thinking about you a lot lately. That's why I'm here.'

'What's the weather like outside?' Albert asked, and again Roland feared he'd lost the old man. 'The nurse told me before that it was raining. Miserable as sin, she said.'

'It stopped about fifteen minutes ago.'

'Would you take me for a walk?' Albert asked his son. 'You and your friend?'

'If it's all right with the nurse.'

'Damn the bloody nurse!' Albert spat out with sudden anger, and for an instant Roland recognized a trace of old Monty Adler. 'I'm perfectly capable of judging whether or not I should go out for a blasted walk!'

With Michael and Roland on either side to guide him, Albert left the house and began walking slowly along the street, head moving from side to side as if he could really see. 'Don't you think it smells so clean after a rainfall?' he asked Roland. 'So fresh. I always liked the rain, it washed away the dirt.'

'Yes, it does.' Roland thought back to Kassler's funeral in Stuttgart earlier that day. Rain had been falling steadily, and the funeral – the meeting afterwards with Peter Hoffbein – had washed away a ton of dirt, swept it right under the carpet. 'I asked Michael to bring me here tonight because I wanted to talk to you. I've wanted to talk to you a long time, but I kept putting it off. Today, Michael and I went to a funeral' – he paused as he felt Albert's hand tighten its grip on his arm – 'and it made me realize how late I've left this meeting with you.'

On the other side of Albert Adler, Michael walked in silence, trying to make some sense out of where Roland was leading. He seemed to have slipped back into that rambling Michael had noticed on the return flight from

Stuttgart, seeming to want to make a point but unable to find the words to do so.

'I remember the first time I met you and Mr Monty, when I brought the sample irons and kettles to your father's office—'

'The office where *you* now work,' Albert pointed out.

'That's right, the office where I now work. I think, deep down, that I was hoping Adler's would go back on its word so I could make the kind of defiant statement I did by selling all that merchandise in Berwick Street Market. I wanted to show you that I was every bit as good as—'

Albert's grip on Roland's arm tightened until it was almost painful. 'Don't bother to explain anything. I know exactly who you are. I've known these past fourteen years. And I know exactly why you acted the way you did.'

'What's all this about?' Michael broke in; he failed to understand any of the conversation.

Albert stopped walking and turned to Roland, completely ignoring his son. 'When you took over Adler's, I realized there was no way I could stop you. You had Michael with you. You'd mounted a successful raid on the shares. All I could do was try to dig up something about you. It was the act of a desperate man, seeking something that might tarnish the image Michael had of you and bring him back to my side. I hired a private investigator—'

'That man who contacted my bank, even my tailor.'

Albert laughed hoarsely. 'I hope to hell he did, for the money I paid him. He also went to Margate, turned up wedding documents, birth certificates. Most importantly, he found a change of name deed.'

'Will someone please tell me what's going on?' Michael demanded again.

Albert turned to his son. 'This man, whom you allied yourself with, is your cousin.'

'My cousin?' Michael stared past his father at Roland.

'My brother's son.'

'That's impossible! Meir died in a car crash in America

610

in 1922.'

'No, he didn't,' Roland contradicted Michael. 'He died in an air raid in Margate in 1940. My father, Henry Eagles, was your father's older brother.'

Michael looked back to his father and was astounded to see tears falling from his sightless eyes. 'Henry,' Albert murmured, 'I had almost forgotten what his English name was. My father always called him Meir, his Yiddish name. Never Henry. And I thought it was just another sign of favoritism, his preference of my brother over me.'

Michael opened his mouth, needing more explanation than this. Roland held up a hand and motioned for him to remain quiet, to give his father all the time he wanted to tell the story in his own way.

'Meir never went to America,' Albert continued. 'Never went there at all. That was the story that we – the family – gave to account for his disappearance. You see, he'd met and fallen in love with a girl . . . what was her name now?'

'Betty,' Roland said.

'That's right, Betty. A Catholic girl. He wanted to marry her. And my father – whose word was always law in our house, in the firm, everywhere – didn't know what to do. He was torn apart, not wanting to see a son of his – especially a favored son – marrying out of the religion. That' – the tears fell more freely now – 'was when I stepped in. The only time my father ever listened to me, and look what misery it caused.'

'I know,' Roland said gently. 'My father told me everything that happened. You poisoned my grandfather's mind against my father, didn't you?'

Albert nodded dismally. 'I knew what Meir was like, I knew what my father was like. Two powerful personalities so similar they could only exist together if they agreed. The irresistible force and the immovable object. If they ever clashed, there would be no quarter given. So I played on my father's old-fashioned values, persuaded him to object to Meir's marriage to this woman. When

Meir learned that Mr Monty was against the marriage, we tried to reason with him. My father refused to change his mind. There were terrible arguments and my father told Meir that if he went through with the marriage he would disown him. And Meir answered exactly the way I knew he would: that if that was the way my father wanted it, that was the way it would be, because he was going to marry this woman come hell or high water. One day . . .' Albert's voice faltered. 'One day he just packed his clothes and left. We never saw him again.'

'He Anglicized his name weeks after the final split,' Roland said. 'He went to Margate with my mother, married her there. I don't think he ever ventured into London from that day, to avoid meeting anyone from the family, anyone he knew. He didn't want to see any of you again.'

'And you and my grandfather dreamed up that story about him going to America?' Michael asked Albert. 'And followed that up with the tale of how he'd died in a car crash?'

'When Meir moved away, people began to ask about him. My father couldn't bring himself to tell the truth, how the family had been split, how his son had disobeyed his wishes. So he made up the story about Meir going to America. And when it became obvious that he wasn't coming back my father killed him off, said he'd died in an accident. We even sat *shivah* for him. Then my father removed all photographs of Meir from the house, cut him out of pictures in the family scrapbook.'

'Except for one,' Michael cut in. 'When you and I cleared out his apartment after he died, we found one photograph there. You said it was of Meir.'

'Except for that one. I think he regretted what he'd done. I know he did. But there wasn't any way he could make it up; he didn't even know where Meir was. And Meir was too stubborn, too bitter, to come back. In turn, my father blamed me for the split. He claimed it was my jealousy of Meir that had forced me to turn my father against him.' He clutched hold of Roland's arm again.

'Take me home now, please, I feel tired.'

They made the return trip in silence. Roland was only vaguely aware of Albert wiping his eyes and face; he was too caught up in his own thoughts to notice. Somehow, he'd always thought he'd be angry on this day, vengeful. Instead, he felt pity for lives that had been ruined by stupid bigotry, by jealousy. Had Albert really enjoyed life once he'd forced his brother out of the family? Had Roland's own father fulfilled himself? What about old Monty Adler? Had any of them reaped a truly rewarding life?

And what about myself? Roland wondered. How much more complete would my life have been had I forced this meeting earlier? How could I have eased Albert's pain? How much more could I have added to Michael's life?

Then, as Roland looked at Michael, he realized he *had* made the reconciliation many years earlier.

'I think I understand now what you meant on the plane,' Michael said as they entered the house. 'About it being justice that an Adler should run the Eagles Group, and an Eagles should control Adler's.'

Roland just smiled and nodded. He had laid two ghosts to rest that day.

Albert Adler died at his home two weeks later, a peaceful passing in his sleep. Roland attended the funeral, and after the coffin had been lowered and the congregation had returned to the chapel, he watched as Michael sat down on the stone bench to receive condolences.

'I think I'll join you,' Roland said, taking the place next to Michael.

'For my father?' Michael asked, touched by the gesture.

'For *both* our fathers. I was too busy thinking about revenge to mourn for mine when he died, and I don't think they ever openly mourned for each other.' He glanced up as a man stood in front of him with hand extended, heard the words of commiseration.

'Thank you,' Roland said, and gratefully shook the hand.

CHAPTER FOUR

Roland sold his shares in the Eagles Group to Michael and stepped down as chairman. Michael was appointed chairman in his place, and Franz Kassler, who had inherited his father's stake in the company, filled the seat vacated by Michael to become, at twenty-eight, the youngest board member. Franz also held his father's shares in Kassler Industries, and was soon caught up in a constant merry-go-round of air travel – until Katherine put her foot down, as Janet had once unsuccessfully attempted to do with Roland. Katherine told Franz she wanted a full-time husband; she refused to be a business widow. Franz, in turn, sought Roland's assistance, reasoning that his father-in-law, who had led such a fast-paced business life, would support him. He was disappointed. Roland sided immediately with Katherine by telling Franz he had to decide what was more important – work or family. He urged his son-in-law not to make the same mistake both his father and he had made. Franz listened, and subsequently sold his holdings in Germany. For the first time since its founding, Kassler Industries had no Kassler on its board.

Roland didn't miss the excitement of a hectic business life at all. He'd long ago achieved his ambition of meeting his father's family as equals, and he was now content to manage the small diverse group he owned. There were no more trips overseas, just the regular journey to Adler's Regent Street store, five days a week, eight-thirty to five. He had more time to be with his extended family; as he approached fifty he welcomed that time more than he ever had.

Although Albert Adler had known of Roland's tie to the Adler family, the revelation came as a shock to everyone else, until they looked back at Roland's actions through the years – the way he had driven Lawrence Chivers in the early days to push the products into Adler's, Roland's distress at Monty's death, his presence at the funeral . . . Then the friendship with Michael Adler, the takeover of the firm, and the courtesy he'd always shown Albert after that. Michael recalled how Roland had even referred to him as family, that time in New York when he'd turned down his request to relocate in the United States. For Michael especially the pieces were finally fitting together.

In June, on Katherine's twenty-fourth birthday, Sally drove Roland to the house in Hampstead for a birthday lunch. They arrived early and Roland grabbed the opportunity to take Henry and Joanne to the pond on the Heath, where they could feed bread to the ducks. He sat with his back against a tree, while Sally broke up pieces of bread for them to throw. One duck waddled out of the water and cheekily snapped at the morsel of bread Henry was holding. The little boy jumped back, screaming in fright, and the duck flapped away in the opposite direction. It reminded Roland of the time a younger Katherine had tried to teach her half-brother and half-sister how to ride and Richard had run away screaming, only to trip and fall into a pile of horse manure. Roland smiled as he recalled Katherine cleaning him off in the pond at Stanmore Common before taking him back to the house.

Katherine twenty-four. It was hard for Roland to believe it – twenty-four years since Catarina had died. He didn't feel any older, although his hair was almost silver now. He still weighed the same, his eyes were as clear as ever. Perhaps he'd inherited the youth of which Catarina had been so cruelly robbed. That same youth which his own sister and brother had missed. A double dose to compensate him for what he'd lost.

When they ran out of bread Sally brought the children under the tree with Roland. 'Doing anything after lunch?'

'What have you got in mind?'

'Fancy a ride down to Aldershot? See my mother? It's been a few weeks and I'm feeling guilty.'

'Why not?' Sally's father had died ten years earlier, but her mother continued to live on the family farm, although other people worked it now.

'Nice day like this we can even put the roof down,' Sally said.

Roland didn't look forward to the prospect. Only two weeks earlier Sally had bought a new red Fiat convertible. He guessed the ride to Aldershot, although Sally cared deeply for her mother, was also an excuse to take a run in the new car.

At midday they returned to the house for lunch and Roland gave Katherine a slender box. 'You always liked it so much, I thought it was about time you had one of your own.'

Katherine opened the gift cautiously, remembering the size-nine top hat she'd given her father the previous Christmas. Was this a practical joke in retaliation? When she removed the elegant gold watch, though, she screamed in delight when she saw the inscription on the back. 'Happy 24th, from Fat Fanny, Boring Dora and Jealous Nat.'

'It's beautiful! Thank you! I love you!' She gave the watch to Franz and ran to her father's chair to throw her arms around his neck. 'Thank you!' she cried again. 'I'll wear it all the time.'

'You do realize, of course, that those three horses were used to glue furniture together at least fifteen years ago,' Roland said, winking at Sally.

'Don't make sick jokes about horses!' Then she laughed and kissed him again before returning to her seat.

'Do you want to give your father his present now?' Sally asked Katherine.

'My present?' Roland looked around the table, suddenly wary. 'It's not my birthday until September, and as it'll be my fiftieth, I'd be grateful if everyone forgot it this time.'

'New tradition,' Katherine answered. 'This time the birthday girl is giving presents as well as receiving them. I wrote to Simon in Paris—'

'What about?'

'About Albert Adler. I waited for you to do it, to tell him what you told everyone else, but you never did.'

'I didn't see any point.'

'Well, I did. So did Sally. All of us. We told him the whole story regarding Adler's . . . the real reason you wanted to buy it. You know he always believed you were only interested in revenge against Albert. You said yourself that Simon could never understand the reason for your ambition. He understands now.'

'So?'

'He replied a few days ago.' Katherine held out a hand to Franz, who pulled an envelope from his jacket pocket. 'Here are some photographs of David. He's eight now.'

Roland took the color photographs, looked at the lean, dark-haired boy with the mischievous brown eyes and felt a hard lump form in his throat. He hadn't seen his son since Sharon was in the hospital after she'd given birth.

'Here's the letter.'

Roland passed the photographs to Sally and took the letter. It began with Simon's gratitude to Katherine for giving him the information about Roland's link with the Adler family, his own feelings of understanding. Then Roland came to a section that read. 'Please tell your father that Nadine and I will do everything in our power to persuade Sharon to allow him to see his son. I fully comprehend how much David means to him – to you as well, Katherine, as he is your half-brother – but we still have to remain very cautious where Sharon's emotions are concerned. On the surface she is well, but any shock,

617

any disruption to the regularity of her life, could prove to be disastrous. David does very well at school and has many friends. Please give our love to your father, and stress that one day we will arrange for him to see David.' .

Roland read the letter through again before handing it back to Katherine. 'I suppose a promise is better than nothing at all,' he finally said, grateful for his daughter's gesture.

At two-thirty, Roland and Sally left for the drive to Sally's mother's farm. Throughout the trip, while the sun streamed down on him and the wind whistled through his hair – he purposely avoided looking at the speedometer to see how fast Sally was breaking in the new car – Roland thought about the letter from Simon.

Simon had never gotten over his notion of revenge, but Roland couldn't really blame him, since he'd never bothered to offer an alternative, substantive reason. He wondered how much of their eventual split could be blamed on that misunderstanding; and again, how much simpler, how much more enjoyable, life could have been for everyone had Roland not played his cards so close to his chest?

Sally and Roland stayed at the farm for an hour, having tea and walking around the grounds. When they left, Roland's mind was still preoccupied with thoughts of Simon, thinking back to the first time he'd ever met the French banker – a day or two after getting out of the army.

'Sally . . . do me a favor.' He touched her arm suddenly and the front of the Fiat twitched. 'Run me by the army camp.'

'Sentimental journey?'

'Something like that.' He sat back as Sally changed direction, heading towards the Aldershot army base instead of the London road. They passed familiar sights such as public houses and hotels mixed with new buildings; the area had changed considerably in twenty-seven years, Roland thought, grown up, expanded.

When they reached the camp entrance, Roland climbed out of the Fiat and approached the military guard on duty. 'I was stationed here twenty-seven years ago. Any possibility of just coming on base for a few minutes to look around?'

The guard looked past Roland at Sally, who remained sitting in the open car. 'Do you have some identification on you, sir?'

'Certainly.' Roland pulled out his driver's license and a number of charge cards.

'What unit were you with, sir?'

Roland told him. The guard went back into his booth, picked up the telephone and made a call. Two minutes later he was finished. 'I think that'll be all right, sir. Will the lady be accompanying you?'

'Want to share this sentimental journey, Sally?' he called to her.

'Love to. Where shall I leave the car?'

The MP pointed to a building. 'By the guardhouse should be all right, miss.'

Roland and Sally signed their names in a book, with their time of arrival, then walked into the camp. 'Changed much?' Sally asked.

'I can't remember it well enough to make comparisons. I suppose I washed this place clean out of my mind the moment I stepped through the gates for the last time.'

'And caught a train and met me.'

'And met you.' He took her hand as they continued walking slowly past the recreational building, past other buildings that all seemed to look alike. Soldiers walked by, some in uniform, others in civilian clothes, off-duty.

'Hard to believe this is an army camp,' Sally said. 'No one drilling, no one firing guns. You know something? The whole time I lived in this area, even when I was writing those wartime human interest stories for the

619

Mercury, I never set foot in this place. Didn't miss very much, did I?'

From somewhere behind came the sound of an explosion, a small pop, not loud enough to startle them. 'Now do you believe it's an army base?' Roland asked. 'Someone just obligingly made a bang for you.'

'What was it?'

'Probably just a car backfiring.' He checked his watch and was surprised to find they'd been in the camp for twenty-five minutes. 'Come on, we'd better be getting back. And can we please ride home with the roof up? I'm too young to die of pneumonia.'

'Spoilsport.'

As they approached the gate they saw a small group of soldiers standing around the red Fiat where it was parked by the guardhouse. Roland felt uneasy. He let go of Sally's hand and quickened his pace. 'Can I help you with anything?'

A beefy, red-faced major with a waxed moustache separated himself from the group. 'Is this your car, sir?'

'No, it belongs to the lady. Why?' He pushed his way thought the groups of soldiers, saw that the trunk was open.

The major waited for Sally to reach him. 'Next time, madam, you'll save us a lot of trouble if you leave the keys to your car with the gate guard. We had to blow open the trunk to see what was inside.'

'You had to do *what*?' Sally shrieked in horror. She ran past the major, through the group of soldiers and saw that the lock of the trunk had been blown apart. The lid was mangled, the trunk wrecked, the spare tire shredded. 'Look what you've done to my new car, you idiot!'

Roland held out his arms and grabbed Sally before she launched herself at the major.

'I'm sorry, madam, but this is standard procedure for unidentified vehicles that we can't properly check. If you remember, we had a big tragedy here not long ago, a car

620

full of explosives planted by the IRA went off and killed a lot of people.'

'But the gate guard! He told us to park it there!' Sally looked toward the booth. The military policeman on duty was a stranger.

'They changed shifts fifteen minutes ago,' the major said. 'The new man called the car to our attention.'

'Never mind, Sally,' Roland said. He was trying hard to keep from laughing. 'I'm sure the insurance covers you.'

'Damn the insurance!' She glared ferociously at the major and the group of soldiers. 'Couldn't you have waited a few minutes before you arbitrarily decided to blow up my car?'

'I'm sorry, madam. Bombs go off in a few seconds, let alone a few minutes.'

'Shit!' Sally swore and stamped her foot. 'Now how the hell are we going to get home? I can't drive it like that. They must have used ten tons of high explosives.'

'Four ounces, madam.' To add insult to injury, the major saluted crisply before leading his men away.

'I'll call up Alf Goldstein,' Roland suggested. 'He can drive out and pick us up in the Bentley.'

Sally seemed not to hear him. She stood with her hands on her hips, staring at the damaged car. Slowly, the scowl of anger gave way to a smile, then she burst out laughing. 'Go on, laugh, you inconsiderate oaf!' she yelled at Roland. 'I can see you're bursting yourself to hold it in.'

Roland put his arms around her and they stood together, still laughing. 'Did you hear what I just said? I'll get Alf come out and get us.'

'No need. We'll get a train back to London. Let Alf enjoy his day off. Tomorrow I'll telephone a garage to see about that.' She pointed to the Fiat and laughed again. 'Do you really think the insurance will cover an act of war?'

'Depends on how they define an act of war. Let's find out the time of the next train.'

Twenty minutes later they were standing on the platform of Aldershot Station. That was when Roland really noticed the difference. Twenty-seven years earlier an old steam train had chugged into the station; now a sleek diesel had taken its place. Nonetheless, the mere sight of the name 'Aldershot' on the station signs triggered his memory. The last time he was there it had been November, cold and dreary. He'd been in uniform, carrying a leather suitcase. Now it was a June evening, bright and clear, and he wore a sportcoat and light wool trousers. But the woman sitting opposite him after they boarded the train was the same woman who had sat opposite him then.

'Bloody useless army,' Sally muttered as the train pulled out of the station. 'Blowing up a brand new car.'

'That was just the army's subtle way of telling you to buy British next time,' Roland answered.

'Soldiers, they're all the same. After my husband was killed at Arnhem, I never did like them. God only knows why I spoke to you that time.'

'Why did you?'

'I was bored. And . . . you looked kind of interesting.' She leaned toward him, inspected the front of his sportcoat. 'Excuse my curiosity, but is that the Military Cross *and* the Military Medal?'

Roland glanced down, expecting to see the two decorations fastened to his sportcoat until he remembered where he'd heard those words before – right here, as they were pulling out of Aldershot Station. 'I came up through the ranks,' he said, remembering exactly how he'd responded. 'For a woman you've got an excellent eye for ribbons.'

'I should have—'

'Yes, I know. You wrote about the war from a woman's point of view. Still wish you were writing for the *Mercury*?'

'No, I don't think so.' She reached out and took

Roland's hand. 'It would have become too stifling in the end. The *Eagle*'s much more fun. What about you? Do you still wish you were coming out of the army that day back in 1947? Would you like to turn back the clock?'

Roland considered it. Given the opportunity would he rectify some of the mistakes he'd made . . . identify himself to his father's family earlier? . . . figure out some way to marry Catarina without forcing the break with her family? . . . avoid Sharon? Or would he go through life the same way, making the same mistakes? He probably would, he decided. Mistakes were part of life. Even Kassler. He would believe Kassler all over again and have to live with learning the shattering truth all over again. Besides, if he *had* learned the truth about Kassler in the very beginning, where would Katherine be now? Would he have two such gorgeous grandchildren? It was like a black cloud with a bright silver lining. No . . . there must be a better analogy than that – black and silver – those were the colors of Kassler's old uniform, the colors of the SS.

'Penny for them,' Sally said.

'For my thoughts? They're hardly worth that much.'

'Okay, if you say so. Then what about when we get to London? Are you still going to stay at that hotel off Leicester Square?'

'I'm not even certain it's still there. How about if I telephone you once I get settled? Maybe we can go out for dinner, to that restaurant in Bayswater? What was it called?'

'Antoine's.'

'That's right, Antoine's. The man who does wonders with the little food the government allows.'

'I'm not sure he's there anymore.'

Roland shook his head. 'Everything's changed but us.' Not long ago he had controlled an international empire, now he was happy to run three companies, all based in London. Once he looked forward to accepting a knighthood; now, he was happy to remain plain Mr Eagles. And once – on the very night they'd shared this same train ride together – he'd had Sally. But that hadn't changed. He still had her. She'd stuck by him for twenty-seven years, her life inexorably entwined with his own, helping him, advising him, even calling him on his arrogance at times.

'You know, I was wondering . . .'

'Oh?'

'I've got a lot of money coming from Michael for those shares in the Eagles Group.'

'Enough to buy me a new car?' Sally asked. Still holding Roland's hand, she stood up as the train pulled into Waterloo Station.

'Enough to buy a thousand new cars with plenty left over for tax and insurance. But what about using that money to start all over again?'

Sally opened the door and jumped down, dragging Roland behind her. 'I think I'd rather you bought me a thousand new cars.' They began to walk toward the exit, where Roland held out the tickets to the collector. 'That way,' she added, 'I might get to see you occasionally.'

'Settle for one new car?'

'If that's your final offer, I suppose it'll have to do.'

Traffic was heavy that evening and Roland took Sally's hand again as they made their way through the crowd to the street, searching for a cab. As they stood together Roland glanced at Sally's profile. For a brief moment he felt that it could have been twenty-seven years earlier. The feeling he'd once had for her must still be there, Roland thought, only this time there was something more – a deeply abiding love seasoned by their many years of friendship. He hailed a cab, and held her hand tightly until he opened the door and helped her inside for the ride home.

THE END